An Immigrant

"The Gorotsuki Club *lies*!" she snarled bitterly. "They set up the entire thing . . . letters, pictures, promises. All of it! *There are no husbands!* And when we get here, we have no choice . . . no money to get back to Japan and no alternative. I—"

She faltered, then the words tumbled on, "I refused, spit in their faces, but they beat me. That's right, Mr. Hoshi, they beat me until they were afraid they'd damaged the goods. And still I refused, and they beat me again . . . and then I knew. I had no choice."

"Why do you stay?" he asked.

"Stay? Mr. Hoshi, I've run away *twice!* But the Gorotsuki reach everywhere like a spiderweb. And when they catch you, they beat you terribly . . . a woman hasn't got a chance."

"There must be some way," he said.

She shook her head, staring at the floor. "None, except death."

CHIKARA!

A SWEEPING NOVEL OF JAPAN AND AMERICA FROM 1907 TO 1983

ROBERT SKIMIN

PINNACLE BOOKS NEW YORK

Grateful acknowledgment is made for permission to reprint "Rouge
Bouquet," from *Poems, Essays and Letters* by Joyce Kilmer.
Copyright 1918 by Charles Scribner's Sons. Reprinted by permis-
sion of Doubleday & Company, Inc.

CHIKARA!

A Pinnacle Books edition, published by special arrangement with
St. Martin's Press, Inc.

St. Martin's edition published in 1984
Pinnacle edition/May 1985

ISBN: 0-523-42488-4
Can. ISBN: 0-523-43458-8

Printed in the United States of America

PINNACLE BOOKS, INC.
1430 Broadway
New York, New York 10018

9 8 7 6 5 4 3 2 1

Dedicated to the Japanese Americans

Special thanks to: Joyce Engelson—my extraordinary editor; Freya Manston—my stimulating agent; Itoko McNully—my astute librarian; Jim Miho—the inspiration; Professor Takashige Mitsui—Library Director of the Japanese Defense Academy; Sen Nishiyama—a perceptive and articulate American Japanese; Jim Sasaki, Barry Saiki, Seizo Oka, Akira Matsuura; my wife Claudia . . . and the dozens of librarians, historians, and other helpful people who made this work possible. *Arigato!*

—Robert Skimin

Though wave after wave of desolation
Has hurled itself upon the city,
The cherry tree still blooms
As in days gone by.

—FUJIWARA SHUNZEI
a poem to the Emperor, 1188

chikara (n.) power; strength; force; might; efforts; resources; capacity; talent

Chikara

PROLOGUE

The master bedroom suite and its spacious connecting study, done mostly in variations of white, were the heart of the villa. It was where the beautiful woman preserved her intimacy, a sanctuary seldom seen by anyone but the housemaid. The study, while enriched by shelves of the books she loved, was bright and airy with a glass wall opening to a pleasing garden of falling water, delicate shrubs, and carefully chosen rocks. She stepped outside as the angry man strode from the suite, his parting words still ringing in her ears. . . . *"This is beyond your prerogative. You are still merely a woman in Japan!"*

Harsh and foolish words for one who knew her so well.

She watched the silvery trickle of water fall over a moss-covered stone and reached out with her finger to capture its sweet taste. A sliver of sunlight caught her blue-white diamond and its brilliance overpowered the water's reflection. Perhaps he was right, she told herself. Perhaps with all her power she was still merely a trickle of water to be obliterated if she dared too much.

She shrugged as she turned the huge gem away from the direct ray of light and again the sparkle of the water flashed back. It was simply a matter of manipulation.

Besides, when had she last been intimidated?

Reentering the suite, she went to the dressing area and quickly changed to a one-piece black bathing suit that accentuated the firm tone of her sleek skin and the trim, shapely figure that had changed little from the days when she had turned men's heads from the Ginza to the Riviera. Over the swimsuit, she donned a brightly flowered *yukata* and, barefoot, ran down the steps to the pool.

1

A refreshing swim would cleanse the touch of smoldering resentment that lingered from the unpleasant encounter. It would also invigorate her for the next step, a move she had anticipated.

Her home was near Nogakogen in Saeki-gun. Forty minutes from the city center, the heavily treed site on which she had built her villa was the result of years of searching for just the right aesthetic combination of land and view. After waiting another year before she could purchase it, she had plunged into the construction and enjoyed every minute of the two years it took to build. What she had accomplished was a marvelous blend of East and West—a superb fusion of stone, wood, glass, and water in a landscape that subtly announced the property of a very special person.

Reminiscent of the old Imperial Hotel, the front entrance was approached by a walkway over a bridge that ran through two huge lily ponds. The entry was a high study in California redwood, adorned by a huge brass sculpture of her grandfather's *mon*, the family crest. To each side, a half-flight of steps ran up to the great room—a striking harmony of rich plants, Japanese and Western furniture groupings, hardwood and carpeting, sculpture and ingenious lighting. At the far end of the magnificent room, rising its two full stories to the beamed ceiling, a massive wall of glass presented a striking panorama of the distant Inland Sea and part of the huge city that fanned out in the foreground below.

Everything else in the main structure flowed from the great room—the dining rooms and kitchen complex in the wing with the servants' quarters and a fully equipped game room. Utilitarian rooms and guest bedrooms with baths were in another wing. Connected, but jutting up to an outcrop of rock ledge, was her private suite with a bath so spacious the housemaid had written to all of her relatives that it contained a white marble swimming pool.

The garage, heated swimming pool, tennis court, and additional guest house were built into the escarpment below and carefully hidden from the main house. Much of the area surrounding the buildings was adapted from Hiroshima's famous garden, Shukkei-En, while the more distant portions of the estate reminded Western visitors of the heavily jammed woods of

Connecticut. But at this time of the year, all of the trees were bare, starkly waiting for spring to course through their branches and make them explode with foliage.

Most anticipatory were the cherry trees, eagerly awaiting their time to burst forth with the most profuse and beautiful blossoms in the world—the spirit, the poetic soul of Nippon.

Following her quick and invigorating swim, the beautiful woman hurried back to her study where she contacted the international operator and said in her cultured Tokyo accent, "I wish to place a call to New York, please."

Twenty hours later in her suite in the Imperial, the hotel hairdresser finished transforming her short, tousled hair into a modified upsweep to go with her Japanese attire, then helped her get dressed. It was seldom that she wore a kimono anymore, and she had brought along one of her finest—a powder blue silk with an off-white brocaded obi. The executives she was about to meet knew of her many years in the West; now she wanted them to realize she was confident in their world, knew their rules . . . and she wanted them to recall that she carried the blood of great samurai families.

And that her name meant *star*.

And finally she was ready. Turning to the grinning approval of the hairdresser, she nodded imperceptibly and placed the simple two-carat solitaire on her right hand. It was time for the confrontation.

The chauffeur of the sleek black Mercedes had the limousine waiting under the covered entrance to the imposing front of the hotel as she reached its doors. Entering the rear of the company car, she thought strangely of how the Imperial Hotel had played such a vital role in her march to this, perhaps her greatest challenge. From its opening day to the present . . .

The driver moved smoothly into the heavy Tokyo traffic in front of Hibiya Park, then proceeded past the vast grounds of the palace toward Akasaka. Shortly, the vehicle stopped in front of a tall dark building that appeared to be all glass, an aloof skyscraper that dwarfed even the nearby New Otani Hotel. A tasteful brass plaque by its entrance announced that this mighty structure was headquarters for the Japanese conglomerate that was most vigorous in challenging America's technological giants for world trade.

Just inside the lobby, a well-groomed man with the bearing of a senior executive bowed deeply as he met her. It was only the third time he had seen this handsome lady and he was surprised to find that she was not exquisitely garbed in her trademark white suit and fur neckpiece.

They stepped out of the elevator on the top floor, crossing thick carpeting in a bright foyer that led past a bowing reception-ist to the chief operating officer's suite. He was already waiting in the doorway, a plump silver-haired little man bowing deeply with a wide respectful smile as she approached. They quickly retired to his sumptuous inner office where hot green tea was silently served by his secretary.

It was finally time for her to see if she had enough trumps.

Forty-two minutes later, she settled back in the soft maroon leather of the limousine's seat and stared out through the darkly tinted window. The clouds that had gathered during her confer-ence now threatened to pour yet another deluge into the already sodden city. Pedestrians and bicycle riders glanced warily up at the sky, reminding her of how Tokyoites had worn the same guarded looks when B-29s flooded the air in that terrible war of so long ago, the war that had torn so much from her. . . .

She pushed the always tormenting memories back into their lair and thought of her meeting. It was just as she had feared—they had been shocked at her proposal and quick to point out its impracticality. Not at this critical time when the company was in such a perilous state of upheaval, she had been told. Yes, they had been most polite and promised to give full consideration to her proposal at some later date, but—

She may have been a star, but she was an intruding woman.

As the limousine waited at a traffic light, she focused on the curious blinking eyes of a small child trying to stare through the darkened window. He was no more than a year old and was slung to the back of a young woman on a bicycle. She smiled softly at him.

Her proposal could have an immeasurable effect on the future of this innocent child, and the rest of his generation for that matter. And all generations. The signs were there, ominous to one with her grasp, obscured to others. The path had been so insidiously and beguilingly seductive that it was all but unrecognizable.

The sudden and horrible blast of inconceivable force and brilliance that had created a mushroom cloud over her father's birthplace had terminated one path and opened the way for the other. This time, however, the generals and admirals were wearing finely tailored suits. . . .

The child began to cry as huge raindrops spattered against his face and his mother pedaled away with the traffic.

She sighed, thinking of her handsome grandfather, of how—if he were watching from somewhere—he would be nodding, pursing his lips, his bright black eyes narrowing in pleased approval of her action. And his full, infectious grin would spread, making it all worthwhile.

For wasn't she part of his great dream?

No, she was more than that.

She was its fulfillment.

BOOK 1

THE IMMIGRANTS
1907–1912

One

Hiroshima, Japan—1907

Sataro Hoshi wasn't certain exactly when he made the definite decision to go to America. The stories of the great western Utopia where riches spewed from the fertile earth like lava from noble Mount Fuji had fascinated him for years. Even going away to find adventure in the recent war with Russia hadn't dulled his appetite for a new life where a man with verve and audacity—an entrepreneur such as himself—could build a fortune.

It certainly couldn't be done in Japan these days. Not only did the postwar depression have the country by the throat, there simply was little opportunity. Only the rich got richer. But these were only factors—Sataro Hoshi *wanted* to go to America. In his tiny cubicle at the store he had tacked a map of California to the wall and a day didn't pass without his studying it and living out different successes. Some nights he stayed on and enacted them at English practice.

And always he would construct the vivid scene of his triumphal return; striding down a gangplank, head held high, the elegant clothes a positive statement of his great riches and conquests. His lovely Itoko would follow, regal as a queen; then his elder son Noboru, confident and ready to become a leader in Japanese commerce; his other son, Hiroshi, the young general, waiting joyously to meet them. It was a magnificent drama.

But snipping the umbilical cord had its problems.

Staring down through the open window of the hillside mission, the exceptionally tall and handsome man felt the fresh ocean breeze on his high cheekbones. He sniffed its salty smell and narrowed his bright black eyes as he wondered how long it would be before he would see this familiar view again. Below, sweep-

9

ing toward the Inland Sea on its six verdant islands and around its seven sparkling rivers, lay the city he so loved. Except for his two years in the army, the entire thirty-four years of his life had been spent in this tranquil blend of water, greenery, and culture. He had always felt a special passion for its beauty, the uniqueness of its fanlike delta and the guardian hills that rose so serenely on three sides. There was even something singular about its people, but he couldn't define it.

Hiroshima had been compared to ancient Rome—its rivers likened to the Seven Hills, Terumoto's magnificent five-tiered castle with its tangerine roofs to the palace of Tiberius, and the vibrance of its culture to that of the greatest Caesars.

The late afternoon sunlight tossed back bright reflections as he tried to paint a vivid canvas for his memory. Suddenly he turned back to Macnamara's office. The sentimentality had gone far enough, he told himself gruffly. In spite of its hold over him, the city just could not help him fulfill the difficult legacy he had inherited at age three. He was the head of the House of Hoshi and it was his responsibility to improve the flagging family fortunes—a high-sounding espousal, his wife insisted.

He had rejected the opening to follow in his father's heroic samurai footsteps as an army officer. It was a simple matter of money. In spite of the giant leaps Japan had taken since the restoration of the Emperor as ruler, military officers were still grossly underpaid. The pitiful pension his mother received was proof of that. Instead, he had opted for the less glorious life of a merchant—a career that ranked well down the status ladder. He opened his first shop at the age of twenty-three; his larger store a year before he was conscripted for the war in 1904.

But he could no longer bear being merely a Hiroshima shopkeeper.

Admittedly, he wanted personal accomplishment—only a hypocrite would deny it. But that was only the foundation, a base from which his greater dream for the family could spring. He had nurtured the plan until it was vivid as reality—one son to America to be educated in the Western ways of trade, the other to renew the Hoshi heritage by becoming a Japanese Army officer. One son a merchant prince, the other a heroic general with all the honors of Nippon. Power in the House of Hoshi! *He could taste it!*

"Sorry to keep you waiting, Sataro," Reverend Macnamara boomed as he hurried into the office. "Are you ready for the big voyage?"

At thirty-seven, Charles Macnamara had been in Japan for ten years, the last three as head of the ambitious Methodist mission. Tall and prematurely gray, with beguiling blue eyes and a commanding voice that had produced more than a few converts through pure intimidation, at times he had the presence of a shogun more than that of a missionary. At other times his compassion emerged, destroying that image. He knew that the ambitious Sataro Hoshi had used him these past years—that his intent from the very first day he had come to the mission hadn't been religious. Sataro Hoshi wanted his family to learn English, and the American House of God was his source. Still, he told himself every time he grew irritated, who knew when a lamb would turn into the fold?

"Yes, except for the difficult part with Hiroshi," Sataro replied in a slight accent that extensive pronunciation drills had failed to eliminate.

Macnamara dropped into the worn chair behind his desk. "I'm still not sure leaving him behind is the right thing. Particularly since Itoko is so set against it."

Sataro tried not to show his displeasure. As he often did when he was irritated or troubled, he fingered the thin white scar that ran diagonally across his right cheekbone—the visible reminder of a Cossack officer's saber blow. In spite of their warm friendship, his family decisions were none of the missionary's business! "Hiroshi's role has been decided," he replied curtly.

Macnamara lit his smelly pipe and puffed vigorously as he made a production of shaking out the match and dropping it into a gleaming porcelain ashtray. He knew better than to push it. With a shrug and a mischievous smile he said, "Very well. How about a last-minute baptism? I hate to lose, you know."

Sataro's expression softened. "You never give up, do you?"

The missionary chuckled. "I may need the credit to get into Heaven myself." He puffed a moment, sobering. "Well, I guess

I've done all I can. You and your family speak English pretty well, even if your souls are in the hands of Buddha. The only thing that worries me is how you'll handle the prejudice. My last letter from Reverend McAllister in San Francisco indicates that it continues to get worse.''

Sataro moved to the window to hide his scowl. This prejudice thing had to be overstated! Weren't immigrants from all over the world streaming into America's open arms? How could a Japan man of good family with money in his pockets be mistreated? Turning back, he managed a calm tone. ''You still don't understand us after all these years, do you? You don't grasp our *gambari*—our special ability to withstand anything. Our Tokugawa leaders practiced it when your Admiral Perry insultingly drove his warships into our harbor fifty-four years ago, and we've been displaying it ever since. Certainly, I can take minor insult in America.''

''Oh, I understand it,'' Macnamara replied with a shrug. ''I just don't know if your precious pride will get in the way.''

Sataro rubbed his scar again. Enough of this inane discussion. He reached inside his *hakama* for the present. Handing over the box with the gleaming new meerschaum, he said gruffly, ''It's time,'' then smiled ruefully and added, ''Whenever it goes out, remember your lost lamb.''

The minister took the gaily wrapped gift with one hand, extending the other. ''Thank you, my friend,'' he murmured, choking back the emotion. ''I'll watch for your letters.''

Sataro shook his hand warmly, then bowed deeply. ''*Sayonara*, Reverend Macnamara. May your God be with you.''

The missionary fished a gleaming oblong disk from the desk drawer and held it out. ''Keep this,'' he said quietly. ''In case your *gambari* fails.''

Sataro thanked him, drew back his shoulders, and erectly walked out. He was halfway down the steps before he glanced down at the shiny gift. It was inscribed with a tiny cross and read, *''The other cheek.''*

Sataro moved along the street slowly as he headed for his house in Shiroshima Kita-Cho, near the banks of the delta's main stream—the clear and smoothly flowing Ota. The beginning of the rainy season had been cheerfully interrupted that afternoon by a clearing sky and the bright benevolence of the welcome sun. Only small, stubborn puddles and a quiet freshness in the air reminded one of the dreary sodden morning.

Sataro stopped to capture the memory of his beloved river as a dark-plumaged cormorant swooped low to the water, dipped its hooked beak with its glutinous carrying pouch into the glaze of water, and jerked up with a silvery fish. As the web-footed predator winged swiftly away, Sataro's gaze settled on a small boat not a hundred feet away. An acquaintance of his was paddling slowly under the bright saffron and gold slats of a tiny square-rigged sail. The slanting rays of the late sun created a brilliant picture for him to store away.

He waved at the rower, then glanced up at the higher ridge of the riverbank on the other side. He thought of the olden days when the samurai dwelt there, separated distinctly from the lower classes on the lower bank. It was said that the banks had been deliberately built that way—so in case of flood, only the lesser caste would be swept away.

He frowned, remembering that his valiant father had helped eliminate such criminal nonsense, then looked with pleasure at a small grove of cherry trees huddled proudly together so that in season their bright pink blossoms could add a rich splash to the colorful palette of the bank.

Now, all he had to do was face Itoko.

At thirty, Itoko Hoshi looked much the same as she had at eighteen when they had married. If anything, a touch of maturity had refined her classic Japanese features. Her figure was as trim as ever, and she still turned men's heads when she was out in public. Although their marriage had been arranged when their fathers were two young idealistic samurai in middle school, their love had begun as excitingly as if they had met accidently and had a vibrant courtship.

If there was a shadow over this couple in the early stages of their marriage, it was the fact that Itoko was an *Edokko*—a Tokyoite who thought the world was enclosed in that huge city. It took Sataro over a year of patient selling to convince his bride of Hiroshima's charm and the fact that he wasn't totally provincial. Itoko's mother, who died of what his wife called a broken heart the year after her father's heroic death in 1904, always claimed that Itoko had inherited *all* the spirit of the Mitsubishi family. Sataro had another name for it—stubbornness.

He had quickly decided she should have been an actress—so easily did she switch roles. Outwardly, she was the epitome of the docile Japanese wife, but in the privacy of their bedroom, she could attack him like a banshee when she was displeased about something. Yet, she worked hard at maintaining a respectful, smooth relationship with his mother, the sometimes less than agreeable Tomi. He thought it was in their fourth year of marriage that she perfected the long-suffering role, which she could play with what he considered consuming relish.

But all in all, Itoko was much of what he thought a wife should be. She was a good mother and homemaker—even though her fanaticism about cleanliness sometimes bordered on the antiseptic—she was witty and challenging, and could turn into the most coquettish and stimulating of lovers when she felt like it. Once he told her she was a reincarnated star geisha with the passion of the Greek goddess, Aphrodite—a role *he* enjoyed.

It was this problem over Hiroshi that was jarring their relationship. Ever since their second-born's birth—when Itoko was told she couldn't have more children—she had lavished most of her love and affection on him. At first this had been understandable, but he thought she carried it too far. And now he was about to take the boy away from her.

He would rather face a *dozen* Cossacks.

"Good-bye, my love." Itoko Hoshi stroked the tiny bonsai tree in the corner of their exquisitely manicured garden as if it were a pet animal. She had planted it only the year before and considered it her baby. She had already said farewell to the rocks, the sand, the other plants, to the short bench where she had spent so many pleasant hours in meditation, and finally to the fence itself. All were vital characters in her proud garden. And all were part of the wonderful life that was being torn away from her.

A small green maple leaf drifted over the wall and fell at her feet. She stared at it a moment, then leaned down to pick it up. Clutching it to her breast, she whispered, "And how did you get torn away so soon?" She thought of how the same dismembering was about to happen to her beautiful Hiroshi, and the cold loathing for Sataro returned. He was her husband and she had to abide by his will. She'd accompany him to this backward, heathen land—but she would *never* stay there, she told herself for the hundredth time. Not taking Hiroshi was the most *insane* crime he could have invented! She could feel the icicles clutching at her heart. What did she care that her fine son would be well cared for by Seizo and his dumpy, barren wife? He was *hers*, he needed *her!*

She tossed the dying leaf away and strode angrily inside.

Ten minutes later, Sataro entered the stone-floored *genkan*, where he slowly removed his shoes. He glanced at the smallest pair of thongs, sadly realizing that they'd never rest in the same spot again. In another fifteen hours, none of this footwear would ever return. Strange, he thought, with so many human lives about to be altered, that it could all be summed up by clogs, thongs, and a pair of shoes silently resting on a low shelf in a dispassionate vestibule.

He shrugged and gathered himself for the storm. Opening the sliding door to the formal room, he saw his mother wistfully fondling the flower arrangement in the *tokonoma*, the alcove reserved for that traditional part of the household. "I've finished at the mission, Okasama," he announced as casually as possible.

Tomi Hoshi looked up, startled. Losing her husband when she was only twenty-one and having to provide for two growing sons on limited funds had made an old woman of her before she was fifty. And twelve years in the same house with the independent Itoko, she liked to tell herself, hadn't delayed the process. Still, it was this ridiculous dream of her tall firstborn that had added the final touch of white to her hair. Trotting off to America and taking her fine grandson along was more than she could bear. She had been shuffling around in a trance all day, unable to face the fact that it was actually going to happen. The tears were past. Like so much in her trying life, she had no control over this sad event. She nodded, trying to smile bravely. "Itoko and the boys are waiting in the *ima*," she replied listlessly.

Sataro patted her shoulder affectionately. Sliding open the door to the parlor, he saw that Itoko had the scene set to play the most emotional role of her life. She stood in the middle of the room like a tenacious lioness ready to defend her young to the last. The wide-eyed Hiroshi stared at his father from her tight embrace, confused and hurt that he was the center of such family trouble. Behind them, an uncomfortable Noboru fiddled with a toy sailboat, not even looking up to greet his father with his customary exuberance. Itoko's eyes glittered angrily as she waited for her husband to make the first move. Tomi glided into the room to watch silently from a corner. She wanted to grab Noboru and hold him tightly. Line up right beside Itoko and tell her son to go alone!

Sataro broke the charged silence, asking quietly, "Is the boy ready?"

There wasn't an iota of affectation in Itoko's defiant last stand. She had never before known such wrenching pain nor such total anger at her husband. He'd pay and pay and pay for this! She crushed Hiroshi more fiercely to her breast, saying nothing, glaring back.

Sataro had seen her violently angry innumerable times over the years, but never before had such naked hurt and total defiance radiated from her expressive eyes. He could see they were painted more darkly than usual around the edges to hide the redness. Her sensual lips were set in a harsh line that told him she was going to fight to the last second. He shifted his weight, feeling the anger mount. He had been over this for weeks and was sick of being treated like a criminal! He pulled the watch from his pocket and glared at it. "It's time," he announced firmly.

Itoko drew in a sharp breath. "No!" she cried.

"Don't make it any worse," Sataro growled. "It's hard enough on the boy as it is. He—"

"*The crime's on your head, Sataro Hoshi!*" she shrieked.

Sataro broke away from her ferocity to glance down at Hiroshi. "Get your hat, my son," he said quietly.

Tears were welling up in Hiroshi's eyes as he started to move from his mother's embrace. She jerked him back. Her grim expression collapsed into naked anguish as she dropped to her knees, crying, "No, no, no!" The stifled tears rushed down her cheeks as she kissed his eyes, his nose, his hair.

Sataro gripped her arm firmly. "Say good-bye to your brother, Noboru," he said to the older boy.

After a final smothering of kisses, Itoko drew herself woodenly to her feet. Closing her eyes, she divorced herself from what remained. Noboru took a tentative, embarrassed step toward Hiroshi, then grabbed him in a fierce hug. The boys looked into each other's eyes for a moment, then stepped back as if on signal and bowed deeply.

Both father and son were silent as they walked the seven blocks to Seizo Hoshi's house. Sataro ambled along slowly, holding Hiroshi's hand, wanting to savor as much as possible of their last moments together. He stared into the brilliant crimson blaze behind the western hills. Nowhere, he thought, could there be such striking sunsets. But such thinking couldn't blot out the heaviness. He glanced down at his solemn son, wishing he could pick him up and carry him, hold him tight the rest of the way. He *was* a beautiful boy! Memories flashed back as if someone were flipping giant pages in a photograph album . . . his first glimpse of the squalling, red-faced infant who had had such a difficult time being born—the first time he had taken him fishing, their first climb in the hills. . . .

"Each time there's a sunset, I want you to think of me," he said softly.

Hiroshi's eyes darted up, accompanied by a quick smile. "I'll think of you more often than that, Father," he replied, obviously relieved at the break in the tension.

Sataro nodded, unable to find the rehearsed words he had been saving.

"Will you think of me often in America, Father?"

"Constantly, my son. You'll always be in my heart." *Where were the gentle, loving words?*

Hiroshi went a few more steps before asking, "And when you come back with all that money—then we'll be together forever?"

"Yes, my son," Sataro replied, squeezing his hand more tightly. He walked for another few seconds before starting the painful part. "Remember, Uncle Seizo will be every bit your father, just as I've been. Obey him in every way and learn to love your aunt."

"Yes, Father, I know. And I'll study hard. You'll see."

"Good boy. Your grandfather's heroic death only grants you the opportunity to attend the military academy. You have to *earn* everything else."

The boy nodded, scowling as a schoolmate ran by with a taunt.

"You're my standard-bearer, Hiroshi—I'm depending on you," Sataro continued.

Hiroshi didn't understand it all. How could he? his father thought. How could a ten-year-old boy comprehend how important it was for the second son to remain in Japan to carry on, to be the next generation's rock while his dream-seeking father went off to a new land?

But Hiroshi instinctively replied, "I'll make you proud, Father," in a voice rich in young bravado.

Sataro cleared his throat as his brother's house came into sight. The weight of the coming moment crashed down on him. He suddenly wanted to turn and run back. What had he done? What sane man would rush off to another world and give up a son he loved so dearly? He stopped and knelt beside the boy, searching the brown eyes, feeling panic. Placing his hands on Hiroshi's shoulders, he spoke gruffly, "Always remember that I love you."

Hiroshi's eyes widened; the lump grew in his throat. He searched his father's wide-set dark eyes, holding back the tears, wondering if his tall, handsome father ever cried. No, he *couldn't* show such weakness! Could he hug him here on the street—just once! Slowly his arms came up and around his father's neck. Throwing his head impulsively against Sataro's chest, he whispered huskily, "I love you, Father."

Sataro held him tightly for a moment, then slowly pushed him away. Drawing himself up stiffly, he cleared his throat and began the last few steps to his brother's house.

*   *   *

Sataro and Seizo left the house at shortly after seven to make the rounds of Sataro's favorite drinking places and geisha houses. Although he had cut down considerably on his drinking since he had washed the taste and some of the memories of war away, Sataro was still an infrequent but popular customer. Quick to buy a drink, often with a new joke, and never settling for less than a twelve-yen geisha, he would be missed. After the third stop, Seizo eagerly asked, "Think we ought to honor a licensed place? It would be a fine way to send you off. I'll buy!"

The sake said "yes," but Sataro shook his head. Even though Itoko had held him off for so long, this night was for good-byes, not sex. "No." He laughed. "You'll get greedy and we'll never get out."

Seizo snorted. "Everyone knows you're the satyr in this family!"

"No," Sataro insisted. "But I read where the famous Yanagibashi geisha from Tokyo are at the Miyume House this week. Why don't you buy us a little culture?"

"I can read about culture at home," his brother grumbled.

They caught a rickshaw and entered the geisha house ten minutes later. The entertainment by the geisha troupe was in the middle of its presentation as they were quickly seated on soft pillows in a crowded corner of the packed Miyume House. The makeshift stage at the far end of the main lounge was brightly lit, while the rest of the room was illuminated only by tiny incense candles on the low, cramped tables. As sake was served, they turned their eager attention to the performance.

The Yanagibashi were doing their small-scale rendition of the Genroku cherry blossom dances, with each member of the troupe dressed and made up as a traditional character. Sataro had read about the production, so he recognized the seller of woodcuts, the haiku master, the flower seller, the samurai—of course—the female Robin Hood, the young hero, the blind minstrel, and others. He marveled at their lithe grace as both the younger and older geisha, whether playing male or female characters, danced and mimed their roles as fluidly as a mountain waterfall cascading over familiar boulders.

He watched their bright laughing eyes, darting around like fireflies on a June night, as their facial expressions ranged from mock anger to elation, from gravity to flirtation, from scorn to ecstasy, as if on command from a master puppeteer. He found them exhilarating, exotic, tragic, as he lost himself in the players rather than the themes. For over forty minutes and more sake than he needed, he was entranced, immersed in the pool of their glowing sunshine.

And suddenly it was over. The bright stagelights went out abruptly as multicolored glass lanterns began to emit a dim glow from the ceiling. Within moments, the cast was mingling, blending its way through the wildly appreciative throng to join tables and share its charm in the primary geisha role.

Before Sataro could stop him, Seizo had lunged somewhat drunkenly to his feet and was reeling toward the thinning cast. And then he was back, leading a village maiden and the poet by their delicate, manicured hands. As his brother made the introductions, Sataro thought soberly of how much even one hour's company with one of these scintillating creatures would cost. But only for a moment. He was soon looking into the compassion and gentility of the poet's wide brown eyes. Her low, silky voice seemed to tumble out of her appealing scarlet lips like the sound of a soft summer wind. Had he enjoyed the performance? she asked.

And within minutes, she had skillfully and professionally started his catharsis, listening to his exciting tale of going to America with the rapt attention of someone who might be sharing the great adventure. When his enthusiasm turned to the pain his day's efforts had produced, her soft eyes reflected her anguish as they welled up with tears. She soothed him with the gentle caress of her warm hand and the purr of her concerned voice. And when he switched to the tale of how he had bribed the passport people to meet the age limit of thirty, she clapped her hands discreetly but gleefully and let her appreciative laugh tinkle out like sparkling crystal.

He had never met such an accomplished, overwhelming geisha! It was the magic of make-believe that even his most imaginative dreams couldn't inspire. When she touched his cheek with her long, delicate fingers and told him she must return to her group, he felt as if he had spent the last two hours in a warm, clean stream of purified spring water.

He was ready to run outside, sprint to the docks, spit on that old tub that awaited them, and dash madly across the Pacific on feet of Mercury that couldn't possibly slow down to sink!

At shortly after midnight, the brothers staggered arm-in-arm, boisterously singing "Roei no uta," the Camp Guards' Song, to the entrance of Seizo's street. As they stopped Sataro broke away in laughter, then soberly bowed so deeply to his brother that he almost lost his balance. Grabbing Seizo's arm, he exclaimed, "Honorable brother, you must uphold the family honor in my absence to the land of the unenlightened!"

Seizo hiccuped. "Yes, honorable older brother, master of the House of Hoshi!" he shouted back. "And you must carry the— the code of Bushido to the imperious ignorant Americans!"

"*Right!*" the grinning Sataro roared, throwing his fist into the air. "*Justice!*"

"Yes, Justice!"

"*And Courage, Benevolence, and,* uh, *Politeness—above all Politeness!*"

Seizo's eyes lit up. "Always, politeness, illustrious brother!"

Sataro rammed his fist high again. "*Veracity and Loyalty!*"

"Right! But you forgot *Honor!*"

Sataro grabbed his brother by the arms. "Above all, *Honor!* Without honor, *hara-kiri!*" He whooped, suddenly dropping to a squatting position and looking dejected. "How will I survive among the barbaric Americans? I hear they don't even have such a code. What shall I do?"

Seizo dropped down in front of him, staring with concern and hiccuping. "You're . . . the one with all the *chikara*," he said, nodding emphatically. "You'll . . . teach them."

Sataro blinked, knowing he would, but wondering how. By exemplary conduct, of course, he said to himself. By example! He leaned forward, almost bumping his brother's nose. "I'll enlighten them," he whispered conspiringly. "I'll set such an example, they'll *have* to join me." He lurched to his feet, feeling the power surge through his muscular form. "And when I've completed my mission, I'll return to my heritage with—'' he burped—''the undying friendship of ten thousand Americans!'' He looked down at his brother who had just tipped over trying to get up. ''And now, it's time.''

Seizo managed to get to his feet to bow. He screwed up his face rigidly as he said, ''Farewell, honorable—oh, Sataro, how I'll miss you!''

Sataro reached out and pulled him to his chest, comforting him as he had when they were young. A tear slipped down his cheek as he held his brother tightly. Damn sake! he growled to himself. ''Goodbye, Seizo,'' he whispered.

Two

Sataro couldn't figure out why the charming name of *Tenshi-Maru* had been given to the old freighter. An angel or cherub signified something pleasant, lovely, young, of mystic portent—none of which could possibly apply to the crew, captain, or the ship itself. He guessed their vessel must have been one of the budding Japanese shipping industry's first coal-burning freighters. Perhaps, he had thought, the old boat needed a *tenshi* to get it to its destination. Or if they made it, the feat in itself would be a mystical result.

He had been tempted to book passage on the nobler *Hiroshima-Maru*, a much newer and pretentious ship, but he couldn't justify wasting the money. Nor, however, would he hear of traveling steerage. Nearly three hundred passengers were crammed down in the hold, packed like tiny oysters in a metal can. Narrow little beds with straw mattresses constituted each passenger's living space; three toilets for the men and two for the women. It was hard enough to imagine sixty fussy females with all their cumbersome attire trying to get by with two, but the thought of all those men lined up in distress made him shudder. And just three large tubs for bathing—how horribly dirty that soaking water must get by the end of the line!

No! If Sataro Hoshi couldn't afford a cabin for his family, he couldn't go!

Of the seven cabins for passengers on the *Tenshi-Maru*, two had the dubious designation of "first class." The others could more aptly be called closets. Six narrow bunks with hard padded mattresses left only a narrow aisle for movement, while the tiny drop desk with its stool and the pitted sink took up the space at the end of the cramped cubicle. Fortunately, the cabin was on the outboard side of the companionway, affording a porthole for some fresh air. But now, Itoko had it shut tightly against the cool wind. Their baggge was stowed on the empty bunks, lined up as if the captain were going to inspect them, and satisfying her obsession for cleanliness and order.

She was lying on a lower bunk as he entered the cabin. As Noboru turned to greet him excitedly from the porthole, Sataro asked, "Would you two like to come up on deck for a final look? The rain has all but stopped."

Itoko remained silent as Noboru scampered down from the stool. "Can we still see Hiroshima?" he asked eagerly. His mother had refused to let him go up in the drizzle.

"Yes, if we hurry."

They had barely reached the stern when the light rain resumed. But off in the distance—as if to offer a final farewell—a blanket of sunshine flashed down on the city. Sataro caught his breath. Hiroshima was lit up like the stage of the geisha house the night before, but none of the characters was moving. "Look, son," he said, pointing. "It's like a brilliant omen sent down from Heaven just for us."

Noboru caught his hand, saying nothing as he stared.

Sataro enjoyed the comfort of the relaxed relationship he had with his elder son. Often, like now, they shared a natural understanding and appreciation of things. At times, they could be together for nearly an hour without speaking; in other instances, they chattered like two playmates. At eleven, Noboru was an extremely bright and collected boy. With traces of his father's strong features and his mother's narrow nose, he showed promise of becoming an extremely handsome young man. And he was already as tall as some Japanese men. Sataro hoped he would have the athletic agility for baseball and the other American sports he had read about. All he could teach him was the use of the sword and the modern form of jujitsu known as judo.

Noboru was standing with his mouth partially open, drinking in the beauty of his birthplace. "Look, Father," he finally whispered. "It's like the gods drew a curtain."

Sataro didn't know if the hole in the overcast had snapped shut or if a rain squall had hurried between them and their precious view. Whatever the reason, the brilliant sight had vanished, replaced by a dull gray mist.

"Father," Noboru exclaimed, moving around toward the side rail. "There's Miyajima!"

Off to the right, the mystical island rose majestically in its mist-shrouded elegance as the freighter plowed farther into the choppy Inland Sea. Cold and aloof in its dark greenery, it truly looked like the dying place of the gods. One would never know, Sataro thought, how warm and beautiful that ominous-looking shape could be in the brightness and happily blossoming flowers of spring. So many times he had visited its remarkable floating shrine and sailed around its famous guardian *torii*. His closest friend, Hirobumi Kaibara, kept a comfortable old inn there, and had served him a sumptuous farewell feast only three nights earlier. It was then that he had forged the final alliance that would bring Noboru back to Japan. He had pledged his son in matrimony to Kaibara's delicate and already beautiful seven-year-old daughter, Haru.

Itoko fell wretchedly ill that night. By midnight she was no longer able to make it from her foul-smelling bunk to the ugly little sink, instead using the porcelain basin Sataro had acquired from the galley. She had never felt so miserable in her life, and Sataro's gentle efforts to wipe her brow and comfort her only made her distress all the more maddening.

What more could he do to her? she screamed to herself. Take her baby, force her from her loving home into this ugly, swaying, bobbing cork to . . . to what? Die like this—it would be a most welcome blessing! The discomfort of the severe morning sickness she had experienced in both of her pregnancies was a distant, almost fond memory compared to this. At least that was over quickly. And Noboru—she had never permitted either of the boys to see her in disarray—how could he stand the sight of her? But he was asleep above her, probably filled with his father's stupid dream and lost in his reverie of bright castles and gold that poured from the ground like melted butter. They were both insane!

She tried to think of pleasant things, of her first sight of Hiroshi in his tiny soft blanket, his tip of a nose separating his bright little eyes. And how the love had burst through her when he first suckled on her nipple and was nourished by her milk. Of his first words and his first awkward steps and his first day in school in his cute little uniform . . .

And finally, she dozed off.

Her seasickness lasted for five days, but it was another three days of forcing down first tea, then soup, and eventually some rice before she felt like fixing her face sufficiently to venture outside for some fresh air. She was certain she would be a wretch for life. But the following day the dark circles around her eyes began to disappear and a touch of color came back to her cheeks. Most importantly, she felt her vital strength seeping back through her veins. She sent Noboru to fetch hot water, soap, and disinfectant. By noon, most of the odor of her sickness had been washed out of the still hideous prison Sataro had provided for them.

That afternoon, in spite of herself, she agreed to go for a walk on deck with her husband. The day was clear and bright, a tonic in itself. And it was the first time she had seen the steerage passengers since embarking on that dreary day. As they worked their way through the mingling groups on the main deck, she stole glances at the women, most of them the picture brides she had heard about. She had sniffed disdainfully at the idea of a decent woman being so unattractive or so desperate that she would get involved in a marriage by mail. None of the conventional, correct arrangements by families, not even a courtship—just the exchange of pictures and letters with a total stranger. She found the idea repulsive!

Sataro had tried to explain that it was the only way most of the poor immigrants in America could obtain or afford a wife, but it didn't change her opinion. It was just another example of how degrading life in this wilderness of savages had become for men who couldn't make a living at home. His statement that they couldn't marry or even mix with American women meant nothing to her. Why should they even want to?

She was surprised to see that several of them were quite

attractive. Obviously, she thought with no thin veil of contempt, something else had to be wrong with them. All one had to do was look at the immigrant men—all village louts or laborers of some sort, parading around in their cheap Western suits.

They had been standing up on the bow, squinting into the cool, refreshing wind for several minutes, when Sataro asked, "Is it too cold for you?"

"Yes," she replied curtly. "But it's better than that dreadful cabin."

He was relieved that she was at least talking to him. "I'll get your shawl," he said quietly. She didn't answer as she turned back to the sea.

Halfway down the ladder leading to the main deck, he was surprised to see an exquisite young lady waiting at the bottom. He hurried the last couple of steps, nodded pleasantly and was about to pass when she asked, "Forgive me, sir, but is it too cool up there without a coat?"

He shook his head and started to answer as he looked into her face. He was jarred by the most radiant eyes he had ever seen! He felt as if he'd been struck by a cannonball. They were amber, wide, with tiny flecks of brown. They made him think of all the colors of autumn blended like bright gold into a pair of amazingly beautiful spheres . . . pleasant, innocent eyes with a touch of humor and mysticism. Was she the Sun Goddess? Eurasian? But no, her face was classical Japanese—the silky, unblemished skin, the inviting rose petal lips, the long black eyelashes. . . .

He managed to mumble, "No, it's cool, but . . . quite pleasant. On the other hand—" her brilliant smile only added to his confusion "—you might take a shawl."

"Thank you," she said pleasantly, gathering her kimono and reaching for the handrail.

He felt his pulse quicken. If he moved, she'd be gone. "I'm Sataro Hoshi," he said, trying to clear his suddenly constricted throat. "Are you one of the picture brides? I mean, I haven't seen you before."

She nodded. The top of her head glistened like black satin in the sunlight. "Yes, I'm Miss Takano," she replied demurely in a manner of speech that suggested more culture than village life could provide. "I haven't been on deck since the ocean illness took me." She glanced meaningfully at the blocked ladder.

He couldn't think of anything else to say. His feet felt as if they were welded to the deck, but he managed to let her pass. Turning as she climbed daintily upward, he drank in the sight of her fully rounded buttocks and shapely calves as the bright-colored kimono stretched tightly with each step.

Noboru's excited voice broke his reverie. "Father! I just talked to a man up on the stern who said he knew you in the army!"

Sataro dragged himself back to reality. "What's his name, son?"

"Togasaki. Come, I'll show you where he's waiting!"

Togasaki! But the man was *dead!* "Are you sure?" he asked, following his son's hurried steps through the milling passengers. The last time he saw Yoshi Togasaki was at the Battle of Uiju on the Yalu River in Korea. That was where he had taken the saber slash in the cheek. He thought back to that terrible day when his battalion was on a small hill south of where the Yalu made a short horseshoe bend. As a corporal of infantry, he wasn't aware of the overall battle scope, only that the Cossack cavalry, riding on magnificent mounts, charged fiercely up the hill and smashed through their outer emplacements. With infantry streaming behind and artillery shells crashing into his company's ranks, it was sheer panic for the defenders. He would never forget the stinging, blinding smoke, the deafening explosions, the acrid smell of bursting powder, and the screams of the wounded and dying.

He and Yoshi, fighting side by side, had killed at least a dozen Russians when the Cossack's horse came flying over their barricade. He could see the officer's black mustache and streaming hair; the bright colors of his uniform and the flash of his saber, the insult on his twisted face as he was jerked out of the saddle to taste the fine Japanese steel of a lowly corporal's sword. It was as vivid as yesterday—the blood spurting from his cheek turning everything a blurring scarlet, the ear-splitting crash of the bursting shell no more than twenty yards away. He would never know how he escaped its jagged, snarling particles of death. Three of his comrades and Yoshi Togasaki didn't.

As he followed Noboru up the ladder to the stern, the thickset form watching him from the rail was immediately familiar to Sataro. The gritty farmer from south of Hiroshima was three years younger, but his naturally rough features, combined with whatever horrors he'd encountered since that terrible day, made him look far older. *"Yoshi!"* Sataro shouted, running forward.

The stocky man's leathery face broke into a broad grin as he bowed vigorously. "So Corporal Hoshi is alive," he said with a short laugh. "I was afraid the boy had the wrong father!" He turned to the beaming, stout woman beside him. "This is my wife, Kimi, the fairest maiden in my village."

Her head bobbed forward in an energetic bow. Sataro noticed how her prominent white teeth were accented by a wide pleasant face that had been darkened by long years in the sunlit fields. Her eyes showed a touch of merry mischief and he guessed she was about nineteen. But the young bride was unimportant at the moment. He turned back to the grinning Yoshi, grabbing his muscular arm. "What are you doing alive, you rascal?" he asked excitedly. "The last I saw of you, most of your leg had been blasted away and the Russians were still coming at us like a thundering herd."

"The gods smiled on me, old friend." Yoshi laughed, limping away a few paces and returning. "A friendly Russian doctor sewed my leg back together and I lived through their terrible prison camp." He lifted his right leg and flexed it. "Not bad, huh?"

Sataro shook his head soberly. "Why didn't you come to see me during all this time? Or at least write and tell me you weren't disappointed in your ancestors?"

Yoshi's laugh seemed to tumble out of a deep cavern. "Because I went to America, my friend. I've just returned now to marry my Kimi." He cocked his head sideways at his smiling wife, then continued, "I have the nicest little house on the finest farm in the world waiting for us."

Sataro was puzzled. "You mean you already own a farm?"

"Oh, no." The cheerful man chuckled. "I work for a big American farmer in the land of marvelous grapes. But someday I'll own my own farm. The boss has promised me." He reached inside his cheap Western-style suit and withdrew two black cigars.

"I've been saving these," he announced, handing one to Sataro and fumbling for a match. "It's an American custom for weddings and other important occasions." He struck the match on the rail and lit them. "But I talk only of me. Is this your first trip to America?"

Sataro was excited as he puffed on the foul cigar. He had heard a hundred stories of America, but this was the first account of success from a man he trusted. "Yes," he replied eagerly. "But I've made a study. I—"

Yoshi's laugh interrupted him again. "A *study?* My friend, America is *there!* And why are you foolishly bringing your family? You should establish yourself first."

Sataro glanced down at the attentive Noboru. "Why don't you take Mrs. Togasaki up to the bow to see your mother. I'm sure they'll have much to talk about." Sataro turned back to his old friend. "I am not going to be a laborer," he said softly. "I have other plans to open a business in mercantile or lodging."

Yoshi snorted. "You and a thousand others. It takes money."

"I'm prepared. But enough of that—tell me about your beautiful land of grapes."

Meeting Yoshi was the turning point in the long, boring voyage. Each day, Sataro listened attentively to his friend's lengthy dissertations on life near Lodi in the San Joaquin Valley above a city called Stockton. It was the home of the Tokay grape, a special flame red specimen that only the peculiar breezes that reached Lodi could produce. He asked eager questions when he found that over two hundred Issei—as the Japanese immigrants were called—resided in the Lodi area. And Yoshi's glowing praise for the weather made it sound like Hiroshima without the mountains.

Kimi was just the right kind of medicine for Itoko. Her bright, pleasant village wit brought Itoko to a semblance of cheerfulness as the two women spent the next few days strolling on deck or chatting in the cabin. The Togasakis were traveling in steerage. Itoko's cheeks were usually bright when she returned from these visits to the deck, and Sataro heard her laugh with Noboru a couple of times. But she still treated him coolly, speaking to him only when it was necessary.

What troubled Sataro most, however, was the effect the picture bride had on him. Ever since their first encounter at the ladder, he found himself obsessed by her striking beauty. His mind wandered to her in the middle of conversations and her face blurred the pages when he tried to read. She smiled through his thoughts when he tried to sleep and floated through his dreams. Each time he went on deck, his eyes immediately swept the groups of young women or darted to a solitary figure. He saw her three times—once to ask about her comfort and prolong the encounter, another time while he was strolling with Yoshi. His friend had noticed his more than casual interest. "Thinking of collecting butterflies, Sataro?" he asked with a knowing grin. He had felt like a child, caught by his mother in the act of doing something terribly wrong.

The third time he saw her he was able to watch her undetected for several minutes. He heard her animated laugh—not like the tinkling of chimes the poets like to write about—but warm, throaty, sensual. The erectness of her carriage and her carefully done hair showed signs of pride and an awareness of her own beauty. But it was her eyes that haunted him most. They gave her an air of innocence, a gentle softness that demanded protection. No, she was no butterfly. The way her lips parted like the petals of a newly blooming cherry blossom, she was the exotic flower herself.

He was totally bewitched!

On their last day at sea, while he sat on the poop deck carving on a statuette for Noboru, he saw her strolling on the main deck with two other picture brides. They were chattering gaily, probably discussing what lay in store for them the next day. He caught his breath at her lovely profile.

Almost as if she had felt his intense gaze, she suddenly looked up at him. Their eyes locked on one another as if hypnotized by some mystical force. He knew he should turn away but he couldn't. For a brief moment, he thought he read invitation or at least a response to his intensity but she quickly lowered her head and turned back to her friends, pretending a laugh at something she had missed. As the little group moved on, she looked back

over her shoulder and smiled. Helplessly, he watched her melt
into the larger group of passengers. He could never remember
being so thunderstruck by anything or anyone. The pocketknife
and piece of wood that he held felt alien and his legs were a
crippling numbness.

This was insane! he shouted inwardly as he slashed the head
from the tiny wooden carving and threw it over the side. He was
acting like an idiotic schoolboy! He folded the jackknife and
angrily jammed it into his pocket, then lit a cigarette with a
trembling hand. Inhaling deeply and holding it for a moment, he
tried to regain control of himself. He stared out at the tiny
whitecaps and fought to conquer the driving urge to run after her,
pull her away from those giggling girls and tell her how he felt.
Pure madness! He looked again out to sea, focusing on another
ship passing far in the distance. But it was no good. He could not
brush aside the image of this amazing young woman. His eyes
wandered back to the center of the ship. She was gone.

"Is my soldier finished yet, Father?" Noboru shouted from the
deck.

"No," he answered. "It split." Now he was lying to his own
son.

"Harry! Oh, my wonderful Harry!"

Miyuki Takano held the wrinkled sepia photograph at arm's
length, thinking he seemed to smile back at her. She liked to
picture him with a warm pleasant smile, instead of the grim,
expressionless image a Japan man always presented when he was
photographed. Crushing the photo to her breast and closing her
eyes, she whirled round and round in the confined space by her
narrow bed. The spin ended as she dropped on her straw-covered
bed with an exuberant whoop! She didn't even look up to see
who might be watching—she didn't care! Holding the photograph
high above her head, she laughed. "Soon, my strong warrior.
Soon, we'll be together!" She hugged his image tightly. Would
he really be as handsome as his picture—or maybe as that
attractive Mr. Hoshi? Mr. Harry Yagana of San Francisco. Her
Harry, she had been calling him. A flood of warmth swept over

her. She could feel his strong arms around her, his lips pressing against hers. It would be so *wonderful!*

She sniffed at the smell of stale vomitus and the musty odor of the hold that never seemed to go away. The annoying sounds that always echoed through steerage were bearable, but the suffocating exhaust of too many bodies jammed together for so long was not. She thought of the slop she had eaten for two weeks and the terrible theft of her privacy at the toilet and the jammed bath. She shuddered inside the clothes that needed a day's scrubbing, feeling dirtier than ever in her life. She had stayed in that tub of filthy water until someone had cursed at her, but it was useless. The first thing she'd do at Harry's place, she vowed passionately, would be soak and soak and *soak* for hours in a luxurious, steaming bath!

Closing her eyes, she drifted back to the comfortable village outside of Hiroshima, where her father's disgrace as an embezzler had ruined her forthcoming marriage as well as chances for another favorable match. For another year she was shackled to the fallen family, doomed to a life in the fields as a farmer's wife at best. And already nineteen! Her childhood dream of a tall, strong warrior was fading fast. Then came the flurry of interest over going to America as a picture bride. Half as a joke and curious to see what responses she might get, she gave her name to one of the girls who was leaving soon for America.

Six weeks later, the first letter arrived. It was from a man named Harry Yagana who owned a hotel in San Francisco. He had been there for eight years, was quite successful, and offered to exchange pictures with her. The joke became a reality—she could actually escape! She had rushed all the way to Hiroshima to get a good, professional picture taken, mailed it off, then waited with overpowering interest for the return mail.

Miyuki held the photograph high over her head again. He looked tall, with a wide jaw and fierce, trustworthy eyes; a big mustache and expensive Western clothes. And only thirty years old! Harry Yagana—she wondered why he had taken an American name.

Suddenly she dismissed her thoughts, sat up quickly and carefully replaced Harry's picture in her purse. Tomorrow, my love. Tomorrow I'll be with you! She hummed gaily to herself as she began to polish her nails.

Sataro was up before dawn the next morning, standing in the chill breeze at the bow so he wouldn't miss the first glimpse of landfall at daybreak. The captain had warned him that it might be shrouded in fog, but he didn't care. Nothing could obscure his excitement! He lit his first cigarette and pulled the lapel of his coat up around his neck. Shaking off a sudden shiver, he smiled at the thought that the *Tenshi-Maru*'s creaking night sounds and foul odor would soon be behind him. The tedious part was over!

No more than three minutes passed until he saw the first break in the velvety darkness to the east. In another five minutes, the sky was turning to a bright peach. And then, suddenly, the top of a huge red-orange ball began to swell until it hung eerily like an invading spirit.

It was the goddess of dawn—*Waka-hirume-no-mikoto*—in all her cosmic power! *How could he forget?* She was the most important of all the deities, the spirit of the Land of the Rising Sun. And the symbolism of her mystic rise on this most important of mornings had to be a marvelous omen!

Sataro murmured a haiku poem, followed by a short sunrise prayer, as the mammoth ball of fire retreated from its illusion to normal size and bright intensity. Below the glare, the hazy distant shadow on the horizon began to lose its violet cast and take form. The captain was wrong, he told himself jubilantly. There was no mist, no fog, only the coastline of the dream. The United States of America with all its opportunity was greeting him!

Three

The *Tenshi-Maru*'s anchor chain rattled from the stern just as its hawsers dropped to the dock. As if to celebrate the fact that the old ship had made it again, the brightly painted tug erupted with a harsh congratulatory blast from its steam whistle, then chugged away with an air of importance. Near the rail close to the debarkation point, Sataro hoisted Noboru up on his shoulders so the boy could get a better view of the scene below. "We're finally a part of America, son," he said excitedly. He looked around to see if Itoko was showing any interest, but she had evidently gone back to the cabin.

"What do you see?" Sataro asked his son enthusiastically.

"Big, hard buildings and many men!" the boy replied eagerly. "Everything's so bright and pretty! And carriages and an autocar, and soldiers!"

Sataro could see some of the teeming activity on the dock. "Those Japan men who look so worried and also so excited are waiting for the picture brides," he explained.

Miss Takano! Was she standing nearby, excitedly searching for her groom? He glanced quickly around, but didn't see her. He was almost glad. He had had a stern talk with himself over the previous day's absurdity and vowed it wouldn't happen again. He was a responsible married man about to begin his destiny, and she was—

"Father!" Noboru shouted. "The soldiers are coming aboard!"

Sataro strained to see several blue-uniformed men in their short-billed caps coming up the gangway. The Caucasian faces looked stern and intent. But they should—didn't they have to examine almost three hundred arrivals? Each person coming in had to be checked for disease—which meant a thorough physical examination. He had heard about picture brides going through many embarrassing indignities, and again thought of Miss Takano. Shutting her out, he switched to Itoko. This coming ordeal was mostly what she was unhappy about this morning—that and the inevitable arrival in San Francisco.

Itoko was furious! Nudity in the public bath was one thing, but to undress and be required to take an unnecessary cleansing in front of these leering Americans was the most degrading thing she had ever encountered. And down in steerage too! She was a lady of quality and position—not one of these farm wenches who had to resort to the mails to find a husband! She glanced around at the wide-eyed apprehension of the clustered nudity. Certainly, traveling cabin class should have *some* advantages!

She watched Kimi Togasaki splashing her sturdy, unattractive body and smiling pleasantly. She liked Kimi, but her cheerfulness over such an insulting ordeal only emphasized the social gap between them. She—

Itoko was startled by a sharp cry to her right. One of the brides had drawn back, her eyes open in shock. An immigration official had reached out to touch her breast. With a rude laugh, he said, "I'm just counting them, honey. We ain't allowed to let any defective ones in."

Itoko shuddered, quickly snatching the towel up over her midsection. The thought of exposing her delicate body to this dirty ruffian made her flinch. Her waist was a bit thicker and the firm little breasts that Sataro had once made so much over were softer after two children, but she was still proud of her shapely form and didn't want it defiled by the lecherous eyes of this approaching beast!

As the man moved to Kimi and began checking her body, Itoko closed her eyes in nervous revulsion. Moments later she jerked stiffly and opened her eyes as a hand slapped her sharply on the buttocks. "Okay, missy, turn around," the harsh voice ordered.

She groped, then found the words. In a heavy accent, she

spoke coldly and resolutely, "I am Mrs. Hoshi, not a bride. We are in cabin three."

The official walked around to her front, glancing appreciatively at her breasts. "Very well, Mrs. Hoshi, you just let go of that towel and we'll get you out of here as soon as possible. You been sick in the last three years?"

Because they were a family and also cabin passengers, the Hoshis' inspection was expedited and they were among the first to leave the old freighter. Laden with the bags that held the balance of their possessions, they reached the dock and dry land for the first time in fourteen days. Sataro looked around the waiting throng, trying to spot the emigration company's welcome man. He saw a Japanese man wearing a white uniform cap talking to several anxious-looking men by the edge of the dock. Telling Itoko to wait, he made his way over to the man.

When the official finally turned to him, Sataro gave him his name, then waited while he scanned his manifest. "Oh, yes," the man in the white cap replied in Japanese, pointing to where a horse-drawn streetcar was waiting. "Take that car up to Van Ness, then get a transfer to Geary. When you get there, turn right and walk four blocks. That's the center of Japan Town. Do you have a place to stay?"

"Yes," Sataro replied, glancing apprehensively at the streetcar. "The Osaka-ya Boardinghouse and Hotel. Do you know it?"

The official shrugged. "Good as any. Do you have any American money?"

"Yes. What do you mean by transfer?"

The official explained, wished him luck and turned back to the troublesome picture grooms. Shortly after the Hoshis boarded the car, it began its laborious climb from the docks to the colorful homes that dotted the city's hills. While Itoko sat stiffly behind them, Sataro and Noboru had to work at curbing their excitement over the sights. In spite of having read several books about this great American city, they gawked at its wonders as if they came from the most remote village on Hokkaido.

Sataro knew all about the earthquake that had nearly destroyed it a year earlier, and that the Japanese government had sent

$225,000 for relief. As the car moved up to Telegraph Hill and crossed Kearny Street, he noticed the half-erected skeletons of several large structures in the distance. He was surprised to see so many buildings still standing and the calm cleanliness of the streets. The abruptness of the sharp incline of Union Street startled them as it crested Russian Hill. Many of the large houses were imposing, but their bright pastel colors, mixing with the balmy Hiroshima-like weather, made him feel comfortable. Noboru commented on the absence of Japanese people, but otherwise continued to point out the marvels, particularly the many motorcars. One block was jammed with shops and busy-looking people. Sataro took it in with a sharp eye, noting the types of businesses.

"There!" he said with animation to Itoko. "Look at that lovely dress shop!"

But she was having none of it, instead glaring at the floor of the car and raging inwardly about the fumigation procedure that had been the final blow before leaving the ship.

After finally making it to Van Ness Avenue and transferring to a southbound car, they headed into the more commercial area that led to Geary Street. Many people had gotten on and off the car by this time, but at California Street a smiling Japanese man stood beside them. He knew by their baggage that they had just arrived and eagerly began a conversation. Eight short blocks later he announced that they were at Geary, dismounted with them, and led them pleasantly up the hill to the west that approached Japan Town.

Their guide noted Sataro's disappointment when they walked over the crest and headed down into the obviously less attractive area of shabby, closely packed two- and three-story buildings. Laundry hung from the upstairs windows and many roughly dressed Japanese men loitered in small groups on the street. "It isn't easy for a Japan man to have steady work," he explained. "Many jobs are not open to us." He pointed to the faded wood front of the Osaka-ya Hotel across the street, then wished them well and disappeared into a nearby laundry.

The new arrivals were soon in a small room, well back on the second floor. Four low narrow beds greeted them, followed by a coffee table with a scarred finish, a worn chiffonier, and a rack for hanging clothes. A yellow print of Mount Fuji was the only decoration on the peeling walls.

Itoko grunted, then sniffed disdainfully as she looked around and remembered her clean lovely house in Hiroshima. "So this is your great America," she murmured coldly.

Sataro sighed, glancing quickly at Noboru, who was peering down at the back alley from the only window. "It's only temporary," he mumbled, sharing her disappointment. Fighting back the feeling of gloom, he backed into the dimly lit hallway, saying, "I must go find Reverend McAllister. When I return, I'll take you out to eat and show you around."

"Can I go, Father?" Noboru asked excitedly from the window.

"No, my son. Help your mother unpack," Sataro replied softly, then turned to get away from the cheated look Itoko gave him as she pulled the long hatpin from her glossy black hair.

The *Fukuin Kai*—the Gospel Society—was located about a block and a half down the street at 529½. Although it was painted white inside, the lack of side windows made the large main room dim, producing more gloom for Sataro as he entered. The tightly arranged wooden benches suggested that the room was also used for services. He nodded to the group of men who eyed him curiously, then asked where he might find McAllister.

Moments later, he was in a small back office shaking hands with a short, sturdy man of about forty-five. The bushy, over-hanging eyebrows and a scraggly fringe around McAllister's ears were all that remained of a once heavy shock of carrot-colored hair. He wore eyeglasses over a pair of intensely blue and heavily pouched eyes that smiled often. And when he spoke his gravelly voice issued from below a graying, walrus-type mustache. After offering Sataro a chair and dispensing with the formalities, the minister asked, "So what are your plans, Mr. Hoshi?" His laugh was short and pleasant. "Are you to become a success for me to crow about to Macnamara?"

Sataro was surprised that he should bring up the Christianity problem so abruptly. "I must get to that when I'm settled, Reverend McAllister," he replied quietly. "In the meantime, I wish to find out where I can best start my new life." Frowning, he added, "My wife is accustomed to better living accommodations than our hotel, so I don't want to waste time."

McAllister studied the letter from Macnamara. Finally, he said, "I see you're well educated and a successful merchant, Mr. Hoshi. Hmmm. Do you have any particular desires? Will you be staying in San Francisco?"

Sataro shook his head. "I don't know, sir."

McAllister stared back at the letter for a few moments, then scribbled a note and handed it to Sataro. "I want you to take this to Mr. Kyutaro Abiko at the *Nichi Bei*—the *Japanese-American News*. He's president of that newspaper and the past leader of this society. He may have some advice for you."

Sataro had to walk through the printing room to get to Abiko's office. Although not normally interested in machines, he stopped three times to watch the process of a newspaper being printed. The Japanese men attending the press glanced up briefly, but went back to their work as Sataro moved on. What a powerful thing to do, he thought, publish a newspaper. The reflection wouldn't go away during the fifteen minutes he waited in the small room outside the president's office, nor as he entered to meet Abiko.

Kyutaro Abiko was stocky, bordering on plump, in his early forties. Already, the well-trimmed hair at his temples was showing touches of gray—an effect that complemented his wide mouth and strong jaw. Sataro had heard of him in Hiroshima; along with the famous "potato king," George Shima, Abiko was one of the most famous of the Japanese immigrants. A community leader, as well as a successful businessman, he had just the year before founded a special agricultural project known as the Yamato Colony. A meeting with him, Sataro knew, was highly providential.

Abiko hurriedly read McAllister's note when the formal bows of introduction were completed. Indicating a chair beside his desk, he glanced up and said in excellent English, "You're a rarity, Mr. Hoshi, bringing your family and resources. What line of business do you propose to enter?"

Sataro sat on the edge of the straight-backed chair and spoke respectfully, "I was hoping you might recommend something, sir."

Abiko snorted pleasantly. "My colony needs a store, but there aren't enough people there to make it a paying proposition yet. Besides, I want them to become members of the outlying community and shop with the local merchants. Do you wish to stay in San Francisco?"

Sataro studied his hat brim for a moment. "I don't know. Are there many opportunities here?"

The publisher snorted again, this time impatiently. "Opportunities are where you make them, Mr. Hoshi."

"I met an old army friend who spoke highly of a fruit-growing community by the name of Lodi. He said that a large number of Japanese had already settled there and more were arriving every day."

"Yes, south of Sacramento." Abiko nodded. "And they haven't had any trouble yet." Noticing Sataro's questioning look, the publisher went on. "Surely, you've heard of the prejudice against our people here?"

Sataro shook his head. "Only a little, sir."

Abiko sat back in his swivel chair. "I haven't the time to explain it in detail. Being Asian, we inherited it from the Chinese. From that point, organized labor, politicians, publishers such as Hearst, and other assorted bigots have built it into such a grave problem that the president of the United States had to intervene with our mayor. You'll learn more each day you're here."

Sataro fingered Macnamara's disk in his pocket. "I don't think it'll bother me, sir."

The publisher shrugged. "You are new. All right—Lodi," he said thoughtfully. "Yes, that might be a good place for an enterprising merchant. Yes, I'd take the train over to Stockton and look around. In the meantime, if I can be of further assistance, feel free to call on me."

Sataro got to his feet. "Thank you, sir. Uh, is there a Japanese newspaper in Lodi?"

The stocky man left his desk, replying pointedly, "I don't believe so, Mr. Hoshi. It takes two things to be successful in the newspaper business—enough advertisers and readers, *and* a knowledge of the business.''

Sataro thanked him, the two men bowed their farewell, and the interview was over. Again, as Sataro walked by the press, he stopped briefly to watch it work.

Miyuki Takano stepped onto the dock, feeling uncomfortable in her new Western ensemble and trying to quell her excitement as she looked curiously around for her handsome Harry Yagana. She moved to a nearby piling and stood hesitantly, trying to shut out the embarrassment of the last few hours. It seemed those hideous inspectors had found one reason after another to delay her departure, probing and fondling her nude beauty as if she were the only attraction on the boat.

She saw only a handful of what might be expectant husbands-to-be left on the dock and none of them looked remotely like her Harry. A sharp chill of fear swept through her as she recalled the stories of old or ugly men sending the pictures of others to the waiting girls in Japan. No! Her Harry wouldn't do that!

She picked up her cloth bag and resolutely stepped away from the piling just as a big black Duesenberg sedan pulled up and stopped abruptly beside her. A thickset Japanese man in a dark brown suit quickly stepped from the front. He held up a picture, glanced at her and nodded. ''You Miyuki Takano?'' he grunted in Japanese.

She nodded, wondering with a start if—

''My name's Howard,'' the man said perfunctorily. ''Get in. I'll take you to Harry.''

She started to ask a question, but the man took her arm and guided her into the back seat. ''Harry couldn't make it,'' was his only explanation as the Duesenberg lurched away into the bright San Francisco sunlight.

Twenty-five minutes later, the shiny sedan pulled up in front of a restaurant in Japan Town. Miyuki stared out the window with a touch of disappointment. Any city excited her, but she had expected more in the way of tall, gleaming buildings—not what looked like a poor section of Hiroshima! The man called Howard led her through a restaurant where a handful of curious male patrons glanced up from their bowls. A flight of stairs led to a heavy door and a large room that looked like a lounge. Passing through, they reached a small dark office, where Howard nodded, grunting for her to enter. Inside, seated behind a huge cluttered desk in the shadow of an oil lamp, was her *Harry!*

He looked a little like his picture, but older, somewhat menacing with dark slits for eyes. There was nothing warm in his rigid expression. He was wearing a hat and a long black cigar jutted from the side of his humorless mouth. She felt like a piece of cheap fabric that might be rejected as his cold gaze wandered from her face down over her body and back to her eyes. Maybe it was the darkness, she thought as he puffed on the cigar.

"Good morning, Miss Takano," he said finally, without rising.

She bowed, replying in a tiny voice.

Harry's tone was matter-of-fact as he growled, "Howard will take care of you."

What could be wrong? she wondered nervously. She had heard stories about how the brides were almost always rushed off to be married the moment they got off the boat. Could it be possible that he didn't like her looks? Maybe she wasn't dressed well enough. Maybe he wanted her to bathe first. That was it, he wanted her to wash off the stink of the ship. She tried to find his eyes as she asked timidly, "The wedding, Mr. Yagana. When—"

His abrupt laugh interrupted her. "I don't believe in marriage."

It took a moment for the words to register as Miyuki stared into his shadowed face. No, she . . . it wasn't true . . . she had misunderstood. Surely, there was some kind of mistake. Her cheeks began to smart, she felt nauseous as her stomach knotted. "But—"

"However," his deep guttural voice broke in, "we have employment for you. Right here, as a matter of fact." He left his chair, walking around the desk into the light. Appraising her from the front and back, he stopped at her face. "Yes, Miss Takano, you will be a superb addition to our business." He turned to Howard. "Show her to her room," he ordered.

Howard nodded. "Come with me, missy," he growled, pointing to the door.

Miyuki turned back to Harry Yagana's expressionless face. "I can't believe this," she mumbled.

Harry said nothing as he disappeared into the shadow behind the desk. Howard tugged at her sleeve, leading her dazedly out of the office and down a dark corridor with several other doors. She barely noticed as a tousel-haired pretty young Japanese woman, clad only in a revealing slip, stuck her head out the fourth door and said brightly, "A new lamb, huh, Howard?"

Moments later, they arrived at a small, simply furnished room with no windows and an American bed. "Are you a virgin?" Howard asked abruptly.

She felt the heat rush to her face as she dropped her bag. "Of c-course," she stammered in a tiny voice. "What—"

Howard grinned. "Then the boss will be down later."

As the truth began working its way through her smarting humiliation, Howard left to be replaced by the grinning face of the woman in the slip. "Welcome to the Mansion," she said pleasantly. "Are you staying here, or going to one of their other houses?"

Miyuki slumped onto the bed. "What *is* all this?" she cried.

"My dear, you're the Gorotsuki Club's newest whore."

Harry Yagana's real name was Kioji Homma, but that name remained in Tokyo when he bought the rigged passport to come to America in 1895. Also behind him were several violent crimes compiled as an enforcer for the *yakuza*. With credentials from his old bosses, it had been no problem to quickly move into the Gorotsuki Club operation—the vice group that controlled the bordellos and loan-sharking among the Japanese on the West Coast. While there were tentacles in Portland, Seattle, and in the small city of Los Angeles to the south, the main operation was in San Francisco. And in twelve years, Harry Yagana had risen to the number-three position in the club. Every bit as handsome and powerful as Miyuki had envisioned him, he had originated the "picture bride" hoax three years earlier and supplied the club's various houses with nearly thirty prostitutes since. His method was simply one of mastery and fear. His village girls lived in such total terror of him that they never dreamed of going to the uncaring, paid-off police, or writing home.

Now, as he made his way down the dark hallway to the newcomer's room, he could feel the excitement building. Nothing, he thought, equaled his coming treat! He stopped in front of her door and heard the soft sobs. Nodding in anticipation, he ground out the cigar, turned the handle, and entered.

Miyuki's hand flew to her mouth as she looked up from the bed. An hour of tears and trying to grasp the reality of her horror had already left her limp and confused. She looked into Yagana's glittering eyes and knew why he had come. She gasped in terror as she edged back on the bed. *This couldn't be possible!*

Yagana laughed. "Get those clothes off!" he snapped as he undid his necktie. She pulled farther back as he tossed his jacket on the floor and reached for his belt buckle. "I told you to get undressed!" he snarled.

Miyuki stared wide-eyed, trying to ward off the growing panic. This couldn't be happening, she told herself, it was all a hideous dream. That was it—she was back home in her own bed and all she had to do was snap out of it! There never was a Harry Yagana, no letters, no San Francisco—

"Now!" he shouted.

It couldn't be like this—not after all those years of dreaming about love! He was naked, but all she saw was a blur of flesh. She looked frantically for a way to escape. His bulk barred the door. She was in a trap without even a window to hurl herself through! He was moving toward her, his eyes boring into hers. She had never seen such a strange look, never been so frozen. She could feel his savagery, but couldn't break away from it. Something about him—what was it? The cobra! Weaving, transfixing its prey as it moved in for the kill. Harry Yagana was a cobra!

His hand was reaching out, the fingers curling and uncurling, his breath short and jerky. She had to tear her eyes away. Yes, turn and curl up in a ball, an impregnable circle. Those eyes. *I will!* she shouted to herself, snapping away from his gaze. The bedspread—that was it! She would wrap it around her like a shield. Then he'd see it was useless. . . .

He jerked the flimsy spread from her hands, tearing it apart and throwing it aside.

His hand was coming back. She wanted to scream, but nothing came out. Her throat was dry, choking. She squirmed backward to the last inches of the bed, rising to her knees as if to climb the wall, afraid to breathe. Her hands flew to her face, but he grabbed her wrist, jerking her forward. A jarring slap rocked her mouth, snapping her head back and producing an instant taste of blood. With a sharp *rip!* the front of her dress and slip was torn away. Her long hair was in her eyes, her mouth, as she groped to cover her breasts. He was on her, panting, twisting her arms painfully behind her back, jamming his exultant face into her chest.

She tried to cry out again. His ear—somehow she got her teeth into it. *Twist it, bite it off!* He was on his feet, roaring in pain, jerking her up and tearing away the rest of her clothes. His fingers were digging into her buttocks. Blood was running down his neck, but he was *grinning!* His face—get it! She slumped, throwing him off guard, then whirled, slashing across his cheek with her nails. He dropped her arm. The door, if only she could—

She was jerked painfully backward as his hand wound her hair into a knot. With a wild roar, he grabbed her around the waist and hurled her to the bed. She had almost made it—*couldn't quit now! Kick, bite, scratch!* The violent scream finally came out—a long piercing screech of agony that came from her soul and ended with a shudder. His vicious backhand slammed into her mouth, knocking away the last shreds of her will. She choked out a mouthful of blood, moaning in numbed defeat as he forced her limp legs apart and began to ram against her. The last thing she remembered was his fingers pawing roughly as a scarlet curtain of insensibility engulfed her.

Four

After taking his wife and son out to eat at a nearby Japanese restaurant, Sataro struck out on a long walk that took him out of Japan Town, back to Van Ness and down as far as Ellis. He felt comfortable, almost nonchalant, in the midst of all the well-dressed, bustling Americans and the busy street traffic. This was why the United States offered such promise, he thought, as he turned to retrace his steps—the *people!* Gone were the restrictions of their past in another world. They had confidence and a license to use it.

As he walked aimlessly back to the hotel, he studied the sights of the interesting streets, again noticing the abrupt change as he reentered Japan Town. The area around Post and Webster, while clean, was highly discouraging to a man who expected an empire. At quarter after four in the afternoon, children ran wildly around in the streets, shouting amid passing wagons, buggies and an occasional motorcar. Men who should be working stood lazily on corners and in front of dismal little shops with signs in Japanese by their doorways or on their darkened windows. While the rest of the city was brightly painted in fresh pastels, Japan Town appeared gray and unkempt. And he didn't see one single garden! How could these proud immigrants fall so low, how could they possibly permit such a pall of indifference to hang over their new life? Suddenly his disappointment turned to anger. *Why?* They might as well be back in Japan! Was this ahead for Sataro Hoshi?

He strode into a bar called The Lion, wondering if *it* had any spirit. But instead of the conventional *tatami*—sitting mats—and low tables, he found a long wooden bar along one wall. A hint of

47

incense was overridden by the stale smell of tobacco. He adjusted his eyes to the darkness as he moved through the stares of several jabbering men to an opening at the crowded bar. A short fat man in a white apron took his order for a sake.

"Welcome to America—again," the helpful man from the streetcar said from his left elbow. He introduced himself as Ito. "Did you get settled?"

"More or less," Sataro replied, signaling to the bartender to refill Ito's cup. He went on to describe his disgust at what he had seen.

"Don't let it inhibit you," Ito stated. "Life here is better than it looks." He was a stocky man with round eyeglasses in black frames and a nasal accent from Tokyo. "It's just that we don't have enough space, and we're not allowed to grow. Landlords won't permit it."

The frustrating anger that had overtaken Sataro made him want to get drunk. "Why is that?" he asked irritably.

Ito snorted. "Because we're Japanese—heathens from the Orient who've come to steal the white man's jobs. Coolies from Nippon, inferior intruders."

Sataro's mouth fell open. "You must be jesting."

"It's nothing to joke about, my friend."

"But the stories? In Hiroshima, we hear nothing but—"

Ito threw his head back and laughed. "You hear nothing but the stories of the Shimas and Abikos, the Morgans and the Goulds, the poor immigrant who grows rich and lives in a palace. I know. It was the same when I came two years ago. Well, my new friend, if you aren't wealthy, you had best put that pretty wife of yours to work for some rich lady and harden your hands for itinerant farm work."

"I'm no farmer," Sataro replied coldly, not ready to tell his new acquaintance everything.

"Then you might find work on the docks for a while."

Ito was part owner of a small laundry. Over several sake, he explained that most Japanese businesses remained viable only because they were supported by their own countrymen. Restaurants, laundries, and the brothels sometimes attracted the *hakujin*, but not sufficiently to expect any future riches. "If one can get into the *right* business where the Japanese population is growing," he reflected, "it could be the key to success." He laughed. "For instance, if a thousand immigrants were to concentrate in one area and a man had the money to open a huge hotel, complete with brothel, gambling, and a bank. Maybe import some real geisha, instead of these imitations we have here. Shaking his head, Ito added, "But then, the Gorotsuki would take over and the investor would be in trouble."

Sataro was listening keenly, absorbing every iota of his free education. "Who are the Gorotsuki?" he asked as he ordered two more sake. He was startled to hear the answer, just as he was surprised to hear that the Japanese underworld had little to do with gambling because the Chinese had that vice under control.

After two more drinks, he thanked Ito and headed back to the hotel. San Francisco certainly didn't sound like the paradise he had dreamed about. He wondered if the other big cities like Portland and Seattle would be the same. Twice, from a short distance, he thought he saw Miss Takano and felt the same quickening of pulse that he had sensed on the boat. But each time, it was a stranger. How long, he wondered angrily, would it take to forget that silly fantasy?

During the next three days, Sataro looked more closely at Japan Town. He talked to proprietors of various businesses and found that Ito's assumptions were basically correct—they were in an economic circle of dependence on other Japanese immigrants. The possibilities of making money off the *hakujin*—the whites— were negligible. He talked to a labor contractor and found that the Japanese migrant workers were also victims, few of them making over thirty dollars a month in spite of rosy promises. The contractor, whose job it was to supply labor for the large farmers, also explained about the peculiar prejudice involving the laborers. "They're good, diligent workers who don't complain and are willing to accept the lower wages. This antagonizes the Irish and other *hakujin* who are competing for work. Add the color difference and it adds up to deep resentment. And here in the city, the politicians get elected by the masses, so they play on the theme."

Sataro read a bigoted editorial in the San Francisco *Examiner*. Abiko was also right! He met Ito in the Lion the next night and listened to the unnerving story of how the mayor—who was under criminal indictment for fraud—had used the earthquake as an excuse to segregate the schools the year before. "Only intervention by the government in Washington changed the edict," Ito explained. "And we don't know what concessions our own government made to Roosevelt. It's rumored that fewer immigrants will be permitted in the near future."

The thought was appalling to Sataro—if a Japanese businessman had to depend on Japanese customers, his growth required numbers. And where would that leave him—in another Hiroshima stymie? He didn't dare tell Itoko.

At shortly after three in the afternoon of the fourth day he was admitted to the office of the assistant vice-consul in the Japanese consulate on Geary Street. The wiry little man of about fifty greeted him pleasantly enough, but Sataro quickly got the feeling he was talking to another bored professional diplomat. Squinting into the afternoon sun streaming through the open window, Mr. Suenaga adjusted his starched wingtip collar and sighed. "Therefore, Mr. Hoshi, your channel for any complaints or affairs that might warrant our government's attentions should come through the Japan Association office nearest your domicile. An official paid by our government is there to be your contact with us, and we prefer that you go through him."

Sataro listened patiently as Suenaga went on to explain that another source of social fraternity could be found in the *kenjinkai*—the prefectural clubs; in his case a Hiroshima *kenjinkai*, if enough people from that area were available to form one.

Suenaga pulled out his pocketwatch, yawned and ended the meeting with, "Just remember that you are a foreigner here, Mr. Hoshi. The ways and laws of the Americans apply and there is little our government can do for you if you have problems."

As Sataro stepped out into the fresh warm air a few moments later, he made his decision. His friend Yoshi would have a curious visitor sooner than he thought.

"Itoko," Sataro said softly. "Are you asleep?"

The lamp had been turned out for some time and Noboru's deep breathing meant his son was asleep. There was no sound from Itoko, but he had heard her turning restlessly in the bed across from him. Kneeling quietly, he reached tentatively for her soft shoulder. "My darling, I have to talk to you," he whispered.

Itoko, wide awake on her side, stared at the wall and said nothing. Sataro stroked her shoulder gently. His fingers moved to her breast as he kissed her neck. "It's been a long time," he murmured. "I've missed you terribly." He felt her stiffen. "I know I've hurt you and I'm extremely sorry. Please try to understand."

His lips moved to her shoulder as his hand stroked her buttocks. "Let me hold you and tell you how much I love you," he persisted. But it was no use—her body was as rigid as a rock. Slowly, he withdrew his hand, moving back to his own bed. What more could he do? he asked himself irritably. One thing was certain—he wasn't *begging* anymore! He strode to the chiffonier, grabbed his cigarettes and matches, jerked the door open, and stormed into the dark hallway. The acrid taste of the cigarette didn't help. He was being treated like an outcast! How far did she intend to carry this stupid revolt?

He walked to the stairs and back, but it didn't help. The anger and frustration seemed to close in on him. He did have his *rights!* he growled angrily to himself. But he would never lower himself to insist on them. Besides, how could it be enjoyable that way? No, he wanted to go back in there, jerk her over on her back and ignite the fires she could *never* put out with animosity! He felt the surge of arousal as he took another deep drag from his cigarette. But that was no answer. No, he should throw on his clothes and go to one of those brothels Ito had told him about. Spend the whole night!

But that wasn't the answer either. There was none!

Inside the room, Itoko squirmed in her hard bed, her eyes closed tightly. She *wanted* him, wanted his power within her neglected body. But more than that, she needed the gentleness that usually followed. She wanted to be held close to his smooth chest and tell him how terribly he had hurt her, engulf him with the river of tears she had been fighting back so long. She wanted her pain to wrench his heart and make him beg forgiveness. She wanted to see the tears stream from his beseeching eyes until they joined with hers, soaking them both and cleansing them of this terrible crime. And then, he'd whisper that he had been wrong and send for Hiroshi immediately.

But she knew it couldn't happen.

She clenched her fists and buried her face in the pillow. But it was useless; the wetness burst through and ran down her cheeks to her ears and neck. She stifled a wrenching sob as she heard the door open and the padding of his footsteps.

The next morning, Sataro packed a small bag and took the early ferry to Oakland. He looked briefly at the city in the vicinity of the railroad station, then caught the Southern Pacific passenger train to Stockton. Sitting by a window, he watched the rich green and thickly forested hills as the engine worked its way north to San Pablo Bay, then eastward along the south side of Suisun Bay. Near where the wide Sacramento and San Joaquin rivers emptied into the end of the bay, the Diablo hills melted into the broadest expanse of valley he'd ever seen.

Although haze and low clouds clung to the far-off Sierra Nevadas to the east, the San Joaquin Valley was clear and bright in the morning sunlight. The still, warm air seemed to be saying "Welcome, welcome, welcome," in rhythm with the engine sounds and the clickety-clack of the iron wheels on the track. He wanted to grin and reach out the windows to feel it. Nowhere in Japan, he told himself with enthusiasm, did an open, thinly populated wonder such as this exist. There, only the steepest of slopes were untilled, while farms and villages jammed the landscape in every direction. He felt a sense of peace and knew instinctively that this massive, restful valley and all its riches would be his home for the coming years.

As if to curb his fervor, an old proverb popped into his mind. *"Rainen no koto o ieba, oni ga warau"*—"Speak of the year to come and even the devil laughs." He must control his emotions and go slowly in his decisions, or the devil most certainly could have cause to laugh! Still, he knew.

Arriving in Stockton, Sataro was surprised to see such an abrupt departure from San Francisco and what he was used to in Japan. The smaller town was spread out, with loads of wasted space between buildings. Standing on the platform as the other passengers moved off, he watched a boy of about Hiroshi's age roll a large hoop to where he was standing and stop to stare. A huge tan and white shepherd dog raced up, barking for the boy to resume their game, but his master continued to look at Sataro with wide eyes. Sataro smiled. "Can you tell me where the Japanese Association is located?" he asked pleasantly.

The boy stared at him for another moment, then rushed away. Sataro chuckled as he stepped down from the platform and headed toward a nearby business street. Seeing a pretentious-looking hotel with a sign reading "Saloon" in large gilt-bordered letters, he decided to try his first glass of American beer. In the lobby, an old man sitting by a brass spittoon looked over his newspaper and gave him a questioning stare as he entered. The room clerk at the registration desk did the same.

The paneled saloon was dimly lit by two gas lamps behind the ornately carved bar, where a portly man with a huge walrus mustache and a white apron around his girth was holding court with four well-dressed customers. Sataro glanced around, guessing that Stockton must be a busy city if everyone was working instead of drinking. He moved to the end of the polished bar and nodded to the bartender, hoping the American beer was as tasty as he had been told. When the men laughed loudly, he wondered if the bartender was a master storyteller.

A moment later, the fat man waddled toward him with a harsh frown on his face. "What do you want?" he asked gruffly.

"Sir, I would like your best beer, please. A glass," Sataro replied cheerfully.

The bartender's scowl melted into a wide grin as he turned back to the other customers. "Hear that, boys? This here slant-eyed fella wants a beer!" His scowl returned as he looked back at Sataro. "You new off the boat or something, boy?" he snarled.

Sataro didn't understand. He heard the men's raucous laughter and turned to see what was so humorous. "Did I say something wrong, sir?" he asked quietly.

"You sure as hell did, Emperor!" the bartender roared. "We don't serve no Japs in here, and you oughta know that!"

Sataro blinked as if he'd been struck by a whip. No one had

ever spoken to him in such a manner—except for perhaps a sergeant when he first entered the army. And then it hadn't been a matter of nationality. He was confused. He had steeled himself against this sort of thing, but in a public place, a business? He felt the sting on his hot cheeks as he balled up his fists.

"What's the matter, Jap, can't you hear?" the bartender rasped with narrowed eyes. "Get the hell out of here and go back where you belong!"

Sataro's rushing anger almost caused him to retort and reach across the bar for the sneering face, but he somehow managed to control himself. He glanced back at the amused looks of the others, then turned on his heel and stalked out. Burning with shame and fury, he went through the lobby hurriedly and stepped out into the glare of the indifferent sun. He wanted to storm back, grab the flabby bartender by the collar and drag him out!

Jamming his hands into his pockets in frustration, he felt Macnamara's silver disk, and wanted to throw it away. He saw a Japanese man in rough work clothes going by in a wagon drawn by two sturdy farm horses. "Hey!" Sataro shouted in angry Japanese. "I want to talk to you!"

The man grinned, hauling on the reins to stop the horses. "Sure!"

"You know where the Japanese Association office is located?"

"Just came from there. Nobody in. The secretary's gone to Sacramento today." The driver glanced down at Sataro's small valise. "You just get in?"

Sataro blew out a deep breath, calming himself. "Yes," he replied. "I'm going to Lodi and killing time before the next train. Is there a place where a man can get something to drink here?"

The farmer glanced knowingly toward the hotel, then nodded. "I could use one myself. Then, after I make a few stops, I'm going back to Lodi. You're welcome to ride along, if you aren't in a hurry."

Sataro showed a grateful smile as he threw his bag in the back and swung up to the seat. "I'm in no hurry."

The man's name was Yego. Muscular, with a wide brown face and a huge mustache, he lookd to be in his late twenties. Sataro thought his accent placed him from somewhere in the south, but found he was from near Hiroshima—a small village where his father operated a fish market. He had been in America four years and worked on a farm north of Lodi. And he knew Yoshi. After a short drive, they arrived in the Japanese section of Stockton, where they tied the team in front of a boardinghouse with a sign that read "Bar." The place was empty at two in the afternoon— the reason being, Yego explained, there was work in the fields in the middle of the growing season. Sataro looked the place over speculatively.

He bought sake for them, then told his new acquaintance about his humiliation in the hotel. The farmhand nodded. "You'll learn the ways," he said softly. "The *hakujin* make the rules. Every one of them is a shogun compared to a Japan man." He leaned forward confidentially. "But it's better than Japan. Here, at least, I can own my own farm someday."

Gambari, Sataro thought. He nodded. There *was* much to learn.

As Yego pushed the big horses along at a brisk pace toward Lodi, Sataro continued to ask questions. The cheerful farmhand responded eagerly, pleased that he could be of assistance to such an impressive newcomer. A man who had money and the courage to bring his family like this had to become important in the great days ahead! He ebulliently rattled off what he knew about the Lodi area. He thought about fifteen hundred or more people lived there, and laughed when he described how the migrant workers loved to come to that town for a good time on weekends. He winked. "One restaurant has the best *jokyus* in the Valley."

Sataro wondered if the bar girls were also prostitutes and if the Gorotsukis ranged this far from San Francisco. Yego knew some of the area's history—that the primary product had once been watermelons, that other fruits and vegetables were still grown, but that the grapes had taken over since the vineyards first matured. With near reverence, he described the Tokay grape that was rapidly making Lodi famous. "Only around Lodi does the beautiful Tokay grow. They are even planning the first great Tokay festival for this fall!'' he announced exuberantly. ''Three days of huge celebration with bands and parades and cowboys and much drinking!''

He went on to tell about the Germans who had first gone to Russia until Catherine the Great persecuted them sufficiently to force their migration to a barren place called North Dakota, then how they had moved west to Lodi and become such successful farmers. He worked for one name Schmitz and was well-treated.

As they approached Lodi, Yego began to pump his passenger about the picture brides. ''Were they beautiful? Young? Strong enough for farmwork and bearing children in large numbers? Honest-looking?'' When Sataro's mind drifted to Miss Takano, his guide announced with a wide grin that he'd be ''ordering'' one within a year.

Sataro asked him about the Japanese businesses and learned that one general store, one fish market, one boardinghouse, two restaurant bars, and a laundry were operating on the east side of the railroad tracks on Main Street. As they drove into town on Stockton Street, Yego drove slowly by that section, pointing out the different establishments. He said he would stop for a drink, but he was already due back at the farm and would catch it from Schmitz if he didn't hurry. Ten minutes later, he stopped the team at a crossroad and pointed out the directions to the Hartley farm, where Yoshi worked. Sataro thanked him warmly. ''If I find what I'm looking for here,'' he said with deep appreciation, ''I'll remember my first new friend. You'll be welcome at my house any time.''

Yego bowed from his seat on the wagon. This new man would be important—he knew it!

And as he watched the wagon pull away, Sataro knew he had learned more than the story of Lodi on this day, he had tolerated his first vivid lesson in becoming a survivor.

The two-mile walk brought him to the Hartley farm just as the dark orange sun was reaching for the western horizon. He was about to inquire at the main house when Yoshi spotted him from outside a small barn and came running over. Grinning through his quick bow, Sataro's former comrade-at-arms asked, "So soon? Come, Kimi is just about to serve supper."

Moments later his effusive host led Sataro into a tiny bright house to the rear of the main buildings, explaining that he had built it himself in the months before going back to Japan to get married. Kimi looked up enthusiastically from the small cookstove in her combined kitchen and parlor, greeting him warmly as Yoshi reached for the sake bottle. "Tell me about Itoko!" Kimi insisted. "Do you have her in a big rich man's house in San Francisco yet?"

"No, not yet," Sataro replied quietly. "But someday soon I may have her in one here."

Kimi clapped her hands gleefully. "You're coming here? Oh, I can't wait!" She pointed a wooden spoon at Yoshi. "All that man does is keep me cooking and in bed. I haven't met one Japan woman!"

Sataro chuckled as he took Yoshi's welcome cup of sake. He had almost forgotten what it was like to be around a vivacious female.

He enjoyed the four-mile walk back into town the next morning. It was a bright, glistening day that matched his buoyant mood. The long talk with the Togasakis the night before provided a strong feel for the Lodi area and served only to quicken his desire to get settled there as soon as possible. Even the neat rows of grape orchards on each side of the road reminded him of the orderly farms of Japan. And the tall, strong palm trees stretching in two straight lines along Acampo Road added a sense of silent security.

The town of Lodi, with its clean wide streets and neatly kept yards around substantial, predominantly white houses, reflected the same serenity as he walked through the outlying portion toward the commercial section. A little boy of about nine, chasing another, stopped and stared at him a moment. Glancing down at his bag, the little redhead with huge brown freckles asked curiously, "You a new Jap in town?"

Sataro smiled as he nodded. As Yoshi had told him the night before, there were worse names. The boy frowned, then dashed on after his playmate. Sataro shrugged, fingered Macnamara's disk in his pocket and moved on down the street. What did he care what he was called on such a bright promising day?

The business section was already bustling at eight-forty-five. Farm wagons, drawn by teams of well-groomed horses, mixed with a number of glistening buggies and a smaller assortment of backfiring motorcars, moved energetically through the streets. Housewives carrying baskets were out in their daytime calicoes and bonnets to catch the early pick of vegetables. The shouts of children, glad to be out of school, mingled with the barking of dogs that were equally glad to have their playmates back. Men smiled as they greeted each other. The town was alive!

He glanced up at the radiant spire of a formidable white church surrounded by tall oak trees, thinking of the difference between it and the squarely built mission back home, then moved on across the tracks of the Southern Pacific railroad to the section of Main Street on each side of Pine known as Japan Town. Beside the shining rails, for as far as he could see, stretched one-story, low-gabled, open-loading sheds. A lengthy freight train stood patiently on a siding, the smokestack on its engine emitting a soft cloud of white steam that drifted lazily upward against the clear azure sky. Busy men hurried back and forth from dozen after dozen of sturdy vegetable-laden wagons and a few trucks, moving their produce to the waiting cars to be shipped.

He watched quietly for a few minutes, rubbing the thin scar on his cheek and wishing he owned a railroad. Turning back to the other side of the street, he saw several relatively small two-storied wooden buildings. Tinted in soft pastels, with two to four windows across the top floor, each had larger windows on the street level. Japanese characters on bright signs denoted the nature of each business. After wandering slowly up and down the street and glancing in each of the six establishments, he returned to the new, pink-painted one that was his destination. The fresh sign by the door read, "Nagoya-ya Hotel."

He drew himself erect, entered and approached the man behind the small desk.

*   *   *

Kajiro Ima leaned back in his straight-backed chair in the comfortable sitting room and stroked his dark mustache. He was a thin, nervous little man, wearing round, black-rimmed eyeglasses and a forced smile over his tired face. "Of course I wouldn't be leaving such a promising business," he recited in a touch of accent that marked his central Japan upbringing, "except for the illness of my parents at home. You're stealing this place from me, you know, Mr. Hoshi."

Sataro gave him a blank expression, concealing his joy at the opportunity. Let the man spend the next fifteen minutes moaning about his misfortunes; he could commiserate. He *was* stealing the place! Eight rooms larger than the one where his unfortunate Itoko and Noboru were staying in San Francisco would accommodate sixteen permanent boarders or who knew what, if he jammed them tightly on busy weekends.

Ima went on. "Within five years, you will be a rich man. . . ."

The front lobby was large enough to keep the two new pool tables and small bar, or to be converted into a store. And the proprietor's two-bedroom apartment, Sataro thought, not removing his attentive gaze from Ima's shiny eyeglasses, was more than adequate. Not nearly as large and comfortable as the house in Hiroshima, but sufficient. The yard in the rear not only held a fine little bathhouse of redwood, but was large enough to put in a vegetable garden or a classical garden.

"I shouldn't be sacrificing for this price," Ima groaned.

It was true, he shouldn't. The newly installed range and sinks in the adequate kitchen, together with the long dining room, the ample storehouse in back and the handsome, sturdy furniture, made it perfect. A ready-made package!

"Only your cash makes it possible," the sad Ima growled.

Six hundred and fifty American dollars would put a severe strain on his available capital, but the income would commence as soon as he took over. And he wouldn't have to make a lease payment for another month. He couldn't wait to tell Itoko! He should find a sign painter before leaving, though—the new "Hiroshima-ya Hotel," under the management of the honorable Sataro Hoshi, recently arrived from that great city in Nippon, was soon to become a reality!

*   *   *

"Did you see any cowboys?" Noboru asked excitedly.

"Yes, two rode into Stockton as I was leaving," Sataro replied.

Shortly after his return to the hotel on Geary, he had brought them out to the tiny *sushi* shop to give them the exciting news. Itoko sipped her tea and nibbled at her rice cake—glad to get out of that terrible room on any pretext—but showed no enthusiasm at Sataro's detailed description of his trip.

"Did they have guns?" Noboru asked.

"No, my son, I think those days are gone. I did see your school principal, though. He's a pleasant man who said they'll give you an entrance examination. Even though you may have to begin with a much lower age group, he said you could move up as quickly as your grasp increases."

Sataro described the American school, then went into a detailed sketch of the Hiroshima-ya, specifically of the apartment. When he mentioned the *tokonoma* and that they might be able to put in a formal garden in the backyard, Itoko's eyes showed a flicker of interest. The pool tables drew a frown, as did his description of the large kitchen and excellent facilities. "Who's going to help me with the cooking and all that other work?" she asked.

He knew she would attack that point. "I'll get someone as soon as possible," he replied. "In the meantime, your strong son here will be your able assistant."

"How far is it to Kimi's house?" she asked coolly.

"About four miles," he replied with a shrug. "But I can arrange transportation."

"Then I'll be as lonesome as I am now."

"Nonsense," he said, holding onto his patience. "You'll meet many people."

Itoko sniffed.as she reached for the teapot. It was her last comment.

Taking a horse-drawn streetcar, Sataro arrived at the bank where he had transferred most of his money prior to leaving Hiroshima. He arranged to have it wired to the bank in Lodi, then wandered around the financial district watching the ongoing construction with interest. He studied the ten-story renovated Crocker Building, then walked to the landmark Ferry Building, which dominated the San Francisco skyline. The *Delta Queen*, the largest and most famous of the delta ferries, was tied up at the dock. He wished he had time to take Noboru for a ride on the stern-wheeler, but they could do it another day. And he bypassed any emporium that served drinks. Once was enough.

Back in Japan Town shortly after noon, he was passing a dress shop on Post Street when he almost bumped into her from the rear. In spite of himself, he sucked in a sharp breath. "Miss Takano!" he exclaimed. She turned abruptly with a startled gasp. "I was afraid I'd never see you again," he murmured, trying to guard his excitement. "Did you meet your new husband all right?"

She brought her hand up to her face as she turned away, saying nothing.

"I never had a chance to ask," he persisted. "What *is* your new name.

She looked at him, sadly, with apparent pain, still not answering. He thought he detected a redness around those magnificent eyes, but knew it was improper to ask. There was also a dark spot on her cheek that looked like a bruise. *Had the devil she married been beating her?* "Will you be living here in San Francisco?" he asked, not wanting to let her go.

As she started to reply, her eyes widened in fright.

"Come, my little queen," a burly, harsh-looking man in an expensive striped suit said firmly as he took her arm. "You've been out long enough."

Before Sataro could say anything, try to introduce himself or whatever would delay their moving on, they were several paces away. A moment later, she glanced quickly over her shoulder like a wounded young animal. It was like throwing a spear at him. His first impulse was to rush after them and tear her away, but he stood riveted by common sense. She was but a passing shipboard fancy having an unhappy beginning in marriage. She'd get over it. Brides through countless ages of arranged marriages had.

Still, he felt cheated and angry. No, he felt guilty. She needed at least a friend and he couldn't be that friend. No, he wanted more than that, but he could never have it. That was the *real* basis for his guilt!

And now, when he was about to embark on his great trip to prosperity, he told himself contemptuously, he was acting like an idiot again! He turned briskly and headed for the hotel. The afternoon train would take them the southern route and be an adventure that would erase such stupid thinking. Still—

He stopped once more and turned for a final look, but she was nowhere in sight.

Five

Itoko pulled her wide hatbrim down lower and shifted the parasol to her other hand to shield off the bright September sun. Squinting up the street toward the elegant Lodi Hotel, she saw the source of her latest irritation. Four across and ten long, forty men in bright white pants and scarlet, gold-trimmed jackets were wielding flashing brass instruments and making the most noise she could ever remember. But what could one expect from the *hakujin* except barbaric music, she thought as she turned to the excited Kimi and wrinkled her nose to show her displeasure.

It was the first time she had worn the new ensemble Sataro had purchased for her in Stockton a week after their arrival. And in spite of the heat, she felt quite grand. Too grand, she told herself, to be wasting it on a noisy, ill-bred crowd such as this. She wiggled her neck in the high collar, glad that the lacy front of her white organdy blouse permitted *some* relief. Sneaking a glance down at her long, blue silk skirt, she wished she could take off the ridiculous high-button shoes and put on her comfortable clogs. Her *damned* feet hurt!

Out of pure retaliation, she had adopted that *hakujin* man's word. And it was the only English word she used. Of course, she didn't utter it around Noboru, but she wielded it like a knife when her husband could hear. As the blast from the shiny instruments drew closer behind the high-stepping drum major, Kimi said something, but she couldn't make it out in the din. People around her were shouting crazily in what she guessed was their barbaric attempt at singing.

"*Yankee Doodle went to town, a-riding on a pony!*"

This was only the third time she had been in the main part of

63

town since their arrival, she thought bitterly. And she wouldn't be here now except for Kimi. It was the last day of the First Tokay Carnival, and Kimi had said she wouldn't go without her. Sataro had also been insistent, but that didn't matter. He could keep her cooking in that *damned* kitchen for all those *damned* boarders seven days a week, but he couldn't make her enjoy herself.

The noise of the passing band was too much for her!

She winced at Kimi again. The arrival of Zenro, she reminded herself, was the only thing that kept her from bundling Noboru off in the middle of the night to San Francisco. Zenro, the poor soul, was the best man cook she had ever seen. Bad leg and all. Pity about the accident, but he was a blessing. And so cheerful and grateful to have a job where his injury permitted him the luxury of saving ten dollars a month.

"Look at that beautiful carriage!" Kimi exclaimed as a gleaming mahogany phaeton, drawn by four high-stepping white horses in sparkling harness, followed the band. On the front seat were the driver in his finery and an elegant woman, while the back seat held the grinning, waving mayor in his high silk hat and the smiling beauty of the carnival—Queen Zinfandel.

She had to admit the waving girl with the lustrous black hair and bright smile was almost as pretty as a Japan girl. But, she sniffed, she was only queen because her father was such a rich grape farmer! The second carriage, led by four shiny black horses, held four pretty young girls, each of whom could be wearing the crown.

"Aren't they beautiful?" Kimi almost shouted.

"Shhh!" Itoko whispered, glancing around. She was still uncomfortable near the *hakujin*, and especially among so many. "Why don't we go back for some tea, Kimi?" she asked softly. "I—"

Kimi shook her head. "Not until the cowboys come."

Itoko frowned as she looked down the street. The men on horseback were at the end of the long parade. She peered across the street to where Sataro and Yoshi stood in the front of a crowd of spectators. She frowned again as she saw they were laughing and enjoying themselves too much in public. They had probably

had too much of the Tokay wine that was being served everywhere!
Damn fools!

Sataro and Yoshi *were* having a good time. Sataro was wearing his best suit and wingtip collar, topped off by a gray fedora
he had just purchased. And he had never seen such a stimulating
parade. The music was strange, but he loved its exuberance! And
the horses—he hadn't seen such beautiful animals since the
Emperor visited Hiroshima. He smiled back at the waving ladies
in the fifth carriage to pass, wondering if any of them denied her
husband his marriage rights.

But he pushed the thought aside. He had too many other things
to be thankful for. Over one hundred additional Japanese immigrants had streamed into the Lodi area in the three months he had
been there, and his hotel was doing famously. He had even turned
one of the rooms into a card room and was raking in ten percent
of the play. Between that, the bar receipts, the boarders, and the
heavy weekend trade, he was netting well over two hundred a
month!

"Here come the cowboys!" Yoshi shouted.

Sataro looked up the street to see ten horseback riders dressed
in chaps and big ten-gallon hats, approaching two abreast. Bright
bandanas adorned their throats and revolvers slapped against their
thighs. Bits of metal threw back tiny reflections from their polished saddles. The horses, curried and brushed to their shiniest,
seemed to be in the spirit of things as they pranced and tossed
their heads.

"Look at that!" Yoshi exclaimed as the crowd cheered.

One of the lead cowboys reared his horse and waved his hat.
"Yippee!" he shouted at the top of his lungs, then followed with
the screeching rebel yell.

Sataro grinned, looking around for the excited Noboru. He
thought he spotted him down the street on the other side with
several other schoolboys. "Why don't you become a cowboy,
Yoshi?" he asked. "You could start a circus and go back to
Japan. You'd get rich!"

Yoshi laughed. "I don't like to clean up the manure."

The lead cowboys were abreast of them now, waving and
nudging their mounts into crowd-pleasing movements. Maybe,

Sataro thought, he would own some horses someday—someday after he bought the motorcar. But already he was the envy of most of the Japanese. Having a Columbia bicycle was prestigious enough for the time being.

As the last cowboys passed, he glanced over to where Itoko and Kimi were standing. "C'mon. Let's go over and join our wives," he said to Yoshi with a smile. "May we can talk them into drinking some Tokay!"

"No," Yoshi replied, "I see a man who owes me two dollars. Go ahead."

Sataro shrugged and started across the street. He hadn't taken more than five steps when something flashed by his eyes and a rope snapped around his shoulders, pinning his arms! He stared up with shock as the cowboy reared his horse and shouted, *"I got me a stinkin' Jap!"*

Staring in shocked disbelief, Sataro saw the rope tighten into a rigid line as the cowboy turned his horse away and jabbed home his spurs. Suddenly, he was snapped off his feet like a rag doll and smashed into the dirt. Dust flew into his mouth as his chin scraped the street. A blur of madness followed—a twisting kaleidoscope of horror in which he seemed at center stage one instant and the only spectator the next. All around him were curious, laughing faces, swimming out of proportion in the glaring sun as if he were totally drunk. He strained to get his face up as a flash of searing pain burned his right knee. Hooves and a long silky tail danced mockingly in front of him as his right hand found the taut rope—only to be jerked away. The same brown dust that was gagging him drove into his burning eyes. Laughter and shouts echoed dimly in his roaring ears as if they had just been unplugged. Again, he tried to reach the rope, as if by some superhuman effort he could jerk the dancing hooves and long silky tail over backward. But his hands seemed frozen! Paralyzed. He was paralyzed! The tail—if he could only reach that tail! Did he hear Yoshi's voice, screaming above the roar? The tail, the rope— couldn't any of those swimming faces reach out and grab him, jerk him off this spinning, crazy nightmare?

Suddenly, the horrible, grisly dream ended as he ground to an abrupt stop. The rope he had so vainly tried to conquer was relaxed in front of him like a dying snake. The swimming faces stood still and began to lose their laughter. The silky tail was gone. The quiet hooves had joined the body of the huge horse. Above, a jeering face shouted, "Gimme back my rope, yellow-belly!"

He spat out the blood and dust as he used every ounce of willpower to push himself to his knees and grasp the rope. He would tear this Cossack down, drive him into the ground and rip him to pieces! But the rope was too slack. He would have to get to his feet and get the Cossack's leg.

Yoshi rushed up and tried to catch him as he lurched to his feet. But he fell backward into an awkward sitting position. His friend's iron grip held his shoulder as the rope was loosened and lifted over his head. From a few yards away, the cowboy scornfully pulled in the lariat and recoiled it expertly. Again, Sataro tried to lunge forward, but Yoshi held him firmly. "Sit still," the farmer growled. "You may be badly hurt."

Sataro felt his throat. The collar was gone. He wiped the blood from his chin and saw his new hat, crushed, lying in the dirt thirty feet away. His bloody right kneecap stared out through a huge hole in his trousers, and he felt burning sensations all over.

"Sataro!" Itoko screamed as she and Kimi burst through the small circle of onlookers. Dropping to her knees, she frantically took his face in her hands. She searched for deep cuts, then pulled his bleeding hand to her mouth and almost kissed it before she caught herself. "Look at what they've done to you!" she cried. "Now you know what the *hakujin* think of you!" She looked around at the white faces and blanched. She hated every one of them! Regaining her feet, she pushed her way through, sobbed, and blindly broke into an awkward run for home.

"Go after her!" Yoshi snapped at the startled Kimi.

"Get the sheriff!" a deep voice boomed as a tall young man shoved his way inside the ring. Pointing down the street, he added, "Tell him to arrest that goddamn cowboy!"

Sataro saw Noboru standing a few feet away. The boy's mouth was hanging open, his eyes wide and disbelieving. His anguish and confusion stabbed into Sataro. He crossed his legs and forced himself to his feet, then slowly reached out to touch his son's shoulder. "It's all right," he said quietly in Japanese. "An accident." He had never felt such shame in his life.

"You all right, mister?" the young man asked anxiously.

Sataro nodded absently, returning to Noboru's pained expression.

The tall young man stuck out his hand. "I'm Baldwin," he scowled. "C'mon, let's go over to my office. I have a first-aid kit."

Sataro sat staring at the floor as Yoshi lit his cigarette. He absently nodded his thanks, unable to erase the numbing sense of humiliation. Baldwin applied the last touch of iodine to his left elbow, then stomped to his cluttered rolltop desk and opened a half-empty bottle of bourbon. Pouring the whiskey into three dirty cups, he growled, "Tokay grapes are for the table, not wine." He passed out the cups. "And horse's asses like that cowboy aren't fit to live!"

Cedric Baldwin was a tall, skinny man who reminded Sataro of a crane. His black bushy eyebrows seemed to grow together over his fierce blue eyes, and a shock of unruly black hair constantly hung down over his forehead. The thick dark mustache over a wide expressive mouth and pugnacious chin tried to, but didn't quite overcome his most outstanding feature—his magnificent beak of a nose. And, at twenty-four, that nose had been into a lot of people's business. Except for a part-time printer who came in from Stockton on Thursdays, Cedric Baldwin was the indignant one-man show of the noisy, but honest, Lodi *Gazette*. All of his combative juices were still flowing as he dropped into his lopsided swivel chair and announced, "You know, it was fellas like you who got me into this one-horse newspaper."

Sataro glanced up dully, not replying.

"Yeah, sure as hell! After years of working on the *Chronicle*, I finally woke up one day when that goddamn bigot, Hearst, was in town and told him to shove his prejudiced newspaper right up his ass!"

Sataro and Yoshi threw each other confused looks.

Cedric leaned forward intently. "You know—anti-Japanese editorials and plain old lies. Christ, don't you guys ever read?" He shook his head and chuckled at his indiscretion. "I'm sorry.

Anyway, if it weren't for you Japanese coming along to be Hearst's private niggers to pick on, I'd still be there."

Sataro sipped the harsh bourbon as he stared at the floor and rubbed the scar on his cheek. None of the newspaperman's words meant anything. All he could see was Itoko fuming over him and the terrible look in Noboru's shocked eyes. *His eldest son, the heir to the House of Hoshi—his proud son who bragged about what a great hero his father had been against the mighty Russians— staring down as Sataro Hoshi sat there in the dirt, disgraced beyond comprehension!*

Cedric Baldwin downed his bourbon and reached for a pencil. "All right, now give me your full name."

Sataro looked with alarm at Yoshi. "For what?" he asked finally.

"The story. I'm going to make an issue of it."

Sataro flinched inwardly at the further shame of his degradation being in print. Subconsciously, his fingers found Macnamara's silver disk, but they rejected it immediately. "Mr. Baldwin," he said quietly, "I'd rather you didn't."

Cedric stared at him in disbelief. "But you were wronged!" he snarled indignantly. "Your people have been abused ever since they started getting off the goddamn boats over thirty years ago! I think the public oughta have it shoved in their face."

A frown knitted Sataro's eyebrows as he shook his head. "No," he said firmly. "It's a matter that relates to Bushido—a point of honor. And I am *samurai!*"

Cedric looked at him in surprise. "You are?"

Sataro nodded. "By blood."

Cedric poured himself some more bourbon. Finally, the newspaperman looked up with a scowl. "All right," he growled. "I think I understand. I'll omit your name, but I'm sure as hell gonna report the shameful incident."

Normally on a night when so many Japanese men were in town, Sataro would help Zenro serve drinks or relieve the man in the card room. But tonight, after losing so much face, he couldn't bear the thought. At least not yet. He stared into his sake cup as the scene with Itoko reached its crescendo.

Her hands were on her hips, her dark eyes blazing as she stomped her foot in front of him. "This is what you get for bringing us to your precious America!" she snarled. "You're now the biggest disgrace in the empire, Sataro Hoshi. And I won't stand for it! I insist that you arrange passage back to Hiroshima at once!"

Sataro poured more sake without answering.

Itoko was livid. "All right, then arrange *my* passage. I will not remain in this barbaric land any longer!"

Clenching his fists to control himself, Sataro's eyes narrowed as he spoke in an even voice. "No one is going back, Itoko. That's enough."

"Huh!" she snorted. "Enough, you say. I would think lying there in that dust would have been enough. Did you see all those people laughing at the proud son of Heigo Hoshi? Well, let me remind you of something—the daughter of Colonel Mitsukuni Mitsubishi has definitely had *enough!*" She glared back for a moment, then whirled and stormed out of the room.

Sataro charged out of his chair in fury, but caught himself. He had never struck her and wouldn't start now. Besides, he told himself, she was fully justified in being upset. He pulled out his watch. Yoshi was overdue.

The scene in the street flashed vividly back to him. He could taste the dust and the salty blood. The faces leering—he wondered how many of them belonged to Japan men? And just as they were beginning to call him *oyakata*, the lower-class term for boss. In just these few short months, he had made himself felt in the Japanese community. He assisted the Japanese Association's secretary, he was a strong voice in the Hiroshima *kenjinkai* and about to become its chairman, and most importantly, the men were beginning to come to him with their troubles. He loaned them money and his little safe acted often as their bank. And now—

Yoshi tapped and entered brusquely. "I found him," he announced. "He's in the Wellington Saloon with some of his friends."

For the first time in six hours, life returned to Sataro's dark eyes. "Good," he replied. "Have Zenro pour you a drink while I get ready.

As his friend left the room, Sataro pulled out the flat package wrapped in brown paper. Already, his abrasions had stopped smarting. The *chikara* was roaring back through his veins, making him whole again. His mind was clear as he pictured what was ahead. In Japan, he would use the sword, but it wouldn't be acceptable here. Tearing the package open, he examined the familiar contents, then quickly ripped off his Western clothes. Grimly, he stepped into the loose-fitting white cotton trousers, then slipped on the strongly woven cotton jacket. The black belt, knotted in front, completed his *judo-gi*. He held out his arms, dropped into a squat, wiggled his fingers to loosen up, then eased into the Randori—the free-style warmup exercises. After ten minutes of strenuous movement, he stuck his head into Noboru's room, where the boy was studying. "Come, my son," he said quietly. "We have an engagement."

The Wellington Saloon was Lodi's largest and most popular drinking emporium. Its owner, an Englishman by the name of Claymore, claimed it held the longest pure oak bar in the San Joaquin Valley and swore that the massive leaded mirror behind it came directly from Liverpool. The huge gas lamps which cast a golden sheen at night were supposed to have been taken from an old Saxon castle a hundred years earlier. He also insisted that the brilliantly shined brass rail and spittoons had been a part of the grandest hotel in London. The massive oil painting that graced the wall opposite the bar was an overpowering scene of the Bavarian Alps—an inducement to make the area's many Germans feel at home. On this, the third and last night of the festival, the tall and burly Claymore stood behind the center of the bar, stroking the tips of his waxed guards mustache as he watched his three efficient bartenders making their frequent trips to the huge brass cash register. He was puffed with pride and accomplishment. Never in his nineteen years in the British Army had he guessed he would make so much money in three days.

His eyes swept the loud throng of assorted city and farm patrons who'd been pouring down drinks since the end of the parade. Even the words of "My Gee from the Fiji Island," blaring from his proud new nickelodeon, were nearly lost in the hubbub. He tossed a glance to where the cowboy who had gotten all the attention over roping that Jap was still holding court with several other cowboys. He'd have to keep an eye on them later—damned rowdies. From ten feet away, he could hear the braggart—Hiram Brooks—go into his spiel again. "No dirty Jap has any right to even *be* in our towns, let alone in our goddamn country," he was announcing to his audience. "We oughta pack them little yellow monkeys up in a big barrel of soy sauce and roll 'em off the goddamn dock in San Francisco! Let 'em *float* all the way back to that skinny little bastard of an emperor!"

Claymore's attention flickered toward the entrance, where a new buzz of interest attracted his attuned ears. There, a strange apparition in white was pushing his way through the crowd toward the bar. Customers were melting out of the way and heads were turning all over the place as a strange hush descended. It was a goddamn Jap! And he was carrying a rope or something. He started to move forward to tell him he couldn't be served, but something in the intruder's eyes and erect demeanor held him back. Claymore didn't even reach for his baseball bat.

Brooks, whose back was to the door, was so busy in his tirade that he hadn't even noticed the swift change in noise level. His voice rang out clearly, like the bray of a single mule when its teammates have suddenly grown quiet. "I shoulda hung the little sonofabitch with that rope while I was at it!"

The cowboy at Brooks's left elbow looked up in surprise as Sataro firmly pushed him aside. Brooks had just gotten his glass back to his mouth when his coiled lariat slammed down on the bar beside him with a loud *thud!* The tall cowboy's head snapped around, as he looked down into Sataro's cold eyes. "Would you like to try this rope on me now, Mr. Brooks?" Sataro asked in a harsh accent that could be heard throughout the now hushed saloon.

The customers who had been inching forward to see the fun suddenly began backing up as Brooks glanced down at his lariat. Glaring at Sataro, he growled, "What're you doing with my goddamn rope, Slant-eyes? What's on your mind?"

Sataro's tone was flinty. "I want you to use your rope when I'm looking—if you have the courage."

Brooks tried to laugh it off: "Naw, you take them silly pajamas and go on back to bed, sonny. This is a white man's bar."

Sataro's black eyes bored into the cowboy as his voice rose so everyone could hear. "Then you don't have the courage to fight me—is that right, Mr. Brooks?"

Brooks glanced around momentarily, seeing the expectant looks in dozens of eyes. As he spit out his wad of tobacco on the floor, Claymore again started to reach for his ballbat, but stopped. He *wanted* to see this gritty little Jap whip the dirty blighter's ass!

Brooks whirled in anger, bringing up his fists and cocking his right. "Nobody calls me a coward, yellow-belly!" he snarled.

The roundhouse right caught nothing but air as Sataro slipped back into the space being swiftly vacated by scrambling, excited spectators. He dropped into a classic jujitsu crouch, holding his open, tensed hands out in front of his chest. As Brooks missed again with a wild left, the taste of blood and dirt returned to Sataro's mouth. He could see the blur of laughing faces, the horse's dancing hooves. But most clearly, he could see Brooks's jeering face. The Cossack. The fury boiled out in a deep growl as his enemy lunged forward with a looping overhand right.

He could not kill him! Sataro shouted to himself as he stepped deftly aside, caught Brooks's wrist, twisted sharply and slammed him viciously to the floor. After a flashing judo chop to the cowboy's neck, Sataro was on his feet like a cat, resuming the defensive position. Laughter and shouts began to echo through the rooms as Brooks climbed angrily to his feet. Wiping his mouth and glaring, he shouted, "I thought you wanted to *fight!*"

"Hey, Brooks!" someone jeered. "Maybe you oughta use that rope again!"

With a furious grunt, Brooks dove at Sataro with his head down, only to find himself flying to the floor from a perfect *tsurikomi goshi*—his target's powerful lifting hip throw. Again, the knifelike hand chopped painfully into his neck. But there was no follow-up, as the white pajamas once more backed away. Brooks tore his head away from the tobacco juice-splattered brass rail and roared to his feet. A sea of taunting faces swam in front of him. It seemed like the *whole crowd* was cheering for this goddamn Jap! In a glare of red, he moved slowly toward Sataro, stalking, shuffling, with both hands cocked. This was no longer a fight—he wanted to *kill* the sonofabitch!

Sataro moved slowly toward him, loose, ready to end it. It was perfect—Brooks's fingers were coming at his throat, finding his jacket, the other arm looping. . . .

In a blur, he drove up hard with his shoulders and hooked Brooks's arm, pivoted counterclockwise, and threw him over his shoulder. The burly cowboy crashed to the floor on his back, screaming in pain and rage. But before he could move, Sataro pounced on him, applying a paralyzing *nami juji jime*—a stifling cross-choke on his throat.

Sataro increased the pressure, staring coldly into Brooks's bulging eyes. The cowboy's struggle ended abruptly as he fought for air. All of his strength and fury drained away in an instant, but still the iron grip continued to force the life from him. Just as his eyes began to flutter, Sataro growled, "Don't ever rope a 'dirty Jap' again," and suddenly released his grip. Getting slowly to his feet, amid resounding cheers, Sataro's gaze swept the crowd until he spotted Noboru's proud smile wedging out between arms and hips. With a slight nod to his son, he pulled his shoulders back and strode erectly toward the door.

Six

Kyutaro Abiko held up the latest issue of his *Nichi Bei*. "Do you think you can produce anything like this without an ounce of experience?" the publisher asked. "Do you have any idea what a newspaper entails?"

Sataro wasn't in the least cowed by the legendary figure. "Sir, I tried to tell you," he replied patiently. "I have no intention of ever approaching your proud *Nichi Bei*. I want only to start a small weekly of perhaps four pages for the Japan people around Lodi. Maybe later, it will include Stockton. In the beginning, there will be little advertising, but I'm prepared to shoulder the expense."

Abiko removed his spectacles. Peering intently into Sataro's concerned expression, he nodded and commented, "I have the feeling this is a vanity enterprise. Is there some other reason you haven't mentioned?"

Sataro found a smile. "With due respect, sir, did any man ever start a newspaper without *some* vanity being involved?"

Abiko got up from his desk and peered out the window for a moment before answering. "All right, Mr. Hoshi," he said as he turned. "We'll print your newspaper every other Friday, meaning it should reach Lodi by train the following day." He made a note on a desk pad. "By the way, what are you going to call your little venture into the precarious world of journalism?"

"The *Shimpo Shimbun*—the *Progress Press*."

The publisher rubbed his strong jaw. "Good name. Are you an admirer of Fukuzawa? His fine paper in Tokyo is the *Jiji-Shimpo*."

Sataro had naturally heard of the great Yukichi Fukuzawa—the man of so many talents and influence, the educator who had

75

founded Keio University and been such a strong factor in modernizing Japan before his death a few years earlier. "Yes," Sataro replied with a sheepish smile. "Maybe he'll be an inspiration for me."

"You could do no better. Now tell me, are you certain this publisher friend of yours in Lodi doesn't resent his possible loss of revenue from advertising?"

Sataro shook his head. In the two months he had known Cedric, the young newspaperman had become the Japanese champion in Lodi. Not only had he and Cedric developed a rich friendship, but the scrappy younger man had strongly urged him to, as he called it, "dip his fingers in ink." "No, Mr. Abiko," he replied. "He gets no advertising from the few Japanese businessmen, and the Japanese community doesn't buy his paper."

Abiko—the man who had made fluent English one of his causes—sighed. "No, most of them can't read more than a few words. Very well, Mr. Hoshi, you have a printer. The rest is up to you."

Sataro jumped to his feet and bowed deeply. "I can't thank you enough, sir."

Abiko's eyes dropped to the mass of work on his desk. "Just make your payments promptly," he said gruffly.

"Would you like a deposit now?"

The publisher broke into the pleasant grin that was known throughout Japan Town. "No. If you don't pay promptly, I'll cut off your source. And I know what that'll do to a fledgling publisher. Good day, Mr. Hoshi. And good luck!"

As Sataro walked out into the cloudy early December day, he tried to imagine how an elated American would jump in the air and click his heels. Because that was just how he felt! The transient trade at the Hiroshima-ya had increased considerably since that unfortunate festival, he had ideas about buying a piece of vineyard, and just might open a grocery store sometime in the near future. But his newspaper was exciting. *His* newspaper— even the term was fascinating!

And it was about to reach reality.

*   *   *

Shortly after nine, following a robust meal, Sataro stood before a cracked mirror in his tiny room at the Osaka-ya. He straightened the new necktie, admiring its diagonal gray stripes. The excitement and anticipation of being with a lovely woman was singing through every nerve. The night was his to do anything he wanted! He was already partially aroused, just thinking about the soft skin of a young beauty in his arms. As he quickly ran a few brisk swipes of the brush through his thick hair, his mind drifted back to another bleak winter day in Hiroshima when he was sixteen. He had had the same sensations then, but had no idea of what would happen.

His friend Hirobumi from Miyajima had set the adventure up with his older brother. "The deflowering," Hirobumi had called it. They had saved up for months to buy those lovely women for an hour's education. And what a great, erotic experience it had been! The young woman had even told him she loved him!

"Ha!" Sataro roared as he tipped the new black fedora down over his forehead in a rakish manner. Of course she did!

He went down the stairs, out of the hotel, and strode firmly down Geary Street. Turning right at Laguna, he found the restaurant with the bright red sign and entered. The manager, a burly man in a black suit, hurried up to ask him if he wanted to eat. "No," Sataro replied briskly, glancing around at the many empty tables. "I want to be entertained."

The manager smiled through his thick glasses and nodded. "Follow me," he murmured in a Tokyo accent, heading toward the back of the dining room. At the bottom of the stairs in the rear, he stopped and asked, "Have you been to the Mansion before?"

"No," Sataro replied as casually as possible.

"We have the finest Japan girls in America," the Tokyo man leered, moving up the steps. A moment later, he opened the door to a large room on the second floor, said something to the man inside, and bowed quickly to Sataro. "Mr. Yagana will take care of you, sir," he said pleasantly.

Harry Yagana was wearing a dark blue suit with a wingtip collar and a red carnation in his lapel. He was also wearing the fixed smile he reserved for men of means. He bowed curtly, motioned Sataro inside and purred, "Welcome to the Mansion, sir. You are in the finest house of pleasure in San Francisco."

Sataro glanced around at the large, dimly lit room furnished with low tables surrounded by large, plush pillows. The walls were adorned with Japanese woodcuts and low music could be heard. A rich incense filled the air. Four men were drinking with girls at different tables, while three other attractive girls were distracted from their conversation to give him tempting smiles. Two of them were wearing revealing, satiny sliplike garments, while the other was traditionally dressed in a bright flowered kimono and obi. All three had their hair groomed exquisitely.

"We have the finest Japan girls on the continent, sir," Yagana announced like a proud father offering his daughters for marriage. "All of them come from the finest traditions in Japan and some have geisha training. Do you have any preferences?"

Sataro nodded, feeling his loins stir as he looked at the taller of the two unattached girls in the provocative slips. She nodded and smiled back, turning to show him a side-slit and a well-shaped buttocks. He took a deep breath and nodded again, saying huskily, "The tall one will do."

Yagana led him to a low table in a corner as he nodded to the girl. She hurried over with a pleasant smile and sat down on a soft satin pillow beside her customer. Sataro glanced down at her bare alluring knees, already sensing his growing erection. She leaned closer, revealing the promising swell of breasts. He barely heard the music as she asked, "Sake, sir?" in a low, husky voice.

"Yes," he managed, not wanting her to move.

He watched her hips dance tantalizingly as she scurried to a sideboard. *By the gods!* He wasn't acting like he hadn't had a woman in months—he was acting like he had *never* had one! A candle's light reflected over the swell of her satiny buttocks as they emerged from her tiny waist and rounded softly into the slit. He'd have sworn he heard a ringing in his ears! And then she was back, melting into a teasing position beside him. He looked into her low bodice as she bent to pour the sake. "My name is Masa," she murmured.

He nodded, downing the sake like a peasant. As she poured

more, he knew he couldn't go through with any extensive preliminaries. Her smooth skin, the erotic smell of her, her touch—*God*, her presence—he had to have her at once! His hand dropped to her silky knee as he took the second cup. "I think I'd like to go to your room now," he said hoarsely.

"Of course," she murmured pleasantly.

He was halfway to his feet when he saw a striking young woman enter from the back. She looked like—the amber eyes flickered back at him. It—it *couldn't* be!

He blinked his eyes as he stood upright and stared. At the same instant she recognized him and quickly turned away. *It was impossible!* As Masa watched irritably, he walked woodenly toward her. "Miss Takano!" he said, still not believing. "Miss Takano?"

She turned, looking at him with those wonderful, wounded amber eyes. "Yes, Mr. Hoshi. How are you?" she whispered.

She was wearing a lacy, apricot-colored chemise; caught at the waist with a thin belt and cut deeply to reveal her shapely breasts. Her hair was swept up in the fashionable style of the time and her rose petal lips were painted a brighter red. Even in the dim light, she was the most beautiful thing he had ever seen. "How? I mean . . . what are you—"

Her eyes dropped as she interrupted. "I'm a prostitute," she mumbled harshly.

"But I thought . . . I mean, your husband—"

"Go with your girl, Mr. Hoshi," she said listlessly, turning away.

"No!" Sataro insisted, clutching her arm. "I *must* talk to you!"

"Then you must pay," Miss Takano replied dully, still looking away as the manager moved toward them. "All prostitutes get paid." She used the word like a leper would describe her disease.

Sataro fished out some bills and handed the tall girl two dollars as Yagana asked, "Is there a problem, sir?"

"Uh, no," Sataro replied, "I just decided I want this girl."

Yagana nodded to Masa, then smiled back at Sataro. "Of

course. I'm sure you'll be pleased by our little Miyuki. She's our
most beautiful princess.''

As the manager moved back to his post by the door, Sataro
looked down into Miyuki's masked expression. "Is there a room?"
he asked hesitantly, beginning to feel like he was having a bad
dream.

She nodded and led him to the back, opening the door to a
small tidy room with a low bed and bright lace curtains. She
pointed to a pillow by a low table and poured two cups of sake.
He seated himself, fumbling for a cigarette. She lit it deftly, then
sat across from him with downcast eyes. At length she looked
up, expressionless, asking coldly, ''Do you want my body now?''

He felt angry and cheated. ''We can get to that,'' he snapped.
''Why did you lie about being a picture bride?''

She looked at him in shock, as if he had struck her.

''Well?'' he demanded.

She sighed deeply, shaking her head. Her voice was barely
audible as a tear appeared. ''I didn't lie.''

''But—''

''They lied!'' she cried out. She jumped to her feet, covering
her face with her hands. She paced a few steps, then whirled
back to him. ''The Gorotsuki Club *lies!*'' she snarled bitterly.
''They set up the entire thing . . . letters, pictures, promises. All
of it! *There are no husbands!* And when we get here, we have no
choice . . . no money to get back to Japan and no alternative.
I—''

She faltered, then the words tumbled on, ''I refused, spit in
their faces, but they beat me. That's right, Mr. Hoshi, they beat
me until they were afraid they'd damaged the goods. And still I
refused, and they beat me again . . . and then I knew. I had no
choice.'' Her hands went to her face again as she slumped on the
bed. ''I gave in,'' she mumbled with a sob. She finally looked up
grimly. *''That's* your lie, Mr. Hoshi.''

Sataro was stunned. His face burned as his anger turned to the
animals who could do such a thing. ''Can't you go to the
police!''

''Ha! They don't care.'' She told him about Yagana.

Sataro was appalled. American discrimination he could take,

but for someone—particularly this beautiful dove—to be made into a *slave* by Japan men was intolerable! "Why do you stay?" he asked.

"*Stay?* Mr. Hoshi, I've run away *twice!* Once, I made it all the way to Seattle. But the Gorotsuki reach everywhere, like a spiderweb. And when they catch you, they beat you terribly . . . a woman hasn't got a chance."

He pictured her lovely back being whipped, her smooth buttocks being slashed; her beautiful face being smashed, blood streaming from her delicate nose. He began to boil! He wanted his army rifle back so he could blast the heads of the Gorotsuki and rip their guts out with the bayonet! He ground out the cigarette that was burning his fingers. "There must be some way," he snarled, wanting to go out and kill Yagana immediately.

She shook her head, staring at the floor. "None, except death."

By the gods! Could she be contemplating suicide?

She got to her feet and began sliding her chemise up over her thighs. "Well," she said with a harsh smile, "you might as well get what you're paying for."

He stared at her smooth flesh and shapely legs in agony. *God, how he'd love to!* "No!" he rasped, grabbing her wrist. "Not like this. Sit down, let me talk to you."

She gave him a strange look as she dropped the chemise and slowly curled up on the bed. He cleared his throat. "I—I noticed you many times on the boat. But you know that. No, I—it was more than that. I was entranced by you. I had this wonderful, overpowering desire . . . this longing that I couldn't even bear the thought of you marrying another man. I think I . . . fell in love with you all at once."

A tiny smile touched her lips. "What about your wife, Mr. Hoshi?"

He frowned. "I—that's why I didn't say anything."

The amber eyes widened, watching him without blinking. Finally, in a soft voice, she said, "I felt the same things."

He stood riveted, lost in her eyes, then broke the magic, kneeling beside her and touching her hand. "And now?" he asked tentatively.

She pulled her hand away, replying dully, "Now, I am a prostitute."

"I don't care."

She turned her head to the side. "Then take me. I know many ways to please you. They made me learn everything. Take me, Mr. Hoshi, then go away."

He was still tempted—oh, how he was tempted. But he was also disgusted. "No," he said softly, "I can't, not here." He took her hand again. "Look at me, Miyuki. Look at me and listen to me." The eyes came back to him, softly, brimming, as he continued, "I'll take you away . . . yes, take you away where you'll be safe . . . take you away where you can forget this terrible thing and learn to love me."

She gripped his hand, wanting to believe him. "I'd like that," she whispered. "But how?"

He shook his head as he leaned down to kiss her fingers. "I don't know yet, but I'll find a way." He looked up fervently. "I swear it! Upon my honor, upon my samurai ancestors, on the soul of my Bushido, I'll take you away."

The fear flickered in her eyes. "They'll come."

"Trust me."

The problem had become more confounding. As the train pulled out of Stockton for Lodi, Sataro stared out the window at the chill dreariness of winter rain. The weather certainly didn't help his bleak mood. During the last hour he'd visited all three Japanese boardinghouses in Stockton to see if anything suitable was available for Miyuki's lodging. But all of them were filled with women-hungry Japan men who would make her stay difficult. Worse, if he came to see her in any of them, the word would spread like the rays of the holy sun that the *oyakata* from Lodi had a mistress. And it would reach Lodi immediately. Stockton was out!

He had immediately eliminated the possibility of finding a place for her in San Francisco. Not only would the Gorotsuki have her back in no time, but he wouldn't be able to see her. And Sacramento, while much closer, certainly had people with Gorotsuki connections, if not the Gorotsuki themselves. No city or town would do. An isolated farm? Certainly not with Yoshi—Kimi would be in Itoko's kitchen before sunset! And he didn't trust anyone else enough. At least for the present, *all* Japan people were out. There was no simple solution, unless it was Cedric's worldly aunt who lived nine miles north of Lodi in Galt. She had winked when they had met and said, "If you hear of a pretty Japanese girl who wants to be a housekeeper, let me know."

It was only a possibility, but it might work. He could easily ride his Columbia that far. . . .

His gloom deepened as a few more miles sped by and the feeling of guilt that he had pushed away earlier in the day returned to trouble him. Having an illusionary love affair with Miyuki was one thing—what he was planning was an extremely hazardous step. Everything in his ambitious American venture was working out beyond his most inventive dreams. With the newspaper and other plans, his status and wealth were sure to continue growing. Could he risk it all for a girl he didn't really know? Be practical, he told himself, pushing aside all emotion. You have everything to lose and nothing but some momentary passion to gain. And what's that in the spectrum of time?

He thought of Itoko. As difficult as she continued to be, she was still his wife and he couldn't bring himself to insult her. His marriage simply had to be preserved. His thoughts drifted back to the vulnerable Miyuki and his pulse quickened. Her beauty swam before his eyes, erasing his practicality with a swift tug. He had never wanted anything so much! In the midst of this torture, the train slowed to stop at Lodi. But Sataro barely noticed the dripping trees and the buildings waiting to greet him.

"When are you going to begin your newspaper, Father?"

Sataro broke out of his troubled thoughts with a start. He hadn't seen Noboru since arriving home a couple of hours earlier. He turned from where he was making an inventory of supplies in the backyard storage shed to greet his son. "Soon," he replied quietly.

"I've just been promoted to the third grade," Noboru beamed. "And the principal said I should be able to go into the fourth by March."

"That's marvelous!" Sataro exclaimed. "I'm very proud of you, son."

Moments later after Noboru had gone inside, the sharp pang of guilt descended like a smothering blanket. What was most important in his life? he asked himself. Why did any Japan man work so diligently to acquire property and position? Why was he here? Family—sons who would become leaders in Japan. It was as simple as that.

And now he was about to toss it all on the table for a fateful roll of the dice. How could he posibly face Noboru if it all blew up in his face? Where would his passion be when that happened? Could he tell him it was that elusive, corrupted thing called love? Could he tell him it was a noble effort to save a poor girl from degradation and misery? And what about Miyuki's feelings—she could be faking, using him as a way out. It was certainly possible. He might bring her here only to be rejected at a later date—and where would he be then? No, he couldn't rush into this matter. There was just too much to be lost.

He threw himself into the inventory, but it was useless. He couldn't count past five without seeing her. Every bottle of sake, every box of produce had her image on its label. Hadn't he given his sacred word? Hadn't he sworn on the code? He was samurai by blood—the obligation couldn't be ignored. Even if he never saw her again, he had to rescue her. A convent—the Catholics would shield her.

He slammed a bag of rice to the floor and angrily lit a cigarette. Who was he trying to convince? It wasn't his honor that was at stake. He wanted her! Her face danced before him—at the bottom of the freighter's ladder when he had been dazzled, when she looked up and into his eyes on that last day at sea . . . when she was hopeful but still doubtful in her room . . . he saw her bare thighs, her graceful smooth legs. And he saw her wonderful, luminous, haunted eyes—and they tore at his heart. The overwhelming desire swept over him, consuming him, driving out house, wife, and sons. It was maddening. Common sense, reality—who cared? He had to have her, he *ached* for her.

Knowing the words could destroy him, he whispered, "I'm coming, Miyuki."

Seven

"You want I should move the car up a little ways, mister?"

"Yes; about fifty feet," Sataro replied from the back seat. He shifted uncomfortably, straining to get a better view of the street. Although the dense fog diminished visibility, it was a blessing. Fewer people would see her enter the rented car. He threw out his cigarette and quickly lit another. He seldom reacted to tension, but he had never done anything like this before. Only a month earlier, he read a story about American gangsters dragging someone off the street, throwing him in a motor car, and speeding off to hold him for ransom. But this was different—he was robbing the Gorotsuki!

He shivered in spite of the fact that his overcoat collar was turned up and the powder gray fedora was pulled low over his eyes. Even though he had worked the plan out to the finest detail, he couldn't take any chances on being recognized. Yagana hadn't been in the Mansion the night before, but his assistant might remember. He pulled out his watch for at least the tenth time: 12:01. Miyuki had been positive she could get away from the Mansion before twelve, but she was nowhere in sight. She should have been working her way down the street by now!

They had gone over the plan until she could recite every step. It was Thursday—one of the two days when she was permitted a couple of hours to get out and shop or just wander around in the fresh air. She said that Yagana even gave them a few dollars a week to spend on what he called their "whore's day out." He also thought it was good for business to have his wares seen on the street.

He looked at his watch again. It was 12:03. Once she was

clear of the building, she was supposed to pull her scarf up over her face and begin window shopping. No hurry, just a casual browse down the street. The pick-up point was the same shop where he saw her when they first came to America—where he had noticed her bruises and been too stupid to question her about them. *Where was she?* Could she have gotten there early and decided he had backed out? Was he too far away? What if she got there and the fog got thicker—and he *missed* her? He leaned forward to the driver. "Will you please drive up another fifty feet?"

The driver shifted the wooden match to the other side of his mouth as he put the Studebaker in gear and it lurched forward. If this slant-eyed nut was willing to pay eight bucks just to be driven to San Mateo, he'd push the damned car fifty feet! Hell, it was his boss's car and gasoline.

As the touring car jerked to a stop and continued to idle noisily, Sataro pulled out his watch again. It was seven minutes after! Could something have happened? Could they have found out? Maybe one of the girls had heard them whispering through those thin walls and told Yagana. He could see the raw, bleeding welts on her naked back, and hear her crying out! He reached for the door handle, but stopped himself. He had to stick to the plan! He could hear his own jerky breathing as his gaze bored into the people walking by the shop.

The driver turned to him. "So this sister of yours gets belted around by her husband, huh? I know some guys who'll improve his manners if you want to shell out the money."

Sataro thought he saw her! "Uh, no," he replied abstractedly. "He'd only make it worse." It certainly *looked* like her! And she was stopping by the store! "There's my sister!" he exclaimed, pointing ahead. "Quick! Drive up!"

The driver ground the Studebaker into gear and eased it forward as Miyuki turned and moved toward the street. Just as the automobile came to a quick stop, Sataro threw the back door open and held out his hand. Miyuki tossed a quick glance up and down the street, then scrambled into the back seat. Sataro tried to pull her into his arms, but she was already twisting to look out the back window. A little cry escaped her lips as she slumped and dropped her face into her hands.

"It's all right, my dear," Sataro said gently, putting his arm around her shoulder as the driver made the turn at Filmore. "You're safe now. The train—"

"No!" she moaned. "He saw me."

"Who saw you?"

"Yagana!"

Miyuki nervously twisted the scarf as the train pulled out. She wanted to take it off, but it was her only shield against the eyes she felt were watching her from every direction. Traitorous eyes that would recognize her, eyes that were connected to a voice that would shriek, *"There she is! There she is!"* Moving her head only slightly, she glanced out the window to where she imagined Yagana was running alongside, trying to jump aboard at the last second. She could see the hate and fury in his eyes as he caught the final handrail and lunged aboard. She knew she'd never get away! She shut her eyes tightly as her hands flew to her face.

"Relax," Sataro said reassuringly as his hand patted her knee. "I watched as we pulled out. There was no one at the station."

She just couldn't believe they'd made it. Yagana could still be outside on the back platform, struggling to get through the door. He'd burst through in a moment, shoot Sataro with a big pistol, then jerk her to her feet and stop the train!

"Look at this."

She opened her eyes to see a small delicately wrapped box in Sataro's palm.

"Open it," he urged.

She glanced around cautiously at the empty seats behind them, then slowly took the gift and fumbled with its wrapping. Inside, a tiny pair of pearl earrings stared back at her. She sighed as she slumped against his shoulder. A tear trickled slowly down her cheek. "They're beautiful," she whispered. "Thank you."

Sataro beamed. "Try them on."

More tears followed as she stammered, "N-no, not now." She couldn't help looking back again. "Are you sure about—"

"No one followed us."

"But the driver?"

He shook his head with a tender smile. "Oakland. It'll take them ages to find him. And he doesn't know anything."

She shuddered. "I wish I had your confidence."

He squeezed her hand tightly. "There's no way in the world I'll let them touch you," he replied passionately. "Even if they knew where to find us. And they *don't!* Now relax and try on those earrings. It's all over."

She sniffed as she brushed away the tears. Smiling weakly, she nodded and reached into the box.

Gently and persuasively, Sataro calmed her over the next fifty miles. He told her funny stories, tender stories, and recited several beautiful old love poems. And each time he touched her, or when she smiled back at him, he wanted to take her in his arms and blot out the world. Finally, about twenty miles from Stockton, she turned from the window with a troubled look. "Do you know the story of O-sichi of Edo?" she asked softly.

"No," he replied eagerly, pleased that she wanted to talk. "Tell me."

A sad smile touched her lips. "I don't tell a story too well, but . . . back when Tokyo was Edo almost three hundred years ago, there was a beautiful young artist named O-sichi whose father took her to live in a temple. Soon after arriving, she fell in love with a handsome young man named Samon—the son of a wealthy samurai who was in the shogun's entourage. But Samon had been promised in marriage by his father and when their secret love was discovered, O-sichi was sent back to Edo. She was broken-hearted and desperate to see Samon again. Then one day, a thief by the name of Kichizo told her she would be reunited with her lover if she would set fire to her father's house.

"Naturally, the idea was repulsive to O-sichi, but she couldn't get it out of her mind. Would Samon come running to take her away? Months of despair followed. Then one dry and windy day, she took a burning stick and started the fire. In no time, Edo was swept by terrible flames, burning thousands of people to death and destroying the beautiful city. But the evil Kichizo wasn't finished. When he was caught looting, he told the police about O-sichi, and when they came to get the nearly insane girl, she readily confessed. Immediately, the people of Edo rallied to her side, saying she was manipulated by the evil demon of love and too young to be accountable.

"But then the terrible Kichizo told the police where they could find a painting that would prove she was the legal age of seventeen. Nothing could be done . . . she was sentenced to burn at the stake. Dressed in her most beautiful kimono, she was placed on an ugly mule and dragged through the streets for three days." A tear slipped down Miyuki's face as she paused. "Then they tied her to a tall pillar in a place called the Wood of the Bell and lit the faggots that surrounded her . . . and—"

Miyuki dropped her face into her hands. "Oh, Sataro," she sobbed. "Last night I dreamed I was O-sichi! Oh, it was *terrible!*"

He put his arm around her gently. "Dreams go away," he said softly.

She looked up with a shudder. "And you were Samon, my forbidden love," she said, the words almost running together. "And because I was a terrible prostitute, I was dragged all over San Francisco on a hideous burro. I was naked with a sign hanging over me telling everyone I was a criminal. And finally, in the center of Japan Town, they tied me to the front of the Mansion and Yagana lit the fire. And when I was hanging there with the flames consuming me, all I could see was your sad face!"

Sataro shook his head. "It means nothing."

"But you *are* a forbidden love. Don't you see—"

"Our love is not forbidden!" Sataro interrupted almost harshly. He squeezed her hand tightly as he looked earnestly into her moist eyes. "It will be the most beautiful love ever known, my darling. I promise you."

Forcing a smile, she whispered, "Then the dream will go away."

By the time they reached Stockton, she was laughing freely and bubbling with stories from her village. Only during their thirty-minute wait in Stockton did she climb back into her shell, and that dropped away once they were safely aboard the train for Sacramento. The stop in the capital lasted only fifteen minutes, but Sataro was uneasy, wondering if the station was being watched.

They arrived in Marysville shortly after dark and walked directly to the Japanese hotel, a relatively new place called the Yokohama-ya. The short room clerk was all eyes as soon as he saw Miyuki. Sataro smiled inwardly, knowing the man would never forget. He dropped a comment about them being on their way to Seattle, just in case the Gorotsuki managed to track them this far.

Miyuki shuddered inwardly as they climbed the steps to their second-floor room. Everything in the last hours—the horrible fear, the gradual relief, Sataro's gentleness and urgent sincerity, even her rush of response—were all blotted out as the moment of truth approached. Yagana's taunting face danced before her, followed by the forms of the faceless ones who had bought her. Could she ever erase their hideous memory? She shut her eyes tightly, shutting them out—just as she had detached herself from her body each time they'd invaded her. How she had scorned them, hated them, even making her body lie boldly to further ridicule them. It was the only way she had been able to preserve that precious portion of self that no man could violate. But had she gone too far?

Could she truly make love to a man, *any* man?

When Sataro burst back into her life, he immediately became a symbol of escape, of gallantry, of what she thought love could be. His handsome, impassioned face became a dream, his promise and words of love a beacon. Sataro's image was no tempting photograph of a criminal, enhanced by girlish infatuation. It was an overpowering part of her. These last hours, his tenderness, his fervor—it was real, and she *wanted* it. His wife meant nothing to her and the future was a thousand years away. She just wanted to love and be loved—totally—for the first time in her life.

But could she?

"It's a nice big room," Sataro said somewhat awkwardly as he lit the ornate oil lamp on the nightstand.

She barely noticed the large double bed, the dresser, or the pleasant curtains. Moving woodenly to the tiny sink, she murmured,

"Yes, a nice room." Glancing in the mirror as she began to unfasten her hat, she saw how drawn she looked. Her heart was pounding in fear. *She had to stop this!*

Sataro carefully placed his fedora on the dresser, sensing the tension. As if her thoughts were shouting at him, he knew what was troubling her. It reached out to him, tearing at him. She was a delicate, beautiful flower that had been horribly bruised, maybe even scarred. How deeply was she scarred? Could she forget? Should he be patient, perhaps wait? Could he? He touched her arm. "Would you like to rest?" he asked gently. "I can—"

"No!" she said sharply, turning to him. She brought his hand up to kiss it. Finding an uncertain smile, she asked softly, "Can we pretend it's our wedding night?"

Relief flooded him as he took her in his arms. Looking into her wide eyes, he could see the hope and lingering fear, her desperate bravery. "Of course," he whispered with a reassuring smile. "You just landed in San Francisco and I've been waiting for you all my life." His lips touched her forehead. "Oh darling, I love you so much. I've dreamed and dreamed of holding you like this, of tasting your lovely lips, of touching your hand, hearing your voice. I—"

She reached up to still the welcome words, kissing him tenderly, then more firmly. Her fingers clasped his neck as their tongues met tentatively, then retreated patiently. She was delicious, warm, exotic, sensual. He wanted to crush her, envelop her, keep her forever without letting go!

Gently, she broke their first kiss. Looking up with brimming eyes, she searched his expression for a moment, then dropped her head to his chest to hide the tears. Slowly turning her face upward, he tenderly brushed her lips with his, saying, "I love you, I love you." He kissed her nose, her moist cheeks, her now soft and unguarded eyes.

Her hands gripped him tightly as she responded to his more demanding kiss and pressed up into his powerful body. His urgent mouth seemed to be a part of her. His strength, his exciting smell . . . she felt it, felt the desire sweeping over her. She wanted him! *Oh, how she wanted him!* It was overwhelming. And it *was* her wedding night!

Her fingers wanted to dig into his shoulders, but she again pulled back. Looking into his glowing eyes, she knew she had never seen such overflowing emotion, never. She kissed the point of his chin, whispering, "We should get undressed."

"Yes," he answered with a touch of hoarseness, lowering his hands to her tiny waist and finally stepping back to smile. She broke the gaze to turn the lamp down to its lowest burning point, then pulled the pins from her lustrous hair and shook it down nearly to her hips. She didn't even have a nightgown, she thought as she began to slip out of her clothes. Every bride should have a nightgown.

Moments later she stepped out of her last piece of lingerie and glanced up shyly. Sataro was already naked and busily throwing the bedcovers back. She glided up and put her arms around him, kissing the smooth skin on the back of his broad shoulders as her arms circled his waist. Her hands moved up to his chest, exploring in wide caressing circles. He was her tall warrior.

He dropped slowly onto the bed, turning and taking her in his arms. Their lips met with the same searching gentleness as the first time. But their tongues soon joined and the intensity grew. Moments later, he broke away, pulling up above her on stiff arms and smiling down at her. "You are even more beautiful than I dreamed," he said in wonder, his eyes straying to her slightly heaving breasts. "Such velvety skin, such—"

"I love you," she whispered, reaching up to pull him back. His face dropped to her breasts, his mouth gently finding the nipples and massaging them softly. She kissed the top of his head as she brought the inside of a knee up to rub against his side. "Oh, how I love you."

He was now more insistent, hungrier, as his lips went back to hers and his hand moved to her thigh. Moving her body in unison with his, she knew this was everything, everything.

They slipped quietly out of the hotel and caught the last train south shortly after midnight. Holding hands quietly in the back of the nearly empty car, they spoke softly as the train rumbled on, catching up on the little things they would have known about each other in different circumstances. A few miles south of

Sacramento, she fell quietly asleep on his shoulder. Without disturbing her, he gently slipped his arm around her and sighed. He had never known such an overpowering feeling. Just her touch, her stimulating smell, triggered an indescribable emotion that wanted to explode in words of love, in tenderness, in passion. He would do *anything* for her!

But as the miles clicked away, his thoughts drifted back to Lodi and Itoko and Noboru, to Hiroshi in Japan, and to his great dream. How could this incredibly wonderful young woman fit in? He leaned down and brushed his lips against her cheek, pushing the troublesome thought away. First, he had to get her safely settled. The rest was unimportant for the moment.

Ellen Murdock's lemon yellow two-story house with its ornate white trim and shutters sat somewhat back from the road. As Sataro led Miyuki toward the front porch, he pointed up at the tall bare oaks and softly said, "In the summer, these trees will grow heavy with a comfortable umbrella of leaves." He twisted the doorbell, adding, "And in the back, she has a nice yard that will be ideal for a pretty Japan lady's garden work if she so desires." He twisted the bell again, hoping Mrs. Murdock could hear it.

Miyuki's voice was soft as she asked, "How many summers will you keep me here, Sataro?"

He inhaled deeply before replying. "The future will have to work itself out, darling. I just don't—"

Mrs. Murdock rescued him by opening the front door with a kerosene lamp in her hand. She was a bright little sparrowlike woman with dancing brown eyes and short white hair that she spent little time fussing over. She squinted over the lamp. "Is that you, Sataro?" she asked in a throaty voice. "Do you have our little darling?"

A moment later, they were ushered into the comfortable sitting room off to the right of the vestibule. Soft hues of slightly worn velvet-covered furniture sitting on a large, wine-colored woven rug greeted them. Staring down from sepia photographs in ornate oval frames, some of Ellen Murdock's ancestors regarded them as they sat stiffly on the edge of a large sofa. A huge black and white tomcat roused himself and arched into an expressive yawn, then moved over to rub against Miyuki's leg as his mistress scurried out to the kitchen to warm up coffee.

Miyuki sat quietly, tossing quick little looks around the room while they waited silently. "I've been waiting and worrying ever since midnight," Mrs. Murdock clucked as she returned and sat primly on the edge of the love seat. She smiled brightly. "I can't wait to hear *every* detail of your dangerous escape, my dear! Oh, I'm so *glad* you could come to stay with me. We're going to be *such* good friends!" She jumped up. "Come, see your nice room." She turned to Sataro with a wicked little smile. "You, too, young man. I imagine you'll be spending some time there also." Her laugh tinkled as she led them to the stairs. "I *always* go shopping on Wednesday afternoons and visiting on Sundays," she added pointedly, then chuckled again as she started up the steps with the lamp.

She was certainly straightforward, Sataro thought, remembering Cedric had told him his aunt was an incurable romantic and that she'd had "more boyfriends during her marriage than closets to hide them in."

Miyuki let out a little gasp of pleased surprise when she saw the bright large bedroom done in lemon and darker yellows. Fluffy, flowered chintz curtains matched the heavily quilted bedspread, on which several dresses were spread out. "I thought we might be about the same size, Miyuki," Ellen chirped. "So I dug these younger styles out of an old trunk."

Miyuki turned to Sataro with wide eyes, then looked back at Mrs. Murdock. After she thanked her in a heavy accent, Ellen nodded firmly. "And we're going to start working on your English right away." As Miyuki held a light blue cotton dress up to her front, Ellen turned to the door. "Save that for later. I think Sataro needs some coffee."

Eight

During the next three weeks, Miyuki became comfortable in her pleasant canary and white hideout. Her relationship with the sprightly Mrs. Murdock continued to develop as rapidly as it had commenced. With Ellen's youthful zest, it was more a girlish friendship than the age spread might have indicated. Miyuki's adoration for her employer—though she received no wages—almost equaled what she felt for Sataro, whom she was growing to love more with each visit. She was able to sweep most of the past six months under the carpet, reliving it only periodically in nightmares. And only in unguarded moments did a chill creep in that the Gorotsuki would find her. To ensure against such a fluke, she left the house only at night and that was for short walks around the house. The big black and white feline—Hercules—soon became her good friend, when he felt inclined. And her English was improving rapidly. She had much to look forward to in the coming New Year.

But on Laguna Street in San Francisco on this cloudy day before New Year's Day, there was little to celebrate in the Mansion. Harry Yagana had been in a dark, threatening mood all week. Losing the lovely Miyuki Takano from right under his nose had been an insult he just couldn't accept. He had even laid the whip to Masa, his favorite, for giving him an impertinent taunt only twenty minutes earlier. Now, as Howard walked into his dark office, Harry leaned up into the harsh light over his desk. "Well?" he growled. "What did you find in Sacramento?"

"Nothing, Harry," his assistant replied cautiously. "She just hasn't been there."

Yagana shifted the black cigar to the other side of his mouth, scowling darkly. "You're sure?"

Howard shrugged. "With her looks, someone would have noticed. Anybody do any good on that Studebaker while I was gone?"

"Yeah, we found it in Oakland yesterday. The driver didn't know anything. Said this guy just came up and offered him eight bucks to drive them to San Mateo. The guy had some kind of a story about saving her from her husband. It wasn't even his car—he's a chauffeur. His boss was out of town."

"You check him out?"

"Naturally," Harry snarled. "You think I don't do things right around here, Howard?"

Howard held up his hands defensively. "No, Boss. I just—"

"We're driving over to Stockton tomorrow. The driver heard this guy mention it while he was approaching the railroad depot in San Mateo."

"But, Harry," Howard implored, "tomorrow is *New Year!*"

Yagana jerked his whip out of a drawer and slammed it down on the desk top as he lunged out of his chair. "We're going to Stockton!" he roared. "I'm getting that bitch back!"

Howard quickly retreated to the door. Turning, he timidly asked, "You get a description of this guy?"

"Yeah, the driver said he's tall for a Jap—with a scar on his right cheek."

Preparing for the New Year had always been an enjoyable, even exciting chore for Sataro. The fifteen-day period when all of Japan exhilarated in a vibrant spirit of jubilation had been a gala time for him since his first memories as a child. It was also a serious time, the season for people to express appreciation of their lives through many customs and rites. During the celebration period that ended with Coming of Age Day on the fifteenth, farmers decorated their plows, fishermen their boats, nets, and other implements—all in appreciation of the tools that helped them earn their livelihood. In Tokyo, a spectacular Fire Fighters parade was always held. In the northern part of the country, the *Koshogatsu* festival was held to drive away evil spirits. But

Sataro always enjoyed the *Sagicho* festival the most because it was the children's festival and the one in which he had first participated. He could still remember how he had excitedly joined the older children in climbing the nearby hills to gather pine branches to go on the huge pile called The Fort of the Gods. He had tried to carry too large a bough and stumbled down a hill in mortifying shame. But it was quickly forgotten when the huge offering was ignited and everyone shouted that the god of the New Year had descended into Heaven to stand guard at the gate. He thought the best part of *Sagicho* had always been the delicious *mochi*—the rice cakes that were toasted over the fire, then eaten to keep from catching colds during the New Year. Overall, even during the war, New Year had never failed to be a gay and lively time for him.

But Sataro hadn't found the gay and lively spirit yet. As he stood in front of the entrance to the Hiroshima-ya, his conscience troubled him. The New Year festival was primarily a family affair and nearly every symbol he was attaching to the door pricked at his guilt. The *daidai*, a type of orange, symbolized long life for the family; the *urajiro* fern stood for purity and fertility, while the piece of seaweed called the *kobu* denoted happiness. As he stood on the chair and nailed the *kadomatsu* above the door, his mouth set in a grim line. The bouquet of pine and bamboo signified stability and righteousness within the dwelling. It was all a sham!

He stepped down to survey his handiwork as Noboru came running around the corner with a paper replica of a huge red lobster. "Hey, Father!" he cried out. "We have to put 'long life' for my generation up there someplace."

Sataro nodded. "You're right, son. I thought you were flying your new kite." It, too, was part of the festival. "We have to show the *hakujin* our traditions."

"Not enough wind," Noboru replied, taking the hammer and a small nail.

Sataro glanced up at the hazy sun. "No, I guess not. Maybe tomorrow."

When the boy finished tacking up his lobster, he patted the

new leather baseball glove his father had given him for Christmas.
"You want to play catch?" he asked eagerly.

"Not now, son. I have too many things to do."

"How about this afternoon?"

"You'll have the papers to deliver." His very first edition.

Noboru grinned. "Yeah, I forgot. I can't wait to see them!"

It seemed he'd done nothing but put his son off since Miyuki
entered his life, Sataro thought with another pang of guilt as he
pushed open the heavily adorned door. On his way to the large
kitchen, he nodded to the group of boarders engrossed in a game
of rotation on one of the pool tables. Pouring himself a cup of tea
from the cookstove, he sat down to sip it and watch Zenro
prepare the *ozoni*—the traditional special rice cake that would be
served the next day. "What time will Yego be in?" he asked.
The farmhand who had given him his first ride to Lodi had been
working weekends and holidays for the last several weeks, running the game in the card room and assisting Zenro with the bar.

"Ten," replied the taciturn Zenro.

"Good. I expect business to start getting heavy around eleven."

"When will you be back?"

"About three. After the papers come in on the train."

The crippled cook wiped his hands on his apron. "I can't wait to
see it," he beamed in what for him was a long sentence. "Particularly the part about me."

Sataro chuckled. One of the features he had decided to include
in each issue of the *Shimpo Shimbun* was a short article about a
local Japanese person. It would not only give him something to
fill space initially, but would start providing a touch of recognition for members of the growing Japanese community. At some
later date he might even begin including pictures.

Itoko came in with a basket of fresh laundry from the backyard.
Placing it on the counter, she poured a cup of tea and asked,
"Will Zenro be working in the bar all day?" Her tone, as usual,
was detached.

"Most of it," Sataro replied.

She nodded. "Meaning I'll be alone in the kitchen."

She had always enjoyed preparing the New Year delicacies in
Hiroshima, Sataro thought—even to the point of trying to ex-

clude his mother from the kitchen. But that was a different matter. She had never felt any resentment toward their holiday visitors at home. Here, they represented the enemy host to her. "Maybe Zenro can get one of the boarders to help," he suggested.

"No, thank you," she replied emphatically, picking up her basket and heading for the apartment. "All they know is how to eat."

Watching the door close behind her, Sataro felt the heaviness that had begun with putting up the symbols. He had wanted so much for his first New Year in America to be a great occasion. On the surface, there was so much to celebrate, so many things to appreciate. But everything was starting off badly, and he had the feeling it was going to get worse. He took in a deep breath. What he needed was Miyuki's sunshine.

Miyuki watched Sataro knot his tie from her curled-up position in bed. In a soft voice, she said, "I wish you could come back tomorrow. New Year won't be the same, stuck alone in this house."

Sataro looked back at her saddened expression through the mirror. He wanted to crawl right back in that canary-colored bed and hold her for the entire fifteen days! He frowned. "I wish I could, too, my sweet one," he said gently. "But I have responsibilities. Many people will be visiting tomorrow and I have to be there."

Miyuki nodded, then swung her bare legs out of bed and reached for the lacy dressing gown Ellen had given her. "I know," she said with a slight pout, "but I'll still be lonesome. Couldn't you just sneak away and come out for a few minutes? I just can't wait to read the newspaper!"

He went to her and brushed her soft lips with his. Picking her up and holding her face close, he smiled and shook his head. "You're nothing but a temptress, do you know that? All right, I'll try—maybe in the early evening. But we'll have to hold hands with Mrs. Murdock."

Her face lit up in a bright smile. "I don't care!" she exclaimed gleefully. "I just want to start the New Year with you. *Oh*, put me down! I didn't give you your present."

She returned from the dressing table with a gaily wrapped little package. She smiled, handing it to him. "I finished it this morning."

Inside was a white linen handkerchief, beautifully embroidered in the lower right-hand corner with the Japanese characters for *ai*—love. He smiled softly and thanked her, wishing the musical jewel box he had ordered from San Francisco had arrived on time. She leaned up and kissed him, then shrugged. "I know you can't take it home, so I'll keep it here for you."

He nodded. No, he couldn't.

Itoko slammed the lid down on the large pot of sweet black beans and surveyed her afternoon's work. Almost everything was ready—mashed sweet potato with sweetened chestnuts, boiled fish paste, rolled seaweed, candied dried fish, eggroll mixed with white fish meat. Now all she had to do was fix the marinade for the seasoned herring roe. "Why did that damned husband of mine have to run off and leave Zenro to tend bar?" she grumbled half aloud. The damned cook ought to be back here helping her get ready for tomorrow's horde of worthless migrants. Or, she thought, further irritated, if he wants them all to think he's such a big man, why doesn't *he* do some of the work?

She sat down on a stool by the small cutting board and brushed a stray strand of hair from her forehead. Oh, how she wished she were back in her pretty house in Hiroshima with her beloved Hiroshi. She reached for a large white onion and began to pick off the dry outer skin. And why this sudden interest in buying a store in Homerville? That place was over four miles north and no more than a crossroad and railroad siding—according to Kimi. And this ridiculous newspaper venture of his was the most wasteful thing imaginable. Who did he think he was—Abiko? He should stick to his damned hotel, get rid of his wild dreams, and quit running around like a damned tycoon!

She reached for the heavy chopping knife and went to work on the onion. And she wasn't so sure all this running around was strictly business, either. She had noticed the change in him these last weeks—total indifference to her, no matter how nasty she got. Maybe Kimi has been right telling her she had better start making love to him. Maybe . . . she would have to borrow a bicycle some of these days and follow him on one of his jaunts up to his precious north! Yes! That was it—there was a damned *brothel* up there somewhere!

Her eyes began to water, and she wondered if it were just from the onion. If he *was* going to a damned brothel, her precious plan was badly threatened. Part of her weaponry was the denial . . . oh, that *beast!*

A tear slipped down her cheek. Wiping it away with the back of her hand, she thought of him poised, erect, and filled with lust—about to plunge into some cheap, dirty whore! She jammed the knife viciously into the cutting board, shattering its tip. *She wouldn't have it!*

Then slowly she collected herself as she stared at the broken knife in her hand. She tossed it aside. She'd never get back to Hiroshima this way . . . no, a new approach was in order. A pot in which some rice was cooking started to boil over with a loud hiss! Hurrying to the stove to move it, she decided it was a timely omen—she ought to let off a little steam, as the Americans said. Coming back to the stool, she wiped her hands on her apron, then slowly ran them up over her breasts. She felt a quickening in her pulse as she imagined that they were Sataro's hands, that he was standing behind her naked by the turned-down bed, with only a shaft of silvery moonlight coming through the window. He would kiss her neck and tell her how he'd gone crazy without her love. And then she'd turn and . . .

Sataro put the day's receipts in the little safe and turned the handle. Going back to the table, he quickly entered the amount in his book and brushed in the grand total for the year. He nodded in satisfaction at the amount. With so many migrants in town for the holiday season, December profits had brought his net earnings for the almost seven months up to over eighteen hundred dollars! More than enough to get started on his new projects.

He poured a cup of sake, sat back in satisfaction, and lit a cigarette. If all went well, he should be able to *triple* that profit in the coming year, he thought with pride. Maybe he could even start buying the hotel, if the owner were willing—

He looked up as Itoko came into the sitting room, deftly whisking a featherduster around at fictitious dust. And she was wearing a thin lacy chemise that he hadn't seen before! He glanced at the clock on the wall. It was almost midnight—what in God's name? And she was even *smiling* at him!

"Thought I'd make sure none of last year's dust carries over into the New Year," she said brightly, moving closer to him.

He could smell a new, heavier scent than she usually used as she brushed up against him. What—

"You know how we must always settle our debts and get a new start," she murmured, dropping the featherduster and touching his cheek softly. He looked up into her glittering eyes in confusion as she ran a hand down over the filmy chemise, forcing it back tightly over one of her breasts. Her fingers stretched and wandered down over her abdomen to her inside thigh before finding their way up to the other breast. She wet her lips with a slow, teasing motion of her tongue, then whispered, "I think we owe each other something."

Woodenly, he came out of his chair as her hands reached behind his neck and she moved up against him.

At shortly after seven the next night, the long, trying opening of the New Year was over. Sataro had begun the festivities just before sunrise when he placed the *wakamizu*—the first water of the year—in a basin for the family and Zenro to wash their faces. Then Itoko had served the first rice cake—and he had poured the family wine, the *otoso*. Well before noon, the lodgers had begun to celebrate. And by midafternoon, over a hundred immigrants had arrived. The few women who came clucked and raved about the assorted delicacies. Two American merchants dropped in out of a sense of courtesy, but stayed for enough sake to depart arm-in-arm, clumsily singing a Japanese song.

The pregnant and ebullient Kimi had helped Itoko—whose sudden vivacity still puzzled her husband—with the food, while Yoshi assisted Zenro with the bar and the cheerful Yego kept the card room going strong. The host had a busy afternoon, proudly greeting guests and listening to their tales of optimism for the coming year. Some paid off small loans to clear the slate for the

New Year, while a few others borrowed. After all, wasn't he their new father in the Valley? But the highlight of the day for Sataro was seeing how excitedly everyone received the newspaper with his name on the masthead. Cedric's praise had pleased him the most. "Be proud, Sataro. It's the beginning of an important contribution for your people."

Now, with the place closed for the night, Sataro was having trouble concentrating on the pool game with Cedric; he had been unable to break away to see Miyuki. Normally, his smooth skill on the table kept the newspaperman reaching into his pocket, so it didn't hurt that Cedric had won three straight games of eight-ball. Sataro leaned over an easy rail shot on the lavender-colored four ball into the corner pocket, but jabbed his stroke and left it hanging.

"Aha!" Cedric chortled with a broad grin. "You're still human." He leaned down over the ivory cue ball and lined up one of the three striped balls left on the table. "Get another thin dime out, you Nipponese capitalist," he gloated. "Your mother could run this table." He made the twelve ball in a corner pocket, then moved around the table for an easy shot on the eleven ball in the side.

Sataro went back to a barstool, chalking his cue tip. He was about to make a comment when he heard Noboru at the front door. A glance behind the bar told him that Zenro must be in the back, so he went to unlock it. His son burst through the doorway exuberantly. "Father, you ought to see the beautiful car out in front! It's a big, shiny Duesenberg! And these nice men told me they'd give me a ride in it!"

Sataro looked over Noboru's head and into the unsmiling dark eyes of Harry Yagana. Behind the brothel operator and also wearing a pulled-down black fedora was Howard. "Mr. Hoshi?" Yagana growled.

Sataro nodded, chilled by a sharp stab of fear. "Yes," he replied blankly.

"I'd like to talk to you."

Sataro quietly told Noboru to go in the back, then showed the two visitors to a small corner table. Cedric glanced up with curiosity from where he was about to make the eight ball, then somberly sat on the edge of the table. As Zenro came back from the kitchen, Sataro told him to bring three cups of sake, then turned to Cedric. "I won't be able to play anymore tonight," he said tonelessly. "I'll come by the office tomorrow."

The newspaperman threw a suspicious look at the corner table, then took his cue to the bar. "No, I think I'll have a drink with Zenro," he muttered. "Besides, you owe me a dime."

Sataro looked up at Yagana as soon as he seated himself. "Well, gentlemen, what can I do for you?"

Howard sat back in his chair lackadaisically as Yagana lit a big black cigar, slowly shook out the match, and exhaled a big cloud of smoke at Sataro. The Gorotsuki leader smiled slightly as he said, "I own a club in San Francisco, Mr. Hoshi, and one of my little doves has flown from her nest. Does that mean anything to you?"

Sataro shook his head, casually replying, "Should it?"

Harry Yagana's eyes narrowed as he leaned forward menacingly. "Her name is Miyuki Takano, Mr. Hoshi, and she was stolen away by a tall Japan man with a scar on his right cheek. The Oakland driver of the Studebaker he hired described him to us." Yagana blew another cloud of smoke at Sataro. "Then, a couple of hours ago in Stockton, a Japan man told us he saw a Lodi hotel operator get off a train with a very pretty young woman on exactly that same date. *Now,* does it mean anything to you?"

Sataro's cold eyes stared back into Yagana's. "Nothing," he stated flatly.

As Howard moved up into a more threatening position, his boss growled, "I want that bitch back, Hoshi!" Getting no answer, he nodded his head and continued more softly, "I like that boy of yours. Be a damned shame if something were to happen to him—like maybe both his arms getting broken, or somebody running a razor blade across his eyeballs . . . maybe even tying him up in a bag and tossing him in the river. . . ."

Sataro felt his eyes stinging as he fought to control himself.

"Tell you what, Hoshi—my associate and I are going to go up the street for a couple of drinks while you make up your mind about that little yellow-eyed whore. We'll be back in forty-five minutes."

Sataro got slowly to his feet and stared at their backs as they disappeared through the door. He was still staring blankly when Cedric sidled up. "They don't change much, do they?" the newspaperman growled.

"Who?" Sataro replied blankly.

"Your everyday Gorotsuki. I could smell 'em. How did they find you?"

Sataro hesitated, then, knowing he had no choice, explained briefly.

"What do you want to do about it—call the sheriff?"

Sataro shook his head. "Wouldn't do any good. They'd be back."

Cedric's eyes narrowed. "Okay, then what are *we* going to do about it?"

Sataro downed his sake shakily, still trying to calm the rage boiling through his body. "Go home, Cedric. This is none of your business," he said coldly.

"The *hell* it isn't!" the newspaperman snapped. "This is *my* goddamn town!"

Thirty minutes later, Sataro withdrew the heavy .45 revolver from the drawer where he kept it hidden and slipped it into his belt. Telling Zenro he would be out for a couple of hours, he moved stiffly toward the door. Outside in the shadow, he looked up and down the nearly deserted Main Street. Only the voices of a few men in front of the Japanese restaurant broke the stillness. The Duesenberg was nowhere in sight. The loading sheds across the street, stretching interminably northward, were bleakly bathed in the cold light of the half moon.

As he stared at the street, he pictured it in daylight. He saw Noboru happily heading off to school with his books nonchalantly slung over his shoulder. And he saw the ominous black sedan pull up, saw Yagana jump out and grab the boy, then slam him into the back seat and dive in on top of him . . . he saw Yagana knock his beloved son unconscious, then pull out a straight razor and slash his eyes . . . he saw Noboru being placed in a gunnysack and saw the gunnysack disappear below the evil surface of the river . . . and he saw Yagana raping his terrified Miyuki, saw him lunging over her with a whip . . . saw the blood on her beautiful back and dribbling from her lovely lips. . . .

Shivering at the damp chill in the air, he fingered the heavy revolver, then fumbled for a cigarette and a match. *He had to control himself!* As the flame illuminated his face, the threatening black Duesenberg appeared at the end of the street. Lumbering slowly forward, it drew up beside him and braked to a halt. Sataro threw his cigarette away, swept the street with a final glance, and stepped through the open backdoor to the silent blackness of the leather interior.

All he could see was the red tip of Harry Yagana's cigar as it brightened and revealed a faint, momentary glimpse of his harsh features in the far corner. "I trust you've come to your senses, Mr. Hoshi," the gangster's rough voice suggested.

Sataro sat grimly on the edge of the seat, leaning forward to Howard. "Turn around and head back north at the corner," he directed in a defeated tone. "Then turn right after three blocks." He stared ahead through narrowed eyes as the big sedan made a U-turn, not trusting himself to even glance at the dark form beside him.

"You'll forget about the little trollop in no time," Yagana gloated. "The kid you'll have forever."

Sataro told Howard to turn left on Stockton Street.

"Of course, you're going to forget this whole episode, aren't you, Mr. Hoshi?"

Sataro grunted, still fixing his stare on the road ahead. "About another three miles," he growled. "She's keeping house for an old farmer."

"How much is she charging *him?*" Yagana asked with a harsh laugh.

Sataro's fingernails dug into his palms as he ignored the question.

Eight minutes later, Sataro told Howard to turn up a one-lane drive to the left and keep going for another half mile. Howard looked back, growling, "This isn't any more than a damned wagon trail. You sure you know—"

"Keep driving!" Yagana barked.

"Up ahead—that turn-in to the left," Sataro said a couple of minutes later. "Through those bushes."

The Duesenberg had trouble negotiating the tight turn, but was soon bumping its way slowly up the even rougher trail. Just as the driver started to complain again, Sataro slumped back in the seat and told him to stop. The big car eased to a halt by a large stand of dark bushes.

Sataro sucked in a deep breath and held it as his fingers found the handle of the heavy revolver and gripped it tightly.

Leaning forward, Yagana grasped the front seat. "Where's this house?" he growled suspiciously. "I don't see—"

The roar of the big .45 under his arm was deafening!

It almost drowned out Sataro's violent scream of rage as he whipped the long-barreled revolver up to Howard's turning cheek and jerked the trigger again. The second blast smashed half of the driver's startled face into the windshield, as the explosion again rocked the interior of the sedan. Sataro whirled, every iota of fury boiling out in another anguished roar! Jamming the barrel into Yagana's slumping mask of disbelief and pain, he smashed his forefinger against the trigger one more time. The face that enticed Miyuki to America disintegrated into a jumble of blood, bone, and brains as the last explosion thundered.

Sataro looked down in contempt for only a moment before shoving the pistol back into his belt and turning to the door handle. As he stepped out into the cold moonlight, Cedric came pedaling furiously toward him in the narrow dim beam of the car's headlamps. The newspaperman jumped off Sataro's Columbia breathlessly, threw the shovels down, and looked closely into his friend's harsh stare. Without a word, he lit a match and leaned into the back seat. After a quick look at the occupants, he stood up with a shudder and nodded his head. "Let's start digging."

Thirty mintues later, with the bodies buried in the bushes and dead leaves covering the shallow graves, Sataro watched Cedric back the big sedan slowly out the path to the trail. As the large headlamps turned and disappeared toward the road to Sacramento— where his friend would ditch the Duesenberg—Sataro heaved a deep sigh of relief. Grimly, he reached down for the shovels, strapped them to his back, and climbed on his bicycle.

Turning the front wheel to the bushes, he leaned over the handlebars and stared coldly at the dark shadow that led to the gravesite. Some would call it murder, he thought. But no samurai would. And the carrion that lay in those damp holes had been nothing but the lowest form of predators—vultures picking at the flesh of their own. And they'd reached for *his* flesh. In another day in the land of his ancestors, he would have used the sword— the soul of Bushido—on them. And he'd have received accolades.

But this was America and their fate must remain forever sealed. There was so much to do, and he'd only begun. The wealth and great honor that would come to the House of Hoshi lay over the horizon. Only the strength and will to acquire it was necessary. It was as certain as the holy sunrise!

He nodded at the dark shadow, saying grimly, "And if a hundred more of you come, *nothing* will change."

Nine

Nearing Stockton at shortly after eleven the next morning, Sataro pedaled the Columbia along briskly and thought about the man he was hoping to see. He had wanted to meet George Shima ever since his arrival in the Valley, but hadn't had a plausible reason before today. From the most isolated village in the cold mountains of Hokkaido to the palace of the Emperor, the story of the Potato King had found its way. He was the most famous of the emigrants and his story had probably brought more poor and adventuresome Japanese to America after the turn of the century than any other factor.

Shima—Kinji Ushijima—was in his mid-forties and had been in the United States about eighteen years. Beginning as a common day-laborer, he soon became a labor contractor, pooling his countrymen into work gangs that ranged throughout much of northern California. Shortly after that, he changed his name and acquired ten acres to farm on shares. By 1900, he had purchased some cheap swampland and had begun reclaiming it for farming. He found the delta land near Stockton and Lodi ideally suited for potatoes, and they became his main crop. It was rumored that he had over four thousand acres under cultivation at the present—and had more money than he could count.

But all Sataro wanted was ten acres of it.

He parked the bicycle against the wall of the bank building and climbed to Shima's unassuming second-story office. He had rightly guessed that the holidays wouldn't interrupt such a successful man's work. Not only was the Potato King in, but he was alone and greeted Sataro personally.

Sataro handed him a copy of the *Shimpo Shimbun*, saying in

English, "While this is only a humble beginning, sir, I'd be honored if you'd accept a complimentary copy of my first edition."

Shima glanced at the newspaper with interest, quickly scanning the front page. Except for his solid build and air of assurance, the developer's only noticeable trait was his effort to speak precise English—just like Abiko, Sataro thought. He would have to get back to his own pronunciation drills.

The Potato King looked up brightly from the newspaper. Nodding approval, he said, "I like it. Particularly the personal interest story about the crippled man. Yes, I like your endeavor, Mr. Hoshi. Now tell me about yourself."

Sataro was brief, ending with, "I'd like to do a feature story on you, Mr. Shima. Something with your personal philosophy about success that might be an inspiration to all Japanese in the Valley."

Shima chuckled. Offering Sataro a cigar, he said, "Then all my migrant workers will want to quit and start their own potato patch. Very well, what do you want to know?"

The interview took thirty minutes as Sataro laboriously took notes with a pencil. Shima's eyes glowed as he spoke of his crops, America, his lovely wife, and his challenging business. Sataro then asked when did Shima expect to have enough money to return to Japan and was startled at the adamant response. "Going back?" Shima replied incredulously. "To stay? Never. *This* is my country now."

Sataro decided not to push the matter further; it was time for the real purpose of his trip. He explained that he wanted to go into the farming business, then told Shima about the parcel he wanted to buy. The only thing that stood in his way was Shima's lease. The famous man leafed through a notebook for a few moments before saying, "That particular piece isn't under lease. I own it."

"Good. How much do you want for it?" Sataro asked directly.

The developer removed his spectacles and looked up from his notebook. "You know anything about farming, Mr. Hoshi?"

"No, sir," Sataro replied quietly. "But I have a friend who does."

"Does he know anything about potatoes—or how to rotate

beans and celery with them? Does he know about the life span of soil for such crops in this area?" As Sataro groped for an answer, Shima nodded. "I thought not. Well, it's a good way to lose your shirt, Mr. Hoshi."

Sataro nodded, but softly insisted. "A man has to learn, Mr. Shima."

The Potato King eyed him speculatively for a moment, then asked, "How much are you willing to pay for it?"

Sataro shrugged. "Whatever it's worth."

Shima laughed abruptly. "I could tell you it's worth a lot of money, but I like you, Mr. Hoshi. That place is about worn out for my crops. You still want it?" As Sataro nodded, he rubbed his chin and scribbled some figures on a tablet. "Tell you what," he went on. "Make it forty-five dollars an acre and send your farmer to see me. I'll tell him how to wring out what's left. Then, if you have the money and patience, you can move into grapes or something."

Sataro had his farm with the dark secret buried beneath the bushes.

Two days later at shortly after noon, Sataro was returning from Cedric's office when he saw a gleaming black sedan parked near the front of the Hiroshima-ya. As a bright reflection from its back window flashed into his eyes, he felt a cold stab of fear. A picture of Itoko and Noboru lying in pools of blood assaulted him. He should have known it was impossible to fight them! Overcoming an urge to stop and get help, he pedaled on, slowly stopping and glancing inside the empty Packard. Evidently, they were all inside. He could still get a weapon . . . but how could he use it if they had his family? The fear and anger convulsed his stomach. Dropping the bicycle in the dust, he sprang for the door handle.

Two burly men in dark suits were getting up from the bar as he entered. Over the rushing in his ears, he heard Zenro say, "Here's Mr. Hoshi now."

The shorter of the two men moved toward him as he braced for the encounter. With a short stiff bow, the Gorotsuki introduced himself, then gruffly said, "I'm trying to locate two of our men,

Mr. Hoshi. Four days ago, they drove to Stockton on a business matter, but we haven't heard from them since. Yesterday, one of our people in Sacramento called to report that their automobile had been found there. I was wondering if they might have stopped in here for information?''

Sataro frowned, unbelieving, then nodded. Coolly, he replied, ''Yes, they asked me about seeing a pretty girl. But I couldn't help them and they left. Said something about going up to the capital. What were their names?''

''Yagana and—''

Sataro nodded again as he interrupted with a smile. ''That was them.''

The gangster scowled. ''They say anything else to you—like who they might be seeing in Sacramento?''

Sataro shook his head, frowning as if he was trying to remember. ''No, sir. They just wanted to know if I'd heard anything. They had a drink and drove off. You think there was foul play?''

A dark look came over the Gorotsuki's face. ''Possibly. But that isn't your concern.'' He turned to his associate and nodded toward the door. ''Thank you, Mr. Hoshi. If you hear of anything, please contact me at the Paradise Club in San Francisco.'' He handed Sataro a card and strode out the door.

Sataro's surprise visits were what Miyuki called her dessert. Wanting to be with him all the time, she jealously guarded her Wednesdays and Sundays as a dieting person would look on two meals a week. Although she never answered the door, the jangle of its bell seldom failed to make her heart skip a beat. And Ellen Murdock never failed to sigh nostalgically as she took her coat from the hall closet and invented a place to go. She liked to tell Miyuki that someday her neighbors would run out of coffee and she'd just have to walk around Galt pretending she was looking for her lost lovers.

Now, as she jammed her hat firmly in place and disappeared out the front door, Sataro swept Miyuki into his arms and kissed her warmly. ''It's all over, my darling!'' he exclaimed. ''We're free.''

Pushing him back, she said, ''What are you talking about?''

He led her into the sitting room and pulled her down beside him on the love seat. "The Gorotsuki came to see me earlier today." Her eyes widened in fear as her hand flew to her mouth. She knew nothing about their earlier visit. "They have no connection with you and me!" He beamed. "The closest they might ever come would be Sacramento, but that would net them nothing. It's over!"

She searched his face. "Are you sure?"

"As sure as the cherry blossoms." He told her about the man from the Paradise Club, making it sound like a casual stop at the end of a hopeless quest. "Oh, I won't be parading you around San Francisco for some time, but they won't be back here."

"Oh, Sataro," she sighed, slumping against his chest, "I can't believe it. I—you don't know how I've worried, how I've dreamed such terrible things. Last night it was you. They were cutting your face and stabbing you with swords."

He drew her tightly into his arms. "I know, darling," he said soothingly.

Her shining eyes opened as she looked into his face. "Oh, I love you so much!" she whispered fervently.

He found her lips and kissed her fiercely. She was safe, his wounded dove was finally safe! And how he wanted her! He brushed her lips again as he got to his feet. Her love was brimming as she came to him with a deep sigh, reaching for his neck. Without a word, he picked her up and headed for the stairs, feeling as powerful as a bull, as intoxicated as a drunk—volcanic!

The next day, Yego delivered the load of rocks to the large stand of bushes by the well in the middle of the potato field. As soon as they were unloaded and his part-time helper left with the wagon, Sataro began sorting out those with the flattest sides to provide the most even surface for his floor. He had considered having Yoshi help him on Sundays, but that would mean an explanation—and he didn't want to burden his friend with the terrible secret. Nor did he want anyone else to know. Cedric, as an accomplice, could be trusted implicitly, but who knew what lay ahead with others?

And how would he justify such a substantial floor for a barn?

Simple—it was a symbol of his first move into empire. His rock.
He moved into the bushes and started placing the first stones so
he could dig precise holes to fit them over the two graves.
Perhaps the barn he and Yoshi would build over them wouldn't
last forever, he thought grimly, but the floor would last until his
great-grandsons had flowing white beards and the Hoshi family
had long ago returned to Japan.

A couple of weeks later, Sataro pulled a wedding invitation out
of his jacket pocket at the evening meal. With a broad smile, he
announced, "We're invited to a wedding. Cedric's."

Noboru looked up from the soup bowl that was hiding part of
his face. "Me too, Father?" he asked excitedly.

"I think so, my son," Sataro replied pleasantly. "I'll check
the American custom."

Itoko said nothing as she kept her eyes downcast and fiddled
with her chopsticks. Controlling her feelings and playing the
game was beginning to gnaw at her nerves. The sex part was
easy enough once she got herself aroused, but Sataro had been
strangely reluctant about *that!* Now he expected her to go to a
damned *hakujin* wedding! And she didn't even like Cedric—let
alone his rich, bouncy, white wife-to-be.

"Would you like to buy a new dress?" Sataro asked pleasantly.

She wanted to scream out that she wasn't going, but bit her lip
and nodded. "I suppose so," she replied casually. "When is
it?"

Sataro glanced back at the engraved card. "A month from
today." He chuckled. "He says she can't wait."

She wouldn't go! She'd find a way—illness or something.

"Do we have to stay long?" she asked quietly.

Sataro reached up and stroked his scar. "Long enough to be
correct Japan people," he stated evenly.

"It'll be fun if a lot of kids are there," Noboru commented.

Sataro smiled back at his son. "Yes, probably so." Then he
turned back to Itoko for a moment before returning to his food.
She was becoming absolutely impossible to understand. "We'll
have to think of a suitable gift, Itoko."

"How about a dinner in one of those fine restaurants we can't get into?" she snapped, unable to stem the bitterness.

Sataro frowned, stopping in the middle of a delivery of rice to his mouth. His tone was edged with thin patience. "This isn't a matter of our being Japan people. He's my close friend." He sighed. "I'll order something from San Francisco."

The Sunday after the Baldwin wedding, all the residents of the hotel plus several other available migrants assembled at the potato farm for the barn raising. Yoshi had already completed most of the framing before the group of twenty-five arrived at shortly after eight. At noon, Zenro and Noboru came with a hearty meal, and at three o'clock the boss opened the sake bottles.

Standing back some thirty feet away, Sataro turned to Yoshi as he sipped. "You've done a good job, my friend," he commented. "That barn will be standing there long after you and I are back in Japan."

The stocky farmer beamed. "It's not very pretentious, but it has the most endurable floor in California." He glanced sideways. "Are you sure you don't have something buried there?" Sataro wondered if his start showed. But Yoshi went on. "Like gold or something? Oh, and I've decided I'm going to become an American citizen. Never going back, except maybe to visit my mother sometime. You know—when I get rich." His laugh erupted.

The barn *was* substantial—some twenty feet wide, thirty long, and almost fifteen feet high under the bracing beams. It would soon be painted a bright red. Sataro felt a tightening of inner resolve. It *was* the beginning of his empire, *and* a symbol—a symbol that he would not be intimidated. He poured some more sake in their cups as he watched the amateur carpenters scampering over the new wood, pounding in final nails, wiping their brows in the warm sunlight, laughing, and enjoying themselves. He chuckled inwardly as he fingered Macnamara's silver disk in his pocket. Why not?

"I think I'll name it 'The Other Cheek,' " he announced with a smile.

Yoshi looked at him curiously. "Why?"

Sataro winked. "Take thee not offense. Don't you know the Christian way?"

The farmer shrugged. "I'll have it painted over the front door."

"In Japanese." Sataro laughed. "I don't want our white friends taking advantage of us." Sobering, he decided the time was right. "Yoshi, I have my plan ready. After the vines are planted here, I'm buying the adjoining ten acres of vineyards and I want you to operate both places."

Yoshi shook his head. "But I won't have the time. I'm within maybe eighteen months of buying a small place over by Schwartz's. He said—"

Sataro grinned as he broke in, "The other ten acres is for you. I'll be your bank. You pay me twenty dollars a month starting next New Year at no interest."

Yoshi sucked in a deep breath as he stared in disbelief. Finally, he managed to whisper, "Do you mean it?"

"When can you start building your house? I imagine you should give your boss thirty days' notice."

The farmer's face broke into a broad grin as he grabbed Sataro's shoulders and spun him around. He shouted exultantly, then danced a short few steps before he noticed he was the center of attention from the new barn. He sobered, moving close to Sataro's face. His eyes were glowing as he said, "Mine will be the first Japan house close to the road."

Sataro knew what he meant. Japan people always lived in the back, in the hired hands' quarters. It was also Yoshi's first step up.

Sataro looked up from the letter he was writing to Hiroshi. Something in Itoko's tone flashed a warning signal. She was looking at him intently from where she was sewing by the oil lamp in the corner of the neat sitting room. "I said, do you have important business that takes you to Galt?"

Sataro replied coolly. "I have business in many places these days. You know that."

He turned back to where he was laboriously writing in English. He still hadn't totally mastered the use of an ink pen.

. . . And so, my dear son, your brother is doing handsomely in school. When the next term starts in a few weeks, he will have caught up with those in his same age group. Naturally, his marks aren't as high as yours, but you are at home where—

"Kimi says she saw you ride out of that town last Wednesday. She was shopping there," Itoko said, watching his face. "Is there something I should know?"

The chill struck at him. *Did she know about Miyuki?* Was she toying with him? No—she couldn't. It was just his pesky conscience jabbing away. No matter how he rationalized, no matter how his heart sang when he was with his beloved Miyuki, it always came back to annoy him. He shrugged, laying the pen down. "You know I seldom discuss business. You have too much on your mind right here. Noboru and the hotel and all."

She methodically placed her crocheting circle on a stand and slowly moved to face him from across the table. It was time, she decided abruptly. For over seven months she had been patient, been the model housewife and hotel keeper, offered her body whenever he'd take it. Yes, any more delay would only further test her already fraying patience.

She cleared her throat as he watched her eyes. "Please tell Hiroshi that I expect to see him soon."

Sataro sighed inwardly. She didn't know anything. "Why should I tell him that?" he replied absently, feeling the relief.

Itoko had rehearsed the line for weeks. "Because I intend to go back to Hiroshima shortly," she announced firmly.

Sataro looked into his wife's determined expression in silence. Finally, he said, "But that's impossible. Maybe in three or four years—"

"He may not be *alive* in three or four years!" she snapped. "I'm going *this* year, Sataro!"

He listened as she stormed on, beginning to see through her recent seductive change of heart. When she finally ran down, he sighed and replied, "Hiroshi is fine. The last letter was clear on that. Now, let's talk about a visit in perhaps two years. Yes, I think we might be able to work that out."

Itoko's eyes narrowed as she leaned down toward him. "I will not wait!" she snapped.

Itoko dropped into the sullen, troublesome attitude she had brought to America. As the days passed, she alternated between total silence and bitter demand. Sataro took it as impassively as possible, trying to point out that Seizo was taking superb care of the boy, and stressing Noboru's need for his mother. But his words were as wasted as raindrops in the ocean.

Shortly over five weeks after her initial ultimatum, he came into the sitting room one rainy afternoon to find a note propped up on the lamp in the middle of the table. It read, "Come up to room nine. Itoko."

Puzzled, he walked to the stairwell and went upstairs. Just as he reached the upper hallway, its stillness was broken by her loud laughter. It came from room nine. Turning the handle, he slowly opened the door to see his wife propped up on one elbow on the bed. She was wearing only a flimsy nightgown that was hiked up to her hips. Beside her, almost naked, a migrant worker named Fueta was stroking her bare thigh. As Sataro blinked, trying to accept what his eyes shouted, Itoko raised her glass and roared with laughter.

"Come in, dear one," she chortled. "The more the merrier!"

The boarder's head jerked up in fright. Dropping his glass, he fumbled for his trousers as he avoided Sataro's terrible gaze. Itoko laughed again. Her hand slid down to her pelvis and rubbed her pubic region as she taunted, "We were just getting to the interesting part."

Sataro raised his hand to slap her, but caught himself. He turned to the frightened boarder in cold rage. But before his angry words could come out, Fueta shrieked, "It was all her idea, Boss! The sake, she told me—"

Sataro's explosive backhand caught him in the mouth, rocking his head backward. "Get out!" he snarled. "If I ever see you again, I'll *kill* you! And if I ever hear one word of this sordid encounter, I'll chase you all the way to hell to kill you!"

Itoko laughed harshly as Fueta nearly fell down scrambling out the door with his belongings. Looking at Sataro with a jeering grin and glittering eyes, she stroked her breasts and taunted, "What about me, Sataro? Are you going to kill *me* for telling everyone I'd rather bed a boarder than my own husband?"

The smile faded from her lips as he edged closer. She had never seen such violence in his eyes. Never— His right hand flashed out, catching her long black hair just behind the nape of the neck. Twisting it tightly, he jerked downward as his face moved to within inches of her widening eyes. His lips barely moved as he growled, "You'll say nothing. Shame yourself, but never disgrace me again." His breathing was heavy as his face moved even closer, his cold eyes boring into hers, the grip on her hair tightening.

She closed her eyes, fearful that he might break her neck, but unwilling to give up. "Now," she whispered hoarsely, "now are you ready to let me go home?"

He released his grip slowly, pulling himself stiffly erect, struggling for the words. Finally, he spoke in a low harsh tone. "If this ever happens again, Hiroshi will be out of your life forever."

She stared back, instinctively drawing her hands up to her face. "Wh-what do you mean?" she asked brokenly.

His black eyes were slits, the muscles on the side of his jaw rigid, the thin white scar on his cheek harshly white. "I swear, Itoko," he rasped. "I swear on my samurai blood, on my father's honor . . . I solemnly swear that you will never see him again."

The following night at shortly after twelve, Itoko slipped into the sitting room and knelt by the safe. Moments later, after she burned herself with two matches, the heavy door was open. She scooped all the available cash into her large traveling purse, then got to her feet and glanced around cautiously. Moving swiftly but silently, she was in Noboru's room in seconds. She leaned down and brushed her lips gently across his cheek. "I'm sorry, my fine son, but you have him," she whispered, then stood and took one final look at his dark shape. "I'll see you in Japan."

She inhaled deeply, bracing herself for the final move. Brushing the tears from her eyes, she slipped quickly out the back door to the shed where her packed valise awaited. Grabbing it, she hurried around the corner to the dark street. She had fifteen minutes to catch the train and eighteen hours before the freighter departed.

Ten

Itoko was thankful for the fair weather and calm sea as she climbed to the bow of the *Haru-Maru* and stood in the cool breeze. Squinting ahead into the reddening ball of the setting sun, she pictured her beloved Hiroshi thousands of miles away in Hiroshima. She could almost *feel* him in her arms, hear his gay voice, his quick joyful laugh. "I'm coming home to you, my baby," she purred softly.

But as if a cloud had thrust itself over the sunset, the guilt that had plagued her thrust itself forward. The face of her elder son stared back at her accusingly and the ship's engines seemed to be throbbing in rhythm, "You deserted Noboru, you deserted Noboru."

Sataro could *rot* in America—he was to blame for everything. Hadn't he forced her into such hideous actions, backed her into corners like a lioness? A short chill caused her to shudder, as if the open sea wanted no excuses. She had behaved atrociously, like no lady from Japan *ever* acted. That abominable scene in the boarder's room—the most hideous, utterly vulgar thing she had ever imagined. Disgusting! Never, *never* again would she so cheapen herself!

She could obliterate those actions, but how could she push away the guilt? Would throwing herself to the deck and begging forgiveness from the dying sun still the voice of the engines? Someday, she'd make it up . . . someday, Noboru. And then, as if cleansed by her fervent resolve, she drew herself erect. Itoko Mitsubishi would win out against all of the forces against her, overcome all odds in making her new life. And her beloved Hiroshi would always be with her!

121

A sharp gust caught the flowered silk hat she had purchased for Cedric's wedding. Turning to catch it, she saw the smiling man who ate at the captain's left grab it as it spun across the deck. Handing it back to her, he smiled again and pleasantly remarked, "Too windy up here for hats."

His voice was deep and cultured—definitely Tokyo, she thought as she took the hat, thanked him and glided away. She wasn't yet lonely enough to talk to strange men. Reaching the ladder that led to the main deck, she glanced up into his whimsical smile. She nodded her head, wondering if she should have stayed for a few minutes. It might have been interesting. No, it would only have led to a game of difficult questions.

Sataro fumbled for the key to the front door, then finally turned the lock and entered. Going tiredly to the back of the bar, he struck a match and lit a kerosene lamp before pouring a liberal portion of whiskey. He sighed as he took a big swallow and dropped to the stool. He hadn't been in bed over eight hours in the last four days and was thoroughly exhausted. He lit a cigarette and sucked in the harsh taste, thinking he should look in the bedroom to see if she might somehow have come back. But he knew she hadn't, not Itoko. She would never—

"Any luck?" Zenro asked, walking out of the kitchen in a nightshirt.

"No. Heard anything here?"

The cook shook his head.

Sataro frowned into his drink. The note was just a subterfuge. "Only four ships left Seattle for Japan in the last two days and she wasn't a passenger on any of them. And I scoured the Japanese community. No one saw her."

Zenro opened a bottle of beer for himself. "And someone would notice a pretty lady like that."

Sataro nodded. "She must have gone to San Francisco. I'll get some sleep, then catch the noon train. How is Noboru taking it?"

"Quietly. He doesn't understand."

Sataro finished his whiskey and headed for the sitting room. "Call me before he sets off for school," he said wearily. "I must talk to him.'' He took a couple of steps, then turned back. "Did Yoshi come in?"

Zenro nodded. "His wife knows nothing."

Two mornings later, Sataro finished the neat brushstrokes of a letter that read:

> My Honorable Brother,
>
> You may be aware of a distressing problem before this note arrives. Itoko has been under severe strain since our departure from Japan, and has now left without permission, stating that she is returning to Hiroshima. I have discovered her ship will arrive October 7. She is to return immediately to me in California. Should she require funds for the return voyage, please advance them. I shall reimburse you. On second thought, permit her to stay three weeks.

After mailing the letter, Sataro pedaled out to the Murdock house. In the backyard, while Miyuki listened attentively from a bench, he explained the full situation. Her joy was hidden behind a calm mask as she quietly asked, "And what if she refuses to return?"

"She must obey the will of her husband," he replied darkly.

It was time to say it. "You have grounds for divorce now."

He'd never looked at her in anger before. "There can be no such disgrace in the House of Hoshi!" he replied heatedly. She dropped her eyes to the ground.

He stopped his pacing and dropped to a knee in front of her. His eyes were troubled as he took her hand and spoke gently, "I'm sorry, dear one. I haven't considered you at all. And I have no solution for our future yet. But this isn't the way . . . a Japan woman does *not* leave her husband in such a manner."

Miyuki watched a golden leaf blow across the ground. Was she to be the eternal mistress? Was she to let this proud man storm about futilely while his shrew of a wife did just as she pleased? It was her life too! She nodded inwardly and made her decision.

*   *   *

Itoko had enjoyed her breakfast. The fantail was thinly populated with passengers on this fine morning and she wished she had a deck chair, like she'd seen in advertisements for those luxury liners. As she started to move to a more open place at the rail, she stepped warily over a stray rope, slipping and losing her balance. A strong hand caught her elbow. "You should remember that a ship rolls on the fairest of seas," the man who had retrieved her hat several nights earlier cautioned. He continued to steady her as they made their way to the rail. "I noticed how particularly lovely you looked at the table this morning. Is today something special?" he asked.

She squinted sideways at him, noting the fine line of his nose. He was definitely from Tokyo, she decided. "No," she replied carefully. "I'm just excited about being another day closer to home."

"Do you make many voyages?" he asked, puffing fruitlessly on his pipe.

"My second. But I was ill on most of my first."

He removed his hat, revealing a thick shock of graying hair. "Forgive me," he said in his deep voice. "My name is Obata, Professor Koki Obata. If I had known you'd be on board I would have spoken to the captain about the seating arrangement in the dining salon."

They both smiled at his allusion to the frugal mess. She noticed the tiny laugh lines around his eyes. "I am Mrs. Hoshi," she replied quietly.

He cleared his throat. "It isn't often one sees such a lovely woman traveling alone on the high seas. Do you have relatives in America?"

She turned from his warm curiosity to the white-flecked wake. He was so handsome—why did he have to ask? "Yes, but I'm returning home to Hiroshima."

He fished out a tobacco pouch and refilled the bowl of his heavy, stained old pipe. When it was lit, he asked, "Couldn't you get direct passage, or do you like rusty old freighters?"

"I wanted to see Tokyo again," she lied.

"And your husband," he persisted. "Is he waiting in Hiroshima?"

Her reply wasn't a total lie in her way of thinking. "I no longer have a husband."

"I'm sorry," Koki Obata murmured, assuming exactly what she wanted him to assume.

"And you, Professor—is your wife waiting in Tokyo?" she asked frankly.

"Yes," he replied quietly. "She's quite ill. I haven't seen her in nearly two years."

Itoko nodded, disappointed. "I'm sorry to hear that, sir. She'll be glad to see you." He had such a good face.

They chatted for another half hour, leaving the fantail and strolling about the deck to the bow—each enjoying the other, each feeling an easy casualness. He was the third son of Baron Utaro Obata, she found out—far down the line from inheriting the title, but apparently also far from any poverty. He taught history at Tokyo Imperial University and had, prior to visiting America, been in Germany visiting that country's universities for a year. It was part of Japan's program of catching up with the modern world, he told her—the Meiji government's method of borrowing whatever was of use. He said he'd be glad to return to his university chair and and sit back to be a casual observer of whatever glory or folly might lie in Japan's path.

Finally he asked, "Do you play *sugoroku?* I have a miniature set."

Itoko smiled brightly. She loved competitive games. "Yes," she replied. "But I haven't played since I was a child."

"Same old twelve black and white pieces." Obata chuckled as he relit his pipe. "We can play in my cabin, if you wish."

It wouldn't look right to go to his cabin. A lady wouldn't— She'd *love* to see his cabin, have some privacy with this delightful man. She gave him a mock frown. "That wouldn't be proper, would it?"

He laughed. "If it'll make you feel better, I'll invite the captain."

She shook her head and smiled. "I don't think that'll be necessary."

*   *   *

The last day at sea was also Itoko's thirty-second birthday and she awoke feeling depressed. Noboru had been haunting her dreams and now she thought of the many years when he had proudly brought her a gift. And the guilt flooded back over her. Fighting it off, she swore to make it all up to him. He was bright, he understood—she *knew* it. He had his horrible father, that was all the eldest son ever cared about—what was a *damned* mother? But she pictured his wide dark eyes as he handed her the package that contained a tortoise-shell comb when he was only eight, and he touched her hand and she'd felt his love.

She pushed him aside, seeing her beautiful Hiroshi waiting, and she threw herself into a radical change in hairstyle to cele-brate arriving back in Japan. It had been a difficult decision, but the shimada lost out to the fashionable low pompadour known as the "penthouse style." Among her meager belongings was a silver inlaid bar for the small chignon and a matching comb to set it off. She wished she had a kimono to wear, but decided on the lavender satin dress she had worn boarding ship. Koki would like it.

Koki. As eager as she was to see her Hiroshi, the more reluctant she was to part company with this compelling man who'd turned the boredom of the sea into an adventure. Except for sleep and a few hours of privacy, they had spent the last three days together. She delighted in his firsthand stories about politics and Tokyo society. What a handsome, invigorating man. Every-thing about him shouted aristocracy, yet his gentle manner never forced it.

She chided herself for feeling a tingle when their hands touched accidently, fighting the arousal she sensed. And the night before, she had dreamed of being in his arms.

She stared into the tiny mirror, knowing she wanted him, feeling her pulse quicken as she thought of his strong stocky body moving against her . . . and her pulsating response . . . his smooth warm skin, his hungry ardent lips on hers . . . strong hands searching, caressing . . . his powerful manhood touching, moving inside, driving. . . .

She jerked to her feet, snapping away from the image and taking a deep breath. What nonsense! How cheap! Her hand trembled as she dabbed at her moist brow. Such preposterous thoughts . . . yet who would know? She knew how much he wanted her, and she'd never see him again—didn't she have it coming? How long would it be before she'd have the discreet opportunity to be with such a man again—*years?* Perhaps she'd be so ostracized it would never happen! She'd seen divorced women before, hoping and waiting for some widower and finally just any available man—often the dregs of the teapot.

Not Itoko Mitsubishi . . . she'd give up love before she'd stoop so low!

She smiled. One night of forbidden, exciting pleasure with a stimulating nobleman on a glistening, moonlit sea that would tell no tales. Why not—wasn't it out of a storybook? She took another deep breath and exhaled slowly. She'd see. . . .

His cabin wasn't much larger than hers, but afforded the luxury of a small table for their invigorating game of *sugoroku*. Koki played the simple backgammonlike game with ease, while Itoko played recklessly and was lucky. As she won the last game at just before eleven, she clapped her hands in glee. "There," she cried exuberantly, "I beat the professor again!"

He smiled indulgently as he picked up the miniature ivory pieces and began to reassemble the set. He chuckled. "But, had this been for money, the outcome would have been different.". He reached across the tiny table, finding her hand. His touch was warm and stimulating to her. "Then I would have to take you shopping before you leave Tokyo."

She tried to keep the alarm out of her eyes. What was he saying? Was he spoiling it all by talking about more than one night of madness, of—

"The ship will be there two days, you know."

She dropped her eyes, confused. Such talk was unnecessary. All he had to do was squeeze her hand more tightly, pull her up into his arms. She couldn't wait . . . all he had to do was take her. "Your wife," she managed.

"I'd break away," he said, his eyes glittering with intensity.

"No, it isn't necessary. I—"

He got to his feet slowly, his eyes locked into hers. She watched without breathing as he came around the table and drew her into his arms. His mouth came down to hers, his kiss sweet, exploring, experienced. She opened her mouth, drawing in his tongue as she reached urgently around his broad shoulders and moved up to him. The aroma of his maleness was as intoxicating as his touch. She felt the hardness of his chest against her swelling breasts as her tongue darted around his. Breaking the first kiss, his lips moved to her neck. "I love you!" he whispered fiercely. "I love you and want you for the rest of my life!"

She kissed his hair, his cheeks. He didn't need to use reckless, passionate words that meant nothing. Her mouth found his. What were words? All she wanted was him, all of him for one wild nights of abandonment. No pretenses, no restraints—just *him!*

His lips were devouring her, his strong fingers working their way down to her swaying, gyrating buttocks. She crushed up against him, moaning, moving away from his mouth to bite at his chin, his ears. Her fingers clawed at the back of his head as his face dropped to her heaving breasts. "Clothes," he gasped, picking her up and carrying her to the bunk. "We must get—"

"No!" she cried, pulling him down. *"Now!"*

She kicked her legs up, fighting the cumbersome skirt and petticoat until they were out of the way. "Oh, Koki, my darling Koki, *now!"*

His mouth found hers as he came to her. Arching up to him, she dug her fingers into his back and smothered his lips with kisses and the wild words of craving. "Oh, yes, yes, *yes!* Oh, I *love* you, darling!"

Eleven

Not far from the edge of the dock, several rickshaw drivers stood around in their short jackets, dark trousers, and conical wicker hats. Itoko motioned to a tall, sinewy-looking old man who rushed up to take her luggage. After giving him the address of Seizo's house in Shiroshima Kita-Cho, she settled back into the rocking motion of the tiny cab to watch the familiar sights of Hiroshima pass by. It was a pleasant fall day with the temperature in the sixties. As the driver ran through the residential streets, she glanced around to see what colors the maple leaves had achieved. She smiled, recalling that the maple leaves always dominated conversation in the fall. How dark were they? How scarlet, how gold? It was *marvelous* to be home!

She leaned up to tell the driver she had changed her mind and gave him instructions to Hiroshi's school instead of the house. Ten minutes later he agreed to wait as she dismounted and strode briskly into the school building. The headmaster greeted her politely, not missing her beauty, and personally led her to her son's classroom.

Her knees felt weak, her breath short. One hand picked at her obi, the other stole up to look for a stray wisp of her silky black hair. She knew her fingers were trembling but she didn't care. Within seconds she would be touching the most beloved part of her life! Standing frozen in the hallway, temples pounding and nothing to do with her hands, she heard the recitations cease, heard some hushed words of instruction, then soft footsteps. And then she saw him . . . taller, even more beautiful. She sucked in a tiny cry as her hand came up to reach out to him. Her heart was bursting.

129

Hiroshi stepped quizzically into the hallway, immediately turning to her. His face lit up in a beaming grin as he rushed the few steps to her waiting arms. "Mother!" he shouted eagerly, clutching her tightly.

"Oh, my darling, my darling!" she exclaimed, crushing his head to her breast as the pent-up tears rushed down her cheeks.

He choked back the words of love that wanted to tumble out and, suddenly remembering the headmaster, pulled back to give her a short jerky bow. "You're free to go with your mother today, Hoshi," he said with an approving smile.

Itoko brushed away a tear and held her son at arm's length. Drinking in the beauty of his straight narrow nose, the square firm jaw, and his misty wide eyes, she sighed. "I had forgotten how handsome you are—and how you've grown!" She pulled him back into her arms. "Oh, how I've missed you!"

Hiroshi hugged her tightly again, then pulled back. "Where are Father and Noboru?" he asked, looking behind her.

She had rehearsed the next lines over and over. "They're still in America, my love. I've come back alone just to be with you. But we'll talk about that later." She gripped his hand tightly and started for the exit.

Thirty minutes after the surprise reunion with Seizo, his wife Setsuko, and Sataro's mother, Tomi, her brother-in-law asked Itoko to accompany him to the garden for a private talk. He stopped by a neatly trimmed azalea bush to light his pipe. Carefully placing the remains of the wooden match in a stone receptacle, he blew out a cloud of grayish smoke and asked, "Precisely how do you arrive without advance notice?"

Itoko assumed his clipped words and cool tone were part of his courtroom manner, and she didn't like them. But she had steeled herself for this moment. Pulling her shoulders back and raising her chin defiantly, she looked him directly in the eye and spoke firmly, "I left without Sataro's permission."

Seizo held her gaze. Slowly taking the pipe from his mouth and controlling his shock at her blatant disrespect, he nodded and asked, "Why?"

"It's between us," Itoko replied evenly, but losing some of her resolve.

Seizo nodded again after a moment. "And how long do you intend to stay?"

"Indefinitely, if possible."

He frowned, sucking noisily on his pipe, and shrugged. Turning back to the house, he said, "It'll depend on Sataro's wishes. In the meantime, Hiroshi is overjoyed at seeing you."

She caught the sleeve of his kimono. "Seizo, please," she implored. "Try to understand. This is the way it has to be."

He looked into her distraught eyes for a moment, then went inside.

Sataro's letter arrived the next afternoon. Itoko saw it on the silver tray by the *tokonoma* and was tempted to grab it, rip it open, and read it. Or throw it away. She followed her sister-in-law into the garden where Tomi was pouring tea, unable to pay attention to their cool conversation. That *damned* letter!

She could understand their coolness. Setsuko, with no children of her own, had learned to cherish the beautiful Hiroshi in the past sixteen months. And here she was—suddenly a threat. And the fifty-three-year-old Tomi, inured to custom and family solidarity, certainly couldn't take her side. Yet when she took a cup of tea from the older woman, she thought she detected a touch of sympathy in her brief smile. For twenty-one years Tomi had been a widow, she thought with a start. God, in twenty-one years she'd be exactly Tomi's age! She sipped the tea, wondering if she'd be an old hag living by some desolate army post with Hiroshi and his wife.

She patted Tomi's hand, actually feeling a closeness with her old competitor. She watched as the long-suffering woman moved to a clipped mulberry bush and smiled down at the glistening back of an orange-colored beetle. Turning with a warm smile that accentuated the deep lines around her dark eyes, Tomi said, "Look, isn't he pretty?"

Setsuko, welcoming a chance to break the stiffness, scurried over to the bush. "Yes, Mother, he's beautiful. If Hiroshi were here, he'd want to put him in a jar. You know how he studies everything so closely. Why, I don't know how he'll ever be a soldier!''

"It's his destiny," Itoko interjected. "Soldiers can also be scholars." *What was in that letter?*

She found out shortly after Hiroshi finished the evening meal and went to his room to study. Seizo looked up from the low table as he filled his pipe. Clearing his throat, he announced, "Itoko, I must inform you of Sataro's wishes. Your husband grants you three weeks' stay here. Then you must return to California. I'll secure your ticket tomorrow."

Itoko tossed quick looks at Tomi and Setsuko, but both were staring into their teacups. She met Seizo's gaze firmly. "I told you, I'm not going back. And I want a divorce."

The women threw her startled glances as Seizo's mouth dropped open momentarily. He collected himself with a deep breath. "You know that's impossible," he said reprovingly. "Good Japan women do not divorce their husbands."

Having entered the deep water, Itoko wasn't backing down. "Then he must grant it," she insisted evenly. "I'm not leaving Japan."

Seizo fought back his anger. She was openly defying her husband's authority and that of the House of Hoshi. He shook his head as he furiously lit his pipe. "You'll do as you're told," he snapped.

Itoko's eyes blazed back. "Tell him I'll bring more shame on the House of Hoshi than he ever dreamed possible. Ask him about room *nine*. Tell him there'll be a *hundred* room nines!" She sprang to her feet and stomped from the room.

Finding Hiroshi in his room, she wiped away the tears and stroked the top of his head. "I must tell you something, my son," she said earnestly, dropping to the *tatami* beside him. Taking his hand and holding it tightly, she went on, "Please try to understand . . . I love you so much I've run away from your father so I could be with you." She explained briefly, ending with, "And regardless of what your uncle may say, remember that our love is all that matters."

Hiroshi nodded soberly, not quite understanding. Getting to his knees, he placed his strong young arms around her shoulders and leaned his cheek against her forehead. *How could this be wrong?* she shouted inwardly. She didn't see Tomi stop momentarily outside the unclosed sliding door. Nor did she see the misty eyes of the older woman.

Itoko was quietly sewing a torn place in one of Hiroshi's *hakama* in the solitude of the garden when the messenger arrived with the letter. Inside, on the embossed letterhead of the Momiji Hotel, Koki Obata's bold brushstrokes read:

> My Dearest Itoko,
>
> You have so overwhelmed my head and heart in the past ten days that I had to find you. I must see you, my darling! I am at this hotel in Room 202. Please come at three o'clock this afternoon.
>
> > Your devoted Koki

Itoko blinked at the words as she reread them. Her breath quickened. It was impossible! A shipboard infatuation, lust . . . wild abandonment in a make-believe situation with a fairy prince. He *couldn't* be here. And certainly with her family problem—if Seizo found out . . . No! It was impossible! Sheer idiocy. She'd burn the note and he'd go away.

Itoko held the fan in front of the lower part of her face as she took a deep breath and entered the lobby of the Momiji Hotel. Now she wished she had worn a Western dress—at least she'd have a hat and scarf to cover her identity. A quick look revealed the stairs and only three men glancing idly in her direction. They must be staring at her! Who would recognize her—a friend of Sataro? What about Seizo, did he ever come here?

She somehow reached the steps and began to climb, certain that knowing eyes were boring into the cerise taffeta of her kimono, recognizing the back of her head. With a sigh of relief, she reached the second-floor landing and paused out of sight of the lobby. She could just walk down the hallway and return. Go back home and never see him again. But the second flight of steps beckoned, leading to her fairy prince, her lover. She touched the bottom step, then floated upward, knowing her heartbeat was echoing throughout the hotel. How many times had she relived that romantic interlude?

And then she was on the second floor—202 to the right. She felt a touch of panic, could still turn back, shop and buy something to justify her coming. No involvement, no more trembling hands. Koki . . . She pulled her shoulders back and found 202 in a few steps. Her knock was tentative, the rushing feeling in her head stronger. Perhaps he had been called away, perhaps she was late and—

Koki's smile seemed to spread over his handsome face as he slid the door open. He reminded her of a child receiving a precious gift as he reached for her hand and said softly, "I was afraid you wouldn't come," and drew her inside the pleasant suite. She glided in, watching his glowing eyes as he bent over her hand and kissed it tenderly. "I've missed you terribly, my dear," he added, looking into her wide eyes.

She couldn't remember him being so handsome! "I shouldn't have," she managed, watching him come closer. "I can only stay a few minutes, then I must—"

He swept her into his arms and found her soft ready lips.

The first thing Itoko noticed on awakening was the silk sheets. She turned, glancing over her shoulder to where Koki was smiling from the side of the wide low bed. Pulling the sheet over her nudeness, she sat up. "What time is it?" she murmured.

"Five-thirty," he replied softly, reaching out to touch her cheek. "You've been asleep for thirty minutes."

She started to get up. "I must get dressed!"

"No, wait a moment. There are some things I must tell you." She pushed up further but he caught her hand. His earnest expression stopped her protest. "I must catch the late train back tonight," he began. "And it may be over a month before I can find another excuse to come back." As the last rays of the setting sun brightened the room, she detected tiny bronze reflections in his serious dark eyes. "I've done nothing but think about you, my dear," he continued. "Every time I see an attractive woman across the room or on the street, she has your face. I—I'm swimming in love for you." Again she started to say something, but the tip of his fingers stilled her lips. "When your problems are worked out here, I want you to come to Tokyo. I'll find a nice place for you to live and—"

"No!" she burst out. "My Hiroshi is here. And you have your wife."

The flecks in his eyes were turning to crimson. "I know you can't leave your son. We can work something out later."

"And your wife."

He shrugged. 'She's very ill, my dear."

"I won't be your mistress."

The flecks were no longer there, only pain. "Trust me, darling, trust me."

She slumped, closing her eyes as his arms encircled her and lowered her back to the sheets. They kissed, sweetly, longingly. Finally she sighed, then whispered, "I'm so confused . . ." Suddenly she saw Noboru with tears in his eyes.

"We'll find a way," he replied gently as his lips moved down her neck.

She stiffened. It *wasn't* a shipboard fairy tale and she *wanted* his promises to be real. She had heard about those "sick wives," but she believed this fine, gentle man. And she wanted a chance, an honest chance for something more than illicit love. "No, Koki!" she cried out, jerking to a sitting position. "I'm still married!"

His eyes clouded briefly as he sat up, saying nothing.

"It was so easy on the ship to let you believe—why should I tell you my troubles? I mean, we were strangers and what difference—"

"Do you love your husband?"

"I loathe him. All I want is a divorce."

He nodded, his dark eyes softening. And suddenly it was more important that he understand than anything else in the world. Her eyes began to fill as the words tumbled out, words of pain, terrible anguish, words of anger and remorse. For the first time since she heard she was going to America without Hiroshi, she had a listener who understood, who offered no judgment, reached out to her in empathy. Her tears flooded his shoulder and chest as her misery erupted and was accepted with warm compassion.

And when there was nothing more to tell, he nodded, his gentle eyes wide and tender as he gripped her hand and said, "We'll have a wonderful life together, you'll see."

Twelve

Miyuki nearly spilled the tea she was pouring for Ellen Murdock as Hercules flew by her on a dead run and threw his black and white form up the trunk of a nearby elm. Ellen chuckled. "Crazy damned cat."

Miyuki glanced up to where the feline was eyeing her balefully from a low limb, his black tail swishing back and forth in rhythm with his mischievous mind. She and the independent Hercules had become fast friends in the nearly eleven months since her arrival, but he still found ways to try her patience. Tasting her tea in the warm fall sunshine, she thought about how much she loved this secluded backyard that she had all but transformed into a Japanese garden. She'd miss it—just as she'd miss seeing her charming and zestful friend every day.

"Tell me again about Nikko," Ellen said.

Miyuki smiled. Her friend loved to hear about the festivals. Although she still had a heavy accent—particularly with her "ls, rs, and ths"—Ellen's daily English drills had produced excellent results. She described the festival of Tokugawa in Nikko at length, ending with, "Remember the old saying—'Don't say magnificent until you've seen Nikko.' "

"Oh, I wish I could go there someday!" Ellen exclaimed. "When Sataro gets rich and marries you, will you take me?"

Miyuki's face clouded momentarily. She was about to reply when Sataro strode purposefully around the corner of the house. As Mrs. Murdock departed to give them privacy, he lit a cigarette and began to pace. Pulling an envelope from his pocket and waving it angrily, he announced, "I just received this telegram from Seizo. Itoko refuses to return and insists on a divorce."

137

Miyuki's amber eyes flicked up to meet his ire as he stormed on. She covered her anxiety with calm as she waited.

Her silence was accusatory, he thought. But the ignominy of a divorce in the House of Hoshi? Unthinkable! He had the great future of his sons to think about—they couldn't be clouded by the scandal of divorce! Yet he knew part of his anger was directed at himself, at his own guilt. And those beautiful eyes he loved so dearly were reflecting that guilt like mirrors of gold. They were quietly saying the door was open, his freedom was there for the taking. But it *wasn't*—there was the dream, the triumphant return to Hiroshima . . . his great sons. It all had to be worked out slowly without scandal.

She continued to watch his distress in silence. If only he weren't such a typical, stubborn Japan man. Why did he have to be so selfishly obstinate? Pride, always pride. Samurai and Bushido. How long would it take for him to change his mind—months, years? Well, she wasn't waiting. The moon was perfect.

She got to her feet and caught his hand. Looking into his smoldering eyes, she smiled suggestively and whispered, "You need to be soothed, my love."

The frost in his expression melted as he took her in his arms. "I'm sorry," he said, kissing her hair. "I don't see you for two days and then come to you whining about the misconduct of my wife."

Her forefinger quieted his lips as she smiled softly into his eyes. "I'll make you forget," she whispered, tugging him toward the house.

Sataro had been trying to write to Macnamara for nearly an hour. Three times he had started and three times he had torn it up. He simply could not get the missionary involved. First of all, he hated to admit that Itoko had left him. Next, he couldn't possibly explain his involvement with Miyuki. And lastly, he was certain Itoko would react poorly to clerical interference from a *hakujin*. As he balled up a fourth attempt, Noboru came into the sitting room in his nightshirt.

"Can we talk, Father?" he asked timidly.

"Certainly, my son." Sataro didn't have to ask if the home-work was finished; the thirteen-year-old Noboru was a top student.

The boy stared at the floor a moment before quietly asking, "Did you hear from Mother today?"

Sataro frowned as he capped the ink. "No, but I received a wire from your uncle. Your mother intends to stay in Hiroshima for a time."

Noboru moved to the *tokonoma* where Itoko's flower arrange-ments had always brightened the room. Only a couple of green plants, which he watered faithfully each day, remained. He swallowed hard, squeezing out the difficult words. "Is she ever coming back, Father?"

Sataro thought briefly of bluffing, but decided it wouldn't be fair. "I don't really know, my son," he replied quietly. "As you know, she hasn't been herself since we left Japan. Perhaps a few months in Hiroshima will help. I know she must miss you terribly."

Noboru frowned, trying to hold back the tears. "I guess she just loves Hiroshi more—I think she always has." He wanted to cry out that it was *unfair*, that he didn't even *like* his brother anymore!

Sataro watched quietly, feeling his son's pain, but not the animosity. What a terrible thing Itoko had brought about, he thought angrily. Divorce? How could she talk of such a scar? He'd write another letter tonight!

Noboru turned away, wiping a tear from his cheek.

Abruptly, his father lurched out of his chair and went to the boy. Taking him in his arms, he held him tightly and whispered, "It'll be all right, son." Clearing his throat, he added brightly, "I think we should go to Stockton tomorrow to pick out your bicycle. What do you think about that idea?"

Noboru tried to blink away the wetness. "Can I have a Columbia?"

Sataro stepped back with a smile that restrained his own tears. "And why not? We can't have the delivery manager of the Hoshi Grocery Company pedaling around the countryside on anything less."

*   *   *

Sataro had the usual mixed feelings as he rode by the red barn of The Other Cheek the next morning—the immense pride at being a landowner, and the concern connected with what lay under its foundation. Pedaling on another hundred yards, he turned into the dirt lane that led to Yoshi's place. The small white house stood out brightly, even starkly in the sunshine. Someday there would be trees. Yoshi had been true to his word about building it close to the road to announce his ownership—the four-room frame structure wasn't over forty feet from the front of the property.

He glanced at the two freshly painted sheds Yoshi had recently completed, marveling at the man's artistry with saw and hammer. The new red wagon stood between them, its bright sign reading GROCERIES in large gold leaf letters.

"You ready to go into the grocery business today?" Yoshi asked with a wide grin as he came around the corner of a shed. "Your new horse is."

Sataro soon patted the rump of the big dapple gray. They had named the placid animal Senyu—fellow soldier. "How is he with the wagon?" Sataro asked as he stroked the horse's velvety, almost white nose.

Yoshi chuckled as he picked up the heavy harness. "I told him he owns it. He'll be fine. If your Yego does half as well selling groceries, you'll have no worries."

Sataro chuckled. Yoshi was jealous of the ambitious Yego. But the man had grown up in the fish market business; certainly he could run a grocery store. Sataro told Yoshi to bring the wagon over when it was hitched up, then rode on to his new venture. Homerville was about a half mile from the farm. It consisted of two long loading sheds by the railroad track, two houses, a building that served as a labor camp for migrants, and the building he had just leased. One house belonged to a man named Smith who owned the huge fruit business and most of the surrounding land. Smith had built the combined store and hotel in hope that more people would move to Homerville, but soon decided that a nonpaying enterprise merely ate up his valuable time. He leased it to Sataro for forty-five dollars a month.

The two-story building was perfect for Sataro's plans. The

long main room in front was shelved and had a big icebox. In the rear was an apartment similar to the one he had in the Hiroshima-ya, while the upper floor housed two large and eight small rooms. He hoped to get some boarders in the off-season, but already planned to turn a section into a bar and game room for Smith's workers.

Everyone, and primarily Cedric, thought he was crazy to go into business out in the country, but he had made a careful estimate of how many families would be wanting the staples and delicacies of a Japanese diet in the next few years. With Noboru delivering in a six-mile radius, and the anticipated arrival of more and more brides, he figured the store alone would net a good profit. And it was closer to Galt.

He rode over the railroad crossing and stopped in front of the building to watch his new manager putting the finishing touches on the bright yellow sign with red characters and letters. In Japanese and English it read, HOSHI, LTD. "Can a man buy smoked eel here?" he asked with a wide grin as Yego greeted him.

On December first, Seizo laid down the ultimatum. Speaking to Itoko alone in the sitting room, he said, "I've arranged passage back to California. You'll depart in ten days, arriving in San Francisco on the twenty-fifth. Sataro will meet you."

Itoko no longer made any pretense of subservience to her brother-in-law. He would do as his brother willed and she had now taken on alien status in the household. "I'm sorry, Seizo," she replied coolly. "I'm not returning."

Seizo tried to light his pipe calmly. He was tired of this situation—the woman was not only totally wrong, she was defiant about it. He had always been impressed by Itoko's beauty and bearing, but they had never been close. He wished Sataro could pull himself away from California and come get his damn wife! Grab her by the damn hair and throw her back on a damn boat! "You cannot disobey your husband," he said grimly.

"I'll get the divorce."

"You haven't got a chance. No judge in this prefecture will grant it."

"After a time one will."

Seizo shook his head. "Not unless Sataro agrees. Not even in modern Japan. You're the one who has deserted your spouse and child."

"But I came back to my other child. He needs me!"

"Hiroshi is no longer your legal offspring."

"He's my son!" Itoko flared. "The adoption was against my will!"

"No such claim was presented," Seizo replied patiently. "If necessary, I can forbid you from seeing him and get a court injunction."

Itoko paled. "You wouldn't do that, Seizo."

He puffed vigorously on the pipe. "If I had to."

"I would take him and run away."

Seizo shrugged. "Then he would never be able to continue toward his military career. You'd break his heart."

Itoko's eyes glittered as she balled up her fists. "I'd find a way."

Sighing as he rose to end the discussion, Seizo said, "The ship departs on the tenth. I don't wish to discuss this matter again."

The afternoon sunlight streaming through the flowered chintz curtains made the bedroom yellows even brighter. As they entered, Sataro caught her hand and drew her into his arms for a long, sweet kiss. Christmas dinner was over and Cedric had spirited his Aunt Ellen off for a buggy ride, leaving them alone for a while. It had been several days since they had been together. "I want you," he whispered, moving toward the quilted bed.

Miyuki pulled away, smiling softly as she went to the dresser. "I have something else for you first," she said as she handed him the linen handkerchief embroidered with *ai* that she had given him the previous New Year. "I keep forgetting you can keep it now," she whispered, tucking it in his shirt pocket. "And I want you always to be reminded of how much I love you."

"Thank you, my darling," he said huskily, reaching for her.

"No, not yet. I must first tell you something." She had rehearsed these words for days and still they sounded harsh. "Sataro, the handkerchief is not the only way I have of showing how much I love you . . . I'm with child."

She held her breath as he blinked, staring at her as the statement sunk in. After what seemed an age, he asked, "Are you sure?"

She nodded. Her eyes were wide and unflinching. "Ellen took me to a doctor."

His gaze dropped to the floor, then back to meet hers. She was still afraid to breathe. He found a smile. "That's wonderful," he said with all the conviction he could muster. He smiled again, searching her eyes. Bastard children were a way of life in Japan, but this wasn't Japan. He should have known it would happen sooner or later. He was going to be a father again. . . .

She had played her trump, now it was time to see if she had won the game. His eyes were clouded, reaching. The scar on his cheek was white. She inhaled deeply and softly asked, "What are we going to do?"

Another moment of truth was on him, forcing him. He looked deeply into the beautiful eyes he so loved, and suddenly he felt glad, cleansed. No more stupidity about Itoko, nothing but a marvelous life with his beloved Miyuki and their children. His great dream could be broadened. Elation swept over him. A slow smile spread into a grin as he took her hands and kissed them. "Why, I think we should get married," he replied happily.

Time, Sataro asked himself, where is the time?

A California divorce for which he was eligible could take months. And he didn't have months—not if Miyuki was to get married in anything but a maternity dress. His eyes fell to the letter he had just finished to Seizo. The words swam on the paper, but the important phrases glared back at him: ". . . Get an immediate divorce . . . Y200 per month settlement for two years. Afford periodic access to Hiroshi . . ."

He slowly folded the letter and placed it in the envelope. He would send a preceding telegram in the morning to get things started. He knew the civil code of 1898 had made most divorces more complex than the old method, known as "three lines and a half," in which the man merely made a public divorce declaration. But even now, with both parties in agreement, all that had to be done was make a mutual statement at the local district office, attested by two reputable witnesses. As an attorney, Seizo would be able to set himself up as proxy.

Now all he had to do was tell Noboru.

Tomi brought word of the marriage to Itoko's tiny rented house in early February. "Her name is Miyuki and she comes from a village not far from here," the white-haired woman announced. Her tone implied disapproval, but Itoko knew she was excited.

Itoko was absolutely astounded, so shocked she almost became nauseous. *Sataro married—the man she was accused of deserting already married?* She didn't believe it! But Tomi wouldn't lie. Maybe *he* lied to hurt her. *How could he do this to her?*

Tomi was rattling on, saying something about the possibility of new grandsons—how fickle could the old crone be? She *had* grandsons! Had she no more loyalty than her unfaithful son? Yes, unfaithful—how else could he be marrying before the ink was dry on the divorce decree? And after all the remorse and shame she'd suffered for leaving him. A *young* country girl—probably couldn't even read. Had the man gone *insane?*

Where had he found her? "Surely he must have said something more," she said as calmly as possible.

"Only what I've told you. Seizo thinks she might be a picture bride, whose intended died or something."

Itoko nodded. "I'll find out!" she snapped. "An old friend of mine, Kimi Togasaki, will tell me everything. I'll write immediately!"

Tomi sniffed. "How can such a young woman be a good mother to Noboru?"

Itoko froze, shocked at the thought. This young peasant, moving into *her* bed, usurping the love of her beautiful eldest son—it was absolutely damned criminal! She turned away to a window to hide her burning cheeks and the chance of a treacherous tear. She might possibly learn to accept Sataro's having a new mate, even a young peasant, but *never* would she be able to—the intruder simply could not take her place with Noboru!

She should write to Noboru. She had been going to write to him every week, but just couldn't. At New Year she had managed half a page and thrown it away. The words were so hollow.

How could she ever tell him of her longing, her wasted time with him . . . her guilt? If only she could hold him to her breast one more time. . . .

Tomi touched her sleeve. "Are you all right, my dear?"

She sucked in a deep breath. "Yes, yes, of course."

Miyuki had looked forward to Ellen Murdock's visit with excitement. Although Sataro had taken her to Galt several times in the six months they had been married, this was the first time Ellen had been to the Hiroshima-ya. Tea and cookies in the parlor was the setting for Miyuki's exuberant stories about how much Sataro anticipated the baby, what a caring husband he was, and how well she had fitted in with both Noboru and the business.

Ellen suddenly jumped up sprightly. "I'm getting a little bored with all this billing and cooing," she said with a twinkle. "Show me where you hide all these lonesome bachelors."

Following a tour through the downstairs, Miyuki led her to the second floor. "And here," she said, pointing to the boarders' rooms, "is where our guests stay. At this time of year they're usually in the fields from dawn to dusk."

Ellen winked mischievously. "How many of these lonely, available men did you say are usually around?"

Miyuki chuckled. "Usually twenty. But on weekends, they're here in swarms."

Heading back down the hall to the landing, Ellen shook her close-cropped white head. "And to think I've been wasting all those years up there in that old house. Hell, I should've bought a boardinghouse long ago."

Miyuki looked back to laugh as she reached the top of the stairs. The rest was a blur. She had no idea how she tripped. With a short cry, she pitched over the first steps, landing on her shoulder partway down. Tumbling almost in a somersault, she came down on her back once, then smashed into the floor below.

"Miyuki!" Ellen screamed, rushing down the steps behind her.

Miyuki was dazed, lying on her side with her head against the wall. She could distinguish Ellen's concerned face and knew Zenro was there. The ringing in her ears drowned out their words. Her back burned and there was a sudden, acute pain in her lower abdomen. As she tried to pull herself up, she felt another sharp pang rip through her swollen body. Falling back to the floor, she heard Ellen shout to Zenro, "Get a doctor quick!" as she slipped into unconsciousness.

She was awakened just over an hour later by a piercing, cramplike pain in her groin. Her scream rocked the crowded bedroom. She bit into her lip as the agonizing contraction grew in intensity. The excruciating spasms continued. Opening her eyes momentarily, she saw the hazy, concerned faces of Sataro, Ellen, and Dr. Kelly. Ellen was dabbing at her sweating brow with a cool wet towel. The doctor's voice seemed to come from another room as he said, "Just as I feared, I'll have to deliver her here."

The baby! she screamed to herself as she tasted the blood on her lips. The horror of her fall flashed before her—the steps rising to meet her, the first stunning bump, the next, the final crunching blow as she came to rest against the wall, Ellen's screams. *But the baby!* She shuddered from fright and pain as another sharp contraction gripped her. When she opened her eyes, she saw for the first time naked fear written on her husband's face.

Doctor Kelly was concise. "Due to a possible lower back injury, she can't be moved. Get plenty of hot water and towels ready. Unless I miss my guess, she's going to spit that baby out in short order."

Sataro snapped a command to Zenro, but he had already disappeared into the kitchen. "You're going to be all right, darling," Ellen said soothingly as she continued to blot the heavy blanket of perspiration.

Miyuki's response was a sharp cry of pain. Sataro took her hand. "I'll be here every second," he said softly.

"I'm sorry," she whispered through the tears.

He brought her fingers to his lips, kissing them gently. "You'll be fine, just fine."

Eight minutes later, the next excruciating labor pain came.

Thirty-five minutes later, their stillborn daughter was wrapped in a sheet.

*   *   *

It was September 29, two months since the accident.

Sataro watched silently as Miyuki cried softly from her kneeling position in front of the small gravestone. The tiny English words on the marker swam in the brilliant sunshine. The sodded grass was green from her watering it twice a week, and the fresh flowers they had brought brightened it. Ellen, she had named her, forgoing any Japanese name for that of her great friend. Little Ellen, who had never had a chance to see the sunshine, never had a chance to laugh and know the meaning of love. The weight tightened around his heart.

Dr. Kelly had said she was a beautiful baby. And in a world of sons, Sataro strangely liked the idea of having a lovely daughter, a continuation of his so lovely Miyuki. But now it would never be—like Itoko, she would never have another child. What a terrible thing for a young woman to face, he thought as he touched her shoulder. And all he could do was ache for her, ache and live with his guilt.

For as surely as the earth turned, he was to blame. Since the day of the tragedy his multiple wrongs had haunted him. The innocent baby and her blameless mother had paid for his pile of transgressions. Just coming to America and tearing his family apart had been a wanton, selfish act. His adultery. His callousness to Itoko. Was there any honor in these acts? Was it his karma to harm those he loved by dishonorable acts?

He gripped Miyuki's shoulder more firmly as a tiny sob escaped her compressed lips. She, too, was torturing herself with guilt. The beautiful love child she had designed for her kind and caring husband was dead because of her greed. Not content to accept the role that had been cast, she had conceived the child as a tool to force his divorce and further her own ends. It was her crime, her terrible wrong against the man she loved that had ripped his child, his beautiful daughter, away. She choked off a final sob, dabbed at her eyes with a moist hankie, and got slowly to her feet. She would make it up to him somehow.

He squeezed her hand as he took it. And they walked slowly back to Japan Town.

BOOK 2

THE MERCHANT PRINCE AND THE YOUNG GENERAL

1912–1941

Thirteen

Tokyo, Japan—1912

A great hush was upon the city—so great that even the insects seemed to be waiting silently to see if the dying man in the Imperial Palace was actually mortal. Business was at a standstill in the muggy July heat while a nation seemed to hang suspended over what it refused to believe. Why should the birds sing or the dogs bark? Was not Mutsuhito—called by the common people the August Son of Heaven—the god of all creatures? Was he not the direct descendant of Jimmu Tenno, who was created by the sun goddess—Tensho Daijin—660 years before the birth of Christ? Hadn't this divine ruler who had rescued Japan from the darkness of the shoguns during his reign of the past forty-five years been the greatest of all her 121 descendants? And the closest to his people?

The city that was larger than London seemed to stop breathing, even though its dense population was being swelled by thousands of pilgrims arriving from all over the islands to pay homage and offer supplication.

In the guest suite Itoko occupied when she visited Koki in Tokyo, she felt the sadness. But as Sataro would have said of her, it was probably a role, a role created by the grief of the nation. For Itoko had overriding concerns. More important than the gloom and sorrow the Emperor's death would create was its inconvenience. The timing angered her. Why couldn't he have waited? Or why couldn't Sataro have made his decision about Hiroshi's school location earlier in the summer?

But that was Sataro, always thinking of himself.

If the boy remained in Hiroshima, he would have to attend that preparatory school and eventually be assigned to a regiment from that prefecture. And she certainly wasn't going to live in Tokyo with Hiroshi elsewhere!

Koki Obata's ill wife had lingered on for over two years, finally passing away in her sleep one night while her husband was spending a weekend with Itoko in Kyoto. Koki had suggested that they marry as soon as a decent period of mourning passed, but she insisted on remaining near Hiroshi until he entered the *yonen gakko*.

Now, she thought bitterly, the mourning period for the Emperor would interfere with everything.

Koki was depressed when he finally returned to his house in the fashionable Kazumi section of Azabu at shortly before five. A high-ranking acquaintance in the police department had gotten him close to the gates of the Imperial Palace and back through the pressing masses of grieving people. He poured a whiskey and sat in an overstuffed chair in the study to tell her about it. "It's the most amazing demonstration of concern I've ever heard of," he said softly, shaking his head. "Thousands of people surround the grounds, trying to get near the fence, wanting to touch it as if to hold off the inevitable. Men, women, and children crouch to pray, weeping openly. In places, they kneel on the coarse gravel. Then, when their prayers are finished, they push their way back to make room for the ever-waiting newcomers. It's simply incredible!"

At forty, Koki Obata's handsome features were normally enhanced by his now nearly white short hair. But tonight drawn lines of sorrow made him look older. "I wonder if the people will ever really know how much Mutsuhito's reign has meant to us as a progressing nation?" he mused. "Crown Prince Yoshihito will assume the throne and all the veneration as if donning a suit of clothes."

Itoko felt his discomfort, wanting to take him in her arms and soothe him. But it could only be for a moment; she had the other matter to settle. Moving to him and softly stroking his cheek, she said, "I think I should see the general tonight."

He looked at her in disbelief. He wasn't too keen about her seeing him at all. "How can you say that? It's an insensitive time to ask for favors."

She stroked his hand. "Because the mourning period will keep him busy. If I wait, there won't be time."

Koki shook his head. "I doubt he'll see you."

She shrugged. "I must try."

Lieutenant General Hidenori Tojo at fifty-seven had come a long way since gaining admission to the noncommissioned officers academy in 1871. Arriving destitute in Tokyo at the time, the opportunity had seemed heaven sent. Little did he dream of his coming heroism in the Fourteenth Infantry Regiment during the Satsuma rebellion six years later—the last opposition of warring shoguns against his beloved young Emperor. None of his aspirations would have included being commissioned a sub-lieutenant a year after the rebellion, or of being a student in the first class of the new War College and studying under the great Prussian, Major Jacob Meckel. And who would have guessed he would graduate at the top of his class, be a lieutenant colonel in the war with China, and a major general in the Russian War?

Now, sitting in the study reminiscing about the times he had seen his dying leader in person, he felt tired and heavy with grief. He looked up in surprise at his wife's interruption and the mention of a name he hadn't heard in years. "Hoshi?" he asked.

"Yes, Hidenori. She says her name is Itoko Hoshi and she is the mother of the grandson of Lieutenant Heigo Hoshi of the Fourteenth Regiment."

The general nodded, snapping out of his gloom at the thought of a dim face from the past. "Yes, he was my lieutenant, Chitose. I owe my life to his heroism back during Satsuma. By all means, show her in."

He got stiffly to his feet as the lovely woman was escorted into the room. Itoko bowed deeply then looked directly into his eyes as she quelled the butterflies in her stomach. "I'm sorry to bother you, great General," she said respectfully. "But I have a favor to ask. In addition to being the daughter-in-law of Heigo Hoshi, I'm the daughter of Colonel Mitsubishi, who died leading one of your regiments in the last war."

General Tojo beamed. "I never thought the day would come

when I could repay anything to those valorous officers. What may I do for you, Mrs. Hoshi?''

Itoko decided to lower her eyes, but spoke bravely. ''My son Hiroshi is about to enter district military preparatory—the *yonen gakko* in Hiroshima. But I would like for him to attend one here in Tokyo so I can be near him, General.'' She *had* to control her voice during the next lines where she would lie by omission.

Tojo hid his frown. He didn't like the idea of doting mothers getting involved in the training of serious young men. He listened quietly as she explained that she would soon be marrying Professor Obata and moving to the capital. ''Yes, I know Obata's father,'' he commented when she finished. Assuming she was a widow, he asked nothing further. ''Very well, Mrs. Hoshi, I will take care of it. Please convey my congratulations to His Excellency the Baron and to the professor. And now, please forgive my abruptness, but the serious matter at the palace precludes any further pleasantries.''

''Yes,'' Itoko said softly, trying not to show her pleasure. ''It's a terrible thing. The professor says our people may never really know his greatness.'' She thanked the general, bowed deeply, and made her exit. On the way out, she bade Mrs. Tojo a respectful good-bye and stepped gaily into the waiting dusk. *Hiroshi would be hers for years and years!*

She sobered as a slender, balding officer nodded to her as he entered the house. First Lieutenant Hideki Tojo, who was about to enter the War College, was returning from a briefing for junior officers about the condition of the Emperor. At the age of twenty-eight, ''The Razor'' had already distinguished himself as a young officer with a keen mind and intense devotion to duty—if not the verve of some of his peers. He resided with his well-educated wife and tiny son in his father's house whenever he was stationed in Tokyo.

Going directly to the study, he brought his father up to date on the latest official condition of the Emperor. When they finished discussing their anguish, General Tojo scribbled on a piece of paper and handed it to his son. ''Here's a name I want you to file, Hideki,'' he said softly. ''The boy is about to enter *yonen gakko* and I'd like for you to keep an eye on him. He's the grandson of my first commanding officer—Hoshi, of whom I've spoken. Watch over him, please."

"Yes, Father," the lieutenant replied. Glancing up as his mother served tea, he asked, "Will you want me to accompany you to the palace when it's time?"

The general stared morosely at the tray. "I don't know. It'll probably be a couple of days before the military is asked to pay tribute. I'll know the procedure at that time,"

"Do you think Yoshihito will be able to fill his shoes?"

The general shook his head. "I don't know. At least the Crown Prince is a well-trained army officer. That should keep him on our side."

Hideki Tojo's eyes glinted. "Then the entire Pacific lies ahead of us."

"Yes," his father replied, thinking sadly that his own illness would most probably preclude his seeing the proud colors of the empire flying from India to Hawaii. "I think he might step up the march."

Itoko lay awake long after Koki fell asleep that night. So great was her excitement that she finally went to the kitchen for a glass of sake shortly after midnight. But it was more than excitement— the old guilt over Noboru was picking at her again. She barely flinched at barging in on General Tojo, but had never been able to summon the courage to even write a single letter to the son she had run away from. She turned off the light and started for Koki's study. It was time. If it took her the rest of the night, she would finish it. And this time, if she had to cut off her damned arms to keep from throwing it away, it would get mailed!

The electric lamp on his huge oak desk was the only light in the book-lined study, a large, comfortable room that always retained some of Koki's tobacco smell. After finishing the sake and making three abortive starts on the letter, she went to his liquor cabinet and poured herself a large drink of Scotch. Soon she forged through the last stumbling point and wrote on. She tried to explain her unhappiness, her leaving, then switched to news of Hiroshi and of her love for Koki and the coming marriage. And finally, baring her soul, she begged his understanding and forgiveness. Another Scotch brought tears.

Reading and rereading it several times, she felt the discomfort of cheating. *It just wasn't good enough!* she stormed at herself as she paced. A piece of paper with hollow words that ranged from matter-of-fact to guilt-ridden. Was *that* how a negligent mother explained away years of disregard?

Sometime after three she returned to bed and cried herself to sleep. A housemaid would find the ashes of Noboru's letter in Koki's ashtray in the morning.

"I'm sorry, Sataro," Cedric said quietly. "The Emperor is dead. My news service in San Francisco called, and his son has already assumed the throne."

Having been at the store in Homerville all morning, Sataro hadn't heard. He went to a stool at the bar. "You know?" he asked Miyuki.

She nodded soberly as she reached for a bourbon bottle and began to pour.

"It'll be a smooth changeover," Cedric said to ease the tension. "I read an earlier *New York Times* account of how it would all be handled."

Sataro barely tasted the whiskey as he stared at the countertop. "You can't know what it means," he finally said softly. "Nothing in America is as dear and inspiring to its people as our Divine Emperor is to us. We aren't permitted to look at him, or to use his given name. He came to the throne at the age of fourteen when they brought him to Edo from seclusion in Kyoto to end the rule of the Tokagawa, and gathered the greatest advisers in the land around him."

He swallowed some more bourbon. "Without him, Japan still wouldn't have electricity."

Cedric thought of the wars with China and Russia, but said nothing.

"He sent our brightest people to every part of the world . . . learning, adopting, bringing back the ways of the modern world. He adapted our government from the British, our army from the

Prussians, our school system from America. The head of our proud navy attended your Annapolis. . . ."

Cedric stood to go.

Sataro held out his hand, still wearing a vacant expression. "I have to write the most important obituary my humble paper will ever carry. I—I hope I have the ability."

Cedric nodded. "You've already started it."

Miyuki followed Sataro into the sitting room where he assembled his writing materials. "Are you going back for the funeral?" she asked softly. "Hiroshi will be entering the *yonen gakko.*"

He shook his head. The compelling idea had occurred to him when he saw from the news release that the monumental funeral would begin in a month, that the procession from Tokyo to Kyoto would make many stops. But he wasn't ready. Much as he wanted to be with the handsome son he had deserted, the great dream was far from fruition. He was not nearly rich and important enough yet. No, not yet, not until the pieces were in place.

But he could write to him, tell him how the greatest Emperor in the world paved the way for Nippon to surge to world leadership, how a young, aspiring officer had nothing but limitless glory ahead. He looked up as Miyuki stroked his cheek. "No, my dear, there is too much to do here," he replied, taking her hand.

Zenro coughed as he entered the parlor. "Boss, many men are coming in. Word has spread like lightning about the Emperor. They want to know if you'll speak to them."

Sataro nodded, thinking of what he could say as he followed the cook out into the main room. It seemed that all of Japan Town was crowding in. Moving behind the bar, he inhaled deeply and drew himself erect as his eyes swept over the expectant faces. He felt a quickening of the pulse—the headiness of being a leader. In his deep voice, he began in Japanese, "A great Emperor has left us with a challenging responsibility. . . ."

At fifteen, Hiroshi was taller than most of his forty-nine classmates. But it wasn't his height that made him stand out, it was his almost classical features. The boyish softness was gone, leaving a square jaw under a wide, strong mouth and prominent nose that suggested aristocracy. His eyes were coal black and wide-set, but it was his high, clean cheekbones that set off his handsomeness. In the two weeks before school began, he received many a flirting glance from the more brazen Tokyo girls, and at his mother's wedding a bright-eyed girl of eighteen had openly suggested that they might find privacy in one of the guest bedrooms.

Yet, Hiroshi found his looks more of a detriment than a blessing. The upperclassman who was in charge of his section of the barracks, Segura, had resented him from the beginning. The thickset son of an army captain was plagued by a continuous crop of irritating pimples and an irascible disposition. He also disliked the fact that Hiroshi's new stepfather was of noble blood and that he had patronage from the Tojo family. He jeeringly referred to him as "Hiroshi Hoshi from Hiroshima" in a singsong voice, and continually found excuses to haze him.

On the other side of the ledger, Hiroshi had a likable new friend. Misao Hosakawa was a bundle of fervid patriotism who jacked up his skinny, uncoordinated body with an intense zest for everything. Short, with large bright eyes that gave him a touch of femininity, Misao had the emotions and experience of a Tokyo alleycat. He studied with more intensity than any of the students and quickly cherished the friendship of his handsome and athletic classmate. Each imagined himself a dedicated samurai of old, each embraced the Bushido code as a zealous religion. And while Hiroshi's destiny was one of family desire, Misao had fiercely dedicated his life to the memory of his two older brothers who had been killed in the war with Russia.

On this early Saturday afternoon, Misao watched wistfully as Hiroshi finished dressing. Fastening the top button of his brown uniform coat, Hiroshi reached for the brightly shined buckle to his leather belt. Next came the white gloves, then the peaked service cap with its tiny star over the visor. He straightened the short sword and came to attention in front of his friend. "Do I look all right?" he asked anxiously.

"You could pass the Emperor's inspection," Misao replied.

"But can he pass *mine*?" Segura snapped as he strode up. "After all, we wouldn't want one of our recruits going off to suck up to the illustrious Lieutenant Tojo looking like an undisciplined civilian, would we?"

As Hiroshi snapped rigidly to attention, Segura walked round him, glaring at every part of his uniform. "Remove your gloves and show me your fingernails!" the upperclassman snapped.

Complying, Hiroshi tossed a quick glance at Misao, hoping his explosive friend would keep quiet. His open contempt for Segura had kept him restricted every weekend since the start of the term. But Misao was standing quietly at attention. Segura's close-set eyes moved up to Hiroshi's face. "Remove your hat," he commanded. When he finished checking Hiroshi's shaved head, which had been cut by a barber only Friday night, he turned to the bunk area. "Your mess kit is improperly aligned, Hiroshi Hoshi from Hiroshima," he announced with a frown. "Now, how can you expect to go out sucking-up when you can't even keep your mess kit in order?"

"I'll correct it, sir," Hiroshi replied calmly. Segura could not keep him from his pass, no matter what he found.

The upperclassman whirled on the straying eyes of Misao. "And what are you looking at, Hosakawa?" he demanded. "I'll return in fifty-six minutes. At that time, you will present to me one hundred written descriptions of the position of attention! Do you understand?"

Misao swallowed angrily. "Yes, sir!"

As soon as Segura stepped out of the barracks, Misao spun to his locker for writing materials. "That bastard!" he snarled. "It's what happens when we get more democratic and let the peasants in. I've heard his father was a sergeant until the war. And now he's being forced into retirement!"

Hiroshi chuckled as he pulled on his gloves. "My father was only a corporal," he said as he headed for the door.

Hiroshi had eagerly looked forward to this afternoon ever since he'd received word the previous Monday. Two weeks after school began, he received a short note from Lieutenant Tojo stating:

Due to my father's one-time service under your grandfather, he has instructed me to provide a limited patronage to you. This in no way means any special privileges for you in

your course of instruction, only that I will keep a distant
eye on you and your progress. I will meet with you in the
near future to discuss your attitude.

Now, sitting beside the lieutenant on the train to Kamakura, he
remained quiet as Tojo stared out the window into the warm fall
sunshine. The officer was about an inch shorter than himself,
slender and quite nondescript. His head was shaved in the customary manner and he wore black-rimmed, round eyeglasses over his
shrewd, masked eyes. Although few words had been spoken
since Tojo picked him up in a rickshaw at the main gate at
one-thirty, Hiroshi had noticed his sharp Tokyo accent.

Finally, Tojo turned, asking abruptly, "Why do you want to
be an army officer?"

Hiroshi answered slowly, "It is my heritage, sir. My father
and uncle were unable to follow in my grandfather's footsteps, so
it was decided that I should."

"That isn't what I asked you," Tojo said evenly, turning his
guarded look into Hiroshi's eyes.

Hiroshi swallowed. "I—I've always wanted to be an army
officer, sir. I feel it's my duty and . . ."

"And what?"

"Sir, I want to lead men as our empire proceeds to its destiny."

"Then you want the glory?"

Hiroshi frowned, trying to understand, trying to provide an
adequate answer. "Yes, sir. I suppose so."

Tojo's eyes didn't blink. "Would you be willing to die for our
Emperor today if I ordered you to?"

Hiroshi was beginning to feel frightened; never had he been
faced with such strange direct questions. He and Misao had
sworn on the code that they'd die in a moment without hesitation,
if duty or honor required it. But this was—

Tojo's expression softened. "Good," he said with a slight
smile. "I'm glad you didn't gush out a stock answer to such a
ridiculous question, Hoshi. There are times to die and times to
question the reason. Now, tell me about Hiroshima."

They got off the train forty minutes later with Tojo quietly
reciting the history of the famous fishing village that had once

been the seat of government and was now a center of shrines. Every schoolboy in Japan knew about Kamakura. They eventually approached the uncovered statue of a giant Buddha surrounded by tall trees that seemed like bushes in comparison. "The Daibutsu," Tojo explained, "was first made of wood centuries ago. But now its massive body is mostly of bronze. It's forty-nine feet tall with a face nine feet long. The eyes are of pure gold and measure three feet each. The silver boss on the forehead weighs thirty pounds, while the circumference of the thumb is over three feet."

Hiroshi stared up at the face of the colossal figure, not knowing what to say, but overwhelmed by the sense of peacefulness and dignity in the expression. "Come," Tojo urged. "Let's go inside and climb to the head. Only there can you truly appreciate the Daibutsu's size."

At the top, Tojo again surprised him with a direct question. "Are you religious, Hoshi? An ardent Buddhist?"

Hiroshi shook his head, replying carefully, "My family is not overly religious, sir. I'm afraid I haven't given it the thought I should."

Tojo nodded. "Being a soldier is a religion. But you should know that."

"Yes, sir. My family is samurai."

"Good. Now we will go to Hachiman."

A short time later, they crossed a picturesque curved stone bridge and came to a long flight of stone steps that led to the hilltop temple. To the left of the steps was an enormous Icho tree with bare branches that seemed to reach to the sky. "This tree is over a thousand years old," Tojo commented as he climbed briskly. "A fitting guardian for the shrine of the God of War."

Soon, they were inside the old temple, wandering slowly around among the ancient religious and historical relics. Tojo pointed to a faded banner. "This was Iyeyasu's war color," the lieutenant explained. "With it, he formed the power of the Tokugawa that lasted until the restoration of the Emperor." Moments later, he pointed to an encased sword. "This belonged to Yoritomo, the first shogun, just before the turn of the thirteenth century."

Hiroshi stood silently staring at the finely crafted sword, feeling the nearness of the past. "It's beautiful," he managed.

"All swords, except those of our enemies, are beautiful," Tojo said quietly. "That is the point of my bringing you here. Look around you and try to feel the spirits of all those who have preceded you in the protection of our great Nippon." He stared into Hiroshi's wide eyes. "If ever you feel doubt about your profession as a soldier, come back here and let them cleanse your spirit. My father brought me here when I was exactly your age and told me the same thing."

Hiroshi felt a sense of power, as if he were indeed joining the great leaders and fighters of the dim past. It seemed that their vague faces crowded the walls and beckoned for him to become one of them. He had never known such an overpowering sensation. He had to ask. "And have you ever come here in doubt, sir?"

"Not yet," Tojo replied thoughtfully.

As they departed, Hiroshi was certain he never would either.

After dining on *sashimi* at an inn in the village, they caught an early evening train back to Tokyo. Reaching the gate to Hiroshi's school, Lieutenant Tojo ended the stimulating outing with, "I've shown you the past, Hoshi. The future is ours. Should you need me for anything so important that you are unable to cope, feel free to call on me. Otherwise, I'll be but another of those spirits from the temple of Hachiman. In the coming years, I charge you as your father did—be the best, Hoshi."

Fourteen

Lodi, California—May 1, 1913

WAR WITH JAPAN?
An Editorial

In May 1907 *The New York Times* published a translation of a German book that predicted war between the United States and Japan. That September, the *Times* carried a story about Japan's designs on the Philippines. Simultaneously, the *New York Tribune* published a serial about that war, and the *New York Sun* determined that war was inevitable. Was everyone clairvoyant six years ago?

Nippon is now angry enough to consider it. Why? Because the proud legislature of the great state of California is defiantly intent on furthering its private racial war against Japanese immigrants. A movement described by President Roosevelt a few years ago as "the wanton levity, brutality, and jingoism of certain California mob leaders and certain yellow journals" will soon bring about the Webb-Henry Bill, also known as the Alien Land Act.

The first step in getting rid of the hated and menacing Japanese will prohibit "aliens ineligible for citizenship" from purchasing our sacred California soil. Leases of land to them are to be limited to three years.

"Aliens ineligible for citizenship" goes back to an archaic naturalization law in 1790. Designed to prohibit slaves from becoming landowners, the law defined those persons eligible to own land as "free white persons." In the 1870s Congress struck the word "white," but it was soon restored to unruffle the

163

feathers of the anti-Chinese agitators. When concern about the Chinese faded out, the law was adroitly applied to the new threat of the Japanese.

Strange, isn't it, that our prized Declaration of Independence and the noble Constitution say nothing about being "white"? And that the Fourteenth Amendment says nothing about being *yellow?*

But our lawmakers and the powers that make them dance are now convinced the Japanese are such a serious menace—the "yellow peril," as the Kaiser calls them—that they can't own land. Goodness, aren't we white Californians fortunate to have such fearless leaders watching over our safety?

And how important is this great act? The Japanese ambassador traipses to the White House to protest in vain. A retaliatory anti-American demonstration in Tokyo attracts 20,000 people screaming for war against us. The Japanese press agrees. But President Wilson cannot interfere and step on our precious "states' rights."

Therefore, are we good citizens of California to gear for war? If our great state has the "right" to incite war with a sovereign nation, has it also the means to fight it? Will it be called the California-Japanese War? Where's our army, our navy? Will our fishing trawlers hold off the imperial fleet?

To date, the South has been able to sidestep the Emancipation Proclamation brilliantly, but not even the vaunted Ku Klux Klan can keep Negroes from owning land. Has the Japanese threat of honest hard work become such a major threat that our legislators should be wearing white sheets?

A source in the legislature states that this new act isn't meant to deprive anyone—merely that it contains a clear message to the Japanese immigrants. What is that message, Senator? Go home and go to war against California?

And what's next, Governor Johnson?

Gonna cut off their water?

How about their air?

*   *   *

Claymore, the burly British owner of the Wellington Saloon, handed the *Gazette* back to Cedric Baldwin. "Pretty sarcastic, isn't it?"

The publisher's dark eyebrows shot up. "Compared to what those bastards deserve, it's a nursery rhyme."

Claymore refilled his beer stein. "What good will it do?"

"I put five hundred copies on the train for San Francisco and had three hundred delivered to the capital and some saloons in Sacramento. It can't hurt."

Claymore had become a casual friend of both Cedric and Sataro in the last few years, often going to the Hiroshima-ya to play pool with them on evenings when he wasn't watching over the saloon. The only block standing between the newspaperman and the ex-sergeant major was the fact that Sataro couldn't drink in the Wellington. But Cedric knew it was a customer demand, and Sataro didn't really care—so he said. "Those people behind this have blood in their eye," the saloonkeeper said with a shake of his head.

Cedric sipped his beer. "So have I. I think I'll write one about the Irish next. They think—"

"So there you are!" a deep voice broke in.

Cedric turned as Charles McBride, the assemblyman from the local district, strode up waving a copy of the *Gazette*. "You must have been full of Claymore's booze when you wrote this damn thing," he said angrily. "What's the matter with you, Baldwin? You want to lose all your advertisers?"

Cedric turned back to Claymore. "You know, I think I hear one of those Irish wolves howling now. Give him a beer." Turning back to McBride with a wide grin, he asked, "What tore you away from the war party up at the capital—you have to come home to get your rifle or something?"

Charles McBride was a large, florid man with lambchop sideburns. He also owned the largest livery stable in town and a Buick agency. "No, my wife had a baby," he retorted, taking the glass of beer from Claymore. "Now, about this editorial—"

"Boy or girl?" Cedric asked nonchalantly, scribbling in his notebook.

"Another girl. Eight pounds, eleven ounces. But that isn't—"

"Her name?"

The assemblyman angrily downed half the glass. "You're way off base, Baldwin. Hell, everybody in town knows you're a liberal idiot, but this editorial goes too damned far. You know as well as I do that the sooner those yellow bastards go home, the better off we'll all be."

The mocking smile faded from Cedric's lips. "No, I don't know that. Now, do you want to talk about your bouncing baby girl, the weather, or baseball? The Yankees won again yesterday."

McBride finished the beer, wiped his mouth and leaned into Cedric's face. "You're making me look like an ass up there, boy. Scattering that damned edition all over the place tells the whole legislature I can't even control my own town. I've got a damned good notion to cancel all my advertising!"

Claymore took one look at the newspaperman's narrow eyes and quickly began refilling the glasses. "The Athletics'll bloody well take their measure next week," he said loudly as three customers moved down the bar to get a better view.

"You know what you can do with your advertising, McBride?" Cedric asked evenly.

"Well, I sure as hell don't have to spend it on a *Jap lover!*"

Cedric's right uppercut caught him flush on the jaw. McBride's eyes glazed as he slid slowly to the floor, trying to catch himself with fingers of putty.

"Now, what the hell did you go and do that for, Cedric?" Claymore shouted as he grabbed his ballbat and swung around the corner of the bar.

Cedric was standing over the big Irishman, fists balled up and ready to continue the fight as soon as his opponent got up. Claymore pushed him back, helping the dazed assemblyman to his feet. "All right, now," he told McBride. "You asked for it. Now, go on home and cool off."

McBride's gaze hardened as he focused on Cedric and tried to swing at him. But the burly ex-sergeant major pinned his arm and waved the ballbat in his face. "Go home, McBride."

McBride struggled momentarily, then lunged for the door. Turning, he shouted, "You'll pay for that, Baldwin! You've had your last damned dime from me. And I'll see to it that my fellow merchants do the same!''

Cedric shrugged as he turned back to his beer. "Now what in the bloody hell did you do that for?" Claymore sighed.

"The power of the press."

Claymore tossed the bat behind the bar in disgust. "He's no one to fool with, Cedric. You just cost yourself a pretty penny."

The newspaperman shrugged again. "I've got a rich wife."

Miyuki told Sataro about the trouble in the Wellington when he returned from San Francisco the next day. "Noboru said it's all over town. The kids at school talk like it was the world's boxing championship."

Sataro sighed as he sat at the parlor table and sipped tea. "I wish he'd keep quiet," he said tiredly. "I hate to think of him getting problems because of me. We'll survive. Besides, it only polarizes bad opinion against us."

"What did you accomplish with Abiko?"

"There's a loophole if they pass the act as it stands," he crowed. "Japanese children who are born here are automatically citizens. Therefore, any Japan man who wants to buy land can put it in his offspring's name."

Miyuki's lovely eyes lit up. "Are you sure?"

"Positive. Abiko's lawyer verified it. There's nothing they can do."

"And those who already own land can keep it?"

"Yes. And a bright Japan man will be able to renew his leases. We'll quietly get the word out as soon as everything settles down."

Miyuki sighed as she stroked his cheek. "Good. I was afraid you might write a troublesome editorial."

Sataro shook his head. "No, this is exactly a situation for *gambari*. As long as we have faith in ourselves and are patient, they have to accept us sooner or later. You know—"

"Yes, the other cheek," Miyuki interrupted with a soft smile.

The leases were a vital point with Sataro. Although he was making good money—nearly $500 per month on his combined

lodging, mercantile, and farming interests—his sights were set on
the rice market. A week later, the day after the Alien Land Act
passed by a huge majority, he visited Marysville. After a wistful
look at the hotel where he and Miyuki had spent their first hours
of lovemaking together, he went to the real estate office of Burns
& Company.

Thirty minutes later, Gordon Burns pulled his new Ford sedan
up on a shallow slope by a clump of trees. Squinting into the
bright sun and pointing out to some spacious acreage to the west,
he said, "I can lease the hundred acres to you for a very good
price, Mr. Hoshi. The owner is a widow in San Francisco who
can't do anything with it."

Sataro nodded as he lit a cigarette. His careful study of rice-
growing in America had included letters to Seito Saibara near
Houston, Texas, where a sizable Japanese colony had developed.
Saibara had many helpful ideas relating to climate and seed.
Previously, the rich lower Sacramento Valley had proven unsatis-
factory for rice because the grain did not mature before the local
rainy season. But some years earlier an inquisitive man by the
name of Ikuta had gambled on some seed he ordered from
Japan—a strain with an earlier maturation cycle. And it had been
ideal for the Marysville area. With Japan unable to produce
enough for its own requirements, a ready market was available.

Burns, a skinny little man with a thin mustache and the
glibness of most real estate salesmen, went on, "Already there
are several successful rice growers in the area, including some of
your countrymen. Although," he added with a conspirational
grin, "none of them have the foresight to think big. You know,
Mr. Hoshi, trouble is brewing in Europe. And if it comes to war,
rice could be a profitable commodity. Your people don't mind
the work and . . ."

As Burns droned on, Sataro nodded to himself. "Stoop labor,"
that was what they called the Japanese. Well, they were right—
his countrymen weren't too damned proud to bend over to make
an honest living. It was the prime reason the farmers wanted
them and the *hakujin* unions hated them so much.

When Burns finally ran down, Sataro asked, "What about the

adjoining land to the south? It doesn't appear to be under cultivation.''

The real estate man grinned. "I can check into it. But I have another parcel of over a hundred acres four miles away. You want to look at it?''

Sataro nodded. He couldn't bite off too much, but he didn't want to miss anything. Besides, he liked Burns's Ford. If he wound up growing rice up here, he might just buy one. Or even something bigger.

At the same moment a small group of men were airing their complaints in a smoke-filled room less than fifty miles away in Sacramento. Present were J. M. Inman, state senator and president of the California Oriental Exclusion League; V. S. McClatchy, the wealthy publisher who was the power behind the League; Thomas McNeil, an official of the Union Labor Party; and Sean Flattery, an official in both the State Federation of Labor and the Native Sons of the Golden West. All were members of the Native Sons, and all were dissatisfied with the modified Alien Land Act. They had wanted more stringent restrictions.

McClatchy, a dignified man with the bearing of one used to being heard, broke into an argument between Inman and Flattery. "We're stuck with this thing for a while and we might as well get used to it. Perhaps in a few years we can put some nails on the coffin through amendments. We should be thankful there was no federal interference.

Flattery's pugnacious jaw thrust itself forward. "I say we mount a strong campaign against leaseholders immediately. Apply some muscle on these landlords.''

McClatchy sighed. "There are hundreds of them. How do you convince them they shouldn't be earning money on the land they own?''

"If we could get enough money in our war chest, we could subsidize 'em," Flattery reported.

The publisher shook his head. "Too much money and too much bad publicity. Besides, we'd be open for suit.''

"I agree with McClatchy," Inman interjected. "Our message

is loud and clear on this bill. Let's move on to something else."
McNeil agreed.

"I'd like to see that goddamn newspaper down in Lodi go
down the drain," Flattery growled. "Somebody oughta teach
that Jap-loving Baldwin a lesson. And there's a yellow-belly
paper down there, too. A smart-assed Jap hotel-owner puts it out.
I had a copy translated and he makes it sound like they're gonna
inherit the damned state. A visit from my boys might make them
see the light."

"No!" McClatchy insisted. "There'll be no interference with
the First Amendment. I have the right to castigate them in my
papers, and they have the right to voice their views. Besides,
who reads them—a few Japanese and maybe a thousand people
around Lodi? What Abiko says is far more important."

Flattery's rough hand moved to the bourbon bottle. If he had
his way, he growled to himself, all the rabble-rousers would go
back on a rowboat—but in pine boxes! Abiko was too big to
touch, but this slant-eye in Lodi might be a good way to get some
action started. It was time to get something new started in the
San Joaquin Valley anyway.

"Remember," McClatchy said as he jammed on his hat and
headed for the door. "Low profile—the eyes of the world are on
us."

Flattery stuck a fresh cigar in his mouth as the publisher
disappeared down the hallway. "You don't call all the shots, Mr.
Moneybags," he muttered.

Fifteen

Itoko looked carefully into the tortoise-shell-framed mirror the hairdresser held before her. Out of deference to the baron, she had changed from the Western-style hairdo to the old-fashioned Marumage-style for the party. Her father-in-law frowned on too much of the Occidental in the women of the family. And she vowed from the day she met the crusty old man that she'd break down his resistance to her. She had made little progress in the seven months of marriage.

She murmured her approval to the hairdresser and nodded her dismissal.

Adjusting her thin cotton kimono, she walked to the open sliding doors that faced the large garden. She still fumed at being slighted as the only member of the family without noble blood. What had the damned Obatas done for their country lately? Their last hero had probably fallen off his horse in fright when Perry brought his black ships. It rankled that her brilliant father's heroism didn't seem to matter any more than being descended from a line of brave samurai.

Koki's two brother's, their uppity wives, and his scrawny younger sister—who had married a weakling fourth son of a count—were irritations she bore only because of Koki. And the only reason she courted favor with the lecherous old baron was for Hiroshi's sake. At least that was what she told herself. Secretly, she was delighted to be a part of the illustrious Obata family, one of twenty-eight that bore the lofty rank of Urin and one of the twenty-one remaining title families that had vast land holdings and a purse with no bottom. Koki had told her shortly after they met that he could give his salary to charity and

171

they'd never miss it, even if they spent forty summers on the Riviera.

She stepped into the bright sunshine in the garden and sniffed the sweet scent of wistaria. To her, the deep reds of the richly blooming azaleas were a welcome variation from the previous month's profusion of cherry blossoms. Nodding her head at a gardener trimming a tree-peony by the tiny waterfall, she sighed deeply. How she loved this marvelous garden that was four times larger than her entire house and lot had been in Hiroshima. But then, she loved this whole estate. She laughed to herself—it wasn't really an estate, compared to many of those around them. But two acres and a fourteen-room Western-style house made of stone, complete with central heating, wasn't exactly poverty either. And with five servants, efficient management was her only chore.

She frowned suddenly, thinking of the invited guests who had sent their regrets. She knew some of the reasons for not attending were merely excuses—the busy cherry blossom social season was over, so it was simply their way of saying that Professor Obata's new wife, the divorced woman, just couldn't move into Tokyo society this quickly, that interlopers had to be shown they couldn't wear the badge of disgrace so haughtily.

She snorted to herself, trying to believe that she didn't give a damn, that her concern was only for Hiroshi's sake. It was his sixteenth birthday and time for him to be accepted. She was about to say something to the gardener when Tomi called out to her from the bedroom. The older woman and Seizo's wife, Setsuko, had just returned from shopping. They had all come up from Hiroshima for the birthday event. Itoko pushed her unhappy thoughts away as she turned to greet them. "Ready for this evening?" Setsuko asked pleasantly.

"She's still fuming." Tomi laughed as the housemaid scurried in with a tea serving and pillows. "She has only two generals coming."

Setsuko chuckled. "The ones with the ugly daughters, I assume."

Itoko frowned as she seated herself and reached for her cup.

"Suiko Goto is one of the most beautiful girls in the city. She—"

The other two women broke into laughter. "See!" Tomi chortled. "She already has a bride picked out for our beautiful Hiroshi—and he just getting rid of his pimples!"

Itoko frowned. "I wish I could arrange it. The general not only has a great deal of money, but he may someday head the army."

Tomi raised an eyebrow. "So why should he consider a betrothal to a pauper from Hiroshima? He can probably find a prince for her."

"He is not a pauper!"

"Koki's money belongs to the Obata family."

"He made most of it himself on foreign investments," Itoko retorted. "And I fully intend to see it doesn't go back to his worthless brothers."

Tomi nudged Setsuko with her elbow. "Our former daughter of the House of Hoshi has big ideas."

Itoko nodded with narrowed eyes. If they only knew.

It took them over an hour to work their way up to the shrine's new altar, so huge was the crowd. Although the general public was out in huge numbers, the compound was jammed with relatives of the dead, especially those who had fallen in Russia. The celebration of the Yasukuni Shrine was an occasion for all the students at the *yonen gakko* to have a two-day weekend holiday. The only requirement was a visit to the shrine on Saturday. Dedicated to the spirits of members of the army and navy who had died fighting for their country, the shrine was the scene of day-long fireworks, wrestling matches, and various military acknowledgments. Uniforms were everywhere. Hiroshi and his friend Misao had arrived with several of their classmates in midmorning, and were just now getting away shortly after noon.

Both were solemn, imbued with a deep reinforcement of their solemn vows of Bushido, as well as a renewed dedication to Emperor, country, and the army. As they caught an electric streetcar for downtown Tokyo, Hiroshi sat silently staring at the people and thinking he would gladly lay down his life that very instant in memory of his two heroic grandfathers.

Misao's ebullient self took over before they were halfway to. their destination. It had been five long weeks since the hated upperclassman, Segura, had let him pass inspection for even a day away from the academy and he was going to make the most of it. Besides, he had a great surprise in store for his friend's birthday present. He continued to chuckle inwardly as they chatted away like two convicts who had just been paroled.

They changed cars twice, finally arriving at the bustling Ginza at one-thirty.

Hiroshi was still not used to the teeming flurry of the business district and was fascinated by it. The narrow dirt streets swarmed with people and abounded in noise. Everything from a baby on its older sister's back to the most ancient of men mingled and wove through wagons, rickshaws, electric trolleys, carriages, and bicycles. Handcarts filled with the milkman's cans, farmboys' fresh vegetables, and every imaginable ware a peddler might sell further clogged the tightly packed streets. The mud from the early morning's rain had already been pounded from quagmire to a rocklike surface by thousands of clogs, thongs, and wheels. With no sidewalks, and open shops abutting the streets in every square inch, there was no right of way except that which one could cleave. "Signboard girls" smiled enticingly and beckoned for the passersby to look at the products of their shops. A stray dog barked now and then and the brash horns of periodic motorcars punctuated the sound of scurrying feet. Overhead, busy birds struggled on their way through the hot May sunshine that beat down through the grotesque, out-of-place electric wires.

After fighting the throng at the Ginza, the boys wandered up and down nearby sidestreets for over half an hour before Misao caught Hiroshi's arm. "Now for my surprise." He beamed, heading up a narrow alley with lesser shops.

Hiroshi had to hurry to keep up as Misao sped off and turned into an even narrower lane of tightly packed houses and hardly any traffic. His shorter friend soon stopped before an older house that was badly in need of paint. With a short laugh, he slipped through a gate and past the smallest garden Hiroshi had ever seen.

Misao announced their presence with a low shout at the door, then quickly removed his shoes. As Hiroshi followed suit with a puzzled look, a woman of about thirty-five, wearing a brightly flowered thin summer kimono, slid the door open and smiled. Moments later, both cadets were seated on pillows in the tiny sitting room. The sisters, who looked enough alike to be twins, called themselves Meiyo and Kaho—Fame and Fortune, the professional names they had adopted when age forced them from the geisha world. Hiroshi was still puzzled as Kaho served four cups of sake and sat close to him with a warm smile. He thanked her stiffly and sipped the wine self-consciously as the two women giggled and waited expectantly.

Pointing to Kaho, Misao bowed his head and beamed. "I give you a fortune for your birthday, my warrior friend." The sisters giggled again.

Hiroshi tugged at his collar, suddenly feeling hot as he realized what was happening. Immediately, Kaho was on her knees, reaching for the buttons, saying something he didn't even hear. *How could Misao do this without asking?* He knew he was blushing, his hand was shaking. It wasn't right! One should mentally prepare for his first time, not have it thrust on him like a sudden shower of rain! How many times had the excitement gripped him in fantasy, dreams, and morning excitement? And now, to be embarrassed like this—he knew Misao had told them, damn him! He downed the sake quickly. He had to get home— his mother's big dinner. She'd smell sake on his breath and—

"Yes, you'd better hurry." Misao laughed. "I had only enough money for one hour."

Kaho refilled his cup with a pleasant smile that convinced him she was laughing at him. "You're a very handsome young man," she purred. "Are you a good lover?"

She didn't know! "That's what I'm told," he managed. She reminded him of his mother—the smooth, lovely features with a few tiny smile lines that the paint couldn't hide. But her perfume was stronger, more suggestive. As her long fingers undid another button, he felt the first urges of excitement.

Misao, who was getting the same treatment from Meiyo, snorted. "Tell her the truth, Hoshi, so she'll know how to handle you."

Kaho touched his cheek gently, murmuring, "Come, my handsome one, let's go where these crude people won't bother us." She stood and took his hand.

He got to his feet stiffly, forgetting to excuse himself as he followed her from the room. He knew his face was burning and the pounding in his ears blocked out his friend's last jibe. What a beautiful, graceful woman—and much younger than his mother, of course. What well-rounded, slinking buttocks, with nothing on but that tight, thin kimono—the most breathtaking rear he had ever seen!

The room was tiny, only four *tatami* mats. He could smell flowers or incense and saw that already a single mattress was spread. As she slid the door shut, he thought he would stifle in the muggy heat. He stood rigidly, embarrassed, afraid to move, wanting to cover the bulge in his pants. She glided to him and took his jacket. "Remove the rest of your clothes," she ordered softly. Slipping out of his shirt, he felt the sweat. He saw her appreciative glance run up and down his torso, and he sucked in his breath. A touch of pride gripped him—maybe she was like the others who flirted with him, hardly able to control her desire. The thought reinforced him and added to his stimulation.

As he fumbled with his trousers, she quickly unwrapped her kimono. He swallowed hard and stared openly as her shapely body was revealed. She was well-rounded, with a flat stomach and firm-looking little breasts that had soft brown aureoles with full nipples. He had seen female bodies in the bath since he was a baby, but never one that was intended for his pleasure. It was *strikingly* different! She twisted coquettishly, running a hand over her lovely buttocks, then turned to caress her black pubic area. "Come, my pretty one," she purred, running her tongue around her open lips. "Come let me make a powerful lover out of you."

He heard his breath coming in short, jerky gasps as he stared at her undulating pelvis. He tried to turn away to hide his excitement, but she caught his hand and drew him down to the bed. The pounding at his temples burst into the ringing in his ears as he touched her. It was overpowering!

Her mouth came to his face as her soft, searching fingers began to run deftly over his body. "Easy, my handsome one," she whispered, pushing him flat. "I'll do everything the first time."

Itoko's party was the most intricate social affair she had ever attempted. It was like staging a coronation—in her mind, the event that would shatter the barrier that stood invisibly between her and the future. In front of that barrier, Koki was a gruff bear, loving her dearly and acting as her buffer. Caring little for family position or the upper level of Tokyo society, he enjoyed his role as a student of history and observer of the new Japan. Yet he understood his beautiful wife's craving for acceptance as well as he did her willful pride. He agreed to be the amiable host and to present Hiroshi in the most favorable light to the generals.

Although he disliked the breach of etiquette in speaking favorably of a member of one's own family, to do so of Hiroshi was natural. He had become extremely fond of the boy and was proud of his accomplishments at the academy. He had first married late and the union with his sickly wife had produced no children. Adoption was considered, but as her illness progressed and his travels increased, it was permanently delayed. Were it possible, he would gladly have adopted Hiroshi at the time of his remarriage. Now, he was content to be just an admiring stepfather.

The banquet, or as Tomi called it, "the grand feast," was a rich blending of East and West. The four entrées should suit any palate: broiled prawns and lobster, wild duck stuffed with rice and mushrooms, roast filet of beef with smoked mushrooms, and broiled sea eel in Marin gravy. Itoko's cook had wheedled the recipe for the baron's favorite salad from his cook—pickled bamboo shoots in a specially marinated dressing of scallions and chopped garlic cloves, served over a special lettuce she had shipped in from Kagoshima. In addition to the embossed ivory-colored menus, place cards for each guest read:

In Honor of the Yasukuni Tribute
for
Colonel Mitsukuni Mitsubishi
and
Senior First Lieutenant Heigo Hoshi
On the Birthday of Their Grandson
Cadet Hiroshi Hoshi
May 7, 1913
The Second Year of Taisho

Itoko inspected each one of them as she checked the place settings at the large table they had rented to seat their adult guests Western-style. Not even the Emperor could be eating better tonight, she thought happily. Nor would many of the ladies at the palace be dressed much better, she assured herself as she smoothed the front of her richly patterned lavender silk kimono. She stepped lightly to the head of the table to check her widowed father-in-law's setting. He was her special target for the night. She was located to his left, with General Goto next to her. It should be a stimulating meal.

The entertainment she had arranged was a masterpiece, she reminded herself proudly. Two of the city's top musicians would play the *samisen* and flute throughout the meal, while another would give a recital on the thirteen-string *koto* afterward. This would be followed by a thirty-minute presentation by the noted Takamura, the famous storyteller whom she had lured away from his theater for a good fee. But the grand finale would be the showing of the highly popular moving-picture film, *Paradise Lost*. As Koki cheerfully described it, that was the *coup de grace*.

The house was a profusion of flowers, producing myriad scents that would obviate any use of incense. Rich roses of every imaginable color, a special breed of early iris, late peach blossoms, chrysanthemums, tree-peony cuttings, and wistaria made the rooms look like a flower show.

She would be a *hoshi* tonight!

Hiroshi had been relieved to hear dinner announced and to be able to break away from the questions the two generals had been throwing at him. He was justifiably proud of his high marks at the academy, but his mind was still on the erotic Kaho. What a magnificent new world she had opened for him. He was somewhat perturbed that Misao had laughed uproariously when he told him Kaho thought he was the best young lover she had ever met. Certainly the experienced, beautiful woman should know!

As he walked into the room where the younger guests were to be served, he wanted to shout out his accomplishment of the afternoon. No longer was he a mere schoolboy—he was a man of the world who was experienced! Surely, these silly children he was about to dine with would be able to tell. If only that arrogant general's daughter, Suiko Goto, had any idea of how such a beautiful courtesan had been pleased by him only a few hours earlier, she'd bring her nose down from the clouds!

He was quickly engaged in conversation with two of Koki's nephews who were about his age. Both were in Peer's school and scheduled to go on to the Imperial University. Although they were reserved with him, their interest in the *yonen gakko* was keen. The older one—who would one day be baron—was named Juichi. Knowing Hiroshi's father and older brother were in the United States, he took delight in castigating the Americans. "The word at school is that we would already have declared war on them if the money had been available in Europe," he stated authoritatively. "They certainly deserve it."

"Yes," Hiroshi replied quietly. "But the countries that might have made the loans available must think of their own war needs."

"What is the military thinking?" the other nephew asked. "Will we come in against Germany?"

Hiroshi's answer was guarded; he didn't want to be quoted. Besides, he was already thinking of these scions of the old autocracy as his future antagonists in Japan's struggle for power. At least one of them would undoubtedly enter the growing bureaucracy, thence becoming yet another civilian stumbling block to stall the military. "Our place is not in foreigners' wars," he replied.

He was saved from expanding on his answer by the announcement of dinner. Moments later, the housemaid directed the placement of twelve elevated serving trays of food. The trays were placed in two lines in the center of the room, so that each diner would have a dinner partner directly across his or her tray. As soon as the last trays were in place, the young guests made a game of finding their place cards. Hiroshi's was near the middle, facing the lovely daughter of General Goto.

As Suiko Goto gracefully seated herself on a silk pillow, she smiled coolly up at him, saying, "I see that I'm honored by being your dining partner, Cadet Hoshi. Happy birthday."

Hiroshi lowered his head in acceptance, then observed her quietly as she began her soup. He had seen her twice before since his arrival in Tokyo, but never this closely. His mother had told him about her—fifteen years old, tall and precocious, a masterful *koto* player, fluent in both English and French, a good lawn tennis player and swimmer, and already an ardent imperialist. She would also soon go to Paris for university study.

He continued to watch her over his soup bowl. Large black almond-shaped eyes with long lashes gave her a special, almost spiritual beauty. Her hair was shiny in the chic *shimada* with the chignon elevated over the crown to denote her high station. Her smooth skin looked flawless, but he guessed her face had been painted in the popular custom. She wore a long-sleeved kimono of cherry blossom pink.

As she turned to cast a sidelong glance at one of the nephews, he caught a glimpse of her sharp profile. Perhaps, he admitted, she had a right to her air of regality. The only thing out of place was her mouth; instead of a pair of lotus blossom lips, it was strong and firm, wide and almost manly. But that departure hardly made her less desirable—he decided he'd like to taste it.

He decided to speak in his excellent English, both to impress her and to try his second language outside the classroom. "I understand you're going to France to study. Is that right, Miss Goto?"

She nodded, daintily placing her soup bowl on the tray. "Yes," she replied in clear English. "After some private tutoring, I will attend the Sorbonne." Her eyes glittered momentarily as she added, "You speak quite well for someone from Hiroshima."

She wasn't so clever, Hiroshi thought. The barb wasn't even delicate. "Oh, yes," he countered, deciding to shock her, "I sharpened it in my tutor's favorite brothel, where everyone spoke the language."

Her eyes widened briefly, then resumed their self-assurance. "Come now, Cadet Hoshi, don't tell me you frequent such places at your tender age," she replied mockingly. "Tell me the truth—have you ever kissed a girl?"

She was not only overbearing, he thought, but positively brazen. If she only knew! He shrugged, saying, "I'm a soldier."

She decided to retreat to safer ground. *"Parlez-vous français?"*

He used the only French phrase he knew. *"Je ne sais pas."*

They continued to spar through the entrées. During the sherbet she abruptly asked, "How can you afford to be an army officer? My mother says your own family has no money."

She was absolutely impertinent! "Oh, and does your mother know that my father is amassing a fortune in California?" he asked coldly.

"Ha! Working as a coolie. I've heard the stories."

He was really growing angry with her. "No, he's a big businessman. His last letter stated that he was placing several hundred acres in rice."

"That's what I said—a coolie."

He decided to end the conversation.

An hour later, as the entertainment was about to begin, Suiko sidled up to where Hiroshi was explaining ballistics to the nephews. Touching the sleeve of his brown jacket with a mischievous smile, she asked, "Kind sir, may I sit beside you during the program? I hear that *everyone* cries during the film, and I want to be near someone brave."

He was about to refuse when his mother interrupted. "I think that would be delightful, Miss Goto. Hiroshi is very gentle about such things."

"I was thinking about playing billiards," Hiroshi said quickly.

Itoko gave him a level look as she said, "Don't jest, my dear. And get an extra handkerchief, in case Miss Goto needs it."

Suiko behaved herself during the entertainment, even smiling sweetly a couple of times when she caught Hiroshi glancing at her. Much as he hated to admit it, her beauty excited him as much as her dainty scent. And when the electric lights were turned off for the film showing, he felt her stockinged foot slip over and rub his leg. Staring straight ahead, he reminded himself that this brazen advance would have excited him tremendously any time before. But a mere toe rub from a slip of a girl who knew nothing about the marvelous world of lovemaking was hardly noteworthy. Not for a man with his experience.

Still, he didn't move his leg.

Ten weeks later, Itoko received Sataro's consent to explore the possibilities of a marriage betrothal via a letter from Seizo. Koki arranged with General and Mrs. Goto to come to their home for tea on the following Sunday afternoon. As Itoko watched quietly, her able husband presented his case, ending with, "Upon completion of his study at the Shikan Gakko in five years, I plan to settle a large enough sum on him to make his family quite comfortable during the years of his lower rank."

The general was polite and pleasant in his response. He reminded his host that Suiko was going abroad to study and stated that he would provide an answer within seven days. As the Gotos departed, Itoko's smile faded into an angry scowl. "He's stalling for richer prospects," she cried out angrily. "I *know* it!"

Koki reached for his tobacco pouch and began to refill his pipe. "Naturally," he replied patiently. "She's a bright, beautiful girl who has everything. Looking at it from their side, wouldn't you do some shopping?"

Itoko's patience had worn thin. Too much planning and maneuvering had gone into this. *Her* selection process was what mattered. "Hiroshi is not a piece of goods!" she retorted sharply. "And I don't know how you can act so casual about it."

A week later, General Goto informed Koki that he had decided to wait until his return to make any marriage arrangements. His appointment as military attaché to France had just been confirmed. And Koki knew what that meant—the Japanese Army wanted one of its finest officers on hand in Paris to observe the buildup to war. If Nippon were to side with Britain and France as was anticipated, his role would be vital.

But to Itoko, it was a major setback. Still, she relaxed. There were many other wealthy young girls, and perhaps she should take an intermission when she could devote energy and love to Koki—something she'd never quite found the time to do. It seemed she had always been at war with someone, conducting major or minor campaigns for her son or herself. It was time for Koki . . . and Itoko.

The next morning she gave her hairdresser instructions to make her more youthful—suitable for an idyll or tryst. She smiled inwardly as the woman tried to hide a look of shock. The result was a soft and lustrous effect in a style called the icho-mage. "It's named after the leaf of the icho tree." The hairdresser beamed. "All the young Kyoto matrons are wild about it." She went shopping that afternoon, selecting among other innovative garments an exotic black negligee that was imported from New York and a summer kimono so filmy she wouldn't be able to wear it in public.

After dinner that evening she asked Koki to walk with her in the garden. They chatted pleasantly as they strolled, finally reaching a small stone bench where she lit his pipe. Dropping to the bench she took his hand and smiled at him with a deep sigh. "I feel wanton," she announced softly. "If we could rent a stateroom on a freighter for the night, I'd forget there was an outside world."

He smiled back with interest. He hadn't missed the buildup—he just wondered what she wanted. But it didn't matter, he always humored her. "What do you have in mind—a game of *sugoroku?*" he asked.

She drew his hand to her cheek. "Maybe . . . at first."

"And after the game?"

"Then I'd make love to my kind and wonderful husband before the ship departed for Bangkok."

"Bangkok?"

She brought his fingers to her lips. "Yes, Bangkok."

"And is there such a freighter?"

"It departs in two days."

Koki pulled her into his arms, his lips brushing her forehead. "Then Bangkok it is. Uh, are you sure there isn't some devious purpose in this?"

She giggled like a schoolgirl as she hugged him. "Not unless the ambassador to Siam is rich and has a beautiful marriageable daughter."

Sixteen

Noboru Hoshi was almost the perfect son that Sataro pictured. At seventeen, he was nearly as tall as his father and almost as handsome as his younger brother. While his jaw was more angular, his eyes were darker and his narrow nose longer. During his more intense moments, his expression was piercing, hawklike. In fact, the players on the Lodi High baseball team—where he was a .350 line-drive hitter as a third baseman—called him Hawk. During the previous summer he had worked hard helping his father set up the rice fields near Marysville, but he was now back to delivering groceries part-time during his senior year.

His relationship with the beautiful, always gentle Miyuki was warm, often conspiratorial as if she were an older sister. She sensed his loss of Itoko, but never stepped into that private world, just as he never mentioned the sadness he often detected in her eyes during unguarded moments. Another never-mentioned feeling was his unwarranted but unshakable resentment toward Hiroshi. He knew it was childish jealousy—that *she* had chosen his brother over himself—but the pique he had sensed following her abrupt departure had festered into a mature case of rancor in the intervening years. Not even one letter. Certainly, she could have torn herself away from him enough for one letter in that time.

Hiroshi's stiff, infrequent letters were nothing.

Another chink in his perfection was the late-night interest Sataro knew nothing about. On this September evening, as Noboru rode the Columbia from the store in Homerville back to Japan Town, his weariness faded at the exciting thought of another encounter with the sensuous Tomoko. Little had he realized how his life would change when a man named Osiriji came from

Oakland the previous year to open a barbershop two doors away from the Hiroshima-ya. In late May, his daughter arrived from the same city, following the accidental death of her husband on the docks. Since she already knew the barbering trade, she quickly went to work in the shop.

At eighteen, Tomoko had just the touch of promiscuity about her to make men get their hair cut with their last quarter. With pouty, promising lips and always a stray wisp of tousled hair hanging down near her saucy eyes, her bouncy familiarity with men was quickly the gossip of the community. And a visit to her barber chair did nothing to dispel the promise of adventure. Tomoko was simply more buxom than was fashionable. And a buxom barber who was more geisha than hair trimmer, more seductive entertainer than young widow, could find a dozen ways to rub her ample gifts against a customer. When Miyuki commented about the long lines at the barber shop, Sataro laughingly replied, "Lodi has the most well-trimmed Japanese heads in America."

His wife's amber eyes glinted as she snorted in reply, "I think I'll start cutting your hair myself."

What neither of them knew, what no one knew, was that Tomoko's temptress role was her private joke. The panting laborers, the dozens of would-be suitors, in fact the cream of the Japanese crop for miles around, held no interest for her. She was simply fascinated by the hawkish-looking son of the president of the Hiroshima *kenjinkai*. The day she first touched his thick crop of hair shortly after her arrival, then found ways to inspect his wide shoulders and firmly muscled arms, she made up her mind. What did she care that he was still a schoolboy—Noboru Hoshi was the young man she wanted.

She watched him ride by on his handsome bicycle, learned his schedule, and secretly observed him in his backyard as he went to and from the bathhouse each evening. The second time he came for a haircut, she fingered the note she had kept ready for days. It found its way into his pocket and was discovered by him that evening when he undressed. It boldly read, "Meet me in the lumberyard at midnight tomorrow night. Love, Tomoko."

Noboru had blinked unbelievingly at the note, then folded it with hot cheeks and hid it in one of his schoolbooks. Since there were no Japan girls near his age in school, and it was unheard of for a Japan boy to have a relationship with a white girl, he was totally inexperienced along that line. Now this—a grown woman, a temptress who had all the men in town drooling—was saying she wanted him. It wasn't possible. He had heard about her humor—was this another of her jokes? He reread the note for the twentieth time. *Love, Tomoko.* He was confused and excited, each reading of the note aroused him. But he knew one thing—nothing could keep him from that lumberyard at the appointed time. Not even an army of samurai!

The lumberyard was only a hundred yards away, just across the street from the edge of Japan Town. It covered an entire block and contained dozens of attractions for the younger children who liked to play there after school. At night it was deserted; the odd piles of lumber providing spooky shapes. After spending the longest day of his life, Noboru slipped out the back just before midnight and hurried over the fence to find out if the note was a sham. His breath was short as he crossed the street and stopped just inside the yard. He'd wait for no more than a minute, then end this nonsense and get back to bed, he told himself, angry at the weakness in his legs.

And then, from the dark shadow of a pile of two-by-fours, she called out as he walked by. She caught his hand and pulled him down to a pile of shavings. The watching moon had been full, providing enough light for him to see her shining eyes. Gone was her impudent air as she stroked his hand and kissed him sweetly on the cheek, telling him how just the sight of him had tormented her. He tried awkwardly to respond, but the glib words he had practiced died in his throat. She filled the void, full of herself, explaining that she had never loved her husband, and that it was wonderful how lovers could meet in America.

They embraced timidly, gently, then passionately.

The next night they became lovers.

Now, weeks later, their flaming love was still a secret that thrilled Noboru even more each day. He sighed, pushing his anticipation away as he found Sataro waiting to share the evening meal. His father was excited. "My editorial on assimilation was forwarded by Mr. Abiko to both the *Tokyo Jiji* and the *Osaka Mainichi* for reprint," he announced proudly.

Noboru remembered the meat of the editorial only too well; it had been run by Cedric in the *Gazette* and thrown back in his face by his detractors at school. Assimilation to his father meant doing everything the American way, but adhering firmly to the roots and customs of the empire within. He knew Sataro sincerely intended that each Japanese who expected to return some day should live as his hosts, but it didn't quite come out that way to those who were considering the idea of staying. And it certainly provided fodder for the anti-Japanese organizations which used nonassimilation as the cornerstone of their defamation.

"That's excellent, Father," he replied quietly. He wanted to be honest and state that holding to the old ways wasn't the concept.

Miyuki served the soup. "Have you told him about the threatening letters?" she asked Sataro.

"No, it isn't important."

Noboru looked up in alarm. "When?"

"What do I care about such threats?" his father snorted. "They come only from cowards and bullies. Besides, my editorials are meant only to stimulate the spirit of our countrymen. When they return to Japan . . ."

Noboru's attention drifted away from the stock finish to Sataro's theme. He thought of how he stood with his hand over his heart every morning when his class recited the Pledge of Allegiance, and how much the American flag in the corner of the classroom had come to mean to him. More and more, his father's great dream of returning to Hiroshima was becoming discomforting to him. More and more, he was forgetting he was different from the sea of *hakujin* that flowed around him. That American flag seemed to be the symbol that made him a part of it; a part that belonged to something more than the hazy memory of another life.

Hiram Brooks had seethed in futile rage for weeks after his humiliation at Sataro's hands in the Wellington Saloon during the first Tokay Festival. He plotted all kinds of revenge but could never get himself to the point of execution. Drinking more and more didn't silence the taunts as he moved from ranch to ranch. After nearly a year, he gave up and rode all the way back to Texas, where he continued to drift and try to drink away the memory of a Japanese ghost. Then, as if he were at the end of a powerful rubber band that was drawing him back, he finally jumped on a freight that took him to California and a ranch south of Stockton. Two months later, he met the plump and lonely widow who owned the Stockton Livery Stable. She quickly ended his life in the saddle by dangling part-ownership of the stable in front of his bleary eyes. And from then on, only two things bothered Hiram Brooks more than running out of bourbon— the decline in the stable business because of the growing number of automobiles, and the fact that Sataro Hoshi still walked proudly around Lodi.

One night in mid-May, a stranger sidled up to listen with interest as Brooks loudly addressed a small bored group of listeners in a local saloon. The topic, as usual, was the takeover of California by the Yellow Peril. When the last of his listeners yawned and departed, the stranger stuck out his hand. "The name's Flattery," the burly man announced warmly. "Sean Flattery of San Francisco. Can I buy you a drink?"

Shortly, the two men were huddled over a quart of bourbon at a corner table. An hour later, Hiram Brooks had a mission. Four months later, he was poised to execute that mission.

The Ford truck rattled its way up to the lumberyard by Japan Town at 12:20 A.M. It turned around and parked facing south, then choked to stillness. Hiram Brooks clambered down from the passenger side, while eight other men climbed out the back. All wore bandanas tied around their faces except Brooks. He spoke in a harsh low tone as the men glanced around furtively. "Ain't no one around at this hour. I told you I been here four nights to make sure. All right now. Get them posters stuck up on all the nearby buildings, like I explained." He pulled out a bottle and took a deep swig before handing it over to his nearest accomplice. "One last drink, then the fun begins."

From the deep shadows of their favorite pile of two-by-fours some twenty feet away, Tomoko and Noboru hastily broke their embrace and stared out at the intruders. The moon was full, bright, and flooding the area with crisp light. They held their breath, wondering at the masked faces. The face Noboru saw looked slightly familiar, like someone he had once seen on horseback. He flashed back to when he was eleven, watching a horror scene in the street. But no, it couldn't be. He strained, trying to hear their words, but couldn't pick up anything logical.

"Who are they?" Tomoko whispered.

As Noboru held his forefinger to his lips for her to be quiet, Brooks nodded his head firmly and growled, "Okay, let's get them damned Japs." Abruptly, he turned and headed into the empty field that backed the main street of Japan Town. Some of the other men followed, while the rest started up the dirt street in front of the buildings.

Hurriedly, Noboru grabbed his trousers and struggled into them. "Stay here!" he hissed.

Tomoko jumped to her feet, adjusting her skirt and hair. "What are they doing?" she asked fearfully as the group in the street stopped to hang something on the front of the corner fish market.

Noboru felt a chill and a sharp feeling of dread. Whatever it was, it wasn't good. The men in the back of the buildings were skirting the backyard fences and soon disappeared from sight. He turned back to Tomoko and motioned for her to remain still, then dropped into a crouch and dashed across the street to the nearest shadow. Hurrying to the front corner, he peeked cautiously around it long enough to see the men stop in front of the Osiriji barbershop, then move on. After another stop, they turned and moved back to the front of the Hiroshima-ya, where they appeared to be waiting for something.

Noboru dashed back to the other corner and crept up the back fences until he saw a match flare behind the boardinghouse. Immediately, something blazed more brightly. He sucked in his breath, afraid his guess was correct.

Hiram Brooks leered at the burning torch in his hand as two of his men splashed kerosene on the back wall of the Hiroshima-ya. The flame flickered on his grimace, highlighting the excitement in his shining eyes. Suddenly, the men stopped soaking the wall and stepped back expectantly. Brooks nodded, bringing two fingers to his mouth. His shrill whistle was followed by a loud *crash* from the front of the building as a huge rock was thrown through the large window.

"Okay, you dirty Japs!" Brooks shouted, igniting the wall. *"Run like rats!"*

Noboru didn't even hear the truck start up behind him. He stood frozen, staring in horror as the flames began to lick up the back walls. *"No!"* he shouted, breaking the trance and bursting into a dead run. *"Father!"* he screamed.

Sataro heard both the whistle and the crash from the front. He threw himself over the side of the bed just as Miyuki reached for him. "What is it?" she cried out.

"I don't know. Stay where you are!" He was already in the parlor when the light from the flames flashed through the back windows. He whirled back to the bedroom. "Miyuki! Follow me!" he shouted. As she scrambled out of bed, the terrified Zenro ran out of the kitchen. "Quick!" Sataro shouted. "Upstairs! Wake everyone!" Whirling back to Miyuki, he snapped, "Out the front! Wake the neighbors!" He darted to the stairs, his shouts joining those of Zenro. Suddenly, he remembered Noboru, but his son was already in the kitchen furiously pumping water into a bucket. He grabbed a huge washpan as his son rushed outside to throw water on the sheet of flames that was now enveloping the wall.

Smoke was pouring into the kitchen and flickering light lit everything as the first fire ate its way through the thin wooden wall. Sataro flung the washpan full of water on it, but he knew it was too late. He turned to the frantically pumping Noboru and caught his arm. *"It's no use!"* he shouted over the growing roar of the flames. "Help Zenro get the boarders out, then stay with Miyuki!"

As his son headed for the stairs, Sataro rushed into the parlor and knelt by the safe. He didn't even look up as the screaming boarders streamed down the steps and dashed for the front. *He had to get that money!* The first try at the combination didn't work. He cursed and whirled the dial again. The flames were now sweeping through the bedroom and smoke was pouring into the parlor. He squinted through the tears, forcing his fingers to go slowly, reciting the combination numbers aloud.

"*Sataro!*" Miyuki screamed from the doorway.

Twenty-six! He jerked the handle and the safe opened. As the fire roared into the parlor, he grabbed the cash box and his ledger, then whirled toward his horrified wife. "Out! Get outside!" he shouted frantically.

The street was already a circus of awakening confusion, cries of alarm and excitement, flying sparks, the flickering eerie light of destruction, and the horrified fascination that always accompanies a growing fire. Sataro quickly barked orders for the boarders to douse the front part of the building. But he knew it was hopeless.

Coming back to where the shocked Miyuki stood staring with an armful of belongings, he gripped her arm to reassure her, then turned as Noboru rushed up. "You seen Zenro?" his son panted.

Shaking his head, Sataro whirled toward the burning building. He *had* to be in there! Without hesitating, he tore into the smoke-filled lounge area. Dashing behind the counter, he saw nothing. Fear gripped him as an image of the crippled Zenro burning to death flashed through his mind. "*Zenro!*" he screamed in anguish, running past spreading flames into the searing kitchen.

Fire was everywhere, an inferno creating its terrible noises and eating everything in its path. The heat was unbearable. The remains of a flaming piece of flooring crashed down from above, just missing his head. Shielding his forehead with his arm, he moved quickly, groping to see. He was about to give up when he heard the moan. It came from in front of the range, and from his cook's motionless form.

Sataro sucked in burning air as he grabbed the unconscious man's arm and threw the body over his shoulder. Just as he spun and darted for the doorway to the lounge, a fiery beam crashed down in front of him. The flames pushed him back, but it was the only way out. His breath was about gone. Summoning all that remained of his strength, he closed his eyes and hurtled through.

Staggering into the lounge, he was greeted by a flashing sheet of cold water from Noboru's bucket. "Hurry!" his son shouted, grabbing his arm and leading him out.

* * *

By the time the volunteer fire department arrived it was all over. The boarders and nearby residents had managed to get enough water on each of the neighboring buildings to keep the fire from spreading, but the Hiroshima-ya was a smoking, still burning pile of embers. All the residents of Japan Town stood across the street by the loading sheds watching the firemen dousing water on the last of the flames. Zenro had regained consciousness, but had been rushed to the hospital to be treated for a head bruise and smoke inhalation. Sataro and Miyuki, still in what remained of their charred nightclothes, watched silently as Noboru rushed up with a copy of the poster that had been hung on several storefronts. The harsh black letters were easily readable in the moonlight:

> NOTICE TO ALL JAPS
>
> GO BACK WHERE YOU BELONG. THOSE WHO
> PREACH ARE THE FIRST. DISASTER WILL
> FOLLOW FOR ALL THE REST OF YOU!

Grimly, Sataro folded the poster, gripping it tightly. His stomach churned, the taste of bile was in his mouth. He wanted to lash out at every white face within reach! Get the sword and *slash!* He squeezed the poster so tightly his nails dug into his palms. But he couldn't use the sword—the blade that had belonged to his samurai ancestors was defaced in that pile of smoking rubble, along with everything personal that belonged to them. Miyuki squeezed his arm. "At least no one was killed," she said softly. "Come, let's get out of the cool air."

Sataro nodded. The barber's daughter had offered their shop and mattresses, but he couldn't break away, standing riveted, staring into the smoldering mess that had been the beginning of his American dream. While the outrage that boiled through him was barely controllable, the sense of loss was crippling, sickening. Pieces of furniture, wall decorations, the woodwork on the bar that he had polished to such a high reflection, Miyuki's flower arrangements, and her needlework all flashed back at him. He saw Itoko and the exuberant young Noboru on the day he brought them from the train station. All the trouble with Itoko, fighting with his conscience over Miyuki. His terrible guilt. The accident. Their love . . .

All wiped out by a bigot's match.

"What the hell happened, Sataro?" Cedric shouted, rushing up.

Wordlessly, Sataro handed him the poster.

The publisher's dark features contorted angrily. "The sons of bitches!" he snarled. "Anybody see anything? Any idea who they were?"

Noboru spoke up. "I was, uh, out for a walk. I couldn't sleep. And I saw them." He described what he had seen, ending with, "I think the leader was that cowboy who roped father that time, But I'm not sure."

Cedric's eyes narrowed. "It won't hurt to see if the bastard is living around here. I'll get the sheriff on it." He turned to Sataro. "We're going to my place. You can stay there as long as you like. I've already told—"

"No," Sataro broke in. "Thank you, but we'll be moving into the Homerville place." He stared vacantly at the shape of a pool table slate in the ruins. "Have to think ahead . . ."

Suddenly it snapped! He was acting like another poor stoop laborer who had been kicked in the face and couldn't do anything about it. Well, he *wasn't!* He was Sataro Hoshi and they could burn him out a dozen damn times, but they could never break him. He grabbed Noboru's arm. "Get everyone in this town back out here, son. Tell them their samurai innkeeper has a speech for them!"

Cedric looked closely at his friend. "You okay? I mean, your brain didn't get sizzled in there, did it?"

But Sataro wasn't listening; he was heading for the center loading platform. Questioning looks from those still present turned into a soft buzz of excitement as other residents began to return. Soon the street was full again. Sataro, who had been striding back and forth on the platform, finally held up his hands for silence. His eyes glowed in the moonlight as the pitch of his deep voice rose. "Fellow Japan people, I must tell you something. . . . Tonight we've seen one of the most terrible examples of prejudice humanely or inhumanely possible. One group of human beings resorted to fire to endanger another group only because of their origin. . . ."

His clear voice grew even louder as he launched into a brief history of what his countrymen had encountered in the past two decades. Finally, after holding them in silence for over ten minutes, he moved into his purpose. He couldn't remember ever feeling so dedicated, so sincere, so powerful, "I will rise from these ashes to live another five hundred years!" he shouted. "And you will be with me—why? Because we have a special gift, a gift the *hakujin* can never take from us . . . We have *gambari!* We can persevere and overcome! We'll win out!"

Sataro stared at them in silence as he paced a few steps. Suddenly, he raised his fist and shouted, *"Gambari!"*

They were spellbound.

Again he threw his fist skyward. *"Gam-bar-eee!"*

The third time, some fists rose in the audience and several voices joined in. By the sixth and final explosion, the entire crowd had chimed in and Japan Town rocked with a yell that was loud enough to be heard in Sacramento. As it died out, Sataro's face lit up with a bright grin that quickly faded into a look of resolve. His life was just beginning. He bowed stiffly and strode off the platform.

Before the vividness of his experience wore off, Sataro wrote one of the most important editorials he would ever print. He recaptured the fire of his impromptu speech following the arson, urging all his readers to persevere against any such treatment they might encounter in the future. And he went on, reaching out to those who might never return to Japan—the Issei, or first generation of Japanese Americans. He insisted that these Issei look to education of their offspring as not only insulation, but a way out of the narrow gauge of their life. If, he maintained, higher education for the offspring—the Nisei—was utilized to the maximum, there could be no holding back the future generations. He added that assimilation would take care of itself.

This done, he returned to his own dream. Optimistically, Lodi was fast becoming merely a passing phase. His busy rice project up near Marysville kept him well occupied and away most of the time. He had finally decided against hiring Yoshi as the foreman because his former army comrade was content with his own grape farm and taking care of The Other Cheek. Besides, several men with American rice experience were available.

The change to Homerville for Noboru, however, was devastating. No longer could he pull on a pair of pants and sneak out to meet his exciting Tomoko a few hundred feet away. It was an eight-mile bicycle ride round trip from the store to the lumberyard, and he soon ran out of excuses for prolonged absences. And there was no way he could tell his father. More and more in the past year Sataro had spoken of the promised bride on faraway Miyajima. He had written periodically to his old friend, the girl's father, and he always passed on any comments about her to Noboru. But at least five years lay ahead of that problem, so Noboru worried only about being in love—madly, insensibly in love.

Tomoko and he met only on those nights when Sataro remained overnight in Marysville, always on Monday and sometimes on Thursday. But being assured of seeing her young lover merely once a week was impossible to Tomoko. From her small savings she purchased an ancient bicycle and scoured the countryside until she found an old, deserted hut on the edge of a farm about three miles equidistant from Homerville and Japan Town. It had no glass in the windows, a rotted door that barely closed, and only three-quarters of a roof. But unless there was a heavy rain, its floor was dry, and there was a cupboard in which to hide blankets, candles, and a small kerosene stove.

Having their own love nest stimulated her to new enthusiasm in their amatory encounters and a carefree disregard for the future. She knew about Noboru's betrothal, but laughed at the possibility that it would ever take place. Confident in her conquest, she gaily laughed and teased her way through her daily routine and fantasized about her nights with him.

One night in early December Noboru arrived ten minutes before their appointed time. It was quite cold, so he lit the small stove and heated some sake from the bottle he had brought a week earlier. By ten minutes after the hour he began to worry; she was always early. Besides, his father was due in on the 11:05

train and he wanted to be home well before then. Just as he decided she wasn't coming, she sang out as she rode up and jumped off her bicycle. She kissed him eagerly, then dropped to the waiting blankets with a deep sigh. The romance of the candlelight flickering on the cracking plaster of the hut's walls pleased her.

"I'm sorry I'm late, dear, but there was a problem at home."

Noboru handed her some sake and dropped beside her. "Anything serious?"

She chuckled. "No. An ugly old day laborer of about forty worked up his courage to ask my father if he could marry me. And I had to sit politely while my father listenened."

A quick chill swept over Noboru. He was in constant fear that she might get an attractive offer and be forced into marriage by her father. "What did he say?" He tried to sound casual.

Her rich laugh tumbled out. "He told me he'd think about it—his way of saying 'no.' He's no fool. He'd have just another struggling barbershop if I weren't there to liven things up." Her fingers stroked his cheek. "Besides, I'd run away before I'd let him marry me to someone like that. Now don't worry your handsome head about it." She leaned up and kissed him warmly on the mouth.

He pushed the troublesome thoughts away, feeling his pulse begin to pound as it always did at their first contact. His excitement mounted further as she teasingly unbuttoned her blouse to reveal one of the newly invented brassieres she had told him was the rage. It made her inviting cleavage more pronounced and desirous. She laughed as she turned and asked him to unhook the back. He loved her full breasts and wondered what could possibly be exciting about the smaller ones he had heard most Japanese women had.

Moments later she pulled his head to an erect nipple. "Ahh, my darling," she sighed, throwing her head back and closing her eyes. She dropped to her back. "Ahh, come and make love to me," she whispered urgently. She moaned as he kissed her fiercely, arching up to him, stroking his broad shoulders. "Oh, how I want you," she cried, pulling her legs up and squirming hurriedly out of her skirt and petticoat as he fumbled with his buttons. Moments later, her insistent arms pulled him into her warm nakedness. "Oh, my strong, beautiful Noboru," she said. "Oh, how I love you!"

"*Tomoko!*" The sharp bark of her father's shocked voice interrupted them like a whiplash. They looked up stunned to see him standing in fury in the doorway.

Osiriji was a short, heavy man, but moved surprisingly fast as he threw an upraised first at Noboru. "You worthless young dog!" the barber screamed, swinging wildly with both hands.

Noboru pulled away, bringing his arms up to shield himself. But Tomoko was on her feet like a cat, throwing herself at her father. "*Stop it!*" she shouted. "I made him come here. I *love* him, Father!"

Osiriji tried to push her aside but she clung to him tightly. Finally he stopped struggling and fixed a terrible look on her. "Get dressed," he hissed. Turning back to Noboru, who was hastily getting into his trousers, he snarled, "If you ever touch her again, I'll cut your head off with my razor!" He whirled to the doorway and stomped outside.

Moments later, Tomoko threw on her coat and tossed a wild wisp of hair back from her forehead. Her face was expressionless in the candlelight. She kissed his cheek. "I guess we'll have to find a new place," she whispered so casually that Noboru just stared at her.

"I must tell you something, Father. I've . . . fallen in love."

Sataro stared at his son as if the words were in an alien tongue.

Noboru blinked rapidly as he blurted out the rest. "I—I've also brought disgrace on our house." His father threw a questioning glance at the quiet Miyuki, who stared at the needlework in her lap. The silence was heavy as he turned back, saying nothing, waiting. The words tumbled out in a stream, as if a floodgate had opened. Noboru rushed through the facts of his relationship with Tomoko, ending with, "But I honestly love her so much I can hardly . . . hardly help myself."

Sataro lit a cigarette, watching his son quietly. Finally he spoke in a low tone, "Many boys your age have infatuations." Again he glanced at Miyuki. "And sometimes they have them when they get older. The important thing is to keep such emotion under control." He blew out a large cloud of smoke as he tried to find the right words—and hang on to his temper. He wanted to shake the boy—shout at him that the *oyakata*'s son had to conduct himself above criticism, not go laying around with some cheap slut of a barber's mistake. But memories of his own indiscretions in Hiroshima pricked at him.

"What you think is love is passion that burns fervidly," he said more stiffly than he wished. "It can be terribly misleading. As you know, you're promised. Absolutely nothing can change that. As far as your indiscretion goes, I can say only that it was wrong. I'm sure the young witch—I mean young woman—enticed you. She certainly has tempted more experienced men than you."

He cleared his throat with yet another look at Miyuki. "I'll see Mr. Osiriji and make the proper apologies. The matter will soon be forgotten. Now I must forbid you to see the woman again in any form of privacy."

Noboru was filled with relief, but stung by his father's apparent lack of understanding. "But I *love* her, Father," he cried out painfully.

Sataro frowned, wanting to end the uncomfortable discussion. "It'll pass," he said gruffly. "I'll have my friend, Mr. Kaibara, send a photograph of your beautiful Haru on Miyajima. That'll help you forget."

Noboru looked bleakly into his father's unwavering gaze. With a deep sigh, he collected himself and replied, "Yes, Father." He was about to willfully disobey Sataro for the first time.

Cedric Baldwin drove the horse and gig inside the open door of the Stockton Livery Stable to get out of the sudden shower. As he swung his long legs over the wheel, the tall manager came out of his dingy office with a nod. "Help you, mister?"

"You Brooks?"

"That's me."

Cedric pulled out a big black cigar and flicked a match to it.

"Uh, I'd just as soon you didn't smoke in here, mister," Brooks said cautiously. "Lot of hay and stuff, you know."

Cedric slowly stepped on the burning match, but puffed on the cigar. "I won't be here long, Brooks. Just want to talk to you a minute." He rubbed his chin as he moved closer to the former cowboy and searched his eyes. "I've been to some saloons this afternoon and I hear you haven't got much use for Japs. That right?"

Brooks eyed him suspiciously, then shrugged. "Who has?"

"Not many. I hear you do something about it, instead of just talking."

Brooks frowned. He knew he had done some hinting, but not even when he was liquored up had he said anything that could incriminate him. "Who are you, mister?" he growled.

"Name's Baldwin. I run the newspaper up in Lodi—you know, where that goddamn Jap got burned out a couple of months ago." Cedric grinned. "I'm planning a big editorial about why they oughta go back where they came from, and I'd like to hear your thoughts. You know, how we oughta do something about it."

Brooks moved to the bay gelding and stroked its flanks. "Nice horse you got here, Mr. Baldwin." He turned back after a few moments. "Yeah, if a little more burning went on, they might get the message," he said with a knowing smile. "All it takes is gumption."

Cedric jammed the cigar in his mouth. "And organization, right? I hear it was a small group of Stockton boys did the job up in Lodi—with a damned good leader."

Brooks grinned. "Yeah, too bad he can't get the pat on the back he deserves."

Cedric nodded, moving closer to Brooks. "Yeah, there oughta be a law for it, instead of against it. You know anyone who could give me a firsthand account?"

The stable man pursed his lips. "Maybe, if his name is left out."

Only Cedric's mouth smiled as his voice dropped into a conspiratorial tone. "You want to tell me about it?"

Brooks was about to fall for it when he suddenly stopped. "I'll ask around," he replied guardedly.

Cedric knew it was over. He took a deep drag on the cigar, bringing its ash to a bright red, then slowly threw it into a pile of straw. Brooks jumped to grab it, shouting, "What the hell you doing, Baldwin? I told you—" Cedric's looping right fist crashed into his face, knocking him into the straw. He looked up in startled hurt and rage. "What the hell—?"

Cedric's face was contorted into a more vicious mask than any pugnacious newspaperboy in San Francisco had ever seen. His voice was low and deadly. "Before I beat you into unconsciousness, I want to give you a warning, you bastard. I may not have enough evidence to haul you off to jail yet, but if you ever show your son-of-a-whore's face in Lodi again, I'll personally hold you while a certain Japanese gentleman chops you to pieces with his samurai sword!"

Hiram Brooks blanched momentarily, then let out a roar and sprang to his feet. Cedric's roundhouse caught him on the side of the head, but the force of his bull-like charge carried him into Cedric's right hammerblow. He grunted as he crawled to his knees, blood beginning to flow from his nose. He was almost to his feet when the newspaperman's left uppercut smashed into the side of his jaw. A series of blows pounded into him, staggering him. One—a roundhouse right—crushed what was left of his nose, splattering blood all over his face.

All Cedric could see was a forlorn Japanese face staring into the ashes of his new life, a noble face that he had grown to love. With the most hatred he had ever known, he locked his fists together and put all of his strength into a final sweeping blow that smashed Brooks to the floor. He stood over the form a moment, heaving for breath, then slowly recovered his broken cigar and walked into the office. There he ground the remains of the Havana into the ledger book and tipped back the open bourbon bottle. Wiping his mouth on his sleeve, he climbed up on the seat of the gig, slapped the reins lightly, and muttered, "The power of the press."

In August 1914, Japan sent an ultimatum to Germany, urging the evacuation of German-occupied territory in northeastern China. When the Kaiser refused, Japan entered what Was called the Great War on the side of the Allies, occupying the German-held Caroline, Mariana, and Marshall islands in the southwestern Pacific Ocean. In 1915 the Twenty-one Demands were submitted to China, requesting mining, industrial, and railroad concessions and a pledge that China would neither lease nor cede any coastal territory to a nation other than Japan. This would lead, a year later, to China's granting commercial rights to Japan for Inner Mongolia and southern Manchuria. The empire was making its first major imperialistic move since annexing Korea in 1910 and renaming it Chosen.

Seventeen

Tokyo, Japan—1915

Hiroshi stood quietly beside the main gate to the Shikan Gakko. He was wet from having walked through the rain to satisfy an undeniable urge to gaze upon the shrine of his dreams. It was one of those gray, drizzling Tokyo days that were often blamed for suicides and usually for any other misfortune. But he didn't even realize his kimono was soaked. His goal lay at his fingertips.

He stared pensively at the striking *kabuto matsu*, the helmet-shaped trees that dotted the grounds of the senior academy. Sataro had sent him a booklet describing the American West Point, but he was sure that far-off institution lacked the heritage and spirit of what lay before him in the former gardens of the Tokugawa shoguns. After all, he thought, that presumptuous country was still a wilderness when the first Tokugawa came to power. He moved to the side where he could see the placid lake that reminded him of the famous Lake Biwa. Even the gray, forbidding buildings seemed to shout Bushido!

Four days earlier, he had completed his six months in the ranks of Tokyo's proud First Infantry Regiment. And he had been commended by his commanding officer, rated excellent in all phases of training, judged the outstanding private in his company, and termed an infantry soldier who should excel as an officer. Two of the four steps to his commission were completed. The course of instruction at the academy had been shortened to eighteen months, to be followed by six months of probationary regimental duty. And with Japan at war—even though there were no major army campaigns—those periods would hardly be changed.

He glanced down at his sleeve. He was now a sergeant, but would never wear the insignia. In ten days he would again be a cadet, subject to the demeaning hazing of upperclassmen. But that bothered him little; Segura wouldn't be there. It was his friend, Misao, that he worried about. His fragile friend had become ill early in their regimental stint and had been able to finish the rigorous training only by superhuman effort. There had been near madness in his eyes at times. What a superb officer he would make.

Hiroshi sighed, staring up at the tall, pagodalike top of the main building just as the clouds parted. A sudden dazzling shaft of sunlight broke through, bathing the red-tiled roof and giving it a special mystique. Even the proud white flag with its bright red ball was illuminated, as if in holy light. He caught his breath, immobilized by the most powerful feeling he had ever known. He thought of Tojo and the shrine of Hachiman, but the feeling was definitely more intense. The sense of honor and promise engulfed him.

As if to welcome him and emphasize the symbolism, the flag—stirred by a momentary breeze—lifted from its pole and waved toward him. Not even in his most profound moments of spiritual training had he been so moved. It *was* a holiness!

He would be the best officer in the entire army!

He reached to his hip for his missing sword. Raising his clenched fist to the sky, he shouted three rousing *Banzai!*

Itoko met him as he entered the house an hour later. After scolding him about getting wet and telling him to take a hot bath, she remembered the note. "One of the Goto retainers brought you a note from Suiko," she announced. "I heard they were back from Paris. The general has an important new job with War Plans."

Hiroshi went to the silver tray by the door to get the sweet-scented ivory-colored envelope. He frowned as he stuffed it into his kimono. The arrogant girl had written to him twice during her absence—each a taunting message in French that Misao had translated for him. The last had come six months earlier, ending with complaints about how the war had cut into her social life. He had burned both.

"Aren't you going to open it?" Itoko asked, unable to curb

her curiosity. She had continued to look for the right match for her son, but nothing as inviting as the Goto girl had turned up. And she had discovered that the general still hadn't promised her to anyone.

"There's an old military classification," Hiroshi sniffed. "It's 'burn before reading.' "

His mother was disappointed in his apparent indifference. "That would hardly be polite," she said reprovingly. "Perhaps I should invite them for dinner to welcome them back."

Hiroshi shrugged; his mother just didn't understand. "Cadets are not even supposed to think about girls," he sighed patiently. "I wish you wouldn't."

Itoko patted his shoulder. "Perhaps during New Year." She'd have Koki see the general again.

Fifteen minutes later, as Hiroshi stepped into the tub, he remembered the letter. "Hand me the envelope in my *hakama*," he told the chambermaid.

The note was in excellent English handwriting on embossed ivory bond. "*Mon cher*," it read, "I am back from my exotic and educational world journey and eager to see if the handsome young cadet I left behind has grown into a man." He snorted, recalling that he had become a *man* the day they last met. The note went on, "I thought of you sometimes during my busy life in Paris, bringing to mind Saigo's ancient poem:

> Did I dream of him because I
> longed for him?
> Had I known it to be a dream,
> I should not have wished to
> awaken.

A rickshaw will be outside the entrance to your home at precisely three-thirty this afternoon. I will see you then." It was signed, "Discreetly, S."

He reread the note, then rolled it up in a ball and tossed it away. Spoiled bitch, he growled to himself. She thinks she can wave her finger and I'll run. She was even more brazen than before her trip—probably due to too much attention from those foppish Frenchmen! How could she intrude on his pure thoughts on this glorious, inspirational day?

He watched as the chambermaid bent to pick up the rolled-up note and place it on his folded, fresh kimono. And why did his mother always pick a cross-eyed, ugly chambermaid? He shouldn't even have come home from the Shikan Gakko—no, a visit to the sensuous Kaho would have been the thing. He thought of the lovely prostitute's attractive body and wondered what the impudent Suiko looked like. He moved vigorously around the tub, thinking of Suiko's flashing eyes.

At 3:35 he sauntered out through the moist air to the gateway. Although patches of blue broke the overhead grayness, he knew the sky had not yet finished its weeping. He spotted a covered rickshaw parked across the road near a stand of huge zelkova trees. Ambling toward it, he pulled out the note he had written in reply. He was about to hand it to the driver when Suiko's head popped out the side of the cab. "Hurry!" she urged. "We haven't much time!"

He shrugged, climbing inside. The cab was tiny, barely large enough for both of them. As he squeezed onto the seat, her fingers gripped his arm. "Yes, as I thought," she murmured. "You're taller and stronger. Let me see your profile."

He turned to her with a scowl. "I'm not a piece of merchandise!" he retorted in a loud whisper. She was a beautiful young woman!

Her laugh was throaty. "You can speak up, Cadet Hoshi. I picked a deaf driver." Her fingers touched his cheek, softly. "You're even prettier than I had hoped. Now—how are your habits? Do you use tobacco? How much do you drink?"

He clenched his fists in anger. "I'm a *soldier*," he growled angrily. "Why these stupid questions?"

Her black, almond-shaped eyes opened wide as she took his left hand. "But I must know these things," she replied innocently. "You enter the Shikan Gakko in ten days, and that doesn't leave us much time."

"Time?" he snorted. "I have plenty. But none for you. The life of a cadet leaves no room for—"

Her fingers stilled him. "Kiss me," she ordered.

He glared at her incredulously. Had the Frenchmen stolen her last remnants of respectability? Her eyes were lidded, her wide and provocative mouth closed and puckered. With the hood of her crimson cloak dropped to her shoulders, she was absolutely striking, he thought in confusion. She closed her eyes, moving her mouth closer. Her lips looked soft, inviting. Suddenly he grabbed her and kissed her passionately for a moment. Pulling back and dropping his hands just as abruptly, he snapped, "There! Is that what you want?"

"Not much polish," she replied, nodding. "But at least I know you're alive. Yes, promising, now do it again. But this time, try not to break my lips."

"What's this all about?"

Her long lashes blinked over the tiny smile. "My father says an eighteen-year-old woman should be betrothed. And you show promise. Now don't ask silly questions and kiss me again." She held her mouth up.

He stared at her, then slowly moved to her lips. He began gently, then applied every bit of technique Kaho had taught him. Surprisingly, Suiko responded warmly and knowledgeably. Damn Frenchmen! he thought as he finally broke away. What else had they taught her?

She took his hand and leaned her head against his shoulder. "I think I'll tell my father I've found a husband," she whispered, her eyes still closed.

He liked her scent, her kiss, her feel. In fact, she excited him. But this had gone far enough. Abruptly, he climbed out of the rickshaw. Sticking his head back into the rickshaw to see her startled expression, he said, "I hope the two of you will have a pleasant life," and turned to go.

"Hiroshi!" she shrieked. "Wait, I want to talk to you!"

But a sudden downpour drowned out any further discussion. He dashed through the entrance and into the house.

Hiroshi was reading Kafu Nagai's latest book on the seamy side of Tokyo the next morning when the chambermaid came to his bedroom to tell him he was wanted on the telephone. Thinking it was Misao, he hurried to answer. It was Suiko. "I must see you this morning," she said. "It's urgent!"

In spite of himself, she had dominated his thoughts the night before. But he couldn't let her know it. "I'm busy," he replied impatiently. "I have to meet my friend."

He detected actual alarm in her voice. "You must change your plans! My whole life hinges on it. I'll meet you in one hour at Aoyama ten-chome. There's a lovely *sushi* shop there." She hung up before he could tell her he wasn't coming.

Itoko walked up with a warm smile. "Misao?" she asked.

"No, another friend," he lied. The chambermaid would probably tell her it was a young woman. "I have to go out."

"Take your umbrella. It looks like rain again."

She was fifteen minutes late—a transgression to him. A general's daughter should know better. Five more minutes and he'd—

"I was detained by my mother," she said breathlessly, dropping to the *tatami* beside him. "I'll have some tea."

He signaled to the waitress, then turned back to her flushed, lovely face. "All right. What's so important" he demanded.

She fluffed out her light pink Western dress as she tried to find a more comfortable position. "That's the only trouble with these beautiful clothes," she remarked casually. "They're meant for chairs. When we rule the Pacific, I'm going to design some for the right accommodations."

It was the first nationalistic thought he had heard from her. But he was exasperated at her evading the question. "You said—"

"That's only one of the changes. Would you like to hear the important ones?" she said with shining eyes. "I want to see a million cherry trees planted in every country we conquer. With the spirit of our brave warriors blooming from China to Hawaii, the empire will never stop growing."

He looked at her in a sudden new light. Could this silly girl actually understand such important things? He started to ask her a question about Manchuria to test her, but she went on. "I understand you're a protégé of the Tojo family. Father says Captain Tojo shows great promise. Have you seen him lately?"

Did she ever stop? "Yes, at graduation," he replied. "He gave me a book by Clausewitz, the great German—"

"Tactician." She smiled brightly. "But I find Lee's defensive moves in the final year of the Civil War more interesting. His Wilderness campaign against Grant's superior numbers was absolutely brilliant."

He was hooked. He didn't care what her problem was. Misao could wait.

Nearly forty minutes passed before she suddenly jumped to her feet. "I must hurry," she announced. "Mother is having guests for lunch."

He caught her hand. "You didn't tell me what was so urgent."

She smiled confidently as she squeezed his fingers. "Oh, that. It's settled. Father doesn't have to listen to any more marriage offers."

As she spun out the door, Hiroshi shook his head. What an amazing new dimension in this confounding and dazzling young woman. But marriage—out of the question. Dazzling. He shrugged as he paid the bill. A visit to the worldly Kaho would wipe her out of his mind.

On the same day that Hiroshi formally entered the Shikan Gakko, Noboru stood quietly with seventeen other young men in a barren reception hall at the Presidio of San Francisco. Except for a few coughs of embarrassment from the ill-at-ease young men, the hall was quiet as a tall captain strode to a low dais and faced them. A large American flag stood just behind him as he began his routine speech. "You men have passed your entrance exams and . . ."

Noboru barely heard the words as his gaze swept past the expressionless face and settled on the flag. The bright red and white stripes draped around the deep blue field of white stars seemed to be nodding in solemn approval. It also seemed to be saying, "You are an American samurai. An American." He inhaled and tried to listen to the captain's words.

The decision to enlist had been difficult, but he had finally made up his mind that his heart was in America and he could never return to Japan permanently. Much as it went against his father's plans, he had himself to think about. And although general pressure against Japanese immigrants had lessened with Nippon entering the World War as one of the Allies, the chance of obtaining citizenship in the foreseeable future was dim. And he had to have it—he couldn't belong one place and be a rudderless vessel in another. A hitch in the United States Army would get him that citizenship.

The captain droned on, "As an infantryman . . ."

He could have enlisted in the navy and been a mess boy, but Hiroshi wasn't the only damned samurai in the family. From the talk and the news, it couldn't be too long before the United States got into it in Europe. And he wanted his share of the glory that came to each generation of Hoshi, not some officers' wardroom on a ship that wouldn't leave territorial waters.

"The United States Army is what you make of it. . . ."

The year at the University of California had been enjoyable, but his heart hadn't been in it. His grades were good and he had made new friends, but being away from Tomoko had been difficult. They had managed to meet every time he went home, and she had visited him twice in Berkeley. Now their separations would be longer.

"You will go to Camp Lewis, Washington, for eleven weeks of basic training. . . ."

While excited about the new adventure, he felt guilty about the way he was embarking on it. His father would be extremely disappointed about the enlistment. That's why he had to enlist first and tell him later. It was far better than direct disobedience, he told himself, knowing it was the same thing. College could be finished later; he had a job to do. He stiffened as the captain told them to raise their right hands.

"I, Noboru Hoshi," he repeated softly, "do solemnly swear that I will bear true faith and allegiance to . . . against all their enemies whomsoever . . . obey the orders of the President . . . according to the rules and articles of war . . ." His voiced caught as he finished the oath, "So help me God."

Noboru's letter arrived just a few minutes before the departure for Marysville. Sataro glanced curiously at the Olympia postmark, then tore it open. His son's apologetic but devastating words seemed to shout at him.

"Is something wrong?" Miyuki asked, seeing his deep concern. He quietly handed her the letter.

When she finished reading it, she patted his hand. "He'll be all right. As he says, college can be finished later. He's a good boy."

Sataro nodded grimly. "A good boy doesn't join the army without getting permission from his father. Not a good Japan boy."

The few people who knew Miyuki well agreed that she was always at her loveliest when her compassion showed. Now, the difficulty of what she had to say brought a soft look of pain. She held his hand firmly. "You must understand that he is not completely a good Japan boy, anymore. He has tried to tell you, but you don't really listen—he wants only to be an American."

The stubbornness clouded Sataro's eyes. "But my great dream—"

"Perhaps it will all work out later. In the meantime, try to understand him."

Sataro shook his head, growling, "A good Japan boy doesn't go against the wishes of his father."

Miyuki knew the stubbornness quite well after seven years of marriage. She brushed his cheek with her lips. "Why don't we leave? I can't wait to see the house!"

Wisely, Sataro had decided to buy a used car. He was too busy with his myriad activities to spend enough time on practice, so his two weeks of ownership had already produced two slightly crumpled fenders. The 1913 Ford sedan was a shiny black with gold-and-scarlet trim lines—a Model T with a two-speed transmission and, most importantly, one of the new self-starters. The starter was a vital element of Sataro's driving skill—without it, he would have spent numerous hours cranking the stalled engine.

"You're getting better!" Miyuki always told him enthusiastically when she rode with him. She wanted to learn. Actually, Miyuki wanted to try almost anything. On the surface, she had an existence that would be the envy of nearly every Japanese woman in America. But the current of new life was flowing around her.

Kimi and Yóshi had three children and babies were being born
out of wedlock throughout the *hakujin* society. But there were no
children for Miyuki.

They had discussed adoption, but it was out. They could not
adopt a Caucasian child, and Japanese children were still not
plentiful. The old-country style of adoption for monetary or
social advantage was out—Sataro had two healthy sons. At twenty-
eight, Miyuki Hoshì was being cheated out of motherhood and
there was no solution in sight.

The house at Marysville could be an alternative.

The house was actually four miles north of Marysville. Gordon
Burns, the real estate man, was busy extolling the advantages as
he drove them out to look at it. "You can call it an estate." He
beamed. "Twelve rooms, three baths, and a guest cottage on
fourteen acres of wooded seclusion sorta puts it in that category
around here, Mrs. Hoshi."

Miyuki smiled, saying nothing. She hoped it had a garden.

"As you know, Mr. Hoshi, the Japanese people are well
accepted around here. And being out in the country in such a
lovely mansion . . . well, no one would say anything . . . if you
know what I mean."

Sataro knew precisely what he meant.

Reaching the impressive tree-lined lane that led to the house,
Miyuki caught her breath. About two hundred yards away, where
the drive circled in front of its columned entrance, stood an
elegant two-story white house. Her eyes grew wide as Burns's
Ford slowed to a halt fifty yards away. Sataro chuckled. "Yoshi
would say it's too far from the road. Everyone would think
we're hired help."

They were soon inside, admiring the brightly polished wood
floors of the large parlor. At the end of the imposing room, a
mammoth white brick fireplace consumed most of a wall. And in
the large formal dining room, a crystal chandelier hung from the
high, recessed ceiling. Burns talked them through the four bedrooms and other wonders, following with the guest cottage.
Miyuki thought solemnly that it alone was larger than her village
home had been.

The carriage house, as Burns called the small barn, had a charming loft with scrubbed pine flooring and a cathedral-type window at one end. "Mr. Hoshi tells me you paint." Burns grinned. "This would make a fine studio—even has north light."

Miyuki smiled at Sataro. It wouldn't be the first time a barren woman painted away her sorrow and tried to create a vast family on canvas or some other material. He grinned back. "Between putting in the best Japanese garden in the county and painting, I won't even get to see you."

She tried to appear casual, but her shining eyes gave her away. "I like it," she whispered. "But isn't it going to cost a terrible amount of money?"

He told her only that the down payment was $5,000. And that the title was going in Cedric's name, as was the mortgage. "Not too much," he replied.

Burns was eager to make the sale, but practical. "How will you be covered if your friend, Baldwin, dies?" The gimmick might help on other sales.

"A special will and a second lien."

Burns nodded as they headed back to the house. "Very smooth. Shall I write up the contract, Mr. Hoshi?"

Sataro took Miyuki's hand. "Do you want it, my darling?"

The amber eyes blinked as she nodded her head. It was a palace! Now, if she could only get some grandchildren to . . .

"Enlisting in a foreign army?"

Itoko nodded sadly, not even seeing Hiroshi. Where had the years gone? It seemed only yesterday when she stole away from the Hiroshima-ya in the middle of the night—and left her fine tall son. Now, brushstrokes of ink were telling her he was going to be a soldier. How? Why? America wasn't at war.

Hiroshi read Kimi's letter. The Homerville farm woman's writings were Itoko's most accurate touch with Noboru and Sataro. Other information filtered in from Seizo, but Kimi's simple, witty exchanges were the most accurate. "The whole idea is ridiculous," he said.

Although he had never told a single soul, not even Misao, the resentment at being left behind when his noble father went off to

America had never totally eroded. It centered on his brother, the firstborn, in an unspoken pique that normally stayed deeply tucked away. But this was a different matter. Noboru was a Japanese citizen, and now he was talking of switching countries. How traitorous! And to enlist in their damned army as a private soldier—absolutely disgusting!

But he couldn't verbalize his irritation as fully as he wished, not with his mother lost in that faraway sadness he sometimes sensed in her expression. "I wonder what's wrong with him?" he said, shaking his head.

Itoko wanted to blame Sataro, but Kimi said her former husband was furious at what Noboru had done. The sharp jab of guilt surfaced . . . if she hadn't deserted her Noboru, he wouldn't be acting so irrational. There it was, the harsh truth. She was to blame—no one else! And now, what if America got into the war? She shuddered inwardly. Would the handsome son she had fled die on some cold European battlefield, in some cold rancid pool of water, without her ever seeing him again . . . without him ever knowing how sorry . . . "I should have brought him back to Japan with me," she murmured absently, holding back the tears.

Eighteen

And when a "Rainbow" forms an arch
And through its portals in the van
I see the Forty-second march—
And lo, the spires of Sedan.

—C. L. Corneille

"Not even a whole year in the army and already a corporal, huh, Hoshi?" The first sergeant shook his craggy head as he scowled at Noboru's records. "You must've been pretty good or they wouldn't have kept you as cadre. I ain't ever heard of a Jap drill instructor before. How many cycles of recruits you run through training out at Lewis?"

"Two, Sergeant," Noboru replied quietly from his position of stiff parade rest.

The first sergeant struck a match, trying to revive the remains of a cheap black cigar. Leaning back in his chair, he growled, "And now you've come all the way to Long Island to train National Guard heroes. Have you ever had anything to do with militia, Hoshi? I mean, they not only don't know their left feet from their right, they don't even know how to find the shithouse! Why, I—" He stopped as a buck sergeant entered the orderly room. "I'm going to let Sergeant Scagnelli brief you so's I don't spoil the rest of my day." Turning to the stocky sergeant, he sighed, "Take this corporal in hand. He's gonna be assigned to the Sixty-ninth with you, anyway."

Mario Scagnelli was more than stocky—his bullet head seemed to grow straight out of his heavy shoulders without benefit of a neck. He was clean-shaven, but his dark whiskers looked as if they might erupt at any time. Under a nearly solid band of heavy black eyebrows, his dark eyes seemed menacing but smiled

215

easily. "Sure, Top," he replied cheerfully. "Want I should put him in my tent?"

"Yeah, then to supply. Get him squared away and give him the tour."

Scagnelli touched the brim of his campaign hat with two fingers. "Right, Top." Turning to Noboru, he wiggled a finger and stepped into the bright midmorning sun. "Welcome to Camp Mills on Hempstead Plain, Long Island, my friend. Within a month all this peace will be shattered by masses of incoming troops from twenty-six states—the temporary home of the scourge of the Hun, the all-new, all-conquering Rainbow Division." Entering a new pyramidal tent, Scagnelli pointed to a cot and asked, "You know anything about this?"

Noboru tossed his bag on the cot. "Nothing, Sarge. I've been on leave in California and then on the train for five days."

"Okay, let's see how much worse the coffee's gotten since breakfast. I'll give you the two-bit briefing."

In the mess tent, Scagnelli launched into the story of the Rainbow Division. "The big shots decided they want a division made up of National Guard units from all over the country to go to France. It's a political thing—you know, the whole country behind the war. That sorta bullshit. So all these outfits are inbound to Camp Mills to be packaged into the Forty-second Division. Trouble is, they're still state militia and most aren't even half trained. That's where we come in. Regular army noncoms are going to give them a fast kick in the ass."

He sipped his coffee thoughtfully, then added, "And we'd better do a good job, 'cause we're going to France to fight with them. As the Top Kick said, you and me are going to the New York outfit—the Sixty-ninth Infantry Regiment. They're also called the 'Fighting Harps' if that means anything to you."

Noboru shook his head.

"Micks, Irishmen—just like I'm a Guinea and you're a Jap. Only thing is, these boys think a fun night is bashing in heads. Okay, back to Camp Mills. The provisional headquarters is that new building with the flagpole. Everything is run by the chief of staff, a colonel by the name of MacArthur, who I heard was only a major a few weeks ago." The sergeant peered into Noboru's face. "Hey, you don't say much, do you?"

Noboru shrugged. "When do the troops arrive?"

"Couple of weeks, I guess," Scagnelli replied with a chuckle. "The colonel doesn't consult me much." He yawned as he got to his feet. "C'mon, let's get your gear from supply. Then I'll take you to town so you can buy me a beer or two. Mineola's a roaring metropolis. Hey, you do have some money, don't you, Emperor?"

Noboru had heard all the names at Camp Lewis. He smiled as he replied, "Only yen."

Noboru spent much of the next two weeks with Mario Scagnelli. Aside from a few training lectures and other minor duties, it was like a vacation. The twenty-two-year-old sergeant came from a tough section of Chicago, but his rough exterior covered an inner warmth that Noboru found appealing. His eldest brother was serving time in Joliet for extortion, and Scagnelli insisted the army was the only thing keeping him out of jail. When he wasn't bragging about his gangster connections, he was asking Noboru about the San Joaquin Valley. California fascinated him.

He wrote to both Tomoko and Sataro. His father had finally forgiven him for enlisting without permission, but steadfastly ignored any talk of his later becoming a U.S. citizen. He had split the leave time between the big house at Marysville and a hotel in Stockton, where Tomoko had joined him.

On the third day at Camp Mills, Noboru was detailed to division headquarters as a runner. Shortly after eleven, he had just come out the front door when an army staff car pulled up. A lieutenant jumped out to hold the door as a tall, immaculately uniformed colonel dismounted from the vehicle. It was the officer Noboru had heard so much about—the erect colonel who was the major force in the Rainbow.

Noboru snapped to attention and saluted as the officers hurried by and entered the building. He had just relaxed when the colonel stepped briskly back into the hot Long Island sun and pleasantly asked, "What nationality are you, Corporal?"

Noboru again jerked to attention, swallowed and murmured, "Japanese, sir."

Douglas MacArthur looked him over, nodding. "I was stationed in Japan briefly just after the Russian War. Where is your home, son?"

"California, sir."

"What are you doing here at Camp Mills?"

Noboru cleared his throat. "Cadre, sir. Infantry."

MacArthur nodded again. "Maybe a little samurai spirit is just what this division needs." Turning back to the doorway, he added, "Good luck to you, son."

On August 20, Noboru and Mario took the train to Manhattan early in the morning. Not only was it their last day of leisure for a while, it was the day the Sixty-ninth New York was heading for Camp Mills. But before that famous regiment caught the ferry across the East River, it had to give a rousing farewell to Old New York. And festive Old New York was wearing its fanciest petticoat and turning out in its gayest holiday mood to respond. Patriotism crackled in the air as huge flags and bright bunting hung everywhere along the route of march on Fifth Avenue. And people were everywhere, jamming the sidewalks, standing along ledges and hanging out windows.

Excitement! Mounted policemen rode along the curbs to keep the massing, animated spectators back. Didn't the whole world love a parade? War for New Yorkers wasn't all rolling bandages, buying Liberty Bonds, and waving their tiny flags. War was sending the city's bright, dedicated young heroes to the trenches to settle the audacity of a spike-helmeted Kaiser who had gone too damned far! America was in it now and the Fighting Sixtyninth was going to smash the Hun to bits! "Erin Go Bragh!" The brave regiment that fought at Marye's Heights, at Bull Run and Antietam, at Bloody Ford and the Wilderness, was on the march!

Noboru and Mario waited near the corner of Thirty-ninth Street, each wearing the newly designed Rainbow patch on his shoulder. As the peppy strains from the regimental band drew closer, Noboru was the first to get a glimpse of the bright flags leading the nearly streetwide formation. It was a wave of brown, sprinkled with vivid patches of color and growing larger. Mario pointed to the regimental colors to the left of Old Glory. "I checked it out. There are eleven streamers designating the regiment's major engagements, and fifty silver furls for its battles."

The regimental band approached, switching smoothly from Irving Berlin's "Oh, How I Hate to Get Up in the Morning" to "The Battle Hymn of the Republic." Noboru watched in awe. What a proud outfit to be joining, he thought. When the square formation of the First Battalion neared, Mario announced, "That's our unit, boy. I hear that major leading it is one tough cookie. They call him 'Wild Bill.' "

Noboru had heard about Donovan. And he had heard about others—the popular chaplain—Father Duffy—and the regimental poet, a sergeant by the name of Joyce Kilmer. He had sent one of Kilmer's poems to his father in Marysville. As the band struck up the rollicking "Gary Owen," he wanted to tell everyone in the foot-tapping, cheering crowd that he was part of this moving segment of American history! The regiment was about to be redesignated the 165th Infantry, but he knew it would never be anything but the beloved Fighting Sixty-ninth—New York's own.

The day the New Yorkers arrived in camp, Major Donovan called a meeting of the regular cadremen. Soberly, he laid it on the line. "I'm known as a hardnose and you noncoms are going to be my whip. We have less than two months to teach the basic elements of discipline and soldiering. If I'm going to bring most of them back to see the Statue of Liberty, you had better do a damned good job."

Noboru was assigned to the second platoon of Company B. At first he was treated suspiciously, but his no-nonsense approach quickly gained the respect of his charges. By September 13, when the last elements of the 27,000-man Rainbow Division arrived, the plain adjacent to the Mineola Aviation Field was a vast sea of tents and bustling activity. It was the first time a national division of militia had been put together—a melting pot of different-colored hat-cords and the accents of many regions.

But the dust that rose from the constant drilling of so many unpolished units knew no regional distinction—rookies were rookies and there were over 15,000 of them. From reveille to retreat, the regular army drill instructors hammered away at them. As one reporter stated, "The field was a small, hellish world unto itself—a drilling, sweating, swearing planet readying itself for the great fight."

For the 165th New York, however, there was an interim fight. Its sister regiment in the brigade was the old Fourth Alabama, made up of grandsons of the Fighting Sixty-ninth's Civil War foes. Redesignated the 167th Infantry, the boys from Alabama flew into battle with the "damnyankees" daily. And the Irishmen had their hands full. Noboru, wearied by ten hours or more of drill each day, stayed clear of the brawls. But every time he was near the engineer troops from California, he had to steel himself.

One night in early October he and Mario were quietly drinking beer in a busy Garden City tavern when a red-faced private came up behind them to stare. Mario finally turned from the bar. "You got a problem, soldier?" he growled.

"Yeah, Sarge," the private replied with a thick tongue and Irish brogue. "How come you're drinking with this here yellow-belly? Out in California, we don't let 'em in a white man's bar."

Mario shook his head. "I don't like your mouth, Mick. Get lost."

The engineer private threw a glance back at his table of buddies, then moved closer, his face darkening. Jabbing his finger into Mario's chest, he snarled, "Get outta the way, Wop, so I can throw this goddamn Jap outta here!"

Noboru whirled, cocking his fists, but he was too late—Mario's right fist smashed into the private's stomach. As the sergeant crossed with a vicious left uppercut, four of the Californian's cronies tipped over their table and rushed forward. Their cries of anger turned every head in the crowded tavern. Female patrons and waitresses screamed as a fist bounced off the side of Noboru's head. He and Mario braced side by side as their attackers crashed into them. The bartender's agonized shouts were drowned by new shouts of glee and rage as several members of Noboru's platoon jumped into the fray. Chairs and tables were thrown aside as the fight spread.

A beer bottle smashed into the heavy plate mirror behind the bar. Another bottle hit the brightly lit nickelodeon, jarring its volume to a thundering rendition of "Over There." Celtic curses and accents rang out as bodies tangled, rolled on the floor, pounded each other, and made blood fly. It was a knock-down, dog-day, Irish soldier donnybrook at its crunching best.

The soldier who'd started it all came flying into Noboru with a wild overhand left, but Noboru sidestepped and slammed the private's head into the bar. Mario pulled himself up from the sawdust with a happy, bloody grin just as Noboru smashed a roundhouse into another attacker's face. Grabbing his friend's waist Mario shouted, "Let's get out of here!"

Noboru shook his head. "Not yet." He grinned.

Mario pulled him away as a police whistle pierced the din. While blue uniforms and military policemen waded into the surging coil of bodies, Mario led them around the bar toward a back door. Outside, Noboru leaned back against the wall and heaved a deep sigh. "Did I ever tell you about my father's 'other cheek' theory?" he asked with a wry grin.

Two weeks later the First Battalion caught a train to Montreal and on October 27 their convoy embarked across the submarine-infested North Atlantic. After landing in Liverpool, Noboru's portion of the Rainbow moved on to Brest, finally joining the rest of the division at Vaucouleurs in Lorraine. Months of arduous training lay ahead before General Black Jack Pershing would consider the raw Rainbow ready for the terrible trench warfare of the Western Front.

But soon there would be no more Eastern Front for the Boche— the Bolsheviks under Lenin were about to seize the bloody reins of Russia's government and pull their country out of the war. Massive numbers of German troops would head for France to make that campaign the most gruesome conflict in history.

And a new war for control of the world would begin.

Nineteen

A. E. F. France
August 4, 1918

Dear Father and Miyuki,

This is the first opportunity I've had to write anything worth mentioning. (And the censors may delete part of it.) The Rainbow, including the 165th, has been in a fierce battle at a place called Muercy Farm. The Irish boys call it "Murphy Farm." It wasn't much of a place—just a house with some small barns and a stone-fenced courtyard—but it stood on a hill and cost a lot of blood.

But then, the regiment doesn't ever dodge a fight. Major Donovan says it's the best one in France. I get to see him quite often now, since assigned to the Intelligence section. He can never be replaced, but I am in the job Sergeant Joyce Kilmer had. He was killed by a sniper seven days ago.

I see General MacArthur now and then, and he speaks to me. It's just a short hello because he's the busiest brigadier in the A.E.F., but it thrills me. He's always dashing around going into no-man's-land by himself. I think he has more medals than any officer in the corps.

I saw General Pershing the other day. (Not close.) Mario and I remain good friends. I'm glad to hear your rice is doing so well. Can I drive the fancy Duesenberg when I get home? I'll bet you are the envy of every Japan man in the Valley!

I hate to ask, but has Kimi had any word from mother lately?

I feel I should send you words from a poem Sergeant Kilmer wrote earlier in the year. It's a fitting tribute to him:

> Go to sleep,
> Go to sleep,
> Slumber well where the shell screamed and fell.
> Let your rifles rest on the muddy floor,
> you will not need them any more.
> Danger's past,
> Now at last,
> Go to sleep!

> Love,
> Noboru

Cedric Baldwin folded the letter and handed it back to Sataro. Nodding thoughtfully, he said, "Interesting. I think you should include some of his information in your newspaper, my friend. He may be the only Japanese American in the Rainbow."

Sataro beamed as he reached for Cedric's bourbon bottle. "Yes, I could call him the Rainbow samurai."

"How's Hiroshi doing?"

Sataro's smile widened. "As I told you, he graduated second in his class from the Shikan Gakko. Now he has just one month of regimental duty left as a *minarai shikan*—cadet—then the regimental officers vote on his final acceptance for a commission."

"That's just a formality, isn't it?"

"Yes, the wedding is already planned."

Cedric hadn't seen his friend in nearly a month. "I imagine Itoko had you right on top of the invitation list." He chuckled. "You going?"

Sataro stiffened. Sometimes Cedric offended him with his indelicate humor. And the man never had learned that Itoko's actions in regard to Hiroshi still came under the domain of the House of Hoshi. In fact, he wondered if Cedric really understood the position of a head of family in Japan. "My son marries only on my approval," he replied evenly. "Of course we're going."

Cedric caught the prickliness, but decided to ignore it. He

thought his friend was taking himself too seriously lately. "When are you leaving?" he asked casually.

"Miyuki and I go to San Francisco in four days."

"Will that rice empire of yours run without you?"

There it was again—condescension. "My foreman can keep it under control for six weeks," Sataro replied coolly. He had intended to ask Cedric to go up and take a cursory look at things in the middle of his trip, but decided against it. What would a country newspaperman know about such things?

Cedric switched the subject. "Bet you'll be glad to see the boy, won't you?"

Sataro nodded. There was nothing he wanted more at the moment. Ever since Hiroshi had sent his graduation picture, the portrait of the dedicated-looking young man had dominated his office, interrupting his thoughts, building his anticipation, and smoothing the edges of his guilt. He *had* done the right thing in coming to America! All that blame he had assumed for tearing the family apart was undeserved—this was his justification, his vindication. "You can't imagine how much it means to me," he replied intensely.

Cedric launched into his idea of Sataro combining his trip into a journalistic effort, of bringing back first-hand impressions of Japan's international outlook and intentions in the Pacific. But Sataro was still thinking about his absolution: It was all coming together, the wealth, Hiroshi . . . Noboru would get his thinking straight and forget this remaining in America nonsense . . . he couldn't be prouder.

"Have you considered what it would mean if we ever went to war with Japan—I mean now that you have a son in each army?"

Impossible, it could never happen. Again, his reply had a touch of stiffness. "I believe there were instances of such a thing in your Civil War, weren't there? Besides, I think all your talk about Japan's purported aggression is nonsense."

Cedric shrugged. "It was just a hypothetical thought." He asked about the ship they would be taking.

A few minutes later, Sataro got to the main purpose of his visit. He told Cedric about a ranch he had found for sale south-east of Marysville. When he finished its physical description, he continued enthusiastically with how he could use Japanese labor to convert part of it to farmland and perhaps later sell it off in parcels. "I can buy it for ninety thousand dollars," he said finally. "Can we use the same procedure of putting the title in your name?"

Cedric frowned. "What are the terms?"

"Fifteen thousand down, twenty annual payments for the balance. It's an outstanding opportunity."

"What do you know about cattle?"

"That's no problem."

"You aren't letting this land baron thing go to your head, are you, Sataro? I mean you're in pretty deep for someone who can't legally own a damn thing."

Sataro's mouth dropped open momentarily. With the rice market the way it was he could buy three *damned* ranches in a few more years! The trouble with this two-bit publisher was he didn't understand the sweep of higher finance. He wanted to reach over and grab him by his grubby necktie and shake him! He could take some of his smart humor, but in no way could he accept this, this being *patronized!* So Baldwin's true stripe was finally showing through—rooted deeply beneath his shiny liberal veneer was a vein of *hakujin* superiority as positive as any red-neck's. He got abruptly to his feet, spilling his whiskey. "There are other ways," he said coldly, drawing himself erect and heading for the door.

"*Sataro!*" Cedric's voice cracked like a whip.

Sataro turned in the doorway, staring back coldly.

Cedric Baldwin's dark Irish eyes were glittering in the sudden anger. "Go ahead," he grated. "Stomp off half-cocked like some slant-eyed yellow-belly who just got off the goddamn boat! I gave you more sense than that. You're playing in the big leagues, boy, and I'm just trying to keep you from losing your ass."

Sataro tensed, his eyes thin slits. He could throw him into the street where all his *hakujin* peers would see him disgraced. In the street, the dust . . . the sun of another day . . . a brass band's blaring music, a horse's hooves, a rope. He bowed stiffly from the waist and walked out.

*   *   *

By the time Sataro looked at The Other Cheek, talked to Yoshi, and had a couple of beers with Zenro and Yego at the store, the edge was fully gone from his anger. And as he headed back for Marysville in the hazy afternoon sunlight, he was able to push even the smoldering resentment away. The excitement of returning to Japan could overcome anything. It had been over eleven years since that fateful departure and it was time he tasted his roots again. He knew he was rich by a Hiroshima immigrant's standard, but he had only scratched the surface of what could be made in this cornucopia.

Title to the ranch would be put in Yoshi's oldest son's name for the time being. If that venture went well and the rice market kept booming, he could be worth well over a half-million dollars in three or four years. Ah, it would be satisfying to visit. The tales he could tell Seizo and others!

The heavy Duesenberg touring car felt good in his hands as he neared the house. He knew it was an extravagance, but he could afford it and wanted it. Now that he had become a competent driver, a powerful automobile was his only vice. He liked the richness of its black leather seats and the brightness of its brilliant dark red finish. As he swung into the majesty of his tree-lined drive and aimed the hood ornament at the white columns of his lovely home, he felt total satisfaction.

Ten yards later, the first chest pain hit.

The doctor's name was Rosenthal. With Miyuki lightly squeezing his hand at the side of the hospital bed, Sataro tried to understand. Dr. Rosenthal spoke slowly, "With this type of heart attack there's no reason you can't recover fully and lead a normal life. But you must be careful during the recovery period. I'll put you on a limited exercise regimen at first, gradually building it up during the next six months. If all goes well, you should be able to do most anything at the end of a year. Do you understand, Mr. Hoshi?"

Sataro stared into the brightly polished eyeglasses. "Travel," he asked weakly. "Can I go to Japan in the near future?" Even a sentence was an effort.

"Absolutely not!" the doctor replied firmly. "Travel is out of the question for some time."

Sataro closed his eyes, but the visions of Hiroshima, of Hiroshi, his mother, brother, and all that was dear to his memory stared back at him. He opened them again. "How soon will I be able to get back to work?"

Doctor Rosenthal scowled. "I don't know. At this point, we want to keep you alive and start making you well."

As she reread the telegram from Miyuki, Itoko was filled with mixed emotions. She felt truly sorry for Sataro, but she was also angry at being cheated. She *wanted* her former husband at the wedding. She *wanted* to show him how she had improved her station in life by leaving him. But as much as anything, she wanted him to see how youthful, attractive, and trim-figured she had remained. With the vindictiveness that lingered with her unhappy memories of Lodi, she wanted him to be painfully sorry about how he had treated her. And she wanted that damned yellow-eyed farm girl he had married put back in her place.

But she couldn't have everything.

Putting the coming marriage together had been difficult enough. Although Hiroshi was respectful and dutiful in every way, he had been balky about the betrothal to Suiko. Koki had finally had a heart-to-heart talk with him, explaining that the union was too vital to permit personal choice. "You know the custom," he had said, flinching inwardly at his hypocrisy, "love always comes *after* marriage." But his personal opinion was that Hiroshi's protests were somewhat less than sincere.

The next three weeks dragged for Hiroshi. It was like sleepwalking for him, going through the motions of being on probation when he knew he was already accepted by the officers of the regiment. The vote had been taken a week earlier. The entire programming of the officers school was a throwback to the darkness of the Tokugawa, he thought. At West Point, St. Cyr, Sandhurst, and other modern academies, a cadet received his commission upon graduation.

With his peers scattered among the various regiments of the

mainland army, there was no specific place for commissioning.
The commanding officer of the First Infantry's barracks near
Roppongi had scheduled a parade for the occasion. Sixteen cadets would receive their commissions; none would be rejected.
Additionally, the powerful Major General Goto from War Plans
would be attending and presenting an award from the Emperor to
the most distinguished cadet.

Well before the long awaited Saturday arrived, the word was
out. Hiroshi Hoshi was to get the award and the general would
soon be his father-in-law. As his friend Misao put it, "It was
nearly as good as being adopted by a prince."

There was no false modesty on Hiroshi's part about being the
distinguished graduate—he was proud of attaining the distinction
through hard work. The other part, having the road ahead paved
by a convenient marriage, annoyed him. He would just as soon
stay in an isolated regiment in Manchuria, and who needed a
wife?

Friday night, after polishing every accoutrement on their uniforms,
Hiroshi and Misao went to the regimental altar to worship for
several minutes. As they slipped quietly away in the darkness,
Hiroshi whispered, "I feel almost holy."

The slender Misao nodded excitedly. "I know. *Yamato Damashii*
overwhelmed me! I wanted to jump up from my prayers and
shout a dozen *Banzai*. I tell you, we are touched by its absolute
essence, the world is at our feet!"

"The world is at Nippon's feet," Hiroshi corrected. He too
had felt the *Yamato Damashii*—the soul of Japan. "We're just her
newest tools, rough and unproven, but shaped in her image."

They walked on in silence, finally reaching their quarters
where a sake celebration awaited. Just as they started to enter,
Misao grabbed his friend's sleeve. "Just promise me one thing,
will you?" he implored with mock gravity. "At the end of the
journey, forty years from now when you command the army and
I'm your chief pimp—please, Hiroshi, *please* make me a general!"

Hiroshi and Misao were up at 0400, attired in their loose athletic
clothing. A brisk run around the parade ground was followed by

fifteen minutes of strenuous jujitsu. Next, they donned their fencing gear, lacquered wooden body armor and meshed metal masks. No last cleansing of the body would be complete without a final *gekken* session. Wielding two-handed bamboo swords, they squared off as they had done hundreds of times in the past six years. "*Ahhyeeai!*" Misao's bloodcurdling scream split the brisk morning stillness as his training blade made a vicious pass at his elusive opponent.

"*Ahrrrayaai!*" Hiroshi roared as he parried and brought his sword heavily down on Misao's shoulder. The battle was joined and would last for a violent and noisy ten minutes. Gasping for air at the end, Hiroshi locked Misao's weapon against his chest and shouted, "What did Mencius say about honor?"

Misao glared into his friend's exultant expression as he panted, "It is in every man's mind to love honor—but little does he dream that what is truly honorable lies within himself . . . and not elsewhere!"

"*Banzai!*" Hiroshi shouted.

"*Banzai!*" Misao echoed.

Dropping their mock swords simultaneously, they grabbed each other in a tight embrace. Fighting the tears, they stepped back to salute each other. Ceremonies and celebrations could come later—this was their consummation, their reality. They knew the last fetters of boyhood had dropped away and they were full of the new responsibility. They thought they would never be closer.

As if on signal, the first bright rays of the rising sun flooded over them to join their precious moment.

Itoko shifted her weight on the hard bleacher seat as she dabbed at the perspiration with a lace hanky. She should have worn Western clothes—at least she'd have the benefit of a wide hatbrim against the boiling sun. On her left, the white-haired Tomi was busily working her fan as she enjoyed the sight of the regimental formation stretched out before the makeshift grandstand. And to her right, Koki puffed quietly on his old briar pipe, wondering about what an impact these sixteen young men would have on Japan's future.

He watched the tall young man who stood at rigid parade rest in the center of the rank of sixteen behind the regimental staff. Hiroshi had everything material—blood, patronage, the marriage, and the money he had provided. Fifty thousand yen wasn't a fortune, but it would keep him independent. There was an old army saying, "*Bimbo shoi, yarikuri chui, yattoko taii*—penniless second lieutenant, somehow managing first lieutenant, just getting by captain." Koki smiled inwardly. With Suiko's rich tastes to contend With, Hiroshi would need all the extra income he could find.

He glanced to where the general's wife and lovely daughter were seated. She was certainly an enticing morsel, he thought with a touch of guilt, wondering if this willful girl had already met Hiroshi in some hideaway and made wild love.

Itoko was so full of herself she had to squeeze her nails into her palms to stay calm. Hiroshi was going to have so much! She hadn't even told Koki about Sataro's twenty-five-thousand-dollar gift—another fifty thousand yen. Blood money! she had snorted when it arrived. She glanced over to where the slender major with the blackrimmed spectacles sat quietly at the end of the first row. She knew Tojo would attend. He should be highly pleased with the protégé who had been thrust on him by the visit of a caring mother to his father. She beamed at the memory of her staunch bravery. She had had trouble controlling her glee all morning, wanting to jump and dance before the whole world! Only the thought of a soldier in France sobered her.

As Hiroshi waited for the bugler to sound adjutant's call and begin the ceremony, he felt the sword against his hip.

Finally, he could wear it! If ever the soul of Bushido, if ever the *Yamato Damashii* had been infused in a sword, it was in this magnificent gift from Koki. Its hilt was of sharkskin and the finest silk, its guard of mixed silver and gold, and its scabbard glistened with a sheen of bright lacquers. But such were merely the fringes of its majesty. It was the blade that made it a sword for a king. When he first drew it in wonder, he pictured the master who had created it—a great artist applying every known element of religion and inspiration to one very special shaft of steel. He could picture the forge, smell the steam as the raw blade was plunged into the water, feel the friction of the grindstone as the master honed its perfect, razorlike edge. Light the color of the sky flashed off its brilliant texture, announcing its indomitable spirit and unconquerable strength. It was a thrill to touch!

He shifted his weight as he looked into the faraway eyes of General Goto. Was the general wondering if he had bet on the right horse? Or was he thinking of changing his mind about letting his new son-in-law serve in the regiment a year before becoming his aide. It didn't matter now. He thought about the Emperor's gift—an inexpensive silver watch, in keeping with the austere life that was expected of an army officer. He would wear it proudly.

His gaze moved to the bleachers, finding Seizo and his Aunt Setsuko. He was so pleased they could come. A shadow crossed his mind—always there was a proxy for his father. If it wasn't his uncle, it was Koki. Of course the heart attack made it impossible for him to be present, but the boats steamed every day. Was the tall, loving figure he remembered a myth, a ghost who would never return? Were his mother's disparaging remarks justified?

The bugler's first clear notes sounded.

No, this great moment wasn't complete without the head of the House of Hoshi.

Koki lit the Havana with a long wooden match, then lit his own. He saw that Hiroshi wasn't too practiced with the cigar, but he could handle it. He raised his glass of cognac. "To your career, my son."

The celebration dinner was over and he would be joining Misao and the other new lieutenants for a party in a Roppongi brothel within the hour, but his stepfather wanted only a few minutes. "Thank you, sir," he replied, sipping his brandy.

Koki walked slowly around his huge desk, stopping to sit on a corner. The study was totally silent. His expression was warm but concerned, as if he were going to counsel a favored but errant student. And what he had to say was perhaps the most delicate subject he might ever broach. Over and over, he had told himself to forgo the talk, but his conscience wouldn't allow it. "My son, what I have to say may be difficult for you to grasp in your present state of dedication and euphoria, but it is most important."

He blew out a cloud of cigar smoke. "As you know, I'm a historian and an observer, not a doer. As such, I can often be objective—and my objectivity compels me to place yet another responsibility on your young shoulders today. It's a warning that I hope you never have to worry about."

His gaze was direct, unblinking, his voice calm in the stillness. "There is a certain hypnotic delirium working its way into the flesh of our leadership . . . maybe into the people. And I'm afraid it may develop into an insidious disease that can destroy us. We've tasted deeply from the cup of imperialistic success in the past twenty-three years, Hiroshi, and it could affect our future in a most detrimental manner.

"As an officer who will surely rise to high position someday, you should try to keep an open mind. It may be that men like you will have to recognize folly disguised as patriotism, and be a brake on its handle."

Koki stood, moving slowly forward, and putting his hand on Hiroshi's shoulder. His gaze was even more intense. "Not only could the fate of the empire be dependent on such awesome responsibility, but your very *soul* could be at stake. His voice dropped to nearly a whisper. "Stay alert to your inner warnings, and heed them. Don't let them be swept aside by the onrushing roar of what may someday be an outburst of that disease . . . true bravery does not always lie in a code or the sword. *It could mean your soul.*"

Hiroshi nodded, drawing on his cigar. What his stepfather was saying was beyond him, a result of his being too deeply involved in his philosophical observation of the trends. But that was the way it was with professors—no practicality.

His soul was Bushido, and he was about to go out and soak it in alcohol and the flesh of a beautiful harlot.

Suiko stood alone before the full-length mirror with a frown knitting her delicate eyebrows. The plain white silk kimono and its heavily embroidered white satin obi with its threads of gold were perfectly appropriate for the old-fashioned wedding. Her hairdo, a *shimada* with the chignon set off by a comb of tiny pearls, was the result of hours of work. The frown was for herself. After all the conniving to arrange this marriage, she wasn't positive she wanted it.

She had known from that night of Hiroshi's birthday party so many years before that she'd have no other man for a husband. And that excited her beyond reason. It was the change in her life she doubted. Giving up nearly complete independence to assume the role of wife to an overly confident man-child with a mother who would relinquish nothing in her powerful grasp was a radical switch.

Suiko shook her head as her mother glided into the room. The battle will soon be joined, Mrs. Obata, she said to herself. "You look perfect, my dear," Mrs. Goto purred. "It's time to go. Everyone is waiting."

Suiko held up a hand mirror to take one last look. There could be no more beautiful bride in Nippon, she assured herself. And she was about to marry the handsomest lieutenant in the far-flung legions of the Emperor. She lowered the mirror—it was time for the *tsunokakushi*, the wide headdress that announced to one and all that she was a bride.

Minutes later she and her mother entered her father's study hand-in-hand and went to where he stood stiffly staring out a window. His arms were folded over the medals of his dress uniform. A twinkle sparkled in Suiko's eye. "Honorable General," she said in an overly humble tone. "Your dishonorable, unfaithful daughter awaits your farewell before leaving the House of Goto forever."

He turned, his sad expression softening. How he had spoiled this magnificent girl, he thought. Young Hoshi had given him a perfect excuse for keeping her home an extra three years. How he loved her. He cleared his throat, but his voice came out gruffly as he said, "All of what you say is true. I'm well rid of you."

She laughed as she caught his hand and hugged him.

The black-lacquered palanquin with its two long poles and festively dressed men carriers stood just outside the front entrance. Brides never rode to their weddings in that old-fashioned conveyance anymore, Itoko had insisted, but the charm had been irresistible. All the old ritual would be observed at *her* wedding! She bowed to her exuberant, waiting friends who would gaily wave their brightly colored lanterns as the tiny procession moved toward the Obata residence, then climbed inside the little cab. Holding her head high, she felt the excitement begin to mount. She laughed at herself—the Goto family wasn't losing a daughter, the Hoshi family was about to undergo a radical metamorphosis!

Itoko, wearing an exquisite kimono of fine black silk complete with its beautifully embroidered design of *goshoguruma* around the lower portion, was herself a result of many hours of hairdressing and grooming. Standing in the screened-off portion of the large parlor that would serve as the wedding ceremony area, she surveyed the rich bank of multicolored chrysanthemums that provided a backdrop for the dais where all the offerings to the gods rested.

For the tenth time she checked the offerings. Two round cakes of pounded rice in the middle; stands of consecrated sake placed in front and on either side, and at the back a stand each of carp and pheasant. Two shiny black-lacquered cabinets with writing materials stood beside a wash basin and tea utensils. Also near the center stood a large flat porcelain dish with legs, in which were planted a miniature pine, bamboo, and plum tree—denoting in order longevity, gentleness, and fidelity in adversity. A crane and tortoise also signified longevity. In the foreground stood an old couple named Takasago with a rake and broomstick—the Jo and wife Uba of native legend.

Itoko nodded in satisfaction. Everything was perfect. As soon as the ceremony was over, the first reception would commence. It was only the beginning of a week-long celebration, but the one she considered the most important. It announced to Tokyo society that her son had married well and would honor the name of Mitsubishi, as well as Hoshi and Obata.

Moments later an outside lookout eagerly announced that the brightly lit bridal party was approaching. As it stopped, the uniformed Misao—acting as *baishakunin*, or go-between—helped the beautiful Suiko down from her glistening carriage. Holding her head demurely low as the occasion decreed, she entered the house and was escorted to a guest room for last-minute adjustments to her toilette. It was time for the groom to be summoned.

On the second floor, in the suite that would be the couple's private living quarters, Koki and Hiroshi shared a toast of scotch. Holding his glass high, the professor smiled. "Between the army and this, your last vestige of freedom evaporates."

Hiroshi nodded soberly as he drank. Homelife with Suiko and Itoko *would* be different, but also exciting. Suiko, in her last note to him the day before, had brazenly joked that she had taken last-minute brothel training to ensure ultimate success in their marriage bed. He snorted inwardly—had she no shame?

Suiko held up her hand for Itoko's hairdresser to stop. It was time. Gliding to where Misao waited, she gave him a bright smile and nodded. He led her to the flower-scented ceremony area where he pointed to a richly brocaded pillow in front of the dais. As soon as she assumed an erect sitting position, the *baishakunin* turned to fetch Hiroshi to a second pillow placed three feet to her right. A tray was placed before each of them and the consecrated sake was poured into a long-handled bronze pot.

The "three times three" ceremony was ready to begin.

Misao slowly poured sake into the top, or smallest cup of a set of three. With the only sound the faint strains of a *koto*, he handed it to Suiko. Slowly, she sipped it three times. Hiroshi then sipped three times from the same cup—after which he was served first from the second cup. Again, it was three drinks each. Finally, Suiko took three long sips from the third and largest cup. But instead of letting the *baishakunin* serve Hiroshi, she turned and handed it to him personally. In a clear low voice she said, "As this cup seals our marriage, my dear Hiroshi, I offer you my most important gift. I shall love you more than any woman has *ever* loved a man."

He stared briefly into the stark intensity of her wide, dark eyes, then took the cup to finish the ceremony with the final three drinks.

As they stood and bowed to each other, Hiroshi smiled and murmured, "Thank you for so honoring me."

He was totally entranced.

Twenty

The Allied offensive to turn the German retreat of early fall into a massive enemy stampede began in late December. The most difficult portion of the overall attack was handed to the American Expeditionary Forces—to smash enemy resistance in the Argonne Forest area. If Pershing could accomplish this extremely difficult mission, break through and capture the vital rail lines that ran from Sedan to the huge German depot at Metz, massive bodies of Boche troops would be forced to surrender.

But General Pershing had his problems. The American First Army, consisting initially of only 200,000 men, was practically stopped in its tracks along its twenty-four-mile front. Inexperienced American troops faced veteran German divisions deeply entrenched in some of the best defensive positions on the entire Western Front. Losses were staggering as confusion reigned. While British and French generals leveled vicious criticisms at Pershing, Black Jack furiously regrouped his fumbling force and readied it to slug forward in mid-October. By then it would triple in strength and its veterans would be back in the lines. On October 11, the Rainbow moved up to relieve the heroic but decimated First Infantry Division—The Big Red One—near the Romagne Woods. Its mission: overcome that strongly fortified sector of the *Kriemhilde Stellung* to its front.

None of this grand strategy, however, meant much to the infantrymen of the 165th New York as it moved into position. The old Fighting Sixty-ninth was down to less than three thousand men and many of them were green replacements. Noboru had just returned to the First Battalion after his stint of temporary duty at regimental headquarters as intelligence sergeant. But instead of going back to his rifle company, he was told that Colonel Donovan wanted him to stick around the staff and "freelance."

Mario Scagnelli stopped by battalion headquarters before reporting into his company the night they settled into a shelled-out farm. He had spent the last month in a rear echelon hospital recovering from an encounter with mustard gas and a minor wound in the left arm. Fortunately, the gas exposure had been brief and the hearty Italian seemed fully healed. The large bottle of Burgundy he pulled from his bag as he and Noboru settled into a quiet corner of the wrecked barn was intact. "What d'ya mean 'freelance'? Hell, that's how you get killed around this neighborhood."

Noboru chuckled as he tipped the bottle back and drank deeply. "You know—" he replied, wiping the back of his mouth with his hand. "Glide around like a geisha and bring back information."

Mario tossed his helmet to the ground as he took the bottle back. "I guess it's not much more dangerous than storming that damned barbed wire. Christ, if I ever see another fence when this damned war is over, I'll lose my mind. What d'ya know about this attack? I mean back in the hospital, it's all over that the war's about to end."

Noboru leaned back against the stone foundation, closing his eyes. "Not here, it isn't. Not over an hour ago, I heard the adjutant telling another officer this is going to be a tough battle— with a lot of dispersement. Lot of individual platoon and squad action. I won't be the only freelancer if that's the case."

"Hey! I got a good idea," Mario said brightly after a few moments. "Why don't you start talking armistice to the Jerrys when you go out into no-man's-land. I mean, tell 'em we're all ready to quit and buy them cases of good wine. I'll bet—"

"I'll have none of that damned talk around here!"

Noboru jumped to his feet as he recognized Wild Bill Donovan's angry voice. Mario followed as Donovan and Father Duffy's faces became discernible in the dim light. "I'm sorry, sir," Mario managed, clearing his throat and holding the bottle behind his back. "I was just joking, sir."

Donovan glared at the sergeant and was about to berate him

when the popular chaplain intervened. "Ah," he purred in his rich brogue, "it's Sergeant Scagnelli from Company C, just returned from hospital. 'Is brain's a bit addled by all that soft rear echelon living, Bill."

Donovan nodded. "Just stow that talk, Sergeant," he said evenly. "It poisons the spirit and gets a hell of a lot of men killed."

"Yes, sir!" Mario barked from stiff attention.

Donovan turned to Noboru. "Sergeant Hoshi, I was just going to send someone to find you. Think you can go out and take a look at the wire about oh-three-hundred? See if there are any weak points we can probe. Be careful. Okay?"

Noboru nodded. "Yes, sir. Any particular place?"

"Middle of B Company. Make sure you check out with their people so you don't get shot coming back in."

"Yes, sir." Both he and Donovan knew any further instructions would be superfluous. He had gone on a dozen such missions in the past two months.

Donovan turned to go, telling them to get some sleep. Father Duffy held back. "Are you a Christian, Sergeant?" he asked Noboru softly.

"No, sir."

The chaplain pulled off his helmet to scratch his head. "Well now, I read a little about Shinto and a lot about Buddhism back when I was in seminary, but I'm afraid I'm not too conversant with either. Would you like to talk to me when we get some quiet moments, son?"

The question of religion had been on his mind off and on since arriving in France. As everyone said, battle did that to soldiers of all kinds. And Mass was part of the day's routine with the Catholic regiment. Remembering some of the teachings of Reverend Macnamara back in Hiroshima, he had quietly sat at the back of a few services to try his hand at praying. He had done the same at some Protestant services and once at a service with the regiment's East Side Jews. "Yes, Father," he replied softly. "I think I'd like that."

* * *

At five minutes before three, Noboru checked out through B Company's center outpost. He was traveling light, with only his Springfield rifle, his bayonet, and a special, sharp-bladed knife that he had used to kill on previous one-man patrols. His face was smeared with black grease and he wore no helmet.

After a week of steady rain, no-man's-land was a soggy quagmire of oozing mud. He had to pick his way forward, finding firm spots around tree roots and rock formations. Although the moon had performed and disappeared, the stars afforded just enough light for him to stay oriented. It took nearly a half hour to navigate the three hundred yards to the first wire formations.

He knelt by a piece of scrub that had somehow managed to survive, holding his breath in an attempt to hear the enemy. But those who were awake behind the fortifications were totally quiet. He could see that the rolls of barbed wire were stacked at least twenty feet deep and held together by heavy iron stakes. He made a mental note that artillery would not be able to dent it—tanks would be required.

Beyond the breast-high wire, he knew the enemy had deep trenches, interlaced with machine gun nests and mines. Since these fortifications had been in place for so long, their fields of fire would be murderous. And still farther back, there would be a widespread network of shallower trenches reaching all the way to the two villages that were the regiment's objective. He toyed with probing the wire, but knew it would be useless and foolishly dangerous. At 0405 he began working his way back.

The attack began on the morning of the fourteenth, but the 165th got nowhere. Noboru, acting as a runner for Donovan and other staff officers, was all over the frontal area that faced the terrible wire emplacements. As he had reported following his reconnaissance, it would take tanks to smash through. And the tanks had managed to stay well mired in the rear. As he was leaving the left flank just as the last rays of the fickle sun flickered across the barren landscape, he caught a brief reflection from the ruins of a shelled-out farm building high on a ridge.

Since the ruins were in a salient where the enemy wire dipped back for a few hundred yards, he guessed immediately what the reflection meant—an enemy observation post. And probably a shellproof one at that, he quickly decided. He could report his estimate and have the ruins shelled, but other interesting possibilities ran through his head. If Jerry had a way out to the observation post, there was a way back into the defensive position. It would be worth a stealthy look under the cover of darkness.

He returned to the battalion command post, ate some hurried rations, and napped while the stalled attack sputtered out for the evening.

Except for periodic harassing fire, things were relatively quiet in the direction of the front lines when Noboru awakened shortly before eleven. After dousing himself fully alert with cold water, he deftly applied black grease to his face, then told the duty officer he was going forward. The captain nodded tiredly, not the least bit interested.

Thirty minutes later, he cleared the left flank outpost and slipped silently out into no-man's-land. There was little cover since the area had been devastated by every imaginable destruction tool during the past years. He crawled to the splintered silhouette of a stubborn tree trunk a few minutes later. He was about to lie back for a short break when he realized he had company. The stench of two corpses told him they had been there at least a day.

He shuddered and moved away quickly, stopping thirty yards farther up the hill in a shell crater. Again, he settled back to catch his breath and listen. The thin clouds broke briefly, permitting a full view of the corpse-littered slope. At least he thought those shapes were corpses—the grim remains of the regiment's earlier charge. They couldn't be Boche bodies; the enemy was safely ensconced in its trenches. He shook his head briskly. Dead was dead, *fini,* as the Frogs said.

He took a deep breath and crawled over the edge of the crater. Another forty yards brought him to a larger crater just as the moon burst out again. He dove into its concealment just in time. The building ruins loomed above him, what was left of the roof silhouetted above the ridge line. How starkly it stood out in the sudden glare—obviously once a prominent house. Two stories and surely a cellar for its wines, a cellar that would connect either by tunnel or trench to the inside of the enemy lines.

He slipped out of the crater as soon as the moonlight snapped off, crawling rapidly up to a rock outcrop. Slightly over a hundred yards separated him from the ruin; he guessed the Boche fortifications began about the same distance farther to the east.

He jumped, startled, as the bright explosion of a harassment shell flashed from behind the Second Battalion's lines. His breath was coming in shorter gasps, the pressure was mounting. It was so still. He seemed to be the only living creature on this part of the world. As the moon again lit the house, he decided he had to get inside. It was just too damned cold to sit still. He rubbed his hands together and began edging toward a smaller ruin—probably a shed or privy.

The smell of his new cover quickly removed the doubt. He crouched by its crumbled side, evaluating what was left of the house. It was only twenty yards away, dark and forbidding. Reality began to assail him—why was he out here in the first place? Playing hero, as Mario called it? What if that moon popped out again when he was halfway there—naked in its floodlight? *Was* the war almost over? What did he care if the place was shellproof—he could just report his sighting and let the artillery and mortars have a shot at it. He could still get back.

Yet, he was so close—

The German soldier cupped a match to his cigarette in what looked like an attached shed. *A sentry!*

Noboru held his breath as the German shook out the match, took a deep drag on the cigarette, and moved toward him. Again, the moon flared out of hiding, showing the sentry in bright detail. He was carrying a Mauser and moving quickly—as if he wanted to make his rounds and hurry back into the warm observation post.

Noboru reached for the long special knife at his waist. Mario called it his samurai sword, but it was just a stiletto. Exhaling quietly, he withdrew the blade and pulled as far back in the deep shadow as possible. The German was only five yards away and coming closer. At a distance of six feet, the sentry turned abruptly and passed the rubble.

Instantly, Noboru sprang at his back, grabbing his mouth and slashing the knife across his throat. In seconds, he had the enemy soldier inside the outhouse ruin. Sticking his soft cap inside his jacket, he donned the German's spiked helmet and broke into an easy lope to the main building. He stopped and held his breath in the shadow. Nothing.

He stood rigidly still, straining for a sign of light or noise that would tell him where to go. He held his breath. And finally, he heard the faint guttural sound of a German voice. Pushing a piece of shattered timber aside, he saw the dark steps to the cellar. Again he heard the German voice as he began to work his way down the stairwell. A faint light flickered against the wall at the bottom.

Nearing it, he tried to control his uneven breath and the tense excitement that gripped him. Ever so slowly, he edged his face around the corner to see what confronted him. And there, by the light of a large candle on a packing case, sat two Germans. He could feel warmth, guessing there was some kind of a stove.

Easing back into the dark stairs, he felt the hand grenade he had fastened to his jacket. It would kill them, but what good would that do? There would just be another team there in the morning. He heard a faint ring. Easing his face to the corner again, he saw one of them answer the field phone. He couldn't understand what was said, but saw one of the soldiers go to a sleeping form to the right. As the form threw off his blanket and snarled angrily into the handset, Noboru knew he had an officer.

The decision was instant. Noboru swung his rifle around the corner. The first shot hit the soldier to the right, the second smashed into the other's chest. The startled officer shouted as he dropped the phone and grabbed for his Luger. But Noboru's Springfield smashed into his knuckles before he could bring the pistol into play. "All right, Captain or Lieutenant, or whatever the hell you are!" Noboru snarled, picking up the Luger and jamming it into his belt. "Up the steps—*schnell!*"

He grabbed the officer's arm and spun him toward the stairs. At the top, he jammed the rifle into his cursing prisoner's back and pointed downhill. A second hard jab of the muzzle put the message across—they started briskly down the slope just as the cloud cover again opened to bathe them in moonlight. They hadn't covered a hundred yards when a rifle cracked from behind them and Noboru felt a searing pain in his right knee. More shots rang out sharply, but the bullets missed. He stumbled, almost falling into his prisoner. A startled backward glance revealed nothing—had he missed someone? It didn't matter.

He dropped the Springfield, bringing the Luger into the German's back. His knee was burning, beginning to hurt terribly. Again he stumbled, nearly falling on his face. The officer turned on him, but he rammed the Luger into his face. *"No!"* he cried. "Get down! Head between your knees! Hurry or I'll kill you!"

The German understood, giving him a final look of loathing before dropping to the ground. Noboru leaned down, feeling his bad knee. It was already getting sticky. He wouldn't last long if the blood was rushing out. He felt some wooziness. Another glance up the slope revealed nothing.

The pain was getting sharper. Not much time . . .

He rammed the Luger into the German's neck. "All right, Fritz," he said through clenched teeth. "I'm getting on your back and you're going straight down that hill until I tell you to stop. You *verstehen?"*

There was a slight ringing in his ears as he made it onto the prisoner's shoulders, but he disregarded it. Hanging on tightly and holding the pistol firmly, he kicked his good leg and gritted, *"Schnell!"*

Donovan was getting one hell of a prisoner.

Five days later, Noboru was evacuated from the Rainbow field hospital to Paris. The rifle bullet had just missed his kneecap, splintering the top of the tibia. The medical determination was that he would limp for some time, suffer minor pain on rainy days for the rest of his life, and soon become a civilian. His war was over; just as it would soon be over for everyone.

Three weeks after his arrival at the hospital at 4 Place Chevreuse, Father Duffy came to see him. "And how is my Nipponese Irishman doing?" the chaplain asked brightly as he approached Noboru's bed. "Are you ready to be baptized yet?"

Noboru grinned. "Wouldn't be practical, Father. A Methodist

missionary has his mark on me if I ever decide. And I may have to get married in a Shinto ceremony." He shook his head. "Too complicated."

Duffy nodded. "Right. Too involved for a simple Mick. When you going home, lad?"

"A few weeks, sir. I understand they're keeping the Rainbow over here for occupation duty."

"That's right. Probably won't get back to old New York 'til next spring. Is there anything I can do for you, lad?"

Noboru looked into the warm, concerned eyes. He wanted to ask the chaplain about mothers who ran off for a favored son, ran off in the middle of the night, and never in all the years took even a moment to write a short note. He wanted to know why, and if the wronged son should at long last reach out. And he wanted to finally tell someone about his sin of feeling jealous of a brother. . . .

But he couldn't.

He shook his head as he thanked the priest and told him to say hello to Mario.

In mid-January, Cedric Baldwin drove his battered old Ford up the lane to Sataro's elegant home. He noted that the trees were bare, but the white house was still impressive. He had only heard the day before about Sataro's heart attack and it made him angry—angry at the stubborn fool for not letting him know, and angrier at himself for not finding out. Since his Aunt Ellen's death the year before, that avenue of information was gone. He snorted—one of them should have made an effort to patch up the stupid damned quarrel at Christmastime. Then he'd have found out. Stubborn goddamn fool!

Miyuki met him at the door, still beautiful in her charm, still a touch of the tragic. She smiled warmly in her brief bow, taking his box of chocolates and saying, "I'm so glad you've come, Cedric. I know how he's missed you." She led him toward the garden where her husband sat under a light blanket. "He's outside enjoying the warm sun."

The heart attack had brought out a rash of gray hairs, but otherwise he was as handsome as ever and showed no effects from the ordeal. He was puffing a meerschaum as he intently studied a drawing. Several other drawings cluttered the rock floor by his recliner. He turned as Cedric greeted him, getting to his feet for a short bow and no handshake. "How are you?" he asked coolly.

"Mad as hell that you didn't let me know you were sick," the newspaperman replied abruptly.

"I thought you might try to tell me how to recover."

Cedric nodded, rubbing his chin. "Is that what you've been saving up to tell me? I mean, I know I was wrong, but—"

"Wrong as hell."

"I apologize. What are you studying?"

Sataro smiled. He had made his point and was terribly glad to see his friend again. And as long as he knew how wrong he had been, as long as he apologized. . . . "I'm trying to decide on a new *mon*," he said. "Something in keeping with an influential House of Hoshi—yet with the flavor of my idol, the great Fukuzawa."

Cedric had always been interested in heraldic crests, but knew nothing about the Japanese approach to them. Sataro handed him a sketch of three symbols meaning star. "This idea appeals, but I don't know whether to go with the lucky three or lucky five in number."

The publisher pulled the framed letter from behind his back. "Why don't you put aside that heavy decision while you figure out where to hang this," he replied with a pleased grin.

Sataro took the frame in surprise, then stared at the official communication.

Headquarters, 42nd Infantry Division
American Expeditionary Forces, Germany

23 December 1918

OFFICIAL PUBLIC INFORMATON RELEASE:
On 20 December 1918, Sergeant Noboru Hoshi of Lodi, California, was awarded the Silver Star Medal for gallantry in action during the Meuse-Argonne Offensive 14–15 October 1918. At that time Sergeant Hoshi single-

**handedly entered enemy territory and captured an
outpost. In spite of a crippling wound, Sergeant Hoshi
brought the officer in charge of the enemy outpost back
to friendly lines as his prisoner. Sergeant Hoshi's valor
was far beyond the line of duty and reflects great credit
upon himself and the United States Army. Hoshi is the
son of Mr. and Mrs. Sataro Hoshi of Lodi and Marysville, California.**

Sataro didn't even see the official signature at the bottom. His
eyes were filled and not only with pride. He pictured the charging Cossack officer back in Korea and fingered the thin scar on
his cheek. The circle was closing. He still didn't understand his
son's enlistment and wrong-thinking, but pride in his valor had
nothing to do with judgment. And how proud he was. "Thank
you, my friend," he murmured in a husky voice.

The beaming Cedric reached inside his coat, withdrawing the
newspaper. The *Gazette*'s headline ran, "Lodi Sergeant Cited for
Heroism in France!" A long and laudatory article about Noboru
followed. "You might want to reprint this in your own paper,"
he said quietly. He knew Sataro hadn't published an edition in
nearly a year.

Sataro looked up brightly. "Yes! And I'll send copies to
Japan!"

If anything could heal him, it was this.

Twenty-one

It was customary for an officer to give a short presentation following the noon meal at the officers' mess each training day. Although no rank was exempt, it was the commander's policy that the newest lieutenants would be heard frequently. Hiroshi agreed that it was excellent training for those who had trouble speaking in front of others. He'd been selected three times in the five months he had been with the Second Battalion and had enjoyed each experience. An officer who was about to become a lieutenant general's aide-de-camp had to be good.

It was Misao who had trouble. Although he was good at teaching his training subject—communications—he tended to freeze when he stood before the regimental officers. Each of his four previous stints had been embarrassing. Scheduled to speak today, he had spent most of the previous night rehearsing his short speech. Now, accompanying Hiroshi to the battalion's dining table, he frowned nervously. "I won't even be able to eat," he growled.

Hiroshi laughed as he looked at his watch. It was 1159; they ate promptly at 1200 and the meal lasted precisely ten minutes. "Just pretend you are addressing some privates. And don't even look at Segura, he's a terrible speaker himself." Of all the first lieutenants in the army, Misao had to get the hated Segura as his executive officer. And Segura was continuing with the miserable treatment he had inflicted in the *yonen gakko*, except it was now more subtle.

Hiroshi glanced around the familiar First Infantry Regiment's officers' mess and got the usual warm feeling. It was barely different from other mess rooms in the army—totally spartan and barnlike. There were rough plank floors without so much as one pad, and three long wooden tables with benches for the officers of each battalion took up most of the room. At the head of the tables was another low table for the regimental staff and battalion commanders.

The only decoration on the whitewashed walls was a huge framed parchment that charged those present to honor the most famous regiment in the army by giving not only their lives but their souls as well. It was written in an ideograph and signed by a former commander who had gone on to become a marshal. It hung directly behind the regimental table.

The barren mess symbolized so acutely the austere life officers had to sustain in their common approach to everyday training. With more and more officers coming from the lower social levels, and insidious communism already beginning to creep into the barracks, it was vital that a familial concept be cultivated within the basic army units. Even the noon meal that the officers had to attend was as simple as the enlisted men's fare—a bowl of rice, pickles, a cup of green tea, and either fried bean paste or some smoked fish.

At 1209 Hiroshi smiled at Misao. "Get ready for the chopping block," he joked.

Misao nodded, inhaling deeply as he tried to drink the balance of his tea. Hiroshi started to say something, but Segura—seated a couple of places away—broke in. "Don't waste your breath, Hiroshi Hoshi. Hosakawa will step on his tongue as usual."

Hiroshi didn't even trust himself to look at Segura. Fortunately, he had been spared the misery of being assigned to Segura's company. He looked up as the regimental adjutant announced, "Lieutenant Hosakawa from the Second Battalion will address us today."

Misao got quickly to his feet and hurried forward. Clearing his throat, he commenced, "Brother officers, today I'm going to speak about morale. I—" he cleared his throat again. "As you, uh, know, the army had no battles and no chance for glory in the past war. It was a naval war, except for the capture of Tsingtao. And even there, the navy got most of the credit."

Hiroshi smiled inwardly as Misao's voice cracked on "Tsing-tao."

Misao went on to briefly list the navy's accomplishments, including forcing von Spee into his ultimate defeat at the Battle of the Falklands. He then hurried into the theme of instilling destiny in the soldier. "We must treat him like a highly bred racehorse that exists for only one purpose—winning the race against our enemies, even if it means dying at the finish line with his last searing breath!

"Gentlemen," he charged with glowing eyes. "The Pacific lies at our feet, but our feet are controlled by the private soldiers of our proud regiments. Excel in everything they must do!"

Misao thrust out his jaw as he turned to bow to the regimental commander. The colonel nodded approvingly, saying loudly enough for all to hear, "A superb presentation, Hosakawa. All officers will take note of its content."

The Obata household was perhaps one of the least conventional in upper-class Tokyo. Its family structure was totally out of kilter. The head of the house was independent of his father and the young man he called son had not been adopted by him. Thus, the position of the new wife raised few eyebrows. Suiko made no pretense of assuming household management, and the beautiful Itoko suffered not an iota of the retiring mother-in-law charade. It was a friendly truce before the first battle cry sounded.

It had been the wise Koki's idea to provide the two-room apartment for the newlyweds, a rare luxury. And the seclusion provided them the opportunity for their ardent lovemaking, a nearly daily session when Hiroshi wasn't kept away by duty or the cycle of the moon didn't interfere.

Hiroshi quickly found that his bride's audacity—from their first meeting until the present—was no act. While it was customary for a young woman of breeding to be discreet about sex at least until her first child was born, Suiko loved it and enjoyed talking about it. At times she was as ribald as the most sensuous and wanton of village girls. But she always knew just when and how to slip back into the ultimate femininity that never failed to stimulate Hiroshi. Their love seemed to rock forward as if it had no bounds.

It had been said by a modern sage that a Japanese wife seldom had an affair because she had neither the time nor opportunity. Suiko Hoshi had plenty of both—and an affair that would never end. She was passionately, erotically in love with her country. And the embodiment of that love was the *aikoku fujinkai*, the Patriotic Women's Association.

Formed in 1901 by a group of socially prestigious women backed by a Satsuma field marshal and a scion of one of the most illustrious princely branches, the Patriotic Women's Association was established primarily to organize and render war relief to the military. Its activities in the Russian War had been so successfully conducted that it received high praise and a commendation from the army and both houses of the Diet.

The PWA, as Suiko affectionately called it, suited her taste as the perfect elite club for well-born and wealthy women to get actively involved in Nippon's march to power. Although it had done little in the recent World War, its ranks had swollen and it was highly visible. It was the perfect instrument for her.

"Mother," she told Itoko, "you'd be perfect for PWA."

But Itoko didn't want any part of it. She had carefully built a position that couldn't be threatened unless she reached too high. "I'll leave that to you young lionesses," she replied with finality. Kimi's letter had arrived only two days before informing her of Noboru's wound, and she wanted no part of anything that even touched on war. Her eyes were still red from the endless hours of grief, guilt, and thankfulness that he was alive. It was also the day she first wrote to Haru, Noboru's intended on Miyajima.

The *setchu kogun*—the infamous annual snow marches—were scheduled for the first week in February, when the weather was normally most severe in the mountains. Like the custom of allowing no special headgear for the hot marches of summer, it seemed the planners enjoyed inflicting the ravages of cold on their soldiers. A Japanese soldier did not wear gloves—even on guard duty or in the most intense low temperatures. And while the common soldier might be excused for complaining about the pain and discomfort, no officer ever considered such a losing of face.

Hiroshi and Misao had collaborated on a paper just prior to graduation from the Shikan Gakko. Its subject—"How Far Will 'Face' Carry the Private Soldier in Battle?" They delved far back into history and fable, calling on the famous story of the forty-seven *ronin* and citing many examples of modern heroism and extreme endurance from the Russian War.

Their not so revealing but personally satisfying findings were that "face" was the ultimate advantage the Japanese soldier had over his worldwide counterparts. While most armies were more polished and a few were as well trained, the one intangible edge of the Nipponese soldier was his ingrained rejection of losing face. And the army honed this edge to the point where he would die first.

Misao Hosakawa, in the frenzied fanaticism that marked his intense young life, should have reported to the medical station prior to the last day's twenty-five-mile full pack march. The cold he contracted upon arrival at the winter training site had blossomed to where his slight body was racked by hoarse coughing, flowing sinuses, and a temperature over a hundred. Hiroshi had purchased a special broth for his friend the night before, but Misao was unable to keep it down. When they arose at dawn, Hiroshi tried to talk him into reporting his problem, but Misao refused. "What would an army do if everyone with the sniffles took the day off?" he asked indignantly. Hiroshi gave up and went on to his own company.

The battalion reached the halfway point of the march at shortly after ten that morning, Misao's company making the turn five minutes later. As the column dropped for a short break, the lieutenant knew he was in trouble. Sweat drenched his uniform, creating tiny ridges of ice in places. Periodic chills swept over him and his legs felt as if they were carrying heavy lead weights. All the water in his canteen was gone, but he wouldn't ask for more. Nor would he eat snow, since it was against orders.

As the column pulled itself to its feet, he staggered, but consoled himself with, "Just twelve more miles." He fought the cough for the first mile, then found enough stamina to correct some of the men who were losing ground.

After three miles, Segura fell into step with him. "You don't look like an infantry officer, Hosakawa," he hissed. "Try to march like one."

Misao didn't respond. A sheet of scarlet fury flooded his eyes. If he had had a loaded pistol, he would have used it on his enemy. Segura taunted him again, then moved on. The weights on Misao's feet returned, heavier, like sandbags. His breath got shorter. He stopped even thinking about the men—just keep the feet, those chunks of ice, just keep them moving. . . .

The severe chills swept back over him, shaking him. He staggered, wondering if they had reached the eighteen-mile point. His eyes were slits that lied to him, creating abstract forms, distorted bodies, and elongated faces that expanded in front of him, then fell back in knowing grins. Horrible faces, rubbery as they tried to ask what was wrong. He heard laughter echoing away. Ethereal lights of wild, swimming colors exploded in his head, then snapped off to bleary whiteness.

The hard, icy ground had flown up to smash him in the face and a sergeant was helping him to his feet. He was mortified.

It gave him the final reserve of stamina to continue on. No officer fell out of a march, *never!* There was no excuse for such weakness, *never!* Pick them up and put them down—the heart-beat of the infantry. Up and down, even if you had to slide them . . . slide, keep moving, stamp them . . . left, right . . . left. . . .

The snow was deep where it rose to cover his face. He choked, spitting it away, feeling its coolness on his cheeks. It was his blanket, his warm blanket that reminded him of the chambermaid's milky back. He was home and she was undressing. The blanket was over him. He—what was the sergeant's rubbery face doing there? It was trying to make noises, but he didn't care. A bad dream.

"You should get a commendation for going as far as you did."

Misao was turned away from Hiroshi, staring out of focus at the small hospital's frosty window. His friend's words meant nothing. He had failed, committed the unforgiveable. The regiment had marched twenty-five miles. Lieutenant Misao Hosakawa had marched twenty-three. He was a disgrace to the army, to his family, and to himself.

"I'll go to the battalion commander myself," Hiroshi added. "He'll understand. No man as sick as you had any business—"

"Disgracing the officers of his company like that!" Segura snarled, stomping into the small room. "Our little baby Hosakawa has brought the shame of the regiment on our heads like I knew he would the first day I saw his miserable face at the *yonen gakko*. You rich babies are all bad for the army!"

Hiroshi felt his nails sink into his palms. He wanted to grab the detestable Segura and slam his ugly head into the wall until it was a bloody pulp. "You knew he was sick," he said evenly. "You should have ordered him to remain in camp."

"That'll be quite enough, Hoshi!" Segura snapped darkly. "Get out of this room immediately. That's an order! I must discuss the company's honor with this unworthy officer."

Hiroshi stared hard at the executive officer. He sensed immediately what he was talking about. "But his honor's unblemished. He's ill! I can't believe—"

Segura's face was red. "If you're not out of here in ten seconds, I'll prefer charges!" he thundered.

Turning to the unmoving Misao, Hiroshi touched his arm and softly said, "You are the most honorable person I've ever known in my life. Regardless of what he says, do nothing foolish. I'll return in the morning, my friend."

Misao didn't even blink.

As soon as Hiroshi departed, Segura rounded the bed and gripped Misao's arm. "You know the answer, Hosakawa," he said coldly. "There's only one way open."

Misao continued to stare. He had never known such terrible loathing for himself.

Shortly before 0200 the medical orderly came to Hiroshi's cold tent to summon him. Hiroshi questioned the man sharply, but he learned nothing; Misao had sworn him to secrecy. But he knew—oh, how he knew. His heart was leaden, his fingers like putty as he dressed, buttoning his ceremonial jacket. It was all a bad dream from which he'd awaken shortly, surely. Woodenly, he fastened his overcoat high against his chin and stepped out into the frigid air. Even the cold stars above seemed to turn away.

Misao was sitting on the side of his bed, his eyes bright and dazed in their dark hollows. The stark light of the single bulb hanging down on its wire exaggerated the pastiness of his skin. He was dressed in a plain white kimono. The kimono was open at the front, revealing his smooth bony chest.

Misao's voice rattled in his throat as he spoke stiffly, "Lieutenant Hoshi, I ask that you assist me in purging my soul—" he pulled his shoulders back as he came rigidly to attention—"by providing its release in the true warrior's ritual of *seppuku.*"

Hiroshi nodded grimly, knowing it was useless to try reason. Segura's poison had done its job. It mattered little, poison, karma—his impressionistic friend was going to perform *hara-kiri* and there was nothing to stop it. "Yes, my honorable friend, if you so insist," he replied in soft words that nevertheless seemed to echo around the small harsh room.

How often they had discussed this most noble rite over their years together, each swearing he would never waver should the occasion arise. But in most cases they had pictured themselves as heroic *ronin*—masterless roving samurai. Youthful romantics. But now, as if wiped away by the swipe of a sudden tornado, the romance was gone.

Misao turned, picking up his *wakizashi*—the nine-and-a-half-inch dagger with the blade of a razor. "Summon the doctor," he said tonelessly to the wide-eyed orderly. He wanted one more officer witness when he freed his tortured soul from its resting place in his belly.

Hiroshi removed his coat as Misao dropped abruptly to his knees, facing the wall and praying. He wanted to reach out and put his arm around his friend's shoulders, wanted to draw Misao's frail form into his arms and tell him it was over. But the Code held him rigid.

The orderly returned with the doctor, a solemn man of forty who made one comment, "I devote my life to keeping them alive and now I have to watch this. It's madness, but I understand." He backed against the wall, staring silently.

Suddenly Misao threw his head back and intoned, "I am unworthy of life." Raising the *wakizashi* slowly above his head, he got to his feet and turned to face the others. After bowing deeply to each of them, he dropped to seat himself customarily with his knees and toes on the floor and his body resting on his heels. Immediately, Hiroshi dropped beside him to the ritual left side.

Misao shook his kimono loose, allowing it to slip to his waist and bare his thin white torso. Carefully, he tucked the sleeves beneath his knees to brace himself against the shame of falling backward. He inhaled deeply, casting a final sidelong glance at Hiroshi. Their eyes met in painful understanding—Hiroshi would not let him fall backward.

Hiroshi knew those eyes, so wide and hurt, would haunt him forever.

Even with his torn and swollen throat, Misao's voice came through clearly, mystically. "Since I lacked the stamina and self-control to complete a simple road march, I am unworthy of being an officer to my Holy Emperor. I now atone by freeing my tortured but innocent soul and I beg those present to honor me by witnessing the act."

Lowering his shining eyes to the *wakizashi*, he reversed the blade and took the handle in both hands. Moving the tip to a point on his left side, just below the waist, he paused a moment, closing his eyes for a final prayer. Hiroshi watched, frozen, as Misao's eyes slowly opened and glazed over.

The blade plunged into his abdomen.

Even before the impatient blood had a chance to spurt out, Misao pulled the blade slowly across to the right side, where he turned it in the wound and made a short slice upward. Not a muscle in his frozen expression moved throughout.

Finally, eyes bulging and blood streaming over his legs, he grunted and forced his head forward with a shudder. As he jerked the blade free with his last conscious effort, Hiroshi caught him and held him in that position for a few moments before lowering him to the floor. Misao's eyes had remained open until the end—the final test of a warrior's strength.

Gently, Hiroshi closed the lids.

The sounds of the waiting locomotive were amplified in the cold air as its puffy cloud of white steam stood out sharply against the clear blue sky. Hiroshi drew himself erect as he stepped down into the soft fresh snow of Kamakura. The weather was keeping all but a trickle of visitors away, a matter of little importance to him. Eleven days had passed since the death of Misao, but this was the first opportunity he had had to come to the shrine.

The Shrine of Hachiman. "If you ever feel doubt about your profession," Tojo had said that day long ago. "Come back here and cleanse your spirit."

Moving along rapidly, he soon reached the curved stone bridge and crossed to the stairs and the monstrous old tree. At the top of the long flight of steps, he paused to look around. The blanket of winter that lay below seemed as unrelenting as the death that had brought him. With a frown he turned and entered the temple, where he wandered slowly among the artifacts, trying to place himself in the past, within the framework of their significance.

A war color from the Satsuma Rebellion had been added since his last visit. It was by this standard that he stopped and knelt. He removed his service cap and tucked it under his arm as he studied the faded orange banner that had fallen to Imperial troops in the last major conflict against the young Meiji. Forty-two years had passed since his grandfather gave his life in that battle. Perhaps he had even had a hand in taking this enemy trophy.

Could his answer be here?

Your very soul will be at stake, Koki had warned.

Suddenly prostrating himself, he tried to shake the numbness of his confusion to recall the core of what was troubling him. After a couple of false starts, the words began to tumble out. "May the gods who linger here, the spirits of war and heroes, join with the souls of my grandfathers in hearing my dishonorable plight," he said forcibly, not caring if he was overheard by a mortal.

But he was alone in the empty temple.

"I am deeply troubled by one of the most heroic acts in the code of the Bushi—that of *seppuku*. As you know, my friend recently performed this noble rite, rashly, in my opinion. Did he not waste his life before bring it to fruition? Were not his vast gifts scattered in his ashes for naught?"

Hiroshi's voice became more intense. "As his rich blood spilled onto my hands, I could only question the sanity of such a code in today's world. And the doubting, in itself, makes me unworthy. Should ties to the ancient Fighting Knights supercede reason?

"Listen to me, Honorable Ones, hear my naked cry. The loss of my comrade has broken my heart and torn my soul. Was his premature death a positive act? Can I continue as an army officer feeling as I do? Or should I give up the life of a warrior? I—"

He stopped, choking up, pressing his forehead into the flooring, trying to force an answer. But none was forthcoming. He inhaled deeply and held it, trying to sustain the intensity of feeling that had gripped him. But it was gone. He had stated his case and there was no reply. He opened his eyes.

The old enemy banner stared back at him as he looked up from the floor. The frayed edges of its bottom seemed to say something. But he knew, of course, they couldn't. What noble voices would waste their breath on him?

Still it came to him—at least a thread. Who was he to employ his personal grief in measuring Misao's act? Where in the overall composition of the jigsaw did Misao's piece fit into a logical place? How many soldiers throughout the army had heard of his dedication and found themselves lacking?

And there it was.

Without the will to die for only the breath of reason, the forces of Nippon would never reach their exalted goals. Faded standards such as the one before him could not languish in humiliation unless Japan's soldiers followed the iron example of their leaders. As long as the fervent young Misaos unsparingly gave their lives—as misbegotten as the decision might seem—the long line behind the Rising Sun would never stop marching into the face of any adversity. It was the key to a discipline that no Prussian punishments could ever equal. It was the key to power that would rule the Pacific!

Hiroshi pushed himself to his feet and replaced his hat. Pulling his shoulders back, he snapped to attention and saluted the Satsuma banner with misty eyes. Never again would he feel anything but the utmost pride in his friend's valiant death.

Twenty-two

Noboru straightened his uniform blouse as he stood by the windy doorway and watched the passing buildings as the train ground to a stop. He tugged his garrison cap down low over his forehead, checking his image in a window reflection. Inhaling deeply, he thought about how many times he had lived this exciting moment in the last year and a half. Regardless of how hideous the nightmare of the trenches became, this picture of stepping off the train in Lodi always carried him through. It was his survival dream.

And now it was eighteen inches away.

Moments later, he dropped his duffel bag to the platform and looked around into the setting sun. The early March evening was warm and hazy, telling him it was glad to have him home. Or so he thought.

It was done. He had served all but a few months of his three-year hitch, terminating it early only because of his medical discharge. His limp wasn't too pronounced and his leg was getting stronger every day. He felt blessed that his wound was that simple—the cemeteries of France were filled with white crosses and the World War's great new weapons had provided many horrible wounds. The row of bright ribbons on his chest included the red, white, and blue Silver Star and the rainbow-colored Victory Medal.

He had served his country well, gotten an education no number of years at Berkeley could have given him, and he felt a deep sense of accomplishment. He was a proud American who had earned his spurs, as the cowboys said. Now, all he had to do was get the citizenship paperwork started. But that could wait.

First he wanted to savor the full flavor of coming home.
Walking down a familiar street, having a curious dog run up and
bark, seeing the stares of people who were thinking, "Oh, look
who's back from the war"; drinking in familiar sights and building the elation of soon seeing loved ones—these were the joys of
a soldier's return. It was something no one else could experience,
a rich proud feeling of having performed a very special duty—
one so full of marvelous and terrible experiences and people that
its events could never be fully recaptured.

Ambling down Main Street, smiling at wide-eyed little boys,
was part of it. Seeing the town end its daylight hours was
another. Inhaling the smells. There was a sign reading "The Lodi
Gazette" painted on a bench. He would see Cedric soon. There
was a new automobile agency, a new drugstore, another saloon.
He'd visit the school soon, walk around the baseball diamond,
and relive enjoyable moments.

Japan Town looked the same, except for the new boardinghouse that had been erected where the old Hiroshima-ya had
stood. This one was painted bright yellow and its sign proclaimed
it the Fujiya. Nothing else had changed. Even a freight train sat
quietly across the street—as if it had arranged to meet him.

Most of his memories were here on this single street.

Seeing his father and Miyuki in Marysville was something
special he was saving. Lodi was his home and always would be.
He shifted the duffel bag to his other shoulder as he approached
the barbershop. Tomoko's last letter had caught up with him
from Paris just before he left the hospital in New Jersey. She'd
be surprised.

He stopped to look through the front window, but the shop was
closed. Moving quickly down the narrow alley to the backyard,
he knocked on the door and waited. Just as he was about to
knock again, the door opened. Tomoko's eyebrows shot up as
she cried out, "*Noboru!*" and flew into his arms, crushing her
body up to his, babbling unintelligible words through her wet
kisses.

At last he held her back to drink in her sensuous beauty. "I
love you." He grinned. "Okay, I called Yego at the store in
Homerville and he'll be here shortly with the truck. You tell your

parents anything for an excuse, but we are going to bed in a nice room at the store, and not getting up until dawn.''

Tomoko smiled as she sucked in a deep breath. "You make it sound so easy."

He shrugged. "It is easy. I spent a year working it out in France. Move, girl.''

Tomoko's face clouded up. "No, you can't wait here. Go on out with Yego and I'll ride my bicycle out later.''

He looked at her closely. "Is something wrong?"

"I'll see you in a couple of hours," she replied, kissing his lips and hurrying back into the building.

Noboru awakened at shortly after three to see her sitting by the bed, watching him in the candlelight. Only a thin chemise covered her lovely full breasts; nothing covered the serious look on her face. She lit a cigarette and handed it to him as he sat up. As he smoked, she slid to the floor and leaned her head wistfully against his knees. She kissed his hand, whispering, "I must tell you something, my darling—something that tears at my heart.''

He braced himself, guessing.

"Four months ago a man came to my father with an attractive marriage proposal . . . that—" She kissed his hand again. "Oh, my darling, how I've rehearsed this, but I can't get it right. I, my father accepted. I told him I'd refuse, run away and wait for you, but he spoke to your father.'' She choked back a sob. "It isn't any use, my darling. You are promised in Japan and I'm not getting any younger. I agreed.''

Noboru sat rigidly. Separation and time had dimmed some of his fascination with her, but why couldn't she have waited a while longer? He felt angry, cheated. She was his woman! "Who is he?" he asked tightly.

"You don't know him. He came to Stockton a year ago and opened a restaurant," she replied tearfully. "He's a good man.''

"How old is he?"

"Only thirty-five.''

"Have you been with him?"

Her eyes were wide as she gripped his hand and looked into his grim expression. "Yes,'' she whispered. "But I don't love him." Choking back another sob, she stammered, "I—I love only you, my darling."

"When's the wedding?"

"In two weeks."

His tone was bitter. "Congratulations."

"No!" she cried, flying into the bed and embracing him. "No! Not like this! Make love to me again, darling. Be fierce and powerful and sweet and tender . . . hold me!"

He couldn't—the shock and anger were too powerful on him.

She sat back on her heels and wiped her eyes with the chemise. Slowly, she lifted it over her head. "All right," she said firmly. "*Don't* be sweet and tender. Take me and treat me like the unfaithful slut you think I am!" She ran her hands down over her breasts and abdomen to her pelvis. "Because that's what I'm going to be." The impudence of the barbershop was back on her face as she tossed her head and taunted him. "I'll be your lover forever, marriage or *not!*"

"This is quite a car, Father."

Sataro smiled proudly as his son parked the large red Duesenberg in front of the house. "Would you like to have it?"

Noboru chuckled as he turned to his distinguished-looking father. "Not a chance. I couldn't afford the gas."

"All right—what kind do you want?"

His son shrugged. "If you insist, how about a Ford roadster? Something light and sporty for an ex-sergeant."

"We'll go to Sacramento tomorrow." Sataro beamed. "Now, while we're on solutions, when do you start back to college?"

Noboru ran his fingers around the large steering wheel. "I don't know, Father. I—I want to go down to Lodi and stay in one of the rooms at the store for a while. You know, maybe sort out what I want to do while my leg mends."

Sataro frowned. "Education is vital," he said firmly, wanting to add that it was imperative to the dream he was still fostering. Now that his strength was back, he was ready to force his will on this errant son who would enlist without permission, and talk of never going home.

"Maybe later. I need some time, that's all." He hoped his father wouldn't bring up the citizenship problem.

Sataro struck a match to his pipe. "The girl is getting married. Do you know that?"

Noboru nodded, staring through the windshield. "I know."

"When will you feel like discussing your Japan marriage?"

Why did he have to bring up all these things at once? He sighed. "I don't want to discuss it yet, Father. I've been in a distant war. Things are different."

Sataro withdrew an envelope from the inside of his coat. "Look inside," he said quietly, handing it over.

It contained a sepia photograph of a beautiful young Japanese woman. "Haru?" Noboru asked.

"Yes, it was taken recently on her eighteenth birthday. Read the inscription from the *baishakunin,* your uncle."

The neat brushstrokes read, "Return safely from the war. Your charming bride awaits faithfully." Noboru nodded ruefully. "She's a beautiful girl." But she was a stranger.

Sataro knew what he was up against. He watched him silently for several moments before saying, "The honor of the House of Hoshi is at stake, my son."

Noboru sighed again. "But Father, it is the old way. This is 1919 in America."

"It doesn't matter," Sataro replied sternly.

Noboru continued to regard the photo. It could be heavily retouched, but the smooth line of her chin had to be real. And the wide, perfect shape of her eyes—that couldn't be false, even with makeup. "I haven't any way of making a living yet. And I don't want to get involved in rice at this point. I just have to get well first." That was his legitimate excuse.

Sataro nodded coolly. "I'll notify the *baishakunin* that you are convalescing."

"How is Hiroshi faring?" Noboru asked, relieved to change the subject, even though his brother's welfare was of little interest. He had written a stiff congratulatory note from France at the time of Hiroshi's commissioning and marriage. Nothing since. And he'd just as soon leave it at that.

Sataro got out, beginning a long account that pleased him so much to relate in detail. "Your brother is the finest young officer in the Imperial Army. . . ."

Noboru drank too much in the next two weeks. He felt guilty about disappointing his father and cared little about the future. Although Tomoko sneaked out to be with him twice before her wedding, their hungry lovemaking only provided temporary relief for his depression. Even the canary yellow Model-T coupe failed to excite him. On the day of her marriage, he drove to San Francisco and spent the night in the Gorotsuki's only remaining brothel. Following a diffident visit to the campus at Berkeley the next day, he drove on back to the Valley. He would have reenlisted if he were sound, but if he were a horse someone would shoot him. He couldn't please his father, his love had been taken away—what was he to do? He didn't want to be another of those veterans with one arm around the bottle. He needed something to occupy his time with no sense of urgency—a place where he could fish without watching the bobber, he thought.

Three days after he returned, he helped Yoshi Togasaki repair his roof. Yoshi, now heavier and deeply lined, plagued him with questions about combat in France. "We're blood brothers." He chortled, slapping his game leg. "Only difference is what armies and where—right?"

That afternoon, Noboru decided. He would ask his rich father for The Other Cheek. The vineyards were maturing well and producing adequate income for a small family with simple tastes. Yoshi would continue to look after the vines and teach him what he needed to know about grapes. But most importantly, he would spend the summer building the house. Yoshi would also help him with the construction. He was finally excited—all decisions would be in limbo while he mended both his leg and his head!

He drove up to Marysville that night.

"I think it's precisely the thing for you to do," Sataro replied with enthusiasm. "The farm is paid for and under legal ownership that precedes the Alien Land Act. It'll be part of my wedding gift to you. After an appraisal is made, based on current market value, I'll make a cash settlement to equal the sum I gave Hiroshi.'' He snorted. ''I'll set it up in a trust fund to make that damned Cedric happy. He thinks I'm becoming an irresponsible gambler.''

Noboru looked up from where he was sitting in front of the fireplace. ''I need only enough money for the materials to build the house. You know, I already have a barn there.''

Sataro nodded. How well he knew. He waved his hand, dismissing further argument. ''It'll be taken care of tomorrow. But you must promise me one thing, my son. You must never sell The Other Cheek.''

Noboru nodded fervently, relieved that it had nothing to do with his promised bride. ''Done. The Other Cheek will belong to the House of Hoshi forever.''

Sataro poured them each another portion of scotch. Now, if only the world rice market would stabilize. . . .

Noboru worked steadily on the one-story, three-bedroom house throughout the summer. Studying some books on Japanese residential architecture, he employed various subtle effects from the old country. The huge main bathroom, however, was strictly American. And so was the spacious kitchen. Miyuki—who drove Sataro down once a week—designed the formal Japanese garden and reveled in the work. Two groups of three locust trees were planted on each side of the drive for luck. It was going to be a charming place.

About twice a month, Tomoko came to Lodi by train from Stockton to spend the afternoon. Her bicycle was still available for a ride in the country, and a picture bride she had cultivated as a friend during the war lived on a farm just a mile from The Other Cheek. The lovers could always use an available bedroom there, or Noboru's solid red barn, where he had placed a firm used mattress.

For Tomoko, their lovemaking had taken on a new dimension since her marriage—the spice of danger. It made her even more erotic in their stolen moments, stirring Noboru to delight in her carnal extravagance and ignore the risk. A woman who had picked him out from all the men in the Valley when he was still a schoolboy had to be rightfully his. He lived for her visits.

Kimi Togasaki's role of intermediary between Itoko and those she had rejected was made all the more intriguing by her friendship with the gentle Miyuki and her position as an unofficial big sister to Noboru. Kimi knew about his renewed affair with Tomoko almost before it began. And although she enjoyed the spice involved and the minor role she played in keeping tabs on it, she soon had to tell Miyuki. Miyuki, in turn, was dismayed not only in compassion and worry for her stepson, but out of concern for what a scandal might do to Sataro. Yet, she said nothing.

As far as the Sons of the Golden West were concerned, the truce was over. V. S. McClatchy, Sean Flattery, and the other leaders of the anti-Japanese movement had kept their antagonism submerged during the war, but now Senator James D. Phelan was bringing white supremacy back to the fore. And McClatchy wanted to revive the Oriental Exclusion League. Phelan's ax was simply a campaign tool for his reelection as a Democrat during a Republican boom period.

At a meeting in late September in San Francisco, it was decided that the hearings by the Congressional Committee on Immigration and Naturalization should be brought to California the following summer. At such time, Senator Phelan would be given high visibility. The second major decision resulting from the meeting was the go-ahead on a revised Alien Land Act—a new approach that would plug the loopholes in the 1913 law. While the ashes of war in Europe were being kicked around by fumbling statesmen, the tiny coals that could lead to another major conflagration were being fanned by the bigotry of little minds that would never comprehend their contribution.

On January 15 it was clear to Sataro that he had made a terrible mistake in not listening to the warning signals. Seated at his desk in the big house at Marysville, he stared at Noboru, barely seeing him. His fingers had been flying over the abacus for over an hour and the result didn't change. He had lost a small fortune.

The world rice market had simply plummeted in the past month. The decline had been gradual but steady since the end of the war, but the last days of the year had been devastating. Since the price fallout had occurred shortly after the harvest, Sataro had been faced with storing vast quantities of the grain or simply selling at a loss. Not wishing to risk deterioration or paying for elevator space, he sold as much as he could and braced for a recovery.

His expression was grim as he announced the facts. "My son, it comes to a loss on the crop of over thirty thousand dollars. My associated investments in the stock market add up to another forty-one thousand." His voice trailed off to almost a whisper. "That's about fifty times as much money as I had when we came to this country."

Noboru had been working part-time with his father since early fall when he had finished the house at Homerville. The rest of his time was devoted to the vineyards and learning everything he could about the marketing of fruit and produce in the Valley. He had a plan for his own wealth and independence. But it would have to wait in the face of his father's disastrous situation. "What are you going to do?" he asked quietly.

"The only thing I can do," Sataro replied firmly. "Be strong. Rice fields that belong to the timid will go unattended this year. Even the big combines will pull back. As a result, the market value will climb again."

"But can you afford it?"

Sataro nodded. "I spoke to my banker this morning."

"What do you have to mortgage?"

"Everything—the house, the ranch, equipment."

"But isn't that too much of a risk?"

Sataro scowled. "I've accomplished almost everything I came to this country for, my son. I'm a respected *oyakata*, newspaperman, and leader of the community. I'm also one of the richest Japan men in America—at least I was. And I will be a year from now. Is it too much to risk? Absolutely not!"

Five months later, as the McClatchy-Phelan machinery moved into full swing in San Francisco, an official letter arrived for

Noboru. Seeing the Immigration and Naturalization Office's return address, he slit the envelope open excitedly. The response to his application for citizenship had taken over a year.

Taking a deep breath, he unfolded the single sheet of paper. His hand trembled slightly as he peered at the long awaited words. There should be a seal. . . . He blinked unbelieving as the words took form and shouted out to him from the page. Typewritten, harsh black letters formed words that screamed:

> Application denied. Applicant is ineligible for citizenship in that he is not a free white person, an alien of African descent, nor a person of African descent.

Noboru blinked as the words swam. There was no way to soften the curt denial—the United States of America had made him a promise and was backing out!

He hurried to Lodi and into Cedric's office, waving the letter.

Cedric began cursing as soon as he read it. "The sons of bitches!" he roared as he reread it. "I don't believe it!"

"But Congress passed a *law!*" Noboru cried out in anguish. "Any person of foreign birth who served in the military or naval forces of the United States is eligible. That's the way it reads. What the hell am I, Cedric?"

The publisher was furious. He tipped the standby bourbon bottle back, spilling whiskey down his chin. "You're *Japanese*, my friend," he snarled. "And those bastards just aren't going to let you be anything else."

Noboru reached for the bottle, shaking his head in confusion. "But I met the requirement. I did everything. How can a law be disregarded like this?"

Cedric picked up a pencil. "I just don't know. I'm going to write the most scathing editorial to ever come off my press. Then I'm gonna send the thing to every son of a bitch I know—every goddamn editor from here to Maine, and every goddamn politician in Washington! Now, I suggest you get that stupid letter up to your old man and see what he can do."

Noboru shook his head. "I hate to get him all upset."

Cedric snorted. "Hell, he's stronger than both of us. Get that old samurai into the act."

Sataro had never accepted the fact that Noboru really wanted to become an American citizen, not even when he came back from the army and insisted. He even expected that his son would sell The Other Cheek when it was finally time for all of them to make the triumphant return to Japan. He still fantasized about it, still saw that vivid picture of his dream. And what was citizenship anyway? But this was a different matter—a Hoshi, his firstborn son, was being discriminated against on a matter of honor. And that took priority over anything! He went to see Abiko in San Francisco.

The old newspaperman was distressed but pragmatic. "I knew when Congress passed that law, it didn't realize Japanese men would serve. And while it didn't matter nationwide, California had to block the door."

"What do we do about it?" Sataro asked.

"Sue." Abiko scribbled a name on a piece of paper. "Herbert Lockett is in Stockton. He's interested in our cause and would be ideal for this."

Sataro and Noboru met with Lockett two days later. A prematurely bald man with a blond walrus mustache, the lawyer looked nothing like the zealot Abiko had described. At thirty-five he was short and fat, sloppy with a shirttail that often hung out, and a heavy smoker who could never keep his cigar lit. He had defended several cases in which Japanese had breached the Alien Land Act, and was a sworn foe of the Establishment.

His eyes gleamed as he listened to the Hoshi story, glancing from time to time at the government letter. Finally he shook his head and snarled, "Even I can't believe it. It makes me want to jump on the next train and go straight to the goddamn White House! Why, it's the worst example of double standard hypocrisy I've ever heard of."

"Then you think we have grounds for suit?" Noboru asked politely.

"Grounds!" the lawyer thundered, pounding his desk. "You've

got a *continent!* Let me look into this—there must be others like you, Noboru. Let me check it all out to see if we have a class action here. If not, we'll go alone. I—''

"We have the money," Sataro interrupted in a quiet tone.

"Good. It may take some time and patience. Suing the government can be the most trying experience in the entire field of law. Of course, they make it exasperating on purpose." Lockett pursed his lips as he read the letter one more time, then stuck his hand out to Noboru. "You have faith in me, Sergeant, and by God I'll see you sworn in as a citizen of the United States if it's the last thing I ever do."

A month later, Sataro summoned Noboru to his study at Marysville. Turning from the window with a frown, he went to his desk and handed over a letter from his old friend on Miyajima. "Haru's father grows impatient, my son," he said coolly. "And I don't blame him. She's twenty years old now."

Noboru said nothing as he fixed his gaze on the envelope.

"And I, too, have been patient," Sataro went on. "But it's time to stop stalling. Your rehabilitation is long over. You barely limp, you have a home for her, and any more procrastination is an insult." He struck a match to his pipe, then picked up another envelope. "And aside from satisfying yourself periodically with that cheap barber's daughter, you have nothing standing in your way. It's time for you to honor the commitment."

Noboru blinked back, angry at the referral to Tomoko. "How do you know what I do with her?" he asked sharply.

Sataro tossed the letter at him. "*Everyone* knows. That's from your mother, wanting to know why you persist with such an affair while your intended rots on the limb."

Noboru stared at Itoko's letter, stunned. It was what he had so wanted all these years, just a letter, just a few words of love, an acknowledgment. How many times had he dreamed of such a letter? And now it had finally come—but not to him, not to the son who missed her so much. No, it came to his father, and it condemned him for his indiscretions. So she thought. She didn't understand, either. How could she—she didn't *care!* He could feel his face burning. Tearing his eyes away from the envelope, he looked defiantly into his father's stern expression. "I love her," he insisted.

Sataro leaned forward over the desk. His eyes glittered. "No," he said evenly. "What you call love is nothing but the excitement of possessing a wanton woman who belongs to someone else. She's nothing, a—"

"I love her!" He had never in his life wanted to strike his father, but he felt his fists balling up. "You have no idea! What do you know—"

"I order you to fulfill your obligation!"

There it was, stopping him cold, the law of the family. He felt suddenly drained, totally incapable of struggling further. The words, the tone—his father had been forced to invoke the law. The alternatives—a son's respect, his love, his desire to please . . . all had been swept aside. It mattered not what he wanted to be, nor where he wanted to live, he was still a Japanese son.

Twenty-three

"A man wishes to see you!" Zenro shouted from the top of the stairs.

"Okay," Noboru replied from his room. He closed the notebook and put it in the top drawer of his small desk. The way he had it worked out, his plan for marketing fruit could hardly miss. He was anxious to get started, but two things stood in his way—helping his father get the huge rice crop in, and the marriage. The harvest was only two weeks away, but the inconvenience of getting married would hold him back until spring. He hated to even think about Miyajima, but he had bowed to his father's will and he would somehow make the best of it. The event was set for late January. Nothing had changed with Tomoko, nor would it. That was out of his father's reach. And no damned island girl was going to change it either. Tomoko had laughed when he told her. "Ha!" she had snorted. "It's *time* you got a housekeeper."

He walked down the hallway, wondering who was looking for him. The store in Homerville had turned into quite a catchall, now serving his sleeping needs when he wasn't in Marysville. The new house was still empty, being gradually readied for its new mistress by Miyuki and Kimi. Entering the storefront he looked up to see the back of a familiar bulky figure—a bullet-head growing out of massive shoulders as if there wasn't a neck. "Mario!" he shouted with pleasure as he darted around the end of the counter. "What in the world are you—"

"Told you I'd move here someday." Mario Scagnelli beamed as he whirled and wrapped his arms around Noboru in a bear hug. "Got any vino around this joint?"

Noboru couldn't believe his friend had actually come. A hundred boasts and promises from a soldier in war are quickly forgotten. "Sit down while I get it," he replied eagerly. They both tried to talk at once as he served white wine from a dusty bottle. Mario was married and had his wife waiting at the Lodi Hotel. Noboru quickly insisted that they stay in the store until they found a house to rent. He raised his glass. "Congratulations, old friend. Now what are you going to do here—open a restaurant, be a gangster, or train Irishmen?"

The Chicagoan laughed. "Maybe a little of everything. I mean, who knows, right? But first, the boys want me to look into the fruit business." He sat on a stool and explained how the mob back in Cicero was certain the shipping and sale of fruit could be an excellent long-range program. "Prohibition will be the biggest moneymaker ever invented, but it won't last forever. Fruit will." He had been given a year and adequate funds to settle in.

Noboru couldn't believe it! What Mario was talking about could be exactly the piece that was missing from his fruit marketing plan. But that kind of talk could wait. Mario's arrival was the most stimulating occasion since his return.

The two ex-soldiers drove up to Marysville the next day so Mario could meet Sataro. On the way back that evening, Noboru launched into his plan. "Not only is the rice business shaky," he explained. "I want my own independent business. Someday my father will go back to Japan for good, and I want nothing that would hold me to the old ways.

"What I have in mind is a combination of services where I become part buyer, part labor contractor, and part speculator. By assembling a pool of laborers, I'd be able to provide year-round services geared to the local fruit crops."

Mario listened closely as he went on. "For instance, let's take the grape crop. If the Tokay is harvested about September first, I contract for certain crops early in June. By contracting, I mean many growers don't want to take a chance on getting hurt by the many problems that can arise in the summer months. You know— bad weather, insects, and so on. I'll speculate what the market price will be at harvest time and try to get the whole farm for the right price. What I'm doing is taking all the risk out of it for the grower.

"There are several seasons for other fruits. Apricots and cherries in May, plums in June, then pears and other season grapes in different locations in and near the Valley. My crews will also pick other crops and prune in the winter."

Mario was nodding his head vigorously. "Sounds interesting. And who do *you* do business with?"

Noboru grinned. "The shipper, of course. The company or guy that buys and ships the produce. The guy with the Eastern contacts. *You*, my gangster friend!"

"Uh-huh! And how does this guy get all of your production?"

"Simple. You act as my bank. Whenever I need any kind of financing—when I miscalculate and get burned on a crop, the money is there to keep me going. I'll always have labor camps full of people to feed."

Mario's eyes narrowed as he stared out through the windshield. There were already over two dozen shippers in Lodi. "How much of a corner could you get on the market?" he asked, trying to curb his enthusiasm.

Noboru shrugged. "I'm not sure, but a substantial amount after a few years. I think it would be a matter of building a reputation for performance and integrity." He nodded his head. "Yeah, a big corner, maybe."

Mario slammed his palms together. "God*damn*, that's it! Stop at the next joint you find so I can buy us a bottle of sake. God*damn*!"

The rain started four days later, on November 3.

By the time it continued for another six days, Sataro was alarmed. It was almost harvest time and too much rain was bad for the crop. His foreman accompanied him around the various leases and subleases in the monotonous gray drizzle. When the tour was finished, they knew it would be close.

Four days later, with an additional five inches of rain having fallen, Sataro returned to the big house with a grim expression. It was early in the afternoon and Miyuki had the sake warmed. She had been braced for the bad news all day, and she could tell by his crestfallen look as he slumped into his favorite chair in the parlor. Staring vacantly at the floor, he told her. "The entire crop will be lost, even if it stops now." His voice was flat as he continued, "I'll lose everything—the house, the ranch, all our savings . . . everything. I—" His voice trailed off.

Miyuki went to him, cradling his head against her breast, wanting to lift him and rock him like the baby she had never had. Her strong handsome warrior had been dealt some terribly unfair blows and was deeply stricken. A chill swept through her as she felt him shudder. *No!* she screamed to herself, *not another attack!*

But it was only a reaction from the revulsion he felt as he berated himself. He wouldn't listen, knew it all. Could have pulled out with a fortune that far exceeded his Hiroshima dreams, even come out rich after dropping that seventy thousand, but no—he had to go back to Japan with at least a half million to brag about. That was the truth, wasn't it-just a matter of playing the big wheel. And greed.

He tasted the bile.

And punishment—retribution for his crime of tearing the family apart in the first place, his transgression of even coming to America. Had he not been so greedy— The stillborn baby Ellen had been one repayment, this was but another.

He felt Miyuki's warm tear slip down his cheek, felt the concern in her warm embrace. How she was paying for his crimes! Had he thought of her feelings even once in this dizzying ride? And now, from being the envy of Japan women throughout the Valley, she'd go to what—a stoop labor storekeeper or something more demeaning?

As if she read his thoughts, Miyuki said softly, "I think I'll enjoy living in Homerville again. The apartment in the store is comfortable, Kimi is right there, and I can stay busy." She kissed his cheek. "Oh, and we'll have a beautiful new daughter-in-law nearby. Won't that be wonderful?" Already she could feel the babies, hear them cry and laugh. Noboru would give her the babies, the grandchildren that would be hers.

The wedding! Sataro had forgotten all about it. He'd miss Noboru's wedding too! And there was positively no way he could go back now. The disgrace of losing so much money was far worse than never having made it. He would neither go back as a lie, nor would he lose face. No, sir! Sataro Hoshi would remain in America, afflicted by his illness, until his riches were recovered. That was it. . . .

He closed his eyes as Miyuki pulled away to get his sake. The sound of rain continued in his ears and he thought he would never again in his entire life hear anything so terribly destructive.

Seventeen nights later, Sataro dragged himself from the Sacramento hotel where he had been holed up for two days of whiskey and self-incrimination and climbed behind the wheel of the muddy Duesenberg. It took him exactly two hours and five minutes to drive to the center of Japan Town in Lodi, but he hardly noticed. Since three days earlier, when the staggering extent of his losses became fact, he had barely noticed anything. All he knew was that Sataro Hoshi, the great and glorious head of the House of Hoshi, was now a great and glorious loser. The stalwart entrepreneur from Hiroshima was broke.

The *hakujin* had a name for him—high-roller—he reminded himself as he slumped behind the wheel and stared at the line of cheap wooden buildings which had been so enticing to him the day he first set eyes on Japan Town. In the faint light of the dying moon, they looked like strangers—not the old friends that were supposed to comfort him and tell him it was all a bad dream . . . or that his plan was intact, that someday his riches would return, that someday it would be all right.

But the dark shapes were as cold as he was in the early winter frost. They didn't care a fig that his heart was broken, that he couldn't go back to the wedding, see his family and friends, and mostly see the handsome son who alone was performing his part of the dream.

He wished he had brought what was left of the whiskey.

His hand pushed the heavy door open and he found himself standing alone in the middle of the cold dark street. Not even a dog barked anywhere. It was as if he had dropped in from another planet and everything was frozen into stillness. He pushed himself around the big car and stared at what looked like the

Hiroshima-ya, but wasn't. And he saw fire begin to lick at the building, and he saw himself standing just outside in a gathering crowd and feeling more defeated than ever before in his life. He could hear the buzz of the crowd, see the tears in Miyuki's terrified eyes as Noboru waited for him to say something. . . .

What was it? Why was that terrible scene haunting him?

He moved forward a few steps, then turned and looked at the loading docks. And he began to understand—not completely, but an inkling. His feet began to pull him to the steps and, finally, up on the platform. And he turned and looked out at the street as the ghostly faces began to materialize. Miyuki and Noboru, yes, and Cedric—all were watching him with bright eager eyes, waiting for the magic words that would make it right.

And slowly, Sataro gripped the silver disk that was in his pocket. He felt the scar on his cheek, then pulled out the disk and raised it to the stars. His voice stuck in his throat, but he could feel the strength begin to return. *"Gambari,"* he whispered hoarsely. He tried it again and it was louder. He inhaled deeply. It would be all right, whatever was to follow would be all right.

Yes, and the faces were smiling, sharing it. The whole town was there below him, raising their fists.

"Gambari!" he shouted.

The excuse Tomoko gave her husband for spending the night in Lodi had something to do with New Year and her girl friend. It didn't matter—he had grown used to letting his young wife have her way. But it mattered greatly to her; she just couldn't let Noboru go off to Japan for another woman without spending a full night with him. Now, at shortly after midnight as she lay sleeping at The Other Cheek, Noboru sipped beer and paced through the house.

Soon, another woman's smell and touch would invade this structure he had put so much of his soul into. A woman who meant nothing to him, a stranger intruding in his life. From her photograph, the young Haru looked quite beautiful, but wonders could be accomplished in the studio of an enterprising photographer. What if she turned out to be a dull fish, a cold lover? What if she

were a shrew? He could still remember some of the terrible
things his mother had done.

His mother . . . finally. He pushed her away.

He downed his beer and opened another. There were so many
things that could be wrong with Haru. After all, his uncle couldn't
do much more than count her heads, could he? How could he
know if she had icewater in her veins?

He dropped into the deep sofa in the parlor.

It wouldn't matter—that part of the marriage would be strictly
Japanese. He would definitely exercise his customary preroga-
tives of drinking out and spending time with other women if he
so desired. Damn right. And just because America didn't have
geisha didn't mean he couldn't find places. He'd damn sure—

"There you are!" Tomoko darted into the parlor and dropped
down naked beside him. Running a finger over the hard muscles
of his shoulder, she sighed deeply. Light from the dining room
touched her soft skin, her smell was on him. She took the bottle
of beer and kissed his fingers. "I don't believe you're really
going," she whispered.

She was seldom soft like this, vulnerable. He shrugged, not
wanting a going away problem. "I didn't believe you were
getting married either. We'll all live through it."

She stiffened, pained by his indifference.

"I don't intend to see you for a while," he said evenly.

Tomoko threw her head on his chest. "Don't talk like that,"
she cried out. "I don't even know how I'll live during those
weeks you'll be away. I want you more than ever! As soon as
you get back, we'll—"

Noboru pushed her away and got abruptly to his feet. "You
don't seem to understand," he snapped, feeling stifled. "When I
return from Japan, my whole life will change. I have a father to
worry about, the reputation of our House to protect. A wife is
nothing. You'll be nothing."

Tomoko knew it would come down to this the last time. She
sat up erectly, recovering her invincible aplomb and inhaling to
draw up her remarkable breasts. Her dark eyes glittered as a
knowing smile settled on her dimly lit features. "Those things
are merely minor details in the eternity that is our love, my

darling." She caught his hand and pulled herself up to him. "We'll *never* stop being lovers." Reaching for his lips, she whispered, "Now, take me to bed again."

At the same time, miles away at Marysville, Sataro ambled around the mansion. Although the huge house held many pleasant memories, it had never actually been warm to him. He had to admit, it was more of a monument than a home. He snorted at the irony—when pride reached too high, the fall was often longer. In the kitchen, he poured a stiff drink from the last bottle of whiskey, then walked to his combination study and office. It too seemed to mock him. There were books he knew he had never read, an expensive phonograph that played music he didn't like, and a rich rug that his bare feet had never touched. All of it would soon be enjoyed by someone else.

He sat at the desk where he had written so many editorials for the *Shimpo Shimbun* and where he had handled the paperwork that built a small rice empire. Even the low flame of the kerosene lamp seemed to laugh at him. Everyone knew a house of that importance should have electricity—even if it was out in the country.

He was lucky a buyer had been found so quickly—saving foreclosure. The whole mess was worse than he thought. Except for the goods on the shelves of the store in Homerville, and the furniture there, he had nothing except a little over two hundred dollars he had managed to hang onto. And he owed more than that in legal fees. The Duesenberg, his proud banner of success, would soon be a memory, replaced by the old Ford truck at the store.

He was so glad he had been able to give the money to each of his sons when he had it. Hiroshi, of course, knew nothing of his plight, and he had refused return of the money from Noboru—just as he had refused the offer to live at The Other Cheek.

Now he had to adjust to the lot of a country storekeeper. He had his paper, his health back. Something would come along, surely. Japan could wait for the time being, yes, wait until something big came along. . . .

He finished the whiskey and turned off the lamp.

Twenty-four

Itoko nervously touched the back of her oiled chignon as she hastily searched the rail of the *Chokutso-Maru*. She gripped Koki's arm as she thought she saw him, but it was someone else. She'd be able to recognize him in a moment. Tomi had sent her a picture of him when he was in uniform during the war, and she had spent hundreds of hours staring at his handsome, hawklike features.

She wished her hands would quit trembling. She had slept poorly for a week, and hardly at all the night before. It had been twelve years since she ran away in the middle of the night, and twelve long years of paying for it. How many letters had never been mailed? And how long since she had even quit trying to write? And never once had she talked about it, bared her tortured conscience with even Koki. Prayer—how she had prayed when he was in France. But that only produced more guilt when she realized she wanted his survival so he could forgive her. But hadn't she paid? Hadn't she gone to the Yakusuni Shrine when she heard he was safe—gone for thirty straight days to prostrate herself before its altar in thanks?

Where *was* he? Could he have changed his mind, gone directly to Hiroshima? He couldn't. She had to have him alone, tell him. . . .

Koki had finally sent the telegram over her name, inviting him to Tokyo before the ceremony to that gentle, unworldly Haru. The island girl was one of the few things Sataro had ever done right—she had to admit that honestly.

Suiko broke the strain. "What do I do with this handsome elder son?" She laughed. "Bow my head demurely like a good

Japanese lady, or play Parisienne sister-in-law and kiss him warmly?''

There were times when Itoko really wanted to gag her flippant daughter-in-law and this was one of them. Couldn't she see how the strain was affecting Hiroshi? The poor boy hadn't seen his brother in so long, and missed him so much. . . .

"I'm sure he'll know you're not French," Hiroshi replied dryly enough for his wife to give him a quick sharp look. She remembered what a lack of enthusiasm he had shown over his brother's coming arrival, but she hadn't mentioned it. They had few secrets—as far as she knew—and his attitude puzzled her.

Itoko again patted her hairdo, certain that something must be out of place. With barely a line in her face, she couldn't *wait* to show Noboru what a beautiful mother he still had. She was only sorry his father hadn't come along—how many times had she relived the scene of parading her well-turned figure in front of him, of flashing her youthful smile at him. Now she'd be old and wrinkled before he ever came back—and he'd *never* be sorry!

Where *was* that boy?

Noboru stood alone in the stateroom he had shared with three others. It was bright and sunny outside the porthole—ideal for a crown prince's majestic return, he told himself harshly. He tipped back the pint bottle and finished off the whiskey. The bitterness was there, along with the anger he was nurturing. Waiting on the dock would be the mother he had tried so hard to push out of his heart, and the little brother who was everyone's shining knight. They were waiting to clasp him to their breasts and tell him how great it was to see him.

He was the first out of the womb, the anointed one to whom they would eventually owe fealty should he ever assume his rightful role as head of the house. And the anointed one had come home to take a bride—a princess selected ages earlier by his father, the king. An island princess, unwanted but consigned.

He threw the bottle into a wastebasket, smashing it to pieces. He should be thrilled about returning to his roots, his homeland. Yes, his homeland—there certainly was no goddamn American citizenship to confuse the issue! He stepped through the doorway;

it was time to begin the charade. He wished he could stay angry throughout. But the slight tremor in his hand told him otherwise.

As the gangway was lowered to the dock, Itoko froze. There, back from those at the rail, a head rose above the others. A head with a handsome, hawklike face. She couldn't describe the powerful sensation that seemed to burst through her body. She waved her parasol and cried out his name, but no sound came out of her throat as his vision swam in her brimming eyes.

Noboru saw the cluster of people that included a tall young army officer and knew it was them. His palms were suddenly moist and his breath jerky. He wished he had another drink. The women were beautiful, particularly the familiar one . . . the woman who looked exactly as he remembered her. He felt a sharp tug, a tightening in his throat. She was waving, reaching out to him, calling out his name. He pressed forward toward the gangplank, suddenly knowing, knowing that nothing in the past mattered . . . that he was returning to his mother.

That night belonged to Noboru. Suiko and Koki plied him with question after question about California and hung enthusiastically on his replies. But Itoko was in love—madly, vibrantly in love with her older son. She hardly took her eyes from him during the entire three-hour dinner at the long table. And what eyes they were—bright, animated, warm, and possessive. She smiled almost constantly, exuding happiness, seemingly breathless at times. And Hiroshi missed none of it, remaining quiet and playing the role of indifferent observer. But as much as he tried to overcome the feeling, the jealousy that had plagued him for years simmered just below the surface.

And when Noboru launched into detailed anecdotes about the war in France, Hiroshi caught himself feeling pure contempt. How could a common enlisted man in an army considered by most professionals as essentially incompetent know so much? Obviously his brother was a practiced liar. It was all he could do to keep from jumping to his feet and setting the record straight. But Hiroshi Hoshi did not win such high standings in everything he did by venting his emotions. He wore his mask well and kept his own counsel, even when he and Suiko retired for the night.

Since Noboru had never been in Tokyo, Itoko recommended that Hiroshi be his guide the next day. They left the house early, driving to the bustling Ginza for a start. Later, the tour included various shrines and the Shikan Gakko at Ichigaya Heights, ending with Hiroshi showing a pass that got them inside the Imperial Palace grounds. Hiroshi was cool and polite, not making a single effort to break down the growing barrier between them. It was his turf and he was already thoroughly tired of his brother's superior airs.

And Noboru was just as indifferent. He thought Hiroshi was even worse than he had expected—a thoroughly snobbish member of the officer class, a conceited ass who would most probably raise his sword and spout Bushido as a tank company was overrunning his infantrymen.

They drove by the inner palace, the palace shrine, and the concubines' pavilion before going on to the Imperial Guards Division compound and stopping at the army club for a sake. The last stop was the Yasukuni Shrine, where Hiroshi dropped his pique and provided a thorough orientation as they wandered through the huge grounds. Reaching the wide altar, Noboru, too, dropped all antagonism to fall to his knees and honor his dead grandfathers. It was the closest they came to bridging the widening chasm between them.

Noboru had liked Koki the moment he met him. The white-haired man of fifty looked absolutely nothing like Noboru's tall father, but somehow he felt the same strength in the man. And he was so learned—and willing to discuss world affairs. Now, as he and Hiroshi sat with the professor over their after-dinner brandy in his library, Noboru listened attentively.

"Since the Emperor's latest health problem—a stroke the public isn't aware of—Crown Prince Hirohito has gradually taken over most of his functions. Within the year, Hirohito will become regent. It's only fair for the country."

"Didn't I read about a problem with his betrothal?" Noboru asked.

Hiroshi snorted. "Rumor has it that every powerful prince in the nation has a daughter for him."

Koki nodded. "But the prince has a positive mind of his own. And his trip to Europe this summer will only broaden his feel for the outside world. If he partakes freely of Britain and France, he'll be more worldly than any of his ancestors. The spirited Edward, alone, will see to that."

After a few more minutes of gossip, Noboru asked, "What is the feeling toward America, sir? I've heard there is heavy animosity."

Koki thoughtfully lit his pipe. Blowing out a promising cloud of blue smoke, he began, "If you are talking about the civilian leaders, they are more incensed with America's immigration policy, her meddling and imperialism in the Pacific, and more specifically—the alleged role of America in stopping Japan's effort to include a racial equality clause in the covenant of the League of Nations.

"If you're talking about military leaders, there are two camps— those who recognize the amazing production effort the United States put forth in the World War—and the major camp that warns Nippon to 'take off her helmet.' This is the faction that espouses the spirit of Bushi and contends that only masterful spirit is necessary to overcome America." Koki nodded toward Hiroshi. "Ask your brother. This attitude is fertilized at every level."

Hiroshi tried not to frown. There were times when his stepfather was prone to tread on hallowed ground. He sidestepped. "A retired general by the name of Sato has written a book called *If Japan and America Fight*. In it, he insists that courage and cowardice are the decisive factors. If several thousand heroic Japanese warriors were thrown in against San Francisco, their faith would be the winning edge . . . and many of our leaders believe him."

Noboru shook his head in disbelief. He had heard this kind of talk before, but never paid any attention. "Is it really that serious?" he asked.

Koki shrugged. "Sato also recommends more military training in public schools, added physical training, and what he calls military spirit education. He sees war with America as inevitable."

Noboru was watching the masked expression on his brother's

face. "And what of you, honorable brother," he asked coolly, "where do you stand in all this? Are you ready to assault the United States?"

Hiroshi looked him calmly in the eye. "No," he replied evenly. "But if the order came, I would obey it in a moment. I'm a soldier—remember?"

The silence was awkward as Noboru held his steady gaze. Finally, he asked, "And what if I were there protecting her shore and your father? What then?"

Before the dangerous discussion could go further, Koki broke in. "I think two champions is the answer. Build a huge stadium halfway between the two countries and let each send its team of all-star baseball players to settle the problem." He laughed. "What do you think of *that* idea?"

Noboru smiled first. "I think I'll have some more of your brandy, sir. I have to think about marrying this strange islander." He shook his head. "Uncle Seizo says she has only one head—I wonder if he counted her arms?"

Hirobumi Kaibara *had* paid the photographer to touch up his daughter's picture. He knew it was an improper thing to do, but he was afraid Sataro's son had become too Americanized to honor the arrangement. And if Haru's photo wasn't extremely appealing, it might be the stone that tipped the cart.

Haru meant spring, and her pleasant sunniness was as fresh and bright as that inviting season. She was a quiet, happy young woman who seemed to commune with Miyajima's abundant nature as if she were one of its wild animals. She had a lovely voice, even though it was quite low for one of her size, and sang often when she was alone. And she was often alone, for she was the Kaibaras' only child.

Her father's fears about her appearance were quite unfounded, since Haru's only abnormality—if it could be called that—was her slenderness. Several inches taller than average, she weighed only about eighty-five pounds. Her face was a bit long, with high cheekbones that protruded slightly more than in the classical sense. But they merely exaggerated her long, soft brown eyes and full lips.

Haru Kaibara had come close to losing her virginity once when she was sixteen and very much infatuated with a young Buddhist priest who came to the island for the summer. A handsome man in his mid-twenties, it was easy for him to meet her on her normal forays into the nearby hills. Glib of tongue, this predator of the cloth tried to convince her that her Americanized fiancé would never come. But each time his kisses and caresses aroused her considerable passion, she was able to tear herself away and fight off the inevitable. Now, four years later, she was more than ever thankful she had. And she was highly excited that her marriage was finally going to become a fact.

The handsome but grim soldier in the photo the *baishakunin* had given her could be any kind of a person, she knew. Her father told her stories about the Hoshi family and repeated everything Sataro told him, and she had even had a most pleasant letter from his stepmother, a woman who called herself Miyuki in a strangely familiar way. The letter explained that they would not live in the same house together, and that she hoped they would become good friends.

Now, sitting high up in her secluded hilltop hideaway, she looked down at the sights that had so long been a part of her life. Closest was the town, followed by the cove that housed the famous expanse of the Itsukushima Shrine. And sitting among the sparkling greens of the incoming tide was the equally famous O-torii—the stately vermilion-lacquered archway that stood guard toward the usually placid Seto Inland Sea. She felt the primeval forest so close around her and towering Mount Misen behind her. Could there possibly be such a place of beauty and peace in America?

The first rays of early morning sun began to sift through the heavy stand of trees. Heaving a deep sigh, the bride-to-be started down the slope toward town. The long wait was over.

There had been much discussion about the location of the wedding ceremony site. Itoko had insisted that her sumptuous home in Tokyo be used, but Seizo had argued strongly that the House of Hoshi was from Hiroshima and that was where the wedding had to occur. A telegram from Sataro settled the matter—it would take place at a shrine to be chosen by the family of the bride on the island.

Haru's mother had opted for the two-storied Taho-to pagoda. Built in 1523 by the Buddhist monk, Shukan, the structure featured a square roof built over a round upper level in a rare combination of Japanese, Chinese, and Indian architectural styles. But Haru and her father agreed instead on the main shrine of Tenjinsha because parties for composing *Renga*, or linked verses, had been held in the shrine for ages. Also known as the Rengado, the ancient shrine was dedicated to Michizane Sugawara—a great scholar worshiped as the Deity of Learning. Since Kaibara was a leading shopkeeper in the town, reserving the shrine was no problem. The ceremony, attended by a Shinto priest, would take place at the warmest time of the day—2:00 P.M. Immediately following, the wedding party would proceed by rented launch to Hiroshima. Friends and other relatives could follow in the ferry.

Noboru agreed to everything; all he wanted was to get the damned ceremony over so he could get on back to America. At his one meeting with Haru at his Uncle Seizo's house, he had been both disappointed and angry. Instead of the appealing beauty her photo showed, she had a horse face! Long and bony, just like her skinny body. He even thought of backing out on grounds of misrepresentation but knew it wouldn't sell. He was doomed to spend the rest of his life with a scarecrow, and that was it.

Life was becoming one long series of lies to him.

His uncle and Koki had taken Hiroshi and him out on the geisha house circuit the night before, and they had all gotten staggering drunk. Now, as they sped back to Hiroshima in the big motor launch, the blur continued for Noboru. At precisely two that afternoon, the lovely *miko* had led them into the shrine—he, dressed in unfamiliar rented Japanese formal attire of a black silk kimono and striped *hakama;* she in a striking wedding ensemble that brought little cries of appreciation even from Itoko and Suiko, the sophisticated Tokyoites. About all he remembered was the white silk of her *uchikake*—the long overdress—and its magnificent gold embroidery of peacocks and the royal carriage. Yes, and he recalled the hilt of her *kaito* sticking out where the *uchikake* closed at her breast. He'd have to ask about the symbolism of a bride wearing a dagger in her wedding attire.

He glanced sideways in the launch, wondering how long she would carry it.

The rest of the ceremony swam by him—the families seated on their respective sides, for some reason his mother the only one he saw with tears; his reading the oath, the Shinto ritual, the altar; the *tamagushi* branches for good fortune, the little stands in front of them. And finally, the three cups three.

He brought himself back to reality as Seizo shouted something to him, then handed him a glass of champagne from the center of the bouncing launch.

For Haru, the ceremony was just the opposite. She had rehearsed in her mind every step and detail of the rite for months. And when it was finally real, it was as vivid as the cinema in slow motion. Two years' work had gone into the *uchikake;* every strand of her high, inverted maidenhair hairdo was shining perfection, and the tiny silver symbols of long life and happiness which she wore like a queen's tiara had been imported from Bangkok. Hers was perhaps the most important wedding on the island in a long time. Wasn't she marrying into the powerful and wealthy House of Hoshi from Hiroshima, Tokyo, and America?

She smiled her thanks to her new Uncle Seizo and sipped the bubbly foreign wine as salt mist sprayed over the launch. Glancing up at her handsome husband's profile, she saw a strange grimness. Was something troubling him? What could possibly be wrong? No, surely she was mistaken—they were going to be so happy! Affection in public—even on a wedding day—wasn't acceptable, but she reached out gently to touch his hand.

He pulled it back quickly, as if he had been shocked. His sharp look was at first startled, then coolly pleasant. "Forgive me," he said stiffly as he brought his hand back to pat hers.

Stating that Seizo's house was too small for the privacy newlyweds required, Koki had added a night in the Momiji Hotel to their many gifts. And he was right—Noboru had to work out his problem.

Everything about the gentle Haru—and he had to admit she

was more than gentle—indicated she was a virgin. And he knew nothing about how to initiate a virgin. Since she was certainly going to be a bony, probably cold specimen anyway, why should he care?

It was himself he was worried about. What if he couldn't perform with this skeleton, this horse-faced skeleton? Facing his problem in the quiet hotel suite, he realized he was still sober, and drank deeply from the flask he had brought. As the fiery whiskey warmed him, he thought about a saying he'd heard in France about skinny women. "The closer to the bone, the sweeter the meat." But he didn't believe it.

He was on his second big swig from the flask when Haru came out of the bathroom in her silk robe and negligee. She was well armed with advice from her mother—of the grin-and-bear-it approach—but she had also read from illicit books the joys she might encounter. Her encounter with the priest had shown her how excited she could become, and already her handsome husband was creating stirrings in her. But she hoped only that she could please him.

Noboru had stripped to the waist, but he still sat on the side of the bed and watched her strangely as she went to the other side and dropped down beside him. "Are you comfortable here?" she asked softly to break the silence.

He shrugged. "Good as any, I guess."

She wanted to reach over and stroke his smooth cheek, his strong jaw, his firm lips she so longed to kiss. She wanted to tell him so many things—how they weren't really strangers, how much she wanted to give him in their life ahead. She wanted to tell him how much her body cried out for him. . . . But she couldn't be forward. Everything had to happen in its due course, she knew that much. She heard him sigh. Could it be that he was bashful, perhaps as uninitiated as herself? No, that would be impossible with such a handsome soldier. . . .

A chill struck her! Had he perhaps been wounded so that he couldn't—

Remembering the old adage, "When a woman wants a man's love, dress for him—not before him," she sat up and turned off the lamp on the nightstand, then slipped out of the robe and back down on the bed.

Suddenly Noboru's anger gripped him. He was a samurai warrior of twenty-four! And here he tarried beside a ripe young virgin whose duty it was to please him. She was but a body in the dark—and he could even imagine she was the erotic and beautiful Tomoko. Yes, that was it! His hand stole over to her side. He was surprised—instead of running into a sharp hip bone, he found a sleek warm thigh. Her fingers touched his arm, softly, inquisitively. He heard a tiny moan as he turned to her. Her smell was of jasmine or something similar. She moved to him, her lips open, barely breathing, wanting him so much. . . .

He found her mouth, warm and delicious, as his excitement mounted.

And most of the anger left him.

Itoko's grand reception for the newlyweds was held the last night of their stay in Tokyo. All of the Obata clan, including the old baron, came, as did General Goto and the rest of Suiko's relatives. Again, Itoko outdid herself with superb food and entertainment. As the last guest departed at shortly after eleven, Itoko drew Noboru into the garden for a private talk. They walked quietly for a few moments before she abruptly asked, "What's wrong with your father, my son?"

He didn't waver from the story he had told ever since getting off the boat. "As I said, Mother, he suffered a relapse just before the New Year."

"I don't believe it," Itoko said firmly. "Sataro Hoshi would have come to this wedding in a wheelchair. He'd have come flat on his back. No, something else is wrong." They walked a few steps. "Is it money, Noboru? Did the relapse have anything to do with the crash of the world rice markets Koki told me about?" She stopped and gripped his arm. "Is that it?"

"He's perfectly all right financially, Mother," Noboru lied evenly.

This was what she needed, Itoko told herself smugly, a way to end it once and for all. "Will twenty thousand yen help?" she asked quietly.

A grin crossed her son's strong face as he took her hand. "That would be like sending a small box of bees to the land of milk and honey." He chuckled. "But thank you anyway. Father said to tell you he'd send about the same amount if there was any problem on this end." One more white lie wouldn't hurt.

Itoko sighed. She'd still like to pay it off in one fell swoop, wipe the slate clean with that stubborn man. At least she had tried. "Are you sure you won't move back to Japan someday?" she asked as she linked her arm in his and headed back toward the house. "There will be great opportunities in the years to come."

Noboru shrugged. "I doubt it, Mother. But we never know, do we?"

Just before reaching the door she stopped and threw her arms around him. A sharp little cry slipped out as she buried her face in his chest. "Oh, my darling, I'm so sorry. I did such a terrible thing to you and—" She sobbed as his finger sealed her lips and he held her tightly. Finally, she pulled away, dabbed her eyes briskly and drew her shoulders back proudly. No matter what, she would always be the stately matriarch of the new House of Hoshi.

Twenty-five

Noboru had completely forgotten the dagger Haru had included in her wedding ensemble. He asked her about it a month after they moved into The Other Cheek. "Oh." She chuckled. "It was just part of the costume. It signifies a bride's dedication to becoming an acceptable and successful wife. There is no returning to her father's house—if she fails, the knife is her destiny."

It was difficult for Haru to laugh at the custom's significance. Although she was being accepted with open arms by the House of Hoshi and its friends, there was still an invisible barrier between her and Noboru. There was nothing she could pin down—he was pleasant, passionate in bed, and undemanding around the house. A model husband from what she had heard. Still, it seemed there was an undefinable coolness, an aloofness that two people who had been married for this long shouldn't have. He was *polite* to her, she decided unhappily.

Was that how marriages developed?

Kimi had immediately become her close friend, creating a next-door bridge between her two mothers-in-law. Now built like a powerful boulder, the ebullient farm woman laughed as she served tea in her kitchen. "So no one plays the lute each time you're together. That happens only in books of romance, I assure you. I don't think my Yoshi *ever* told me he loves me. The closest a Japanese man comes to that is a wild grunt when he finishes making love. The poets lie."

Haru had also been immediately clutched to the breast of Miyuki. Although only thirteen years older, Miyuki sensed at once that this bright, gentle flower from Miyajima would be the closest thing to a child she could have until the grandchildren came. And what a wonderful sharing that would be! In the meantime, she considered herself a shield for her vulnerable daughter-in-law.

When the afternoon English lesson was over, she listened patiently as Haru tried to find the words to express her insecurity. Her heart went out to the young woman, but there was little she could say. Her relationship with Sataro had been so abnormal, so tempestuous and adulterous, so passionate and romantic that a simple scheduled marriage and its problems of adjustment seemed ordinary. But she knew Noboru hadn't gotten Tomoko out of his system.

She patted Haru's long slender hand. "Give it time, my dear. What's it been—a few weeks? He's busy getting his new business going and has many things on his mind."

Noboru did have much on his mind. He had a small crew of six men pruning vineyards on a large spread halfway between Lodi and Galt. It was a losing start; in order to get it, he had had to underbid his cost. The way he had it figured, if the men worked full speed he would lose two dollars a day. But he had to get his foot in somehow. And he had to get a start with the laborers. He could last just so long as the son of Sataro Hoshi, the great newspaper and rice entrepreneur. And it wouldn't be long before he'd have to bid his first speculations on fruit crops.

But that wasn't what was bothering him.

Mario Scagnelli had rented a nice yellow house on Eden Street, just off South Stockton, and the Italian had really been exerting himself learning the buyers' and shippers' roles in the complex Valley fruit and vegetable business. His connections back in Chicago still hadn't committed on a full financial tie-in with Noboru, so that security was still hanging in thin air. And he hated to use any more than absolutely necessary out of his operating capital that Sataro had given him before the rice market crash.

Still, that wasn't what was disconcerting him. Living a lie was eating away at him, and sneaking around for assignations with Tomoko was a major part of it.

He sat up on the bed and inhaled deeply from a cigarette as he reached for the bourbon bottle he had brought along. Being in this damned farmer's bedroom while the man's wife discreetly went shopping at the Hoshi store wasn't the most comfortable or unexposed of arrangements. But it was the only haven for them— short of going to San Francisco or Sacramento. They couldn't be seen together in Stockton's Japan Town. Lodi was absolutely out. It was all one gigantic problem.

How he had anticipated this reunion. Almost ten weeks away from her was more than he could bear, he had thought. But parking his conspicuous Ford behind the barn had been the first act of this surreptitious arrangement that made him uncomfortable. Oh, he had thrown caution to the winds as he ran into the house and into Tomoko's waiting arms, but now it troubled him. He tipped the bottle back again.

"Don't you get drunk on me, my beauty!" Tomoko warned as she ran back into the bedroom and took the bottle from him. Her eyes sparkled under her tousled hair as she stroked the small patch of dark hair at her pelvis. "We have another hour and I intend to enjoy every minute of it in beautiful, tender, wild, marvelous lovemaking with you!"

He laughed as he shook his head. She was so wanton, so earthy, so round and soft. Not skinny—no, he didn't want to think about it. His wife had no place in this strange bedroom, she was alien. *This* was love, *this* was passion. All the rest had to be blotted out when his captivating, stimulating Tomoko was with him. Her educated fingers were already stroking the inside of his thigh as she dropped to the bed and began to squirm toward him with glittering eyes.

"God!" she cried out. "I want you even more now!"

He ground out the cigarette as she straddled him.

That night he began playing in the poker game in back of the tavern in Japan Town. He would frequent the game for the next six weeks, playing until after midnight and making no explanations to Haru about his absences. In that time, he met Tomoko five times and made love to Haru just four times. He knew he was drinking too much and felt as if he was on the same out-of-control slide he had been on when he first got out of the army.

"Everyone knows why she comes up here. It's that Noboru Hoshi!"

Haru glanced up from where she was looking at some material for a dress when she heard the familiar Japanese accents. Two women she didn't know were speaking with gossipy animation behind a dressing screen where one of them was trying on a robe.

"I hear that yellow car of his is a rolling hotel room," one of them snorted. "Do you think he's got something special?"

The other woman laughed. "She thinks so!"

Miyuki was startled by the terrible look on Haru's face when she walked up a moment later. "Are you all right?" she asked with concern.

Haru raised an index finger to her lips for silence.

"I understand she's been nothing but a brazen jade ever since she came here," the other woman remarked acidly. "I told my husband to stay away from that barbershop long before she ever got married."

The other woman shook her head. "Some of these days, that husband of hers is going to wake up. Then young Hoshi'll be more careful!"

Miyuki moved swiftly around the screen. "Good afternoon, ladies," she said coolly, looking each directly in the eye. "Did I hear my name mentioned?"

The women threw startled glances at each other. They hadn't expected to have their Japanese understood, let alone by the *oyakata*'s wife! "Uh, no, Mrs. Hoshi," one of them stammered. "We were talking about your stepson's new business."

Miyuki nodded, eyeing each of them again, then bowed and bade them good day as she turned to the ashen Haru. "They are idle gossips, my dear," she said softly, taking her arm. "Come, let's go where we can talk."

Moments later they climbed into the battered pickup truck. Haru stared ahead as Miyuki hit the starter with her foot. The engine cranked and sputtered, then died, but Haru didn't even notice. Her cheeks were burning, her breath was jerky, nausea threatened her. She knew he couldn't have come to her without experience, even infatuations—but *this!* A woman, a married woman. How could he—"Who are they talking about?" she asked Miyuki in a tiny voice she didn't trust.

Miyuki gave up on the engine and turned to her young protégé. It was better to get it out and air it than leave the poor girl hurt and thoroughly confused. The girl was just too bright and sensitive for anything else. She laid it out as gently, yet directly, as possible, ending with, "He's basically a wonderful young man, my dear. I'm afraid you'll just have to wait and be patient. He's too upright to continue like this."

Haru continued to stare blankly through the windshield, tears slipping down her cheeks. That was why he was so cool with her—*he loved someone else*—always would. How could she be patient, how could she wait . . . if it might be—"How long?" she asked. "How much time will it take?"

Miyuki wanted to take her in her arms and hold her tightly. Her child, her baby. How she loved this innocent from Miyajima. She tried to sound confident as she replied, "As long as it takes. Or as long as your love holds out." She had told Haru about her harrowing beginning in America. "I had to suffer the unhappiness of being a mistress, you know," she added softly.

Haru shook her head. "That was different. You knew he loved you."

Miyuki gripped her arm tightly. "It wasn't that simple. Now listen to me. Like most Japan women, you have little alternative. What you do—how well you handle this—will determine the course and happiness of the rest of your young life. Please, my dear, try to find the patience to, to—" She threw her arms around Haru and hugged her tightly. "Oh, darling, I can't tell you what to do!"

The next day Sataro parked the truck in front of the station at four o'clock. He had just returned from Walnut Grove, where he had done some politicking and promoting his newspaper. Although he was already saving a little money from the store operation, he had to get more income from another source. He had to be ready when any new opportunity arose—the break, the big break that would get him back on the road to his dream.

His explanation to the curious ones who showed concern about his return to the Lodi area was succinct: "My friend, the crest of a wave is slippery."

For the present, making the *Shimpo Shimbun* back into the proud publication it had once been was his biggest challenge. Not only was the Japanese population in the Valley continuing to grow, it was now more stable with growing numbers of families. And they needed a paper like his, one that knew their roots and dreams, that could touch their pulse. It was *good* to be back!

He saw the train was on time, impatiently pausing for its 4:08 departure. But he didn't see Cedric or Lockett—the lawyer who was handling Noboru's citizenship suit—anywhere. Just as he was about to get back in the truck, the newspaperman jumped out of a taxicab, suitcase in hand. "Couldn't get my damned car started!" he panted as he ran up on the platform. "You see that goddamn shyster anywhere?"

"Here!" the stocky Lockett shouted from a door of the train.

Cedric waved, then turned back to Sataro as the train's whistle shrieked. Sticking out his hand, he said, "Take care of the old rag, my friend. I'll be in touch from Washington."

Sataro nodded as the newspaperman turned and hurried into the car. Next to buying the *Gazette* many years earlier, this trip to the capital and wherever else it might take him was the biggest venture of Cedric Baldwin's life. He was about to cast his irascible charm on the waters of "bigotry and governmental irresponsibility," as he called it, to write a daring exposé of the Japanese American problem. And Herbert Lockett was going to run interference for him, in the hope that it might build interest in the case.

Sataro waved as the train began to move. Over his protests, Cedric had insisted he run the *Gazette* for the time he would be gone.

Cedric accomplished about as little as he expected in Washington— key members of congressional committees were difficult to reach and gave him only lip service when he did get to them. Orientals owning land was a trivial matter, just as immigration and naturalization policies were subject to constant change. Still, he gathered enough material to write four discerning articles. Three weeks from the day he departed, he was back in San Francisco where he interviewed Abiko, the abrasive Sean Flattery, and managed to get an appointment with V. S. McClatchy. The publisher, now divorced from his newspapers, had gone to Japan for a visit in 1919 and was now concentrating his energies against the California Japanese in a businesslike manner.

McClatchy, Cedric found when he interviewed him in his plush San Francisco apartment, was urbane, shrewd, and everything he had expected. "You see, Mr. Baldwin," he began patiently over cups of tea. "One must look at the overall impact of a foreign group that is difficult to assimilate. The Japanese are so productive, so intelligent, and quick to improve on existing methods—particularly in certain areas of agriculture—that one must look at the overall effect of a massive influx as eventually disastrous. You must admit, sir, that the Chinese experiment had its drawbacks. Admittedly, the Chinaman was industrious to a fault and just as honest. Fortunately, he lacked ambition—one of the most formidable of the Japanese traits."

As McClatchy continued with his superbly developed line of reasoning, Cedric found himself being lulled into a degree of agreement. His arguments were so smoothly constructed and polished that the listener, like a lover of music, soon found himself tapping his foot to the beat of an obtrusive melody. He was never derogatory, always easing the implication of shortcomings into strengths. He casually dropped the names of men like Abiko, whom he had had to his dinner table and considered equals in his own realm. But regardless of how well his views were presented, an astute audience such as Cedric could boil it down to a simple bottom line—the Japanese could not be equals and did not belong as such in California life.

All in all, the Lodi newspaperman found him sincere and courageous in his convictions, and promised to return sometime for dinner.

The wealthy Senator Phelan—who had charged before the Committee on Naturalization and Immigration the summer before that the Japanese were an "immoral people" and that the state was headed for "mongrelization and degeneracy" because of them—was out of town, so Cedric collected all of his degrading public statements from copies of the Hearst papers in the public library. And he went to see the more than cooperative Reverend William McAllister, Sataro's old acquaintance from the *Fukuin Kai*—the Gospel Society.

The minister, grayer in the hair but still hearty, had just returned from two years in Hiroshima, where he had relieved Reverend Macnamara for a sabbatical. McAllister claimed to have gotten his finger on the pulse of the country and to have been privy to inside government information. As he launched into it, Cedric decided it bordered on gossip, but was still unable to believe his good fortune at getting an inside on Japan. It gave his series an added twist.

"The Emperor is quite off his rocker, you know," McAllister went on. "And the military faction headed by old man Yamagata rules the country. And while there is a certain discontent among the people due to the postwar recession, the taste of imperialism is on their lips. I look for a move on China within the next fifteen years."

Cedric scribbled rapidly. "What do you know about the crown prince?" he asked after the clergyman had discussed Hirohito's coming appointment as regent.

"A very alert young man, from what I hear," McAllister replied. "Quite Westernized and inquisitive. Yet, as long as he is only regent, he'll most probably go along with the generals and admirals. And he already has a kitchen cabinet composed of uncles ranging from ten to fifteen years older than he is—each married to his aunts—daughters of the Meiji. They're also military people."

"Boy, oh boy!" Cedric exclaimed. "You preachers would make great spies. Who else is strong behind the prince?"

"Prince Saionji, a seventy-one-year-old former prime minister who represented Japan in Paris during the peace talks. He has impeccable taste, plays the lute, and excited French society with his beautiful young mistress named Flower Child. He is supposedly the only major power near the throne who is not enthralled by conquering the Orient. In fact, he's a staunch liberal and could be a profound influence on the new Emperor.''

The Lodi newspaperman still couldn't believe he had stumbled onto such inside information from behind the bamboo curtain. He'd have Sataro check it out, but it looked like an amazing scoop. Nothing of such import ever came out of Japan!

After another session with McAllister the next day, he took the train to Lodi. He was elated, knowing he could go from a good, incisive story to something much bigger—possibly something worthy of the new journalism award, the Pulitzer Prize.

Two days later, Sataro summoned Noboru to his small office at the store. Zenro had found him in the daytime poker game in Japan Town at shortly after noon, nearly sober and losing only a little money. Sataro turned from the window as his son entered the room. His expression was stern and Noboru knew what was coming. Except for their long discussion about his wedding trip following the return from Japan, this was the first time they had met privately and Sataro was furious that it had to be for such a purpose. His eyes were cold and his voice harsh as he said, ''I thought you had become a man.''

Noboru said nothing, waiting, fixing his gaze on his father's thin white scar.

''Instead, I seem to have a wastrel for my heir. A drunkard who makes the House of Hoshi the butt of jokes while he chases another man's baggage around the countryside. Isn't that right?''

Noboru swallowed, not answering, unable to look into his father's enraged eyes.

''Have you no tongue? Surely you must need it to tell your wife why you are never home, or to arrange your adulterous meetings with *that* woman! How many years has that bitch been coming between us, Noboru? Huh, how many? *Seven?*''

Noboru tensed, his cheeks stinging. This was the second time in a year his father had talked to him like a child and he was getting damned tired of it!

''This is the last time I ever want to discuss the matter, do you understand?'' Sataro rasped. ''I forbid your seeing her again and I order you to get your own house in order.''

Noboru felt the heat as the unfairness of his father's interference struck him like a wave of searing flame from an open furnace. He was a grown man with a business of his own and a life of his own! The old ways of Japan—his father could shove them and get out of his damned life! He blinked his eyes to hold back the words he'd regret, but it was useless. The beers he had drunk before arriving were now in command. "I think my private life's my own affair," he snapped angrily. "I—"

Sataro's still powerful fist crashed down on the top of the desk, his voice cracking like a high-powered rifle. "When your actions are detrimental to the House of Hoshi, you'll do as you are told! And if this displeases you, there's only one alternative." He ground his teeth together, hoping his strong son wouldn't force an issue that would break his heart.

Again, Noboru was still a Japanese son. The thought of being cast out of the family dulled the edge of his anger. Yes, he knew he was wrong with Tomoko, even though she belonged to him, even though fate had foiled them at every crazy turn. But many things in life were wrong. And *damn it,* he couldn't get her out of his system! How could his father understand anything so deep, so overpowering? He looked into the unwavering expression. It was all so unfair. There were things yet to be said, heated words down inside him—comments about forced marriages and the twentieth century. But he knew bringing them to the surface would only seal his fate. He stood, his hawk's face as rigid as Sataro's. "I will conduct myself honorably, Father," he said coldly, then turned and strode out.

The anger and humiliation burned his cheeks as he reached the door. He can lead me to water, he growled to himself, but he can't make me drink. For at least a while he'd forgo Tomoko and some of his other activities. He'd just throw himself into his new business. After all, Mario's Chicago deal had just come through and it was time to get rolling after his own damned fortune.

But no edict from his father could make him love his inherited wife!

Four months and two days later, Miyuki handed Sataro a telegram. Watching him with wide eyes as his fingers fumbled with the envelope, she saw him peer intently at its contents for a moment, then smile and hand it back to her. It read:

At 0214 today, Suiko gave birth to Sachiko, a beautiful six-pound, three-ounce girl with already a healthy voice.
                                                                Hiroshi

She smiled, thinking of how much happiness there must be in Itoko's house in Tokyo, and was happy for those strangers who meant so much to her Sataro. She touched his hand as she handed the telegram back to him. "Congratulations, Grandfather Hoshi," she whispered, wondering when her beloved Haru would produce *her* child.

Sataro took the message, gripping it tightly, feeling a surge of power. *Sachiko!* Why did it seem so natural that his first grandchild should be a girl? And hadn't he known all along, ever since Hiroshi informed them of her pregnancy, hadn't he been positive that the child would be a bright-eyed, lusty little female. It was his little Ellen, most certainly, only her name was Sachiko and she was going to be a modern goddess, at least a princess. Yes, that was it—Amaterasu, the Sun Goddess and ancestress of the Imperial family had provided him with a princess! He could feel his heart pounding, his breath was short. The House of Hoshi had a princess! Never before in his entire life had he felt anything so strongly; his hand shook. Delirium? Of course! He could almost reach out across the seas and touch her beautiful little face . . . yes, that was it—she was a part of him! He could hear a ringing in his ears as the power surged through his body like an electrical shock. They should have named her *Chikara!*

Even Noboru was surprised at the number of fruit growers who had jumped at the opportunity to have a Japanese labor contractor sweat out the crop and market for them. He was the first such speculator in the Lodi area. He bought so many crops that summer that he had trouble lining up enough fieldhands. But word quickly spread that the "young *oyakata*" was paying good wages and treating his people well. Work with Boss Hoshi could be permanent. As he passed several harvests profitably and no weather problems presented themselves, it looked to Noboru as if he would make it without falling back on Mario's Chicago insurance.

One night in late August, the two former members of the Rainbow sat in Mario's office drinking wine and telling war stories. Suddenly Mario said, "Hey, Emperor, when you gonna have me and the wife over for teriyaki or something good. I mean, you ain't never invited us. What are you doing—keeping that beautiful wife of yours locked up? You know, I've seen a lot of Japanese women since I came out here, but she's absolutely the best-looking one of the bunch."

Noboru laughed. Except for the inner social circle, no one came to his house. He replied that something would be arranged, finished his drink, and drove home. He had other things to occupy his mind. But as he turned off the roadster's engine in the front yard of The Other Cheek, Mario's words about Haru came back to him. He sat there in the dark, pondering them. Was there something he couldn't see? Had her skinny face changed, those protruding cheekbones—had they receded? What intrigued him? He had to admit she was an exceptionally good wife—if keeping a clean house, not ever asking for extra money, not plying him with annoying questions about the business . . . hell, not hardly talking to him at all.

He had caught himself sneaking looks at her lately, wondering how to perhaps find a little more, a bit more friendliness to share. That was it, he just wanted some friendship . . . casual, nothing demanding, just like a close army buddy maybe. They had sex once a week, always on Saturday and after he had had several drinks. And that wasn't nearly enough. He had almost gone back to Tomoko several times, but his fierce pride held him back. He had made a vow.

But it was more than that. Haru's gentleness and habit of not complaining had begun not only to make him feel guilty, but—he couldn't define it—feel *protective* in a way. There were times when he wanted to gather her in his arms and shield her from the harsh world. But then the guilt would come seeping back, saying *he* was the only one causing her pain. And his foolish pride would step in the way.

He stared through the windshield at the low light in the kitchen. She'd be there writing English or doing needlework—whatever she did to keep herself busy. Was she really the most beautiful Japanese woman in the Valley? She didn't really have a horse face, and her eyes could be hauntingly soft and expressive. He had seen them hurt enough when he came home drunk. And what beautiful teeth . . .

He thought of how smooth her ivory skin was to his touch, and how—skinny or not—how it warmed to his touch. He opened the door, feeling a slight tingle of excitement. She *was* his wife . . . there was more than just crawling inside in the dark. . . .

Haru had heard the Ford pull into the yard and had gone to the cookstove to add some coal in case he wanted anything to eat. A stew was warming. She looked up at the wall clock. It was only eight-thirty. Maybe he would stay up a while tonight—he was usually so tired he couldn't. Just a few words of casual conversation was all she wanted, any touch of warmth, of knowing she was alive and more than . . . She had sworn she'd stick it out if it took fifty years, but she was weakening. He had been softer lately, she thought. But not enough—

Noboru tossed his straw hat on the counter by the door. But instead of his usual cool greeting, he stood there staring at her. He started to say something but stopped. Taking a tentative step toward her as her eyes met his and widened, he reached out and took her hand. "I—I want you to do something for me," he began awkwardly.

She didn't reply, holding his look, wondering and barely breathing. He looked so confused—had something gone wrong at work? His grip was tightening on her hand, his strong man-smell pulling at her.

He came closer and put his arm around her, drawing her close to his chest. His lips moved against the top of her head, murmuring, "I want to go to the bedroom with you and—" He kissed her hair. "I want you to light some incense and a soft candle, and . . ."

Her face tilted upward as she closed her eyes tightly, hoping he was going to, afraid to let the excitement—the love that had been stifled inside her ready to explode or die—afraid to believe what might—

"I want you to undress your lovely body in front of me and make love with me," he finished huskily as his lips moved hungrily to hers.

Already tears were slipping down her cheeks as she threw her arms around his neck and moved into his strong embrace. Was that all he wanted? *She'd tear her clothes off right here in the kitchen if that was all!*

A few minutes later, the graceful Haru disrobed somewhat bashfully but quite happily in front of her excited husband. He took in her delicate, lovely breasts, her tiny waist, her smoothly rounded hips and slender, shapely legs as if he were opening a long delayed Christmas present of the greatest value. He went to her slowly, trancelike, and in the midst of his fascination, he shook his head at his own stupidity. He wanted to kiss each enchanting part of her exquisite, exotic body. And his first words of love began to tumble out.

Twenty-six

Tokyo—September 1, 1923

The driver knew just how to swing the army staff car through the thinning traffic as he sped into the Kazumi section of Azabu. He should—he had been there often enough to get Hiroshi or bring the general to see his daughter. It was a fine Saturday—an excellent day for the formal opening of the finest new hotel in the Orient, Hiroshi thought as he lounged back against the rear seat of the open touring car and ignored the stares of the many pedestrians hurrying to a noon meal. It was also hot and muggy and he wished he could stay home in a thin summer kimono the rest of the day. But the women had been planning this special excursion for over a week.

Because Hiroshi had to arrange a dinner party for the general, the manager of the hotel had most graciously offered a private tour of his new marvel, the talk of Tokyo. Japan had decided it wanted a stately Western-style hostelry in its capital, and Frank Lloyd Wright—the innovative American architect—had designed the magnificent structure. And no lesser name would suit it. It was the Imperial Hotel and it was majestic. It was also close enough to the Imperial Palace for people from the provinces to think it was part and parcel.

The project had become viable a decade earlier when its committee first contacted Wright in New York, but the war had intervened. Earthquakeproof was the boast of its founders and its imaginative architect who had utilized cantilevered construction with a foundation floating on a soft bed of mud to supposedly absorb the 150 or more earth tremors that touched Tokyo each year.

This would be one of Hiroshi's last social duties as an aide-de-camp for his father-in-law. General Goto had promised he could go back to his regiment by September 15, and the orders had been issued. And none too soon—a dedicated young officer belonged with troops, not running around opening doors for generals.

The sedan pulled into the Obata driveway and stopped. Hiroshi nodded to the driver as he got out and entered the house, hurrying to the garden where he heard his mother and Suiko laughing. Stepping out into the bright sunshine, he quickly saw why they were enjoying themselves. His lovely daughter Sachiko was gaily scurrying around a bush, evading her scolding governess. He watched quietly a moment, then jumped out and grabbed the squealing little one. Swinging her high above his head as she cried out with joy, he let out his loudest swordplay roar.

Itoko shook her head in mock dismay. This tease of a granddaughter of hers was the most mischievous little charmer in the city. But it was time to go and nothing was going to interfere with her seeing this amazing hotel she had heard so much about.

Suiko also hated to break away from her delightful child, but she didn't want to fall behind schedule—she had an association membership meeting at two and had promised to meet her father at four. But lunch at this grand new hotel was such a departure, a lark. Seldom did Japanese women do such a thing. And if it weren't for the Western philosophy of the hotel, they wouldn't be doing it now. Someday, she was going to help break some of these ridiculous shackles on Nippon's womanhood, it was a solemn vow!

Hiroshi handed the squealing Sachiko over to her governess, then turned to the smiling women. "Well, ladies, shall we go?" he asked cheerily. A glance at the silver watch he had received from the Emperor told him they had little time to spare if they were to be at the hotel at eleven-thirty.

Genro was a descriptive title conferred on the surviving members of the Meiji's oligarchy. Although it actually meant founding elder, the term denoted prime minister–maker when applied to the seventy-four-year-old Prince Saionji. Before long, the handsome, gallant prince would be the sole *genro* and senior political adviser to Hirohito. But for now, he had only to maintain his intelligence sources. And Koki Obata was indirectly part of that procedure.

Impeccably dressed as usual, the prince was finishing his point about the regent's desire to find a military successor for the recently deceased premier. Koki nodded his white head. Many years earlier, the urbane Saionji had provided the professor with a temporary French mistress during his stay in Paris. And although over twenty years separated their ages, they had become friends.

Periodically, Saionji called on Koki to get his usually sound advice and to test the current of the academic world for dissension. They also had a running game—the prince would select one of his most tempting young concubines and proffer her to Koki. But always, Koki laughed and remarked that he had his own temptress at home—one who had such powerful appetites that any wandering on his part would bring unmitigated scorn upon his head. And always the prince solemnly offered to relieve the problem.

Koki listened politely as Saionji continued. He knew the discussion was running late, but there was nothing he could do about it. But while he could tour the new hotel some other time, he still wanted to join his family for lunch. Finally breaking away from his charming host, he looked quickly at his watch. It was eleven-forty and the Imperial Hotel was a twenty-minute drive in the new white Buick sedan he had purchased only a few days earlier. As he swung behind the wheel, he wondered how long it would take to put a new cabinet together.

Lieutenant General Goto nodded his handsome head at the statement by the Shikan Gakko's commandant. He, too, believed firmly that Admiral Yamamoto was a logical choice for premier—as long as the army's goals were fully understood and the budget wouldn't be affected. He looked at the wall clock: 1149. It was time to head for the mess hall, where he was to be the honored guest at the noon meal of the corps of cadets.

At Imperial University, the graduate student on duty at the seismograph casually glanced at the instrument at 11:54, just as he felt the shudder of an earth tremor begin. What he saw as the shock increased made him gasp in disbelief—the instrument was going crazy! Could it be erratic due to a malfunction? The force of the vibration as it increased violently in the next few seconds was his answer.

In a special Imperial Hotel dining room, the assistant manager who was escorting General Goto's party stopped in the middle of a sentence as he was seating Mrs. Obata at an exclusive table draped with the finest of new linen. The crystal glassware and ornate silver at the place settings had suddenly begun to bounce around and make noise. A vase of fresh yellow roses toppled over.

Itoko threw a startled look at Hiroshi. *The table was dancing up and down!*

Hiroshi grabbed Suiko's hand as her mouth flew open in fright. Up and down—not sideways. The sign of a violent one! Sharp creaks of sound turned to a rumble as the manager stood riveted to his place, trying to mumble something about the structure being earthquakeproof. All four faces turned fearfully upward, eyes racing over where potential cracks might appear in the ceiling. And everything continued to shudder up and down.

General Goto was just entering the large mess hall when the first violent shudder struck. He and his party were bounced sharply up and down as they grappled for each other in sudden horror. The walls in the entryway split open with a roar. The general caught his balance momentarily, but his arm came up too late to ward off the shattered heavy beam that crashed into his skull. He didn't even hear the frightened screams of the trapped cadets inside. Nor did he see the flames that flashed up as large over-turned ranges in the kitchen poured their coals into oil and created an instant inferno.

Similar tragedy was striking all over the city and down the seacoast. Braziers filled with hot charcoal for the noon meal created instant fires in hundreds of thousands of flimsy wood-and-paper buildings. There was no gradual breaking up of more substantial buildings—many were instantly torn apart, crashing to the ground in thundering clouds of dust. Everywhere, people who were conditioned to tremors were dying suddenly or screaming in agony from injuries. And at the center of the chaos the shifting wind fanned the blaze of a giant spreading holocaust that would render millions homeless.

As the hungry flames and disintegrating buildings reached out to slaughter the citizens, so also did the panic of small and large mobs trapped in narrow streets of jammed shopping districts take its toll. The main business district of Nihonbashi was soon destroyed. Gas mains ruptured and contributed to the mounting flames. Sheared electric wires joined the havoc. The noise was deafening. The frantic cries of tiny children torn from their parents weren't even distinguishable in the screams and terrible sounds of devastation that shrieked above the death-dealing wind.

Over seven hundred persons were killed when the twelve-story tower at Asakusa fell. Explosions continued to rock the city and there was periodic flooding when the city's water system was destroyed. From Senju at the northern tip of the city to Shinagawa on the south end, Tokyo was fully ablaze. All the bridges were rendered useless, the major railroad stations damaged severely. Transportation froze as trains were derailed and destroyed. Communications within and to the outside were obliterated.

Along the shore, thousands tried to escape the furious flames by diving into the water. Fire broke out in the Imperial Palace. In Kamakura, the Daibutsu—the giant Buddha where Tojo took Hiroshi when they first met—shifted and cracked. A massive tidal wave struck the coast southeast of Tokyo. Yokohama was almost annihilated, as was the connecting city of Yokosuka. The latter's huge naval base spilled out thousands of gallons of oil into the bay where masses of survivors from the land fires were bobbing desperately about, trying to comprehend and struggling wildly to stay alive. When a blaze flashed over the huge oil spill, it was as if hell had risen through the ruptured crust of the earth and blown its execrable breath over everything.

Inside the Imperial Hotel, there was terror but little panic. The grand opening luncheon wasn't scheduled until twelve-thirty and many of those planning to attend had not yet arrived. Still, hundreds of people responding to the primary rule of earthquake discipline—get outside—rushed to the main entrance immediately after the initial shock. Reaching the huge main lobby, Hiroshi spotted the crush of people at the front and told the wide-eyed Suiko and Itoko to wait by the reception desk while he tried to find out what was happening outside. One look at the madness in the street in front of Hibiya Park eliminated that possibility. In fact, a man who looked like the hotel's manager was directing a flow of outsiders *into* the lobby. Hurrying back to the reception area, Hiroshi studied the still intact arched ceiling and made his decision. "We'll stay here!" he shouted to the waiting women, pointing to a safe-looking corner.

Suiko's eyes were shouting her fear as she cried out, "Hiroshi, the baby! Call the house—you've got to see if she's all right!"

A sharp chill stabbed at him as he saw the same naked fear in his mother's eyes. They had *all* forgotten about their precious Sachiko! Hiroshi tried to stay calm, telling himself the tremor could be localized. Yes, probably just a severe local shock. Nothing to worry about. And even if it did encompass Kazumi, the house was so strong . . . and the governess would die before she'd let anything happen to her baby. He cleared his throat, trying to sound confident. "I'll try."

As he suspected, he was unable to get through on the telephone. He returned to the women, shaking his head. "No luck," he stated grimly. "But the house is probably much safer than this place." As if to confirm his statement, a thunderous explosion from outside rocked the huge room. Suddenly more people were running inside, screaming, filling the lobby with more terror. Hiroshi pushed the women behind a tall potted tree.

Itoko shuddered, smothering the fear that was convulsing her. Closing her eyes tightly, she forced out all thoughts of her beloved little Sachi. Another numbing fear gripped her—*where was Koki?*

Suiko looked at the frantic people pushing toward them. Hiroshi was right. She inhaled deeply, squaring her shoulders and reaching for Itoko. "It's all right, Mother," she said with all the forced calm she could muster. "It's all right." It was the first time she had ever held the advantage over her headstrong mother-in-law and it didn't even matter. Tightly holding Itoko's hand, she turned anxiously to Hiroshi. "Isn't there something we can do?"

Another deafening explosion sounded from outside. "Not yet," he replied loudly. "But I'd better think about getting back to headquarters. I've got a hunch the army's going to be extremely busy."

Itoko shook off her crippling fear and grabbed his arm. "*No!* You can do more good here!" she insisted. Pointing to the milling, frightened people hemming them in, she pleaded, "Look! You can take charge."

Hiroshi nodded, knowing she might be right. He went back to the main desk.

Koki was four blocks from the hotel when the shock began. First, the view through his windshield began to vibrate. Then the new Buick started to jump and buck like an unbroken horse. He saw a building collapse to his left, heard the loud noises and saw the horrified looks of terrified people in the streets as their distorted features swam around him. Fighting the wheel, he tried to get his foot on the elusive brake.

A motorcycle with a wild-eyed driver smashed into his front fender and went flying past. A moment later, a truck sideswiped him from the left and careened away. Everything in sight was bouncing and vibrating crazily as he tried frantically to stop. People were everywhere. He shouted futilely as a woman with a baby fell in front of the car. He was frozen in horror. The wall of a four-story building crumpled to his right front, smashing pieces into the hood and right side of his cracked windshield. Swerving left, the Buick ran up over a downed telephone pole and slammed to a stop, its front wheels still spinning. Koki stared in horror at the live, sizzling electric wire that fell toward him. The last sound he heard was the brassy blare of the Buick's stuck horn.

Hiroshi broke away from his mother and Suiko at 12:35. He had been unable to call anywhere from the hotel's switchboard, so he guessed all intracity telephone lines were out of commission.

Organizing relief activity within the hotel could be handled by others—he had to get back to the military somehow. The general was at the Shikan Gakko, but getting there was surely out of the question. And his office was most probably impossible. But the palace wasn't too far away—certainly, he could be of value there.

The streets were a nightmare. Fire was everywhere or had already made its flashing visit. Bodies were all over—black smoking bodies, scorched beyond recognition, many still burning. The stench and smoke were so bad he tied his handkerchief around his face. The living ones were running, pushing, struggling to get somewhere. Many carried what remained of their earthly possessions in wrapping cloth and other containers over their shoulders. All had bleak, hopeless looks in their eyes, or stark fear. Some appeared to be mad.

A few hundred yards from the hotel, he came upon a screaming woman in the middle of the street. She was tearing madly at a pile of rubble. As he started by, she clawed wildly at his arm. "Save my baby!" she shrieked. Hiroshi looked to where she was pointing and saw a child's arm moving. Instantly, he sprang to the pile of mortar and began to rip pieces away. Moments later, the child's spitting, screaming head appeared. It was covered with blood, but very much alive. He jerked more debris from its body, finally pulling the terrorized little girl free. He handed her to her babbling mother, then hurried on. *His beautiful Sachiko, his darling Sachi, just had to be safe!*

Moving against the flow of the hysterical mob, he picked his way in and out. Several times he saw looters—excrement rising to the surface of a sewer, he snarled to himself. He had seen only one police uniform since he left the hotel and that was on a dead body. The sooner martial law was declared and troops deployed, the sooner there would be an element of sanity.

In the middle of the next block he saw what he thought was a white Buick hung up on a light pole or something. It looked like Koki's new car and its horn was blowing. But it was only one of dozens of wrecked vehicles. He didn't even look inside.

The smoke and dust continued to tear at his lungs as he hurried along. Near one intersection, he saw a tall man unbelievably strike a little old woman and rip away her bag full of belongings. He wasted no time, furiously jerking his sword from its scabbard and rushing after the thief. *"Halt, dog!"* he roared.

The fleeing man threw a startled look over his shoulder as he dodged through the crowd. But he was no match for Hiroshi's rage—in less than fifty yards of wild pursuit, the furious lieutenant caught up. With a thunderous bellow that outdid any of the thousands of practice shouts over the years, Hiroshi rammed the gleaming sword through the predator's side with all his strength. As the man fell, his eyes already glazing in death, Hiroshi disgustedly placed a foot on his hip and jerked the bloody blade free. He wanted to jump in the air and scream to all who could hear, "Death to all looters and dogs who pick on the helpless!" But all he could do was grab the old woman's bag and try to find her.

Twenty minutes later, he arrived at a gate to the Imperial Palace. Pushing through the huge crowd clamoring at the iron fence, he caught the attention of a captain. "I'm Lieutenant Hoshi!" he shouted. "General Goto's aide. Let me in!"

Cedric rushed out to the Homerville store as soon as he saw the Sunday morning edition of the San Francisco *Chronicle*. It was possible that the Hoshis had heard the terrible news on the radio, but he doubted it. Parking in front, he rushed up on the porch and pounded heavily on the door. Moments later, Sataro was staring at the huge black headline—"EARTHQUAKE AND MASSIVE FIRE RIP TOKYO AND YOKOHAMA; MILLIONS HOMELESS." He felt crushed as the words swam before him.

Hiroshi! His beautiful little Sachiko!

He rushed on to the smaller type. "Inhabitants rush to find refuge in harbor ships—Severed railways prohibit survivors from fleeing—Epicenter in Mount Fuji . . . Regent Hirohito safe in burning palace, Emperor safe in mountains . . . 500,000 casualties, 300,000 homes burned in metropolitan Tokyo—Food and water at a premium—Famous Japanese isle and two villages disappear . . . Thousands trampled to death in greatest calamity of modern times. U.S. Navy to speed relief, American Red Cross asking for millions . . . .

Cedric had dropped into a chair. "Unbelievable, isn't it?" he said softly as Miyuki brought coffee.

Wordlessly, Sataro handed her the *Chronicle*. He couldn't trust himself to speak. All those people—what wrath the gods? The paper said the only news was coming by shortwave radio from a Radio Corporation of America station, so there was no way to find out about survivors yet. He pictured his little Sachiko again and his hand shook. *It couldn't be!*

He had to snap out of this, get busy. Much to do—the paper, that was it, daily editions, so many Japan people didn't read English. Big special edition immediately. Get a collection started. Noboru had over two hundred men in his crews. The *kenjinkai*, the association, the merchants—everyone would give at least pennies!

God! he thought. If he were still the rice baron, he could send tons! Surely there'd be food riots if relief wasn't immediate. Why didn't he have all that money *now?*

Miyuki was trying to read the newspaper through brimming eyes. He went to her and took her hand. "Why don't you go help Haru. She'll want to fix things for the crews to eat when they come." His eyes went back to the headlines as she handed him the *Chronicle*. "There's so much to be done," he whispered.

The next ten days, while terribly trying, were far better for the Obata household than for most in the ruptured city. Due to its sturdy construction and location, the building had escaped serious damage. And not only had the bright little Sachiko escaped harm, the servants were unhurt. Following Hiroshi's orders, Itoko and Suiko not only armed themselves and the servants, but they took turns remaining awake in case of attack by the marauding bands of thieves, food rioters, or madmen who still roved the city. Fortunately, there was enough food in the house to sustain a strict ration.

Hiroshi tried to check in daily, but having volunteered to serve with the Imperial Guards Division, he was on duty night and day. Returning to the house Sunday just before midnight, he brought the sad news to Suiko that her father's body had been identified at the mess hall of the Shikan Gakko. She shuddered at the news, trying to stall off her severe grief by thinking of a way to tell her mother. Hiroshi held her tightly, whispering, "I'll take an escort to get her in the morning. She'll be better off here for a few days."

Suiko nodded blankly, hiding her tears in his chest. But a vivid picture of the general in his dress uniform on the night of her wedding refused to go away. How like their love that one occasion had been.

Itoko could hardly comfort her; her own concern for Koki overrode every emotion. She sat and stared for minutes on end, not moving a muscle, unaware of anyone as she remembered the warm and loving things that marvelous man had done for her throughout the years—how he had managed to love her so intensely in spite of her selfish ways. And she prayed—for the first time in many years, she prayed fervently that he would walk through the door, smile that generous smile of his, and take her in his arms. Never again would anything be more important to her!

But as the days passed, she knew it was hopeless. If he even had the breath to talk, her Koki would send word.

Hiroshi used all the influence he could wield with the undermanned City Police and the army units that were clearing bodies from the streets. Finally, he heard that a white 1923 Buick was located a few blocks from the Imperial Hotel. Inside was the partially decomposed body of a white-haired man. Since he bore no identification, it was assumed that looters had robbed the body. Hiroshi sadly rushed to identify what remained of the cheerful, benevolent, and loving man who in many ways had been more than a father to him.

An hour later, Itoko watched her son's tight expression as his mouth formed the words to confirm her worst fears. Inhaling deeply, she stared down at her tightly clasped hands, noticing that the knuckles were whiter than they should be. How abstract. She didn't want to hear the words, refused to listen to any of the details. He'd never be gone, she wouldn't permit it. No, a worn old freighter crossing the Pacific, a hat blown off a spiteful young woman's head . . . a warm bemused smile from a handsome, aristocratic stranger—

She gasped as Hiroshi's arms encircled her and drew her tightly to his chest. She couldn't fight the ice that was clutching at her heart, but she couldn't let herself break down. She sniffed, almost smelling the aromatic tobacco of his pipe as the image of his strong face forced itself through her tightly clenched eyes. Koki, oh, my darling Koki . . .

The night after Koki's funeral, Major Hideki Tojo came to pay his respects. At thirty-nine, the Staff College instructor was beginning to show his age. A short haircut exposed his growing baldness and his clipped mustache was grayer than when Hiroshi saw him after Tojo's return from Europe. Thin-lipped and basically humorless, Tojo's eyes seemed ever hard and penetrating from behind their round, horn-rimmed spectacles. But Hiroshi knew his mentor's success lay in his intensity and addiction to hard work. It was rumored that the major had only two friends in the entire officer corps, and that was too many. Tonight he seemed tightly wound and pleased to have a listener. Seated in an overstuffed chair in Koki's book-lined study, Tojo sipped his coffee—he didn't touch alcohol—and unlimbered random thoughts. A chainsmoker, he lit another cigarette as he said, "I don't believe the new cabinet will last, but it doesn't matter. All that counts is the military budget. We can't let the politicians cut us down."

Hiroshi listened attentively as his patron continued. He knew from being a general's aide how distasteful appropriations for an army that didn't fight were to the public.

"We're going to need everything we can get to build for the coming struggle," he went on. "Regardless of the limitations placed on us by the Western powers at the Washington conference, we must never slip back into second-rate power status." His voice took on a conspirational tone. "There are important people who have set a timetable for our progress."

Hiroshi listened carefully. Was there a special cabal whose machinations were outside the knowledge of the War Plans department—or had his deceased father-in-law just not mentioned it in front of him? The word "timetable" implied something specific. He could feel his breath quicken. He wanted desperately to ask about the timetable, but Tojo had moved on to criticisms of America. On the way home from the European assignment, he had crossed the United States, only to be highly disappointed in comparing its attitude to that of the Prussians in Leipzig. The Americans were to him far too casual, impolite, and geared to material riches.

"The United States has absolutely no business coming over here dictating, arbitrating, or interfering in Asian differences," he stated emphatically. "They expand in Cuba, Hawaii, and the Philippines, then lecture us about Korea, Manchuria, and China. They preach from a lofty perch and stick their greedy hands in the Oriental purse without compunction. And Britain has always been guilty of imperialistic greed." He got to his feet, lighting another cigarette. "Russia is our primary enemy and we must never forget it."

Halfway through his second cup of coffee, Major Tojo suddenly turned to Hiroshi's new assignment. "I know you want regimental duty—all young infantry officers do. But a far better opportunity has presented itself. An opening has occurred for a brilliant young officer in a special branch called Strategic Analysis. They want a lieutenant with connections who isn't actually a member of the aristocracy or any of the wealthy commerce families. I recommended you."

"But I don't actually have any real connections," Hiroshi replied, trying to conceal his excitement. He had heard about the new branch—a special intelligence entity, rumored to be headed by a prince of the blood.

Tojo blew out a thick cloud of smoke as he stood to leave. "You will, Hoshi, you will."

A few minutes after the major's departure, Hiroshi returned to the study and sat back in the overstuffed chair with a glass of scotch whiskey. The excitement was still on him and he couldn't wait to tell Suiko at an appropriate moment. He was about to take a step that could later place him at center stage in the path chosen for Nippon's glory. Power struggles within both the army and navy were as normal as the strife between the two services. But an overall conflict was brewing. The dominant, conservative side of the entire military was geared toward an eventual showdown with Soviet Russia, while a dissident faction was just coming out of its embryonic stage to espouse attacking south against the Western imperialists in their possessions.

And there were those who were licking their lips over the vulnerability of China in its continuing civil war. Already in 1896, Nippon had wrested the island of Taiwan and the peninsula of Korea from her huge Oriental neighbor. And on the tiny Kwantung Peninsula of southern Manchuria a fiercely independent Japanese army plotted against both China and Russia. Known as the belligerent Kwantung Army, it would surely play a major part in forthcoming aggressions. Big things lay ahead if Japan were to find growing space for its surging population. And this new course of his would certainly place him directly in the mainstream of whichever route was chosen to get it. In spite of the sadness that still gripped the household, he tingled with excitement. His glory beckoned and he liked its siren song.

And he totally forgot Koki's warning about losing his soul.

Twenty-seven

The Japanese school was a rented house in Acampo—not ideal, but adequate for the twenty-one students who attended for two hours after their regular day at an American school. Like many such schools, its objective was the teaching of the Japanese language as well as history and customs—an effort by the elders to instill more of the old country's heritage into their offspring. Often it merely took the learning edge off a child who yearned to be outside playing or anything else, after a full day of being cooped up.

Miyuki taught full-time, while Haru helped, insisting that it couldn't hurt her pregnancy. Now, as the last child ran outside at the end of the day's session, she slumped wearily, spread-legged on a chair. Brushing back a loose strand of hair, she sighed deeply. This schoolwork right up to her time was but another of the activities that kept her fully occupied. She believed doing so would help her baby be healthier and more zestful. And she wanted this baby to be magnificent—added cement in the improving union with her husband. For over a year she had been certain he loved her, but just a week earlier she had seen that woman of his in Lodi. His poison, as Kimi called her. Had it ended? If not, would it ever? She couldn't ask him. Suddenly she felt extremely tired, then a sharp pain struck her abdomen. "I think I'd better go . . . home," she said weakly. "Don't feel so good."

Miyuki was around her desk in an instant. Her child was coming! She took Haru's arm and headed for the front door. The old pickup was right outside. Her child was coming, her child, finally. Haru was finally bringing her long delayed child into the world. It was time! she shouted to herself. Soon she'd have a tiny live bundle of warmth and love clutched tightly to her breast. And Haru was so healthy—it had to be a splendid child she was providing. Never, anywhere in her life, had she felt such a rush of excitement!

Haru settled uncomfortably into the right side of the seat as Miyuki closed the door and ran to the crank to start the engine. Haru could feel sweat forming on her brow; her face was hot. Tired, terribly tired. She closed her eyes as the engine caught and sputtered out. Noboru had promised to teach her how to drive after the baby—

Noboru had traded the Ford roadster for a used two-ton truck soon after he knew his business would be successful. There was so much hauling to be done—tools and workers. With so many jobs going on he had soon added an additional truck for his foreman so the juggling of workers from crew to crew could be expedited. But he *was* successful; word of his trustworthiness had spread and he was now one of the leading contractors in the Valley. Ninety-two men working this year—a huge family to be responsible for. He had lost on only a few bids, part of the learning process, and had managed to avoid getting money from Mario's people in Chicago.

Mario looked up from where he had been slouched under his hatbrim in the right front seat of the truck as Noboru drove through downtown Lodi. "Hey, you given any more thought to that bootlegging idea of mine?" he asked abruptly.

Noboru's hawkish look became more pronounced when he thought about something that troubled him. And the danger of making bootleg wine involved plenty of trouble. It was a matter of the Chicago tie-in, local gangsters, and the law. The Feds were far from stupid and the Valley simply produced too many grapes for the area not to be closely watched. Furthermore, the suit for his citizenship still hung in abeyance and he couldn't take any chances. He shook his head. "Nothing's changed, Mario. I simply don't think it's worth it. We're doing all right."

The chunky Chicagoan threw his cigarette out the window. Shaking his head, he growled, "Yeah, but there's a lot of big money we could be getting in on. I been thinking about maybe setting up a winery just over the state line in Nevada. What would you say to that, buddy?"

Noboru shook his head as he swung the truck into the driveway of Mario's large yellow house. "I'll think about it, but right now I—"

"*Noboru!*" Mario's wife Teresa shouted as she ran toward them from the front porch. "Go home! Haru had the baby—a seven-pound boy!"

Mario stuck out his hand as his wife reached the truck. "Congratulations, buddy. Get your ass home."

"I just got the call ten minutes ago," Teresa said loudly. "I didn't know where you—"

Mario affectionately clapped a hand over his wife's pretty mouth as he stepped out. "Call me later." He was about to add something about the Nevada idea, but he'd have been talking to air. The truck was already spitting dirt as Noboru jammed the accelerator to the floor. Billy Hoshi was waiting to meet him!

The Other Cheek became the center of everything that mattered to the American Hoshi for the next couple of days. Billy—there was no fooling around with formality, Noboru wanted a name as American as possible—Billy Hoshi was holding court during the brief periods when he was awake. He was the firstborn of the firstborn, and the only grandchild Sataro could see, touch, and smell. There was none of the great closeness he felt to the granddaughter he had never seen, but he adored Billy from the first moment he saw him. Perhaps this new Hoshi would someday inherit the House and consolidate its *chikara*, he thought hopefully as he jiggled the bassinet.

And already the Japanese community from miles around was coming to pay its respect to the newest *oyakata*.

But no one, including the proud parents, felt the bursting love for little Billy that overwhelmed Miyuki. She had waited all her adult life for this very special child and she didn't want to be away from him even for a moment. She did everything he needed done and happily did it over at the slightest provocation. And when he was asleep, she sat by the hour, joyfully adoring his peaceful little face. The only problem had come when Haru nursed him for the first time. Miyuki felt a sharp pang of jealousy that she had to trample immediately—and a jolt of reality. She could fantasize just so far. But even so, a huge part of him was hers. It was not only due, but a reward for her patience. She smiled to herself each time she looked at him—yes, it was a private love affair.

However, the birth of his majesty the baby passed and life resumed its other priorities as the weeks went by. Noboru continued to withstand Mario's obsession with the bootlegging venture, but the stocky man couldn't be talked out of it. In mid-December he returned from a trip to Chicago, where he had tried to interest his connection in the wine venture. But the gangsters had flatly turned him down, sending him angrily back to California to tend to the fruit business. But on the way, Mario had made a fertile contact. The Androtti mobsters in Denver liked the idea and were interested in dealing with him.

Mario was elated as he stepped down from the train in Lodi. There was an out-of-work winemaker named Otto in Sacramento who would be more than glad to start fermenting grapes again. Most of his experience related to his home industry in the Black Forest of Germany, but he was adamant about making a good fast Zinfandel—or Dago Red—from local grapes. The conversion from wine to high spirits—brandy—would take only a month longer. And for variation, a touch of brandy could be added to the Tokay to make it a desirable dessert wine.

Transportation over or around the Rockies could easily be worked out. The only remaining problem was the location of the winery.

Noboru shook his head firmly. "I just can't get involved, Mario."

They were drinking homebrew beer in the Hoshi backyard the night after Mario's return. "Okay," Scagnelli said patiently. "I know all the reasons. I just want you to find me a couple of vacant barns big enough to put in thousand-gallon vats and still have room for the crushing. That ain't such a big deal, is it? I mean, you got something going all over the Valley, right?"

"Have you really looked at the consequences?" Noboru asked. "Not only is the fine huge, but you can spend a long time in jail.

And from what your friends in Chicago said, they could get pretty mad about your freelancing, right?"

Mario shrugged. "They'll get over it—besides, I'm gonna cut 'em in after it starts to roll. I'm telling you, buddy, we'll make a fortune! We'll—"

The loud *bang!* of the extra-live bottle of homebrew jolted him as he opened it. Noboru laughed. "That's just what's going to happen to you when the prohibition agents get you."

Wiping off the front of his jacket, Mario shook his head again. "I'm gonna get started somewhere pretty damned soon, so you might as well find me a barn."

"Okay, I guess that's the least I can do for you."

"And I can use some labor."

Noboru shook his head emphatically. "Absolutely not! I'm not setting any of my people up for jail. Get yourself some round-eyes."

Mario was about to retort when Haru called out from the doorway, "Herbert Lockett is on the telephone from Sacramento, Noboru."

It had been over two months since Noboru had heard from the attorney, and last time was to ask for a hundred dollars. Entering the house, he eagerly picked up the receiver. But the news was crushing. "A lot of words are in the decision," Lockett explained over a good connection. "But here's the meat . . . 'It has been the settled policy of the United States not to allow the naturalization of any person unless he is a free white person.'

"It then covers the same old hogwash about African nativity or descent, then gets to the military part. As you know, we based our case on that fellow Toyota from Massachusetts getting his citizenship in 1921 for military service. Now the Supreme Court has even wiped out that precedent. The ruling states in effect, 'The contention that a different rule applies to persons of Japanese birth who have army or naval service would appear to be valid. However, based upon current policy and law, this contention is denied.' " After a short pause, Lockett said softly, "I'm sorry, Noboru."

Noboru stared at the black mouthpiece of the wall telephone as if it wasn't there. It was impossible. A voice simply could not come out of the wall and say, *"You cannot—no matter what you do for your country—be a citizen."* The wall blurred as he slowly hung up. An American flag danced on it and faded. He heard music, saw a parade—a regiment of proud New Yorkers marching jauntily down Fifth Avenue. The crowd was cheering as the music got louder and he saw the flags. He felt the mud under his feet in the French trenches and remembered a dying Irishman reaching out for his hand for solace. Wasn't he one of them?

How could a small group of old men in black robes say, "This . . . is denied?" He swallowed hard to fight down the rising sense of betrayal, but it lingered, and with it, the terrible taste of sour bile that accompanies sickness. He turned, walking blindly past the waiting Haru and Mario toward the bedroom. Reaching the bassinet, he reached tentatively down to touch the sleeping Billy's soft cheek. "At least they can't take it away from you, my son," he whispered.

Hiroshi's beginning with the secret Strategic Analysis Branch was inauspicious. The highest-ranking officer he met on the job in the first four months was a major. And in that time he did little more than bury himself in research ten hours a day or more in a cryptlike room deep in the Imperial GHQ building on the northwest side of the Imperial Palace compound. His special area of study was China and its warlord leaders. By late January he was beginning to wonder about Tojo's cryptic hint that he would have some high connections. Then one day a note arrived from his patron. It said simply, "Saionji."

Three days later, an invitation came for dinner at Prince Saionji's townhouse in Aoyama. It was richly engraved and delivered by an aloof old servant who had undoubtedly been with the prince most of his life. Inside was a note to Itoko that read, "I considered your late husband a valued friend. Please forgive my taking so long to invite you to my humble table." The event was scheduled for February 3.

To Suiko, who stayed eternally busy with her association work, the forthcoming dinner was an intriguing idea because she had heard so much about Saionji's hedonistic life. To Itoko it was a majestic summons from the solitude of mourning. She had come to grips with Koki's death and was ready to get on with life. Her connection with the boring Obata family had served its purpose and she was glad to be finally free of it. She had everything in order—a lovely home, as much prestige as she needed, and plenty of money. Income on her estate totaled nearly fifty thousand yen per year, if she never touched the principal.

The only thing missing was a man and she had learned to accept that void. With custom the way it was, the chances of her finding another husband—in spite of her youthfulness—were nearly nonexistent. Life for Japanese men involved young women. Seldom was a mistress beyond thirty. And their outside life in the teahouses and other haunts involved almost exclusively younger females like the geisha—unblemished young flowers of porcelain and rose petals. And finally, the poor people on the farms and in the villages seemed to have a never-ending supply of young daughters to send into the brothels.

Oh, she could have gigolos, but she'd never cheapen herself or her family by such atrocious behavior! She had a rich full life without a mate, and she could get along just fine without such services. Hadn't she proved she could do without lovemaking back in America? The thing that troubled her the most was becoming another of those practically faceless ancient women who were such a fixture in Japanese society. She simply would *not* ever be one of those dependant apparitions!

"Oh, Mother!" Suiko exclaimed as she entered the large bedroom. "How divine! No wonder you wouldn't tell me what kind of an ensemble you were having made." She pursed her lips as she fingered the fine gold thread of the intricate peacock design in the navy silk kimono, then admired the complementing needlework in the white damask obi. "You'll be the most beautiful woman there." She pouted.

"Ha!" Itoko snorted, adjusting a tiny platinum comb in her lustrous hair. "Not as long as my beautiful daughter-in-law is there to turn heads. Don't you feel a bit ill to be going?"

They both laughed as each made a final adjustment in the mirror and turned to go.

*   *   *

The townhouse was brightly decorated for the first affair Prince Kinmochi Saionji had thrown in the city since his beautiful Flower Child had given birth to a young lover's child and been banished. Saionji spent most of his time at his villa in Okitsu, using the comfortable Tokyo mansion for such occasions and spending the night when it was necessary for him to come to the city. Tonight, his newest mistress, the cultured and exotic O-Hawu—Miss Lotus—was acting as his hostess.

The premier and his wife were present, but would leave immediately after the meal because of the tenuous condition of his cabinet. Two elder princes of the blood were there, as were a lieutenant general and a vice admiral. One of those cabinet members and two older members of the House of Peers rounded out the list of important persons. A few more guests were of little significance to the intrigues of rule, but in one way or another filled a particular niche in the prince's order of manipulation. For as the head of the Fujiwara—the great family that had forever been charged with the protection and wisdom of the throne—his responsibility knew no bounds and would end only when he ceased to breathe. And he was also the last of the statesmen who had served the Meiji in bringing about the Restoration.

He was particularly attentive to Itoko and her party when they first arrived, then left them with the general, an old friend of General Goto. Shortly after the long and sumptuous meal was served, the guests broke up into groups for an informal period prior to the scheduled entertainment. Hiroshi, wearing his mess dress uniform with the magnificent sword he had received from Koki, was caught up in a discussion with a professor who had known his stepfather at the university. Their brandy had just been served when Nakagawa, Saionji's private secretary, bowed to Hiroshi. "The prince would like to speak with you, Lieutenant Hoshi," he murmured.

Hiroshi nodded, excused himself, and followed Nakagawa to a small, secluded, book-lined study, where the tall figure of Prince Saionji stood glancing through the pages of an old book. Erect, with white hair and eyebrows, clean shaven and dressed in a well-tailored black tuxedo, Saionji spoke in a deep direct tone, telling his guest that he was an old friend of Koki's and quickly dispensing with other trivia.

After giving Hiroshi a fine Havana and waiting for him to light it, the prince began, "When you leave this room, your life will be different, my son." Saionji then moved around his subject deftly before abruptly saying, "In short, I believe you are capable of seeing beyond the samurai maunderings of knighthood and sacred codes. Is that correct, Hoshi?"

Hiroshi tried not to blink. He had grown used to high rank, but the regal *genro* was intimidating. He was ridiculing all that was sacred. Before he could stammer an obtuse answer, Saionji went on, "What I mean, of course, is there are often better ways to serve than dying uselessly in battle. In short, Hoshi, your Emperor can be served politically. And that is why you're here."

Hiroshi held the prince's steady gaze. "But I have no political training, Excellency," he replied carefully.

"Which is one of the reasons I selected you," Saionji replied crisply. "As you know, we will have a new Emperor in the near future—a divine ruler placed on this earth to guide Nippon in perhaps its most ambitious period . . . more ambitious perhaps than that of the Meiji." Saionji's eyes began to shine as he cupped his hands. "Within his grasp will be technology such as we have never known and can't yet imagine. And within Nippon's reach will be power to rule the Pacific, if that be her wisest course."

The prince's tone became more intense. "I have observed and taught our great prince since his early youth and there is nothing that will not be within his divine reach . . . in the right time. Unfortunately, there are forces which are unwilling to wait for that propitious timing. And they will be waiting—are waiting—to propel him and the empire into dire positions."

Saionji's fierce gaze seemed to bore right through Hiroshi as if he weren't there, as if the prince had forgotten he was speaking to a mere lieutenant. "Already there is a cabal of intimates, including princes of the blood, who are extremely close to him. And if they have their way, we could be at war with Russia, China, and the Western powers, all possibly at once and within my lifetime."

Saionji's black eyes blazed as he moved closer. His voice cracked through the silence of the study like a whiplash. "I do not believe we can win such a war, and I do not believe such a war will be in the best interest of our people, and therefore His Imperial Highness!"

Hiroshi caught himself holding his breath as he waited for the prince to continue.

The *genro*'s voice dropped suddenly to a whisper. "I believe that I alone have the position, the power to obviate such a destructive course."

Hiroshi was entranced, waiting.

"But I must have help, must have information. I will need an organization so elite and so condensed that it can be neither fully compromised nor infiltrated. I, the empire, will need you, Hoshi. As an intelligence officer, you will encounter information of distinct value to me, and you will give it to me."

Hiroshi tried to tear his eyes away from the prince's narrowed gaze. He sucked on the dead cigar. There it was! He knew Saionji was a pacifist, but such a plotter? Was the old liberal plotting some kind of a coup—overcome by some form of senile madness? He looked back into Saionji's now relaxed expression. No, if ever a man was in control of himself, it was this majestic old prince. His voice was hushed as he replied, "That would be disloyal, Excellency."

Saionji smiled suddenly, brightly. "I expected precisely that word, Hoshi. But loyalty and disloyalty can require interpretation. There are those who would die in an instant for His Imperial Highness, but their doing so would place him in jeopardy. I'm asking that you pass on information which in your conscientious opinion will best serve the Emperor in my able hands. For instance, there will be terrible events in which plots of severe implications may come to your attention. These, my son, are what I should have."

The *genro* was the third most hallowed man in the empire, and soon, when the regent became the Emperor, he would be the second. But still the idea of being unfaithful to his military superior, no matter what his persuasions, violated his principles so acutely he wanted to shudder and smother the thought. *He could not be a party to such dishonesty!* But it began immediately as he lied to the prince. "I will consider it, Excellency."

His oath as an officer and a member of the Bushi came first. He thought painfully of Misao. Never could he be unfaithful to the army to satisfy the political whims of an old power-seeker—no matter how high his position or exalted his goals.

But he would tread carefully.

Hiroshi did not stop to consider with any seriousness the message behind the old prince's words, a message of warning very like that given him on his wedding day by his stepfather. It would be many years before the import of such wisdom was to come clear to him. By then there would be little time left.

The millions of dollars raised by the American Red Cross for earthquake relief motivated the closeness that existed between the United States and Japan in the period following the calamity. But it was a kinship born of disaster and the romance didn't last long. The California Exclusion League was in the forefront as Congress formulated sweeping revisions to U.S. immigration policy in 1924. As a result of incomprehensible ineptitude, *all* Japanese were excluded by the new law. When President Coolidge signed the bill into law, to take effect in 1925, the Japanese press protested vociferously. An unthinking American government, with its head buried deep in the sand of protective discrimination, had slapped the face of the strongest, most easily affronted nation in the Pacific. The kinship born of disaster would crumble to create calamity that would far overshadow the results of a mere earthquake.

Twenty-eight

In the middle of Christmas morning, 1926, a speeding motorcade with lights flashing and sirens howling roared up to the gates of the Imperial Palace and hurried on through the grounds to the small forest where the Imperial Family shrine stood. Doors to the gleaming black limousines opened immediately, disgorging dignitaries in formal attire. From the third vehicle, with two royal princes and two other nobles in attendance, the bespectacled and studious-looking Crown Prince Hirohito moved briskly to the shrine. Entering alone, the twenty-six-year-old regent began the ritual that would proclaim him as Emperor to all the spirits of the realm. It would be a year before the official crowning in the ancient capital of Kyoto, but for the worshipful Japanese, Nippon had its new spiritual leader. Calendars would immediately proclaim that a new year had commenced—Showa One. Hirohito had carefully picked Showa—Peace Made Manifest—as the name of his reign. The capitals of the world would withhold judgment on that selection until its meaning was justified and truly manifest. And more than one seasoned diplomat caught himself taking a deep breath and wondering what path Nippon would follow under the grandson of the Meiji.

Having heard an hour earlier while in the office of the inspector general of military education that the Emperor had just passed away, Lieutenant Colonel Hideki Tojo knew what the motorcade implied as it roared past him at the steps to the War Ministry building. But he had no idea it would make him modern Japan's shogun, nor that eventually it would lead him to the gallows.

The venerable Prince Saionji received the word in his villa at Okitsu. By prior arrangement, he was having nothing to do with the ceremonies. Walking in his superb garden, he paused to look at an Aralia japonica bush and pondered again the possibilities the Showa reign would face. At this point, Hirohito was as well prepared as any of his predecessors. And part of that preparation carried the Saionji stamp. Other aspects of the new Emperor's makeup were a keen military awareness and a gentle scientific curiosity. He was certain about one thing—Hirohito would be more than a mere deity. Now, if only he had the perception to avoid the jingoism and saber-rattlers. . . .

Since it was Saturday and the beginning of the New Year season vacation from the Army Staff College, Hiroshi was home in Kazumi that morning. It was exactly one year since his promotion to captain, a fact that mattered not at all to his willful and precocious little Sachi. Laughing gaily as she ran around the study trying to entice him into a game of tag, she stopped and made a face when the phone rang just before ten.

It was from a prince who was one of his classmates, informing him of the death of the Taisho. With Sachi following him around as if she sensed the gravity of the moment, he paced around the study. There would be little change in his life under the new Son of Heaven, at least not in the near future. After all, the Taisho had been essentially dead for years. No—he would continue as a student at the Staff College, most probably graduate near the top of his class, then be posted to a foreign attaché job. Since he was so proficient in English, London was a strong possibility, but Berlin was perhaps more realistic.

He wondered what Saionji was doing. Had he made specific plans for the young Emperor, would he sit back and depend on his influence to hold, or take on a stronger role as the manipulator?

Twice he had been contacted by the prince—once by note to inquire about the Kwantung Army in Manchuria, and once to ask a question about the Chinese Kuomintang's apparent strongman, Chiang Kai-shek. Both times, he had carefully cleared release of the classified information through his superior, and in the last case presented it in person verbally during lunch with the *genro* at his villa on the seashore. He was proud of not letting the prince's considerable charm sway his decision to remain free of political intrigues.

He had told the women and now looked up as Suiko brought a tray of green tea into the study. "What do you think will mark the age of Showa?" she asked in her usual direct manner. "Will Nippon begin to assert herself, take her noble place of power?"

Hiroshi nodded pleasantly. "I believe those militarists close to the palace will become more aggressive. From what I've been able to deduce, I doubt that His Imperial Highness will condone any strategic rashness, but clever men have their ways when they are intimate with the top."

Suiko gave him a quizzical look as she served his tea. "Are you saying we'll finally start marching some of these days?"

Hiroshi nodded solemnly. "We'll march."

Two nights later on an isolated farm twenty-eight miles east of Stockton, Mario had just wished Otto a happy New Year and watched him drive away. Turning back into the old isolated barn, he nodded with satisfaction as he surveyed his hidden winery. The three huge vats in the middle of the large floor of the barn were in different stages of fermentation. All had Zinfandel working in them, utilizing the dark red skins that gave the wine the rich color that marked its popularity in Colorado and the Portland area.

With two locations going full tilt, he was making a small fortune—enough to make his fruit-shipping business with Noboru and the Chicago crowd a joke. But he needed it as a front, at least until he made his move. He figured to go back to Chicago in late January and make his demands. After all, hadn't he put the operation together without their consent—and then gone to them at Thanksgiving and handed over 25 percent of his profits for the past year? Why they oughta give him—

"Put your hands over your head!"

Mario jerked around at the harsh shout. Three men, two of them pointing shotguns at him, were moving forward from the doorway. The one in the middle, in the dark suit, waved his pistol as he snarled, "United States Treasury Department, Scagnelli. You're under arrest for violation of the Volstead Act."

* * *

"Lockett says he can get me off with two years and a two-grand fine. But I only have to serve about ten months, maybe a year."

Noboru looked up from his kitchen table at The Other Cheek. They were alone and he was uncomfortable about what was coming. "You're lucky, Mario," he said quietly. "I hear they're going to stiffen the penalties."

The Chicagoan waved his huge slab of a hand. "Aw hell, they're all crooked at the top, so what's the difference? I could probably have bought my way out right at the barn if I had waved enough paper in that bastard's face."

Noboru sipped his coffee. "Yeah, and it might have gotten you ten more years. You ever think of that?"

Mario grinned. "Yeah, just before I made the offer."

Noboru snorted. He wished his friend would get it over with.

Mario lit a cigarette and inhaled deeply, watching the smoke rise toward the electric light fixture. He hated to do it, but it was the only way. And besides, he growled to himself, what are friends for? Wouldn't he do it in a minute if things were reversed? He looked Noboru defiantly in the eye. "Will you keep the bootlegging business going for me while I'm away?" he asked gruffly.

Noboru held his gaze, then angrily got to his feet. "You know what you're asking me, don't you?" he said tightly.

Mario stared at his cigarette. "Yeah, I know," he replied quietly. "But all I want is to keep the new place producing enough to get one shipment a month to Denver and Oregon. Otto will take care of everything but the money. You don't even have to go near the place—not once!"

It was unfair! Noboru shouted to himself. There was just too much at stake. He was a leading contractor now, with a name as important as his father's. And a lot of people depended on him—the huge family that was his labor force. And he was doing well—hadn't he netted almost twenty thousands dollars in the past year? And there was still the matter of his citizenship; Lockett said it was far from dead, that there was a former Japanese American sergeant major named Tokie Slocum who had pledged his life to getting a reversal. Any kind of a prison record could be the end of his chances there.

Mario's dark eyes were pleading. "All you have to do is make a trip to each destination once a month to collect. Then meet Otto some place safe and give him the month's operating money. That's all there is to it, buddy."

Noboru shoved a cigarette in his mouth, struck a match, and puffed hard. He barely tasted it. Just one little slip-up, that's all it would take. Just one, and he'd be right there in prison beside the very friend who was asking him to stick his damned neck out! "Those Treasury men aren't stupid," he said evenly. "They know we've been in business together, and they'll see me supervising your shipping operation. Why don't your Chicago people send someone out? It's their money too."

"No dice. The Feds would be all over them like flies."

"Then shut down. It just isn't worth it."

Mario Scagnelli jerked to his feet, his eyes blazing. "Look—we been all over that! I didn't want to say it—but if it weren't for me, you'd still be a one-crew picking operation, buddy!" He scowled hotly into his friend's troubled expression. "Now I'm asking you—you gonna do it or not?"

Noboru had known all along—he didn't even know why he had argued. There just wasn't any way out. His eyes glittered momentarily before he shrugged, then managed a short smile. "How else can I keep your family out of the poorhouse?"

The trial was handled swiftly and Lockett was right—two years and a two-thousand-dollar fine. Mario started serving time in the federal prison in Atlanta immediately. And three weeks later, Noboru started breaking the law of the land he so much wanted to belong to. He was extremely careful about collecting and disbursing the money—setting up meetings as cleverly as possible. Once in April, he thought he was followed to Portland. But he quickly caught a train to Seattle and spent the night in that city's Japan Town. He never saw the man again. He thought he was tailed to Denver a month later, but he merely changed the meeting place with the payoff man from the Androtti mob.

He met Otto in a different place each month; once in Stockton, once in Sacramento, in Walnut Grove, and the rest of the time on different trains. As far as he knew, the transfer of the money went undetected, but that wasn't his only problem. In early June, he stopped by Mario's office in the back of a building on Main Street to complete some paperwork relating to the shipping business. Two burly men in dark, double-breasted suits were waiting in a parked car in the alley. It was just after dusk.

"Hey, Slant," the taller one in the wide-brim hat said menacingly as Noboru turned the key in the lock. "We got a message for your buddy in Atlanta."

Noboru inhaled quietly as they swung out of the car. He knew something like this had to happen sooner or later!

"Yeah," the taller one continued, "tell your buddy to shut down his operation like we told him, or he might come out of the slammer feet first."

The shorter one moved closer, glaring into Noboru's face. "Yeah," he snarled, "and lots of other people can get hurt, too." He jabbed a forefinger into Noboru's chest. "Startin' with you, yellow-belly!"

Noboru's eyes hardened, but he held his temper. "I don't know what you're—"

The taller one slammed a fist into his stomach, doubling him over. "Just send the message!"

By the time Noboru recovered his breath, their car was gone.

The next day he wrote to Mario and reported their visit. Three weeks later, the Chicagoan's terse reply arrived: "They're bluffing. Practice your old man's *gambari*."

Noboru doubled his stealth, but never quit sweating it out.

Twenty-nine

"So I'm gonna interview a real live Japanese Army officer, huh?"

Sataro nodded, swishing some of the Baldwin office bourbon around in his glass. He still couldn't believe the marvelous news that Hiroshi's letter had brought:

> "Finished second in my class at the Staff College . . .
> Going to Europe as attaché for one or more years . . . Will
> cross the United States as an observer for sixty days,
> visiting military installations and major cities, including
> Lodi, where I will visit my beloved family. . . ."

"You suppose he'll tell me the truth about what's going on over there?" Cedric asked. "Goddamn, I could really scoop the *Chronicle* if he'd give me an inside story on those supposed war plans. Hey, old man, you think he's on some kind of a spy mission?"

Cedric still had the ability to make Sataro angry, and he was using it now. "My proud son will be honoring his father with a visit," he replied stiffly. "And his tour of this country is educational, not something deceitful. Nippon has been sending her sons out like this since the Meiji was a boy. You should know that!"

Cedric chuckled. "Take it easy. I'll show him every respect."

Sataro shook his head and went back to the whiskey. The son he hadn't seen since that long-ago day in Hiroshima had recently turned thirty. He saw the picture of the small boy holding his hand and walking into the setting sun, the scene that had burned in his memory, and pricked at his conscience all this time. And now a crusty editor was promising to be respectful to that boy. . . . Where had it all gone? The time, the dream—and only that little boy was doing his part.

Was he finally going to see him? Or would another cruel twist of fate jerk yet one more reunion away? "I just don't know what to tell him about my diminished means," he said quietly. There certainly wasn't any way to hide it.

"Tell him the goddamn truth," Cedric snorted. "You've got more to be proud of than any rich rice merchant in the world."

Still as handsome and trim as he had been ten years earlier, Sataro had no trouble fitting into one of the expensive suits he had salvaged from his financial crash. And the exact cut or width of a lapel no longer meant anything to him. He lowered the gray fedora and adjusted the formal wingtip collar as he watched the *Mikoto-Maru* sitting under slack steam as it was secured to the dock. It was a warm bright early September day. What a contrast, he thought, seeing the freshly painted colors of the clean ship stand out against the clear azure sky as white gulls swooped noisily around its fantail.

Yes, what a contrast the big clean ship was to the drab little freighter that had landed just a few berths away twenty years earlier. He looked from where he stood near the descending gangplank, slightly apart from others meeting the ship, toward the streetcar stop and saw that little had changed there. No more horses in front of the cars, but the same pastel colors surrounded them. He drew himself even more erect as he turned back to the ship and saw the debarkation was about to begin. Already his breath was getting jerky.

Hiroshi had stated that he'd be carrying a leather diplomatic pouch for the consul and would be immune from a customs delay.

Sataro stretched his neck, trying to free it from his sticky collar. It wasn't hot, so he shouldn't be perspiring. He pulled out a handkerchief and dabbed at his brow. His hand was shaking. All these years . . . twenty years of desertion, of not being there when his fine neglected son might have needed him. Twenty years. Would it be all right? Anyone could be polite in a letter. . . .

He felt a trickle of water run down the middle of his back. He had looked at Hiroshi's picture—taken when he had been promoted to captain—for hours on end. Every detail of his handsome features were burned into his memory. But would he recognize him in civilian clothes? Why couldn't he have worn the uniform that meant so very much to his father? He stilled his hand by busying it with the handkerchief again. How glorious it would have been—to see him for the first time as a man in the Emperor's proud uniform. His future general, one half of the dream. Oh, yes, he hadn't given up yet. . . .

There! The tall young man in the panama hat and black suit! He was certain! Automatically his hand came up to wave, but he caught it and returned it to his side. The head of the House of Hoshi had to restrain himself! He stared as the strong face began to descend the steps toward the dock. Broad shoulders, alert eyes, a firm jaw—it was him! But the image was beginning to swim . . . how could this happen to him— He blinked back the moistness as Hiroshi smiled and hurried toward him. His son.

Hiroshi's week-long visit to Lodi evoked different feelings in different people. Sataro was so enthusiastic he could hardly sleep at night, and Miyuki so adored him immediately that she dreamed of ways to please him. Only at The Other Cheek was an edge of reservation apparent to anyone who knew Noboru well. The stay was an abrupt departure from anything Hiroshi had seen. He had traveled extensively in the Orient, but hadn't been anywhere with such space among the *hakujin*. And what a difference in people. He sensed it even in his own family and those close to it. While their politeness and consideration reminded him strongly of home, there was a vibrance, confidence, and casualness that was refreshing. Actually—he realized with a touch of guilt—most of what was American appealed to him immediately.

Tojo had spoken of individual selfishness and the lack of discipline he saw in America, but after all, Tojo had only recently broken off a dazzling infatuation with the Prussians when he passed through. What Hiroshi felt in this prosperous state that was roughly the same size as all of Japan, was a deep-seated sense of power, an almost perceptible rumble of something that could break out at any time and roar at the world. And he had not seen her great industrial cities yet. He must keep careful notes.

For Captain Hiroshi Hoshi *was* a spy. He had undergone an intensified orientation during the month preceding departure. France, Germany, Britain, and Italy were covered in as much depth as the United States—customs, military, industrial centers, politics, everything Hiroshi was to observe and report on. He was to record every single impression he garnered. They wanted all of it back in Strategic Analysis—every grain of information that might produce intelligence. And they were particularly interested in the California Japanese.

Hiroshi was also adept at speaking to groups and extricating himself from dangerous ground when being questioned. The first test in this vein came when Cedric Baldwin questioned him closely for an in-depth *Gazette* feature. The second came the next night when he spoke to the largest meeting of the Hiroshima *kenjinkai* that his father could remember. Japan Town's street was full and attentive as he spoke of how Nippon had to remain in Manchuria and keep Korea as buffers to the Soviets and the growing communist danger in China. He then launched into a description of the palace compound and some of its routines— always an exciting subject for laborers who had never been to Tokyo and had been in America since the Son of Heaven was a small boy.

Sleeping in an unassuming room at the store, he was up and going through his martial arts exercises by the time his father awakened each morning. Several times, they were off to the river with fishing poles in hand before the sun cleared the Sierra Nevada hill mask off to the east. To Sataro's questions, Hiroshi was less artful, and at times totally frank. "Don't you think the army might be getting too much power?" Sataro asked him on the fourth morning.

Hiroshi shifted the fishing pole to his left hand, pointing to his breast with his right. *"Koko ga sabishii,"* he replied quietly. "There are no medals. It's been a long time since there was a real war for our army, Father. Even Colonel Tojo didn't see live combat with Russia. It's difficult to explain, but when an army lives on such a strict diet of glory, it has to be fed now and then.''

Sataro nodded, sucking his pipe and fingering the scar on his cheek. There wasв't any shortage of combat when *he* was in the war, he snorted to himself. And he could understand about professional military men wanting medals, but— ''That isn't what I'm talking about. I'm concerned that the country will have to follow the whims of military leaders, whether they're logical or not.''

Hiroshi hid his frown. This was the kind of dangerous talk that someday would not be permitted in Japan. He certainly didn't like hearing it from his own father. They just didn't understand that only a powerful Nippon could attain its justifiable goals. ''It's always difficult for civilians to understand, Father,'' he replied smoothly.

Sataro bit down on his pipe stem. He read four major Japanese newspapers and several periodicals. If anything, he was better informed and capable of understanding than the average citizen at home. Japan was getting ready to put on her helmet. ''But won't it lead to wars the people don't want?'' he asked softly.

Hiroshi sighed. ''Possibly. But except for the beginnings when impetuosity runs rampant and patriotism shrieks in wild passion . . . do the people ever really *want* war?''

Sataro turned, looking directly into his son's eyes. ''How about you?'' he asked quietly. ''Do you want it?''

Hiroshi stood, stretching and lighting a cigarette. ''Yes,'' he replied slowly. ''Yes, I do, Father. There is unbelievable greatness ahead for the empire—world leadership. But it won't come without a struggle. To achieve this greatness, I want whatever is necessary . . . and that is war.''

Sataro could see his son's eyes were unfocused, staring west and glowing with the light of fanaticism. Hiroshi went on, telling him how the young officers were being inculcated with the *kokutai* principle—the semi-mystical values of nationalism that bound them to their Bushido and the Throne. And he told of being converted from the popular Shinto worship to a form of Buddhism called Nichirenism—an approach that was highly nationalistic, somewhat apocalyptic, and had as its goal a single mission that embraced all the people of the world from its heart in Japan.

Sataro felt himself caught up in his son's missionary zeal, sensed the allure, the powerful tug of jingoism that placed the empire in the center of the universe. It was enchanting, as hypnotic as a swaying cobra. It was more than Nichirenism or Shintoism, it was the all-devouring chant of nationalism that could be irresistible in powerful doses. And he understood it for what it was. It was the Englishman, Kipling, in a kimono; it could be the Kaiser.

And he wanted to tell this brilliant, impassioned son of his.

But he couldn't. Not now, not yet.

Noboru had no such compunctions about his brother's opinions, but out of respect to his father and to the custom of politeness afforded any visitor, he kept his silence at the meals and other occasions when he was thrown into Hiroshi's presence during that week. Even during the evening when he had to be the host, he managed to hold his tongue. But it made him extremely uncomfortable. In his eyes—and he knew it could be a holdover of petty jealousy—Hiroshi was the gifted but pampered product of yet another breed of samurai, the tool of yet a new form of shogun eager to endanger the Orient—and maybe the world.

He arose early on the last morning of his brother's stay, and went out into the rows of now mature Tokay trunks. Smoking his first cigarette of the day and walking slowly through the still, dew-covered orchard, he was startled to see Hiroshi spring out in front of him in a judo stance. For an instant, he wanted to respond, but he merely sighed and asked, "What brings you here at this hour, honorable brother?" He hoped the sarcasm was apparent.

Hiroshi relaxed, producing a grin. "I just wanted to talk to you alone, honorable elder brother." He hadn't missed an iota of Noboru's thinly veiled antagonism throughout the stay, and he owed it to his own honor to say what had been troubling him.

Noboru shrugged, dragging deeply on the cigarette. "We have freedom of speech in America," he said coolly.

Hiroshi nodded, standing spread-legged and facing his brother from a few feet away. An early ray of sunlight struck his face as he replied, "So I've heard. But if that's the case, why don't we go have breakfast in Lodi's best restaurant so you can tell me about it? I know we won't be served, and will most probably be forcibly removed from the premises, but will they afford us free speech first?" He laughed as he shifted his weight from one foot to the other. "Or why don't you exercise your right of free speech to tell me why you haven't become a citizen here, *Sergeant* Hoshi?"

The stark fact of what he was saying struck Noboru like the sharp lash of a whip. He almost recoiled. "There are problems yet to be solved," he replied quietly, controlling his urge to lash back.

Hiroshi couldn't stop now, the words had been coiled up inside him for too long. "If you wish to continue in your treason, I can only label you for what you are," he said coldly. "But why do you encourage others to remain and be a part of this hideous lie they call a democracy? Why do you use your hold over our father to keep him here as a lowly storekeeper, when he could be a prosperous leader in Japan? Why, Noboru? Tell me what selfish blindness makes you do this."

Noboru stared at his brother, not believing what he'd heard, boiling inside. He dropped the cigarette to the ground, grinding it out with his heel, and wordlessly strode back toward the barn. Hiroshi followed. Now that he had commenced he couldn't stop. "You're all living a lie, brother. Stop now, while everyone is young and healthy enough to return and enjoy Nippon's coming glory." He followed hurriedly as Noboru entered the barn and stopped in its center.

Whirling, Noboru glared at him through glittering eyes. His voice was low as he pointed to the stone floor and said, "Do you know what's under this?"

Hiroshi shrugged, staring at the stones his father had so meticulously fitted together twenty years earlier.

Noboru didn't blink as he continued to point. Finally, he said, "When your father, the man you call a lowly storekeeper, first came here so many years ago, he had a dream and the spirit to accomplish it. And what's under this floor is part of it."

Hiroshi continued staring at the stone floor, wondering when his foolish brother would get to the point.

"This floor covers the first piece of land he acquired, and it still belongs to the House of Hoshi." Noboru's anger made his mouth dry. His voice was harsh as he continued. "From this floor that he laid himself, he went on to become one of the most successful Japanese men ever to come to America. And as far as I'm concerned, he still is. Now you take your stories of glory, Captain, and tell them to someone else. I have no doubt that you will be a great general some day, and he'll be proud of you. But I want no part of it."

Hiroshi's cheeks stung with sudden anger, but his brother was already striding past him, not even acknowledging his presence as he left the barn.

It was not until Mario came out of prison in early February that Noboru found out he had made a deal to keep the competitors off their backs. "But now," the Chicagoan told him emphatically, "the payoff is over." It mattered little to Noboru, for now he could get out of the whole worrisome mess. His business was doing well and there were good times in America, Japan, and around the world. *No* illegal activity was necessary.

August 25 was little Joey's fourth birthday. Joseph Sataro Hoshi had followed close on the heels of his older brother, with merely eleven months separating them in age. Sataro was beaming proudly at the boy's birthday party, for not only had he received a neatly brushed note from his beloved little Sachi, but a letter had also arrived from the busy Hiroshi:

Stuttgart, Germany
July 24, 1928

My Honorable Father,

Thank you for your letter of May 21, which finally caught up with me at our embassy in Berlin. My European tour continues with Stockholm next. In Italy, I attended a reception for Benito Mussolini and met him. He has a strong following and, I believe, definite tastes for African expansion.

France and Britain are tidy and frugal in peacetime. To the east, the Russian Bear rumbles in its communism. This is Nippon's eternal enemy. I find it hard to believe that I am so far from home and yet so close to the Soviet's other border. How can she be so huge?

I just completed a week's stay in Munich, where I became intrigued by the political fervor. An energetic party is the National Socialistic German Workers led by a fanatic with a compelling hold over his followers. His name is Adolf Hitler and his intents are spelled out in a book he wrote in Landsberg Prison. It is entitled *Mein Kampf* and makes some daring propositions.

My tour will end after Scandinavia. I will return to Tokyo, assigned to the First Infantry Regiment. Colonel Tojo is in command and most probably will be a stern taskmaster. After all this staff duty, I relish the thought of being back with troops where the true spirit is.

Suiko joined me on the French Riviera in early May and she has thoroughly enjoyed our journeys. But she is getting anxious to be back with the children and her job as vice president of the Women's Patriotic Association.

> Your Respectful Son,
> Hiroshi

In October 1929 the New York stock market collapsed, triggering a severe worldwide depression. In spring 1930, a naval conference was held in London to determine allowances for various types of ships Britain, the United States, and Japan would be permitted. But the restrictions were a farce—Japan's shipbuilders continued secretly to build more of the new aircraft carriers and heavy cruisers that were more like pocket battleships. In China, Chiang Kai-shek was busy consolidating his forces in the KMT—the Kuomintang Party—and struggling to get along with his adversaries. And in Manchuria, a warlord known as the Young Marshal remained aligned with Chiang and deployed his raw militia against the threat of a rumored Japanese adventure from Kwantung. On September 19, 1931—one month to the day after Hiroshi was promoted to major—a masterfully contrived "attack" against Japanese troops provided the excuse for the Kwantung Army to make its long-awaited move and spring into action. When the smoke cleared, Japanese forces held Mukden and would soon create a new Nipponese puppet state from Manchuria. It would be called Manchukuo and would be a springboard for more ambitious ventures into China by the imperialistic planners in Tokyo. To much of the world, what would be called the Manchurian Incident in some quarters was little more than another Oriental squabble. To the carefully watching Western nations with huge investments in the western Pacific and Indochina, it was more. Their colonial empires could be at stake. And a young military genius by the name of Ishiwara was developing his Final War thesis. But all that mattered to most of the California Japanese was survival in the hard times.

Thirty

"Things are so bad I'm afraid to walk into my own bank," Noboru said with a shake of his head as he stepped down from the truck. "They're liable to close up while I'm in there."

"If you'd been smart, you'd have listened to me years ago," Mario admonished, walking around the front bumper. "Then, instead of having a couple hundred people to worry about feeding, you'd be rich and carefree like me." He looked around the side of the large red barn that served as his newest bootleg winery, wondering who the strange yellow Buick belonged to. "Even if they do repeal Prohibition next year, it won't hurt. Hell, I made my pile and I won't ever have any worries."

Noboru nodded, thinking his friend just might be right. Mario had to be worth a fortune, and who cared how he made it? Hell, everyone drank. Still, with the strong possibility of veteran's citizenship getting closer, a clean slate was all the more important. He had dreamed of standing up in front of that bright flag and being sworn in so long it was reality . . . and he was even wearing his old uniform! He pointed at the big yellow sedan. "Your winemaker running around in limousines these days?"

Mario frowned as he pulled open the small door to the barn. "That's not Otto's car."

"No, it ain't!" a burly man in a dark blue pin-striped suit barked as he sprang out into the bright sunlight. He was the same gangster who had come to the old bootleg site when Mario was in prison—the same one who had attacked Noboru. And he held a Thompson submachine gun in his hands. "Come on in, Scagnelli. And bring your yellow-belly buddy with you."

Noboru tensed as Mario snarled, "What the hell's going on?"

The other gangster, the shorter one, stepped around the corner of the barn waving a big .45 automatic. "Inside and shut up, you bastard," he snapped. "And hurry up!"

The interior of the barn was darker but there was no mistaking the lifeless body of Otto sitting grotesquely propped up against the larger vat.

"You sons of bitches!" Mario shouted, swinging wildly at the closest one.

The butt of the machine gun caught him alongside the head, smashing him to his knees. Noboru pushed forward, but the short one swung his pistol up. The roar of the .45 was deafening, the blast blinding. Noboru was thrown backward as the huge slug tore off part of his ear. He blinked, barely able to see as Mario let out a wild roar and hurled himself at the man with the Thompson. He stared, horrified, blood streaming down his neck, as the submachine gun blasted and blazed at Mario's charging, bull-like form. His old friend jerked to a stop, convulsively, the rage dying on his lips.

It seemed that time froze for Noboru as he saw Mario's thickset body crash to the barn floor. And suddenly he flashed back to a vivid picture of his friend grinning in the bright sunshine of Fifth Avenue as a proud regimental band played "Gary Owen" while it marched briskly down the broad boulevard. He could almost hear the music. The shiny instruments glinted, the festive crowd cheered its encouragement! Mario clapped him on the back, again grinning broadly, saying something humorous.

Vaguely, he saw the little man with the big automatic pistol moving toward him, waving its ugly black snout. There were words spilling out of his twisted lips. . . . "You guys just wouldn't listen, would you?"

And suddenly he saw Haru in her wedding finery—wide-eyed, wistful, trusting as she held up the third cup . . . not even guessing how she repelled him . . . and he saw her coming to him that first night he realized he loved her, gentle, desirous in the soft light of their bedroom . . . his beautiful, gentle Haru. *God, how he loved her!*

The pistol came up, pointing at his face.

His fine sons . . . his noble father. He saw the handsome face as it stared into the smoking ashes of his hotel—God, how he wanted to reach out and touch his strong hand!

This was outrageous!

His ears rang, the side of his head burned. He smelled incense and heard the notes of a *samisen*. Whittling a toy soldier on the deck of a shadowy ship's fantail. In the midst of salty sea spray with his noble father . . . the great and powerful father who defeated the terrible cowboy as a small son watched in the Wellington Saloon. He could see it now, hear the shouts of the smelly, excited men. . . .

The racketeer's eyes glittered over the oblong snout of the pistol.

How could anything so totally insane be happening? This grotesque nightmare had nothing to do with the proud House of Hoshi—no, nor the huge family he'd adopted. There was so much to be done. . . .

They couldn't do this to him!

He lunged forward as the pistol exploded in his face.

Eighteen minutes later, Mario dragged himself over to Noboru's prostrate form. He forced one look, then with a wrenching sob managed to throw an arm over his best friend's lifeless form. OH GOD! he screamed to himself, WHAT HAVE I DONE? And the salty tears slid down to join the blood trickling from the side of his mouth.

It was the largest Japanese funeral in the history of the Valley, with people coming from as far away as Marysville. Counting buggies, wagons, and bicycles, there were over a hundred vehicles parked around the Lodi cemetery by the time the graveside service began. At 2:50 the religious part was over and the military honor guard from a Stockton National Guard unit raised its rifles to fire the ritual salute. A few feet away, poised over the open grave, a flag-draped casket awaited its interment. The beautiful colors were stark in the bright sunlight, contrasting the white against the vivid reds and deep blue. Almost glaring.

The family was grouped on the other side of the grave, touching each other at moments, its members lost in individual grief. A rigid, unseeing Sataro held the elbow of the erect Haru as the rifle volleys rang out, splitting the blanket of silence. As the last shots faded away, the flag detail stepped forward to fold the colors. In front of Miyuki, blinking back tears of pain and confusion, Billy threw off Joey's clinging grip and thrust his stubborn chin forward. Like the jibes he heard once in a while at school, this terrible thing was connected with the bad things the *hakujin* did to them. *They* killed him!

Haru watched the soldier's hands as he folded the bright red and white stripes, baring the somber gray coffin. That was what Noboru wanted, that flag. She stared, remembering not the re-paired face that was inside, but the hawklike handsomeness of the young man she had been destined for since she could first recall . . . the wonderful man she thought she could never keep. It was all so wrong, that terrible Mario always using him like that. . . . She reached for Sataro's hand, trying to push away the suffocating pain, stifle the disrupting sob that was overwhelming her.

They had reached the blue and white section, the stars. . . .

Sataro still didn't believe it. It reminded him of his heart attack—impossible, crippling. The noble, handsome son who was so much a part of his great dream, the inheritor of the House of Hoshi, the marvelous boy he had shared so much with . . . torn a mother from—that pained as much as anything, remembering the brave young son hiding his hurt when she was forced away. The son whose compelling desire for America he couldn't fully understand, yet in a way shared . . . his merchant prince. Was it retribution? Did the Gorotsuki he had murdered to save his son reach out from the grave and finally destroy him? His merchant prince . . .

As the young officer handed the triangular-shaped flag to Haru, Sataro tightened his grip on her arm and didn't even try to stop the tears that slipped down his cheeks. There was the sound from the bugle; mournful, the chilling notes his dead son had once said were the most stirring of any ever played. He felt Miyuki's touch. It was over. Everything he'd . . . it was all blown away in those fading tones from that single bugle.

*   *   *

They knelt side by side at the altar of the Yasukuni Shrine to the war dead. There seemed no more appropriate place to either of them—the mother and brother who felt an overriding guilt in their grief. Hiroshi couldn't push away their final quarrel in California, knowing it was his fault. And he didn't know why he had to be so arrogant with a brother whose memory he had so fondly clung to during all those growing years. What wonderful things they might have shared had he only followed the way of wisdom and reached out in warmth. . . . And now it was too late. And what of his father? How he must grieve, how this terrible event must have wounded him . . . his dream. But that dream wasn't totally dead. Now, more than ever, he had to earn a general's stars, had to present them to his father. Yes, that would help make it up. . . .

Itoko stared at the carved chrysanthemum in the teakwood altar a few feet away from her face. *He* had caused this, just as surely as *they* had committed the horrible act. Her hated husband and the despised *hakujin* had conspired from the very beginning so long ago to steal her beloved firstborn, and now it was done . . . done, final . . . she'd never see him again. How often she'd planned to do so much more for him . . . why even her proposal for him to bring his whole family over the next year for a visit—his darling wife and the grandsons she'd never met. What a rich visit it was to have been. They hadn't had the time during his hurried wedding visit, but next year, just next year, she would have spirited him off to the mountains and have had him all to herself for days. . . .

The tears slipped down to her black kimono, making her wish she had worn western attire so she could hide behind a dark veil. Yes, they would have had *days* together to walk in the woods and hills, perhaps sit by a quiet stream where she could pour out her love for him . . . convince him that she really hadn't deserted him, that he mattered as much to her as anything in her entire life. Yes, she could see them hand-in-hand . . . and then she could see him playing catch with that first baseball glove in the street in—in that terrible place where he was killed.

The sobs racked her as she lost control. Turning into Hiroshi's chest, she wanted to scream that it wasn't her fault, but all she saw was the sleeping face of a beautiful boy as she leaned down to kiss him good-bye in his tiny bedroom in a far-off place.

Hiroshi's wire converted to just over one thousand dollars. Noboru's life insurance policy was nearly four thousand dollars after paying back the loans he had taken out against it to keep his oldest employees in rice. Haru could make it for a few years by continuing in her austere ways, and her in-laws were just down the road, just as Kimi and Yoshi were right next door to help in any way. A telegram from her parents urged her to return to Miyajima, but she firmly rejected the idea. Her sons' birthright was The Other Cheek and her beloved Noboru had built the house with his own hands. Besides, there was the matter of the citizenship, *his* precious citizenship.

The weeks passed slowly for Sataro. After a few days of staring into nothing at the store, he busied himself in the vineyards with Yoshi and tried to find reason in his son's useless death. And each night, he spent an hour speaking Japanese with his grandsons before returning to Miyuki's gentle solace. Exactly a month after the funeral, Noboru's foreman came to him asking if there was anything to be done for the remaining crews. After digging into his savings for a few rice dollars, he watched the man ride away on his bicycle thinking there must be *something* that could be done with good hard-working men who were almost artists with the ground.

The bull-like Mario lingered in the twilight of life and death for ten days following extensive surgery and the removal of all but one single bullet near his spine. He had one physical effect from the tragedy—he would never walk again. The mental receipt was a sense of terrible guilt and loss over Noboru. Seven weeks after the ambush a grave Sataro came to see him in his bedroom in the large white house he had bought only a few months earlier. Sataro quickly reassured the Chicagoan that there was no bitterness, then launched into the purpose of his visit. "You want to know what you can do for the family, Mario? I'll tell you. His *big* family—his workers—are without employment and needy. And there is a solution, a way for you to help them and make up for any wrongdoing that may be on your conscience." He paused as the big man leaned forward from his cranked-up hospital bed with a glint of unmasked interest.

"There are dozens of farms here in the Valley rotting after foreclosure. Just sitting there. Now, I've been talking to Noboru's foreman and he assures me we can keep the weeds away and a number of crops under cultivation for a minimum of money, enough to keep food on the workers' tables and minor supplies."

Mario lit a cigar, saying nothing. This could be a way to make some of it up.

Sataro clasped his hands to control his intensity. "You know what, Mario? Those damned bankers can't operate those fore-closed farms and no one has any money to buy them. . . . Now suppose someone came along and said, "See here, Mr. Banker, I'll give you ten dollars down and so much a month for those farms. And I've got a good labor contractor who'll keep the farms in good shape in case I default. I pay him and your collateral stays productive. Your bank doesn't go broke and I get some good farmland for investing the money."

Mario nodded, exhaling a big cloud of smoke. "How much money you talking about?"

"I'm not sure. Maybe a hundred dollars a month per farm, and that would include total upkeep and mortgage payments. Ten farms would cost twelve thousand a year, more or less. Twenty— double that."

"You think big."

Sataro stared down coolly. "I always have."

"What do you get out of it?"

"Half interest in all the properties and their profits when these hard times slack off."

Mario blew out more smoke. "That's a lot for not putting up any front money."

"It can't be done without an *oyakata*."

"Japs can't own land."

"I have two grandsons who are American citizens, remember?"

Mario studied the older man. He was Noboru's father and perhaps the most respected Japanese in the Valley. And not only did he owe the Hoshis, he needed some goddamn interest in *something*. Hell, he might even wind up as a land baron . . . yeah, *Don* Mario. Yeah, he decided, why not look into it? "How soon can we get started?" he asked.

Sataro reached inside his jacket for a small notebook. "I have a list of prospects right here—all with fine land and empty, waiting for good caretakers to move in. Herb Lockett has some papers drawn up and will be our agent with the banks. He'll set up a corporation right away."

Mario nodded. "Okay, Mr. Hoshi. Send him over to see me."

As Sataro left the house, he felt buoyant for the first time since before the tragedy. Not only was he going to be useful and energetic again, but maybe, just maybe, part of his dream could still be accomplished. After all, he thought brightly, who was more capable of handling the big gamble? Maybe he'd even have his brother raise some money in Hiroshima to buy some more on his own—those repossessed farms were lying out there like gold nuggets waiting to be panned! Yes, the old entrepreneurial juices were already gushing. Why, thirty farms in just a few years could be worth a fortune. Forty—

Sataro poured himself into the farming operation, leaving the store completely to Miyuki and Haru, who often helped. That income combined with the rental rooms, bar and card game proceeds provided enough money for the Hoshi needs. The newspaper broke even. Both the Democratic and Republican parties campaigned on Prohibition repeal platforms and when Franklin Delano Roosevelt took office in January, the changeover began. Grape growers again had a legal wine market and financial relief for them was in sight. Under Yoshi's loving care, the vineyards of The Other Cheek would soon provide Haru with a secure living.

At ten, Billy Hoshi was the only internal problem in the family. Even before his father's death he had been a highly strung child, temperamental and prone to get into trouble. Following the tragedy, his conduct grew even worse and was marked by frequent outbursts against his white peers. He got into fights at school and was manageable at home only when Haru exerted her utmost patience, or his grandfather meted out discipline. And every time he needed an excuse, he fell back on his father's murder. And whenever he wanted comfort or someone to hear his complaints, Miyuki's warm heart, blind love, and welcome arms awaited. On one occasion this prompted one of the most serious disagreements she and Sataro had ever had. By the time Billy finished the fifth grade, his conduct began to visibly change into a stage of less explosiveness and more quiet contempt. At least that was how it appeared to the concerned Sataro, who was nevertheless quite pleased with the nearly perfect grades the boy brought home from school.

But by then Sataro's schedule left him less and less time to deal with a problem that would undoubtedly work itself out. Mario's confinement had combined with the availability of properties to make the business a live monopoly game with him. The more he bought, the more he wanted. And apparently he had made more money in those bootlegging years than Sataro had dared to guess. One whole new room in his house was now a huge mapboard of the Valley, around which he moved in his wheelchair with a light rake changing symbols that represented different values and stages of crops. He was the president of Nob-Star Corporation, and as he grew fatter and balder, he relished it more and more.

Again Sataro was the big *oyakata* to whom everyone came for help and advice. Now, he controlled more land than even at the height of his days in Marysville. Yet not an iota of pretentiousness crept into his everyday living. That could wait until the Great Depression ground to a halt and he went back to Hiroshima, dream in hand—the changed dream, he would always remind himself sadly.

In the summer of 1935, his other dream was realized. Escorted by a teacher from her school, his beloved granddaughter was coming to Lodi! With a promise from Haru that Billy could go two years later to spend the summer with his uncle's family in Tokyo, Hiroshi had made the decision. She was to arrive in mid-June. Once more Sataro dressed in his World War I finest and went eagerly to San Francisco to meet the child who had totally captivated him since the moment he had heard she was born.

But this time, the ever beautiful Miyuki went with him for their first holiday in years. Even she was caught up in his exuberance and the fantasy that this lovely granddaughter who wrote such exquisite letters was actually their reincarnated Ellen. At least it made an enjoyable and fascinating reverie. Yes, she could pretend their Ellen had been off to school in Tokyo and was finally coming back to them as a stranger, yes, but their beloved daughter. She knew most certainly that though he didn't say it, the same idea was pounding through Sataro. She hadn't seen him as excited since the corporation acquired that big farm up near Sacramento.

For fourteen years he had waited!

Sataro couldn't explain it—he hadn't felt this way since he had come to the big city to spirit Miyuki away from the Gorotsuki. It was more than just excitement, it was . . . total anticipation that something magnificent was about to happen, that this vision he had practically worshiped for so long was about to become a part of him. His palms felt sweaty and his heart was pounding like a schoolboy's the first time he meets a pretty girl.

For the umpteenth time he pulled her photograph from his coat pocket and stared at it. Would he know her? Had she changed? Would she reject him . . . dislike him? As when Hiroshi came, he stared at the early debarkations. Hiroshi had arranged for her escort to bring a diplomatic pouch to ease them around customs. They should be among the first, he knew it! He squeezed Miyuki's hand as he squinted into the afternoon sunlight . . . a woman and a pretty little girl. *There!* he saw them. He drew in a sharp breath as he pointed for Miyuki.

But the one he thought was the pretty little girl was the teacher. The taller arrival, wearing a finely tailored white suit, a wide-brim hat and high-heeled pumps, was Sachiko Hoshi—Sachi to everyone close to her. Not yet fifteen, she was already full-figured and had been turning men's heads for a year. Her mouth, although full and ripe, was less manish than her mother's and her voice was already lower, huskier. And while her large, expressive eyes with their full black lashes were much the same, they exuded a merry brightness that implied warm pleasure in everything they perceived. Sometimes they even looked as if they were enjoying a special secret or were about to divulge one.

Coming down the gangplank, her breath caught as she fixed her gaze on the Japanese couple, particularly the tall man who was staring at her. It was he, the distant grandfather she had known but hadn't known ever since she could remember . . . a man, a special something that always seemed to create a unique feeling within her every time he sent her something. Even her father's old photo of him when he was young and so vitally handsome had thrilled her since she first saw it. She had kept it in her room for years. Her heart pounded as they drew closer . . . it was hypnotic! He was so tall, erect, and handsome with his gray hair. So dynamic, she could *feel* his magnetism. . . .

And then she was in front of him, bowing as he spoke, feeling his *chikara,* seeing his hand come out in the American custom to touch hers. His warm dark eyes were shining, brimming as his strong voice welcomed her. She had to finally tear her eyes away to greet Miyuki.

The following weeks were a daze of happiness. It was just as Sataro had known—they were as one without ever considering it. Their temperaments were identical, their tastes similar, even their humor seemed to dance along on the same keyboard. A glance from one to the other was an understanding, often generating a nod, a smile, or perhaps a slight frown. When he told her about Noboru, she reached out for his hand and cried silently—not for the uncle she had never met, but for him, for his grief. And once, when they were walking together in the woods, she found a tiny dead squirrel and cried. And tears came to his eyes, accompanied by an overwhelming desire to comfort and protect her.

Often she accompanied him on his daily jaunts to the farms, and always she was exhilarated by the open vastness of the Valley. She could pluck a cherry and exude that special brightness of hers, drop to her knees and find joy in a leaf of fresh lettuce. And though she liked to practice her excellent English, often while riding in his Model-T truck, or eating a picnic lunch under a tall old oak, they would sit in silence, singularly comfortable with each other.

Miyuki watched their unique closeness, and in spite of herself, felt a periodic twinge of jealousy. But she always pushed the hateful emotion away with a sense of guilt when the sparkling Sachi would bounce in to eagerly share some tiny joy she had encountered.

It was enough that her beloved Sataro had a light spring in his step and a song in his breast. Not since the days in Marysville when he was at the peak of his financial power had she seen him so lively, nor as loving. He was as lusty as when they first met. And though he didn't mention it, she knew his dream was again vibrant with a new dimension, again rounded.

But this time with a princess.

And he never saw the only cloud that touched his princess on her visit. It happened just one week before her departure for the return trip to Tokyo when she was sitting in the old rubber tire swing in the backyard of The Other Cheek on a warm afternoon. Billy had been at first smitten with her, finding excuses to be near her, and watching her with cow eyes when she wasn't looking. But when she continued treating him like Joey, from a friendly but reserved position, he began to resent it. Now, standing before the swing, he bared his bruised feelings. "You really think you're the cat's meow with Grandfather, don't you?" he said cuttingly.

She didn't understand the American slang, but his tone and scowl were unmistakable. "He's the most wonderful man in the world," she replied brightly. "I think he loves you very much, Billy."

Billy wasn't about to be sidetracked by her charming lies. "Love is for sissies," he replied gruffly. "I'm talking about twisting him right around your stinking finger, that's what!"

Sachi hid the hurt her cousin's sting produced. Disentangling herself from the old tire, she decided the best thing to do was just go in the house. But she stopped, turning back to him. "Tell you what," she said pleasantly, "when you come to stay with us in Tokyo, you can do the same to Grandmother, okay?"

He just glared at her and stomped away.

She watched him sadly for a moment, then shrugged and went inside. Sataro was taking her fishing in a few minutes and she didn't have time for such silly nonsense.

It seemed the world paused to collect itself in misery during the 1930s, but it was only steeling itself for far worse than the Great Depression. In Germany, Hitler came to full power and the potent Nazi military geared itself for action. In North Africa, Mussolini's jutting jaw thrust over backward Ethiopia. And having walked out of the League of Nations when censured for her China exploits, Japan pushed its legions through the Great Wall and moved toward a major conflict with Chiang's masses of militia. But all was not well internally for Japan. In spite of the massive profits generated by producing the tools of a huge war machine, certain elements of the powerful *zaibatsu*—usually family-owned monopolies—were against the military juggernaut. Under the leadership of Saionji, they were the only protesting voice. On the reverse side of the coin were the ultra-nationalists who wanted to rush madly at Russia and overpower the Orient. They selected February 26, 1936, to detonate one of the most savage and stunning coup attempts in the history of the empire— the Young Officers Revolt. But the bloodbath was quickly pushed aside when an excuse for full-scale war with China was sought for the eyes of the world. It was known as the Marco Polo Bridge Incident and involved a minor clash outside the ancient capital of Peking on July 7, 1937. Full operations against Chiang began shortly after. However, in the months following it became obvious that Chiang's porous forces would not be easily conquered. And there was highly secret talk in the army's top echelon of creating an example—an example so devastating that all of Nippon's enemies would think twice before refusing her will. Nanking lay in the advancing army's path.

Thirty-one

China? There lies a sleeping giant. Let him
sleep! For when he wakes he will move the world.

—Napoleon Bonaparte

"I want you to go to Shanghai, Hoshi, as my special liaison
officer to General Matsui. It is reported that the old man is
friendly with Chiang and wants peace. Go with him to Nanking,
then return directly." At fifty-three, Lieutenant General Hideki
Tojo was again Hiroshi's chief. And while Tojo had made an
incisive name for himself as a provost marshal, he was becoming
interested for the first time in the murky politics of a warring
Japan.

After leaving his tour of duty under Tojo in the First Infantry
Regiment in 1931, Hiroshi had gone to the Kwantung Army as
an intelligence officer shortly after the Manchurian incident. And
he had spent a tour in Shanghai, going to Jehol and Inner
Mongolia when those operations took place. Another tour back in
Manchuria when Tojo was chief of staff in the Kwantung Army
was followed by home duty in the elite Operations Section of the
General Staff. He had been actively involved with Colonel
Ishiwara—the proponent of the Final War philosophy—in put-
ting down the Young Officers Revolt, and had personally warned
Prince Saionji that he was on the assassination list in time for the
aged *genro* to escape from his villa in Okitsu.

When Hiroshi's plane landed in Shanghai at five-thirty that
night, he was met by a captain from Matsui's headquarters and
driven to the Lotus Hotel—a small hostelry Japan's Central
China Command kept for visiting VIPs. He was told that a full
briefing would be provided at 1000 the following morning. It was
Saturday, December 11, 1937.

Following a long bath, Hiroshi, now a lieutenant colonel, decided he wanted some Western food and conversation. He dressed in a light civilian suit and took a rickshaw to the Devonshire Hotel, an inn that was known for its international trade. Walking into the busy lounge he quickly found a place to stand near the center of the bar.

Two slow-moving overhead fans did little but redistribute the heavy tobacco smoke that enveloped the packed room. For some reason the place was sweltering and many patrons had loosened their ties and removed their coats. The motif of the Devonshire was strictly British, but in the irritability of the heat, voices with a half dozen accents were trying to overpower each other. It reminded him of a Friday night he had spent in a saloon on East Fifty-seventh Street in New York during his trip through America.

A ruddy-faced man with a huge walrus mustache and a loud voice was carrying on close to him. "I say we oughta blow the bloody bastards off the face of the earth!" he announced emphatically. "*Nobody* fires on the Union Jack!"

Being so tall and able to speak both Chinese and English so well, Hiroshi had no trouble passing himself off as other than Japanese. Now, he affected a Chinese accent as he asked the man next to him what the excitement was all about.

The man was slightly drunk and his English showed a Dutch accent. "The bloody Japs fired on two British ships up near Nanking late this afternoon. Didn't you hear?"

"No," Hiroshi replied. "I was en route to the city."

The Hollander nodded angrily. "A ferryboat and the gunboat *Ladybird*. Killed a British sailor, the bloody bastards. Nothing's sacred to 'em anymore."

The news astounded Hiroshi, but he remained noncommittal and calm. Why hadn't the captain who met him at the airport told him? And what idiot could have possibly attacked a British gunboat? He asked more questions, most carefully guarding his accent. After he had gotten as much information as possible, he decided he was stretching his luck to remain in that atmosphere. A Chinese dinner suddenly sounded most delectable.

*   *   *

The briefing at headquarters the next morning was a monotonous description of the divisions and their commanders who were already attacking the ancient walled city of Nanking. Chiang Kai-shek had already moved his capital to Hankow several days earlier and it was believed that the former KMT hub would fall by that night. Hiroshi tried to find out what its disposition would be, but all he was told was that General Matsui's orders were explicit—every standard of chivalrous conduct would be observed. It was to be a highly honorable victory, demonstrating to the Chinese that the two nations could live together in pan-Asian coprosperity.

He was also told that the *Ladybird* incident was an accident.

That afternoon Japanese planes bombed the U.S. gunboat *Panay* and two American tankers! Hiroshi was dumbfounded. An artillery colonel without authority had attacked two great nations in two days! It could mean war—a war that Japan could not yet possibly win!

But as the next two days passed suspensefully, that probability diminished. While Britain lodged a formal complaint with Tokyo, President Roosevelt sent an indignant demand direct to the Emperor. And as Hiroshi waited hopefully, the government in Tokyo took immediate steps for apology and indemnity to both nations. He was able to breathe more easily. The pressure eased further as the destroyer carrying General Matsui's victory party to Nanking departed late Thursday afternoon.

During the trip upstream, Hiroshi busied himself with a draft of the report to General Tojo about the scorched earth that marked the path of the army that had marched on Nanking. He discussed the noncombatant zone in the center of the fallen city, noting that of all the foreigners, the ones who remained were mostly Germans—apparently secure in the anti-Comintern pact between Japan and Germany.

He hoped the report would get more interesting. Alas, it would.

General Iwane Matsui looked tiny atop the fine chestnut stallion that had been provided for him to ride triumphantly into Nanking. Only five feet tall and thin from his tuberculosis, he looked as if his samurai sword and medal-covered tunic would be more than he could carry. Behind him, his staff and subordinate commanders were also mounted and plodding along to the cheers of troops lining the main boulevard. But the general looked troubled. Where were the curious Chinese faces waiting to see their beneficent conqueror?

Hiroshi had arranged for a staff car to take him directly to Matsui's headquarters for his two-day stay. Checking into the stately old Metropolitan Hotel, he found its Chinese staff acting strangely nervous. He stopped the bellboy as he was bowing out of the room. "Why are you so frightened?" he asked in his fluent Mandarin.

The man shook his head as if he didn't understand, then scurried off down the hall. Hiroshi shrugged, assuming his imagination was working overtime, then went out on the veranda to watch the entourage arrive. It was a sunny but cool winter day, and as he flexed his shoulders to stay warm, he saw that he was standing beside Hill, a hulking Associated Press reporter who had ridden up on the destroyer with them. Hill was still angry over the *Panay* incident, but he was pleasant enough with Hiroshi. "I don't see anyone passing out the keys to the city," he growled. "Doesn't something smell fishy to you, Colonel?"

All Hiroshi could do was shrug as the generals arrived.

A strict curfew that included everyone in General Matsui's party was set at dark and everyone was restricted to the hotel. Hiroshi, still troubled over the oddities he had encountered since arriving in the city, sat in a corner of the bar after the evening meal. As he was finishing his third drink, Hill entered complaining about a provost marshal major he had had an argument with when he tried to slip by the hotel guards to nose around the area. Hiroshi shrugged, listened to his complaints over another drink, and went to bed.

General Matsui and his party were kept busy and well contained seeing what Hiroshi recognized as a tightly arranged tour of the city the next day. While visiting the tomb of Sun Yat-sen on a high hill east of the city, Hiroshi learned from a staff colonel that

Matsui was both hurt and angry that his order about keeping a minimum of Japanese troops inside the city was being disregarded. "Does it seem to you that we're being treated like schoolgirls wearing blinders?" Hiroshi asked.

The colonel shrugged, but admitted privately that he thought the whole reception was disconcerting. Hiroshi wondered about the colonel.

Again that evening, a tight restriction was imposed on the visitors in the hotel. Hiroshi retired early to draft his impressions and itinerary for the day in his report, then lay awake wondering if the sick little general was being used as some kind of a scapegoat for something. He was still troubled.

At ten the next morning, just before the party was due to depart for its destroyer on the Yangtze, Hill burst wild-eyed into Hiroshi's room. He was white-faced and out of breath. *"You bastards!"* he shouted.

Hiroshi was startled by the big man's violence. "What's wrong?" he asked.

"I just came from the Safety Zone," Hill hissed. "I slipped through to see if I could get another slant for my story. And you know what, you know what, you sonofabitch? *The whole god-damned thing is a grotesque fucking lie!"*

Hiroshi continued to stare as Hill gulped in some more air. "Half this city," the journalist continued in a voice half broken with misery and half overcome with rage, "half this goddamned city has been murdered, robbed, or raped. It began four days ago and was halted only for this sickening production I've been watching like a high school sophomore." His head dropped to his chest a moment, then jerked up. "You lying, murdering bastards . . ." he muttered, his eyes clouding up.

Hiroshi's anger had surfaced. "Are you drunk?" he demanded.

"Drunk?" Hill asked coldly. "Drunk? I'll show you drunk." He strode to the door. A moment later, he pulled a young Chinese woman into the room. "This is Mei-ling. She's the daughter of a wealthy merchant and a schoolteacher. She refused to flee with her family." Turning back to the young woman, he said, "Tell the colonel about it, Mei-ling."

She was basically attractive, about twenty-five, and spoke English quite well. Her hair was in wild disarray, she wore torn old clothes and her face contained several hideous sores. Her voice was a low, expressionless monotone, her eyes at times dull, at other times angry. "Last Tuesday, the soldiers descended upon the city, thousands of them. First, they began to round up men of army age. These, they herded like cattle to pens along the riverbank. Later, they were machine-gunned, bayoneted, chopped to pieces with swords, covered with kerosene and burned. I've heard they killed many thousands."

She dropped her face into her hands and shuddered. Raising it moments later, she thrust out her jaw and glared at Hiroshi. "And at the same time . . . Japanese soldiers all over the city were getting drunk and raping. They broke down doors, bayoneted husbands who were forced to watch, slaughtered children . . . I—I saw at least a dozen babies' heads skewered on swords or bayonets like melons. Many girls had been tied to posts . . . for anyone to have, over and over until they died."

Tears were streaming down Mei-ling's cheeks. She sobbed, then reached to a horrible-looking sore beside her nose. With a brisk movement of her forefinger she smeared it. "This is the only way to save oneself," she explained. "Make it look like you are the most diseased person in the city. And be dirty. But that hasn't even stopped some of them . . ." Her voice dropped to a whisper. "I've only been ravaged once."

Hiroshi had been thunderstruck throughout her narrative. Twice, he almost shouted that it was an impossibility. *It couldn't be!* There was always some plundering, some killing, and a few rapes when an army took a city—but this, this horror was just not possible! "But the officers wouldn't allow it," he finally protested. "They—"

"A major raped me!" Mei-ling screeched. "A fat pig of a major who laughed and told me he was the provost! He took me to his office before I was able to look like this. He, he was a terrible beast!"

"That sounds like the one I met out in front the other night. Provost marshal by the name of Segura," Hill snapped.

Hearing that hated name, Hiroshi's eyebrows shot up. "Did he have mean, close-set eyes?" he asked.

"That's him."

Hiroshi reached out to tentatively touch Mei-ling's worn sleeve. "I'm sorry," he said slowly, knowing the words were hollow. "I don't know what has happened to the control here. All I can do is apologize for the Japanese Army and His Imperial Highness. This is the work of madmen."

"We know something has been going on here, Hoshi, but it isn't prudent to deal with it at this time," the colonel said evasively. "It's time to depart."

"I'm not leaving yet," Hiroshi announced firmly.

"No, Hoshi, you are attached to our headquarters. You must return to the destroyer with us."

Hiroshi shook his head. "I've contacted General Tojo. A plane will come for me tomorrow morning, Colonel." Why should the colonel be acting this way? he wondered. And suddenly he knew. "Thank you for your hospitality," he added.

The colonel shrugged as an orderly came into the room to get his bag. "Very well. It's out of my hands. Oh, do me a favor, will you, Hoshi? Send me a copy of your report."

Hiroshi's reply was curt. "That will be up to General Tojo."

Hiroshi's plan was vague. Although he didn't doubt Mei-ling's story, he wondered about the facts. It was quite possible that it was highly exaggerated. He still couldn't believe such madness—had Attila the Hun returned? Or was this all several wildly overinflated coincidences? He had to know—not for Tojo, not for any logical reason. *He had to know for himself.*

Hill had stayed in his room until the command party departed, so he was an added responsibility. But he owed him some protection, he figured. And while debt was on his mind, the thought of confronting Segura—if it were the same Segura—consumed him. He would never forgive the pig for Misao's *seppuku*. Never!

He waited until 1400 to go with Hill through the streets to the edge of the Safety Zone where a committee composed of a

British Anglican missionary, an American surgeon, and a German doctor wearing a swastika armband angrily presented their case. It not only corroborated Mei-ling's story, but exceeded it. The old missionary, who had been in China for thirty-eight years, stated that the pillage should net millions of pounds, the rapes should exceed 4,000, and the deaths approach 60,000—unless they continued, in which case they could *triple!* Hiroshi simply couldn't believe it.

Hiroshi carefully took notes, but they looked alien. He and the distressed Hill returned to the hotel, where the protesting journalist agreed to wait. At four-thirty Hiroshi walked a few buildings down the street to where the provost marshal's office was located. Entering the four-story office building, he heard female screams from above. But when he queried the surly desk sergeant on duty in the reception room, the NCO just laughed. "Interrogation," he replied.

"I'm here to see Major Segura," Hiroshi stated coldly, showing his identification.

The sergeant was back shortly to lead him to Segura's office at the rear of the first floor. A lavish two-room suite that looked as if its real owner had conducted more than business among its erotic murals, it seemed out of place for its occupant. Wearing suspenders over a dirty shirt of underwear, the fat, pig-eyed Segura sat behind an ornate mahogany desk waving a bottle of scotch whiskey. Three frightened Chinese girls in their late teens stood behind him.

With a loud belch, Segura shouted, "Look who's here—little old Hiroshi Hoshi from Hiroshima!" He threw his head back and roared with laughter. "And a colonel already, too!" Rising unsteadily, he grabbed the arm of the closest girl. Jerking her along, he lurched around the desk. "Here, Hoshi," he sneered. "Have a conquered enemy." He laughed again, then suddenly tore viciously at her tattered blouse, ripping it from a bruised shoulder. The girl whimpered, staring at the floor as Segura laughed again. "You can have her right here, Hiroshi Hoshi from Hiroshima. She's all yours."

Hiroshi fought to control the rage that was sweeping over him. His gaze flicked to the other two girls. One had a swollen jaw,

the other a blackened eye. "No," he snapped, afraid he'd kill
Segura if he got too close to him. "I want you to answer some
questions."

Ten minutes later, nearly out of control and seething with
disgust, he lurched out of the building. It was all true—on order,
unbelievable brutalities and wanton crimes had stopped for the
visit of Matsui. Segura had snorted in contempt when he said the
death toll was easily over 100,000. Now, the lid was coming off
again.

As Hiroshi blindly headed for the hotel, he heard a scream
from an adjacent alley. Spurting into the narrow street, he saw
three soldiers tearing the clothes from a middle-aged woman.
"What's going on here?" he shouted, jerking his pistol free from
its holster.

They acted drunk and out of control as they shouted and
laughed, ignoring him. The corporal in the middle jerked his belt
loose and dropped his pants as his cohorts spread the woman's
legs. Her pleading and whimpering gave way to another scream
as the corporal dropped over her.

Hiroshi's pistol roared, the explosion rocking the cold, darkening alley. *"I'll kill you with the next round!"* he bellowed.

The suddenly wide-eyed corporal turned as the other two men
backed off. Waving the pistol menacingly, Hiroshi moved toward
them. "Report to your company at once!" he barked.

They eyed him tentatively, continuing to edge away as the
corporal secured his pants. Then suddenly they broke and ran
down the alley. Hiroshi quickly knelt beside the whimpering,
babbling woman, saying in Chinese, "It's all right, madam.
They've gone."

She opened her eyes, showing the naked fear, then scrambled
to her feet and hurried out of the alley. He decided she couldn't
have been under fifty. Gulping a deep breath didn't help. The
revulsion was draining him. It was all so clear. The aged and
highly respected General Matsui was in China as window-dressing
to the Japanese public, a simple pawn. He slumped against the
wall, wondering what animals could even permit such a travesty.

And for the first time in his life, he doubted his destiny.

Then he leaned over and retched.

Thirty-two

"You want to open a *winery?*" Mario turned from where he liked to sit in his wheelchair by the window and watch the street through the venetian blinds. He now weighed nearly 300 pounds and required a special chair. "What the hell's wrong with you, old man? You want to be the richest Jap in America?"

Sataro chuckled inwardly, waiting.

"I know you're making over a grand a month from the farms, your hotel and store are the center of Japanese commerce outside of Japan Town . . . where you also own a store. Your paper is doing well, and I know damned well you've got an unofficial savings-and-loan operation going on out there. Why a winery?"

Sataro shrugged. Lean and still handsome at sixty-seven, he was the most familiar figure in the Valley. "There are over two hundred Japanese outlets in Los Angeles and San Francisco alone to get it to the public. You see, Mario, you've got to understand the Japanese American consumer. He buys Japanese when he can. It all goes back to the mutual support survival system from the early part of the century. Give them a wine with a Japanese name and label, and they're going to buy it."

"I don't like it," Mario said quietly. "It brings back too many bad memories."

Sataro nodded. The Chicagoan had never forgiven himself completely. "I understand, but this would be *legal*. With your expertise, we can put out a good product—both an inexpensive table wine, and perhaps something a little heavier. Maybe even wind up making our own sake some day. I tell you, we can make a fortune."

371

Mario's eyes narrowed. "I thought you were going back to Japan soon."

"So then you get rich all by yourself," Sataro replied with another shrug.

"What would you call it?"

"*Tani*—means 'valley.' Valley Wine. A Japanese specialty."

Mario frowned. "I don't like it." He hadn't tasted a glass of wine since that day—

Sataro opened his battered briefcase, withdrawing a sheet of paper. "Here are my initial estimates. You work out the logistical requirements—site, vats, labor, and such. And I'll get it started. I suppose a good wine man would be the first acquisition, wouldn't he?"

Mario nodded, heaving a deep sigh. "I'll make some calls."

Five weeks later, the first complimentary cases of the new Zinfandel, called Valley Wine in Japanese and English lettering on the label, were delivered to a few selected outlets in each city of any size from Seattle to San Diego.

It was October 1940.

On November 2, a letter arrived at the Homerville store from Seizo Hoshi in Hiroshima. After some basic commentary, Sataro's brother wrote:

> "It is difficult to explain to one who has been gone so long, my brother. Our beloved empire seems to be caught up in a breathless fervor that disguises its doomsday possibilities in a blind addiction to destiny. We are bombarded by what I'm sure is not always the pure truth in the newspapers and on the radio, but if the Co-Prosperity Sphere in Greater East Asia is a workable program, Nippon will lead the Orient to dazzling heights. Best you come home soon to join in this glory. . . ."

Sataro discussed Seizo's letter with the gentle Miyuki at length that night when they retired for the evening. Although she had lived with his dreams, his successes and his sorrows for nearly thirty-four years, the thought of returning to Japan had become such a vague concept that it had long before lost its reality. Here, she was the wife of the *oyakata*, and here she had her beloved

Billy . . . yes, and Joey and Haru and Kimi and all the others who were such dear friends. She was kept busy in the store and was happy in her lovely garden. Even Haru's vineyards had become a natural part of her enjoyable life. As she listened to Sataro speak of going back in glowing terms, she felt uneasy, sensed the discomfort of one who was secure and happy within the perimeter of proven routines. To trade it all away for unknowns—no matter how appealing—at this stage was unsettling to her. Yet, her rich happiness was wrapped around this vibrant, daring man who made dreams come true, and it was only right that whatever he desired be what they should do.

As his reasoning drew further toward the return, she told herself that they wouldn't even be here if it weren't for his dream.

"It won't be as much money as I once thought," he said quietly, "but surely enough to give us a rich life and the great respect of everyone in Hiroshima."

She wanted to ask him how many people who mattered would still be alive and interested, but she didn't. She would *never* cast one shadow on his vision. And she couldn't ask him if just an extended visit would be sufficient . . . a triumphant tour and a warm return to the Valley that had given them so much . . . a joyful return to everything she held so dear. . . .

"Just think, my darling," he said enthusiastically, "how wonderful it will be to have our lovely Sachi practically at our fingertips. And Hiroshi can introduce me to statesmen and generals like Tojo, and perhaps I can publish some kind of a magazine or newspaper! And just imagine the *investment* possibilities!"

And she knew from the glow in his eyes that he was about to complete his dream.

"You're crazy to even think about it until this damned war is over," Cedric said, pouring more bourbon in their glasses. "Absolutely loco. Why, it could begin anytime, and then where would you be?"

Sataro didn't want to hear logic, and he was convinced there was too much sense in Nippon's leaders to ever attack America. "You're just worried about drinking alone, Cedric. Besides, you'll be over to see me within a year anyway."

*　　*　　*

"Goddamn it, you just can't go, old man!" Mario stormed. "We've got an empire right here in these *farms* and you know it! Christ, as soon as this damned war starts, we'll be rich as Midas, rolling in money!"

Sataro nodded. "All the more reason for you to meet my price, Mario."

"Who the hell will run them for me?"

"The same man who runs them for *me*. You know damned well I never get dirty."

"You'll get your ass shot off over there."

Sataro laughed. "I'm not going to a rifle range—I'm going to the most beautiful, peaceful city in the world. Mario, it's a place that the gods will protect forever."

"And what about that goddamned wine company you talked me into? Huh? What about that, old man?"

The wide smile was still on Sataro's face. "It's already off and running. I'd hang onto my half, but I want the cash. Make it an even ten thousand and I'll not only get you a top-notch sales manager from Little Tokyo in Los Angeles, but I'll make a full swing up and down the coast before I leave."

Mario jammed a big cigar into his mouth. "You old bastard, you got no business even thinking about this. Tell you what—I'll increase your take on the farms ten percent."

Sataro flicked his lighter to the cigar. "No dice, Mr. Scagnelli." He laughed. "But you can add ten percent to the sales price if you wish. You never lifted your hand on the deal anyway."

"No, but I sure as hell lifted my checkbook. Now what else might dissuade you? Tell you what, you just stay three months and I'll pay for the whole damned trip—lock, stock, and barrel. What do you say?"

January 1, 1941

Sataro had risen just before sunrise to draw the *wakamizu*, the first water, from the kitchen faucet. And one-by-one, Miyuki, Haru, and the boys followed him in washing their faces from its

basin in the traditional New Year ritual. The *ozoni* and *otoso* had
been served soon after, and then everyone but Sataro returned to
The Other Cheek to continue preparations for the massive reception that would begin at noon. By nighttime several hundred
people would have come in celebration of the New Year and to
say farewell to the *oyakata*. For on the following day he and his
lovely Miyuki were departing for Hiroshima.

Today, before the festivities, Sataro had his own farewells to
make. The end of a stay that had spanned a third of a century had
its gateposts. He and Miyuki had been feted for weeks, but now
it was time for his private snipping of the cord. And although he
still didn't believe the war talk, he somehow felt a sense of
finality in his leavetaking. He stepped on the starter of the new
Ford sedan he had just purchased for Haru and the boys, and
smiled at the purr of the smooth engine. He had shipped a big
white Cadillac sedan on ahead a month earlier and could hardly
wait to ride down Hiroshima's streets in it, nodding and smiling
to the people as they stared and wondered who the strange
important man might be.

He chided himself for the vain thought, but smiled inwardly.

Soon he was cruising down Acampo Road nodding farewell to
the tall palm trees, then it was north to Galt, where he found the
old house in which Miyuki had lived with lively old Ellen. He sat
there for several minutes, thinking of the torment and great
passion when he made those trips up on his Columbia bicycle.

And now he could buy a hundred Columbias, even a hundred
Fords!

He had driven a hard bargain, but Mario was convinced America would be at least in a war with Europe inside another year
and that the price of farm products would go sky high. He had
moaned like a wounded bear as he pushed his wheelchair around
his lair, but he finally agreed on $93,000 in cash for Sataro's
interest in the corporation's farms and the fledgling wine business.
Adding what he had netted from the corporation's operational
profits since the Depression began to slack off, plus his share
from the farms Seizo's group had financed and his own savings
from the other ventures, Sataro had another $31,000—not as
much as he had once accumulated in the rice market, but still a

magnificent sum to take back to Hiroshima at the end of such hard times.

His next stop was the river, at a place where he had often brought Noboru to fish in the early years. He stared at the water, picturing a twelve-year-old boy laughing brightly with excitement as he hauled in a flashing nine-inch beauty. It pleased but also sobered him. It was the one awful gap in the otherwise perfect story.

And then it was back toward Lodi. Again, he had missed a marriage. His delightful Sachi had married a handsome naval aviator named Korin Koga the previous summer when she returned after spending a year at Vassar College. But he'd make it up when he was back in Japan. After purchasing the impressive house he planned to get, he would throw a reception that would really make Hiroshima sit up and take notice! He couldn't *wait* to see her!

The sun was just beginning to sift through the cold morning fog when he reached Japan Town and parked in front of the barbershop. He remembered catching a glimpse of the brazen barber's daughter at Noboru's funeral, standing alone on the edge of the crowd. But she had been an outsider and her grief didn't count. And now in his farewells, he wished he had had the decency to send her just a single word of comfort.

He walked to the corner and glanced at the old lumberyard before beginning his last stroll up the street that had once meant so much to him. Few people were out this early, but he knew the card games were already going strong in the boardinghouses. He crossed the street and climbed up on the loading platform, staring at where the bright Hiroshima-ya had once stood. . . . Could it be so long since a shiny Duesenberg stood in front like a dark coach of death? And then he saw flames and smoke, and a crowd of people awed by a fire in the middle of the night . . . a scorched sword. And involuntarily his fist started to come up.

Where would he be without his priceless gambari?

"I knew you'd be here."

He turned at the sound of Cedric's voice as the tall newspaperman walked up behind him. All he could say was a quiet, "Yes."

"You trying to drum up some Gorotsuki to liven up our night?"

Sataro shook his head. "I've been wondering if I should tell anyone about it—the boys maybe. You know, clean the slate before I leave."

"Still bothers you, doesn't it?"

"Yes."

Cedric knelt beside his friend, lighting a cigarette, and staring across the street. Exhaling, he said, "It would serve no purpose except to disrupt Haru's life. They'd tear down the old barn, you know." He paused. "Tell you what . . . I'll tell everyone on my hundredth birthday." He grinned up at Sataro. "How's that, old friend and partner in crime?"

Sataro nodded. How would he ever get along without this ridiculous man? "I guess that'll set it straight," he replied.

Cedric's grin widened. "You know, you've done a hell of a job here, old man. You want to go over to the Wellington and shoot a farewell game of pool?"

"I still can't go in there."

Cedric thrust his jaw out as he got to his feet. "Want to *bet?*"

Haru had refused to return to Japan with them, insisting that she would eventually get the citizenship that Noboru had so prized. "Someday when all this silly war talk is over it'll happen," she insisted. "Americans are really a fair people, you know."

Billy groused, wanting to go with his grandfather. The summer in Tokyo with Hiroshi had filled his impressionistic head with grand ideas of Japan's nationalistic destiny in the Pacific. He had even started wearing his defiant *hachimaki*—the white headband on which he'd embroidered "Bushido" in Japanese characters—to school when he returned. At seventeen, he had his father's hawkish good looks and height, with a gangling skinniness from his mother. He seemed to frown constantly, keeping his sensuous lips compressed and ready to hurl back any assumed affront. He was the only Japanese boy in Lodi High School history to be suspended for dirty play in sports. Still, Sataro was convinced the boy would come around.

Joey, in turn, was just the opposite—the quiet, normal Nisei boy who got excellent grades and behaved impeccably. The only time he ever seemed to get in trouble was when he was trying to keep Billy out of it.

Sataro took both boys out into the vineyards of The Other Cheek at shortly after eleven. He gave them a synopsis of family history—facts they knew, but hadn't heard lately, then concentrated on Billy. "One of these days, my son, you will be head of the House of Hoshi—a position of grave responsibility." He pulled the silver disk from his pocket, rubbing its brightness and familiar touch. "I want you to have this to keep until such time as you pass it on to your own son," he said softly. "It would have been your father's . . . I can't tell you what it has meant to me."

Billy bowed his head, taking the disk. He noticed the English letters and felt a wave of revulsion. American religion even! Well, he wan't carrying this white man's amulet out of any feeling of respect, that was certain! No, he'd have a hole drilled in it and wear it around his neck as a reminder that they had once dragged his noble grandfather in the dust, and killed his brave father! It would symbolize his hate.

"Thank you, Grandfather," he murmured.

"Akemashite Omedeto Gozaimasu."

Hiroshi bowed deeply as he opened the door to greet his surprise visitor. "And a Happy New Year to you, also, *Sensei,*" he replied warmly as Tojo slipped out of his overcoat and handed it to the waiting maid.

It was early for a visitor, but Hiroshi knew his patron would have an extremely full New Year between his huge family and the requirements of being war minister. The Hoshi household had observed the traditional early morning rituals and was preparing for the busy day ahead. Sachi's husband, Korin, had arrived the night before from his combat assignment in China, so the entire family was together.

Telling the maid to bring hot coffee for the war minister, Hiroshi led his visitor into the small formal room that was unblemished by Western furniture. They passed pleasantries for several minutes before the general said, "Summon the members of your family, Hoshi. I wish to see them."

Itoko and Suiko had, of course, met the general on many occasions and Sachi had met him twice. But it was the first time for the greatly awed Korin. While the rest bowed and murmured greetings, the naval fighter pilot snapped out of his bow to rigid attention. "I'm deeply honored, Excellency," he said passionately. The war minister was perhaps the third most powerful man in the government.

Moments later, Tojo announced the purpose of his visit. "In addition to wishing a fortunate New Year," he said in his quick manner as he reached in a pocket and withdrew the shoulder boards of a full colonel, "I have a promotion to announce." Turning to Hiroshi, he handed over the new insignia of rank. "Your date of rank is today. Now you can quit pestering me about a battalion to command. You'll have to start looking for a regiment." His smile was warm as he nodded to Itoko, saying silently what they both knew—it was a long way from her visit to his father on the night of the Meiji's death.

But as Hiroshi stared at the new rank, he couldn't help thinking with revulsion of Nanking.

Sataro wished the big noisy China Clipper were a ship so he could go to the bow to watch his homeland rise to greet him. The excitement at arriving had been building in him for the last hour and had been literally bursting out in the minutes since the flight steward had announced that they were approaching Tokyo Bay, with Yokohama under their left wing. He had been eagerly describing the fascinating scenery below to Miyuki since spotting their first landfall at the tip of the Boso Peninsula when the huge flying boat began descending.

Below was Nippon, the Land of the Rising Sun, his great homeland!

Stopping in Tokyo first was perhaps taking the edge off his long awaited return, but they had to see Hiroshi and his family. And his wonderful Sachi had written with exciting suggestions about the things they could do together during the stay. What a marvelous time they'd have!

"Look! There's *Fuji-san!*" he exclaimed. In all the photos and paintings he had seen of the magnificent sacred mountain, none even suggested the majesty of seeing it like this, from several thousand feet in the air. He guessed it was an atmospheric phenomenon, but the white-topped peak seemed to overpower everything from only a few miles away. It was mystical, overwhelming!

But Miyuki had her eyes tightly shut in the seat next to him. She was still deathly scared of the aircraft's letdown and was busy swallowing to relieve the pressure in her ears. He patted her knee affectionately and turned back to the compelling view of Mount Fuji. It was just wonderful to be back!

In spite of heavy pressure from everyone, Itoko would have no part of the big reunion. There was no doubt that she still ruled her house, and her final word was clear—the rest of the family could spend all of its waking moments with her former husband and that "new" wife of his, but they could not bring them to the house in Azabu.

Thus, Sataro and Miyuki were booked into one of the Imperial's finest suites for their week in Tokyo. And what a week it was. After the warm meeting at the aeroport on the edge of the bay when the Californians met Suiko and Korin for the first time, their suite became a flurry of activity that resulted in sightseeing trips, luncheons, exquisite dinners, investment discussions, a meeting with Tojo for Sataro, and an expensive buying spree in the Ginza for the fascinated Miyuki. Except for the one kimono she had made just before the trip, she had no Japanese wardrobe at all. Suiko and Sachi were more than delighted to take her to several of the fine shops to outfit her still graceful and shapely figure. Warning them that she had lived an extremely frugal life and would balk at spending the exorbitant sums the Ginza's top seamstresses might ask, Sataro gave them carte blanche and told them to keep the prices a secret.

There was no more striking trio of women in all of Tokyo as the three laughed and gaily scurried around the noisy and richly colored Ginza. For a moment, one could see them and forget there was a war on with China and many things were becoming difficult to buy.

Aside from Sataro's fascinating trip to the war minister's office, the most enjoyable part of his visit was the morning Sachi took him to the Meiji Shrine. Being with her was just the same as when they had been together back in the Valley a few years earlier, but now she was a striking young woman with a strong sense of her own identity. The touch of adolescence that had softened her girl's face in 1935 had been replaced by the clean lines of a firm chin and added refinement in her high cheekbones. Only her perfect skin was the same. Though troubled by the war and talk of its escalation to the West, she was able to push it away and vividly discuss her world of books and beauty. And their ability to share unspoken joys such as the shrine's tall trees and clean pebbled pathways after the early morning rain was still a part of their natural relationship.

When it was finally time to leave, he spoke again of his dream and asked the important question. "Will you come down to Hiroshima with us? Just for a few days. It would mean so much to me—an old man's fantasy."

Her bright dark eyes danced. "And what role will I play in the triumphant return of the great king? Shall I carry your trail of ermine, or cast chrysanthemums in your path as you greet the multitudes?"

He laughed as he took her hand. "No, my dear. Just be there."

Bowing suddenly from the waist, she replied, "Your humble subject would be delighted, great king."

And finally it was time for the triumphant return to Hiroshima. They departed on a coastal steamer that took nearly two days to pass Osaka, Kobe, and finally to approach the delta city through the calm Inland Sea. It was clear and balmy, as if even the weather knew the exultant son was returning. Though it was still early January, the distant hills appeared green and friendly in their custody over the vibrant city of rivers.

Sataro couldn't hide his excitement as the steamer drew closer. And how could he with his heart pounding the way it was? He felt eighteen! *There!* off to the left was Miyajima, gleaming richly in the bright sunlight. In his dream he always pictured it as misty and forbidding, as when he departed.

Almost thirty-four years. He gripped the rail and inhaled deeply as he noticed a huge battleship anchored off to his right. It was the greatest ship he had ever seen, dwarfing even the nearby aircraft carrier. Sachi saw his awe. "It's the *Yamato*," she explained. "Admiral Yamamoto's flagship."

The city was bigger than he knew it; many more smokestacks to fuel the military needs, his brother had written him. It looked so alien.

But it was his city!

He inhaled deeply, wiggling his fingers to keep them from shaking. But he could feel the incessant pounding in his temples as they drew nearer the dock.

Here he was . . . resplendent in new, finely tailored clothes . . . with papers proving his wealth and success tucked in his breast pocket. The dream—parts of it had changed, but a beautiful loving woman stood just behind him, and another part of him, an exquisite extension, stood beside her . . . the general would be along. And it tasted even sweeter than he had ever thought.

He drew himself erect and felt the roaring in his ears as he saw his brother's figure on the pier. *He had done it!*

He turned and reached for Miyuki's hand.

The next few days were busy with looking up old acquaintances, reliving memories, and visiting parts of the city, getting interviewed by the newspapers, and house hunting. He wanted a structure that bespoke his success yet wasn't overly pretentious. One Marysville was enough. On the second day, he climbed the hill to the old mission to see Reverend Macnamara. Asked by the aged housekeeper to wait in the study, Sataro was thrust back to his departure as he stood by the window staring down at the fanlike delta. While the guardian hills remained serene and the seven sparkling rivers still led to the Inland Sea, it was vastly different—too large, too modern, and busy.

"I send away a handsome young man and look what comes back."

Sataro turned his nearly white head sharply at the sound of Charles Macnamara's deep voice. The missionary was standing in the doorway to the study, still tall, now bald, ever commanding at seventy. A broad smile creased his still handsome face as he strode forward, hand extended. "How is my old lamb?" he asked zestfully.

The amenities were hurdled quickly as they sped on to summarize events that hadn't been mentioned in recent letters. Macnamara was one of the few remaining Christian missionaries in the prefecture, definitely the last of the Methodists. "What is a coming war to me?" he asked with a shrug. "The question is—why should *you* return at this time?"

Sataro shook his head. "There will be no war with America."

Macnamara snorted. "My friend, *I* sell faith . . . *you* are blind."

The man from the stock brokerage smiled broadly as he bowed. This could be the single largest purchase of stock not only in his career, but by an individual in recent weeks in the prefecture. He still couldn't believe his good fortune in being found by this highly successful returning expatriate.

Later over tea, he finally asked if Sataro had found something of particular interest in the different issues he had recommended.

"No," the erect man in the finely tailored suit replied. "But I've selected some others for the time being." He smiled briefly, showing emotion that most certainly came from being with the Americans too long. He held out a slip of paper with three stocks listed in strong writing.

Now Mr. Hoshi's smile was more of a grin. How uncustomary!

"As you can see, I'm partial to the last one."

The stockbroker had trouble maintaining his own composure when he saw the number of shares Hoshi wanted to purchase— 48,000!

Sataro watched him with an inner chuckle. He wanted to take the little man by the hands and swing him around like an American square-dance partner. His new investments could hardly miss! But instead, he pulled a cigar from inside his coat—an expensive Havana, naturally—and handed it to the man as he

calmly said, "Please get the quotations as of this moment so that
I may write a check for the total."

The driver stopped the taxicab by the gate of Saeki Air Base.
Korin was waiting and climbed eagerly into the rear as Sachi
opened the door and called out to him. Kissing her fingertips, he
asked, "And now, my love, what kind of a nest did you find?"

His voice seemed to rumble, but carried a slightly musical tone
when one listened closely. He was of medium height, slender,
and with an expressive mouth over which a well-trimmed thin
mustache provided a slightly rakish effect. While he seemed
indifferent to care, Korin Koga was one of the navy's finest and
most intense fighter pilots when at the stick of one of the superb
new Zeros. The son of a Tokyo silk merchant, he had been a
navy pilot for seven years and had served briefly in the famous
Commander Genda's flying circus before recently shooting down
six Chinese aircraft and two Flying Tiger P-40s on the mainland.

Sachi loved her cocky pilot with the fervor of a schoolgirl who
worshiped a matinee idol. They had met on the tennis court three
years earlier and disregarded all the stiff conventions of custom
in their relationship from that day on. The sixth time they met,
Sachi knew there would never be anyone else and unabashedly
went with him to an inn near Ogikubo to make love. The next
day she told her mother they wanted to marry. Suiko had at first
been dismayed, but quickly remembered that Sachi was her
mother's daughter and agreed to join forces against any resistance
from Hiroshi or Itoko. They both, however, liked Korin and gave
in quickly. All they asked was that she go on to Vassar for a year
first, but the separation had done nothing but intensify their ardor.

Sachi laughed. "I found a deliciously expensive house and a
housemaid who would satisfy the Empress." Ignoring the driver,
she kissed her husband's cheek.

"Good! How far away?"

"Fifteen minutes by bicycle, but I think Grandmother will buy
us a car."

He squeezed her hand. "Very good—and the ransom?"

"Too much, but that's why we have allowances, right?"

He shrugged, replying, "For a few months, who cares?"

The fear instantly chilled her. As the daughter of the prominent Colonel Hoshi and his dynamically patriotic wife, she was immune to war talk in Tokyo, but when she thought of her beloved Korin flying in prolonged air battles, all her sophistication crumbled. "Did you hear something?" she asked softly, trying to sound casual.

He shook his head. "Couldn't tell you if I did, you know that. But it'll be sea duty before the New Year."

A few months! she shouted to herself. Crazy war-happy world! She ground her teeth together as she turned to the window. She'd handle it. Sachi Hoshi Koga could handle anything! Even her grandmother had told her she was more forceful and willful than *any* of the rest of them. She would take it a piece at a time, and like they said in Poughkeepsie, the rest could go straight to hell!

The visit to her village had been nostalgic, but other than that, just something that had to be done in life's framework. Both her parents were dead and she had long ago outgrown that life. Riding back to Hiroshima on the train, Miyuki quietly stared out the window at cramped rice fields and bending backs. Most of the backs on the hillsides and in the silent little valleys belonged to women—and that was just where she'd be if she hadn't escaped . . . the picture bride. She grimaced inwardly, still unable to get over the horror of that grotesque hoax.

Nearing the outskirts of the big city, she heard a soft snore and turned to see Sataro's chin on his chest. Taking his hand, she smiled softly. What a fine life this wonderful man had provided since those terrible days. Not having children had been painful always, but her Billy and Joey had been superb substitutes, more than any woman should ask. And now he was so happy, even talking of producing a small magazine and having Sachi contribute to it—anything to include that delightful child!

If only that stupid war with the West would stay away, they could have the most wonderful new life in Hiroshima. As if to confirm her point, the sun suddenly burst out on a small village just up a steep valley. Or it seemed to . . .

Suddenly the village disappeared, no, it was there. No, it was a blur of hazy red. She shook her head briefly, but the blur didn't go away. It seemed to be on the right side, or— She closed her right eye and she could see the buildings again—spotty, but there. It must be some kind of a trick! She'd close both eyes for a while, then everything would be all right.

Moments later, she cautiously opened them. The village was gone, but the blur remained. Something was dreadfully wrong! She reached up to—*her right hand wouldn't move!*

"Sataro!" she cried out, but it didn't sound right.

He awakened to see the starkest of fear in her expression. "What is it?" he asked, fully alert in an instant.

"I can't see or move my arm!" The words were slurred and hard to finish.

Fear knifed into him as he swung fully around and gripped her arms. "When did this happen?" he cried, searching her frantic eyes.

"Just now—a few minutes ago." Still slurred, slower.

"Can you see?" he asked, trying to hold down his growing panic.

She stared straight at him, nodding, trying to hold back the tears. She brought her left hand up to touch his cheek, but the blur was larger. Her darling Sataro.

The train was slowing to a stop. Throwing a frenzied look outside, he said softly, "We're in the city, darling. We'll get off as soon as we come to a halt, then go directly to a doctor. You just close your eyes and relax. You'll be all right in no time."

He slid out of the seat, holding out his hand to help her. She gripped it tightly, following, following the blur and pressure. She tried to say something, but it wouldn't come out. He was lifting her toward the aisle . . . she'd just put her foot down and stand up and all this nonsense, this bad dream, would go away.

But her leg wouldn't hold her.

Sataro . . .

Sataro stared at her still restful features pillowed so gently in the soft white satin of the casket. He could still hear the hushed whispers of those who had come to pay their respects and peeked uneasily at his lovely Miyuki. "It looks just like her . . . like she's asleep."

But she wasn't asleep! he shouted to himself. She was dead! His beautiful, gentle Miyuki would never open those doelike amber eyes of hers again—never would they radiate the love and joy that always seemed to shine through their beauty.

She was still so young and gentle. Why couldn't it have been him?

He knelt, leaning his head against the cold surface, seeing her in a montage that began with the ladder of an old freighter, led to a cheap room in a grim whorehouse, and wound up in a simple but comfortable country store. He saw her frightened young face in a getaway car, the excitement of her bright smile when he rode out to her in Galt, the agony of her miscarriage, the joy of her grandchildren, her gentle caring . . . the years of her friendship and passion. Her precious love.

Japanese men didn't cry, but the tears weren't his.

They belonged to her.

He shook his head. Why, Lord Buddha? Why, God? Why this gentlest of all souls, this gracious flower, this blossom? *Why?* A sob tore from deep within. Tomorrow You will take her away forever. But tonight I have her shell, her lovely tragic chalice, the grail that one or both of You used as her form . . . this dove, this angel whom you so mistreated. Oh, dear Power above, *why?*

Sachi watched her grandfather from the doorway. She saw his body shudder and heard the sounds of anguish, and she knew that no one could possibly grieve more. And it worried her.

Her worries were justified almost immediately. As soon as the funeral service was over, it was obvious that Sataro was not normal, that he had either suddenly lost his zest for life or retreated somewhere within himself. He was listless and uncaring. He dropped the idea of buying a house, seeming vaguely content to live with Seizo. A chauffeur was hired to operate the Cadillac so he could go for drives, but he wouldn't get behind the wheel himself. Even the magazine idea failed to affect his seemingly enervated condition. Reverend Macnamara worked full-time with him, employing his considerable talents as a missionary. Seizo brought a Shinto priest to the house, and then a Buddhist, but no one got through. Three times during the busy months that followed, Hiroshi flew in for a couple of days—and twice Sachi broke away from Korin and spent a whole week. No change. It was as if a part of him had been buried with Miyuki, and the rest refused to function fully. Thus, as the critical months of 1941 sped by, he had no concept of the frantic rush toward world destruction that was going on around him. Nor of his son's proximity to its core.

Hiroshi hung up the telephone at shortly after ten o'clock the night of October 17. Staring at it blankly, he barely heard Suiko ask, "Is something wrong?"

His voice was low as he blew out a deep breath. "Tojo has just become premier."

Her eyebrows shot up. "But he had no plans for it—is there something you didn't tell me?"

Hiroshi shook his head. "I had no more inkling than he had."

Itoko appeared in the doorway to the study. "What has happened?" she asked, noticing Hiroshi's solemn expression.

He explained, adding, "I feel sorry for him somehow."

Joy was already coursing through Itoko as she quickly thought of the many social possibilities. "Why could you possibly say that?" she asked, unable to disguise her excitement.

Hiroshi shook his head. "I don't know exactly. It's just that so much has been put in motion that no man at the top can survive long. He has also kept the war and home ministry portfolios."

Suiko jumped to her feet. "*I* think we should celebrate!" she announced brightly. "We finally have a leader who's decisive and persevering enough to lead us to our destiny!"

"Yes," Itoko exclaimed. "A *shogun!*"

At 1615 the next afternoon Tojo found time to see Hiroshi while he was cleaning out his desk in the war minister's office. The new premier was tired from lack of sleep and Hiroshi sensed the tension in him. With a cigarette dangling from his thin lips, his speech was as rapid as ever. He quickly got to the point. "I haven't forgotten my promise about a troop command, Hoshi. However, I need you more than ever on my personal staff. Still, the decision is yours."

Hiroshi nodded, having guessed he'd be placed in this difficult position. He bowed his head slightly, replying softly, "Excellency, I am a soldier. While I deeply appreciate the honor you bestow on my unworthy head to share your glorious mission, I must humbly ask for the command."

Tojo ground out the cigarette, nodded and turned back to the papers he was gathering. "You will be given a regiment in General Homma's Fourteenth Army. Good luck, Hoshi."

Hiroshi came rigidly to attention and bowed deeply. Homma would be in on the long-awaited strike south if war became a reality. In the recent war games map exercise, the Fourteenth Army had conquered the Philippines.

And he knew Admiral Yamamoto's wild and dangerous scheme to strike across the Pacific at Hawaii was gathering momentum rapidly. In fact, a great task force was mustering to put to sea, should final efforts to bring Roosevelt to the conference table fail.

Departing the war ministry, he glanced up at the leaden, forbidding skies. The walk would do him good, perhaps ease his worry. He knew the timetable, and how it had already been adjusted. He knew what Tojo faced, and knew the general would do everything possible to avoid that final, sacrificial step. But wasn't the machinery in place, and all the well-oiled moving parts forcing the conveyor belt forward?

How many Nankings would there be? How could he explain it to his father? And what if the success were great—what if he, through some quirk of fate, should be in command in California and have to deal with his own nephews?

He shoved his hands in the pocket of his coat and stared ahead. He was going back to the infantry, where there were no politics and strategic tones . . . back to a regimental family where integrity mattered, and the Code was vital . . . where he could still the voices that troubled him. But the clouds had gathered.

Sachi stood apart, back toward the short rise of steps, watching as her husband knelt in front of the altar. He was among several young men in uniform and a handful of assorted civilians praying at the massive Yasukuni Shrine for the war dead. This temple portion, where the wooden altar stood nearly outside the huge dark building with the ornately carved, jade-colored roof, made her shiver. She wanted no part of its connotation of death. No! she wanted her dashing pilot to *live*, not join these ghosts. All she ever heard about was war—the past wars, the present war, and the coming wars. She was sick of it!

The slanting rays of the setting sun cast a rich gold blanket over those at the altar, giving them an aura of the supernatural, she thought, shivering again. Why did war and dying have to be so damned *holy?* she asked herself bitterly. Why did the most beautiful husband in the world spend so many hours learning how to kill so well in the air, then come to this chilling place to pray for his companions who hadn't returned? And what about the Shinto gods of love and joy—did they look down on such a place of hideous import with approval?

Something surely had to be wrong with the whole thing.

Korin smiled softly to her as he got to his feet and turned. Reaching her, he took her elbow and started down the steps, saying nothing, squinting peacefully into the brightness of the sun's rays. He felt a special warmth, a holiness, that his beloved but troubled Sachi would never understand. It was the same purity that he had known when her father took him to the shrine of Hachiman in Kamakura just before the wedding—the true *kokutai*, the national essence of the warrior. No, somehow his magnificent wife was misplaced, a misfit moving uneasily within a family of dedicated patriots in an empire headed for glory.

War—his livelihood, his spirituality—was the one major subject that she refused to discuss. And particularly on this last night of leave. Soon he would desert her, soon he too would be hailed and rewarded. Added to his air victories in China, the new conquests would surely vault him to high rank before Nippon's rising sun ended its march.

They were through the tall inner gate and headed toward the towering black *torii* when Sachi finally spoke. "I want to go to that inn near Ogikubo," she said suddenly. "The one where we first made love."

Korin glanced at his wristwatch. "But your family is expecting us within an hour."

"I don't care!" she insisted, grabbing his hand and hurrying. "It's *my* last night with you—not theirs!"

He stopped, holding her arms and staring quizzically into her glittering eyes. Suddenly he chuckled. "All right, my pretty one, but let me take you to the finest hotel in the city. That's it—we'll go to the Imperial?"

"No!" she stormed. "No, no, *no!* Don't you understand? I want to—never mind, we're going to Ogikubo!" She broke away and into a run, thankful that she wasn't wearing a kimono. Paying no attention to the stares that followed them, she turned out through the nearest exit toward Uchibori Street and hailed a passing taxicab.

Twenty minutes later they were standing in front of the somewhat isolated inn where they had first explored the wonders of each other's bodies. It was a very old three-story building surrounded by a high wall as if it had once been the mansion of someone important. But they knew the inn's highest peak had been when it was a First Division's officers' brothel after the Russian War. Since then, it had been mostly an assignation house.

But to Sachi it was tragic. They walked through the main gate of the wall and past a garden with its unraked maple leaves. Shortly, a tiny bent woman with the wrinkles of a century on her beaming face led them to Room 207—the site of their first time. She watched coolly as the woman splashed fresh water into a large porcelain bowl and laid out clean towels, then hummed a low tune as she deftly spread a mattress on the *tatami* mats. She emitted a toothless little cackle as she pointed to an old erotic scroll hanging on the wall, then turned down the lamp. Bowing deeply, she stepped outside and slid the door shut without the wide smile ever leaving her face.

Sachi went to the low table in the corner, noticing the thin, black-lacquered vase that held two freshly cut fall roses of a deep crimson color. How long would their sweet-smelling petals survive? The didn't even have a shrine for their dead, she thought bitterly. Her anger began to churn. Turning to Korin's amused expression, she saw he'd removed his uniform cap and coat and was unbuttoning his shirt. "And what now, fair virgin?" he asked with a rakishly raised eyebrow. "Shall I begin the seduction?"

She reached for the pins that held her hair in the twist on her neck, moving close to him, watching his eyes. As her shoulder-length tresses shook out, she slipped out of her light fall coat, dropping it to the *tatami*. Her soft white sweater heaved as she drew in several deep breaths and held his gaze. "No," she replied, moving against him. "I'm doing the seducing tonight."

She reached for his mouth with the tip of her tongue as her hands slid down to his buttocks. Pulling her head back briefly, she murmured, "Just pretend it's a hundred years ago, and I'm Edo's top geisha who is madly in love with her admiral." Her fingers worked around to the middle of his thighs and to his already growing erection. Her tongue found his mouth again, running around it and finally entering as her hands slipped up over his flat stomach and chest to encircle his neck. Arching up to him, she ground briefly against his erection, then suddenly pulled away and ran her fingers sensuously over her breasts and groin.

He caught her hand, emitting an urgent groan as he dropped to the bed. But she twisted away, finding the zipper to her well-tailored wool skirt. A moment later, she slipped the sweater over her head and quickly followed it with the slip. Her eyes continued to flick toward his bright gaze as she swiftly gained full nudity, then dropped to the foot of the bed and pulled off his socks. Kissing his ankles, her hands slid up to his now surging erection and to his belt. But his strong fingers were already there, tearing at the buckle. "No!" she cried. "I want to do it all!"

Two minutes later, she climbed astride him and began to rock. Her hair fell over her face as she gritted her teeth and increased the tempo, crying out wildly, then choking back the sound of her misery. All the fear and anger that had been welling up in her for days was turned into savage animal eroticism and pain as she tried to smother, smash it, consume it.

Two hours later, she wiped away the last of the tears and slipped out of his loose embrace to crawl to the low corner table. Reaching out to the black-lacquered vase, she withdrew the red roses and carefully placed them in her purse.

BOOK 3

THE
FALLING SUN
1941–1945

Thirty-three

The Americans think a battleship is the
mightiest weapon of war. Sinking as many
as possible might cripple their morale. . . .

—Vice Admiral Yamamoto, 1941

It was impossible for Korin to quell the knot of excitement in his
abdomen as he watched the aircraft in front of him jerk away and
disappear over the end of the flight deck. Quickly, his hand went
to the white silk *hachimaki* that he had wrapped around his
helmet only minutes before crawling into the cockpit. He had
nearly forgotten about the samurai scarf Sachi had made for him
during their carefree idyll at Saeki Air Base. His hand returned to
the throttle as he braced himself for takeoff.

Above the hum of the idling engine, he could feel the pitching
of the huge carrier as it continued to fight violent seas and a
turbulent headwind. He flicked a last glance at the clock—
0603—and in spite of himself, felt his legs stiffen as his toes
struggled to remain gentle against the rudder pedals. His fingers
tightened around the throttle, white-knuckled inside the heavy
leather gloves, as he saw the takeoff flag rise, hang suspended a
moment, then flash down!

Smoothly, he pushed the throttle handle to full power, feeling
the Zero respond with an overwhelming roar. Almost immediately,
he surged forward, the faces, objects, and other parts of the great
ship becoming a blur as he headed straight down the ever so short
deck like an arrow from a crossbow. In a split-second it was time
for back pressure on the stick—just the right amount to suck the
fighter plane's heavy load off the deck, yet not enough to pull it
up too high into a murderous stall. All he saw was a flash of
whitecaps and dark spray as the Zero staggered through that

momentary mushiness that meant instant life or death when it cleared the bow and dipped toward the angry waves.

And then the aircraft bucked through a jolting gust and snarled up into a soaring climb. He heaved a sigh of relief as he picked up the lights of the dark aircraft ahead of him. His one fear about this great raid had been that he'd miss it because of engine trouble. Glancing back at the carrier as he continued his wide climbing turn, he saw that all five of his flight group members were airborne and following him. The first gray touch of light to the east broke through the busy darkness, announcing that finally the great day was about to become a reality.

In another fifteen minutes all 183 aircraft of the first wave from six carriers had formed up at their assigned altitudes and had turned toward Hawaii—some 210 miles away. Korin felt like an honored guest in the royal box of a majestic theater as he looked around and down at the great armada that flooded the morning sky like a vast collection of fireflies and glinting reflections. Just ahead of his six aircraft, leading all of the forty-three Zeros at 14,000 feet, was Commander Itaya in his lemon-marked fighter. The next layer below the fighter cover contained fifty-one of Takahashi's dive bombers, while a thousand feet lower, Commander Fuchida—the brilliant strike leader with the Hitler mustache—led his group of high-level bombers. Murata's four groups of torpedo bombers carrying the attack force's knockout punch made up the bottom element.

As the dawn's bright pinkness increased, Korin was able to detect the orange markings of Fuchida's Betty bomber below. They had flown together on several missions in China, and he felt only Genda himself could be a more masterful leader. He nodded with satisfaction to each of his wing men as they tightened the formation. It was time to tune in on KGMB, the Honolulu commercial broadcast station that would provide a friendly radio beam for them to ride all the way to the target. He had preset the frequency prior to takeoff, so it was just a matter of fine tuning with the tiny crank. Moments later, the strains of "Stardust" greeted him, but he quickly turned the loop antenna to the silent nul position. He was one of only four Zeros with radio equipment; Fuchida was controlling the strike visually.

After all the dry runs, the attack should be nearly reflex action anyway, he told himself as he thought of the scout planes that were thirty minutes ahead of them. *The U.S. fleet just had to be there!*

Twenty minutes later, the first gleaming rays of the sun flashed over the horizon and through the broken cloud cover. Again, Korin looked around and down at the brilliant expanse of Nippon's finest aircraft speeding along in concise formations—the individual elements of a power violent enough to destroy a modern city, combined into a synchronized whole, into the greatest aerial production ever to grace the skies of the Pacific. He sighed deeply and whispered a short Shinto prayer, remembering the vows his pilots had taken back on the carrier *Akagi* the night before. "At the slightest malfunction of my aircraft," they had sworn. "I will proudly crash into the most important target I can reach!"

He switched the frequency of the two-way radio to the channel on which the scout planes would report—if they weren't shot down first. There was nothing but intermittent static. He thought back to his first long-range mission in China, but reliving it couldn't hold his attention. The sharp edge of nervous anticipation that had gripped him ever since he arose at 0350 was now more intense. Could they possibly pull off this massive gamble?

He wiggled his extremities to keep his circulation working in the heavy flying suit. A chuckle followed. How many young silk merchant's sons could afford a winter vacation on a huge luxury yacht with airplanes in the northern Pacific? He laughed aloud, then through habit swept the skies around him with a sharp glance. What a terrible thing it would be to get jumped from above at this point!

His gloved hand rose to his forehead, touching the white *hachimaki* under his goggles. A sharp pang of sadness struck him as he thought of Sachi—so grave and tight-lipped when he left her. How could he convince her that he wouldn't be one of those spirits of the Yasukuni Shrine in Tokyo? That he would return? Even with the solemn vow of death he had made with his pilots, he knew he'd return. The highest honors of the empire awaited those who smashed the enemy fleet!

Those scout planes had to be there by now!

As if in answer, he heard in simple code and static that the great U.S. fleet was indeed still at Pearl Harbor! Nine battleships, several cruisers, and clear air over the entire naval base! And only twenty minutes away! He nodded with a smile at each of his wing men, giving them the prearranged signal that the target was waiting. Then he took a deep breath and occupied his excited mind with a full cockpit check.

Eight minutes later, Korin caught his breath. Dead ahead, as he squinted into bright rays of sunshine, he could see through a break in the clouds what had to be Oahu! It was almost as the training officers had described it—mystical lavender mountains rising to be shrouded in feathery clouds. And surrounding their bases stretched a subdued emerald collar bordered by the white-edged tabletop of an unending seascape. A fascinating sight!

Immediately, his eyes swept the sky again. If enemy pursuit aircraft were aloft, they could be lurking anywhere from this point on. Nothing. They were nearing the northern tip of Oahu and nothing was in the air but the Emperor's magnificent armada! He looked forward to Commander Itaya's aircraft, but it was boring on with no sign of action. Dropping his attention to Fuchida's bomber four thousand feet below, he wondered what was happening. A signal was supposed to—

There it was—a black dragon rocket! The single signal meant total surprise—they had brought it off! But wait—a second rocket signal after a pause. Not total surprise! Immediately, he looked sharply around, but there was nothing foreign in his part of the sky. An error? At once the whole formation began letting down in a wide arc around the main island to come in on the target area from the south where Pearl Harbor and the military airfields were located. It was 0748. He wiggled his fingers and took in a sharp breath. Soon . . .

The attack signal, *to, to, to,* crackled through his earphones.

Years of training, honing the edge in China. . . . Itaya was leading them wide so their speed wouldn't cause them to overrun the dive bombers. They flashed past Fuchida's high level bombers. At 8,000 feet Korin sucked in another sharp breath as he saw the magnificent entirety of Pearl Harbor break brilliantly into the clear. Bathed in warm sunshine around Ford Island and lined up like stationary targets back in Kagoshima Bay, America's massive circle of battlewagons and other ships innocently blinked back shifting reflections as if in welcome. They looked like great gray-white sharks sleeping beside lesser fish on the surface of a deep ultramarine lagoon, a lagoon that surrounded a dark verdant isle to which they were tethered.

As the descent took the formation of fighters through 4,000 feet, Korin took one more look. The statuesque superstructures of the battleships took regal form and he thought he recognized one as probably the 32,600-ton *California* or the similar-sized *Arizona*. Another looked like the princely *West Virginia*. And still they remained silent, as if they were giant models of fighting royalty, waiting to be moved by a massive hand. It was the most stunning sight he had ever seen.

Itaya was beginning to zigzag—the signal to break off for independent flight action. As they slashed through the minor turbulence at the broken cloud level, Korin waggled his wings to his other pilots and veered sharply off toward Hickam Field. Simultaneously, Fuchida's excited voice burst through the earphones, *"Tora! Tora! Tora!"*—the vivid code words that announced to the Imperial Navy everywhere that its victim had been caught.

But Korin had no time to relish anything—the moment had arrived. Down, down, he streaked toward Hickam's flight line, where assorted pursuit aircraft were lined up side by side like sitting ducks. P-40s and P-36s were bunched close together, while the large new B-17 bombers were more spaced out. He began to level off at 150 feet, screaming three *Banzai!* as his finger mashed the trigger and his blinking machine guns began pouring lead into the parked aircraft. One pursuit ship erupted into his path as it exploded in a towering cloud of roiling flame and black smoke.

Pulling up, he banked left and quickly turned his head to watch as his last two flight members streamed down the flight line with guns blazing. More aircraft were burning, tiny figures were scurrying around, vehicles ran about indiscriminately, and smoke was beginning to create a cloud of death. He could see the explosions as some of Takahashi's bombers smashed away at the vulnerable hangars and other base buildings. As he peeled off from nine hundred feet for another pass, he saw one huge hangar erupt like an exploding balloon. Again, he squeezed triumphantly on the trigger and slammed home a destructive stream of twenty-caliber bullets. And once more an airplane exploded in front of him. On the next pass, he was sure he crippled at least one B-17 to the point where it would never fly again, but he couldn't understand why it didn't explode. Neither could he fathom why the pursuit aircraft were parked so close together, nor why someone didn't try to get at least a handful of them in the air.

Was *everyone* on the golf course?

After two more passes, with more bombers over Hickam, Korin decided to freelance it and give Wheeler Field a shot. He waggled his wings at his other pilots and gave them the sign that released them for private hunting. Moments later, he streaked in over Wheeler at fifty feet, finishing the run through a geyser of flame from yet one more exploding target. That was enough for the moment—he wanted to save some ammunition and also take a look at what was happening at Ford Island.

Climbing swiftly to 2,000 feet, he banked back toward the middle of Pearl Harbor, warily watching for other aircraft. A midair collision was the last thing he needed at this point. Below him, the earlier scene of placid beauty had been corrupted into a maze of destruction partially obscured by smoke and rendered surrealistic by the glare of the sun. One battleship—possibly the *Arizona* from the look of her superstructure—was down on her side, belching steam and black smoke. Another had made a complete turnover so that only her hull showed. All the other battleships and cruisers were burning or seemed to be in some stage of damage. Few appeared to be fighting back. The bombers must have done a magnificent job! He felt exultant!

One huge wagon that was of *Nevada* type appeared to be limping away from Ford Island with some return fire activity spouting from her decks. Korin immediately made his decision, peeling off and diving straight for her bridge. At 1,000 feet, he gripped the trigger fiercely, letting his guns erupt. For once he wished he were a bomber pilot, slamming his powerful phallic payload into the enemy queen below. But he had to settle for raking her with knifing bullets that tore into her nerve center. Twenty-millimeter shells screamed by him. A brilliant proximity shell exploded just off his right wing, but apparently caused no damage as he bore on through the severe turbulence. And suddenly he was on her, jerking the stick back at the last second and banking sharply away from the front of her superstructure. It was magnificent! *Aaayeeee!*

Like a show-off in the old days with Genda's circus, he couldn't resist a snap roll before pulling up sharply to the left. Leveling off at 1,200 feet, he looked around for the slim chance that an enemy pursuit plane might have gotten off somewhere and was waiting for a lesson in gunnery. All that was missing from this magnificent victory was a personal shootout with a top American pilot—an encounter that would mark the silk merchant's impostor son as a modern samurai knight.

But he saw nothing. Suddenly, the adrenaline stopped pumping, leaving him momentarily spent. He was acting foolish. A glance at the clock told him it was 0821, time to climb to the rendezvous point and find some bombers to escort back to the task force. The second wave could mop up.

Cedric Baldwin wondered if someone thought it was the Fourth of July or Chinese New Year when he heard the distant explosions rumbling through the open window of Room 319 in the Niumalu Hotel in downtown Honolulu. He rolled over and looked at his watch, seeing it was nearly eight o'clock. Another glance told him his new blond friend was still sleeping soundly at his left elbow. And he saw a few lines in her face he hadn't noticed the night before. But then after the seventh or eighth drink he seldom detected such things—or at his age, cared.

Divorcée from Dallas, she had said as he looked at the big diamond on her right hand. Fifth day in Honolulu and lonesome. It was his first time in the islands, but he guessed she was a typical stateside tourist looking for a change of scenery, waving palm trees, aloha music, and someone to haul her ashes. Name was Genevieve or something—Gwenivere! He remembered he couldn't spell it.

Goddamn that infernal racket!

He swung his long legs out of bed, testing his headache at the same time. A few cigarettes were left in the crumpled package on the nightstand. He lit one with his battered Zippo and inhaled deeply, savoring the first biting taste. What he needed was a cold beer, he thought as he got up to close the window and shut out the noise. The damned artillery ought to have more consideration for tax-paying civilians on Sunday morning, he snarled to himself. Service practice? Maneuvers? He stared off to the south. Sounded like they were going all out. He could even see the damned smoke.

"What's goin' on, darlin'?" Gwenivere was propped up on an elbow, squinting around a strand of blond hair. Her Dallas accent was thicker when she was sober. Covering her full breasts with the sheet, she giggled. "You're sure cute without any clothes on, darlin'."

Cedric hurriedly got his shorts from the floor and stepped into them. Frowning back at the scene to the south, he finally replied, "I think something bad's happening down at Pearl Harbor."

Wrapping herself in the sheet, Gwenivere headed for the bathroom. "What do you mean, bad?" she asked over her shoulder.

Cedric's black eyes narrowed as he growled, "Maybe some unwanted visitors." Suddenly he turned to the telephone on the nightstand and asked for the Associated Press number. After five rings, a tired voice came on the line. "This is Baldwin," Cedric said. "The publisher from California. What the hell's going on down at Pearl Harbor?"

"Beats the hell out of me," the voice replied. "I heard the Japs are bombing it, but there's no confirmation. Christ, the phones are ringing off the wall!"

Cedric slammed the receiver down. *He knew it!* That was exactly why he had laid over on his trip to Hiroshima—he knew *something* was going to happen. Christ! What a close call. He looked back at the distant smoke. And the sons of bitches would have to do it on a Sunday—a sneaky goddamn Sunday hit! He hurried to the radio on the dresser, snapping it on and quickly turning the knob to KGMB. An excited announcer was exclaiming, *"I repeat, the island is under attack! This is the real McCoy!*

Since shortly before seven this morning, massive waves of Japanese bombers have been dropping their payloads on the greatest ships of our fleet. One report states that several have been sunk. . . . Sneak attack . . . No word from Washington. Both the army and navy are refusing official comment. *This is the real McCoy!''*

Gwenivere stepped out of the bathroom, her face white, her eyes wide. "Is that real?" she asked in a tiny voice.

Cedric was staring at the blaring radio. "I'm afraid so," he said angrily. The sons of bitches. The *sons of bitches!*

At seven-twenty Tokyo time, Sachi was a few blocks from the house taking a brisk Monday morning walk to start the day. It was part of a physical conditioning regimen she had decided would help ready her for motherhood. She wasn't certain she was pregnant, but she was late with her menstrual period—and she had certainly exposed herself on her ovulation days during Korin's final stay.

Turning briskly into a commercial street with many shops, she was surprised to see a crowd gathered near a local police station. The words of an excited voice tumbling out of a loudspeaker rushed toward her. ". . . So His Imperial Highness's rescript about the war will be read just as soon as we receive it later in the morning. Again, this is Tateno Morio at NHK. To repeat the bulletin, the army and navy divisions of Imperial Headquarters did jointly announce at six o'clock this morning that our military forces have commenced hostilities against British and American forces in Malaya and Hawaii earlier today. Although the details are not known at this time, it has been suggested that a great naval victory has taken place. . . ."

Sachi stopped, feeling as if someone had smashed a fist into her stomach. She felt instantly ill as pictures of a flaming Zero swept over her. *It was true—they had finally done it!* She moved close to a fence and grabbed at a post, thinking she would vomit. All this talk since she had been a tiny child, all of it had been real—her mother's and father's conversations about war with the West, the buildups, the stories in the media and in the movie newsreels, everything Korin had told her. . . . It was all reality.

She passed her hand over her flat stomach. What would this fine child have to face someday? What would happen to the wonderful life she had always known? Surely it would all change. Her mother's face rushed by her—it was smiling and flushed with excitement over the news. Maybe they didn't know at home yet. She wouldn't tell them when she returned. No, they'd know. And there would be a celebration back at the house—most probably in all of Tokyo, all of Japan. She'd go to her room and be ill, that's what. And she would stay there until, until . . . A tear slipped down her cheek.

"Korin . . ."

"Boys! Come quickly—the radio!"

Billy and Joey stopped their game of catch in the backyard at the urgency in their mother's voice. Billy was the first to reach the door. "What's wrong, mom?" he asked, seeing her ashen face.

She was rigid, her eyes wild as she shook her head. The voice of an announcer from a Stockton station filled the kitchen. ". . . cruisers. Admiral Kimmel, the naval commander in Hawaii, has made it official with a message sent at eight A.M.—ten our time—that curtly announced, 'AIR RAID ON PEARL HARBOR. THIS IS NO DRILL!' Therefore, it has been official for over two hours now. . . . *The Japanese Navy has bombed Pearl Harbor and destroyed most of the capital ships in our Pacific Fleet!* Even the residents of Honolulu were startled and unaware of the sneak attack until a bomb killed fifty of them.

"It was immediately reported that Japanese citizens were in on the raid and were about to take over the government. . . . Another report stated that a huge arrow pointing directly to Pearl Harbor had been cut in a sugar cane field. Further, extensive acts of sabotage were being effected by more local Japs. . . ."

Billy and Joey stared at each other, then at their stricken mother. "I don't believe it," Billy managed. "It has to be some kind of a lie."

The telephone jangled. It was Mario wanting to know if they had heard. Haru softly replied that she had, but couldn't say any more.

The words continued to blare out of the radio.

"What does it mean?" Joey asked with wide eyes.

"I don't know, my son, except that nothing will ever be the same."

At 0905 Taiwan time, the staff car carrying Hiroshi pulled up to the compound that held his new command. It was thirteen miles south of the city of Taipei—enough distance to keep his new troops out of trouble, he thought. They would be restricted for the ten days before departure. He tried to quell the excitement as he returned the sentry's salute at the gate. But then it had been a stimulating morning. He never had believed that Yamamoto's crazy longshot at Pearl Harbor could work—or that it would ever be attempted. But what an audacious, fascinating victory it had produced! He had heard about it over the aircraft radio just before landing in Shanghai.

And so the long buildup was over. The road to victory lay ahead.

He had spoken to General Homma, the Fourteenth Army commander, just prior to leaving Tokyo. The regiment he was to command was the Twelfth Infantry, a seasoned China unit that unfortunately had been at Nanking. There would be almost no time for familiarization because the regiment was scheduled to join the Philippine invasion force. But he didn't care—it was a troop command.

The sergeant major hurried to the door as Hiroshi entered the headquarters building. Saluting and bowing, he quickly led the way to the commander's office. The thickset figure of a lieutenant colonel turned from the window as he entered. Memories of Misao's *hara-kiri* and Nanking whirled before Hiroshi's eyes as he met the gaze of his executive officer.

It was Segura.

Thirty-four

. . . Now that Japan has instituted this attack upon our land, we are ready and prepared to expend every effort to repel this invasion together with our fellow Americans.

—Japanese American Citizens League to
FDR–December 7, 1941

At shortly before ten o'clock the students of Lodi High School were assembled in the auditorium where a table model radio was set up in the center aisle. The principal quickly strode to the middle of the stage and announced that the entire nation was listening to a solemn moment of history by Franklin Delano Roosevelt. Then right on cue over light static, they heard the rapping of a gavel in the chamber of the House of Representatives as Speaker Sam Rayburn's firm voice announced, "The President of the United States."

Quietly, the radio announcer explained that the president was walking slowly with assistance from his son, James, a Marine captain. And then he was at the podium, opening a black notebook, and looking gravely down through his pince-nez glasses. The chamber was utterly silent as he began in that solemn but captivating voice the nation knew so well, "*Yesterday, December 7, 1941—a date which will live in infamy—the United States of America was suddenly and deliberately attacked by naval and air forces of the empire of Japan. . . .*"

Eight rows from the rear, sitting with two friends from the baseball team, Joey Hoshi slid down in his seat, feeling as if everyone in the place were staring at him. He fastened his gaze solidly on his interlaced fingers, wanting to bolt from the huge room and go somewhere to hide.

"*Last night Japanese forces attacked Hong Kong. Last night*

Japanese forces attacked Guam. Last night Japanese forces attacked the Philippine Islands. Last night the Japanese attacked Wake Island. And this morning the Japanese attacked Midway Island. . . . Always we will remember. . . ."

Joey ground his teeth together. Everyone would always remember. He felt his cheeks burning—what shame, what agony that they had even done it so, so without honor. How he suddenly hated that handsome uncle his grandfather had always raved about—and his daughter, that smiling Sachi! She had probably been spying while she was supposed to be a damned student. He hated them all!

The emotion was charged in the president's closing statement. *"I ask that Congress declare that since the unprovoked and dastardly attack by Japan on Sunday, December 7, 1941, a state of war has existed between the United States and the Japanese Empire."*

The roar of applause from a cheering House was quickly joined by the faculty and student body of Lodi High School as everyone jumped to his feet and began to cheer. Joey's shouts were as loud as anyone's—they voiced his pain. His best friend, Bert, pummeled him as he shouted through tears of passion. He had already said he was enlisting immediately. At that instant Joey made the decision to go with him. As soon as the pandemonium quieted, the three ballplayers made their way out through the excited students. Just as they reached the door, Joey stiffened as a voice shouted, "Hey, Jap, where you going—to bomb San Francisco?"

The taunt sliced at Joey, tearing at his stomach. He lowered his head and hurried outside. Bert's hand caught his arm two strides later. "Hey, pal, don't pay any attention to jerks like him. C'mon, let's get a soda—I'll buy."

But Joey barely heard. The only words ringing through his ears were, "Hey, Jap!"

At one-twenty they strode into the Stockton recruiting station only to find the place full of noisy, bright-eyed young men in the process of enlisting. Joey saw no other Japanese faces and was surprised. Waiting in line, he ignored several hostile stares as he tried to stay occupied with Bert's running banter. Finally it was Joey's turn. A staff sergeant with a leathery face and short gray hair shook his head. "Sorry, sonny," he said abruptly. "We ain't taking no Japs today."

Joey squirmed inwardly but stood his ground in front of the desk. "But I'm an American citizen," he replied softly.

"Don't make no difference," the sergeant replied coldly. "Them was the captain's orders first thing this morning. Said it came from Washington."

Billy had been home from college at Berkeley since the Thanksgiving holiday. He told his mother he had been discriminated against and would select a different school for the new semester. But he had merely dropped out and come back home when he ran out of money. Joey knew it, but Haru pushed the truth away. Her poor Billy always had a tough time with the tide. Now, with the war and all, it didn't matter in the slightest because the future suddenly was hanging in abeyance for everyone with Japanese ancestry.

On the afternoon of the twelfth, Billy answered a knock on the front door.

Two tall men wearing double-breasted suits were there. The one in front held up a badge. "Peterson, FBI," he said evenly. "I have a presidential warrant for the arrest of Noboru Hoshi. Is he at home?"

Billy's quick temper flared. "What's the charge?" he snapped.

"He fits a number of categories relating to national security," Special Agent Peterson replied stiffly. "He's a leader with over fifty men working for him, his father recently returned to Japan after publishing an underground newspaper, and his brother is a Japanese Army officer."

Billy's face was livid. "And for these ridiculous lies the President of the United States would *arrest* him?"

"Is he at home?"

Haru caught Billy's fist and moved him partially out of the doorway. "My husband has been dead for over nine years," she said quietly.

Special Agent Peterson turned to the other agent in sudden dismay, then returned to Haru and searched her face. "I'm sorry, ma'am. The records, you know, they—"

"You want to arrest *me?*" Billy taunted.

Peterson's eyes were hard. He didn't ever like to be wrong or get embarrassed. And he certainly didn't want it rubbed in by a punk Jap when he still didn't know the fate of his brother on the U.S.S. *Arizona.* "Don't push your luck, kid." He touched his hatbrim. "Good day, ma'am."

Herb Lockett had been placed on a supervisory retainer by Sataro when he left. He was sort of an unofficial guardian to Haru and the boys, and when he stopped by The Other Cheek six days later, he brought disconcerting news. "The reports that Japanese in Hawaii created all that sabotage and such are being discredited, but it doesn't make any difference here in California. Here, you're still the yellow menace. They're shouting 'Remember Pearl Harbor!' and hysteria is the name of the game. The politicians are going to make hay out of this—and the fertilizer is going to be Japanese bodies. Frankly, I don't think they'll stop until everyone on the West Coast with a Japanese surname is behind barbed wire."

"Are they locking up any German or Italian aliens?" Haru asked.

"Are you kidding?" Lockett replied. "They're white."

Haru shook her head. This was all impossible. In a way, she was glad her beloved Noboru wasn't alive to hear such a thing. But she still had faith in the basic fairness of her adopted people.

Douglas MacArthur at sixty-one had become an enigmatic power since his days as a flamboyant brigade commander in the Rainbow in France. The former medal-hunting specter of no-man's-land had returned to active duty just a few months earlier after having retired in 1935 to accept a field marshal's baton in the Philippine Army. As commander in chief in the South Pacific, he was now fighting an unsupported delaying action and almost certain defeat in the archipelago he so loved.

In the fourteen days since the war began, the Japanese onslaught had rushed to victory after victory. The mighty British warships *Prince of Wales* and *Repulse* had been sunk by brilliant bombing after heroic maneuvering by their gallant commanders.

Japanese forces were rushing toward the crown colony of Hong
Kong and the British stronghold of Singapore. Guam had fallen
and the ominous shadow of Japan threatened the entire Pacific.
Only a handful of brave American marines and civilians on tiny
Wake Island heroically withstood the onrush, and they would pay
the price of that audacity a few days later.

Standing off from the shores of Lingayen Gulf on the west
central coast of the main Philippine island of Luzon, the huge
Japanese invasion flotilla began to disgorge its troops at 0200 on
December 22. Aboard the transport *Kami-Maru*, Hiroshi was told
that the first wave had encountered high seas, but no enemy
resistance. And he was glad to hear that the enemy had with-
drawn south toward a rugged peninsula called Bataan—he needed
all the time he could get to become familiar with his new
regiment.

With so much happening so quickly, Hiroshi had pushed aside
the fact that the officer he most detested was his executive
officer. While Segura remained aloof, he was an efficient second-
in-command and coldly complied with Hiroshi's wishes. But
Hiroshi kept an eye on him.

Thirty-five

We're the battling bastards of Bataan;
No mama, no papa, no Uncle Sam:
No aunts, no uncles, no cousins, no nieces;
No pills, no planes, no artillery pieces.
. . . And nobody gives a damn.

—Correspondent Frank Hewlett

Cedric Baldwin watched grimly as the pilot tossed a phosphorous grenade into the cockpit of his wrecked P-40 Tomahawk and ran back several paces as it burst into flames. He thought of the grisly humor of the fictitious note that had been sent to the White House: "Dear Mr. President: Please send us a P-40. The one we have is all shot up."

Cedric's application with Associated Press had been accepted immediately and he had arrived in Manila in mid-December as one of the oldest correspondents in the Pacific. But his scrawny fifty-nine-year-old body was still hard as nails and after all those years in Lodi, he was as adventurous as a cub reporter. His present predicament was typical. He could have gotten away from Luzon on several occasions, and he could still relax during the capitulation and be exchanged in perhaps a few months. But there was something about the doomed underdog lot of the beleaguered FilAmerican force on Bataan that had appealed to him from the very day he joined it, and he wasn't about to leave its doomed fighters until the last gasp.

When asked why, he always had a gruff answer. "That's what being a journalist is supposed to be all about." And he loved it! Except for that flirtation with the Pulitzer back when he threw himself into the Japanese-American discrimination series, this was the first time he had really gotten down into the meat of

being a "real goddamn newspaperman." And now he was going
further—he was going to fight until the damned thing was over.

He had just two hours earlier left General King after he
announced that, in spite of orders from the departed MacArthur
and the besieged Wainwright on Corregidor, it was time to end
the inhuman struggle and salvage as many lives as possible.
Approximately 80,000 soldiers and civilians would be surrendered,
but Cedric Baldwin wouldn't be one of them.

"She was a good old bird," the pilot said sadly as the flames
crackled.

"Yeah," Cedric replied. He shifted the Garand M-1 rifle to a
more comfortable position on his shoulder. It was time to head
for the one truck that had been allotted the escapees. If they were
lucky, they'd join up with Filipino guerrillas before their meager
bits of food ran out or the malaria did them in. He strapped the
round steel helmet over his unkempt hair and swore as he lit his
last cigarette. He also swore he'd come back to this godforsaken
place named Cabcaben someday, someday when he didn't have
dysentery or malaria, someday when he wasn't hungry—yes,
he'd sure as hell come back with the forty pounds he had lost and
eat a juicy steak two inches thick and drink a whole bottle of
bourbon while he pissed on the red ball of a goddamn Japanese
flag!

They didn't reach the Mariveles cutoff until well past daybreak
due to the heavy congestion on the east road, the highway that
ran down the coast. The bumper-to-bumper traffic included every
type of military vehicle imaginable, as well as most of the
civilian relics that could still move. And on each side of the
dust-choked road, the forlorn, half-starved hikers straggled along,
heads hung low, hoping there was substance to the rumor that
boats awaited at Mariveles to ferry them over to the safety of
Corregidor.

The truck was driven as far as possible into the jungle before
the party struck out on foot, working its way up the massive
mountain toward the northwest. Their escape group consisted of
two pilots, five enlisted men, and one Filipino Scout sergeant.
Their plan was sketchy, simple, and dangerous. They had to pick

their way north through Japanese lines to fight a hit-and-run war of unknown duration, or until they could eventually escape from Luzon. Simple. The going was tiring to their weakened bodies, so at 0855 they dropped in a tiny clearing on a ridge overlooking the bay and immediately fell into a fitful sleep.

At 1110 the Filipino awakened Cedric. Pointing down to where parts of the highway could be seen, he said softly, "I wonder if it was worth it."

Shaking out the sleep, Cedric first took in the majestic beauty of Manila Bay as it stretched out in its grandeur of deep blue-greens, rimmed on the near shore by a thin line of white beach and foaming breakers. Three miles away, the kidney-shaped form of Corregidor stood up defiantly, announcing that there was one place the Japanese could not demolish. Cedric wondered how long it could hold out.

"So it is the end," the sergeant said sadly.

Cedric shook his head, focusing on the road where white flags hung from nearly every vehicle he could see. His hand went to his shirt pocket for a cigarette, but there were none. The long snake of chalky white vehicles down there didn't belong to him, he thought. He was free. The date made him think of the Civil War. April 9, 1865: Appomattox. Thousands of ill and starving Confederate Americans shuffling around, waiting as their gallant and broken-hearted general did the only humane thing possible.

Only those Southern boys were going home to peace.

He was angry and humiliated. Was everything he believed in, was willing to die for—was it in vain? What the hell kind of a country could write off an entire army? So what if it was 80 percent Filipino, it was all American! He wanted to vomit but there wasn't anything in his stomach. He sipped a few drops of water from his canteen, then got to his feet and joined the others.

Exactly one hour and four minutes later, they ran straight into the huge Japanese patrol.

"All prisoners, Filipino and American, are to be killed."

Hiroshi stared at the message Segura handed him in disbelief. "Who did you say gave you this order?" he asked his executive officer.

As usual, Lieutenant Colonel Segura's flat face was a mask. "Colonel Tsuji from Tokyo. He's at field headquarters."

"And you didn't question the validity of the order?" he asked coldly.

Segura shrugged. "Why should I?"

Hiroshi looked out at the small mesa where the prisoners were being assembled some ninety yards from his command post. At an hour before sunset, they were still being brought in by the dozens. Already there were over nine hundred of them. He turned back into the tent and directed a sergeant to get Colonel Tsuji on the line. Moments later, he was talking to the staff officer. He spoke evenly, keeping the anger from his voice, "By what authority do you issue such an inhuman order, Tsuji?"

The colonel's voice came back on a weak connection. "Imperial Headquarters. Why do you question it, Hoshi? As a mere regimental commander, you—"

Hiroshi's voice crackled as it cut in, "I want it in writing, Tsuji. Over General Homma's signature."

"Do you question me, Hoshi?"

"In writing!" Hiroshi hung up, turning to the frowning Segura.

"Do you think that was wise?" the executive officer asked. "Prisoners are costly and we don't even have enough food for our own troops."

Hiroshi's anger boiled over as he pictured Segura with those poor Chinese girls in Nanking. He wondered how many thousand deaths the former provost marshal had been responsible for in that tragic city. How could he be in the same army with the Seguras and Tsujis? But he chopped off the violent words before they were uttered and just walked away. Moments later, he turned to his sergeant major and quietly said, "Have the officers separated from the other prisoners."

As the sergeant major hurried off, he went to his tent, where he kept a bottle of scotch. Pouring himself a small portion, he sipped it and tried to push away his disgust. No officer of any quality could possibly consider such a decision. He was samurai, and no man of honor could so violate the code of Bushido. How could this be happening? Had Nanking been but the writing on the wall? Was the whole war to be conducted by barbarians? Was *he* a barbarian?

He finished the whiskey and strode out of the tent, finding Segura at the headquarters tent. "Colonel," he announced tightly. "I'm releasing the prisoners."

Segura looked as if he had been slapped. "You can't," he murmured. "The order—"

"There has been no legal order! And I will not be a party to such butchery. The prisoners will be released just after sunset. Disseminate the word that they will be unmolested within the regimental sector."

Segura thrust out his jaw. His voice was belligerent. "I can't permit such an irrational rebellious act, Hoshi. These prisoners are nothing but dirt—pigs of Filipinos and arrogant Americans. They deserve to die!"

"You have your orders, Segura."

The violence on Segura's face subsided into a look of pleasure. "You know of course that I must report this. You're finished, Hoshi. They'll have you back in some rear depot counting socks."

Hiroshi turned away before he did something violent.

Ten minutes later, Cedric Baldwin looked up from where he was discussing the surrender with the officers of his escape group. A tall, erect Japanese officer was approaching the group of about forty officer prisoners. A guard shouted "Attention!" with a bad accent as the colonel and his adjutant stopped close by. Cedric blinked as the colonel stood silhouetted against the bright slanting rays of the sun.

The tall Japanese spoke in nearly flawless English. "At ease, gentlemen. I'm the commander. Please listen carefully. In twenty minutes, all prisoners of this command will be released without harm. You may do as you wish about escape, but when I finish my adjutant will brief you on the location of other Japanese Army units. This should make your task easier. . . ."

Cedric narrowed his eyes. There was something familiar about the colonel, something in his erect carriage, his voice. And what was he trying to do? What was this sudden reprieve all about? The Japanese just didn't do things like this. He had already had most of the contents of his pack taken, his Bulova ripped from his wrist, and a rifle butt jammed viciously into his kidneys. Who was this gallant knight—or was it just an act to get everyone shot in the back while escaping?

Hiroshi finished his short explanation and came smartly to attention. "Good luck, gentlemen," he said as he saluted them and strode away.

Instantly Cedric recognized him. "Colonel Hoshi!" he shouted.

Hiroshi turned back to where a tall, gaunt man was waving his arm excitedly. Old Baldwin!

Moments later, Cedric stood outside the tent trying to decide how he felt about this sudden development. He'd like to smash his fist in the bastard's eye, but mostly he wanted to find out about Sataro and Miyuki. He didn't have long to ponder. "Come in, Mr. Baldwin," Hiroshi said pleasantly, handing him a glass with scotch whiskey in it. He pointed to a pillow on the floor. "How is my father's oldest friend from Lodi?"

Dropping to the floor, Cedric sipped and eyed Hiroshi coolly. "Trying to stay alive and out of your stinking prison camps, Colonel. What the hell is this act you're pulling?"

Hiroshi shrugged as he sipped his scotch. "No more than what you heard."

"Why?"

Hiroshi didn't want to tell him about the order to kill prisoners. He shrugged again. "A military decision, sir. How is my family in California?"

Cedric's eyes glittered. "Ashamed and frightened. They're ashamed of being Japanese and afraid of the coming retaliation. At least that was the last I heard. What about your father?"

Hiroshi shook his head sadly, then told Cedric that his father was still in a deep state of shock over Miyuki's death. "The last letter from Uncle Seizo stated that he hadn't improved," he said quietly.

Cedric slumped, momentarily overcome. He couldn't imagine his noble friend walking around in a daze. They had said he hadn't recovered from the tragedy, but nothing about how serious it was. Why hadn't they told him when it happened? Surely he could have gone to Japan earlier, possibly helped. . . . He shook away the shock. "Please send him my best wishes and tell him—'' Cedric swallowed, unable to speak for a moment. "Tell him everything is the same between us."

Hiroshi nodded. "I will, Mr. Baldwin. Now, you had best rejoin your group. They'll be wanting to move out with what's left of the light." He stuck out his hand. "Good luck."

Cedric pulled himself to his feet, tossing down the rest of the whiskey and leaving without shaking hands or thanking his host. Turning a couple of paces from the tent, he looked into Hiroshi's eyes and nodded.

Later, some three miles southeast of Bagac and nearing the west road they hoped to take up the coast, the trail Cedric's group was following under the bright moon ran into a major road. Sitting in the center of the intersection was an armored car—part of the Japanese patrol that recaptured them. They were about to commence one of the most brutal and gruesome marches in the history of modern warfare. When it was completed at wretched Camp O'Donnell several days later, thousands of prisoners had been savagely murdered in one of the most inhuman examples of barbarity a captured force ever endured. It finally became known as the Bataan Death March.

Thirty-six

Three days later, when Tokyo had just finished celebrating the fall of Bataan like so many other of her victories, Suiko arose early and hurried outside into the garden to enjoy the beauty of the cherry blossoms in solitude. How she loved this time of the year and these magnificent bloomings, so very fresh and softly vibrant. She took a thin branch lightly between her fingers and moved it to where she could brush it with her cheek, thinking of how soon it would pass through its life cycle and fall to the ground, dying, with thin brown edges. Automatically, she drew her kimono more closely about her throat. The cherry blossom, the warrior. And she thought about Hiroshi's poem.

She sighed deeply as she moved on, touching another tree's flowers. How she loved her handsome warrior. And how she wished she could be on Luzon helping to ease his mind. She had admitted long ago that he was really the weaker one—hadn't she even manipulated their marriage?

She laughed at the memory of their first kiss in a silly rickshaw.

And now, when the empire was just beginning its trip to world power, her poor darling was feeling qualms. She understood and agreed with his shock over Nanking years earlier—she, too, had been revolted. But in war against the West, one had to think about the magnitude and keep doubts and minor quirks of conscience in perspective. After all, hadn't Alexander once said, "To know and worry over the individual soldier is to emasculate a general, but to do so over the enemy is to emasculate an army"?

Sitting on a short stone bench, she closed her eyes and imagined Hiroshi's strong arms around her. She reached to his lips and smelled his invigorating scent, thinking that there might be a way for the association to send her down there. Chuckling, she scolded herself for interrupting even her fantasies with association activity. And how she could fantasize these days—it seemed the older she got, the more her fires burned. Her hand crept up to touch her breast.

"Good morning, Mother."

She looked up at the bright smile on her pregnant daughter's face, thinking that Sachi was getting more beautiful each day. But then, it was a family trait—hadn't she been at her radiant best after the six-month stage of pregnancy?

"Good morning, my dear. I was just enjoying the beautiful blossoms and thinking of your handsome father." She patted the bench. "Come sit with me and talk."

Sachi sat down slowly. Although she remained strong, she was quite large in the belly for this stage. This morning, she had had some of the sickness—a rare occurrence. "I don't think I want to go with you to the factory today, Mother. I don't feel too well."

Suiko frowned inwardly. She liked to show the workers how a young pregnant war hero's wife came out to contribute to the war effort. It reminded them that one could always do and give more, no matter what. Soon, there would be more women workers in the factories—not just the maids that had fled households like the plague for the higher paying jobs. Oh, there were so many juicy possibilities for the association on the horizon, all the political implications, the improvement of rights. The idea of going to Manila to speak to the Filipino women—while farfetched—was worth developing. Didn't those women need guidance just as their men needed the spirit of the Rising Sun to bring them back into the proper Oriental sphere? And in Malaya and Siam, Indochina, the Indies—there was *so* much to be done! She really ought to see Premier Tojo about the theory of military commissions for the leaders of the association, and about a formal budget. No, he'd frown on that—one of the values of the association had always been its self-supporting and charitable aspect. "How about the hospital visit at two-thirty?" she asked. "Do you think you'll be able to make that? The poor wounded men like you so much!"

Sachi smiled tiredly as she patted her mother's hand. "Maybe. I think I'll feel better later. Why don't you swing by and pick me up after your speech at the factory?"

Suiko nodded with a bright smile. "Good. You're a brave soldier. Maybe mother will go to the factory with me." Itoko had grown more involved with the association since the outbreak of war with the West, but she wasn't too keen on these factory appearances. She was at her best recruiting older women and extracting yen from the tight fists of dowagers. My, the drive that woman had—and she didn't look a day over fifty!

Suiko got to her feet and stretched languorously.

"You remind me of a sleek, satisfied cat," Sachi said with a touch of envy. "Aren't grandmothers supposed to be dumpy little old women?"

Suiko laughed as she headed for the house. "Tell that to yours."

Itoko never knew whether she was comfortable sitting on the platform while her daughter-in-law gave a speech. As a girl and young woman, she had always been confident in turning men's heads and getting an envious look from women now and then. But sitting on a chair in front of them was a different matter. Besides, she told herself glumly, she was *old* now. And—she felt—above being an object of curiosity for a bunch of village girls and a sprinkling of condescending men who stuck their noses into the meeting. Still, giving something of herself was the *least* she could do.

She shifted her position and turned her attention from the wide-eyed curious faces below the tiny dais to Suiko. There were sounds to the east almost like someone shooting off fireworks. She leaned forward a fraction to hear better.

"We are invincible," Suiko was saying, standing proudly to her left. Her fist was raised dramatically. "The sacred land of the Rising Sun has produced warriors from the beginning of time, and now they reach out, immune to enemy. . . ."

Several heads turned to whisper as the explosions grew louder.

*   *   *

Sachi finished her light lunch of chopped lobster and Brussels sprouts at 12:25. She had plenty of time to change before her mother picked her up with the car at two-thirty, so she went out to drink in the fresh warmth of the garden and smell the bright cherry blossoms again. As much as she loved the pinkish beauties, she couldn't help feeling a touch of resentment. The warrior flower—a short life of splendor. Why couldn't a thistle have been picked? she asked herself angrily. Why did Korin have to be a beautiful cherry blossom instead of an ugly weed? She thought of his short leave after the great victory in Hawaii, his medal, his great pride—and his damned eagerness to get back into combat. She shuddered. Fools!

Sounds sifted through her anger. . . . What could anyone be celebrating? Another victory? Small explosions? She was struck by a sharp chill.

Premier General Hideki Tojo leaned close to the window to look down at the Shimbashi Station section of metropolitan Tokyo as the pilot turned the aircraft onto a long final approach for landing. Off to his right was the huge expanse of palace grounds—so green and rich, so powerful and impenetrable. He seldom bothered thinking about himself, but a feeling of satisfaction warmed him now. It was a long way from his father's humble beginning to being premier of the greatest empire in the world. And now the three-year timetable for total victory looked secure. Success after success followed his forces wherever they attacked. Only that stubborn island of Corregidor held out in Manila Bay, but it couldn't last more than a couple of weeks more. His wife was so proud— What were those bright spots, like explosions, like fireballs? He asked his military aide.

Lieutenant Colonel Jimmy Doolittle, in the first B-25 to arrive, eased back slightly on the steering column as he noticed a twin-engined aircraft off to his left. No slowing down now, he told himself excitedly as he banked slightly to go directly over the Imperial Palace. There it was—all green and confident, waiting to be blasted! Arrogant! But orders were orders—no palace today. He pushed the nose down. There was no order against letting the bastards know he was here! He roared onward, gritting his teeth and pretending he had a whole bay full of bombs to unleash. At two hundred feet, he leveled off; crossing the moat, and giving the engines one short blast of power to complete the buzz job. Then it was off to China. *It was finally a two-way street!*

Tojo felt the aircraft rock as another airplane swept past. He blinked as he caught a glimpse of the markings. An American fleet had been reported eight hundred miles away that morning, but everyone knew the Americans had no bombers that could fly from a carrier! Where had it come from? How—

The pilot shouted that they were diving to land.

Sachi ran frantically from the Obata house. Instinctively, she knew what the explosions meant—she had been dreaming about them for months! A stab of fear gripped her stomach. *She had known all along, tried to tell them—these fools and their holy, valiant war. . . . She knew the enemy would come!* She shut her eyes so tightly they hurt as a B-25 thundered by a mere two hundred yards away. As she lost consciousness and slumped to the ground, the image of a bleak funeral procession marched before her.

The sound of large engines on a low-flying aircraft roared into the factory's crowded courtyard only a split second before the bombs crashed into the building! Itoko remembered jerking her head up in time to see a brown airplane of some sort roar overhead. It had red, white, and blue markings—

One element of the incendiary cluster struck high on the wall of the two-story building behind them. A piece of it tore into the top of Suiko's skull.

Hiroshi had been in a quandary about what to do with Segura. The executive officer had filed his charges personally with Homma's chief of staff in Manila five days after the prisoners were released. Upon his return a day later, Hiroshi had given him an implicit order to remain clear of the headquarters until such time as reassignment orders came through for either one of them. Now, on April 19, he had just returned from inspecting a battalion headquarters when he saw a staff car from army headquarters parked near his command tent. His stomach knotted briefly. Had Homma come down to relieve him personally?

Moments later, a lieutenant colonel jumped up as he entered the tent. "Sir, I'm Gotanda from Manila," he said softly. "Is there a place where we can have some privacy?"

Hiroshi glanced at his watch. "Yes," he replied. "The mess tent will be empty."

An orderly brought tea as soon as they seated themselves at the low staff table. And then they were alone, the obvious seriousness of the situation hanging like heavy incense as Colonel Gotanda reached into his briefcase and extracted an envelope. "I'm most sorry, sir," he murmured, handing it over.

Inside was a message form stamped with a receipt at Fourteenth Army Headquarters. It was addressed to him and read: "It is my most grievous duty to inform you that your wife, Suiko Hoshi, was killed performing her patriotic duty during yesterday's sneak air attack by the Americans. I am most deeply sorry and will ensure that she receives a funeral with full honors." It was signed, "Tojo."

Hiroshi stared, blinking as he tried to read the swimming words again. "Air raid?" he asked absently.

The staff officer nodded.

It was impossible. Suiko couldn't— "How many were killed?" he asked softly.

"I don't know, sir," was the reply. "It's being kept secret for the time being. But it will be a terrible shock to morale."

Hiroshi stared back at the message, seeing SUIKO HOSHI WAS KILLED jump out at him from the blur. He turned away, catching the sob that nearly betrayed him. His heart was a slab of ice, stiff, compressed. His ears rang, but he wouldn't have heard Gotanda slip outside anyway. He saw her laughing eyes over the finest dinner money could buy at the Imperial Hotel that last night before he left, saw her bright smile as she leaned down over him in bed afterward.

He slumped to the table as the ringing increased, dropping the message.

Scenes struggled against each other, fighting to stab him, break him . . . a flippant pretty girl with too wide a mouth at a party, a rickshaw, a wedding of love; a lovely mother holding her beautiful baby . . . her silky black hair widespread on a pillow . . . a brilliant, strong partner . . . her face, so soft in tenderness, so . . .

In spite of himself, the low moan escaped.

Sataro looked up at the orange-tiled roof of Terumoto's Castle— they called it Hiroshima Castle these days—and had a warm feeling. Like so many of the sights and points of interest that he visited on his long daily walks, the tall old edifice brought back parts of his memory. And now that spring had returned, he seemed to recall more and more . . . even seemed to feel some enthusiasm. The bright freshness of the cherry blossoms and all the new greenery of other plants rushing into the growing season stimulated him as if he were a bee or butterfly darting from flower to flower. He felt some of the buoyancy of childhood, some return of his old awareness as he walked the riverbanks and climbed the hills.

Or at least he had until that terrible plane with the bomb killed poor Hiroshi's wife. Yes, his Suiko. A beautiful young woman, the mother of his wonderful Sachi. He remembered how it had struck him when his Sachi called from Tokyo. Hiroshi's Suiko dead like his beautiful Miyuki? More piercing pain, more confusion. The curtain of uncertainty that had been parted seemed to slide back and forth, creating misty edges on his clarity.

He looked at his watch. He had promised to be back before this.

She was coming.

Yes, it seemed to come and go. He had to push it aside somehow. Yes, something down there was trying to fight its way through, trying to break out into the open and tell him something, something important.

He had to hurry, had to get home immediately because she was coming!

*   *   *

Sachi turned from the edge of the red-lacquered bridge. Her black kimono seemed to accent the dark hollows around her eyes as she stared into the large pond that was called Takuei. "You have no idea, Grandfather," she said softly. "For anyone to even think there was a chink in our armor—in our divine invincibility— was pure heresy. And Mother would have been the first to admonish them for such impure thinking." She didn't know if he fully understood, but it didn't matter. Just being with him here in this peace, just feeling his presence was worth the long trip. And she knew that deep down inside somewhere he knew. She told him more about Tokyo and how food rationing was already becoming a major imposition, and how her grandmother was making her demanding presence known with the *yami*—the black market. "Grandmother should be a general," she added.

Sataro always felt comfortable in the serenity of the Shukkei-en, the famous Garden of Condensed Scenic Beauty that dated back 300 years to the Seventh Lord of Hiroshima. Its ingenious planning that encompassed ten islets, tea ceremony rooms, arbors, groves, and footpaths while borrowing scenery from the Kanda River and Futaba Hill had been one of his fondest memories through all those years in America.

And now his Sachi was part of it. He nodded. "When will your child be born?" he asked gently.

She reached out to touch his hand. He knew; how wonderful. "In June," she replied, smiling brightly. And she hadn't smiled brightly since . . . since the raid. Yes, she had known he was the medicine she needed. "I want it to be a boy so I can name him Sataro."

That was pleasing, the idea of another little boy. And named for him. Yes, but then, didn't she always please him? "I'll teach him to whittle little soldiers," he replied with a quick grin. And he knew instinctively that she wouldn't like that. "No, I'll teach him to whittle little doctors."

She nodded. "That would be nice."

He also nodded. It was coming out, that something was coming out. And it was telling him that there were things to do, that he had been asleep or something. Yes. And his Sachi was in such deep pain and sorrow.

He took her hand, hoping he could help her.

The day after Sachi left to return to Tokyo, Sataro went to see Reverend Macnamara in the old hillside mission. Except for a handful of his most devout converts coming to a small weekly service, the testy Methodist was practically shut off from the world. And he would most probably have been interned had not Seizo assumed legal responsibility for him. Now he saw part of the old Sataro was back, and troubled. And he was again a man of the cloth. "What do you remember about the past months?" he asked softly.

Sataro walked to his favorite open window. "It's like a quilt you Americans make," he replied. "It's called patchwork, but some of my patches are missing." He sighed as he watched a large aircraft carrier working its way into the bay. It seemed so alien. "I want to find a place of solitude so I can sort it out. Perhaps then, I will find peace."

Macnamara rose from his chair and picked up the Bible. Holding it out to Sataro, he said, "This is peace, my friend. The Word of God. Take it to your heart and it will pacify your mind. Come stay with me here in the House of God, Sataro. Stay as long as you wish."

His friend's offer was tempting, but what was plaguing Sataro required more. "I'm sorry," he answered at length. "But I think my peace is far, far away and will require a search of perhaps never-ending extent."

The monastery sat on the side of a hill overlooking the end of the floating shrine of Itsukushima on the island of Miyajima. Across the small inlet, the top of the orange-lacquered five-story pagoda could be seen distinctly, and of course, further out in the water the famed O-Torii stood majestic guard. One could also see the mainland through a small break in the heavy foliage that enclosed the wall, as well as the white ferryboats that plied their way back and forth from the southeastern edge of the city.

The monastery seemed smaller than Sataro had pictured, yet its entry garden with its green moss-covered rocks and carefully trimmed trees and shrubbery spread out to form a courtyard of sorts. In the center to the rear of the grounds, the largest building, the meditation hall, seemed to dominate everything. Other buildings ran around the inside of the wall to provide a fortresslike appearance. Black-robed monks were busy at different tasks in several places. All walked in a meditating position when they weren't at labor.

Sataro watched the figure of the monk who was leading him to the master's quarters. Tall and skinny, his height accentuated by the high wooden *geta* he wore on his feet, he seemed to jerk as he walked.

His black robe of flax was caught at the waist by a white cord and stopped short of his knobby knees. The sleeves were wide and flappy. Sataro guessed he was in his early twenties, but his shiny bald head made him look older. Soon, they were behind a small cluster of trees, where the monk silently pushed aside the door and indicated that the visitor should enter.

Inside, erectly seated in a double lotus position on a cushion near the far wall, was an older man in a light gray robe. His translucent skin and white eyebrows indicated that he might be over eighty; his bright black eyes suggested a quick brain. At sixty-nine, Sataro was seldom intimidated by older men, but this Zen master was one of the few priests who were called Roshi—a fully awakened one to whom the "transmission of the lamp" ceremony had been administered years before. It was he who controlled every element, nearly every thought of the monastery's population. Sataro inhaled deeply as he removed his shoes. It was so vital that he say the right things.

Entering, he stopped several feet from the master, bowed deeply, then dropped to his knees and held forth the customary five-yen offering "for incense." The master accepted the money, tucking it into his robe as he asked in a deep but quiet voice, "Why do you wish to place your shoes before our door?"

Sataro looked directly back into those glittering eyes—alert for any sudden shout, attack, or tricky question that he had heard was often part of a Roshi's repertoire. He saw nothing but glowing anticipation. "I have traveled far and I am troubled," he said carefully. "My full brain has been absent for a period, but now has returned to cause me extreme discomfort. If possible, I would like to find enlightenment . . . if not, I wish to find a degree of peace within myself." The short response should please the master.

The Roshi nodded slightly, waiting to see if there was more. As Sataro held his gaze in silence, the master nodded again, saying, "Yes, you have walked a long path—to America, I hear. And that, in these times, should give you extensive cause for discomfort. And now you've come to the right place. Here, the enlightenment—the *satori*—can be found, but only through extreme dedication. You are old to become a disciple, and our ways are rigorous—perhaps beyond your physical capability."

He sighed slightly as he nodded. "But I find you acceptable, providing you will stay either for a minimum of six months, or until you cannot possibly take the regimen any longer. In that event, you will be the loser."

"I can stay for the rest of my life," Sataro replied, fascinated by those intense eyes.

"Such a commitment is unnecessary and impulsive. Our day begins at three in the morning and ends at eleven in the night. We meditate considerably, and you will be subject to criticism and seemingly needless rebukes from monks young enough to be your grandsons. I am told you have been deeply exposed to Christianity."

Sataro nodded. "Yes, *Sensei,* for many years. But I never accepted it wholly."

The eyes widened, containing a glint of humor. "It is no hindrance. I once read part of the Christian Bible and found that someone had written the way of our beloved Buddha."

Macnamara would like that, Sataro thought as he nodded.

"Our diet is that of a stringent vegetarian, and your private area will be far more austere than that of any army private. But your greatest problem, other than teaching your old muscles to endure the lotus sitting position, will be staying awake. You will, at first, doze incessantly—creating a familiarity with the *keisaku,* the warning stick, which will be applied abruptly and smartly to your person."

Sataro nodded again. It would be a matter of will.

The master went on, "Can you push away your family ties? Can you afford three yen per month?"

"Yes." Sataro couldn't believe the insignificant cost.

"Then you are acceptable. Are you prepared to join us today?"

"Yes, *Sensei*. I have meager belongings with me."

The bright eyes softened. "Good. Now tell me about America."

Sataro was not billeted in the meditation hall with the monks, but in an empty room in a storage building next door. The room had a single electric light bulb in a wall socket, a mattress, and one low table that badly needed painting. There were three large nails on the wall for hanging things. There was no means of heat. It would need a thorough scrubbing and most likely a good dose of lye. He sniffed at the odor, remembering that Zen was supposed to create awareness.

The head monk, who acted as administrator, had given him a thorough briefing after he left the master's quarters. Every fifth day was cleaning and bath day. Water was used with austerity— each member was authorized three cups per day for washing. He was issued a bamboo cup. Blankets and pillows were not used; the mattress was doubled over to provide warmth. He would be first assigned to work at the gardening. The head monk ended with, "You will learn meditation."

For thirty minutes prior to lights out that night, he practiced sitting erect. He had been using chairs for a long, long time, and going back to the floor wasn't easy. The full lotus was impossible for him; the half lotus quite uncomfortable. He decided those argumentive muscles would never get past the half—and that would be at their own painful schedule.

He twisted the light off at exactly eleven and fell quickly asleep.

When the rising bell awakened him at three A.M., he wondered if he had made the right decision. He hurried into a turtleneck sweater and one of the two pairs of black pants he had brought along, then rushed outside with his bamboo cup to wait until he could dip into the community basin. Like a tomcat, he dipped the fingers of his other hand into the cup and quickly rubbed water over his face. They had three minutes to get from bed to the meditation hall. He ran a comb through his almost white hair as he took a deep breath and entered. Nodding to the head monk seated near the door, he hurried to the altar in the center of the hall, where he bowed deeply to a shrine of Manjusri, the Bodhisattva of wisdom. Moments later, he was sitting erectly on the meditation pillow that had been assigned to him. His legs were already stiff from the previous practice, but he managed to lock himself into a position that might hold up for the first twenty-five-minute meditation period. By the end of the second meditation period, his legs felt like pieces of ice, but he held on until he was summoned to see the master again.

Early on this spring morning, the master sat in a single lotus and, while his bright eyes were full of life, there was no time for talk of faraway places. "You may have heard of the *koan*," he said in his deep, almost musical voice. "The *koan* is a concentration subject the master gives the student. You will live with a *koan* until it becomes a part of you, and until I decide you have the answer. At that time, you will be given another *koan*." The touch of humor returned to his eyes. "Novices are always given a big *koan* . . . meaning one that will occupy your meditation for an extended period. Yours is 'What is the sound of one hand clapping?' I will see you for a short period each day. When you think you have an answer, you will tell me." He nodded and rang the tiny bell beside his knee. It was the signal for Sataro to go on to the next phase of his new day.

Heading for the dining hall, he shook his head and muttered, "What is the sound of one hand clapping?"

Although the Doolittle Raid succeeded in lifting the sagging American morale, nothing could stay the sure hand of the anti-Japanese forces in California. So powerful was their propaganda that elements of it would be the basis for argument over forty years later. The press, both print and broadcast, was almost universally rabble-rousing in its treatment of the problem. Westbrook Pegler in his Scripps-Howard column cried out, ". . . to hell with *habeas corpus*." Another columnist, Henry McLemore, shouted in print, "Herd 'em up, pack 'em off, and give 'em the inside of the badlands." Conversely, Hearst's Chester Rowell in the San Francisco *Chronicle* stood up for the Japanese and campaigned against evacuation. Ernie Pyle wrote a column in warm support. But Executive Order 9066, signed by Roosevelt in late February, illuminated the path to the United States' own particular brand of infamy.

Thirty-seven

"How can I possibly leave this?" Haru cried aloud as she slumped to the edge of the bed, dropping its rumpled sheets to the floor. A hand went to her forehead as she tried to blink back the tears. Stripping the boy's rooms had been bad enough, but this room, this bed, was where the stranger she had married had brought her when they arrived in this heartless country. She stared through the tears at the still unpacked wedding picture sitting on the dresser. A stern Noboru—she could read the disappointment and rejection in his grave expression—glared back from the old brown photograph. He reminded her that even the beginning of her life in America had been star-crossed. *She should never have left beautiful and safe Miyajima!*

A deep moan wrenched from her breast as she threw herself face down on the bed and pounded her fists, smashing them into the mattress that had long known her innermost secrets . . . her fears, joys and pain, her grief and utmost happiness . . . the screams of her childbirth. It, more than any other object she was about to leave, represented the life of Haru Hoshi in the great democratic United States—the Cradle of Liberty! *Now she wouldn't be a citizen of anything!*

Another moan escaped, but she didn't care—not for these few moments of private misery did she care about anything. Later, she would have to put on the brave front of the strong Hoshi woman; now she was a frightened child. She shuddered, swamped in tears, drifting back to her mother's arms, even that tempting young priest . . . a tiny tame deer. Oh God, why had she ever left Japan?

She sat up, reaching for a sheet to wipe her face. It was all so

432

unfair! Just four years after Noboru's tragic death, the law had been rectified to make the deserving Japanese veterans eligible for citizenship. And her sons were both citizens by birth. How could they possibly lock everyone up?

She was so worried about Billy.

But she'd protect him. That's what would carry her through, she reminded herself with sudden resolve—being the rock. She knew all about the famous Hoshi *gambari*. The terrible whites could rip her from her beautiful home, they could break her suffering heart and tear away all her possessions, but they would not, *could not*, keep her from holding her proud family together. No matter what!

But the resolve was fleeting. A fresh batch of tears erupted, followed by another deep moan. She wasn't that strong, she knew it!

The sound of Teresa Scagnelli's voice brought her hands to her face to hide her shameful breakdown. "I've brought you some more coffee, my dear," the big woman said tenderly as she knelt to take Haru in her arms. "But maybe you need my shoulder more."

Haru tried to stifle another moan, but she didn't quite make it as racking sobs shook her and she poured tears onto Teresa's huge bosom.

It was May 11, 1942, the infamous day of evacuation.

Billy, wearing his freshly laundered white *hachimaki* around his forehead, was striding up and down the rows of vines repeating the code of the samurai in a harsh monotone. This was his land, his home, and his vines they were leaving—most probably to be stolen while they were imprisoned. As firstborn, *he* was heir to this property. He would be the third Hoshi to own it, by God, not some red-neck white who might try to get it for back taxes! He didn't even trust old Mario when it came to that.

Rich old fat Mario. He had made all his money off the Hoshis, that was a fact. And now he was supposed to watch over The Other Cheek and old Yoshi's place next door. Well, if he didn't do as he promised, he'd get his damned head blown off when this was all over. He fingered the silver disk in his pocket. He swore it!

A few minutes later, Haru pinned on the last hat she had bought before Noboru's death. It seemed only fitting. The fog was breaking, allowing bright diffused rays of sunlight to flood the yard. She took in a deep breath as she stepped through the doorway and watched Joey carry the last duffel bag out to the road and sit on it. Oh, how she hoped the right things were packed to see them through whatever horrors lay ahead. . . . Teresa gripped her arm. "Quit worrying," she soothed, trying to sound casual. "I told you I'd check everything at least once a week. I have the key to the barn right here. Your things will be perfect the day you get back, I promise."

Haru nodded dully, wanting to believe it. "Please, Teresa, above all, don't let my vines get neglected. They're all I'll have left to build on when we return . . . our roots."

The loud horn of the Greyhound bus ended the conversation.

The San Joaquin County Fairgrounds at Stockton looked as if a small ugly city had sprung up in its midst overnight. Inside the broad oval of the racetrack, ten separate blocks of tarpaper shacks—each block containing a mess hall and other facilities—was a streaming mass of humanity looking for assigned places to live. The Hoshis were given 24445 as a family identity number, then assigned a room designated 4C1. When Haru saw it, her hand flew to her mouth. It wasn't any larger than her living room! There was one window and no partitions—just a bare, dirty room. "We can get it clean, but what about privacy?" she asked in a tiny voice.

Billy frowned. Numbers and now a cell—a family cell.

"I'll get a blanket for a divider," Joey offered.

Soon Billy began his tour. He had heard there were well over 4,000 evacuees to be held five to seven weeks—until the permanent camps could be completed. He had been to the fairgrounds on several occasions, he recalled as he made his way through the throng of confused, troubled people. But betting on horse races and throwing balls at wooden milk bottles, eating cotton candy, and riding Ferris wheels had nothing to do with incarceration.

And the crowds hadn't been guarded by soldiers with loaded rifles, either.

He looked into the crude latrine and standard old army mess hall, where he was told to expect two dozen different recipes for Spam by a Nisei cook from Turlock. Walking outside the housing area, he found a large building near the hog barn had been set up as a hospital, while horse stables along the backstretch were saving their aroma for the nonfamily evacuees and couples without children. A long line of people with mattress bags was queued up outside a feed barn, waiting to stuff them with straw. A tall fence topped by three strands of barbed wire that sloped inward was dotted with manned wooden guard towers which overlooked everything.

The sense of injustice flooded over him like a red sheet. Nearly two years earlier, Nisei boys were getting drafted! And in the last year, many had been discharged purely because of their ethnic origin. Now the same boys were going into prisons just like this!

He walked on, furious. Across the racetrack, the grandstand stood like a towering mother hen surveying her cluttered barnyard. He climbed to the top row and sat down to observe the teeming scene below. There had to be something he could do about this terrible thing. . . .

Joey found him twenty minutes later. Climbing up, he saw that his brother was still wearing his *hachimaki*. He dropped to a bench a couple of rows below Billy and heaved a big sigh as he wiped his forehead. "Quite a mess, huh, big brother?"

"Yeah, they got us all penned up good, the bastards!" Billy spat out. "I may just break out of here and work my way down to Mexico."

Joey not only had more of his mother's gentle looks, but much of her cool patience. "Then what?"

"Oh, I'd go to Ensenada or some place and catch a damned boat back to Japan."

"And then what?"

"Well, I wouldn't be a damned prisoner, that's for sure."

"No, but you'd just make it awful for Mother. You know that, don't you?"

"She'll live. Besides, soon as this war's over in a few months I could send for her. Then we could all be together spending Grandfather's money in Hiroshima, where we belong."

"We don't even know if he's alive," Joey said sadly.

There were those in the school system who were concerned that some of their top students were being cheated out of their high school diplomas by the evacuation. One forceful Stockton teacher had already arranged for a classroom where tutors could ensure the seniors would finish. Following the school meeting the next afternoon, Billy spotted a fresh box of chalk and swiped a full piece on his way out. Then he went to the maintenance shed to volunteer for repair work. The supervisor scowled and told him all such assignments were being made through the personnel department.

As Billy left the shop, his fingers closed on a pair of pliers and slipped them into his pocket.

But as hard as he looked, he couldn't find an isolated piece of fence; he had to settle for a short span by the backstretch where no direct rays of the floodlights would strike the wire. He studied it carefully that night as darkness fell and decided it was his best shot, then feverishly went to work with the cutting slots of the dull pliers. Sweating profusely after only a few minutes' work, he quickly found that it would take hours to make even a small hole—and he wasn't sure if the soldiers would conduct bedchecks or not. He angrily stole back to the quarters, slipping inside with a casual comment to Joey about the long wait at the latrine.

For the next two days he had trouble keeping his secret, twice nearly trying to recruit an accomplice. He wanted to shout at the top of his lungs, wanted to jerk every young Nisei he saw into the shade and order him to come along. He wanted to openly taunt every soldier he saw, spit on every Caucasian who came near. When he finished work the third night he stopped in the dark shadow of their mess hall on the way to the barracks to pull out the stick of chalk and print in large letters "TO HELL WITH AMERICA" on its wall.

At 10:28 the next night Billy finished with the last strands of wire and carefully edged his broad shoulders through the hole as a searchlight's bright beam moved past. It would work! He reached back into the darkness for the small bag of belongings and food. He was elated! By the time his absence was detected he'd be a good twenty miles away. He—

"Hold it right there!"

He jerked, startled, spinning around to stare into the glare of the flashlight.

"Raise your hands!"

He slumped, scared, his stomach churning. The voice of the guard bore into him. "I could've just let him go a few steps and blasted him, Sarge."

They took him to the guardhouse, where he was held until the next afternoon. Since his was the only attempted escape in the short time since the evacuation began, the camp commander considered Haru's plea and the fact that he was the grandson of a former leading citizen in the Japanese community. He was released to her custody with a warning that another attempt could mean being sent to a federal prison such as Fort Leavenworth.

The Rising Sun showed few signs of ending its high roll. Corregidor had fallen on May 5, and three days later the Imperial Navy escaped with a draw after being ambushed at Coral Sea. And while Yamamoto's ships virtually controlled the Pacific, the new U.S. Pacific fleet commander, Nimitz, was nursing his wounds and treading water until America's industrial might could begin splashing new fighting ships down the ways. But the gambling Yamamoto had an ingenious plan for a knockout punch—to entice Nimitz into a massive trap at Midway Island. The stage was set. On June 3, Yamamoto made a feint on the Aleutian Islands far to the north. But Nimitz had cracked the Japanese codes, and intelligence pointed to Midway. With great heroics, seamanship, and perseverance the U.S. force took advantage of the phenomenal luck it encountered in the face of equally tenacious bravery on the part of Yamamoto's vastly superior armada.

Thirty-eight

Lieutenant Korin Koga had been involved in a busy morning. Flying escort on the first strike on Midway, he had gotten two kills on American fighters—a Buffalo and a new F4F Grumman Wildcat. And after returning to the air following refueling, he had just shot down two U.S. Navy Avenger torpedo bombers as they hurtled hopelessly toward his carrier group. Flying low over the water, he saw with relief that both crew members of the last one were bobbing about safely. He considered it unlucky to think of the numbers, but this one brought his total to twenty-one. He stood a good chance of being awarded the—

His quick reflexes told him more visitors had arrived. From out of the sun a large number of enemy dive bombers were heading straight for the carriers that were right in the middle of refueling! With all that aviation fuel and armament on deck, the ships were infernos waiting to be ignited! Slamming the Zero's throttle forward, he pulled the responsive fighter's nose up into a sharp climb. He caught a glimpse of other Zeros swarming after him, but he knew they'd never reach the steep glide path of those Douglas Dauntless bombers in time.

Roaring up through 3,000 feet, he spotted another wave of dive bombers—perhaps fifteen or twenty—coming in from the opposite direction. Was the entire American naval air arm opposing them? He headed straight for them on a collision course. Larger and larger the enemy dive bombers loomed as he continued to snarl toward them. And now they were dipping over to begin their dive. Closing at nearly 500 miles per hour, he could almost read the numbers on the bomber's tail when he squeezed the trigger and saw his twenty-millimeter cannon shells tear the canopy away. Banking sharply into a dive to his right, he was about to blast another one when two .50-caliber machine gun bullets crashed into his cockpit. The second one hit him in the left eye.

Itoko was using all her willpower to control herself. Having just heard over NHK radio that the accursed Americans had thrown all West Coast Japanese into horrible concentration camps, she had cried most of the morning over Haru and her grandsons. Now this swine, this secret police *swine* . . . "I believe you should check with Premier Tojo," she replied icily. *Thought police*, they called them, she fumed to herself. They could arrest you for thinking wrong, as the saying went. She had read about Hitler's Gestapo, same damned thing!

"But," Inspector Oishi replied coolly, "your granddaughter's comments were extremely unpatriotic."

Itoko sighed, saying, "She's an extremely pregnant young woman who recently lost her mother in an air raid that wasn't supposed to happen. Whatever she might have said came from severe grief. Now as I said, call General Tojo's office if you have any further questions."

Oishi didn't like this haughty rich women with military officer connections. They could rot in a cell just like so many others who had crossed him. And they could be tortured just as easily. He jotted a note in his small book. "We don't like use of such implied connections, madam," he replied. "I must make a note of it for your dossier."

Itoko didn't know how much more she could stand. "My dossier?" she asked incredulously. "Why should there be one on me?"

The inspector's eyes narrowed. "Because you are suspect, madam. I—"

Fear or no fear, the Itoko of old exploded, her voice cracking like a whip. "Get out of my house! And if you ever come back, I'll have you sent to Siberia!"

Oishi shrugged coldly. "I would suggest, madam," he said as he turned to the door, "that you watch your activities carefully."

He nodded to the bald-headed major-domo. "And that your servants also be especially careful."

Itoko whirled as the man departed. She would personally go to Tojo's—

"What's the problem, Grandmother?" Sachi asked as she came out to the entry.

"I didn't want to wake you, dear," Itoko replied smoothly. "It wasn't anything important." With the baby due any moment, she didn't want anything to further distress her granddaughter.

Hata, the elderly major-domo who had been with them for so many years, moved to answer the door as Sachi shrugged and turned to go back inside. She felt particularly big this day and wondered if it was finally time. "May we have some tea?" she asked wearily. "I need to be entertained."

The visitor was Lieutenant Colonel Dobana, one of the premier's military aides. Entering solemnly, he bowed deeply to the women. Both of them sensed immediately that something was wrong. *Hiroshi!* Itoko cried out to herself. *No!* Sachi shouted silently. They moved to the parlor as Hata went for tea.

A few minutes later, Colonel Dobana ended the amenities with a clearing of his throat. His voice was low and toneless as he looked gravely at Sachi and said, "Your husband, Lieutenant Korin Koga, became a great hero at the recent Battle of Midway, Mrs. Koga. He reached the most glorious plateau of shooting down twenty enemy aircraft and will soon be awarded the Order of the Golden Kite, First Class."

Sachi stared frozen into his eyes, knowing there was more. Itoko held her breath.

The colonel cleared his throat again. "The premier has asked me to relay his personal interest in informing you that Lieutenant Koga met a proud and glorious death in this same act of outstanding bravery. His Imperial Highness has been told of your husband's great contribution and has expressed his pride."

Sachi continued to stare at this stranger, this puppet mouthing words which she could no longer hear. His head moved and his eyes tried to say something—but he was a robot. What was the drivel coming from his lips—her Korin had been instrumental in the great victory? Already, she had heard a commander's wife whisper over tea that something was wrong with the victory proclamation they had heard over Radio Tokyo. *Lies! Everything was a lie!* she screamed to herself as the colonel's features and those of her grandmother became wavy, floating forms. *Korin was a lie! Her mother—and most probably her father off on some crazy island! All lies!*

Her grandmother's hand was stretching out to her, her eyes coming closer, waving, huge, dark, lying. . . .

"Ahhyiee!" she screamed, throwing her head backward and slamming her fists into her eyeballs. *"Aaayeeee!"* Falling to the floor, all she knew was the terrible pain. The noise was gone, but the scream was stuck in her throat forever.

Her daughter was born fifty-eight minutes later.

The next two days were detached, disconnected scenes of distress for Sachi. The pain of the childbirth was vivid, but scorched with hate . . . the parade of faces . . . Itoko . . . the doctor . . . the servants . . . others, the faceless woman with the bare breast who was nursing the red-faced, terrible little baby. Why didn't the woman just be gone with the bawling thing? Take it wherever she lived and never come back. Why did her grandmother keep shoving the little lie at her—couldn't they understand that this, this red-faced *thing* was part of the lie—part of Korin's crazy, horrible lie? If Korin wasn't real, how could this thing be?

The only way to beat the lie was to stare at the wall.

At times, Korin would come and go, seeming to entice and taunt her as he enveloped the room. Once, she was certain she experienced the physical joy of making love to him. But each time she tried to crush his beautiful head to her breast, he slipped softly away like a specter . . . winking at her as if she'd been in on the joke all along.

On the fifth day the bitter anger returned. Now the great Tojo—even the Emperor—were saying his dying was a remarkable feat. A medal for a holy religious act? How far had these mad generals and admirals come on this path of self-destruction? How far ingrained was this insidious insanity—was it the preeminent device to ensure military victories at any cost? Glorious death—what would be left when Nippon had been denuded of all her sons?

And her father—wasn't he one of them?

She shuddered and dropped back into her dull, uncaring state. She'd just lie there and ignore them, particularly that lie they kept telling her was her baby daughter. She ground her teeth together—they were even calling her Mitsu, the name she would have given to her own dear baby. Korin's own dear baby . . . if he and she weren't lies. . . .

Swinging down from the Betty bomber that had brought him to Tachikawa Air Base from Manila, Hiroshi glanced around to see if anyone was meeting him. But no one knew he was coming, he remembered as the crew chief grabbed his bag and hurried toward Operations. In no time, the duty officer had arranged a staff car and the long ride to Azabu began.

It was past ten and quite dark as the driver worked his way past the many bicycles that were still out on this rainy night. He wasn't used to seeing that many, then recalled that gasoline was severely rationed. And the tiny villages they passed through— they were dark except for a few bright paper lanterns hanging in front of the teahouses and eating places that were still open. It was almost a war zone, he thought, then remembered the Doolittle bombers with a chill.

At first, after hearing of her death, he thought he'd never want to see Tokyo again—just finish the war out and perhaps retire to the hills somewhere around Hiroshima. Maybe Miyajima, like his father. Anywhere to find peace, to bury himself away from the sorrows and horrors of the world. But he had his duty. . . .

He thought back to the daze of that first few days after he was notified of her death. He barely noticed that Segura received orders transferring him from the regiment, insisting up to the last moment that he would get even—that a court-martial would still come of the prisoner release on Bataan. Not that he cared. With the specter of her death hanging over him like a shadow, they could reduce him to captain and it wouldn't matter.

He could have come home on leave before, but he didn't have the courage. Now he was being reassigned, with temporary duty in Tokyo, so there was no way around it. He caught his reflection in the window as he stared at two drunks waving from a few feet away. He had tried that too, including the last three days in Manila. He leaned back against the cushion and closed his eyes. And that was exactly what he was going to do when he got to the house.

After a quick warm embrace with his mother, such thoughts were immediately wiped away as she told him about Korin and Sachi. "Come," she said, dabbing her eyes. "Come meet your granddaughter."

Numbly he followed Itoko to the room where the midwife was sleeping with the baby. Moments later, Mitsu Koga was blinking wide eyes at him as he held her awkwardly in his arms. "And you say Sachi hasn't accepted her once?" he asked, feeling a flood of tenderness and a memory of another young mother sweep over him.

"Not once."

He smiled into the baby's lopsided yawn, then handed her back to his mother. He nodded. "I'm going to Sachi now."

"She's probably asleep."

"She's been sleeping too long."

A minute later, Sachi stirred in her fitful halfway world. A tall dark figure carrying a small incense candle had entered her room and stood beside her bed. He was the god of darkness who had come to take her away and punish her for being part of the lies. She fixed her gaze on the candle as it was placed on the nightstand. Would he drag her away or carry her? It didn't matter—she must go. . . . his hand was moving up to her face, lingering an inch away, as if making up its mind. There was something about it, a smell . . . she was a small girl again, a child basking in the comfort of being loved. . . . The fingertips touched her cheek and she wanted to kiss them.

The words, they sounded like her—no, it couldn't be.

"Wake up, my darling," they said tenderly. "Your father has come to take all the pain away."

She opened her eyes wide as she sat up. His strong arms encircled her and she knew. A tiny, fearful smile came to her lips as he rocked her slowly back and forth, murmuring soft words she couldn't even understand. Then slowly, the first tears began to slip down her cheeks, and suddenly the great blanket of crushing darkness and pain burst loose and was torn aside. A deep moan of relief escaped her lips as she gripped his shirt. "Father?" she asked tentatively.

"Yes, my little flower," he replied softly as his hand caressed her matted hair.

"Will you stop the lies?"

He brought her cheek up to his. "Yes, the lies are finished. And now I have a most precious present for you."

She smiled through the tears. "Oh, how nice."

Picking her up, he held her tightly as he carried her past the worried Itoko and on to the baby's room. A single lamp was on, creating a soft light. He shook his head for the midwife to be still, then gently lowered Sachi to the floor. As she watched with wide, curious eyes, he handed her a tiny, warm, doll-like bundle that moved as she took it in her arms. And then its bright black eyes opened wide and stared back at her. "What a beautiful baby," she whispered.

Hiroshi reported to the General Staff Operations Division the next morning. Inside the Plans Section, a colonel took him to a huge map of the South Pacific and pointed northeast of Australia to the Solomon Islands. "When you finish your leave, Hoshi, you are to absorb everything about this group of islands. We are certain the Americans will soon be very interested here." His fingertip was resting on a smaller island named Tulagi and its larger neighbor—Guadalcanal. "You'll depart by air on July twenty-sixth for Ribaul, where you'll be assigned to General Hiyakutake's Seventeenth Army headquarters."

Hiroshi's next stop was the premier's palace, where Dobana arranged an appointment for him to see Tojo briefly two days later. After Dobana mentioned Korin's coming medal, Hiroshi asked him about Midway. "How come it was declared a major victory when we lost four carriers and Yamamoto's invasion force was driven away? Don't we have enough victories without fabricating them?"

"It's the propaganda people," Dobana sighed. "Even the general can't control them. And in this case, the navy reported it that way."

Hiroshi nodded grimly. "And we can't let the people know we lose now and then."

Dobana nodded. "You said you wanted a favor?"

"Yes, an Inspector Oishi from the political police has harassed my family for no apparent reason—even threatened my mother. Will you see that he finds . . . other duties?"

The aide scribbled in his notebook. "His chief will be reprimanded."

He found his mother watching with pleasure as Sachi nursed the baby in her bedroom. "Ah, lunchtime," he said pleasantly as he entered the bright room. "And how are all my ladies today?"

Sachi smiled up happily, quickly returning her attention to her busy daughter. Itoko got to her feet and glided through the door, motioning for him to follow. When they reached the warm, sunlit garden, she said, "It's amazing! Her rejection of the child is gone, but she's still in some kind of a daze—as if she has reverted to some phase of her childhood."

"What does the doctor say?"

"He thinks the confusion will pass and she'll soon be back to normal."

Hiroshi's expression darkened. "Yes, with her grief." He paced a few steps before adding painfully, "Mother, I want you to do me a favor . . . take me to the factory where . . . where she died. I—I want you to describe her last moments."

Itoko nodded. "She was a glowing, vibrant young patriot, my son."

He stared at a tree-peony Suiko had so loved. How well he knew.

Sataro looked up from where he was weeding turnips as the head monk called out to him. Squinting into the sun, he had trouble making out the features of the soldier. Normally visitors had to be received in the waiting room, but it might be— He jumped to his feet as he saw it was his son! In a moment he was pummeling Hiroshi's hand in the American fashion.

"You may take the rest of the day off," the head monk said pleasantly.

It took only minutes for Sataro to change into his clean pair of pants and a fresh shirt, then it was off down the hilly path toward town. Hiroshi said little, waiting for his father to take the lead. Finally, Sataro smiled and said, "You're wondering if I'm sane yet, aren't you, son? Well, I suppose I'm as well off as many and as lacking as a few. Do you understand Zen?"

"Only its basics, father."

"I'm undergoing a rigorous search."

"That's what Uncle Seizo told me. Are you making progress?"

Sataro smiled, stopping to point at a nearby bush. "See those blossoms? See the butterfly?" He smiled again. "That butterfly looks brilliant to me—I can see every single hue and tint in its breathtaking colors. I'm vibrantly aware of so many things I never noticed before. I could rush back up to the master and shout that I've discovered something new and vital!"

Hiroshi nodded. He had heard about the goal of detachment. He watched the peaceful expression on his father's face as he continued to study the butterfly. He looked trim. The closely cropped white hair gave him a military look—as if he might be an elder field marshal tending his garden while his armies gathered. Would he be able to do this someday, would he be able to reach so serenely into his own enlightenment, shed forever the terrible loss of his beloved Suiko?

"Why do you come, my son?" his father asked as he again headed down the hill. "I feel there are troubles. Is it the war?"

"Yes, Father." Hiroshi told him about Korin and Sachi.

Sataro slumped momentarily, then pulled out an old pipe and lit it with a wooden match. How terrible that she had suffered such a dreadful blow. The part of him that was her grandfather was pained; the part that was learning to overcome self tried to shut out the news as some distant happening to strangers. They walked on. Finally Sataro murmured, "I know it's of no solace to you, my son, but the Buddha has said everything is temporary and will die. Life is suffering—that is always the way of it. Even what we consider happiness is suffering because such feelings are limited in time and will end."

The fine gravel path flattened out as it led into the wider thoroughfare by the inlet near the Daigan-ji Temple. A small spotted deer ran up to see if they had food to offer, then gave them an accusing look and decided to go elsewhere. Miyajima was utterly silent as Sataro smiled at his tall son. "Come, let us go to the inn where you can buy a curious old man some rich crab and warm sake. And perhaps you can tell me about California."

Hiroshi stiffened. Surely his father remembered that Noboru's family were the enemy, and now supposedly even the enemy of the United States. He decided not to mention what he'd heard about the concentration camps. "I've heard nothing, Father," he lied gently.

Sataro nodded. His zen wasn't yet strong enough to shut out the pain over Sachi.

Thirty-nine

"Is this the Forty-sixth Regimental Headquarters?" Hiroshi asked the blank-faced captain. It looked like perhaps a company command post. As the stocky officer nodded curtly, Hiroshi asked, "Where's Colonel Nigata?"

The captain pointed to the stump of a huge gnarled tree forty feet away in the undergrowth. In the dim light of dusk, Hiroshi made out the form of a figure squatting in a double lotus, staring straight ahead. He hurried over to the meditating commander. "Sorry to bother you, Nigata," he said brusquely. "But you've got to get this regiment on the beach for pickup tonight."

The colonel was wearing a torn, filthy kimono and a blank expression on his worn face. "Who are you?" he asked in a hoarse voice.

"Hoshi—from Seventeenth Army. Deputy chief of staff. The destroyers are coming down the Slot to get us tonight and it's their final trip."

Nigata stared straight ahead. "I won't retreat another step. Two-thirds of my men are dead or unable to move and I won't dishonor them."

Hiroshi had heard the same story over and over. After six months of desperate combat and starvation on this rotten island, almost every commander wanted to at least save face by a final *banzai* attack against the hated Americans—not take his defeats home with him. Guadalcanal had been one of the most desultory, emasculating blunders in the history of Japan. Even against staggering losses in the outlying waters, the Americans had hung on and continued to resupply the mad marines who protected Henderson Field. Eventually, the Americans were so well sup-

449

plied that their major problem was what to do with their huge stock of condoms—or so it seemed to the diseased, starving Nipponese soldiers who faced them with such futility from the depths of the rotten, stifling, malaria-infested jungle.

Japanese soldiers, while trained to live on a cup of rice a day, were forced to survive on roots, insects, and whatever else they could force down their gullets. Out of 38,000 proud troops that had eventually landed on this fetid piece of the Solomons, they'd be lucky if they could get 13,000 out safely. "Colonel Nigata," he said tiredly, pulling out a written order. "I come directly from General Hyakutake on the beach. You will do as ordered."

Nigata moved his shoulders slightly, then stiffened. He had said his last word on the matter. Sensing this, Hiroshi moved in front of him. Swatting a mosquito on his cheek, he growled, "Very well, Colonel, you're relieved from command." Whirling back to the watching captain, he barked, "I'm assuming command of the regiment. Get runners off to the battalion commanders immediately that we are withdrawing to the beach in one hour. And have the executive officer report to me at once."

"Sir," the captain replied quietly, "I'm the executive officer."

The First Battalion remnants began their leapfrogging withdrawal fifteen minutes later, but Hiroshi had trouble getting the other two battalions moving. After prodding the Second into motion, he reached the command post of the Third at 2125. A young captain led him to the emaciated major commanding. The man was tall, but couldn't have weighed over ninety pounds; his forehead was swathed in a filthy white headband and his too-bright eyes were vague. Hiroshi wondered how long it had been since his malaria had been treated. He repeated the withdrawal order, but got no response. Immediately, Hiroshi relieved him and appointed the young captain temporary commander. "I want this battalion on the beach in forty minutes," he ordered grimly.

Hurrying away, accompanied only by the grizzly sergeant who had been his bodyguard since leaving the beach, he rushed back to make sure the Second was still moving. The oppressive jungle was now blanketed in total darkness and the eerie sounds of the myriad forms of life that made it so miserable. The faces of the worn soldiers—unshaven and hollow-cheeked, bewildered and betrayed—seemed to stare back at him in the periodic flashes from the pale moon breaking through the overcast. He wondered if most of them would be sent directly to a China command to recover—like the survivors of Midway. Maybe the Philippines, anywhere to keep the truth of defeat from reaching the people.

Forty minutes later, he walked heavily up to the forward beach area boundary. His legs were about gone, his own malaria the culprit. He wanted to slump to the sand and let someone else, anyone else, take over. But he couldn't—he had to get back to headquarters. There was so much to be done to meet the destroyers. And surely, the Americans would soon start raising hell with—

He saw the brilliant flash and heard the thunderous explosion as the shell exploded and tossed him into the air like a rag doll.

Joey settled down on the edge of the roof and watched as the dissidents tested the loudspeaker. Billy's words still rang in his ears. "There'll be a special event at kitchen twenty-two this afternoon—and be there early so I don't have to explain why my little brother is a *hakujin* lover." His tone had been condescending, as it usually was since their arrival at Manzanar and his association with the troublemakers.

Most of the reactionaries were Kibei—Japanese Americans who had gone back to Japan for some extended period of time and had been treated to a strong dose of nationalism just as Billy had been during his brief stay with Hiroshi in 1936. They continually exhorted violence and tried to coerce the camp population. Unwilling to accept any form of passivity, they held that the JACL—the Japanese American Citizens League—and other middle-of-the-roaders were *inu*, dogs of informers. And via loudspeakers, they read so-called "death lists" to intimidate everyone.

Joey had no use for them, but couldn't curb his fascination. Usually wearing white *hachimaki*, they often paraded and shouted Bushido sayings. Today was to be their most forceful demonstration, and they had hinted that it might even grow into a camp takeover. A cook who tried to organize a union after charging the assistant camp director with selling the sugar ration had been arrested and that was the point of their dispute. Tomorrow it would be something else.

Joey turned up the collar of his jacket as a chill wind picked up and blew the infernal, ever-present white dust of Manzanar into his mouth. It was December 5 and they had been in this godforsaken new prison—one of ten so-called concentration camps the government had built—since late August. Located in the Owens Valley thirty miles west of Death Valley, the camp rested in the shadow of towering Mount Whitney, which many of the internees compared to Mount Fuji. Forty blocks of tarpaper shacks to house 10,000 people. School, infirmary, recreation halls, and places to eat and perform body functions; called relocation or evacuation centers, or projects, but regardless of name—barbed wire enclosures that stole one's most precious possession: liberty.

Joey never ceased to flinch when he thought about the Pledge of Allegiance being recited in the schoolrooms. ". . . liberty and justice for all."

"Death to the inu!"

The first speaker was beginning his harangue to the gathering crowd as the appointed hour approached. By the time the second shouter had taken over the microphone, at least a thousand people were packed into the area around the mess hall. More listeners edged in, jamming shoulder to shoulder, flooding the roofs, pressing forward. More Kibei speakers took their turns, screaming about the sugar fraud and roaring for the union organizer's release. And with each agitator's added invective, the crowd grew more and more restive. Joey even found himself being caught up in the fervor.

He saw Billy near the microphone, raising his fist for emphasis.

By now the crowd had become a mob of vituperative, violent strength. Joey guessed there were over 2,000 people in it, all incensed, the flames of their pent-up frustrations and craving for retribution fanned until they were ready to burst into a fireball. Suddenly three thundering *BANZAI!* exploded over the area. The mob had broken loose and was surging like a flood around the buildings and down the streets toward the jail. It was bedlam as Joey jumped from the roof and joined the current.

Deciding he had to get near the front to see anything, he broke down a side street on a dead run. Dodging a big yellow mongrel that barked loudly at him, he went over another street and then turned, paralleling the mob's course. In a couple of minutes, he cut back toward the street leading to the jail in time to see the head of the mob column pull up in front of a cordon of armed military policemen. Stopping as they stared into the muzzles of assorted rifles, shotguns, and machine guns, the front ranks of the mob tried anxiously to decide what to do. Joey gulped in deep breaths, trying to spot Billy as a sudden silence overcame the crowd.

An MP captain brandishing a tommy gun stepped up to a microphone. In patient terms, he asked the people to disperse and go back to their home blocks and cubicles until order could be restored and logical agreement reached. He hadn't even finished when a song began to swell from the center of the mob. Whatever hope the captain had for a sane solution was dashed as the words of the Japanese national anthem swelled in an open taunt: *"Kimigayo wa chiyoni yachiyoni, sazareishi no iwao to narite!—* We Japanese wish the Emperor longevity through all ages, as a pebble grows up to a massive rock covered with lichens."

More *banzai* followed and then the first stones. Jeers and more stones came after that. The captain shouted the order for the tear-gas grenades. And a blanket of fizzling grenades sailed over the front ranks of the mob, igniting in its midst, bringing screams and panic. Many rioters rushed forward toward the startled, angry soldiers.

Gunfire roared.

Joey watched, horrified, as bodies slumped to the ground. He looked frantically for Billy. Now the screams of the gassed mingled with those of the panic-stricken and wounded. He heard the captain's command to cease fire just as he felt a wave of nausea.

He couldn't believe such a terrible thing had happened!

Billy was neither hurt nor among those arrested as riot ringleaders and shipped out of Manzanar to more secure facilities. But while the Kibei movement was broken, he still continued his private fuming against his captors, and looked for ways to retaliate.

Christmas and New Year arrived and passed, adding activities of interest as the internees of the camp settled down to their restricted life. Babies were born, teenagers learned to jitterbug to popular swing tunes, and couples ran out of ideas for finding privacy to make love. Billy continued to flirt with trouble by running an after-curfew craps game in kitchen fifteen, and Haru wrote often to Teresa Scagnelli to check on her beloved home.

For years Joey had carried on an active correspondence with a young fellow his age from Hawaii. Although they jokingly referred to each other as Pineapple Jack and Mainlander Joey, the island Japanese was a "Buddhahead," while Joey was a "Katonk." Now they enjoyed using the terms in disguised ways in case they were being censored. In late January, a letter from Jack arrived that began: "Buddhaheads and Katonks to wear khaki in samurai regiment." He then went on to explain that an all-Nisei combat team was being formed, and that it was to include Katonks. Uncle Sam had now reversed himself and wanted Nisei to volunteer for military duty! Jack had already decided to enlist.

The word shot through camp like wildfire. Of those Nisei kept on active duty after the war started, most were serving as intelligence interpreters. And in Hawaii where there was no relocation, a Nisei battalion of National Guardsmen was shipped to Camp McCoy, Wisconsin, given brooms for drilling, and designated the 100th Infantry Battalion. Now there would be the 442nd.

A recruiting team headed by a captain visited the camp in early February and made its pitch. When the recruiters departed, Joey joined his friends at the newspaper office. One, a press mechanic, said, "They've already thrown me out once." A writer added, "If I'm a damned spy, they can shove it!"

One copy editor said, "I can see it all now—they have this form where you have to list your home address and I write down 'Manzanar Prison, California.' "

"Yeah," a girl with a journalism major from UCLA chimed in, "and if they get a whim to ship us to Japan, you can apply for home leave, care of Tokyo."

Joey laughed at all of the justified jibes, but said nothing. He couldn't wait to enlist. Like Pineapple Jack and so many other smarting Nisei, he wanted a chance to prove that he was just as good an American as anyone. And joining an outfit with all those other guys, particularly those fun-loving Buddhaheads, sounded like one big party.

Billy sneered. "You crazy, man? Those bastards do this to us and you want to join their army? They're our *enemies*, you know." He refused to discuss it further.

And that left only Haru. From the moment she heard about the change in policy she knew her life would never be the same again. This hateful, dreadful war that had torn her away from her beautiful home had already created a chasm between her sons, and now they would be leaving her. What was fair about anything anymore? Billy was still the beautiful baby that she had shared with the lonesome and loving Miyuki—perhaps that was part of his problem. They both wanted him so much they started spoiling him even before he was born. And for all his faults, the thought of his going into the army simply tore at her heart. Joey was different, he was a good boy and could survive without her. Billy *needed* her.

On Washington's birthday, Joey told her he had enlisted.

Billy sucked in a deep breath as he raised the window sash. Another quick glance behind him confirmed that the coast was still clear. He hoisted himself off the ground and up through the opening. Silently sliding to the floor inside the large dark showroom, he reached out for the counter that held men's underwear and steadied himself as he drew out the penlight. He didn't want to use it until it was absolutely necessary, but he didn't want to run into anything and make a noise either. If they hadn't moved anything since just before closing time, he had it down pat. That was when he had slipped open the window lock.

Softly, he moved around the counter and down the aisle to the manager's office on the right side of the building, just outside the showroom. It was locked, just as he figured. He cursed under his breath, even though he had been certain getting cash would be impossible. The first counter to the left was the glass case that held the men's wristwatches—his alternate target. It was locked, but he instantly put a screwdriver to work and soon had it open. Without wasting a moment, he scooped up the watches he had decided on earlier in the day—two Elgins, three Gruens, and four

Bulovas. Shoving them in his pocket, he hurried to the cosmetic counter and grabbed a lipstick. He grinned as he jerked off its cap and hurried back to the watch case. Then, in large red letters, he wrote on the glass "Down with American Fascists—A. Ronin."

And with a satisfied smirk, he tossed away the lipstick and hurried back to the open window. Once outside, he laughed. A. Ronin was a beautiful touch—a masterless samurai.

Since thievery was not normal with the Japanese, it was the first time the camp's main store had been broken into. But because of the lipstick taunt, the military commandant decided to treat it as a major incident before something similar occurred. He called in a criminal investigator from the military district, a sergeant who had been a robbery detective in Denver before he was drafted. Then he made a statement for the camp newspaper stating that he would pull out all the stops to catch the burglar.

Billy smugly laid low for a week, then casually dropped one of the Bulovas into his craps game the next night. Since jewelry often found its way into the game, the watch was barely noticed. Billy pocketed fifteen dollars for it and chuckled to himself. Two nights later, he unloaded an Elgin, and the night after that a Gruen. Then he held off for several days before going to the craps game over in block thirty-six; there, just before it shut down for the night, he sold another Bulova.

Six days later, the investigator found that the first Bulova was being worn by a cook from kitchen fifteen. After questioning, the cook admitted he got it in the after-hours craps game, but couldn't recall from whom. The sergeant understood—in a craps game the action was fast and furious. Several days later, when he discovered that a Gruen had come out of that same game, he called in the game's operator for questioning.

Billy was calm as he entered the interrogation room, having expected it since hearing that the first watch was discovered. But after over half an hour of parrying the sergeant's questions, Billy finally lost his temper. "Listen, soldier boy," he snapped. "I can get a dozen witnesses to swear that over a thousand dollars worth of jewelry has passed through that game in the past few months."

The Falling Sun: 1941–1945

457

"Yeah," the investigator replied harshly. "Well, I'm convinced you're my crooked little slant, buddy boy. And I'm gonna sit on you like sweat until I nail you. You got that? Like sweat. This isn't any little Chinese checker game you dealt yourself into, boy. You're going to Leavenworth."

Two days later, after noticing that the sergeant was following his every step, Billy Hoshi enlisted in the United States Army to become an interpreter.

"The trouble with you stateside Japs is you need leadership, that's all."

Joey snorted as he looked up from where he was scrubbing the floor near the water fountain. Pineapple Jack Fuoto was into his favorite line about the supremacy of the Hawaiian Nisei. "You see," Fuoto continued, "you guys even had to be stuck in jail 'cause you weren't bright enough to quit spying. And then when Roosevelt realized the fightingest damned bunch of guys on the face of the earth was sitting over there in Hawaii just waiting for him to say the word, there was no way to keep you out of it. You see, that would have been discrimination. So that's—"

He ducked as Joey threw the brush full of soapy water at him. It was the sixth Friday night that Joey had been at Camp Shelby and the fifth Friday night they had thrown a GI party—that hated, traditional scrubbing of the barracks before Saturday morning inspection.

Fuoto threw the GI brush back at Joey from where he was mopping around the center aisle rifle racks. "What I can't understand," he said in mock dismay, "is why the prez even considered you screw-ups. I mean, it's like throwing extra weight on a perfectly honed racehorse."

Joey laughed as he grabbed the brush and thrust it into the pail. He liked his pen pal more in person. In fact, he liked most of these Buddhaheads—in spite of their cockiness and seemingly endless supply of bubbling patriotism. There wasn't any doubt in his mind that the 442nd Regimental Combat Team was going to be the best unit in the army. Not only were these little dynamos bright, but they thought they could lick the world—and had proven they were willing to try on several occasions when white troops had insulted them at the PX or other common mixing places on the post.

"You ukulele players need mainland stability," Joey gibed back. He started to say something else, but the platoon sergeant strode into the squadroom barking, "Okay, knock it off. I got something to tell you." As everyone gathered round, the NCO went on, "A couple of things about tomorrow for those of you who get by inspection and go on pass.

The sergeant scowled patiently as he waited for them to give him their full attention. "Okay, first about the fighting. I know it's tough to take that crap about being sneaky Japs, but I want you to suck it in. No fighting off post. Save it for those red-necks here on campus, boys. . . . Number two: you all know about the decision on Southern segregation here in the Camp Shelby area. When you're in Hattiesburg, you're white. Use the white facilities whenever they're separated. And even if you have to stand up, you don't go to the back of the bus. Got it?"

Two hours later, Joey was sitting on a toilet writing a letter to his mother when Pineapple Jack came in to brush his teeth. "You know, Jack," he said, "I'm having trouble with this black and white thing in town."

"What's the big deal?"

"Well, there are all kinds of places on the West Coast where we can't get inside the door any better than these Negroes down here . . . and suddenly they tell us we have to come in on the white side, that's all."

Fuoto brushed vigorously, responding with grunts as Joey told him about the things a West Coast Japanese American couldn't do. When he finished rinsing his mouth he turned and shrugged. "You don't have to tell me about the *haoles'* rules, Katonk. We been living by them our whole lives back home—and we aren't even the natives. You oughta ask *them!*" He bowed deeply. "Now, if you'll excuse me, a poker game awaits my deft hand over in Fox Company."

Joey turned back to his letter. " . . . So it bothers me. Since I'm in the army, I'm a citizen again. And down here, I'm a white citizen. But back there, you are considered nonwhite and noncitizen. Down here I can go into places where a Negro would get beaten for entering. And I could go on, but you know what I mean. I know now I did the right thing by enlisting with this great bunch of guys, but somebody's sure got to sort this mess out while we're over there proving we're Americans. Love, Joey."

The surgeon held Hiroshi's latest X rays up to the light of the open window and nodded. "You're a fortunate man, general," he said as he made some notes on the chart. "Millions of men have died from far less serious wounds. Had the facial wound alone been a few millimeters deeper, you'd have been killed instantly or lost part of your face." He shrugged. "And the arm, well, that may be why we have two." He nodded to the other doctor that he was finished, then bowed to Hiroshi. "Enjoy Tokyo. I wish I were going back."

Hiroshi watched them leave the small room, then swung his legs out of bed and walked to the window. A rain squall had left Rabaul wet and muggy, but he was lucky to be alive anywhere, just like the doctor said. The white slash across his left cheek merely made a Hoshi out of him; the loss of his left arm was another matter. He didn't even know why the gods had chosen to save him. In these months of healing, more and more of him had seemed to erode. In his worst moments of drifting between the real and unreal, he had seen the jeering faces of Koki and Saionji—his stepfather talking about his soul, and the old prince, dead finally at ninety-one, warning him and talking about the folly of war. And he had seen inside his shallow, one-armed form and found nothing but a massive ulcer crying out for reprieve, for a chance to redo. But the pulsating, hideous lesion was surrounded by leprous faces soundlessly crying out to him that there was no reprieve. Just one of the faces had a voice, the one of the Chinese girl pointing to her hideous sores. And its words were unintelligible, though their meaning was clear.

They had given him another medal and the star of a major general. Since he had been a tiny boy hearing about the exploits of his grandfathers, he had wanted that star. And oh, what it meant to his father. But things had changed—now that it was a reality, he simply didn't care. It was nothing wihout her. . . .

Staring down at the wet streets, he saw a woman hurrying

along with the same gait as his beloved Suiko. He started to call
out, but caught himself. His eyes bored into the woman, causing
her to turn and smile up to him, permitting her to have the bright
loveliness of his wonderful . . . yes, it *was* her and she was
shouting for him to wait, that she'd be there in a moment, come
to him and hold him, love him. . . .

"Excuse me, General. Is there anything I can do for you?"

He turned to see a pleasant Japanese woman of about forty
smiling at him. She was wearing a Red Cross uniform. "Yes,"
he replied after staring vacantly into her eyes for a moment.
"Can you get a letter through international channels to the United
States?"

The Woman nodded. "Perhaps—if it's personal. I won't guarantee it."

"I understand. I want to write to my nephew." He told her
about Lodi.

She frowned. "I hope he's alive. If he's in that concentration
camp where all those prisoners were killed in December, there's
a chance—"

"What do you mean?" he snapped. He could still see all those
dead prisoners on Bataan, and a cruiser captain that had been in
the hospital with him had told him he had seen American B-25
pilots strafing survivors of sinking ships. Had all decency been
obliterated?

"It was in California," she began, then unfolded the story of
the Manzanar riot that Japanese propaganda had built into a
major massacre.

He balled up his fist. Was that what the great Americans in all
their damned sanctimony did? Maybe he was wrong after all,
maybe his sense of right was twisted into something unrealistic.
Maybe he should turn into the harsh kind of a leader they had
trained him to be. He blew out a deep breath. No . . . no, no,
no! That was the kind of thinking that made beasts out of fine,
considerate farmboys. Besides, it was too late. "Please send the
letter to Mrs. Noboru Hoshi, in care of the Lodi *Gazette*," he
began quietly.

At least he could tell her he was sorry.

Forty

It was April 18, the second anniversary of her mother's death. Stepping down from the dilapidated trolley car, Sachi wondered how Suiko would have liked her drab Tokyo in 1944. Nowhere was there a sign of gaiety or hope. The hordes of people hurried back and forth with dreary expressions through the bleak and dingy city, reminding her of a colorless sea of sheep—seven million sheep pushing and forever waiting in line for even the most trivial requirements of their hopeless lives.

Even their clothes marked them as sheep—the women in their baggy pants often made from the remnants of old clothes; the men in tawdry khaki uniforms of ersatz materials. How proud she was to still wear her bright, quality kimonos whenever she left the house. It was a point of honor with her—a sign to one and all that she had not joined the war effort, *their* horrible war effort. At times they stared at her as if she had slipped out of the amusement quarter of Akasaka, but she didn't care. Only the baby on her back mattered.

She stopped for a moment to adjust her germ mask.

She seldom ventured out and positively would not be a part of any of the activities so popular with senior officers' families. No factories, no morale, no teas, and no Red Cross. The only reason she was out today was her daughter's diphtheria shot.

Nearing her house, she thought of her grandfather and envied his solitude on peaceful Miyajima. Then she thought of how terrible it must be to meditate all day. She'd have to go down and see him again soon.

As she turned into her driveway, she failed to notice a man standing in the shade of some shrubbery across the street. Inspec-

461

tor Oishi from the thought police watched her quietly, his black eyes glittering in dislike. This younger Hoshi woman was no better than the cheapest prostitute!

The army sedan wove out of Tama River Funeral Park at 0935 and headed for the premier's palace. Deep in thought in the back seat was the one-armed Major General Hiroshi Hoshi. He had just visited the shrine of Admiral Yamamoto, shot down one year to the day after his own beloved Suiko's death. April 18 seemed to be an unlucky day, he decided as he flicked a lighter to his cigarette. The grim lines in his handsome face relaxed slightly as he reflected.

He had first met the brilliant Yamamoto early in 1941 aboard his flagship and he remembered clearly the admiral's pragmatic words, "I can rule the Pacific for six months—and after that, if we have not won, it will be only a matter of time."

Yet, like himself and seventy-five million others, the flamboyant Yamamoto had been caught up in the powerful jingoistic tug of the tide.

And somewhere along the line, the state had stolen their souls; it had certainly stolen their minds. And what was this state—people? He knew Tojo had been hesitant about the final step of war. Was it the other admirals and generals, the *zaibatsu*, the ruling class? Perhaps, but not any one of them singly. Was it a religion like Nichirenism, the Shinto beliefs, the fanaticism of Japan's warrior past?

Hiroshi stared out the window at the faceless ones, rejecting all positive answers. Somehow, the state was all of these things, the sum. And only the people would suffer, just as only the survivors would inherit the guilt.

Soon America's might would tell—giant fleets would shell Nippon's shores, and thousands of aircraft would fill her skies and devastate her cities. As deputy chief of strategic intelligence on the General Staff, he had it all on paper. Time would soon run out, and then there would be no more great battleships or carriers moving anywhere. And then MacArthur and Nimitz could bring their gigantic invasion forces and storm the beaches. Two million untrained boys would then join with Nippon's veterans to hurl themselves in front of the American juggernaut in a violent, all-consuming, last-ditch butchery.

How much time, Yamamoto? A year, eighteen months . . . and then what?

Twenty minutes later, he was alone with Tojo in his huge private office. The premier stood staring out a tall window, the light illuminating his nearly bald head. To Hiroshi, his figure seemed to slump either from weariness or the enormous load he had been carrying for twenty-nine months. He turned slowly, sighing deeply. "Hoshi," he said quietly, "I've about finished the run. I've only yesterday been informed that my role as premier will be finished in a few months." He blinked as he lit a fresh cigarette. "I've presented an image and now I must retain it. I'm the terrible shogun, the dictator who has led Nippon to the brink of disaster. This is all classified, of course, but there is a peace faction thinking ahead to salvaging whatever possible." He inhaled deeply. "I am not salvageable."

Hiroshi was shocked. He had heard a murmur of something involving a peace faction, but nothing about Tojo becoming a scapegoat.

Tojo went back to the window. "You see, Hoshi, someone has to take the blame, and perhaps that's the highest of all honors . . . after all, isn't that the supreme sacrifice—dishonor in the face of crumbling walls?"

Hiroshi blew out a deep breath. Honor! He was being used—they had picked him from virtually nowhere to head the wartime government, and now that the war that never could have been won was being lost, he was to be the whipping boy. What was going on? He had heard much about the Final War theory years before—*had someone finally decided this is not the final war, that the horns should be pulled in for another effort someday?* Absurd! "What can I do, Excellency?" he asked quietly.

A softness touched Tojo's face for but a moment. "Nothing, my son. In five months, it will not be in your best interest to be aligned with me. I wanted you to know, because this may be the last time we see each other."

Hiroshi inhaled and held his breath, wanting to go to his old mentor, go to him and hold him as he would his own father. How vividly he remembered the lieutenant who came to take him to Kamakura so long ago. "How can I thank you for so much?" he asked.

Tojo turned, erect, his eyes shining. "You have many times over, Hoshi. I am proud." And with that, he bowed deeply and the meeting was over.

Biffontaine, France—
October 1944

The tall replacement stopped to ask a question as he tried to light a damp cigarette with his worn Zippo.

"Hey, Hoshi, there's a guy here looking for you!" Pineapple Jack Fuoto shouted from his makeshift lean-to.

Several yards away, Joey looked up from the M2 carbine he was trying to clean to see a somehow familiar figure in a helmet and poncho standing in the mud and drizzle. The figure's hand came out of the poncho as he moved forward. "You've got a leak in your goddamned roof, Sergeant," Billy said with a broad grin as they hugged each other.

"Yeah," Joey replied, glancing ruefully up through the shelter-half that was stretched over some low-hanging branches. "I plan on doing some fixing up next spring. New paint, curtains—the whole thing. Hey, man, what the hell brings you over here? I mean, the big intelligence sergeant, fat cat instructor—weren't you supposed to be going to the Pacific for some soft job?"

Billy looked around disdainfully. "Yeah, well you see, I punched this smart-assed *hakujin* captain and they court-martialed me and sent me here. The way you guys been getting shot up, I guess they figured that was just like the firing squad. I'm assigned to battalion intelligence."

"Yeah," Joe replied quietly, "not too many of us originals left."

Billy peered through the rain, picking out Joey's men in their holes and whatever they could find in the way of cover. Looked like a big squad, but he had been told at the company CP that it was all that was left of Joey's platoon—just seventeen men. And it had no officer, only a twenty-year-old buck sergeant by the name of Hoshi.

They sat down and lit fresh cigarettes as Joey gave him a quick rundown on the "Go for Broke" outfit. The heroics of the Nisei unit had already made a big name for its sawed-off fanatics in Italy, and now it was trying the impossible—the rescue of a battalion of cut-off Texans from a tenacious and well-fortified enemy. The First Battalion of the 141st Infantry from the Texas Thirty-sixth Division had been surrounded several days earlier and stopped cold in trying to break out. The 442nd, in support of the Thirty-sixth, had been ordered to bring them out—if possible. Now, after two days of ferocious fighting and devastating fire from the Germans, the 442nd was still a thousand yards away from the dying Texans. And the Nisei had taken nearly as many casualties.

"What do you think about the chances of getting them out?" Billy asked.

The crash of a German eighty-eight shell exploding in the trees off to the right rear drowned out Joey's reply. He repeated it. "We'll get 'em." He rubbed the stubble on his chin. How could he explain all this to a brother who didn't understand? And he knew Billy hadn't changed much. But then maybe serving with these fun, gritty guys who were the best damned soldiers in Uncle Sam's army would shape him up. It had sure been good for himself—they had even put him in for a battlefield commission, which he would probably accept. Hell, he might even stay in and give his grandfather a general on the other side of the family . . . when this madness all ended.

Pineapple Jack came over to join them, meeting Billy. "You didn't volunteer for this crap, did you, man? Your brother could've sent you one of his medals, you know."

Billy grinned, starting to reply, but they all hunkered down as the German artillery stepped up its fire. It was a drab, wet day in the Vosges Mountains of eastern France—a good day for finding a warm fire. The visibility was limited, almost foggy, sharpened only by the shattering explosions of bursting shells. Many of the splintered trees stood like eerie skeletons, and the damp chill permeated everything.

When it quieted down, Pineapple Jack said, "Man, if only those chicks back in Moiliili could see me now . . . living it up with these beautiful French—"

"Sergeant Hoshi!" The company commander's urgent call interrupted.

"Yes, sir!" Billy replied, springing to his feet as the officer trotted up.

"Think you can get your guys moving again?"

"I don't know, Captain. I'll sure try." As the officer moved on, Joey turned to Billy, sticking out his hand. "Nice seeing you, big brother," he said, already having turned back into a combat leader. "Now, you had better get your ass back to battalion. Okay, Jack, get the guys out of their holes. We're gonna make like superman again."

Billy wanted to say something else—tell him how glad he was to see him. Something more. . . .

But Joey was shaking his head and already checking his grenades. Tossing a "thumbs up," he trotted off to the right with words of encouragement for his battle-weary men. What sounded like a heavy mortar shell crashed overhead, not more than eighty yards away. Billy just stared up as a small piece of shrapnel rattled against his steel helmet. The gaunt remainders of the forest seemed to shrink further into their trunks. And somewhere off to his right, he heard a faint, "Go for broke."

And then he heard it again, closer and louder. "Go for broke!"

The last he saw of Joey, the sergeant threw his arm forward in the signal to move out. And gray shapes in light packs grimly followed him into the mist.

Nearly four hours later, the eleven men remaining in the platoon were pinned down below a ridge line so steep the German gunners couldn't hit them. Joey, still panting heavily from the mad dash he had just completed to determine what they were up against, glanced at his torn map. Heaving a deep breath, he said, "If they haven't moved, those Texans ought to be just over that next hill by this creek."

Pineapple Jack pulled out a cigarette and flicked his Zippo into enough blaze to light it. "With them Jerrys sitting up there with everything but the kitchen sink, they might as well be in the next county," he replied softly.

Joey nodded. As near as he could tell, there were at least three machine gun emplacements on the hill above them. And unless he missed his guess, their fields of fire would be perfectly interlaced, creating an absolutely impassable roadblock. And off to his left, another steep slope made a flanking move impossible. He blew out another deep breath. "Well, we can sit the war out here or see if there's a chink in their armor. And I forgot my deck of cards."

"Where you going?" Pineapple Jack asked Joey as he checked the long magazine in his carbine and switched it to automatic.

Signaling to the others to stay put, Joey slipped out of the cover of the crevice and began to edge back in the direction they'd come from. "I'm going to look around. If I holler *'Banzai,'* come up and give me a hand. If you hear three *Banzai,* move out—okay?"

Pineapple Jack started to move after him. "I'm coming along."

Joey's hand shot up. "No! Do as you're told."

Minutes later, he found another crevice where a trickle of water was running down the side of the small cliff. Working slowly and quietly, he reached the top of the crest in four minutes. Stretching up a few inches, he sucked in his breath sharply. He was looking directly into the back side of a sand-bagged gun position where three burly, gray-uniformed Germans were busy manning a heavy machine gun. Some fifty yards to the east and higher up the hill, another emplacement pointed sixty degrees away from the first. It was more of a bunker and he guessed it held two guns.

He looked back down the short cliff. Eleven men couldn't take those positions, but one just might be able to. Shrugging, he muttered, "Go for broke, baby," and slipped the safety off his carbine. The first emplacement was about sixty yards away—180 feet, just a good line throw from centerfield to the plate. But that was with a baseball, not a fragmentation grenade.

The slope was open with no boulders, just soggy grass that

might reach to his knees in spots. Maybe a bit of concealment. Squirming over the edge, he began to crawl forward on his elbows, keeping the carbine ready. After ten yards, he stopped, staring at them. The noises of battle on both sides drifted through the mist, ebbing and building constantly. He wondered if the rest of the company was doing better. Moving on, he squirmed through another fifteen yards before he stopped.

He could hear them talking, saw one light a cigarette and laugh. He thought he had killed seventeen Krauts personally since they landed in Italy; these three would make an even twenty. Wasn't that a fair start at making up for the fact that he was a goddamn Jap? He moved silently forward another twelve yards to where there was a higher patch of grass. From his location, it was a good seventy yards to the bunker—and he'd have to make most of it after his first grenade went off. Uphill.

No sense waiting—

Pulling the grenade's pin, he threw it straight into the middle of the gun emplacement, at the same moment jumping to a crouch and sprinting up the hill. He timed the explosion perfectly, hitting the ground and rolling to avoid any stray shrapnel. Back on his feet and on a dead run, he jammed back on the carbine's trigger, spraying automatic .30-caliber fire into the surprised faces of the bunker's inhabitants. He saw the blast of something shooting back at him just as something burned his left shoulder. There was a thud in his right side, as if someone had punched him, but still he continued up that slope, firing steadily. At twenty yards, his right leg was smashed out from under him, but he already had a grenade in his hand when he hit the ground. Rising to his left knee, he jerked the pin loose and held it long enough to make sure no one would throw it out. Then he used the last of his strength to heave it through the dark sandbagged entrance.

The last thing Joey saw was the explosion.

Pineapple Jack was holding Joey's head and rocking slowly back and forth when his brother walked up the slope. Billy had met over thirty muddy gray-brown Texans in the last few minutes, some wounded, others helping them along the slippery path.

They looked like they had just come back from hell, and they had. The last one he saw, a staff sergeant, shook his head and said, "Them little sons of bitches did it. We was dead for damned sure." They all had glazed looks, like they didn't believe it.

Billy knew the moment he saw Pineapple Jack.

Stopping, he stared down at the bloody head in Jack's arms.

"He had to do it all by himself," Jack whispered, tears running freely down his cheeks with the rainwater. He told Billy in halting phrases what he knew. "And we had to go on . . . had to get over that next hill . . . and I couldn't get back here until—"

Billy dropped to his knees, reaching for Joey's hand, and for perhaps the first time in his life felt true grief.

Forty-one

People of the Philippines, I have returned. . . .
—Douglas MacArthur,
October 20, 1944

"U.S. armored units hope to . . . Manila . . . February first . . ."

Cedric Baldwin squeezed his shaggy gray head closer to the makeshift radio, but all that was coming through was static. "Goddamn it, straighten that thing out, Eddie," he snapped at the radioman.

"What the hell do you expect from baling wire and toothpaste tubes?" the radioman retorted.

The group of prisoners crowded around the radio set drowned out the static as they all tried to talk at once—a whole shackful of emaciated, diseased skeletons of American fighting men who had managed to stay alive for almost thirty-four months through the ravages of a hell that might never be washed from their minds. They were the survivors—the white survivors of Bataan, Corregidor, and Camp O'Donnell, where as many as 250 captives a day had died at one time. And they were the survivors who for one reason or another had missed the death ships that took other prisoners to the mines and various forced labors of Imperial Japan. Counting a small number of British, there were 512 in this maze of bamboo, barbed wire, filth, and stench known as Pangatian or Cabanatuan, after the nearby town.

Cedric, deciding their information had ended for the evening, strolled back to the end of the shack where his bedridden friend, Hoover, lay in his misery. It wasn't just the radio—they had heard battle sounds and seen distant flashes for several nights now. And they had spotted dozens of bombers with those new markings that were definitely American. It had been over three weeks since Major Takasaki, the wily commandant, had gathered up his guards and left them to shift for themselves. Cedric guessed they were trying to save their asses when the good major announced that there was a thirty-day supply of food, including the remaining animals on the large farm outside the compound.

What a gorging they'd had—swilling five hundred cases of milk, cramming down rice bread, and finally getting to the livestock. A pilot in the compound took charge of butchering the Brahma steers that had survived, stretching them over a pit covered with bedsprings. How the aroma of fresh barbecued beef had attacked their dormant taste buds! It had been a virtual feast.

But their brief idyll ended abruptly when the remnants of an infantry battalion moved into the stockade and interrupted their freedom. Now, though they were allowed to move around the compound much as they pleased, they were confined prisoners again. It was January 30, 1945, and a new game of survival faced them.

Cedric sat down beside the filthy cot that held the feverish Hoover. "Looks like MacArthur's kicking hell out of them," he said brightly. "Tanks roaring into Manila, twenty divisions pouring in from Lingayen Gulf. Hell, man, we're gonna be out of here in nothing flat."

Like Cedric and many of the others who had missed the lists of those shipped to Japan, Hoover had amoebic dysentery, which the Nips were afraid to ship to the main islands. Only Hoover's was close to killing him. The bombardier weighed just about seventy pounds, twenty less than the camp average. "What's going to happen to us in the meantime?" he asked weakly.

They could be hit by advancing American artillery or tank fire, by bombs, or killed by the fucking Nips when they pulled out, Cedric wanted to tell him. But he squeezed his shoulder reassuringly and found a smile. "We're gonna sit right here and get ready for all those nurses they're gonna send out to greet us—the oversexed ones I've been telling you about."

Hoover tried to smile, blinking his recessed, too-bright eyes. "I don't think I could—"

Automatic weapon fire tore through the stillness!

Before Cedric could even turn away, grenades exploded nearby and rifle fire cracked! The unmistakable chatter of tommy guns joined in. It was right outside! He grabbed Hoover's bony hand. Was this finally the end—were they just shooting everything up? Hoover whimpered and closed his eyes tightly. More grenades exploded, throwing the flashes of their bursts inside the shack. Cedric dropped to his knees, cowering. *The sons of bitches!* He heard other cries of fright, but his own fear tore at his gut worse than any dysentery. Why couldn't they at least—

A tall form holding a tommy gun on his hip stepped into the open doorway. As Hoover cried out, an explosion outlined the form in bright light for a split second. He was very tall—

"All right, youse guys," the form shouted in unmistakable Brooklynese. "We're Yanks! This is a prison break!"

Cedric stared—it was an apparition, a terrible taunting dream. He felt Hoover's nails dig into his palm—

"I say again," the form barked as it moved inside. "This is a break. Now, we haven't got much time, so everybody out!" More forms followed him inside. "Okay," he went on, "I got some big strong farmboys here to carry those what can't walk. Youse guys just holler out and we'll piggyback you out. Now sound off! We ain't got all fuckin' night!"

Cedric blinked unbelievingly as he pulled himself to his feet. "Over here," he said in a voice he didn't even recognize. "Here's one." He started to say more as a huge corporal stopped in front of him, but he couldn't. He knew tears were starting down his cheeks. "Are you really—" His voice broke.

The corporal whipped out a pack of Luckies and shook one out. Quickly flicking a light from a Zippo and holding it out, he replied in an East Texas twang, "Sixth Rangers, old buddy. I got some chocolate, too, but it'll have to wait." As he picked Hoover up like a dirty shirt, he added, "Right now, we gotta haul ass. There's carabao carts awaitin' and a long hike to them trucks."

Cedric hoped he wouldn't choke as he sucked deeply on the cigarette. The bitter, dizzying taste was fantastic! He blinked back the tears as he hurried around the cot. Oh God! he shouted to himself as he joined the other dazed skeletons. *Oh God!*

*   *   *

Going through the narrow back entrance to Intramuros, the walled town that dated back to the sixteenth century, was like going through a tunnel. The brown walls were nearly forty feet thick at their base. Inside, Hiroshi looked around in the moonlight. It was as if he had stepped from twentieth century Manila into a city in ancient Spain. As he gazed at the extensive stonework, he noticed arches, a fountain, and other traces of that civilization. He was standing in front of a church with its high twin belfries and closed front door. Was it turning away souls? he wondered. There were enough of them still about—aside from the soldiers and sailors wandering through the street, several Filipino men were hurrying somewhere. Yet it was quiet, as if everyone recognized the pall of death hanging overhead.

And it was hanging there. The final stand in the defense of Manila would take place within these walls in a very short time—possibly as early as daybreak. And there would be no escape for anyone still there.

The master sergeant who had brought him in nodded for them to proceed, keeping as much as possible to the dark shadows of the buildings. He had guessed what was in Hiroshi's mind and wanted as little attention as possible. Turning a few moments later down a wider street, Hiroshi stopped momentarily to glance at a Catholic convent standing cold and bluish white inside its walls. The front gate was open and he could see a tall statue of the Virgin.

For some reason he thought for an instant of old Reverend Macnamara on his hilltop in Hiroshima. What would he say if he knew the mind of the small lad he had tutored so long ago? And how was he—as a man of God—dealing with the slaughter of his adopted flock by his countrymen? Or, for that matter, did religion make *any* difference? That statue that had been worshiped by so many for so long would most probably be smashed to pieces before the last shot in Intramuros died out.

Moving on, he shook his head. He still couldn't imagine what insanity had occurred in the navy General Staff. General Yamashita had wisely decided to pull back to the hills around Baguio to set his final defense against MacArthur's advancing hordes—leaving Manila an open city to be spared from destruction. A sensible move, considering that the war could be over in another year or less. But just as Yamashita withdrew—leaving 3,800 service troops to destroy the vast stores of equipment and the various munitions dumps—Rear Admiral Sanji Iwabuchi landed a force of 14,000 sailors and marines. Since then, the admiral had made good his vow to make the enemy pay dearly for every inch of Manila—many of the finest parts of the city had been reduced to rubble in the violent house-to-house fighting.

As the sergeant headed up a darker street, Hiroshi shook his head again. This whole last-ditch Philippine operation was futile. No *Banzai* charges nor all the *kamikaze* pilots in the empire could change that fact. General Yamashita—the Tiger of Malaya—had been exiled to the Kwantung Army for disagreeing with the wrong people after his brilliant campaigns early in the war. Now, he had been thrust back into the role of savior. After several days with the old bull-necked general, Hiroshi was about to go back to Tokyo when Segura's name came up.

As he had listened with growing rage, Yamashita had explained how Segura—now a colonel in the *kempei,* the secret police—was almost certainly guilty of profiteering in Manila. "Filipino works of art are his special interest," the general grunted. "I ordered him out of the city when we pulled back, but he didn't come."

Hiroshi immediately volunteered to get him. Yamashita refused, stating that he couldn't possibly permit a general officer—he didn't say with one arm—to do anything so dangerous. But Hiroshi had been adamant, insisting that there were already too many stains on the officer corps. And finally the tired Yamashita had sighed his permission.

Now he felt the tension prickling as they neared the old mansion where his nemesis was holed up. The master sergeant who was his guide was Tateno, a criminal investigator from the provost marshal's office who had been probing Segura's activities. It was Tateno's opinion that Segura had made a deal for negotiable gems and would be fleeing the city just before it fell.

Hiroshi knew he had overreacted, but there was no way he could be objective about Segura. With all the lack of order and human decency he had been forced to overlook in the past few years, he simply could not permit this swine, this murderer . . . this *vulture* to go any further.

Four minutes later they were inside the old two-story house following an old Filipino down a dimly lit hallway. Hiroshi knew his hand was trembling, but there was nothing he could do about it. The road to this moment had been too long. "I'll arrest the colonel privately," he told the sergeant quietly.

Tateno nodded grimly, unslinging his submachine gun and releasing its safety. He had known all along.

Hiroshi closed the door to the high-ceilinged room where Segura stood smoking a thick black cigar near a huge carved desk of dark wood. The room was dimly lit by two oil lamps, but the area around Segura's face was bright enough for Hiroshi to see the evil he remembered so well. Segura was wearing a dark kimono and was grinning at him. "Well," he said scornfully, "if it isn't Hiroshi Hoshi from Hiroshima. I heard they made a mistake and gave you a star. They wouldn't listen to me." His eyes glinted as he stared hatefully into Hiroshi's cold gaze. "All right, we've had our tender reunion. Now get out, Hoshi."

Hiroshi moved closer, staring grimly at the face that had plagued him since he was a cadet. He saw the pimples, the fat, the close-set eyes narrowed in a domineering expression. He saw little Misao fuming and being ridiculed, saw them together in the hospital room the night after the tragic winter march . . . and he saw his emotional little friend brace himself for the ritual of *seppuku*—goaded by this killer. "You are under arrest, Segura," he said hoarsely.

The glinting eyes blinked in disbelief, then narrowed. "For what?"

"Crimes against mankind."

Segura snorted. "Have you been drinking, you fool?"

Hiroshi's hand went to the automatic on his hip. "Officially," he rasped, "for disobeying an order."

"From whom?"

"Yamashita. I'm here on his authority."

Segura finally moved, going to the desk where a bottle of scotch whiskey stood among several things he was packing. He laughed as he picked it up. "A cripple from Tokyo has no authority whatsoever . . . particularly when his family is involved in criminal conduct."

Hiroshi unsnapped the flap of his holster.

"You forget I'm a *kempei* officer, Hoshi. I've had a special police inspector watching your family for years now. One word from me and your daughter in Tokyo will be arrested for—"

The poison in Hiroshi's stomach was boiling. "Do you wish to change into uniform?" he managed to grate.

Segura laughed again, twisting the top from the bottle. "—be arrested for various acts and words of sedition. In short, for being a disloyal young whore!" He tipped the bottle back, drinking deeply as his eyes remained riveted to Hiroshi's. Whiskey spilled down his chin as he held it out. "Here, Hoshi, drink to your dear old mother—the rich bitch who tramples policemen. I'll have her in prison before—"

The Nambu's bullet smashed through Segura's mouth.

Forty-two

They stood alone at the rail like two lovers, leaning into the cool breeze and watching the cloud-shrouded island as a heavy rainstorm obliterated the little town and its guardian O-Torii. The water was choppy with dancing whitecaps, the noise of the ferryboat's engine all but muted by the wind. They hadn't spoken in minutes, each not wanting the visit to end.

Suddenly Sataro broke the silence, taking her hand and leading her to a bench. During the entire day he had been vibrant and witty, generating a strength even she hadn't seen before. At times Sachi thought she was with a holy man; at others he could have been her brother, her loved one, just her dearest friend. Now the full intensity of his presence bore into her, dominated her as he gripped her hand more tightly. "My dear," he began in a gentle tone, "I've told you much about my existence today, as well as the long story of my life that may have bored you mightily. Now, I shall tell you about its balance."

His eyes were dark, sparkling.

"Only recently," he continued, "have the pieces begun to fall into their proper places. But now I think I have it together, this maze called life. And the most important of its elements, that which has eluded me for so long, is now obvious."

She had never known his voice to be so vibrant.

"I know so little of the war and that's just as well. Yet, I cannot shut it out completely for you've been so terribly hurt. Your father is deeply involved . . . and perhaps my grandsons in America. And it grieves me acutely. But what distresses me most is my own shallowness, my meaningless pursuit of a frivolous dream for most of my adult life."

He released her hand and turned toward the island. "My superficial dream of material success and great accomplishment was no different than that specious dream that has seduced Nippon. And now, as my beloved empire will also come to realize in time, I know there is more. . . ." He turned back to her and his eyes were glowing. "I see and feel it in my deepest, brightest meditation. . . . It's my nirvana, my enlightenment . . . but it's elusive, slipping away each time I reach out to capture it."

He was back from the rail, kneeling at her feet, looking up into her wide eyes with such force and beauty that she hardly breathed.

"My dear, I now have a genuine dream of true merit, of such significance that the rest of my life will be devoted to it. It is peace. All the time in the monastery has been a search for my own peace, and now I know that journey won't be complete until I've done everything in my power to establish it between my two beloved countries."

He took her hand and led her back to the rail. Miyajima was spreading out before them. The town, the ferry dock, the glistening green hills—all were clear after the refreshing rain. The clouds were suddenly breaking, a shaft of sunlight striking the brilliant vermilion O-Torii.

"And soon I'll come out and begin to pursue it," he said softly, staring ahead. "Will you help me?"

She had never known such a powerful tug of emotion. "Yes," she whispered. "Oh, yes." And there was nothing more she could say.

Haru adjusted her hat and pinned it firmly in place. It was the same hat she had worn the day of the evacuation, and if it had been torn apart in the past three years, she would have worn it anyway. It was the fourth of March and both she and the Togasakis were going home together. The Greyhound bus that would take them was due to depart at noon, but all her belongings had been packed since shortly after dawn. She wasn't taking any chances.

But before she could go, there was a ceremony she had to attend.

"You look just fine," Kimi Togasaki said with a soft smile.

Yoshi didn't say anything as he stood in the door and sucked on his cold pipe. He had said little for three years, worrying about his priceless vines and trying to practice his old friend's *gambari*. Fortunately, two of their children had moved east to New York and weren't involved in the relocation. And the other had gone with his family to Topaz in central Utah, where he was now out of camp and working.

Her dress was dark gray and plain, not the kind one should wear home on such a day. But there was the ceremony to attend. Haru was even thinner but amazingly unlined, considering the grief and misfortune she had been through in her forty-five years. And only in the past few months had the gray begun to infiltrate her hair. She looked around the cubicle where her sons— She turned and drew her shoulders back, fighting the emotion. There were other friends she should see to say good-bye to, but she didn't feel up to it. There was the ceremony.

They had almost forgotten to schedule the ceremony, but at the last minute one of the officers remembered the medals.

The martial music could be heard as they stepped outside the tarpaper shack and started for the recreation field where ceremonies were held. There were curious looks from passing faces, but they were just a blur as she marched on. It was only five blocks, past the mess hall and a recreation hall where she had watched movies, but it seemed further on her wooden legs. The music was getting louder each step. And then she could see all the people and the bright reflections of the brass horns, and an honor guard of soldiers in their OD uniforms, with their rifles. Noboru would have enjoyed it so.

Why did the music have to be so loud?

It seemed that everyone left in Manzanar was there. Parades broke the monotony. Ceremonies could stir the emotions. Or they could be shrugged away like so many other things. The Issei, the old ones, watched everything. Many of them still didn't understand after three years; some didn't even want to go home—if they still had a home. Some, the troublemakers, had been shipped to Tule Lake and would be repatriated to Japan when the faraway war was finally over.

Faraway? Not with the ceremony.

Haru didn't remember much else—more loud martial music, the soldiers moving, the national anthem, being led to a place in the middle. Words over the loudspeaker, a tall man with a big shiny eagle on his hat and a bright silver star on each shoulder . . . more words . . . "Sergeant Joseph Sataro Hoshi . . . Biffontaine, France. October . . . gallantry above and beyond the call of duty . . . did single-handedly attack. . . ."

She held her thin body rigid, her head high, but the tears slipped down her cheeks. She stifled the pain and stared straight ahead.

". . . resulting in mortal wounds."

And then the general was looking at her sadly and fumbling with a medal dangling from a bright red, white, and blue ribbon. He finally managed to pin it to her dress. It was her second Silver Star medal.

It was shortly after six when the Greyhound bus stopped in front of The Other Cheek. Stepping down, Haru blinked as she took in the picture that had helped sustain her in her worst hours in the camps—the fine house, the trees, the shrubbery that she'd soon subdue again . . . the sturdy barn that she'd have painted, and the vines in the background. Yes, it would all keep her very busy. The best cure.

The door opened and Teresa Scagnelli hurried out. Following a hug and exclamations of reunion, she took Haru's bag. "I tried to put everything back as you had it," she said excitedly. "And I have a surprise for you. No one else has lived here, not a single soul. What you thought was rent money came from Mario. He insisted. And even your car works fine." She bubbled on as they went in the back door to the kitchen where Haru had spent so much of her time.

It was the same! Even the smell of tea brewing. Moving on to the other rooms and softly touching things, she nodded silently. Her home. She stopped at Joey's room, gripped by the returning grief, then forced herself through the doorway. Reaching inside her purse, she removed the dark blue box that held the medal and placed it on the nightstand.

And finally she entered her bedroom, and looked at the dresser.

Noboru's face still stared out grimly from the wedding picture, but then perhaps he had sensed something forbidding, she thought. No, that was farfetched. She smiled at Teresa as she sat on the bed and leaned back.

Yes, this was her home.

Except for broken windows, the sturdy Western-style house that Koki had brought Itoko to in 1912 remained intact from the bombing. The fires that had destroyed so much of Tokyo— particularly following the massive raid during the high winds of March 9 that killed over 70,000 people—had merely licked hungrily toward them as they destroyed thousands of flimsy homes in the nearby area. With a solid shelter built beneath its sturdy floors, they never rushed away when the air raid sirens wailed. Sachi snorted at the folly of going to crowded shelters under bridges or into the open space of nearby Shibya Park. It wasn't the small incendiary bombs that killed so many people, she had emphatically stated when the massive raids first blanketed the city, it was the searing flash fires that followed. Nearly every raid, to some extent, was like an aftermath of the 1923 earthquake. And proud Itoko agreed completely—the idea of sitting fearfully in a crowded, sweating shelter was extremely unappealing.

It was a mad, alien world that spun around their small estate in Azabu—seldom any electricity, no new clothing, limited medical care, limited everything. The chase for food was an unending nightmare, with only a trickle of rice filtering to them. They seldom left the area, relying on the local black market sources. With the value of money diminishing daily, Itoko continued to up the ante, letting it be known that she was willing to pay even more than the unscrupulous *yami* operators wanted.

The 1943 government slogan, "Strength through skinniness," had long lost any trace of sense. But most slogans had suffered the same fate. It was said that the government had played on the lowest level of the public's ignorance and succeeded. No longer were the scandals of monstrous graft in the *zaibatsu* of interest, only day-to-day existence.

The millions of ordinary people who still remained in the city, ever moving like the ants Sachi compared them to, adjusted their gauze masks over their bleak expressions and struggled to keep from starving. Not knowing what to believe, either from the newspapers or radio, they were a vast sea of automatons vainly waiting for the fruits of the great victories about which they had been told for the past three-and-a-half years. Only their beloved *kokutai*—their national essence—and their unshakable faith in the Emperor kept them going.

Sachi had steadfastly refused to work in a factory, even though school children were now working four days a week. It was part of her still angry protest. As to her father's role in the war, she remained silent. The two servants they had managed to retain and feed were simply too old to be forced into the factories. And now the running of this precarious household was about to fall on her shoulders.

Itoko had packed her two large bags four times and still wasn't satisfied. "I can't come back here for more," she kept explaining as Sachi patiently helped her repack. "And who knows what I'll be able to find in that backward city." For the past two months, the obsession to leave devastated Tokyo until the end of the war had plagued her. And now, deciding that Kyoto would be struck down in a massive bombing raid before the other untouched city, Hiroshima, she had made the decision to go back to her one-time home.

Sachi had resisted her grandmother's persistent persuasion to accompany her to the southern city, insisting on remaining in Tokyo as long as her father continued in his assignment there. She chuckled. "I'm sure you'll find whatever there is. Do you have the diamonds?"

Itoko patted the lining of the kimono she'd wear on the train in the morning. "Of course." Twenty months earlier, she had had the foresight to convert money into small, quality jewels for barter. "And you know where the remainder are hidden."

"Yes, Grandmother."

"And you'll keep a careful watch over the other things?"

Sachi patted her hand tenderly. "Everything's under control, Grandmother. Both pistols are loaded."

Itoko suddenly turned away, darting quickly for the garden

door. Sachi saw her shoulders slump and heard the sob as she stopped and stared outside. It was the first time she had ever seen her grandmother break down. Rushing to her and embracing her tightly, she said the soft words that she might use with her beautiful little Mitsu. No longer was her grandmother the regal, still beautiful matriarch with a will of iron; she was merely a vulnerable woman of sixty-eight whose world was crumbling about her. "Come, darling," she said gently, "let me fix some tea."

Itoko dabbed at her tears, trying to find a smile. "I'm sorry," she whispered. "I, it's just . . . I remembered the first time Koki brought me there . . . and I thought it was a place I'd never leave." She glanced around as she followed Sachi toward the door of the bedroom. Her voice broke as she admonished, "You be sure and do as you promised, young lady. I don't expect one thing to be out of place when I return."

Sataro bowed deeply from the waist, then knelt before the master. The older man's bright black eyes exuded warmth instead of their usual dynamism. It wasn't the normal visit of disciple to master; Sataro had requested a special audience for the middle of the morning. "I've come to ask your permission to leave the monastery," he said calmly, his voice breaking the stillness.

"I know," the master replied.

Nothing about the amazing master surprised Sataro anymore. "I feel it's time," he said. "My few months have turned into over three years and there are perhaps positive things I can accomplish outside."

The master nodded his gleaming head. "Yes, I understand. The war."

Sataro shook his closely cropped white head. "No, the end of the war. My brother told me about it on his last visit. I have a family to reunite, a House to repair."

The master pushed out cigarettes and an ashtray, then slipped out of his double lotus position to get tea and sweet cakes. Sataro watched his movements with a deep sense of attachment. Seeing this great man—even if only for the few minutes he was allotted each day—was the most fulfilling part of his life. He held himself erect in the lotus, sensing the strength that coursed through his hard lean body. He would miss him considerably.

The master sipped his tea. After a moment he asked, "And your *koan*—have you solved it yet?"

Sataro was on his fourth *koan*. "I have years for it," he replied. "I'll save and relish it. Although one might say I have an additional *koan*—the rebuilding of my house that I mentioned, the House of Peace."

The intense black eyes glowed as the master nodded. "Not an easy task, but too specific to be called a *koan*. You will be too involved. Remember, detachment is ever the key. This has been part of your closeness to enlightenment—your mastery of detachment. Compassion and detachment—you must keep them foremost." He tasted the sweet cake. "And when do you depart?"

"Tomorrow, if it is permissible."

The master nodded, replying, "Of course." His eyes burned into Sataro's for a moment before he continued. "We shall miss you . . . I shall miss you. You've been perhaps my most rewarding disciple . . . one who could have become a master in time. Possibly a great one. Now let us speak of pleasantries. . . ."

It was July 16. At seven-thirty that night a cryptic message was delivered to President Harry S Truman in Potsdam. It announced the successful detonation of a powerful new weapon in the desert near Alamogordo, New Mexico.

It was called the atom bomb.

As the summer of 1945 sped by, it seemed that Nippon was frantically gulping in huge draughts of air as if trying somehow to find a pure strain of oxygen for survival. The savage battle for Okinawa ended on July 2, following massive casualties. And the skies over Japan were filled with American bombers. Japan had made an overture to Russia for an extended peace treaty and a request that the Soviets act as intermediary in a peace feeler with the Allies. Independent peace efforts were also underway in Sweden and Switzerland. Tojo had long since been replaced and old Admiral Suzuki—shot through the heart and genitals during the Young Officers Revolt—was the premier who was trying to ride out the insanity of the last great battle that could kill an inestimable number of Japanese. But Russia had its own plan to rush into war with the staggering Japan so that she might gorge herself on the spoils. And there were top officers insisting on national suicide before acquiescing to the Potsdam proclamation that demanded unconditional surrender. The demand was dropped in leaflet form on July 27. It emphasized that the Japanese people were not considered the Allies' enemies, only the military leaders. "The alternative is prompt and utter destruction," it stated. But Nippon still had its legions and over 8,000 *kamikaze* aircraft.

Forty-three

The shiny soldier
The bright cherry blossom.
A flash of glory,
A withered stem.

—Cadet Hiroshi Hoshi, 1916

Itoko was highly pleased with her decision to move to Hiroshima. The city, while much more heavily populated now, was as lovely as ever in its rich green delta. The hills and balmy weather were still enjoyable, and food was more plentiful than in Tokyo. There was even a touch of casualness in the sight of young people boating and laughing together on the Kyobashi River, near her rented house. What a change from the bleak horror of Tokyo and its daily rain of death from the open bays of a never-ending stream of hateful enemy bombers.

The house, while not as elaborate as she desired, was considerably larger than the one she had lived in following her return from America. It was in superb condition, with an airy garden and an old housekeeper who came with it. Located a mile southeast of old Terumoto's Hiroshima Castle, it was just a fifteen-minute walk to Hiroshima Station. And the trains were far less crowded than in the capital. She had toyed with contacting Seizo, if for no other reason than to express her sympathy over the loss of his wife earlier in the year, but there was still discomfort involved with him.

On the third day of August, she felt vigorous but lonely as she trimmed a japonica bush in the garden. She wished she could talk Sachi into coming down, but the trains were restricted to essential military travel now. Maybe Hiroshi could break loose. For some reason, Noboru's handsome hawklike features came to her.

And her mind wandered to the past—two small boys and a choice—a terrible choice. She hadn't heard anything from Haru since before the war. Were her grandsons still in that terrible American concentration camp? She forced the horrible thought from her mind as she squinted up at the sky. Why didn't the planes ever come over Hiroshima?

Going inside for a drink of water a few minutes later, she discovered that someone was at the front door. Wondering why the housekeeper hadn't answered, she sighed and removed the broad-brimmed straw hat as she opened it. She blinked into the sun. Standing a few feet back was a tall, erect man with short-cropped white hair. He was wearing an old black suit and holding a red rose in one hand. There was a serene look on his tanned face. Her eyes widened as her hand flew to her open mouth.

"Good afternoon, Itoko," Sataro said pleasantly.

It was simply a matter of wrongs, Itoko fussed. He had wronged her and she retaliated. He had no right to show up at her front door like this! So strong and healthy-looking, so untroubled. His eyes seemed to actually glow with some kind of warmth that seemed to reach out and say, "I care." It wasn't right for any man—let alone her horrid former husband—to do this.

She adjusted the open collar to the cotton dress—most of the best clothes she had left were Western in style. And now he insisted on taking her for a walk. A walk! She should have been more firm, told him she was busy. But he would have merely laughed. He was so damned sure of himself.

Why were her fingers not behaving? And her hands—why the tremor? He was just a silly old man who belonged back in the monastery—that was it, he should be wrapped in monk's clothing and praying for his terrible sins.

Brushing back her short gray hair, she remembered she hadn't been to the beauty parlor for a rinse yet this week. She usually looked better—why did he have to pick *now* to appear? A walk—if it was merely a walk around the block, why did he make it sound so important? She glanced in the mirror again, pushing back another wisp of undisciplined hair. She would have to teach the housekeeper how to do her hair. She thought back to

the days before the war when there was a maid for everything—
hairdressing, sewing, housekeeping, nursing, everything. And
now all the young farm girls who had always worked as maids
were in the factories getting wages that would forever ruin house
servants. *Why was she being so particular about a piece of
jewelry?*

A touch of perfume at the earlobes . . . might as well. In all
his fervent Buddhism he wouldn't possibly notice. Would he see
how trim and still shapely she was after all these years? They
said Zen improves awareness. Oh, why didn't he come during all
those years when she was still so beautiful, when men's heads
still turned wherever she went? No, she really wasn't shapely.
Chic, pert—those were the English words that were so popular in
Western fashion magazines before the war. She was pert!

She found him in the garden, intently studying a chrysanthemum bush that was just beginning to bloom. He turned his head
at her footsteps, smiling gently. Cradling a fresh white blossom
in his fingertips, he said, "It isn't for the Emperor—not enough
petals."

Petals, why—oh, yes, the imperial chrysanthemum had sixteen
petals. Why did he have to look at her like that? So disconcerting.
"I'm ready for this important walk," she announced tightly.
"But it's extremely warm."

His smile returned as he moved toward her. She could barely
make out the old Cossack scar on his cheek. "Have you seen
Hiroshi's scar?" she asked. "The one from Guadalcanal?" She
knew it was a stupid question the moment she uttered the words.
Hiroshi came down to see this old man who had deserted him
whenever he got the chance.

"I've never seen a blemish on our son," he replied as he took
her arm and started inside. "But tell me about my Sachi and her
beautiful daughter—I want to hear everything!" He thought about
their new dream. Soon, maybe.

Itoko began to relax as they departed a short time later. It
seemed so *easy* to talk to him, to chatter on about anything.
Passing the nearby firebreak, where hundreds of people were
working at the removal of houses in preparation for possible air
raids, she heard him interrupt and say, "I was told that over

twenty-five thousand children above third-grade level have been evacuated to the country. And I hear the bombing of Tokyo is terrible. Tell me about it.''

And she talked. It seemed that something about him was totally relaxing, some new element of his seemed to give one energy, enthusiasm. Made one forget. She barely noticed when they reached Hiroshima Station and he bought tickets. Finally, when they were on a platform waiting for a worn, puffing train, she asked, ''Where are you taking me, Sataro Hoshi?''

He took her hand and held it gently as the train hissed to a stop. ''You are the first beautiful woman I've touched in many years,'' he replied softly. ''I'm taking you away to a place where we can talk in peacefulness and learn to know one another.'' He smiled as they touched going through the door. ''You are in safe hands, I assure you.''

She knew it. She hadn't felt so free in years. Who was this strange, handsome knight who had dropped in from a place in the sun and told her he was an old lover of another era? Surely, she'd wake up on her cold bed, shivering from loneliness, and he'd be gone—gone back to the world of make-believe from whence he had come. Standing close to him as he hung onto a strap in the crowded car, she felt the firmness of his thigh and her breath quickened.

Forty minutes later, they got off at a village with a name she had never heard. It was a small village with only a handful of shops, a few curious people on the dirt street, and a small number of bicycles leaning against walls that had been freshly scrubbed. The sun was just touching the hills high to the west as he led her up a long rise on a gravel path. Ahead stood a two-story building of old but clean white walls and a tangerine-colored tile roof that had been shedding water since well before the last shogun was born.

She breathed deeply as they stopped by its entrance. A graceful white bird with a long neck painted on a large sign announced the inn's name. She squeezed his hand as she smiled up at him. ''How delightful. How did you ever find it?''

A skinny chestnut-colored mongrel wagged its way up to lick Sataro's hand. ''They have a son who was in the monastery for the first two years I was there," he explained, rubbing the dog's ear. "At first, the boy helped me learn the routines and did little things to ease the problems of an over-age novice. And then, in his last year, I began to help him. But finally one day, he decided the church was not for him and he ran away to join the army. I find that just being here in this restful fragment of another day is equal to a week's meditation. Come, meet these fine people."

The mother lined up her four stairstep daughters, each with a wide grin and a penchant for Sataro. Once they had been introduced, they scattered and it was time to order. "Do your best, madam," Sataro said pleasantly. "This is an important anniversary."

The woman bowed deeply, her worn face creased in a wide smile and many wrinkles. As she darted away, Itoko asked, "What anniversary?"

Sataro took her hand and smiled gently into her eyes. "Our first, my dear. I intend for us to have many more."

She looked at him in fascination. It was all so mad and she loved every minute of it. What magic had this marvelous man acquired? They were seated at a low table on worn *tatami* mats in a small room just off the entryway. Low-burning oil lamps had already been lit, even though an open screen still admitted bright fresh air. She could hear the birds. As the oldest girl bowed her way into the room with a tray of herb and seaweed soup, Sataro said, "Tell me about your husband. Hiroshi said he was a fine man."

Itoko would have thought telling his stranger who was also her former husband about a man she had loved dearly would have been difficult. It wasn't. The words flowed swiftly through the slices of boiled eggplant served in bean paste, on through the tasty *sashimi* and boiled sea eel. She hardly noticed that the rice hadn't been boiled with barley. And throughout, Sataro listened with glowing eyes and soft appreciative words. Finally, when she stopped to finish her small cup of mirin, he said, "He must have been wonderful for you. I wish I could have met him."

She didn't even ask about his Miyuki, it just didn't matter. All that troubled her was the fear that this marvelous fairy tale might end. When the last dish had been cleared away, she sat quietly looking into the gentleness of his thoughtful expression. And she realized she had never stopped loving him. She tried to shove aside such a ridiculous thought, but it wouldn't go away. She found his hand and held it tightly until he excused himself a few minutes later.

When he returned shortly, he reached for her hand and pulled her to her feet. "Our room is ready," he said softly, holding her close.

Excitement that she hadn't known in decades coursed through her as she gripped him tightly. "Will you keep me there forever?" she whispered.

"Forever," he replied firmly.

Three mornings later, Sataro returned from an early cup of coffee with Reverend Macnamara and his brief visit with Seizo at shortly before eight o'clock. Itoko was up and puttering around the garden. She smiled brightly as he stepped outside into the fresh early sunshine. Cushions and two small tables were placed on the small wooden porch that extended a few feet from the house. "I thought we'd have breakfast outside," she announced cheerily.

He nodded, coming to her and taking her hand. Brushing her fingers with his lips, he said, "I invited both of them to dinner tonight. I hope your black marketeers can come up with enough food. If not, I can get some fish in the village at Miyajima when we go over this afternoon."

Itoko smiled her agreement. She hadn't seen the mystical island since Noboru's wedding and she was looking forward to it. In fact, she was looking forward to doing *anything* with this wonderful new Sataro of hers. It hadn't yet been three full days since he had popped out of the sky, but it seemed like eons— eons of pleasure and warmth that were like fantasies. And there were so many marvelous things ahead—why, with both of them enjoying such robust good health, who knew . . . maybe as many as twenty years?

The "all clear" sounded in the distance. The air raid sirens had shrieked just before Sataro's return, but there had been two previous false alarms since midnight and she had given it no thought. Heavens, after a whole war in Tokyo, what was another siren?

Nineteen miles southeast of the city, at an altitude of 31,600 feet, the *Enola Gay* led two other B-29s toward the center of the Ota's bright green delta at a speed of 287 miles per hour. At the controls, but about to turn the huge aircraft over to his bombardier, was Colonel Paul W. Tibbets, Jr. The *Enola Gay* had begun the bomb run four minutes out, and most of the crew members were getting ready to cover their eyes with the dark glasses they had been issued. Inside was the strange black weapon that was ten feet in length and twenty-eight inches in diameter.

Below Tibbets, in the nose compartment, Major Thomas Ferebee peered intently through the Norden bombsight and began to pick up the familiar landmarks that he had studied so intently prior to the mission. Sliding up fast were the six islands, the hills, the docks. He spotted Aioi Bridge—his aiming point—just as he pressed the intercom button and announced, "I've got it." They were one minute and fifteen seconds from drop.

At that moment, near the Kyobashi River, Sataro stared up from Itoko's garden at the clear blue sky. Squinting into the sun, he remarked, "I think we'll have a beautiful day for our little journey." Off to the left of the sun, he noticed a sudden reflection. "Some day I'd like to fly around the world," he mused. "Have you ever flown, my dear?" He stroked her hand as he smiled warmly.

Itoko shook her head. "No, and I have no intention to." She started to pull away from him. "I'll have the breakfast served."

He tightened the grip on her hand. The reflection had turned into three aircraft—several miles high. "Do you know what kind of planes those are?" he asked, suddenly feeling a vague apprehension.

Itoko squinted upward, snorting, "I should! They're B-29s."

"Shouldn't the air raid sirens be blasting?"

"What difference would it make?"

He pulled her toward him. "Look! Something is falling from one of them!"

She didn't want to look. Hadn't she seen enough massive sticks of bombs fall? Still, she glanced upward, feeling her breath catch. The lead aircraft was diving and turning. Parachutes had blossomed far up. Instinctively, she moved even closer to him. *What was wrong?* A sharp stab of fear caused her to shudder as she stared at the tiny chutes. There was something. . . . "Sataro!" she cried out softly. "Sataro!"

His eyes were riveted to the parachutes. And suddenly a tiny dark object was falling fast below the chutes, an ominous speck that was growing larger by the second. How could such an insignificant object create such alarm? Its rush to earth was mesmerizing him!

He jerked his eyes away, finding terror in Itoko's upraised face. Her nails dug into his palms and suddenly all that mattered was protecting her. Yes, she was part of him and he knew for certain he still loved her . . . it had never ceased. No, deep down, somewhere it had somehow remained alive like a spark. And now it was flooding over him like a wave, rushing like that dark thing. . . .

He had to tell her, now! "Itoko, I—"

The dark object abruptly disappeared in a blast of such intense brilliance that its vivid colors ranged from purple to blue-white, from gold to pure white. It would later be estimated that the following fireball contained for a fraction of a second a temperature of nearly one million degrees. Its piercing heat instantly incinerated everything within several hundred yards of its hypocenter, and almost as quickly ignited all that would burn within two kilometers. The shock from the titanic explosion flattened much of the city as if its buildings were fragile matchsticks. But the savage gray cloud which followed, coupled with the white mushroom cloud which boiled to nearly 40,000 feet, were never seen by most of the victims. Nor would they see the black rain and the utter devastation. For many—and all those close to the hypocenter—the colossal explosion was never even heard.

For Itoko and Sataro, clinging tightly together in their last moment, death was instantaneous.

Forty-four

Hiroshi looked down at what had been the city of his birth as the plane made a wide circle prior to landing. After frantically trying to get factual information ever since he had heard about the holocaust two days earlier, he had finally convinced his superior to let him ride along on this flight with Japan's leading nuclear physicist, Dr. Nishina. Since the United States had announced that the devastation had been caused by an atomic bomb, the war minister wanted an opinion from the man responsible for Japan's own atom bomb project.

What both men saw from a thousand feet wasn't much different from an aerial view of many parts of Tokyo. But the knowledge that it had happened in one split second was terrifying. Here and there in the debris, the remains of a more sturdily built temple stood up starkly; the rest of the surface of the six islands looked like the remains of a charred tinderbox. He located the section where his Uncle Seizo lived—more of the same. He forced his gaze to the area between Hiroshima Castle and the fork of the Kyobashi River, knowing what he would see, but hoping that somehow—

He guessed her house would have been about 1,500 yards from the hypocenter—that was what Nishina called the center of impact. Obliteration blinked back at him. He knew it, she should never have rented that flimsy Japanese-style house! He shook his head, trying to ward off the knot in his gut. There wasn't any chance. Nishina had also told him about radiation and some of the amazing effects that had been reported to him the previous day.

As the aircraft turned on final approach to a field near the waterfront, Nishina leaned over and nodded. "I believe them," he said vigorously. "It could be one atomic bomb."

"Do you think they have more?" Hiroshi asked.

"But of course."

Hiroshi nodded grimly. "Then tell them it's time to quit."

The professor gave him a blank look as the aircraft touched down. How could a general make such a statement?

Hiroshi found the remains of the house with the help of a young lieutenant who knew the residential area. "If your mother was there, it's possible that her body has been moved or incinerated," a Red Cross official had tiredly warned him. He was staring at the sight, hoping that he would have reason to look further. But his heart sunk when he saw what was left—pieces of metal, such as the stove; rocks and the charred stumps of small trees in the garden. Thinking he saw something that resembled a leg, he brushed aside a blackened beam and found a woman—a short fat woman, burned beyond recognition. With a quick sigh of relief, he realized it couldn't be his slender mother.

The other rooms disclosed nothing.

"Out here, sir," the lieutenant said softly. And he knew.

The smell of death was in the garden. He saw the slender form of a woman, face down in the remnants of a burned kimono by a seared shrub. And close by was the body of a tall man. But he had no time for strangers. Staring at the slender form, he edged closer, breathing lightly. It took all of his will, but he forced himself to kneel over the woman and look at her face. Slowly, he turned her head and sucked in a sharp breath. It was his mother. Her face was a dark brown, as if she had a severe sunburn or tan. He shuddered as he lifted her form and held it closely, trying to hold back the sob that was tearing at his heart.

The lieutenant stood by the other corpse, looking through a wallet that had partially survived the fire. He waited until Hiroshi lifted his head. "General, these papers say this man's name is Hoshi."

Hiroshi stared, trying to comprehend. His uncle? Slowly, he lowered his mother's remains to the ground and crawled over to the man's corpse. The eyebrows and part of his white hair were gone, but a thin white scar on his cheek showed through the same type of dark stain that his mother had. He reached slowly out and touched the strong jaw of the man who was his father—and had become his friend in the past four years. And this sob could not be contained.

Gently, he touched his father's corpse and moved it close to his mother's. When he looked at the lieutenant, the young man was holding a handkerchief to his nose. "What should I do now?" he asked like a confused child.

The lieutenant looked away. "All bodies are to be cremated, sir. It's an order."

"But where?"

The young man pointed to the remains of a nearby house. A small group of people were standing around a cloud of smoke. "Wherever there is something that will burn, sir." He gulped.

Hiroshi stifled a scream of agony when he realized what he had to do.

It was the last scream he had in his soul.

The following day was August 9. The Russians had declared war and another atomic bomb had been dropped on the beautiful city of Nagasaki. But neither event made much of an impact on Hiroshi's numbed thoughts. He arrived on Miyajima by ferryboat at two-thirty in the afternoon and made his way slowly to the monastery on the other side of the inlet. There he spoke briefly to the head monk and handed him the two small urns. The monk agreed. One year later, on August 6, he would place the ashes in an appropriate final resting spot. Hiroshi gave him all the money he had left and departed for the city. An hour later he was winging back toward Tokyo.

The shabby old Ichigaya Heights auditorium that had served thousands of cadets was filled at 1157 on August 15. Hiroshi guessed more than three hundred officers were assembled to hear the Imperial rescript that was to be broadcast to the nation and all overseas installations where the powerful NHK station could be heard. After four days of stubborn delays by the military leaders, the saddened Emperor had been forced to make the decision for the failing Suzuki cabinet. There would be no last-ditch sacrifice of millions of loyal subjects. Though there would be die-hards, the majority of the Japanese people would be able to lay down its arms and the wrenches that built the war machine.

A hush was over the huge room.

Like the others, Hiroshi wore his dress uniform, complete with his full array of medals and his prized dress sword. A gold safety pin held his left sleeve neatly in its folded position. His face was cold, expressionless, as he listened to Lieutenant Colonel Dobana whisper of General Tojo's plans for surrendering himself to the Americans as soon as they entered the city.

He was interrupted by the solemn voice of Chokugen Wada, Nippon's leading radio announcer as it came over the loudspeaker. "This will be a broadcast of the gravest importance. Will all listeners please rise. His Majesty will now read the Imperial rescript to the people of Japan. We respectfully transmit his voice."

Over six hundred heels clicked sharply to attention in that auditorium as the national anthem played. There was a short pause. Then a thin voice employing the strange, nearly Chinese words and expressions of ancient imperial language began: *"To Our Good and Loyal Subjects. . . . After pondering deeply . . ."*

Hiroshi stood rigidly, already deeply moved by the voice of his Emperor. He pictured the millions of people throughout the empire—anyone old enough and sufficiently healthy to get to his or her feet—standing and listening to words they might not understand, but with a meaning that was as clear as the peal of a bell on a winter morning. And as he felt his emotions begin to take over and his eyes moisten, he knew that they, too, had begun to weep. In every city, every hamlet, on every stopped conveyance, every ship, every military installation . . . in every temple, hospital, factory, school and home . . . the people were standing with heads bowed, crying silently.

". . . Our Empire accepts the provisions of their Joint Declaration. . . ."

The only sound in the auditorium was the voice—the Voice of the Crane, as it was called. Hiroshi knew by now that many of those standing around the empire had dropped to their knees, shrieking in anguish . . . perhaps some in relief.

"We have resolved to pave the way for a grand peace for all the generations to come by enduring the unendurable and suffering what is insufferable. . . ."

There it was—his father's precious *gambari.*

The Emperor's voice was almost a whisper as it ended with, *". . . the innate glory of the Imperial State and keep pace with the progress of the world."*

Tears streamed down Hiroshi's cheeks, while all around him there were open sobs. He nodded to Dobana and headed for the exit. It was over.

The drive to Kamakura was difficult with all the bad roads and the milling, stunned crowds, but the driver made it in just over four hours. Leaving the staff car, Hiroshi first walked to the giant Daibutsu. There he began the reenactment of a young cadet accompanying a solemn lieutenant up to its head. After a moment's pause, it was off through the quiet streets to the Temple of Hachiman.

Climbing the stone steps, Hiroshi glanced back to his left to see if the thousand-year-old tree had been bothered by the folly of another thirty-three years. It hadn't. He climbed the last dozen steps and entered the temple. Standing with his hat in his hand, he looked at the faded war banner of Iyeyasu, the great shogun. Again, he saw the young Tojo and heard his words, "If you ever feel doubt, come back here and cleanse your spirit." The words seemed to echo at him from every corner, *feel doubt, feel doubt.* He remembered the rush of power he had felt that day, but now it was replaced by a sapping revulsion.

Dropping to his knees, he ignored the stares of the handful of nearby people. "Oh, God of War," he whispered, "I've given my life to you, tried to live by your great code, and served my empire in spite of misgivings. I know there is nothing you can do in my immense grief, but I beseech you to understand . . . I am finished."

Silently, Hiroshi got to his feet and withdrew the sword from its scabbard. Raising it high above his head in his powerful right hand, he let out a piercing cry of anguish and rage as he rammed the tip into the floor and shattered it.

At exactly ten o'clock Hiroshi went to his granddaughter's room and stood silently by her bed for a few moments. Then he found Sachi reading by a candle in the study. He placed a warm container of sake on a low table in front of her. "I think we should drink to our philosophical union," he said quietly as he poured the strong liquid into two small cups.

Sachi looked at him quizzically. Philosophical union? A general and Nippon's most bitter pacifist? She had seen very little of him since his tragic return from Hiroshima—*God, she could still hardly utter the name!* Just the thought of her grandparents . . . all he would tell her was that they perished immediately and that he had made the funeral arrangements.

He looked so tired, so sad, she thought. But then he was undoubtedly morose over the rescript . . . the Emperor's *words*. She noticed those words hadn't included anything about *surrender*, only to stop fighting. But she had to push aside her bitterness, her father needed her on this, Nippon's most ignominious night. She smiled softly as she sipped, waiting for him to go on.

"Yes, our union, my dear. For tonight, we are one. We are joined together in violent pacifism." He stared at his cup as he emptied and refilled it. "But I don't want to talk about that," he said, shaking his head. "I want to talk about your mother." He smiled sadly. "Did you know that she once spoke to me only in French?"

Sachi chuckled. How she wanted to hold her sad, wounded father close to her breast. "Really? Why did she do that?"

Hiroshi sighed, remembering his sixteenth birthday party. "She was a very impertinent girl. Did you know she launched a campaign to capture me that would have made Napoleon look like a corporal?" He pictured her for Sachi, quoting von Clausewitz to him.

Sachi's eyes widened. "I didn't know that. She told me something about making you wait while she played the bon vivant in Paris."

Hiroshi smiled. "And I doubt that she ever mentioned trying to seduce me in a rickshaw."

"Father! *My* mother?" She stroked his hand, seeing how quickly the joy fled from his eyes. Perhaps the capitulation had hurt him even more than she thought. "Tell me more about her," she urged gently.

He went into other stories about Suiko—tiny bits of loving memory that had been locked inside him for what seemed forever. And warm memories of his mother, and the trials of school, of Koki. And his father. "I never seemed to give enough of myself to him, particularly after Noboru's death," he sighed, shaking his head again. "I was too busy marching to glory." He pushed the bitterness away. There was no more time for it. Only his beautiful Sachi mattered. He told her of how much he doted on her when she was a tot, how she was one of the main reasons he pulled through the Guadalcanal wounds, and other private recollections.

And soon she was crying against his knee and smiling bravely up through the glistening tears. What a magnificent child he had fathered, he thought as he touched her cheek. He hated for it to end.

Even at eleven-thirty, the vast ground of the Yasukuni Shrine were still occupied by many mourning people. And now, how could these poor grieving people reconcile the deaths of their loved ones with defeat? How long would it take for them to recover from being party to such a mammoth and hideous fraud? He parked the bicycle near the broad steps at the southwest entrance and began the long walk to the altar. There was enough moonlight to illuminate the wide gravel pathway that led to the enormous black *torii* which marked the first stage of the shrine. He moved erectly, looking neither right nor left, seeing no one.

He was wearing the traditional black ceremonial kimono with the Hoshi *mon* embroidered over the breast. The left sleeve hung loosely at his side. He stopped at the massive *torii* and looked up, wondering for some reason if it were as tall as the one in the water at Miyajima. Now he would never join his father to find peace on that quiet island. He moved on through the next *torii* to the main part of the shrine. Here, it seemed that all the weeping people were old—tiny, shriveled old people mourning sons and grandsons who had died so hopelessly. But they would never know they had been betrayed—they just provided the forage of war. He moved quietly up the few steps, advancing to the wooden altar and depositing his coins.

He wondered what they'd be worth in a few days.

Dropping to his knees, he stared at the carved chrysanthemum on the altar, concentrating on its wooden petals as if they might reach out to comfort him and tell him it was all a hideous nightmare. The sharp lines blurred as he thought of his attempts at religion. Nichiren, did you bring this all about—or were you just part of the salesmanship? Lord Buddha? Christ? The great Western God? Where was Heaven and what was Nirvana?

He inhaled deeply, seeing Koki beside him in the study. His stepfather was smoking a cigar and speaking with such deep concern, ". . . true bravery does not always lie in a code or a sword. It could mean your soul!"

He saw the regal Prince Saionji moving toward him with blazing black eyes, his voice cracking like a whip, "I do not believe we can win such a war. . . ." Why hadn't he listened to that magnificent old man—gotten out of the army to serve him, given him all the information he requested, anything? Why didn't we listen to you, oh wise one? *Why?*

And he saw the feverish eyes of little, tempestuous Misao—courageous, gallant, and the very core of the Code. He stiffened, barely able to choke back the overwhelming revulsion, the gripping urge to smash the giant flower. Even his splendid friend had been nothing but a faceless tool in the grotesque sham. . . .

And so it had come to this, the final accounting. And on the giant abacus he was guilty, guilty of the tragic act of omission. Had he and those like him listened as Koki had warned, listened to their inner voice of conscience, just possibly a way might have been found to stop it. . . .

The chrysanthemum blurred and he felt the final tears on his cold cheek.

And voices were already saying, "This is not the final war."

Only minutes remained of this most ignominious day, only minutes for his final belch of disgust and shame.

Faces danced before him, a blurring kaleidoscope and sudden stills. And always it came back to the terrible march in the snow. Cold snow. With blood. A bleak light bulb in a barren hospital room. There was only one act of purity, nothing left to be done except free his tortured soul from his guilty belly. Forever.

Slowly he shook off the black kimono, baring his upper torso. Then carefully, by custom, he tucked the sleeves under his knees to keep from falling backward. There was no one to hold him erect except the will of the Hoshis once the stroke began. His hand went to the hilt of the sharp dagger, the ceremonial *wakizashi*, as he again fixed his gaze on the carved chrysanthemum on the altar. The face that replaced the petals was that of his father, wearing the robe of a monk. It was expressionless, waiting. . . . He moved the tip of the *wakizashi* deliberately below the waist on his left side and gripped the handle firmly for its plunge into his abdomen.

His final words were, "Free me, Father."

And his blood spilled onto the Shrine of the War Dead.

BOOK 4

THE MERCHANT PRINCESS

1945–1983

Forty-five

Sachi would never forget the violence of her decision, nor the grim vehemence of her vow. Whenever it rained on her face, the savagery of it all rushed back with vivid accuracy.

It happened less than minutes after the trip home from her father's funeral—a daze of waiting, riding, and stumbling from a forbidding graveyard through the grisly wasteland that was Tokyo one day after the unofficial end of World War II. She had escaped the waving sea of confused, hopeless faces attached to bodies that suddenly had no meaningful place to go. And just as Japan was a void, so was she.

Not wanting to face even her daughter, she slipped into the unkempt garden and slumped down on a stone bench. She gazed dully at the corner of the house where a bomb had caused some severe damage just ten days earlier, and she didn't even care if it got fixed. She didn't know how long it was until the first raindrops fell coldly on her bare head, but it triggered an explosion. Her mouth suddenly tasted bitter as a violent rage washed aside the pain and added hot tears to the cold rivulets of rainwater. And the more drenched she became in the sudden downpour, the more furious she became. She closed her eyes tightly and suddenly all the pain and futility of over three years boiled out in a wild, agonizing scream.

And the heat was suddenly displaced by a cold realization.

She had to survive.

She was a woman in a broken world where women didn't count. A little girl, an innocent child who could easily starve, depended on her in love and the blindest faith. There was one servant left, an old man who had somehow to be fed. It made her think of her grandfather and more angry tears streamed down her cheeks. His great new dream had vanished in the ashes of a terrible new weapon. Peace—what was that, a hollow illusion, a mockery? Survival was the goal now. And then insulation, protection from the animals who made war.

The House of Hoshi had a new head in Japan, and nothing would keep her from prevailing, from jerking them free from the clutches of madness. Nothing! The answer was simple—

A flash of lightning illuminated her wet face. It was followed by a violent boom of thunder.

She threw up her fist. That was it—*power!* The only answer, and she'd stop at *nothing* to get it. Turning her face upward into the now driving rain, she shouted, "*On the honor of my families, I swear it!*"

September 8 was the day of the feared MacArthur's arrival. Arising at dawn, the curious Sachi dressed quickly and made her way to the not too distant American embassy, where the conquering hero would reside. His motorcade was supposed to arrive from Yokohama, so she found a place to observe from a block away. Already the area around the front of the embassy was crowded with a squadron of tall soldiers wearing shiny helmets and white leggings. On their shoulders, a huge yellow patch with a diagonal black line and a horse's head announced that they were cavalrymen. Later, she heard one of them say, "Seventh Cav out of the First Cav Division. Little Big Horn, old buddy."

Sachi had examined every possibility carefully. Hearing the GIs talk brought back memories of Vassar, New York, and California. She thought of her pleasant stay in Lodi and wondered how all those people had weathered the war. She had begun to polish her nearly perfect English by extended daily practice. Years earlier her father had told her a talent for languages ran in the family; now it might pay off.

At twenty-four, she knew the impact of her beauty would be a factor in the difficult road ahead. But for now, she hid her full figure in the popular baggy pants that she had scorned through the war and in oversized shirts. A wide-brim straw hat concealed much of her face when she was on the street. And she wore no makeup. She was curious about this powerful American general whom her father had described as a god to the Filipinos.

At shortly before eleven o'clock, the military band from the horse soldiers struck up a lively tune. Leaning forward from her position at the front of the small crowd, she saw Japanese motorcycle police with lights blazing, leading only a few large black sedans. Other Tokyo policemen scanned the crowd anxiously, trying to detect any possible trouble. Except for the martial music, it was unusually quiet in the bright early fall sunlight as the motorcade approached her position. Straining to look into the back of the first gleaming vehicle, she thought she saw him. A sharp, handsome profile under a light tan marshal's hat. And just as the car passed, he looked out toward her. She thought she saw a touch of curious warmth in his calm look.

"That was him!" the man next to her said excitedly. "I've seen his picture."

There was more music, then as the little motorcade entered the embassy grounds, a bugle began to play. More music followed, and then silence. When the bugle once more sounded, she could see the stars and stripes of the American flag reaching the top of the embassy's flagpole.

What she could not see was the emotion that softened even the scowling face of the unforgiving Admiral "Bull" Halsey, nor the grim look of dedication in the eyes of the man whom the Japanese would soon consider their own new god.

During the next two weeks, as the American occupation force moved into the city, Sachi explored every avenue of employment with the Americans. She could easily get a job as a maid or in some other domestic capacity; her English would open doors to nearly any office job, and dozens of interpreter positions would soon open up. But all of these possibilities were dead ends. She needed something where she could make contacts, have some flexibility, and yet remain submerged. And for what she had in mind, she needed a new identity.

Already, she had procured a new ID card that changed her name to Sachiko Yukai, and had developed her new cover story. In it, she had worked in a library in Hiroshima, departing just days before the atomic bomb blast, when all of her relatives were killed. And she had spent summers in California with relatives, and had even once been to New York. The fact that her new name meant "pleasure" in Japanese added to the allure.

Informed that the mighty Imperial Hotel had been designated a senior officers' billet where mostly generals and admirals would be staying, she did some needlework on a tasteful tweed suit that had been in mothballs since 1942, cut her hair short to her best advantage, and prepared for the first step on her path to *chikara*.

The institution that became famous on its opening day in the 1923 earthquake had withstood the war quite well, considering the devastation that visited so much of the surrounding area. With the exception of fire bombing that had gutted some 150 rooms in its south wing as well as the fancy Peacock Hall ballroom, the stalwart structure was merely a bit shabby around the edges when its new tenants arrived. Rumor had it that Frank Lloyd Wright had been invited back to rebuild, but the famous architect had refused. Some people felt he had done sufficient damage the first time.

The Imperial was a paradox—an imposing, expansive structure with long, horizontal lines of design, but no elevators or dumb-waiters for room service. While it had a monstrous main lobby, one almost had to duck when entering through the entrance lobby. It was also rumored that Mr. Wright had spent the week in a geisha house at the time of color selection; in his absence an undertaker conjured up the tones of the lobby's interior walls— morbid brown brick trimmed with *oya*, a volcanic rock that was ash gray and had the texture of Swiss cheese. In fact, the Americans quickly named it "the morgue."

Possibly the most practical description of the edifice came from the Imperial's new American manager when he said its north and south wings looked like two huge claws sticking out from the center dome giving it the appearance of a giant crab working on a stick of chewing gum.

To Sachi, regarding it in awe from across the street in Hibiya Park, it was intimidating. Only the red, white, and blue water lilies covering most of the hotel's giant protective pool softened its starkness. After watching for several minutes, she sighed deeply and started across the street. Someone who was going to become a powerful woman couldn't stand around with feet of clay. Besides, wasn't she a Hoshi?

Going around to a service entrance, she asked for the manager of the cocktail lounge and was directed to a small cubicle where two young women waited for interviews. Now it was time to control being a Hoshi—she Was Sachi Yukai from Hiroshima, and she badly needed a job. She smiled inwardly at the ease of her role; it was what the Western writers liked to call "the inscrutable Japanese smile" and she was directing it at her own people.

"We'll give you a one-week trial, Miss Yukai," the bar manager said abruptly when she finished telling the smooth story she had rehearsed to perfection. He then went into a detailed description of her duties, ending with, "This is the most prestigious lounge in the empire, Miss Yukai. Please conduct yourself appropriately."

She bowed her head as she replied, *"Hai."* It was the first step—she was a bar waitress.

Her day began at 1030 when she changed into the uniform she had taken home to alter the day before. It was a white blouse with a black string tie and a flared skirt of black cotton. Her locker in the employees' dressing room was next to that of another cocktail waitress, an attractive bubbly girl named Ume. Sachi liked her the moment they met.

Ume chuckled as she handed Sachi a card with drawings of the different officers' insignia of rank. "You find they're nice to know, but mostly these are what you'll see." She pointed to the eagles of a full colonel and the one and two stars of a brigadier and major general. Touching the five little silver stars in a circle, she smiled and said, "Makassar, but he never come."

She was nervously waiting at the waitress station in the middle of the bar when an older brigadier general and a colonel came in and took a table close to the bar shortly after eleven. Ume smiled encouragement as she turned to wait on her first customers with a bright smile.

The general looked her over approvingly. "Well, well, look at our new girl, Harry. I could forget Pearl Harbor in a big hurry at this rate." He smiled at Sachi. "Bring us a couple of Jap beers, honey. Kirin, I guess."

Sachi bowed her head demurely as she murmured, "Yes, sir."

It was going to be easy.

Four nights later, after going off duty and changing into her street clothes, Sachi stopped in the kitchen to collect her main perquisite—a plate of meat and potatoes from the evening menu. As she stood by a chopping block eating, she became conscious of someone watching. Glancing up, she saw a Japanese man in an American Army uniform staring at her. He was a technical sergeant and an inch taller than she. In a New York accent, long ago familiar to her, he asked, "You like American food?"

She nodded over the edge of her plate as she continued to chew.

He moved closer, asking in Japanese, "Are you new here?"

She smiled as she swallowed, then replied, "Yes, but I speak a little English, if you please." She carefully said, "ritter Engrish."

He looked her up and down with a big grin, then shook his head. "You're something else, honey. What's your name and what do you do around the Ritz here?"

She finished the last bite of roast beef. "Cocktail waitress. Name of Sachi. Who you, Sergeant? I no see before."

"I'm Charlie Asaka, Technical Sergeant Charlie Asaka, baby. And I come here once in a while to see that Buddhahead sergeant who works here. You know—Madakoro, who supervises the kitchen? But to hell with him—you look like you just got off work. You want to go somewhere? I mean, maybe there's some place where we can go to dance or something." He glanced down at her chest with a grin. "You do dance, don't you? You know—boogie-woogie, baby?"

One of Sachi's most enjoyable memories of her weekends in New York City during that year at Vassar was her jitterbugging lessons. She had gotten quite good just before leaving. "A ritter bit," she replied, continuing with the game. "But dance place no good for Japanese girl. Only men go there." It was time she made some contacts. "But you can buy me *sushi* if you have enough money and know place."

"No sweat, honey. There's a little place—kind of an intimate type—just a few blocks from here. And don't you worry about money. Old Charlie never has that kind of a problem." He turned to a cook, telling him in Japanese to tell Madakoro that his plans had changed, then grabbed Sachi's elbow and steered her toward the exit.

Charlie Asaka was from Manhattan and loved the Yankees. He also loved nearly everything about his big city and spent most of the next hour and a half talking about it. He was twenty-five, had worked as a cook in a Japanese restaurant near Carnegie Hall just before the war, and tried to make it sound like he owned the place. He had a long pleasant face that was interrupted by the shadow of a mustache he was cultivating over his ready grin. Except for his touching her too much, Sachi was amused and enjoyed being with him. Suddenly, he said something that sharpened her attention. "I don't understand," she interrupted with a perplexed look.

He shook his head. "I said a smart guy could make a million bucks in this town with the right connections and a little working capital. Why, the food that gets spilled in my mess hall alone is just a starter." Lighting a cigarette, the intensity in his eyes grew. "You know, there's a thousand guys just like me who've got their fingers on stuff: Like these cigarettes, but that's nickle and dime." He sighed. "Yeah, baby, I wouldn't be a mess sergeant very long if I could lay my hands on some loot."

She nodded, saying nothing as the waitress brought more tea.

Charlie grinned at her. Reaching for her hand, he said, "But you don't want to hear that stuff, baby. Let's talk about where you and me can go to be by ourselves."

She blinked innocently. "What you mean, Charrie-san!"

"You know. How about your place?"

She smiled bashfully, then looked down.

"C'mon, baby—where do you live?"

She shook her head without looking up. "I go now, Charrie-san. Late for streetcars."

He glanced at his watch. "Yeah. Well, c'mon. I'll take you."

She looked up firmly. "No, Charrie-san. I go home alone."

"But I—"

"I go alone. Meet you here tomorrow two o'clock." She started for the door.

He threw some yen on the table and followed her hurriedly.

The next day was Sunday, her first day off. Charlie was waiting when she arrived at the *sushi* shop. She had decided to continue with the broken English ruse and keep the hard-breathing Charlie at a short distance. They walked toward the palace in the warm late September sunshine, she listening and he chattering away about how he could be the richest soldier in the Orient if he had a stake. They wound up back in Hibiya Park across from the Imperial. Dressed in her street garb of wide pants and the straw hat, she dropped to the worn grass and smiled at him.

She steered the conversation to his black market thinking. "How much money it take for *yami*," she asked innocently.

"Ha!" He laughed. "Depends on how rich you want to get. There's hundreds of guys willing to sell a little here and there. Put it all together, you got a bunch, baby!"

"You know Japanese *yami?*" she asked quietly. "How you sell this things?"

Charlie snorted. "Hell, baby, there's all kinds of smart cookies out there starving. I'd set up my own distributors." He shrugged his shoulders and made a wry face. "On the other hand, it might not hurt to work with something established too. Depends on how bad they're going to rob you. Yeah, I'd say make it a combination at first, then go independent." His eyes glowed. "Yeah, make a million."

They talked on for another hour. Aside from any food, Charlie thought the most desired items were any kinds of sweets—candy, sugar, and saccharin—cigarettes, penicillin and other medical supplies, soap, and whiskey. At least for starters. Clothing and blankets, too, but they were bulky items. Finally, he took her by the shoulders and asked, "Just why are you so damned interested in the *yami*, young lady? You got a gangster daddy or something?"

She got to her feet. It was close to five and she had to get home. She had found a big carp and promised her daughter that they would have a special supper. She smiled in answer to his question. "No, but I have uncle who might be interested."

Charlie's eyes lit up. "Hey, really? God, that's great, baby, just great! When can I meet him? I mean, the time is *now!*"

Sachi shook her head. "You can't—not now. I do." She moved more swiftly toward the trolley stop.

Hurrying to keep up, he grabbed her arm. "Hey, where you going? I'm just getting started. I know this place, it's a small hotel—"

Sachi broke into a run, throwing him a final smile as she swung up on the last inches of the streetcar platform.

She knew he would be waiting in the kitchen when she got off work the next night at nine o'clock. And she guessed he'd be angry. He was scowling over his coffee in Sergeant Madakoro's office near the storeroom when the first cook handed her a plate of chicken and green beans. Madakoro wiggled a finger for her to come to the office just as she started to eat. He had a big grin on his face. "This mainland idiot thinks your pidgin is pretty good, Sachi. Come give him some of your library culture." The Hawaiian Nisei had read her file.

"Yeah, baby," Charlie growled. "Let me hear you say 'look at the large balloon.' "

Sachi grinned sheepishly.

"Trying to con a con, huh, baby?"

Sachi ate silently.

Madakoro threw his head back and roared with laughter. When he finished, he said, "I love it, Miss Yukai. Teach these hotshot New Yorkers a lesson. I wish I'd put you up to it."

Sachi lowered her head in a bow, but when she looked up she smiled at Charlie. "I apologize, Charlie-san," she said in her best English. "Will you take me to your favorite *sushi* shop for some tea?"

Charlie scowled as he nodded. "And what about after that— you going to pull that fade-out at the streetcar again?"

Calmly, Sachi replied, "I certainly will."

Madakoro laughed again, but Charlie just shrugged. "Okay, baby, one more time."

Outside a short time later, Charlie took her arm as they walked away from the Imperial. "Good idea." He grinned. "Putting up that front with that Buddhahead. After all, you work there. Now, I told you, I've got this nice little hotel—"

She stopped and turned close to his face, saying evenly, "Charlie, there will be no hotel. Friendship and business, that's all."

Charlie looked into her cool dark eyes and read something he wasn't used to seeing in a young woman—particularly a young Japanese woman. And he nodded. "Okay," he replied quietly. "Let's talk business. What did your uncle say?"

Sachi began to walk. "I'll tell you at the *sushi* shop."

"Okay, baby. I've been waiting." Charlie stubbed out his cigarette in the ashtray as the waiter finished pouring the tea.

Sachi reached inside the oversized man's shirt she was wearing. From the special little pocket in the seam of her left arm, she pulled out a small packet of white tissue paper. Carefully unfolding it on the table, she reached for its contents—a tiny blue-white diamond of over one-half carat that Itoko had paid the equivalent of $2,600 for three years earlier when she began to convert her savings.

Charlie whistled when he saw it. "Wow," he whispered. "Is that real?"

"It's supposed to be flawless, a special stone. It was appraised last week for forty-five thousand yen—three thousand dollars."

Charlie's eyes were wide. "I might be able to get more for it from the high rollers—the guys in the big card and dice games. Man, with a start like that, your uncle and me could get things rolling. Yes, sir!"

Sachi had been over it and over it, finally deciding to play the "uncle" routine all the way. If Charlie or any other men got the idea that she was doing this by herself, the good old Japanese male chauvinism would become a factor—or, even worse, they might just rob her. "He's a difficult man, Charlie," she said. "But you won't have to deal with him." She rewrapped the diamond in the tissue and replaced it in her shirt. "All of your dealings will be through me."

Charlie nodded, his mind already buzzing with ideas. "I've got a guy—a one-armed Jap soldier I met. I know I can trust him and I can start getting some stuff moving his way immediately. I—" He saw the fleeting look of pain cross her face. "I say something wrong?"

One-armed soldier—she still couldn't take off-guard reminders of her father. "No, it's all right, Charlie. Go on."

He cleared his throat. "I'm jumping the gun here. First, we gotta sell that rock. No, first, you have to make up your mind if we're going on with this thing. I'll sell the rock, then pay your uncle back three-quarters of the money and cut him into the operation for one-eighth. That way—"

"No," she broke in. "You don't pay anything back, and it's fifty-fifty."

Now Charlie had a pained look. "No dice, baby. I do all the organizing and take all the risks—and you get half? Huh-uh."

Sachi shrugged and started to get up. "We have risks too."

Charlie caught her hand. "Sixty-forty?"

Sachi shook her head firmly as she turned to go. He squeezed her hand. "Okay, *okay!* Fifty-fifty. Now, what do you want to do about the rock? I can't very well bring these guys to you."

She had already decided. This one diamond was just a start for what she had in mind. She had to start taking chances somewhere, and before long the *yami* would be too well organized to get in. She pulled the diamond back out and handed it to him. "All right, Charlie Asaka," she said coolly as she stuck out her hand for an American handshake. "We're partners. Now, the first rule is that you are never to see or speak to me at the hotel. Understood?"

Charlie looked into those unwavering dark eyes as he shook hands and knew that not only was he never going to get in bed with this woman, he was never going to have the upper hand.

Forty-six

"The Russians want you again." Ume chuckled as she nudged Sachi with her elbow.

Sachi shook her head as she picked up the cocktail tray and started for their table. Two Russian generals and one admiral lived in the hotel, but they never came to the lounge together. General Karalenko was the one who was the most difficult— getting more insistent that she favor him each time he came in. A heavy-shouldered, bulky man with a thick neck and a gleaming bald head, he had thick Slavic lips and a chestful of medals. His aide, a major who looked like he was stamped from the same Ukrainian cast, liked to repeat the story that Karalenko was practically the savior of Stalingrad. They were seated next to the wall in the far right corner of the slightly crowded bar. It was just after happy hour on the fourth Friday night following Sachi's deal with Charlie Asaka.

The general leered at her as his aide ordered double vodkas for both.

She was about to go back to the bar when Karalenko caught her wrist. "You are very beautiful tonight, my dove," he said in poor Japanese.

She bowed her head, giving him the bright, stock smile, then extracted her hand and glided away to get their order. When she brought the drinks, it was more of the same; the general kept talking in an embarrassing manner. Finally, she broke away again and stayed busy with her other tables until the major intercepted her and ordered another round. Placing it at the bar, she sighed and shook her head. "Hey, Ume. How about delivering this?" she asked. "I'm going to the restroom."

The other waitress rolled her merry eyes. *"Hai,* and I get pinched instead of you."

Sachi took as long a break as she dared, then shrugged and headed back to the lounge. She was worried though, having heard how difficult these senior Russian officers could be with too much alcohol in them. Ume quickly informed her that the general was impatient for her to return. But before she could go to the table, the major strode up and glared at her. "The general wishes for you to be his personal waitress only," he announced in heavily accented English.

Sachi shook her head. "But sir, I can't do that. I—"

"You'll do as ordered!" the major snarled.

Sachi took a deep breath. How could this be happening?

"I'm afraid that's impossible, Major," a youthful-looking American colonel with several rows of ribbons said. "This young lady is coming with me to serve a private party." He turned to Sachi and smiled pleasantly. "Are you ready to depart, miss?" He took her elbow and started for the door.

The Russian major grabbed his arm. "Whose party?" he asked belligerently.

The colonel glanced coldly down at the major's hand. "General Eichelberger's," he replied quietly. "Now take your goddamn hand off me, Ivan, or I'll feed it to you."

The Russian pulled his head back as if he had been slapped. Immediately, the colonel firmly continued toward the service door with Sachi. As she blinked her surprised eyes, he propelled her through the storage room right on out into the kitchen, where he finally stopped and looked around. Sergeant Madakoro looked out from his small office with a start. As he got up from his desk, the colonel asked, "Who's in charge around here tonight, Sergeant? We've got a problem."

"Uh, I think the captain's around somewhere, sir. What's the problem?"

The colonel quickly explained, adding, "The only answer is to get her out of there before we have an incident. And she's the only one who'll get hurt."

Madakoro shook his head. "No sweat, sir. She can take the rest of the night off. We don't have to bother the captain with it.

Those damned Russians think they can get away with murder, don't they, sir?''

Sachi had made a quick clothing change and was walking down the crowded street with the colonel almost before she had time to realize what was happening. All she knew was that she couldn't have trouble and lose her job. The Imperial was her ideal haven. A half block from the hotel, she stopped and asked, "Where are we going, Colonel?"

He laughed as he leaned down to look under her straw hat. It was a surprisingly boyish laugh. "I'm taking you to my favorite snack bar for a GI hamburger. Oh, by the way, my name is James Forster and I'm from Washington, D.C."

She nodded her head in a short bow. "I'm Sachi."

He chuckled. "I know—I saw your name tag."

A brisk ten-minute walk brought them to the snack bar in the Dai Ichi Hotel, a field grade officer's billet. The snack bar was small, with plain white walls and low lighting. No other customers were present. Forster ordered two hamburgers with french fries and two chocolate milkshakes as the waitress gave Sachi a quick disdainful look. At that moment, Sachi decided to keep a decent dress in her locker. She gave the colonel a soft smile. "What will happen with the general?" she asked, not quite keeping the worry out of her voice.

"I work for General Thayer," Forster replied. "He's a strong major general and after I tell him what happened, he'll have Karalenko's superior straighten him out. There won't be any problem." He smiled. "I used Eichelberger's name because he's a three-star. Don't worry about it. In fact, don't worry about anything and take that silly hat off so I can see your pretty face."

Sachi smiled in agreement as she removed the hat and brushed back a short lock of hair. She liked her rescuer immediately. Except for a few tiny wrinkles around his wide greenish eyes, the only sign of age was a single line an inch above his eyebrows. Even the deep cleft in his chin failed to disturb the youthfulness about his face. His soft brown hair was cut just long enough to comb, and he was another tall American. She smiled again as she studied him from across the table. "How old are you?" she asked innocently.

"They call me the boy colonel," he replied. "But I'm thirty. There are a couple of other ones from the Eleventh Airborne who are real whiz kids—twenty-eight."

She had trouble restraining herself when the food arrived; it had been her favorite meal in America. The food was from the army field ration mess and the milkshake was thin, but it tasted to her as if it had come from the Waldorf. Forster watched with amusement. "Forget your dainty Japanese manners." He chuckled. "And dig in."

By the time they finished and she had consumed two cups of coffee and a piece of cherry pie à la mode, she felt she had known him for ages. She couldn't remember when she had been able to relax so. When she mentioned having visited New York, he told her about being a West Pointer. That was the most difficult part of the meal for her—not being able to tell him about Vassar and how she had been smitten by the handsome gray-clad cadets who came down to nearby Poughkeepsie every weekend. She had dated one just before she left—an aggressive halfback on the football team who had claimed it was her duty as a foreign student to make love to him.

Finally it was time for the snack bar to close and for them to go. Before a discussion about her getting home could arise, she stated simply that she would catch a streetcar. He was casual about it as they walked to the trolley stop, asking as a car arrived, "When may I see you again—away from the Imperial?"

Without any hesitation, she blurted out, "Sunday at one o'clock in front of the Russian embassy." Her house wasn't far from there.

He nodded, smiling. "Is that supposed to mean something?"

She pulled the wide-brim hat down tighter as she shook her head. "No, don't bring your vodka-drinking friends." For some reason, Sunday seemed a long time away.

Not having to go to work until four the next day, she met Charlie Asaka at three at the *sushi* shop. As she waited, she wondered if there could be a problem—she always worried when he was late. Between them, they had been able to get a team of over two dozen people peddling or acting as middlemen for the myriad items that were available and in demand. They had three retail outlets—those little newsstandlike boxes near railway stations that had sprung up like mushrooms since the war. Just as she pictured him being arrested, he hurried into the shop. "Sorry, baby," he panted. "But I had to wait on this guy over at Tokyo Station. He's from Kyoto and he thinks he might know of a good warehouse we can rent down there. That's just what we need, you know."

She nodded as the girl served his tea.

"And I got a navy guy from Yokosuka meeting me at four o'clock in front of the Dai Ichi building—a chief who's a medic," Charlie went on eagerly. "Sounded like he's got his finger on a bunch of stuff." He withdrew an envelope from his OD Ike-jacket. "Here's the weekly summary." He smiled. "As you'll see, we made over three hundred bucks this week and it's still only peanuts. If we only had some more capital—"

His eyes darted to the piece of tissue paper she pulled from her shirt. With a slight smile, she handed him two more of Itoko's diamonds.

Charlie looked around furtively as he opened the tissue. He whistled. "Christ, where did your uncle get these?"

"I don't ask," she replied. "But apparently he thinks you're trustworthy now. The larger one is worth about thirty-six hundred, the smaller one around twenty-five. Can you get a good price for them?"

Charlie nodded eagerly. "Sure can!" He looked at them again, then wrapped them back in the paper and buttoned them in his Ike-jacket pocket. "Man," he said softly, "this ought to get us moving."

"What about your money, Charlie—did you figure a way to get it back to the United States yet?"

"No, not exactly. But I'm not up for discharge for another three months. And then I'm not sure about my points. I'm thinking about leaving it all here—if these banks settle down. And I heard Mac's going to make them as solid as a rock."

He was referring to MacArthur's recent shutdown of nearly all of the nation's banks—merely one of the stringent controls that had taken place since the nation got over the shock of hearing that their Imperial Emperor had gone politely to visit MacArthur, instead of the intruder coming to the palace. "Or," Charlie added, "I could maybe just take my discharge over here."

Sachi's heart jumped. The terrible problem with this arrangement was Charlie's impending departure. Although the operation could run without him, it would be quite difficult for her. "Would they let you stay?" she asked hopefully.

He grinned. "It's about time I went back to college. Maybe Tokyo University—who knows? Or maybe I might just reenlist." He winked. "The recruiters are saying the army's a place for opportunity."

Sachi was glad about one thing from the war—staying home continually, she had learned how to sew well enough to consider herself an accomplished seamstress. The dress she was wearing had been torn completely apart and rebuilt from her mother's size to her own. It was of light blue taffeta and had a stand-up collar. Fortunately, both her mother's and grandmother's shoes fit, so finding matching pumps was no problem. And she had brought along a white jacket, in case the warm October day turned otherwise. In short, this American colonel who had somehow excited her was not going to see a tawdry little cocktail waitress. She had tried to quiet that stimulation, but hadn't been successful. For the first time in years, her heart was fluttering like a giddy schoolgirl's. She had told herself it was ridiculous—that as much as she violently hated war and its makers, it was utterly incongruous that she should be attracted to Forster. So much so that she was actually worried sick that he wouldn't show up.

The American jeep parked directly across from the Russian embassy silenced her fears immediately. Lounging in the driver's seat in his OD uniform, Colonel James Forster looked quite out of place in the Sunday foot traffic. As she crossed the street diagonally, he spotted her and hopped out with a warm grin. "Good afternoon," he sang out cheerily. "I rounded up a set of wheels."

"So I see," she replied as he helped her into the passenger's seat. She liked the warm strength of his hands.

He drove slowly through the area, eventually heading northwest.

"I thought you might like to get out of the city," he said casually as he expertly handled the jeep. She thought about the two automobiles in their garage and wondered if they would ever work again, once there was enough gasoline.

"Have you ever been to Tachikawa Air Base?" he asked as he slowed for a traffic policeman.

She almost said yes, but caught herself. "No," she replied, getting used to the stares. "Is it far?"

"Not too far. Do you have to be back early?"

"By five." She started inwardly, knowing she had a problem. He would want to drive her home!

"I think it's great the way the people are picking away at the wreckage and rebuilding. It's imperceptible—a piece here, a fragment there. All these people who fled to the country coming back and starting with these little shacks." His hand came over abruptly and touched hers. "I'm sorry. I didn't think that you might be living in one."

She said nothing, wishing she hadn't come. But a couple of glances at his warm, curious smile as he drove on made her change her mind. She pictured him in his gray cadet uniform, looking even younger and more handsome as he stood waiting in the lobby of her boardinghouse at Vassar. He was holding a green plastic wrapper with a half dozen light yellow roses that were just coming out of their buds. And they went out in the bright sunshine and got in his Ford convertible. . . .

"There are many people from Hiroshima living in America," he said, evidently thinking about the story she had told him. "I had a terrific Nisei interpreter with me on Leyte. His parents came from there." He paused. "He was killed."

"Oh, I'm sorry," was all she could manage.

Thirty minutes later, after driving in the country for some time, he swung into a gate with a small guardhouse. A tall MP stepped out and saluted smartly. Eyeing Sachi, he briskly waved them inside and saluted again as they passed. Shortly, Forster stepped in front of a new Quonset hut and parked the jeep. "It's a temporary officers club," he announced as he jumped out and came around to help her down. As she looked up, he was still standing close, gazing intently into her eyes. Leaning down, he brushed her lips with his. "I heard these fat-cat pilots were flying steaks in from the States," he said as he took her hand and led her inside the round-roofed structure. She blinked, still tasting his lips. He was the first man to kiss her in almost four years.

There was only a handful of other people in the club—a couple of officers drinking at the short bar, and two others with Japanese girls sitting in a living room arrangement near the center of the hut. One more was playing some kind of a machine standing against a far wall. Forster pointed to an overstuffed quartermaster sofa in a corner. He went to the bar, returning shortly with a beer and a glass of dry wine for Sachi. "How would you like your steak?" he asked pleasantly.

"Oh, I don't know," she replied softly. The last steak she had eaten—and that had been teriyaki style—was before the baby was born. "You order it for me." She sipped the wine as he went back to the bar to order.

"They're barely open," he explained. "But the good old air corps sure knows how to get the stuff. . . . C'mon, you ever played a slot machine before?"

She shook her head, and moments later was looking at the spinning reels a nickel could put in motion. She put the second nickel in the machine and pulled the handle, awed by the speed and noise of the thing. Two cherries spilled some coins into the metal tray at the bottom. "You won!" Forster exclaimed with a smile. "Now, let's hit a jackpot and make these guys sorry they stole this thing from Reno."

She couldn't remember having more fun since before the war. When the three bars fell into place and dozens of nickels splashed out of the tray a few minutes later, she shrieked and danced with the pure joy of a child. Forster had trouble getting her to the excellent T-bones the cook had broiled. And when they finished eating, he put some nickels in the jukebox, selecting mostly "Stardust." They managed to get in a few steps on the tiny linoleum dance floor, but mostly Sachi enjoyed relaxing in his arms.

And too soon it was time to go. "Do you absolutely have to get back?" he asked, holding her hand and searching her eyes.

She nodded with more emphasis than she felt. It would be so easy to stay, but she couldn't weaken, just couldn't.

Moments later they were in the jeep, but he made no move to start the engine. Putting his hand gently on her shoulder, he said, "I'd like to take you somewhere so I can hold you, Sachi." His voice was soft, his deep green eyes wide and compelling.

She knew what it meant and without any doubt knew that she wanted it to happen just as much as he did. But she just could not get this involved. She shook her head and pushed his hand away.

Parking in front of the Russian embassy, he said, "This is nonsense. Just tell me where you live and I'll drive you there in nothing flat."

But she quickly swung her legs out the side and got to the street. Leaning back, she put her hand over his and shook her head. "I must do it my way. . . . Oh, thank you, James Forster. I can't tell you what a wonderful time I had." She smiled brightly, gave him a short bow, then hurried away.

Shortly after arriving at work the next day, the captain who ran the Imperial called her in to ask about the Friday night incident. Apparently Forster or someone else had called him and there had been no complaint from the Russians. When five o'clock—the end of normal duty hours—arrived, she caught herself watching for the colonel. But she was back into perspective and tried not to think about it. To him, she was a Japanese barmaid. He knew little more about her—except for the cover story—and was interested in one thing. On the other side, she was the head of the House of Hoshi with much to accomplish. Any involvement at this critical stage of her initial move toward the power she so emphatically wanted was foolish. But deep down, she knew the foolishness was there.

When he didn't come in by eight o'clock, she looked at it more logically. He couldn't even think of being involved with her. He mentioned being in something like civil intelligence and, after all, he was a full colonel. She shrugged away her disappointment. She had more important things to think about. One was a licensed house for officers. It might not be as quick a source of profit as the *yami*, but it would give her a base. She would have to think of a way to get someone who knew the business.

When Forster didn't appear for three more days, she knew the previous Sunday had been just one major production for a bed partner. She should have known—yet there was something about him, something that said this man was more sincere than that. And besides, she told herself, sex was available from the girl standing in the doorway begging to do it for a pack of gum, or from the polished geisha who wished to do more than entertain. A big production wasn't necessary.

Friday night just after six, she had just placed a big drink order with the bartender when she heard his voice behind her. "How's the jackpot girl tonight?"

She whirled, unable to mask her pleasure. "I'm fine, thank you," she replied with a broad smile and a short nod.

It was crowded and noisy at the bar. He stepped back to let a brigadier get through. "Any Russian problems?" he asked as he moved closer. She shook her head. "I've been out of town," he added loudly. "Had to go down to Osaka Monday and just got back. Can we—"

She shook her head, the bartender was telling her to mind her business. When she returned from serving the round, Forster was waiting with a drink. "Is there someplace where we can talk?" he asked quickly.

She shook her head again. Her hand was trembling.

"Okay, can you meet me tomorrow night? Are you off? I want to take you to a nice place." He was like a schoolboy. "I have to go somewhere to a reception now."

She thought quickly, nodding her head. "Yes and yes, and in front of the Russian embassy again. Six o'clock all right?"

He grinned as he nodded his head vigorously.

"But Japanese women don't go in such places, James," Sachi protested as they entered the Komachi-en. She could feel all the eyes turning in her direction.

"Nonsense," Forster replied. "MacArthur's going to give you

girls the vote as soon as he can. A little suffrage in restaurants isn't out of line.''

She shrugged as they were led to a plush private *tatami* room. Westerners just couldn't understand certain things. She looked around approvingly as she took her pillow. Obviously, they had just refinished the gleaming woodwork—an indication that the war hadn't meant the end of the world to the owners. The Komachi-en was a combination restaurant and geisha house in Omori, partway between Tokyo and Yokohama, which Forster had explained was a favorite place for officers who liked to go out on what was called ''the economy.'' Secretly, she was glad to finally see such a place in person.

They had nearly finished the plate of excellent *sashimi* when the door slid open and a regal-looking geisha descended on the colonel. ''Ah, Forster-san,'' she exclaimed happily as she knelt gracefully beside him and poured beer into his glass. She was wearing the traditional bright kimono, obi, and high hairdo, and her beautiful face was painted white. Sachi watched in quiet amusement as she produced a tiny silk napkin and delicately brought a piece of the raw fish hors d'oeuvres to his mouth, clucking soft sounds constantly. Her next movement was to tap a free lock of his brown hair back into place. Then she patted his hand and scurried through the door without once having looked at Sachi.

Forster shrugged. ''That was Ayako. She's the head geisha here. I'm sorry.''

Sachi chuckled. ''Don't apologize, Forster-san.'' She came up on her knees and emptied the bottle of beer into his glass, then touched the knot of his tie to straighten it. She clucked a couple of soft sounds, then happily watched with an attentive mocking look.

He laughed. ''Okay, I got the message.''

The sukiyaki was prepared in front of the table on a small hotplate, while the huge shrimps had been boiled earlier and were served cold. Sachi was drinking the sweeter and less potent mirin, instead of the sake that Forster switched to for the main course. It was the best food she had eaten since shortly after the war started.

Forster talked about politics and his genuine interest in her people. "I doubt that communism took anything but a major setback," he said as they reached the end of the meal. "Stalin's unheard-of deceit in turning the three-hundred-and-seventy-five-thousand-man Kwantung Army in Manchuria into Siberian slave laborers has to be the biggest crime of the postwar era."

She paid little attention to the news. Between working, giving her little Mitsu as much time as possible, and handling her new venture, there just wasn't time. Besides, the news only brought her hates out of their uneasy purgatory when it related to the war. But she was a good listener—even tonight, when she wanted to touch him more than hear his words.

As soon as the meal was finished, Ayako opened the sliding doors again, bowed to Forster, and clapped her hands lightly. The entertainment began immediately as drum beating and *samisen* music accompanied a high-pitched geisha's voice in an age-old song. Two other geisha began their graceful, postured dancing as the lovely Ayako dropped beside Forster and poured him another tiny cup of sake. Sachi soon became bored and found herself wondering what would follow. And she studied Ayako—who most surely must have been one of the area's top geisha before the war. Now, most probably in her middle to late twenties, the woman had to protect her territory at the end of her career. It made Sachi shudder inwardly to think of such a well-trained, beautiful creature becoming obsolete so early in life.

Finally, when Ayako started to pull Forster to his feet to learn the *Tokyo Ondo*, a folk dance, Sachi decided she had had enough. Quickly rising to her knees, she caught the geisha's wrist and smiled coolly into her white mask. In Japanese, she purred, "The party is finished, beautiful woman. I shall care for his every need the rest of the evening."

Ayako nodded, her expression never changing as she bowed to both of them and murmured, "*Sayonara*," and slipped away.

"What was that all about?" Forster asked as the door slid shut.

Sachi leaned close and touched his lips with her fingertip. "I just told her you were mine and we wished to be alone."

His hand slipped up behind her head as he moved to her lips and kissed her long and gently. It was then that she was sure.

Forty minutes later, he pulled the covered jeep into the parking area of his hotel—the Dai Ichi, where he had fed her the hamburger the night of the Russian trouble. He took her hand, saying, "I thought you were magnificent back there at the restaurant." Drawing her close, he brushed his lips against her cheek as he spoke softly, "Now, I want you to come to my room so I can hold you close—shut out everything else. . . . God, how I want you, Sachi."

She felt the surge of excitement, the desire. She liked his smells, his touch, his strength—and she wanted all of it.

They had to go to a side entrance. Since Japanese Nationals weren't allowed in the living quarters, he had done some bribing prior to going out that evening and they were able to go up the stairs with no problem. He had a two-room suite with a small bathroom on the third floor. She stepped inside as soon as he unlocked the door and waited while he turned on a table lamp. "Would you like a drink?" he asked. "I have a sweet Benedictine you might like."

She felt nervous, like a young girl. "Yes," she whispered.

He pointed to an overstuffed chair. "Here, please sit while I pour."

She followed him to the table where he kept his liquor. Just as he uncapped the bottle, her hands slipped around his waist and she leaned her cheek against his firm back. Quietly replacing the bottle, he turned, taking her in his arms. She leaned up to his lips, whispering, "Yes, James Forster, hold me as close as you can."

His lips hungrily explored hers before his tongue flicked into her mouth. Her open jacket fell to the floor as she stretched up to him and pressed herself into his tall sinewy body. When they finally broke, he smothered her face with quick moist kisses, reaching her ears, her neck, her throat. She couldn't suppress a tiny moan—it had been so long. Already she could feel his erection moving against her pelvis, so large, so powerful.

Demanding. She ground against it as she moaned again. How she
wanted him!

His hands gripped her buttocks, slipping to her thighs and
under her skirt. Throwing her head back, she closed her eyes
tightly, feeling almost faint as his mouth found her breasts. And
then it reached her nipple, biting gently, pulling, sucking urgently.
She wanted to wrap her legs around his hips and climb right
through him.

And suddenly he pulled back, roughly reaching under and
picking her up, lifting, kissing her mouth, mumbling words she
couldn't even understand—and then they were by the bed and he
was jerking off his tie, ripping open his shirt, urging her to hurry.
Her skirt came down in a single motion, freeing her hands to
struggle with the blouse buttons. And in a moment she was nude,
her breathing short and harsh. They reached the bed together, his
mouth going directly to her rigid nipples, her hand finding his
surging penis. Smothering the top of his head with kisses, she
pulled him up, spreading wide and arching against him, guiding
his penis's demanding head inside, surrounding it, devouring it,
and following it back as it rocked to charge again. She cried out
and threw her legs around his buttocks as he stroked deeper and
harder, over and over until she felt the onrushing roar of climax.
And it began, the overwhelming, shuddering washing away of
everything. And it lasted for several moments until he exploded,
increasing her arousal even as it had begun to subside.

It was nearly twelve when she awakened from her short nap and
hurried into her clothes. It was too late for the dilapidated
streetcars; she would have to find a taxi or walk all the way
home. Fortunately, more and more taxicabs were to be found
every day—"*kamikaze* cabs" as the GIs called them for their
drivers' recklessness. How she wished she could stay in this
wonderful man's loving arms, make love again and again. But
she had to go, go to the other side of her identity and her
responsibilities. And she didn't want to—for a brief, nearly
frightening moment, she didn't care about it. The flash of being
this man's wife and no longer struggling was overwhelmingly
attractive.

She got to her feet, reaching for her jacket. She *had* to go.

He saw her in the crack of light that came from the bathroom, immediately swinging his legs over the side of the bed and awakening fully. "Hey," he said, startling her, "where do you think you're going?"

She smiled as he opened the door, saying softly, "Home, of course."

He shook his head. "Not without me. What do you think you're doing?"

She caught his hand. "Please listen, James. This is the way I must do it. I come and go alone." Her dark eyes pleaded into his face. "I absolutely must insist on it, or I can't see you again . . . even if I do think I love you."

He nodded as he took her in his arms. "All right, I won't fight it. I'll be dressed in a moment to get you a cab."

Forty-seven

"Next to our Imperial Emperor," her mother had loved to say, "is our beloved Fuji-san. He is the soul of Nippon—Fuji-san is the heart."

Mount Fuji, Fuji-san, or Fuji-no-yama—it didn't matter, the magnificent mountain that rose in supreme white dignity to an elevation of 12,389 feet like a spiritual cone seventy miles southwest of Tokyo was the sacred peak of the universe. After all, hadn't Fuji-san burst from the great plain and risen in all its majesty in just one night?

Sachi vividly remembered her other trip up this splendid mountain. It had been on her twelfth birthday, and she had shared it with her zestful parents. How exciting it had been—not only a vigorous outing fraught with bugs, scratches, and sunburn, but one of laughter, love, and sharing. They must have visited a dozen mountain shrines and temples in those two days, and she would never forget reaching the final shrine at the summit. She had turned as her handsome father pointed at the distant patchwork of the plain below, caught her breath, and felt like she belonged to the gods.

But her young legs were used to running around tennis courts in those days. Today, on Christmas 1945, they were complaining. And due to the bad weather, they had gone only partway to the top. She sighed with relief as she spotted the rest station hut where the jeep was parked.

Forster laughed. "You look like you just saw the end of the rainbow."

"I did," she replied. "And it's got a beautiful hot bath in it."

He leaned down to kiss her rosy cheek. "And more than that, my love."

She smiled back, nodding. Oh, how she knew. Below, after two more stations, lay the village of Fuji-Yoshida where they were going to spend their first entire night together. Just the thought of being in his arms all night was stimulating—no jumping up and running home like Cinderella, no strain about where she lived, just their love to share. As if in recognition of her anticipation, the little town down in the gathering darkness began to blink a welcome with its first lights of evening.

The ride down the rest of the hill was slow and uneventful. She watched Forster's deft handling of the jeep for a bit, then her mind drifted back to Tokyo. She now had a middle-aged widow as Mitsu's nurse, and the repair job on the house was gradually coming along through the efforts of an old carpenter Hata had found. The business was doing superbly, with the previous week's profits outdistancing even Charlie's vivid imagination. And now that he finally had the number of points necessary for discharge, Charlie had made his decision. He would take it in Japan and register as a student. That would give him much free time, make him far less vulnerable with the army, and enable him to broaden the operation. Everything looked good.

Except for the problem—she was totally in love with this tall, boyish man from America. And her resolve was beginning to weaken.

As if he had read her feeling, Forster moved his mittened hand over to pat the inside of her thigh.

Somehow he had gotten a room with a Western bed in it, and its foot was laced with bedwarmers when she returned from her long bath shortly after seven. He watched her quietly as she placed her things in her small suitcase. "I ordered dinner for eight o'clock," he said, finishing a glass of beer. "That gives us, my darling, plenty of time to hold each other." He grinned as he produced a small gift-wrapped box. "But first, merry Christmas."

She forgot the chill in the room as she eagerly sat on the bed and pulled off the bright red ribbon. Inside was a black velvet jewel box that held two tiny pearl earrings. Holding them up to the light, she guessed they were of the finest quality and let out a little cry of surprise. She ran to the small wall mirror and quickly placed them in her lobes. Even in the low light of the table lamp they seemed to glow and please her. His arms came around her from the rear as his lips nibbled her neck. Turning, she arched up to him with a mock look of distress, whispering, "Japanese girl have no gift for her lover. She—"

His mouth sealed off the words as his lips found hers. Simultaneously he undid the tie of her robe and slipped it off her shoulders, dropping it to the floor and leaving her naked in his arms.

Exactly three weeks later, after finishing work at six-thirty, Sachi met him at a new restaurant that had opened near the Sanno Hotel in Akasaka. He was seated Japanese-style at a low table in a corner and struggled to his feet to kiss her cheek as she glided up. He indicated to the head waiter that he wanted the sake container filled. As they seated themselves and disposed of opening comments, she could see by the brightness of his eyes that he had had much more to drink than one container of sake.

He was strangely silent throughout the excellent lobster dinner, barely responding to her lively anecdotes about the happenings at the Imperial. Finally, he reached across the table to take her hand. "I have to tell you something," he said quietly. "Please try to understand."

She watched his pained eyes and felt a quick jolt of fear.

His grip tightened, almost hurting her fingers. He started over. "Please try to understand, darling . . . I . . . my orders to the States came in today. I though it might be another four or five months at least, but—" He shrugged, tried an embarrassed smile. "You know how that goes."

The room was suddenly filled with one of those utter silences that seem to accent an awkward pause between two people. She held his troubled gaze as the reality of what he was saying began to sink in. She didn't breathe.

'It's kind of a shotgun thing. I'm leaving in six days—going to Command and General Staff School at Fort Leavenworth, Kansas. Nine months' school . . ." His voice trailed off.

She nodded silently, waiting.

He squeezed her hand even more tightly. "*I*, well, I don't

know how I'm going to get along without you, darling. I love you so much.''

It was what she dreaded so fiercely that she had never faced it. Their idyll was supposed to go on and on until they married and drove off in his jeep into the glorious sunset. She blinked back the coming tears, still trying to watch his wide eyes. She barely heard what he was saying as he talked of them going to Kyoto for a couple of days.

A couple of days in Kyoto? *He was talking about leaving Japan!* No! She couldn't bear the thought. Her charade had to end. She had resources. ''Can I meet you in Kansas?'' she asked fearfully, ready to pour out the truth. ''What has to be done for me to come?''

His eyes dropped to the table, then came up with a look of consuming pain. ''You can't . . . Sachi . . . Sachi, I'm married. I wanted to tell you before, but I couldn't. I thought I'd have more time . . . Sachi, my darling, I love you too much to hurt you. I—''

She closed her eyes hearing nothing more. The roaring in her ears obliterated everything as she got woodenly to her feet, fighting the tears, trying to control herself, numbly realizing the futility, the shame of being used. He jumped to his feet as she struggled into her coat. ''Wait!'' he pleaded. ''Let me take you home, darling. I must talk to you.''

She stumbled into a run toward the exit, her head down, burning with shame and anger. And suddenly, just before she reached the door, she stopped and drew herself grimly erect. She would leave as a Hoshi.

Sachi sent word that she was ill to the hotel and stayed out for two days. And she *was* ill—for the fourth time in four years a man she loved had been taken from her. But in this case, it was a matter of deceit. James Forster had deceived her by not telling her he was married, and she had deceived herself by never questioning or facing reality. Even Ume had told her she should find out.

But hindsight had nothing to do with the pain she was suffering. She ate little and slept in snatches, remaining in her bedroom and seeing only her daughter. The third day was Sunday, her normal day off. At just before midnight that night she went out into the cold, moonlit garden to where she had made her vow only a few months earlier and grimly renewed it. The path was clear again—no more moping and no more of that agony known as love. It would be all business from here in!

She got her first test at noon the next day when Forster came into the lounge wanting to talk to her. "I'm sorry, Colonel," she said coolly as she continued to wipe a tabletop. "I'm working."

"That's not good enough, Sachi," he insisted. "I won't let you shut me out this way. You have to understand that I love you—that none of this was a cheap game with me."

She stopped. Turning and looking into his troubled eyes with all the disdain she could muster, she replied, "It no longer matters, James. Go home to your wife and forget me. You mean nothing to me."

He studied her expression for a moment, saw nothing but rigidity, and finally shrugged. "I'll never forget you," he whispered as he turned to go.

"You see, Charlie, my uncle wants to do certain things without you. It has no bearing on our relationship whatsoever. All I want you to do is find a buyer for this last diamond so we'll have some cash for the enterprise."

Charlie didn't even whistle as he held the sparkling stone to the light. He just sucked in his breath. "How big?" he asked softly.

She had checked Itoko's list again after she selected it. "It's one-point-two. And again, perfect. Do you have anyone in mind?"

The former mess sergeant nodded as he rolled it back up in the tissue paper. "Yeah, there's a high roller over in the Seventh Cav—a master sergeant who's been running a big craps game. This is an easy way for him to sneak some of that money home. What's your bottom price?"

Sachi knew what made Charlie tick. "Since it isn't going in the company, you get a ten percent commission," she replied smoothly.

He grinned as he nodded.

They left the *sushi* shop that was still their rendezvous a few minutes later, Sachi hurrying to catch the train to Omori. She hoped to get there before noon for her appointment.

The small park was just exactly two blocks from the Komachi-en geisha restaurant, as she had been told. Since it was one of the first really warm days of spring, many people of varying ages were there. She looked around, but the party she was to meet hadn't arrived. Watching two little girls skipping rope, she thought it might be time to teach Mitsu. Her poor little girl, shut off from other children her own age. Too bad. But it wouldn't be forever—the nurse would see to that.

Many other children were playing in the park—a sure sign that Japan was on the mend. Only six months earlier, she had read where dozens of vagrant starving little beggars had been picked up by the police in Tokyo's Ueno Park. But then, Premier Prince Higashikuni had said they would have to endure the unendurable when he surrendered the government to MacArthur. And millions were. Seeing one little girl about Mitsu's age wearing a ragged sweater and clogs that were almost worn to the ground, she called out to her and handed her a hundred-yen note. The little girl's dark eyes grew wide as she studied the bill and stared back at Sachi. Suddenly a broad smile lit her face and she bowed deeply before running away.

"Konichiwa."

Sachi turned to see Ayako looking at her calmly. The geisha seemed strange—another person—without the heavy white makeup on her face. Her high formal hairdo was covered by a scarf and she was wearing a well-tailored but slightly worn gabardine suit. Yet, Sachi was satisfied—she was still a strikingly beautiful woman, although a bit older than she had thought. "Thank you for coming," she replied. "Is there a place where we can talk nearby?"

Ayako nodded, turning to the street and indicating that Sachi should join her. They walked in silence to a small nearby tea room, where they took a corner table. After ordering rice cakes and tea, Sachi asked her about her job. The replies were reserved, defensive. "I was the number-twelve geisha in Tokyo when the war began," she said quietly. "I was mistress to one of the most important admirals and always in demand. This Komachi-en is nothing compared to my former work, but one must take what is available, right? By the way, where is Forster-san?"

"Like all men," Sachi replied quietly. "Gone."

"Too bad. Handsome man."

They chatted on through several more cups of tea, working up to the point of the meeting in evasive Japanese style. Finally, Sachi said, "I've been thinking of opening a place of entertainment for officers in Tokyo. It would be an especially attractive place of quality. The entertainers also would have to be of top quality in order to charge the prices such a place could demand." She smiled. "What do you think of that?"

Ayako nodded. "Would it be a place of full entertainment?"

Sachi held her gaze. "Yes, with a geisha influence. Run by someone who could train and supervise young ladies, a beautiful woman with a good business mind who has been a top geisha herself."

Ayako pursed her lips as she nodded her head. "I'm trying to think of such a person. Would she be able to share in the profits of such an interesting place?"

Sachi nodded, frowning. "If she were trustworthy and willing to dedicate herself . . . most definitely. And without a cash investment."

"I see. And when would such a person begin such a venture?"

"In five weeks."

Ayako nodded thoughtfully. "I will see if I can think of such a person."

Sachi had a manager for her new brothel.

The house was two-storied and had supposedly belonged to a count at one time. It was located on the edge of Aoyama in the direction of Roppongi, and had somehow missed major damage from the bombing. Several factors made the place desirable from Sachi's point of view—it had many bedrooms and a huge Western-style living room, a tall brick fence gave it superb privacy, and it was available and could be licensed.

Sachi didn't have the money yet to finish it as handsomely as she wished, but parts of it could be closed off and opened as the cash came in. Besides, it was about time to use some of the *yami* money; it was coming in by the barrelful. It would all be in Hata's name, and although the old major domo would have no part of its operation he would be an effective screen for Sachi. She laughed each time she thought of the perfect name she had selected for the place.

It would be known as "Madame Butterfly."

Forty-eight

Hata was out so Sachi answered the door.

"Excuse me," a young man with an American accent said, "but I'm trying to get some information on the family that once owned this house. Are you Mrs. Yukai?"

He was tall and looked somehow familiar. "My name is Yukai," she replied guardedly.

The brightness of the late afternoon sunlight made it difficult for him to see into the house. "Their name was Hoshi, and I'm a cousin from California. Any information would help me. I can't find out where they went."

It was Billy, her cousin!

"Can you help me? Anything at all. He was a general and—"

"Come in, Billy," she replied in English. She was delighted to see him!

He peered back momentarily, then moved through the doorway. "Sachi?"

"Yes, Billy. The name is a temporary thing for convenience. I'll explain later. What are you doing in Tokyo?"

He bowed abruptly, then grinned and reached for her hand. "Wow, are you beautiful!" Glancing around, he added, "What a layout! And this was Grandmother's house, wasn't it? I'll bet it was really something before the war, huh?" His Japanese was excellent and he hadn't planned on using English at all, but this reunion with his lovely cousin was another matter.

A few minutes later over tea he explained that he had gotten a job as a civilian interpreter and was working in one of the subagencies of civil affairs in the military government department.

"It was a way for me to get back to the fatherland," he added. "Where I belong."

Sachi thought this remark a bit strange, but ignored it as she asked eagerly about his mother and Joey. He bitterly recounted Joey's death, vehemently capping the account off with, "But don't worry, they'll pay for it someday."

It was then her turn to relate the tragedy of the family in Japan. It was the first time she had gone through the pain of telling anyone the entire story, and she had a difficult time. The horrors of Hiroshima and her father's *hara-kiri* were the most trying.

"Our grandfather at least realized his dream," Billy said when she finished.

It was the first time she had thought of it in a long time. Hiroshima had obliterated even that. Hiroshima and her subsequent resolution. No, her grandfather's dream—his richer dream—had never been fulfilled. He never had the opportunity. She looked away, fighting the tears as she remembered their fervent ferryboat ride . . . when she promised to help.

She pushed away the memory to discuss more pleasant recollections. They talked on, and through the Sunday evening meal, discussing prewar family activities and whatever else each felt the other should know. Sachi remembered his hawklike good looks from before the war, but now he seemed almost too handsome, too sure of himself. There was something about his easy smile that was disconcerting, but she shoved the feeling aside and enjoyed the reunion. She invited him to stay with her, but was relieved when he said he had government lodging. It was enough that he was one more person from whom she would have to hide her activities, without having to worry about it daily.

Strolling casually away from the house at shortly after nine, Billy was immensely pleased with what had transpired. He had found his family—or what was left of it—and had established that he was the only remaining male Hoshi. And even his pretty cousin was a widow. It would take time and a great deal of patience, but everything in his hazy master plan was possible now that the first big step was complete.

He had worried about not being accepted in this government job because of his court-martials, but apparently they had just looked at his honorable discharge and then sped on to his ample qualifications. His position in the large business conversion section could provide some ideal contacts for later use. In the meantime, he intended to submerge himself off duty, going totally native, and learning his new role.

The tea houses would be a good start. Perhaps there he could find young men of persuasion who were still angry with America. After all, His Imperial Highness had only mentioned that Nippon should "stop fighting," not surrender.

A short time later, Sachi opened her gift store near the U.S. Army–operated Sanno Hotel in Akasaka. Its display room was the corner of a small partially bombed-out office building that had been repaired. In the rear, there was adequate space to expand and store whatever goods she might decide to handle. Her other business interests were of such a precarious nature that she needed a fully legitimate enterprise to act as an umbrella. And she picked a good one. American wives were descending on Japan like locusts waving military scrip and yen in each fist. Anything Oriental—all fabrics, silk screens, ceramics, prints, lacquered wooden items, jade and other jewelry; fans, combs, brassware—it was all in demand and highly profitable. Sachi and Ume, her new manager, had listened carefully. And when Ume had her grand opening, it was done in high American style—free fans, soft *samisen* music played by one of Ayako's smiling geisha, seductive incense, bite-size tempura, and warm, resolve-weakening sake.

Ume seemed born for her retailing management role, giving Sachi one more loyal and capable lieutenant for the place she named the Velvet Chrysanthemum.

In spite of the rigid control she exercised over herself in regard to the other businesses, she simply could not stay away from the grand opening. Wearing a high wig and traditional Japanese dress, she also donned softly tinted glasses and browsed for thirty minutes without speaking to anyone either in English or at any length in Japanese. She loved it! Finally bowing to Ume at the door, she happily made her exit. This business alone could make her a very rich woman.

She did not see Inspector Oishi raise his small camera and snap several pictures of her as she walked away. He looked like any other Japanese resting on his bicycle.

At age forty-three, Inspector Oishi had been a policeman for over twenty years, including his four years in the army in the early thirties. Later, when his shrewd mind and willingness to stop at nothing while working a case was demonstrated repeatedly, he became a full inspector. Following the war, it was a simple matter for him to join the intelligence division of the Tokyo Metropolitan Police Force. Not only was Victor Hugo's Inspector Javert his favorite literary character, but Oishi had for years begrudged the wealthy their money and had been looking for the right opportunity to share it.

"The garden should have no prying ears," he said peremptorily as Sachi greeted him coolly. When Hata announced that the inspector wished to see her, she had been struck by a sharp stab of fear that shattered her usual calm. It was exactly one year since she gave that first diamond to Charlie Asaka, and not once had there been a problem. Even Charlie was beginning to speculate on when the ax would fall. Now, she guessed, it was time. She remembered the sinister-looking, fat inspector from when he had harassed her grandmother.

She bowed her head slightly, leading the way into the warm, midday sun of the garden. He looked around appreciatively, commenting on the condition of her shrubbery, then obliquely began his approach. Finally, he got to the point. "Mrs. Koga, I've been extremely interested in your family for a number of years. Your outspoken criticism of the regime brought you to my attention when the war broke out, and later a Colonel Segura from the *kempei* ordered me to keep a close eye on your family—a chore I've continued to this day."

He pulled out a thin cigar and lit it, blowing out a large cloud of smoke with a sigh. "Of course," he went on, "I enjoyed the assignment. You see, your father used his rank to make things difficult for me until Segura entered the picture. And since the end of the war, the pleasure has been all mine, madam."

His voice took on a sharper edge. "I'm more than familiar

with ex-sergeant Charlie Asaka and his dealing in the *yami*, just as I know who owns Madame Butterfly and the Velvet Chrysanthemum. The latter is, of course, presently legal and reputable. The others are derogatory and one can land you in prison for many years."

Although Sachi remained outwardly calm, she was certain her heartbeat sounded like a pounding drum.

"Mrs. Koga, please permit me to be direct," Oishi continued with a trace of oily smile. "You have three problems—prison, disgrace, and the *yakuza*. Surely, you didn't think our underworld would stay ignorant about your participation for long, did you? It will be only a matter of time—six months, a year, two years. But I assure you, madam, they will get to you." He blew out another cloud of smoke. "Unless you are protected."

Sachi held her breath.

Oishi leaned forward with gleaming eyes. "It can all be handled for a paltry sum for one so rich, for one who wishes to avoid all the pitfalls, and for one with such a lovely daughter and fine name to protect."

Rage was building up in her, but she remained grimly silent.

Oishi chuckled. "And I have it all documented in a safe place, marked for delivery to the superintendent in the event of my death—in case you are thinking of any violence, madam." He paused, then nodded. "I see. . . . Very well, my fee for this service is fifty thousand yen initially and four thousand a week—about a thousand of your precious dollars per month." He chuckled again. "And the sum also includes silence about your personal indiscretions, Mrs. Koga."

If she had her father's sword, she would kill him. But there was no sense in denying it, nor of ignoring his demand.

Inspector Oishi jammed the cigar in his mouth and headed for the house. "I shall call on you tomorrow night at ten for the initial sum. Good day, madam." He waved his hat and walked airily inside.

Moments later, she slumped to a bench. Charlie had told her she was naive about the *yakuza* and she knew he was already making small pay-offs, but something of this scope was staggering. The man actually had her life in his hands!

And she had a feeling it would be that way for a long time.

* * *

Billy, who had given himself the name of Heigo after his heroic paternal grandfather, normally came for the noon meal on Sundays, a day when Sachi seldom worked at the Imperial. He had quickly discovered Sachi's deep aversion to anything nationalistic, so he had to refrain from discussing anything about the interesting people he was meeting in the tea houses, particularly some disgruntled young former officers, and the son of a leader of the infamous Black Dragon Society that had meddled in right wing activism between the wars.

Instead he talked about MacArthur's activities. He personally detested the general as the personification of all that he hated in the whites, but again he had to soft-pedal any criticism because Sachi, like millions of other Japanese, seemed to be caught up in his spell. But his comments about how MacArthur was dealing with big business totally fascinated her—particularly how the huge Houses were circumventing the general's programs.

"MacArthur will never be able to totally demolish the *zaibatsu*," he explained. "Each one has a single remarkable feature—a holding company at the top which shelters innumerable subordinate companies, like a royal family sitting atop a giant pyramid of smaller firms. He is cutting off the head, removing the ruling families, confiscating their fortunes—he thinks—and forbidding them to conduct business. But it won't work."

On this particular November afternoon, Sachi was in high spirits. Charlie's report for the previous month of *yami* activities had netted her over $14,000, and she had been thinking of future investment possibilities all morning. "What are they doing with their money?" she asked, trying to sound casual.

"Dozens of subterfuges, mostly set up before the capitulation. But this money will surface in a few years, when MacArthur and his minions are gone, and it will be business as usual. Mitsui, Mitsubishi, Yasuda, and the others will be just as powerful as ever—most probably more so because they will have picked the American brains. And there will be tremendous opportunity for small new companies. I translated for a Harvard professor today who predicted that within a decade a thousand household operations will surpass the million-yen mark in gross business for a year.''

Sachi's eyes were shining. "What a marvelous opportunity for investors that would be," she said, wondering if there would be any way to enter the field of finance once the occupation controls were over.

"Yes," her cousin replied. "There is already a new name for the *zaibatsu*—the *zaikai*, literally the 'financial circles.' And the men at the top of the *zaikai* will rule not only the economy but Nippon again some day not too far in the distance."

Sachi shuddered inwardly. Such power would be merely a step away from another march to war. Yet she found herself wanting to be part of such a heady challenge. *Her* power would be a deterrent! And again she thought of her grandfather's rich new dream, the dream that was still her responsibility. Yes, she had been dodging that fact, but she *had* agreed to share it with him—

As always when she thought of him too vividly, as when they were on the ferryboat going to Miyajima that day, she was overcome with emotion.

"Are you all right?" Billy asked, touching her hand.

She turned away momentarily. "Yes, I was thinking about Hiroshima." She cleared her throat. "Yes. And where does a lowly American interpreter and his cocktail waitress cousin fit in?"

Billy's expression hardened. "Don't say such a thing!" he said harshly. "We're *Hoshis!* Just as soon as this goddamn American yoke is thrown off, we'll rise to our proper station again." Then he told her that he was going back to the States as soon as his year was up, and returning to college. "And when the time is right," he went on, "I'll return to my destiny. It's time you knew, I intend to be part of the new Nippon some day, the Nippon that will—" He stopped, seeing her cool look. "Yes, I have a dream also."

She saw the fire in his expression completely exposed for a fleeting moment, and recognized it. A similar look on a hand-some face was stored away in her memory forever—but it belonged to an enthusiastic naval fighter pilot.

Billy quickly acted casual as he added, "I intend to make our noble grandfather's accomplishments insignificant. And by the way, he brought quite a bit of money back to Japan. Do you know what he did with it?''

She shook her head. Billy seemed so cold. ''I have no idea,'' she replied quietly. If only he could gain some warmth and sincerity, he just might be the answer. After all, no woman in Japan had ever done the thing she had been dreaming about. Yes, the two Hoshis—who would be able to stop them?

On New Year Inspector Oishi called at shortly after one to pick up his monthly payoff. Each time she saw him, she thought he looked like some different kind of vile animal. On this day, he reminded her of a lizard as his tongue licked his thick lips. Standing by Koki's old desk in the study, he frowned and announced, ''I have added expenses, Mrs. Koga. And at the same time, your income increases weekly.''

Sachi watched him coldly.

''I'm afraid I must double the cost of your protection, madam. Let's call it an even thirty thousand yen per month.''

''I can't let you do this to me,'' she replied evenly.

Oishi licked his lips again. ''I'm afraid you have no choice. The *yakuza* is becoming more difficult for me to hold off. Would you like for me to give them my dossier on you so you may deal directly? They have the opinion that a woman meddler isn't even worth the effort of negotiation. And that an American ex-sergeant would be better off without a head.''

Sachi felt the strength drain away. ''When will the next increase come?'' she asked tonelessly.

Oishi shrugged. ''Who knows? It's simply a matter of expenses with me. With you, it's simply a matter of percentages. Without me, you have nothing, perhaps not even a pretty daughter.''

Forty-nine

> The son of a bitch isn't going to
> resign on me! I want him fired!
>
> —Harry S Truman

April 16, 1951, was a cold clear morning in Tokyo, but that didn't bother the over 200,000 people who lined the route from the U.S. embassy to Haneda Airport; many of them had arrived hours earlier in the hope that they might catch a final glimpse of "Makassar."

The first touches of bluish gray light touched the eastern horizon as the Japanese driver of the Associated Press sedan turned south of Tamachi along the waterfront. In the back seat Cedric Baldwin—who had just flown up from the Philippines—read the morning Tokyo papers while Sachi stared out at the patient faces of the waiting people. Six and seven deep in places, they held small American and Japanese flags and banners that read, "Good-bye, Liberator," "Sayonara, General," "We love you, MacArthur," and dozens of other good wishes.

"Listen to this," Cedric said, reading from the *Mainichi*, " 'He was a noble political missionary. What he gave us was not material aid and democratic reform alone, but a new way of life, the freedom and dignity of the individual.' " He pointed to the Nippon *Times*, "And this—'Mere words can never describe . . . all he meant to this nation.' And finally, the *Ashai* says, 'Japan's recovery must be attributed solely to his guidance. We feel as if we have lost a kind and loving father.' "

Sachi nodded as she continued to stare out of the window. "I know," she replied. "Even I, the ultimate cynic, have grown to revere him in some abstract way." She noticed a tiny, white-haired woman, bent and holding a chicken she evidently wished to give the general as a going-away present. "I still don't know why he has to be jerked away like this, Mr. Baldwin."

Cedric shook his head. "It's a play on egos. MacArthur actually believes he *is* God, and Harry Truman can't stand it. Additionally, there are other hatchets in Washington who got into the act. . . . You know, Sachi, I'm a journalist and as such I'm far from a MacArthur fan. I think he's an arrogant bastard who has made a second emperor of himself over here. I've seen his phony show business both here and in the lines in Korea, and I don't like the old son of a bitch."

He lit a cigarette. "And he blew it in strategic planning after his brilliant Inchon landing. Still, what he has done in this country is positively amazing—the results he has achieved in five and a half years most probably are in the realm of a miracle. Actually, it's so positive it scares me. He's unleashing a new power on the world, a lurking potential that even Nippon doesn't yet realize. You know, somebody said China was a sleeping giant that shouldn't be disturbed. Well, I think it can be applied right here, also."

Sachi didn't want to get into his philosophy. "But why, how can such a great man be treated this way?" she persisted.

Cedric sighed. "Because we live in democracies. As such, the governing bodies and the executive branches have the final word over military leaders of any stature. And thank God. MacArthur far overstepped his bounds. He disobeyed orders and went against the will of his commander in chief. He had to go. The way it was done was bush league, but then, sometimes democracies have a way of installing bush-leaguers as leaders."

They rode on quietly for a couple of minutes before Sachi said, "I hear General Ridgway, the new commander, will live at the Imperial for a while."

"Yeah." Cedric chuckled. "I hear you once worked there. Maybe you can get them to take you back so you can wait on him."

She smiled. She had stopped the cocktail waitress game in early 1948, when the business required her full attention and a cover was no longer necessary.

Cedric liked this beautiful, assertive young woman. He was so glad Haru had insisted he contact her. He remembered how Sataro could never quit talking about her—now he knew why. God, he thought, if he were even thirty years younger and had his dark hair back he would take a run at her. ''I saw the Buick. Looks like your grandmother's investments are getting better and better, huh?'' he said.

That was her cover story, although the Velvet Chrysanthemum—which she now ran full-time following Ume's marriage to an American captain—generated enough profit to justify any minor show of extravagance. Additionally, her operation now included two less exotic brothels and a restaurant, as well as a small gambling house. She nodded, replying, ''They're doing very well. I'm thinking about going abroad for a while.''

Cedric's eyebrows shot up. ''And just when investment possibilities are going to pop up like mushrooms here. Why?''

She shook her head. ''I think you're premature on this big financial explosion of ours. Besides, I don't have to be here to invest.'' She couldn't tell him that Oishi's growing greed and the very real threat from the *yakuza* had combined with stress from years of illegal activity to make her weary of the whole thing.

''Billy's the one who told me—last time he came home from school. Personally, I don't give a damn, young lady. I'm like MacArthur. Soon as I get back to Lodi and write this last big story, I'm going to settle down and report the local bridge scores.''

She laughed, but thought of Billy finishing his master's degree in business at Stanford in a few months.

As they pulled into the packed Haneda Airport, Cedric pointed eastward and shouted, ''Look!'' One small cloud had momentarily obscured the bright orange sun as it climbed above the horizon, creating a fan of bright extending rays. ''Do you think Mac could've ordered that rising sun effect specially for the occasion?'' he asked, not totally in jest.

They were soon on a raised platform reserved for the press. Not that it mattered, but Sachi turned up her coat collar and wore her dark glasses before Cedric introduced her to some of the older journalists. That was a reflex that she would certainly be able to stop once she got to Europe, she thought. No more worry —just the pleasant life of a wealthy widow.

The correspondents were in a good mood, but the jocular noises were merely a mask for the nervous realization among all these members of the fourth estate that a great moment was almost upon them—that regardless of their personal feelings, a giant was about to pass them, a giant who had created a shadow that would endure most probably beyond their own lifetimes.

Sachi felt it also as she looked around at the thousands of Americans and Japanese who had managed to get inside the airport and as close to the general's plane as possible. Vehicles of every description, together with hastily erected stands of anything that would provide elevation, ringed the area of ramp that composed the departure area. And every single inch of that outside space was filled with camera-laden and sign-carrying humanity experiencing the gamut of emotions. There were people ready to cheer, to salute, and to cry. Even the hundreds of white-gloved Japanese policemen seemed in awe. In the middle of the tarmac stood the general's trusty Constellation, the aircraft that only the day before had been rechristened the *Bataan* in fresh bright letters. To one side, an army band waited quietly next to a spit-and-polish, chrome-helmeted honor guard, while on the other side of the aircraft a group of Japanese dignitaries waited tentatively. As his carefully programmed moment of arrival neared, the entire area seemed to be blanketed by a wave of skittish silence.

And then the lights of the lead motorcycles flashed as they turned into the departure area. Leading the motorcade, directly behind the policemen, was the sleek black 1941 Cadillac that was so familiar to anyone who frequented the general's route to and from his office. If anything, it seemed even shinier; its fender flags snappier; and the five tiny silver stars around the license number "1" on its blue plates much brighter. The band immediately broke into a medley of military songs ending with "Army Blue." Quickly, MacArthur dismounted and returned the salutes of various American senior officers led by General Matthew Ridgway. Then it was quick farewells for him and his wife with senior Japanese and American officials. And just as the emotion began its march to a crescendo, the battery of howitzers fired the first rounds of its booming salute. Overhead, the flyby of eighteen jet fighters surrounding four B-29s roared by.

It was time. As the band blared "Auld Lang Syne," the general and his family hurried up the steps to the open door of the aircraft. At the top, MacArthur paused and turned for a final wave. Moments later, as the huge aircraft prepared to depart, the massive, silent crowd remained immobile except for the drying of frequent tears. An era was over.

Three hours later, Charlie Asaka met Sachi in the plush office at the Velvet Chrysanthemum. Removing a beer from the small wall refrigerator, she uncapped it and handed it to him. "Did you make up your mind?" she asked.

He nodded his head as he dropped onto a huge velvet sofa. "Yeah, but I think you're crazy to fade out now. These *yakuza* bastards don't worry me the slightest. I've got too many connections for them to mess with us."

"How about the money?" she asked quietly as she sat at her ornate desk.

He shrugged. "It'll take a few weeks. I'll wire two hundred thousand to your account in Switzerland, and the other eight hundred thousand to your account in Hong Kong. But you're letting me rob you for a million bucks, baby. With all the action we've got over in Korea—if that war lasts just one more year—you'd make that much easy."

She shook her head as she fiddled with a gold letter opener. "No, I've been too lucky for too long, Charlie. It's time. And the *yakuza* means business this time—I'm sure of it."

Charlie laughed. "When you get sick of playing the European scene, I'll be right here making a ton, baby." He sobered. "Oh, are you sure you don't want to unload this place? I'll give you a good price for it."

Shaking her head vigorously, she replied. "No, it's part of my roots."

"You got somebody to run it for you?"

Sachi's smile was secretive. "Yes, a former geisha."

At almost nine years of age, Mitsu was showing some of the independence of her female forebear at just the age when the pampering of early childhood in a Japanese offspring was supposed to be turning into ready obedience. It was somewhat understandable but not excusable, Sachi thought, because of the lack of a male parent most of her short life. Life abroad wouldn't change this problem, but Sachi thought it should give them an opportunity to spend much more time together.

Again she worked out a name change—this time reverting to Hoshi for both her and Mitsu. Her plan was flexible, including stays in England, France, and America, with room for other extended visits on the continent. The time frame had an open end and held a contingency related to the activities of Oishi. She knew the blackmailer wouldn't accept her disappearance easily.

In their absence, Hata and a housekeeper would maintain the house in Azabu. The nurse would accompany them abroad.

They arrived in Honolulu by plane three weeks later, then took a ship through the Panama Canal to New York. After a vigorous reunion with the great city that had so intrigued her during the year at Vassar, they moved on to England aboard the S.S. *America*. Five days later, they were in London moving into the small but pleasant townhouse she had leased in Chelsea. One of her contacts there was Master Sergeant Madakoro, the mess sergeant from her early days at the Imperial. He had transferred to the air force and was mess steward of the officers club at Lancaster Gate. She met him and his British wife a week later for lunch, and arranged for Mrs. Madakoro to become Mitsu's private tutor.

At the same time, a man who had been trying to locate Mrs. Sachiko Koga for over six years—and had in fact three times been turned away in perplexity from her house—marked her file "whereabouts unknown" and placed it on hold for another year.

Five weeks after that Sachi received a telegram from Ayako at the Velvet Chrysanthemum. Charlie Asaka's body had been fished out of Tokyo Bay.

In the summer of 1952, extensive lobbying by the JACL brought into law the Walter-McCarran Act that eliminated race as a factor in American immigration and naturalization. The old Alien Land Act was struck down. Nisei who had migrated to the great inland or eastern cities often remained in the friendlier climates, even though California was outgrowing its discrimination. The patience in the camps, the unequaled heroism of the 442nd, and the perseverence of the JACL combined finally to achieve all the basic human rights goals and reversed much in popular attitudes. Nisei began to successfully climb the social and economic ladder. Although stubborn pits of bigotry would remain, the doors to assimilation were finally opening. Within thirty years, the Japanese Americans would become the second-highest-earning ethnic group in the United States.

Fifty

The federal district courtroom in Stockton was packed. While only a handful of applicants were taking part in the procedure, dozens of the former Hoshi employees—both Noboru's and Sataro's— were present. The benches were full, with the remainder standing along the side walls and in the back. Even one of Noboru's former high school teachers, a thin white-haired woman, was there.

Part of it was a result of Cedric's moving editorial in the *Gazette* a week earlier. Singling out the Hoshi family as an outstanding example of the courage and patience of Japanese Americans, he announced that it would be a fitting tribute to attend the swearing-in ceremony for Mrs. Noboru Hoshi, her deceased husband's surrogate. He ended the editorial with the citation of Noboru's decoration.

Haru sat quietly along the other applicants in the front row. Although she had splurged with a new organdy dress of dark blue, the dilapidated old hat she had worn going into the camps and the day she came out was firmly pinned to her head. If it had been in shreds she would have worn it. It had been to her beloved Noboru's funeral.

Behind her in the second row, Cedric Baldwin sat with Teresa Scagnelli and Herb Lockett. Next to Cedric, Billy sat quietly, staring coolly ahead. The balance of that row was filled with those closest to her in church and the *kenjinkai*.

The red, white, and blue of the national colors seemed to swim down at her from behind the high bench, joining the curious sunshine that had worked its way past the Valley's early morning fog. Her throat felt dry. She heard the low hum of quiet talk and whispers, but nothing mattered except—

"All rise!" the bailiff's voice demanded loudly.

The judge in his black flowing robe seemed to enter the room in slow motion from the left, moving to the bench and tediously announcing the purpose and procedure. His features blurred as did his voice while the flag behind him seemed to jut forward, its stars and bars blotting him out, reminding her of a casket at graveside, of rifle volleys . . . a folded flag being handed to her. Noboru had been so proud to raise the flag each morning at The Other Cheek.

"Hold up your hands and repeat after me . . ." She was standing, staring at the judge. She remembered Noboru telling of his embarrassment because he didn't know the Pledge of Allegiance when he first started elementary school, how he had stood so much taller than the other kids. . . .

Voices of the other applicants joined hers in repeating, "I hereby declare, on oath, that I absolutely and entirely renounce and abjure all allegiance and fidelity to any foreign prince, potentate, state or . . ."

She could feel Billy's strong presence behind her, picture his cool mask, perhaps even a touch of the smile that he presented to the public. He had been totally against her forswearing her Japanese citizenship for what he called the "archaic, misguided obsession" of his father. Sometime in the near future, he would return to Japan and renounce his American citizenship. And where, he argued, would that leave her? Certainly she would wish to join him so he could take care of her and establish her in Japanese society. He troubled her so with his inflexible dislike of the Americans. And now she was about to become one.

". . . that I will bear true faith and allegiance."

He couldn't understand that this meant so much to her. She was the surrogate. She had inherited this responsibility from her beloved Noboru. The Other Cheek was her life, not some hazy island or teeming city in Japan. But he couldn't grasp that. He never had learned to truly love the vines.

She gripped Noboru's Silver Star medal tightly in her left hand

and pictured him smiling at her, approving. And the tears came to her eyes.

". . . that I take this obligation freely without any mental reservation or purpose of evasion. So help me God."

It had been a mistake to leave Ayako in charge of the Velvet Chrysanthemum. As strong as the former geisha was, *any* woman would eventually weaken under Oishi's constant pressure. And now she had to give up and move away from Tokyo. But if anyone could understand, it was Sachi. Providing her friend with a handsome bonus that would buy a home in Kyoto was no problem; finding a replacement manager was. Still, that alone didn't require her presence in Tokyo—the investment matter did.

To ensure that her location in Europe was kept secret, she did all of her communicating through a post office box in Madrid. Three weeks earlier, a letter had reached her from her Tokyo attorney. He knew of a young electronics company that might be of interest to her and suggested that she make at least a brief visit to meet with its founder.

It had been just over two years since the peace treaty became effective and full sovereignty returned to Nippon in April 1952. And, as Billy had predicted, the old families had returned to positions of power in the new *zaikai*—the money circles that were the government behind the government. There was a powerful thrust in Japan's business world, and it was time for anyone with confidence and the capital to wager to get in the big game. The ground floor would soon be occupied, Billy advised from his job with World Technologies, Inc., in New York. He had been with that company for two years and soon expected to be transferred to WTI–Japan, in Tokyo. He hoped to remain with the huge American company's Japanese operation until the right opportunity came along, continuing to acquire as much of its expertise and technical knowledge as possible in the process.

This new electronics company might be their opportunity.

She had checked into a small hotel in Akasaka only a few blocks from her shop upon arrival. Although she didn't expect anyone to be watching for her to show up after all this time, she stayed away from the Velvet Chrysanthemum and interviewed

the woman her attorney had recommended in the hotel. When she
ventured out, it was in a broad-brim hat and large dark sunglasses.

The summary of the electronics company read: "Kishi, Ltd.,
an electronics firm that has been in existence since 1949, manu-
factures vacuum-tube voltmeters, oscillators, and small screen
black-and-white television sets. The latter are produced on a
limited basis. The company has grown since its origin to employment of twenty-one technicians and operates out of an old building
in Ogikubo. Its main strength lies in the brilliance and inven-
tiveness of its founder, Taku Kishi (no relation to the politician).
Kishi, 41, graduated from Waseda University with a degree in
electrical engineering, rising to the rank of major during the war
as an army communications officer. He worked with Matsushita
Electric before and after the war. Programs for new develop-
ments are most interesting. The only restraint for Kishi is capital
limitation."

As the taxicab stopped in front of a dilapidated three-story
building in Ogikubo, she stared at the Kishi sign on the cracked
wall with wide, unbelieving eyes. *It was the very inn of her
lovemaking with her darling Korin!* Her hand flew to her mouth
as she flashed back to the tenderness of their first time together
. . . and the violence of their last. Old red roses pressed inside a
book . . . old tears, long dried but never forgotten. Was it an
omen? Could she even go inside to see cold machines tended by
indifferent strangers oblivious to what had once been? Could she
be rational about an investment? She closed her eyes and blew
out a deep breath. *Yes!* It was a good omen—repayment for a
great loss. So fateful it could bode nothing but good fortune!
Surely.

Forcing away the last painful memory, she frowned and left
the taxi. Inside, she saw a short, wiry man wearing thick spectacles and a white jacket hurrying toward her. His hair was a shock
of unruly gray and his piercing black eyes seemed to bore into
her. His quick smile was warm as he bowed and introduced
himself, hiding his surprise that she had come alone. He was
Taku Kishi. Indicating a small office to his right, he said,
"Please come in for tea, Mrs. Hoshi. Forgive the mess, but I

never get around to hiring a secretary to pick up and serve
guests.''

She sat in a hard-backed chair by his cluttered desk as he gave
her a more detailed history than the summary had provided.
Pouring more tea, he plunged ahead, speaking in nervous spurts
as he strode around the small office. ''There are exciting things
ahead in the electronics field, Mrs. Hoshi. Bell Laboratories in
America have developed the transistor, an electronic amplifying
device that uses single crystal semiconductors. Unless you are a
scientist, I'm afraid you have no concept of what this can mean.''

His eyes glowed brightly through the thick glasses. ''I can see
these transistors as the key to dozens of applications that will not
only miniaturize, but provide unlimited capabilities.''

Sachi nodded as she sipped her tea. ''And what does that mean
to a woman who doesn't know any more about electricity than
the off-on switch?''

Kishi stopped in front of her and dramatically raised his hands.
''It means tiny portable radios, small television sets, advanced
hearing aids—to name a few applications. And amazing computers.''

Sachi could already feel a tingle of excitement. ''What is a
computer?''

''An information storing device with infinite applications. It is
even whispered among us engineers with electricity running through
our veins that the computer could someday *think*, even replace
man.'' He suddenly smiled. ''But it will never replace a beautiful
woman.''

She liked this highly charged little scientist, liked him personally and liked his enthusiasm. But mostly she liked the idea of
being part of something with such exciting potential. ''And what
part of these applications could your company perfect—or should
I say develop into a profitable enterprise?''

His eyes bored into hers. ''Mrs. Hoshi, if I had the capital, *all*
of them would be strong possibilities. The computers *fascinate*
me, but even the strongest baby first has to crawl. I think a great
profit awaits what could be termed the transistor radio.''

It was time for the customary talking around the subject, but
both of them instinctively knew the other was eager to get to the
point of the meeting. Sachi, with her long experience in the

Western way, finally asked the abrupt question, "Mr. Kishi, how much money do you need to begin making these little radios?"

He stroked his chin. "There's the matter of purchasing patents, arranging for marketing . . . advertising would be vital. I would say the equivalent of ninety thousand dollars would give us a sound beginning. Yes, I think that would be a logical sum, Mrs. Hoshi."

He waited quietly by his desk as she paused, then replied, "I would have to discuss such a large investment with my colleagues. How much ownership in the company would that provide the investor?"

Kishi didn't even blink. "Fifteen percent, and an option to buy another fifteen at the market rate at such time as the stock might go public."

Sachi kept her voice calm. "We'll need a full financial report."

The engineer picked up a brown cardboard folder and handed it to her. "It's right here. You'll see that there are some outstanding debts, but I've included their elimination in the investment sum."

She took the folder but didn't open it. "Do you have other interested investors?" she asked directly.

A hint of a smile touched his lips. "One always has interested investors," he replied. "But how serious is their money? I spent two months in America last year and learned one thing in defiance of an old custom of ours. . . . 'He who hesitates too long in *ringi* is lost.' "

She nodded. *Ringi* was the time eater—the consensus process of decision-making that could take an interminable period, a Japanese business custom on major commitments that one British executive had told her was the single most exasperating problem in dealing with Nippon. "I'll soon be leaving the city, Mr. Kishi. I assure you the decision will be made before that time. Now, may I see your operation, please?"

Kishi's nod was more of a deep bow.

As she followed him from the office, Sachi could hardly contain herself. Her thoughts rushed ahead. Billy would soon be in Tokyo to keep his eyes on Kishi and perhaps funnel off some of the huge WTI expertise. Yes, the possibilities were unlimited

. . . if only Taku Kishi was as much of a genius as everyone thought.

Sachi Hoshi Koga was in the technology field.

She chuckled to herself. How's that, Grandfather?

She called the corporation Lodi, Ltd. The name sounded Japanese when pronouncing the "i" in the Nipponese way, and it tied into her beloved grandfather in a manner that pleased her. She was the only shareholder other than Mitsu, but not even Billy would know that. Nor was she going to divulge to him or anyone else the terms of the investment. Four days later, she had her attorney notify Kishi and he formally accepted. That same day, she arranged for the transfer of funds from one of her Hong Kong accounts. And the next night she regretfully left the city on a TWA flight to Honolulu. It was time to go back into exile.

Four days later, the man searching for Mrs. Sachiko Koga again renewed the "whereabouts unknown" status of her file and replaced it on hold.

Fifty-one

New York City—1959

Sachi loved New York—there was no way around it, she was disgustingly wanton about her feeling for the city. It was a case of unabashed adoration that wiped out all but the fondest memories of the City of Light, sunny Athens, even the delightful little Palma de Majorca. London and Frankfurt both had some of the bustle, but they seemed to be breathing more easily—as would befit dowager queens. The empress of the New World seemed to tug at her undergarments, straining and short of breath while she bounded forward seeking new excitement.

Yes, to her it was that single element above all others—that sparkling potency that made a walk down Fifth Avenue an act of experiencing and sharing that was unequaled. On a warm spring day, or even a chilly fall day, just three blocks of that broad, famous institution was an experience to treasure, to package and flaunt, to keep as a memory of total exhilaration. She could shop for an entire day and feel like she had barely gotten up. The museums, galleries, and libraries were vast treasures that were to be savored briefly and sweetly like a rare dessert. And the subways that took her to far reaches were much more interesting than those in Tokyo. Where else in the world could one see a person become almost invisible behind a newspaper folded to the width of a single column?

She bubbled to Haru in a letter: "Yesterday I walked down Sixth Avenue (former mayor LaGuardia renamed the beautiful boulevard the Avenue of the Americas, but New Yorkers are slow to change) from Central Park to Forty-second Street, then from Times Square down Broadway to the unique Flatiron building at Fifth Avenue. Times Square—a showman named Billy

561

Rose called it 'a triangle full of squares running around in circles.' I love it! And ah, the music, entertainment, and dining—Manhattan is positively the world's capital, just as it surely must be the horn-blowing center of the universe. I think I shall never come home.''

Sachi had been in New York for nearly a year, having arrived in time the previous summer for Mitsu to enroll at Brearly—the exclusive private school for bright girls. She had taken an apartment at the fashionable Meurice on West Fifty-eighth, just a block and a half away from Carnegie Hall and a block from the southern edge of Central Park. Although Mitsu had just turned seventeen, her amah, Teru, remained with them as a general maid and cook. Now, tall and willowy, Mitsu had already acquired the grace of an exquisite model. And exquisite was the right term—the general beauty of the Hoshi women was enhanced by delicate features that she had evidently inherited from her dead aviator father. Softly and perfectly curved lips could easily turn a mischievous smile, while her large brown eyes could widen into a look of the utmost concern or innocence. In three hours, she was going to join a classmate at Grand Central to catch a train to Boston. Then they would be off to a farm in the lower New Hampshire countryside for the summer.

Dressed in a powder blue cotton sheath appliquéd with white organdy scalloping, she had turned as many heads as her mother when they were seated at "21" for lunch. Sachi had been difficult to convince in regard to the summer plan, and now as she happily shared such a pleasant lunch with her daughter, she again had reservations. Besides, it was only until mid-August, and she could go up for a weekend visit whenever she felt like it. "Oh, you didn't tell me, dear. Are there tennis courts available?" she asked as the waiter served the chocolate mousse.

"Not on the farm, but her friend has one," Mitsu replied. "She says—

Both looked up as a tall figure in uniform stopped at the table. "Is that you, Sachi?" James Forster asked incredulously.

She looked up at the handsome major general in the beribboned green uniform and saw the same boyish expression that she thought she had forever purged from her memory. Except for a few fine lines around his eyes, Forster was little changed by the thirteen intervening years. He shook his head. "It is you, isn't it?"

She blinked, startled, swept up in a rush of emotion she couldn't control. "Yes, General Forster," she replied in a hushed voice she didn't trust. Breaking away from the intensity in his green eyes, she managed, "This is my daughter Mitsu, General."

He bowed slightly. "My pleasure, Mitsu. You are a lovely young woman." He glanced ahead to where another officer was waiting. "Excuse me a moment."

He was back immediately. "May I join you?" he asked, smiling back into Sachi's eyes.

Sachi nodded, angry at herself for not being able to give him the icy treatment he warranted. After further amenities he explained that he was in New York on a special assignment from the Pentagon and would be there for several weeks.

"Is your wife with you?" Sachi asked quietly.

"No, she's visiting her family in Dallas," he replied smoothly. "For the summer."

"And your children?"

"We have no kids, Sachi." Turning to Mitsu, he asked her about her schooling.

"Private Continental and Brearly," she replied with a coquettish smile. "And although Mama thinks I'm going to Keio University back in Tokyo, I'll be attending UCLA in another year."

A few minutes later, she excused herself for a trip to the powder room. Immediately, Forster turned earnestly to Sachi. "I've done everything possible to track you down, but Sachi Yukai is some kind of a myth. I even used military intelligence channels. . . . But that's history." He touched her hand. "Sachi, you look absolutely marvelous—every bit or more beautiful than on the day I saved you from a panting Russian."

"Thank you," she replied, withdrawing her hand to her lap. "And the years have also been kind to you, James Forster."

His intensity returned. "You aren't married, I can tell. I must learn everything. When can we get together—this afternoon, tonight? Sachi, you don't know what seeing you does to me!"

She knew better—oh, how she knew better—but she replied, "I must put Mitsu on a train for Boston, but I'll be free tonight."

He quickly withdrew a notebook. "Address and phone number, please."

She had been tempted to do the apartment in Japanese art and furnishings, but she had so many fine things from Europe and to whom did she have to advertise that the Hoshis were Japanese? On a permanent basis, it would be a different matter. In the large living room, the carpeting was a light beige sculptured pile, on which rested elegant crushed velvet overstuffed groupings in pure and off-white. The table lamps were two huge Grecian urns she had acquired on the island of Andros. One wall was filled with smaller paintings and original prints from various countries where she had lived, while the open spaces of the other walls remained blank in stark contrast.

Forster arrived sharply at six-thirty, bearing a dozen red roses. "Is this too ostentatious a start?" He grinned as she opened the door.

She sipped white wine while he drank a scotch. His first question was, "How in the world does a mysterious little cocktail waitress that I loved and left in Tokyo wind up in Twenty-One having lunch?" He shook his head in wonder as he asked.

"There are things which are not explainable," she replied. "My daughter, my widowhood, and the fact that my grandmother's investments became quite valuable, are sufficient."

It was the year of black and her trim figure looked striking in the silk crepe sheath dress with a trumpet skirt. A string of fine pearls accented her cleavage in the deeply scooped neckline, while her ears bore the tiny earrings he had given her on that Christmas in the mountains so long ago. She still wore her hair short, with a tousled effect. She looked approvingly at his conservative dark gray suit, so well tailored over his still athletic frame, and knew their entrance in any establishment in Manhattan wouldn't go unremarked.

"I have tickets to *Once Upon a Mattress*, the Off-Broadway musical with that zany young actress Carol Burnett," he announced as it approached time to head for the theater.

Following a most enjoyable performance at the Phoenix Theatre at Second and Twelfth, they caught a cab to El Morocco on East Fifty-fourth. After ordering steaks for supper and sipping a cocktail, the moment she had dreaded arrived. Joe D'Orsi's orchestra eased into a medley of old songs led by "Stardust," and Forster held out his hand. To this point, she had been reserved and very much in control, but as she slipped into his strong arms and blended against his body for the smooth dance steps, her resistance began to erode. His smell, the touch of his lips brushing her hair, his fingers firmly holding the small of her back—all were destructive. On the last number, a soft rendition of "Blue Moon," he whispered, "I've never stopped loving you, Sachi. Never."

She wanted to believe him, so very, very much. The years in Europe had been busy and not without men, but none of the suitors or philanderers had sufficiently excited her or lived up to her requirements. Once, after a whirlwind affair with a wealthy and charming Italian count, she had given marriage serious consideration. But it also wasn't enough. Now she knew why; in spite of everything, her love for this tall boyish man whispering words of endearment in her ear had never destroyed itself.

She led him back to the table when the medley ended. Enough was enough for the first taste and the initial course of their delightful meal awaited. By the time they finished the steaks, he had brought her up to date on his career. He had recently completed command of an airborne division and thought he stood a good chance of making a third star in another couple of years. He was still a whiz kid at forty-five.

"And your wife?" she finally summoned the courage to ask.

"We just had our twenty-second wedding anniversary," he replied uncomfortably.

"Is that all you have to say about her?"

A touch of pain crossed his eyes. "How can I tell you how much I love you and talk about her?" he asked quietly.

She looked at her plate. How could he?

They returned to the Meurice shortly after one, and after being admitted by the doorman, took the elevator to her floor. At the door, she said, "Thank you James, for a totally delightful evening."

"May I come in?" he asked softly.

She shook her head as she fumbled with the keys. When the door opened, she turned to say good night. His arms went around her as his face came down to hers. Her eyes widened as his lips drew close. "No!" she whispered, quickly turning her head aside.

He straightened, releasing his grip. "I'm off for the weekend," he murmured. "I'll call about ten. Better yet, I have my car. Why don't we drive up to Connecticut for lunch. It's lovely in June, you know." He smiled. "And it's not a jeep."

She nodded, her face a mask, thinking about those lips she so much wanted to kiss.

"Pick you up at ten?"

She nodded her head briskly and went inside. Closing the door, she slumped against it. None of this made any sense, she told herself irritably. He was still another woman's husband! Going to a chair and dropping into it, she closed her eyes and felt the misery of long ago flood over her. Wiping away a tear, she sighed deeply. She was going to risk it.

They reached Ridgefield at shortly before one, stopping at a beautiful old colonial house that had been converted into a charming inn. The spotty showers they had encountered on the trip up from the city had worn themselves out and left a sunny freshness that wafted into the bright but small room they had to themselves. "This is Revolutionary War country," Forster commented after he had ordered their Yorkshire pudding and began sipping his beer. "There were little skirmishes all around this area. You know, we're only about an hour's drive from West Point."

"Oh, good!" she exclaimed. "Can we drive over when we finish lunch?"

"Sure," he replied. "We can have dinner at the Thayer Hotel tonight."

Her smile was whimsical as she softly said, "I haven't been there in almost twenty years."

It took a moment for that to sink in. His eyes opened in surprise. "You were *here* twenty years ago?"

"Yes, when I was attending Vassar."

"Vassar?" He was looking at her funny.

"Yes, Vassar . . . in 1939 and 1940."

"But I don't understand. You—"

"I lied," she said softly, reaching for his hand, watching his expression stiffen. "I'm the daughter of a Japanese general and have lived in Tokyo most of my life. I'm also the widow of a Japanese naval hero who bombed Pearl Harbor and died at Midway. Mitsu is his daughter."

He shook his head slowly as he searched her eyes. "But why the story, the secrecy? The war was over. And the cocktail waitress thing?"

Sachi shook her head. "Until the war, I never wanted for a thing. But you know how it was in Tokyo in '45—no food, no medicine. I had to—"

"How did you get to a plush Manhattan apartment?" he asked tightly, withdrawing his hand from hers. "Lunch at Twenty-One, private school. Rich jewels . . . it all adds up to a hell of a lot of money, Sachi."

She wanted to break down and tell him all of it, but she just couldn't! "I told you," she replied evenly. "My grandmother's investments. Actually, they were diamonds she left for me. And I invested them in several businesses that paid off handsomely. Things boomed after you left Tokyo, you know. And I've done quite well in world markets since then . . . your high-flying WTI for one."

He frowned, unable to conceal his annoyance. "What kind of businesses in Tokyo—black market?" he asked sarcastically.

She smiled coolly. "Of course, and I ran one of the top brothels too."

He snorted, slowly finding a sheepish grin. "*Sure* you did. Okay, it's really none of my business anyway." He recovered her hand. "Now tell me more about your family . . . and don't tell me your father's name was Tojo. I don't think I could take it."

She laughed. "No, not quite."

They chatted on through the meal, engrossed in each other and the conversation that sprang from their stimulation. As the waitress served the burnt almond parfait, Forster asked about Mitsu's college. Sachi didn't mention that she still didn't feel comfortable about going back to Tokyo to live, but replied, "It's time for her to get back to her roots. Besides, there's a great deal of Japanese language that she hasn't learned. If she's to become a movie or TV star, she must become thoroughly Japanese again."

"She's lovely enough. Can she study acting in Tokyo?"

"Yes, but I promised her Pasadena Playhouse or something like it—if she gets through Keio University and doesn't change her mind."

They drove through the Thayer gate from Highland Falls at 3:40. A light rain was falling, but the military policeman at the gate directed them through briskly, rendering a stiff salute. "I have an officer's sticker on my bumper," Forster explained. They proceeded slowly down the winding hillside street to a large group of buildings where he found a parking place. "I know how you abhor war," he said as he opened the door for her. "But this museum is also part of our history." Back in the car later, they drove on around the huge athletic fields on Cullum Road to a small parking area. Although it was still cloudy, the rain had stopped and she could see a marvelous view of the Hudson River as they stood beside the ancient black cannon of the Kosciusko Monument.

A few minutes later, she stared northward at the broad expanse of the Hudson from beside the Sedgwick Monument. "Old John Sedgwick was a Union general who was killed at Spotsylvania during our Civil War," he explained.

She shuddered. Why did they always build monuments to someone who died in a terrible war? "Oh-oh, Retreat," Forster said as four military policemen approached the nearby flagpole. As if in answer to her silent question, he added, "This is what this place is all about." She watched him come to attention and stare silently ahead as a record played the bugle notes and the flag came slowly down the pole. There was a softness in his face as he turned when it was over and the flag had been folded. "It never fails to touch me, but when I'm able to share the ceremony here at its heart, I tend to get carried away,'' he explained with a sheepish smile.

The rain grew suddenly heavy, so they hurried to the entrance of the Thayer Hotel. ''I'm not dressed very well for this,'' she said glancing down at her paisley print shirtdress with its wide skirt as he parked the car.

''Nonsense,'' he replied. ''You look great.'' Leaning over, he kissed her cheek. ''You'll be the most beautiful woman here.''

She glanced up with wide eyes at the intimidating portraits of several old generals staring down frostily as the headwaiter led them to a corner table in the high-ceilinged formal dining room. Thick carpeting, old silver, and crisp linen tableclothes and napkins added to the sense of quality she felt as she glanced at the huge menu. Only bright sprays of fresh June flowers softened the effect.

They were halfway through the veal parmigiana when a man in a tweed sports jacket came up to the table. ''James!'' he said enthusiastically. ''What in the hell brings you up here? Last I heard, you were down at Bragg.''

Forster got to his feet, quickly wiping his mouth with his napkin. ''Hello, Harry,'' he said warmly as they shook hands. ''I want you to meet Mrs. Hoshi, a friend of mine from New York.'' Turning to Sachi, he said, ''This is Colonel Harry Leveret, an old classmate of mine. He's hiding out as a dean here.''

Sachi couldn't miss the cool smile on the colonel's face as he bowed his head, ran his eyes quickly down her front and returned to her eyes. ''It's a pleasure, Mrs. Hoshi,'' he said, then turned back to Forster for more animated conversation.

A tiny shaft of red light from the garish motel sign beamed itself around the edge of the drapes and made a small pattern on the wall. Sachi thought it looked like a rose. She sighed as she slid out of bed and went to the scarred dresser for one of Forster's cigarettes. Lighting it with his Zippo, she dropped into a faded armchair and inhaled deeply. Maybe she should take up smoking, she thought. No, that was silly. She thought of Tokyo, wondering if it would be safe enough to go home in another year . . . or if her gamble with Forster had a chance of paying off. Tonight at the Thayer Hotel had been but one indication of the odds against her.

"What are you doing?" Forster asked drowsily from the bed.

"Thinking about your friend, Leveret," she replied quietly.

He sat up, slipping into his shorts. "Oh, don't pay any attention to him. He's known my wife since we were cadets, and he lost his best friend on Okinawa."

She nodded, taking another drag on the cigarette then snubbing it out. "I understand the last part, but how do I cope with the first? How often will we run into old friends and what do I do—bow my head like a dutiful geisha?"

He took her hand and pulled her up to his chest. "Don't worry about it, my darling," he replied softly as he kissed her hair. "We'll work it out."

What else could she say? All the love she had known in Tokyo had flooded back over her like a monstrous, uncontrollable wave. She kissed his shoulder, whispering, "Take me back to bed, my darling."

The next two weeks flew by for both of them. General Forster was working out of First Army Headquarters on Governors Island and had VIP quarters there. Twice he was able to meet her for lunch in Manhattan; he came into the city every night. They saw Rodgers and Hammerstein's *Flower Drum Song* with Pat Suzuki at the St. James Theatre, and Tennessee Williams's *Sweet Bird of Youth* with Geraldine Page and Paul Newman at the Martin Beck. On those nights they had late suppers at the Cub Room of the Stork Club; on other nights they enjoyed Les Elgart's orchestra at the Roosevelt Grill, and Milt Shaw at the St. Regis.

It was a mad, dizzy whirl of buying and wearing lovely clothes—she haunted Bergdorf's and all their competitors in the daytime—and of being escorted to shows and some of the finest restaurants in the world by a handsome and gallant young general who loved her vigorously and tenderly. One weekend they went down to the Jersey shore at Long Branch; the next it was out to Southampton for tennis and a relief from the late June heat of the city. And it was more—she felt irresponsible and youthful, fulfilled, robust, zestful. She enjoyed his flowers and books and other little thoughtful gifts. And she savored, vigorously reveled in loving Major General James Forster.

On the following Tuesday, after he had met her at the nearby Russian Tea Room for a quick serving of its famous borscht, she returned to the apartment shortly after two to find a man had called and left a number. She looked at the name with a chill. It was Oishi.

They met an hour later in a small restaurant bar a few blocks east on Fifty-eighth. Oishi's oily smile hadn't changed, only his looks. He was much thinner, almost skeletal, and wore shaded glasses. He was sipping a Kirin beer in the middle of the empty restaurant portion in the back of the place when she walked in. As she took a chair across from him the same fear gripped her that she had felt at the apartment.

She numbly ordered a Scotch from the smiling waiter.

"How nice of you to come, Mrs. Koga . . . or should I say Mrs. Hoshi," he said casually. "Very clever to change the name, but Hoshi really wasn't very bright. And I had trouble with the Greece and Spain parts of your long journey. In fact, Mrs. Koga, I've spent nearly my entire savings finding you." His eyes glinted. "But it's worth it. You just have no idea how enjoyable it is to see you, and to find out what a fine luxurious life you have here."

She tried to keep the fear and hate hidden. "What do you want, Inspector?" she asked in a cold voice.

He waved a finger at her as the waiter brought her drink. "I haven't finished my story, Mrs. Koga. A year ago, an unfortunate incident forced me to resign from the Metropolitan Police Force and I had neither anything interesting to occupy my time, nor a regular income. You see, I wasn't eligible for a pension—" He grinned. "And you had been gone so many years I had little of that money left . . . So, I combined pleasure with business— traveling abroad and finding you again."

He lit a cigarette and sipped some beer. "You see, I couldn't wait to go back into business with you. You're so prompt with payments and so reasonable. And you have the same lover, don't you, Mrs. Koga?''

"What do you want?" she managed.

The cigarette dangled from his mouth, its smoke drifting up past his eyes, causing him to half close one as he drummed his fingertips together. "I'm a reasonable man, Mrs. Koga. I believe, since you have no illicit income that I'm aware of, that four hundred dollars a week should adequately take care of my simple needs."

"For what?" Sachi whispered.

His oily grin was wide. "Silence, my dear, golden silence. You have family, friends, and business in Tokyo. And such a lovely daughter here. And a fine combination of good names, and last of all—a lover who's an American general. I should not wish to discuss any of your past with them or the newspapers anywhere."

She took in a deep breath. "I—I can't afford it."

"Oh, come now," he snorted. "How much did your old partner, Asaka, settle for before those bad fellows killed him? Must have been at least a half, maybe three-quarters of a million dollars. Probably much more. And I didn't tell you I need an advance. Five thousand dollars within a week."

"I can't possibly raise that much cash."

"Oh, you will, Mrs. Koga. Or I'll begin with the director of your daughter's school—Brearly, I believe."

Twice during the next two weeks she continued to put the inspector off, two weeks of worry and stress that were difficult to hide from Forster. She kept hoping some kind of a miracle would happen, an accident, a stroke . . . but no, that would merely serve to release his damaging information.

She glanced at her watch, knowing the dreaded phone call would be precisely on time.

Even so, she jumped when it rang moments later. "If I don't get that money by tonight," Oishi growled, "I'll release the information in all areas first thing in the morning. I swear it, Mrs. Koga. You've stalled enough!"

She stared numbly at the telephone. It was over. She had

considered every approach—hiring someone to do away with him, even bringing someone in from Japan, but it couldn't be done. She would only be open for more blackmail. Her voice was expressionless as she told him she would have the money and where to meet her.

"But why there?" he asked, annoyed.

"Take it or leave it."

"I'll be there at eleven."

Sachi slumped into a chair by the phone, then collected herself and called Forster's office. Finding him out, she told the secretary, "Tell him please that Mrs. Hoshi called and had to cancel the plans for this evening. Thank you." Again she stared at the phone. When would she ever have time and a clear head to bore on with her campaign to win James Forster away from that ghost of a wife who haunted her? She loved him so much she ached! What had he said the night before when they ate at Le Pavillon? "You'll love Washington in the fall," that was it.

She ate a snack at six, then complained of a headache and retired to her bedroom. A few minutes later, Teru stuck her head inside to say good night. She was spending the night with a friend—a widow from Tokyo who worked as a seamstress at Hattie Carnegie's.

Sachi left the apartment at nine-thirty, catching a Seventh Avenue IRT Number Three train for Brooklyn. An hour later, after getting off at Clark Street, she left the subway station in the St. George Hotel in Brooklyn Heights and walked down to the Promenade. Following it to a point near the intersection of Atlantic and Columbia, she looked down over the edge of the iron railing to the middle of the Brooklyn Queens Expressway—the BQE. She nodded, noting that traffic was still heavy.

It was a hot, clear night with bright stars but no moon. Just an even mile away, across the East River, the skyscrapers of lower Manhattan rose majestically, their compositions of lights like the glow of a million fireflies. It was one of those nights of illusion, when the buildings loomed much closer and seemed overpowering, hypnotic—surreal. Up to her right, the lights of the unmistakable Brooklyn Bridge rushed toward the huge beckoning buildings above Wall Street. And immediately below, with its masts blocking a bit of the view, a dark freighter sat quietly in her berth in the Brooklyn docks.

It was strangely more quiet than usual. She could hear a soft melody from a radio drift up from the ship, somehow cutting through the sounds of traffic on the expressway below. And behind her, a large dog's angry bark wafted down from Henry Street. An inevitable horn honked. But mostly she heard her own breathing and the sound of her heart beating. Just as she looked at her watch and saw that it was two minutes until eleven, she saw a short man walk up and knew it was Oishi. The Promenade was deserted except for them. "Inspector," she said loudly enough for him to hear.

He moved closer, peering through the dark. "Is that you, Mrs. Koga?"

"Yes."

"Do you have the money?" He pointed a lit penlight at her. "Why are you wearing men's clothing?"

She held out a package, a brown paper bag. As he reached for it, the end ripped open and four .32 slugs smashed into his chest. The silencer on the barrel held the explosions to nearly inaudible buzzes. As he groaned and started to slump, she caught him and glanced around. Their part of the Promenade was still isolated. Quickly she emptied his pockets, getting his wallet and apartment key. The next move was the most difficult, requiring perfect leverage. Placing one foot on the second horizontal bar of the iron railing, she heaved suddenly with all her power and tipped his body over the side.

Not being able to see the form fall into the speeding traffic of the expressway, she watched the lights and listened. Immediately, the sounds of blaring horns and screeching tires shouted up to her. Headlights of cars and trucks swerved and more horns cried out. With a satisfied nod she imagined the inspector being tossed from bumper to bumper, smashed and torn by the wheels of at least a dozen vehicles.

She pulled the brim of the man's fedora down over her face and strolled back toward the St. George, where she would catch the next express to Manhattan. The revolver and silencer, which had cost her $300, would be pitched over the rail of the ferry to Liberty Island the next day. Its serial numbers had been filed off.

Seventy-three minutes later, she bent to open the door to Oishi's small apartment in southern Harlem. By telephone contact and Western Union delivery of the private detective's fee, she was able to retain complete anonymity while he had traced Oishi to this address. Four minutes after entering, she found her carefully catalogued dossier in a black leather folder. It was amazingly detailed—as if the terrible Oishi had made her his life's work! She nodded, certain that this would be the only copy. Oishi had been in a foreign city and totally secure in believing no one knew where he resided. She carefully closed the folder and made one final search. Then, with a deep sigh, she tightened her gloves and left.

They were in a small Armenian restaurant just off Fifth Avenue, as usual attracting the glances of the curious. Forster was in his green uniform, having just concluded a late morning presentation from the military specialization branch of WTI. He smiled when he finished giving her a thumbnail sketch of it. "This first generation computer program of theirs is something else," he said shaking his head. "Even I can't conceive what's ahead—it's overwhelming."

Sachi nodded pleasantly. She wondered if Billy still had his inside sources of information at WTI, and also if Taku Kishi even needed that kind of industrial espionage; supposedly his brilliant planning for the computer was moving as scheduled. But she should certainly buy some more WTI stock.

"Someday we'll see computers in tanks, on artillery, even in the cockpit of fighter planes," Forster continued. "Hell, it might even come to replacing the common soldier with a little black box someday."

"That intrigues me," Sachi replied quietly. "Can a black box be invented to do away with the armies and war?"

He shrugged. "Only when politics, greed, and aggression have been eliminated from life." Sobering, he sipped his beer and stared at the curling blue smoke of his cigarette.

"Is something wrong?" she finally asked.

"Yes," he replied quietly. "I'm finished here, darling. It's time to pack up and head back to the Pentagon. I—I leave the day after tomorrow."

She watched him silently, not even moving her wide eyes. It was time to look at the dice, to see where the little white roulette ball had landed. She held her breath.

"Will you follow me down to Washington? It'll be a marvelous place for Mitsu to spend a year . . . so much to do, to see. And you'd love it. Why, it would take you a year just to get through the Smithsonian. And that's just the beginning."

She still waited for the words she was dying to hear.

"You could find a good apartment, or perhaps invest in a house. Real estate has always been a good place to put your money. McLean is really something."

Breaking his gaze, she sipped the white wine. He was telling her.

"Doesn't that sound great to you?"

She nodded dully. Not one word about the subject they never had discussed in their six-week trip through Wonderland. He reached across the table for her hand. "Darling, I love you so much," he said gently. "We'll have such wonderful times together."

She smiled softly. A whiz kid with three or four stars in the offing couldn't get divorced and marry his Japanese mistress at this stage, could he? The dice had come up snake eyes and the tiny roulette ball had landed in what the German croupiers in Baden Baden called *Null*. She had lost the big one . . . did she want to stay in the long-range race, just taking what she could . . . or fold her tent and move on to a new campground?

She got to her feet. "I have to call my daughter," she replied softly. "It's about time we went home."

Fifty-two

It was shortly over a year after Taku Kishi made the deal with Sachi's corporation that he first needed more money. Not yet in position to go public with his company stock and still too unsuccessful to acquire a lower interest loan from the standard commercial or local banks, he contacted Sachi's lawyer.

Kishi's projections had fallen short in his plan to get the new, ultra-small transistor radio on the market and he needed $21,000. From London, Sachi first tried to purchase more stock with the money, but Kishi refused. She then agreed to the loan at an interest rate of four percent, at that time far below anything he could have gotten from any other source.

In effect, she was loaning money to herself, but she had a plan.

Then in 1958, with the tiny radios highly successful, Kishi decided to plunge directly into computer research and development while also producing an electronic calculator. Again he needed money, and once more Sachi gave him a low-interest loan. His next need, that for money for the new factory near Ogikubo, was met when Kishi, Ltd., went public and made a large sum from the stock sale in 1963. This action netted Sachi a substantial profit that made up part of the purchase price of the additional fifteen percent of Kishi stock she was eligible to purchase under the original agreement.

It was then that a specific bank became part of Kishi's future needs.

The Japanese government had been easing the borrowing of capital for proven industries for nearly a decade by various attractive money acquisition methods and tax benefits through the banks.

Under the system, doing business with one particular bank for a company like Kishi was attractive simply because it could then dictate how much money it needed, and the bank would go out and find it.

Sachi, back in Tokyo since late 1959, was now eager to open a bank. In fact, she was obsessed with the idea. With a major interest in what could someday be one of the world's largest technological firms, a cousin who was both well-educated and qualified in the field, and a personal fortune of her own—all she needed was a bank to round out her power structure.

Yes, she could taste it! She had read everything she could find out about banks, talked to numerous bankers and even taken some university courses in banking and finance. Now was the time and she knew how she wanted to do it, but there were problems. Primarily, she didn't know how her background would hold up under tight scrutiny. It had been merely twelve years since she got out of her illegal activities, and even if that part of her life were to remain obscured, there was still the matter of her money. It had been well-laundered through international banks and holding companies, but there was still no logical source for it. Also, the other investors willing to join the venture wouldn't wait forever.

It was then that the sure hand of Sataro entered the picture—in the form of a man from the company that had been marking "whereabouts unknown" on her file for so long.

Sachi looked up from her huge desk in the plush office of the Velvet Chrysanthemum as the man from the brokerage entered. Following a short bow and accepting the offer of tea, he sat beside her at a coffee table and said, "Mrs. Hoshi, you have no idea how hard we've searched for you over the years. Of course, we first looked for Mrs. Koga, but were told your home had been sold to another family after the war. And after several years, we assumed you were dead and that there were no living members of his family."

Sachi nodded. "Yes, I understand."

"The estates of the Hiroshima victims have been a terrible mess."

Sachi nodded again.

The man opened his briefcase and withdrew a sheet of paper. "Your grandfather made various investments through our firm prior to the war, and on August 5, 1945, just one day before the horrible catastrophe, mailed a copy of his new will to us. It designates you as his sole heir, Mrs. Hoshi."

She waited quietly as he went on, "While Mr. Hoshi invested in Yawata, the huge steel company, and in Mitsubishi Heavy Industry, his largest block of stock was in the *Yomiuri*, the daily newspaper which has nurtured the giant Nippon Television. And, Mrs. Hoshi, his investment was substantial for those days. Nearly eighty thousand dollars. Can you imagine what it's worth today?"

Sachi shook her head. It could be—

"It totals just over twenty-five million yen!"

Sachi drew in a sharp breath. About $720,000! How absolutely amazing! She thought of his original dream and wondered what he'd say if he knew. "What do you need from me?" she asked softly.

The man rose, holding out the sheet of paper. "Call us when you are ready to accept the money. There are certain forms, of course. . . ."

Sachi flew down to Hiroshima two days later. The address of the building was not far from Hiroshima Castle, near the River Ota, and close to where her grandfather's house had been in the days when her father was a small boy. The building she leased was a modern one-story structure that was both unassuming in appearance, yet substantial—exactly the face a quiet new bank should present. Standing in the large empty room that would serve as its lobby, she could already feel its strength, sense the flow of finance that could become a viable cog in the *zaikai* someday. She inhaled deeply and drew herself more erect—savoring the sheer power.

Sataro's money was her answer—the nucleus from an indisputable legal source. The fact that she would add a substantial amount of her own funds to insure control was immaterial. The bank was Sataro Hoshi's memorial, founded by his fortune and dedicated to his dream. And the other directors had been handpicked. No one would even bother to question her now.

Already she could see the bronze sign that would read, *"Hoshi Heiwa Ginko*—the Hoshi Peace Bank."

She turned, looking to the right of what would be the main entrance. There, where no one could pass without seeing it, a huge oil painting of her grandfather would hang—already the finest portrait artist in Tokyo was working from photographs.

She nodded, picturing him in his wingtip collar and the finery from his days of being the rice baron. Yes, the bank would give her the power to finally pursue his rich dream, to at last begin work on the promise made on a ferryboat so long ago. She closed her eyes and recalled the cool breeze, the mist, the fervor in his glowing eyes as he charged her with sharing his beautiful new mission.

She didn't know where she would begin. There were organizations, but she knew it would be more than that, something personal and trying . . . something that would require the strength. Already there was unrest in the cities, right-wing talk of a more active military, jingoism in the marketplace. Of old Ishiwara's Final War that her father used to talk about.

She nodded. Even the idea of moving to Hiroshima, the center of the peace movement, was appealing.

She nodded to the leasing agent and walked out.

At forty, Billy Heigo Hoshi was one of the most handsome and well-groomed men in Tokyo. His piercing good looks were now more refined and set off by a touch of gray at the sideburns. And his tailor-made suits fit his tall, lean body in a casual manner that suggested a male model.

The polished side he showed to the public and most of his colleagues was that of the sophisticated, well-educated Nisei who had returned to his homeland as a loyal citizen of the empire. Urbane and witty, he spoke Japanese as flawlessly as he spoke English. He was married to the beautiful daughter of a wealthy Ginza department store owner and lived with her and their tiny son on an old estate in the still fashionable Kazumi section of Azabu. And most importantly, since company affiliations were becoming such a vital key in Tokyo society, he was international sales manager for Kishi, Ltd., the vibrant electronics firm that was the talk of the stock exchange.

Within the company, his reputation was that of a reserved person who could suddenly be quite charming. His exceptional grasp of marketing technique, particularly in the American and European areas, went unchallenged. He was also held in a degree of dread by some of the company's senior and middle management people because of the razor sharp ruthlessness he could display on occasion. But to Taku Kishi he was the answer to a scientist's dream—an entrepreneur who could not only successfully market, but share the excitement of the drawing board.

The personal side of Billy Heigo Hoshi was well guarded. While his salary with Kishi was substantial, his tastes and commitments were expensive. He had moved his family into the Obata house with Sachi as soon as she returned from America. And although she had moved out to a lavish apartment in Akasaka a year later, she still paid the household maintenance costs. The most expensive item in Billy's budget was the apartment he kept in Kioi-cho for his extramarital affairs and private meetings with the small group of people who were dedicated to his cause. There were seven of them at the present, each recruited carefully for special leadership potential within either the government or business world of Nippon. Caring neither for the political left or right, he had met four of them at anti-American demonstrations during the spring of 1960 when the Japan–U.S. Security Treaty was coming up for renewal.

He called his little group the *Sakurakai*—the Cherry Society— after the small semi-clandestine nationalistic movement that had been active during the prewar period. They met two nights a month, discussing their philosophy, affirming their patience and reinforcing their commitment. One of their intermediate goals was to infiltrate the influential *zaikai*, but this would require more position and recognition than any of them had yet attained.

Rising and hurrying to meet his cousin, Billy bowed and motioned for her to be seated at a low couch in his efficient office at Kishi headquarters near Ogikubo two weeks after her visit to Hiroshima. After hurrying through the graces and having their tea served by an attractive secretary, Sachi smiled brightly. "I remember when your boss had to serve the tea himself."

He flashed his dazzling smile at her. "Times have changed, my dear. What was urgent enough to bring my lovely cousin here?"

"I am the wise woman from the East, bearing great gifts, my lord," she replied quickly. Reaching inside the thin white briefcase that matched her tailored suit, she extracted an envelope which held the title to the house where she had been born and raised, the Obata house of her grandmother. She handed it to him silently.

After staring at the document a moment, he looked up in genuine surprise. "Why?"

"I've had the use of grandmother's jewels to gain my fortune, and now it's only right that you get her house." She wasn't telling him about Sataro's estate, not until sometime in the future when he might share the rich profits.

He lowered his head in a quick bow. "Thank you, pretty cousin."

"And one other item," she said quietly. "A group of people is putting a bank together in Hiroshima and I've nominated you as a director. The position includes five percent of the bank's stock, with an option to buy more."

She had never seen him so disconcerted. It took him at least five seconds to slip the mask back over his face and ask, "Why a bank?"

She shrugged. "It's time you began acquiring status outside the company, don't you think?"

He nodded. "Absolutely. Yes, of course." *It was the vital step he needed!*

And then she told him about naming it after Sataro.

And when she finished, he could barely control his excitement. *It would even be named Hoshi—indicating to the* zaikai *and all others that it was his family bank!* He'd have an additional set of calling cards made immediately!

Her father had told her about Seoul, but she had somehow always pictured the huge city as more like Tokyo than a massive, colorless collection of tired-looking people hurrying grimly along a municipal survival path. Except for a sprinkling of new Western-style hotels, the drab skyline was mostly monotonous, futile.

She smiled, thanking the attractive Korean bar waitress for bringing her scotch and water and thinking back to the Imperial. How many times had she bowed her head as she served drinks? How many times had she smiled away the passes of men who wanted her body? And then she remembered that Nippon had long occupied Korea and she wondered how many times Japanese officers had done the same with these lovely Koreans. Her own father? No, surely not. Her mind drifted back to the Imperial. A boyish young colonel and some nasty Russians.

How would she have ever guessed it would lead to her sitting in this Eighth Army officers club waiting for a handsome American general? Her forbidden love, the delightful man she couldn't have but couldn't do without. Once, twice, three times a year; Paris, Honolulu, Bangkok, London, San Francisco—it didn't matter. She would go by dogsled or rowboat if necessary. Just a few days with James Forster kept her young, vibrant, alive! And this year with his Korean assignment it would be once a month—more if she wished.

She smiled ruefully to herself. She could buy a Korean *hootch*-one of those one-room dwellings with a charcoal stove that was the center of existence—and wait for her soldier to come to her each time he could get away. Forster had told her about the girls who lived a year at a time with a succession of soldiers until they were too old—often by age thirty—to attract anyone. None of those promised GI marriages and no return to normal Korean society; outcasts in a land purported to have the highest female suicide rate in the world.

Her smile was replaced by a shudder.

She was so fortunate. So what if her love had to be grabbed on the periphery in snatches? She had it, and it was beautiful. And there was always the chance that something would happen to his wife, maybe that he would even divorce her someday. *Anything* was possible when two healthy people loved so vigorously!

Her sense of humor returned. She could build a hotel to be her *hootch!*

And then she saw him at the entrance to the lounge—tall, erect, handsome in his faded green fatigues and the bright buckle of a general's belt. He looked around and blinked as she gaily waved her hand.

And in spite of herself, she drew in a short quick breath as he hurried toward her.

Fifty-three

Saeki-gun, Hiroshima Prefecture— January 28, 1973

Sachi liked to arise early and walk around her grounds. Even in the heart of winter the place never failed to stir her emotions. The now barren trees still harbored birds and little animals, the new wood of the house promised to mature with grace, and the shrubbery that her gardener had so carefully transplanted vowed to make its marriage with the rocks and water a highly successful union. And the final element of any successful Japanese landscape—the background from which any architect worth his salt always borrowed—spread out around its seven sparkling rivers below and in the distance.

Stopping at the observation point above the swimming pool, she looked through the shiny new telescope. Even in the bright glare of the early morning sun, she could pick out the shape of Miyajima and other land masses around the edge of the Inland Sea. A gleaming reflection announced the arrival of a ship, perhaps a freighter, working its way into the harbor.

"Nothing has changed, has it?" Mitsu asked with a chuckle.

"Yes, the city grows larger each day," she replied softly. Having her beautiful daughter with her on such a glorious morning completed the rich, full feeling she had on this wonderful day. She inhaled the fresh moist air. This would be one of the most remarkable days of her life and she wanted to enjoy every single minute of it.

"Do you suppose those men who will sign the peace treaties are walking around any such tranquil setting in Paris this morning?"

Sachi shook her head. "There is no place like this, not even in glorious Paris. Isn't it the same time there?"

Mitsu nodded her head briskly. "Just a day earlier." At thirty-one she had matured into an alluring combination of her mother and grandmother, only more willowy and effervescent. She had survived a broken, childless marriage and was working in broadcast journalism and film at NHK in Tokyo. "What do you think it will mean?" she asked.

Sachi sighed as she moved the telescope to find the Peace Park. She had given it so much thought—visited Saigon on several occasions, met with other peace delegations in Bangkok, in New Delhi. Economic influence had been tried. "I don't know," she replied softly. "Hopefully, some of our discontent will lessen. America has massive internal wounds to be healed. . . . The main thing is for the war to be over."

Mitsu had been working on a documentary about Vietnam. "But the fighting won't stop until the communists have what they want. Isn't that right? What about Cambodia and Laos? Won't they—"

"Hey," Sachi broke in, taking her arm. "Don't start ruining my beautiful day. A war is ending, we're going to have the finest reception in the history of the *gun*, and—"

"What time is your handsome general getting in?"

Sachi sighed again. "Not until two-forty."

"And how long will he stay?"

"One day, then back to Saigon for a brief period. He'll retire in Washington."

Mitsu chuckled. "Why don't you bring him back here and find a place to chain him. I think he'd go well with the design. Or better yet, send him up to Tokyo. I'll—"

Sachi pointed sternly toward the main part of the house. "You tend to your own business, young lady. And right now it's breakfast."

Billy looked at his watch as the captain announced their approach into Hiroshima International. Closing his briefcase, he inhaled deeply from the cigarette and looked down through the window of the aircraft. He shouldn't even be taking the time to come down to this damned thing, but he didn't want to displease Sachi and there were a couple of things he could accomplish. He wanted to sound out the man from the huge Mazda plant in Hiroshima—he'd be at her housewarming. And there was a former member of his Cherry Society to see before he left the city.

Through the amazing growth of Kishi, Ltd., during the past decade, as well as his determined jockeying for high position in the management associations, Billy's rise had been almost unbelievable for one of foreign birth. He had come up through the *Nissho*—the Chamber of Commerce and Industry—to an important finance committee in the *Keidanren*, the powerful federation of economic organizations. And though he lacked the vast wealth of most of the *zaikai*, he had played golf with two of them at the exclusive Koganei Golf Club where he had spent a large sum for membership. He had also been invited to a few fringe social activities.

And while he carefully avoided voicing his anti-American sentiments, he found that he was not alone in possessing them, nor far from singular in his ruthless approach to world trade.

He wasn't sure how this peace treaty that was being signed in Paris would affect American business thinking—there could be a letdown, or WTI could make an aggressive move on world markets to make up for its loss of wartime sales. And there was a rumor of something coming up in the oil market in the Middle East. All of it could have a definite impact on the use of computers and Kishi's highly profitable semiconductor chip programs.

His Cherry Society now numbered an even dozen people, including his current mistress—an attractive political science professor at Keio University. Many of the members had already assumed positions of increasing importance in policy-making areas. And he had only recently recruited a young editor of a major newspaper. The next few years should do it—

"Please extinguish your cigarette, sir." The pretty stewardess smiled pleasantly as she pointed to the lit No Smoking sign.

*   *   *

The U.S. Air Force T-39 Sabreliner pulled into the parking area of Pan American's main gate at 1437 and shut down its twin jet engines. Shortly, a tall man wearing a flight suit and a green service hat with scrambled eggs on its visor hurried down the steps and strode eagerly toward the terminal. The epaulets of his jacket each carried three white stars.

Continuing to the reception area, Lieutenant General James Forster quickly spotted the waiting Sachi in her black trenchcoat. Smiling, she lowered her head slightly in a bow. But that wasn't enough for Forster. Disregarding the curious looks, he pulled her quickly into his arms and kissed her soundly on the mouth. Looking up into his still boyish grin, she said, "You look very good, General."

He laughed, putting her down as the crew chief brought up his valpac. "I *am* very good, pretty lady. And all ready to be entertained in this new palace of yours."

Several minutes later she was swinging the white Datsun sports car deftly through traffic, heading northwest. "So how does it feel to win a war?" she asked quietly.

He didn't take his eyes off the cigarette he was lighting. "I was under the impression we just lost one," he replied quietly. "But I suppose it will take the world a couple of decades to understand that. Can't we talk about something more cheerful like whether we have time to make love before your shindig starts?"

Her hand slipped over to his. "I'd like that, Forster-san, but there is much to be done and the night will be very long and intimate."

He kissed her fingertips. "Very well, reject me abruptly, Dragon Lady. I'm sensitive, you know."

She laughed. "Yes, and I know all the places. When's your retirement date?"

He stared through the windshield, not seeing anything in particular. "Last day of next month. They'll have a parade at Fort Myer, give me a medal, then snip off my buttons, and break my saber."

"Can I come?" She had never been to Washington—that was his wife's staked-out territory.

"Of course."

She turned onto an expressway. "You're too easy. I pass. Besides, I cry easily when they turn old bulls out to pasture. Do you know what you're going to do?"

He nodded. "Yeah, I'm gonna play golf for one month, then report to the headquarters of WTI in New York. Seems they have so much money, they can afford to keep an old soldier around as a consultant. What do you think about that? You still own WTI stock?"

She had made a fortune on it over the years and still held a substantial block. "Yes, and I think it's a good idea, James. Something about keeping old bulls busy, or busy fingers out of trouble."

He chuckled. "I just didn't want you to get upset about my joining the archenemy. How did Kishi do last year, by the way?"

She turned, throwing him a quick bright smile. "Very well, sir. Very well indeed." If she counted her dividends at the bank that were related to major Kishi development loans, her total income from the company for 1972 would be over four hundred thousand dollars. Yes, Kishi did well.

It seemed that Sachi's extensive travels had been one long gathering of architectural effects that she might someday use in her own exquisite home—although calling the grounds, buildings, and their combined beauty a home simply wasn't adequate. She had finally settled on "villa" as the best label for her residence, since even "estate" lacked the aesthetic value of what she felt.

And now, after years of searching for its location and finally seeing the extensive construction completed, she was putting it on display. Guests would approach the front entrance over an arched bridge that ran through two lighted lily ponds. They would remove their shoes in the entry that was a tall exhibit of striking California redwood where the Hoshi *mon* in massive brass looked down upon them. On the next level, they would become a part of the great room—a striking harmony of rich plants, Japanese and Western furniture groupings, subtle hardwood and carpeting, sculpture and ingenious lighting. At the end of the magnificent room, rising its two full stories to the beamed ceiling, a massive wall of glass presented a striking panorama of the faraway Inland Sea and part of the famous city that fanned out in twinkling lights in the distance.

The guests would number over seventy—mostly bright and successful members of the business and banking worlds, artists, and members of the boards of various peace and civic organizations.

Sachi's own kitchen staff was bolstered by cooks and waiters from the city, and two portable bars would dispense drinks of every nature. The food would be a nonstop barrage of hors d'oeuvres made from an imaginative spectrum of international tastes. And later, the entertainment would consist of a concert by Eri Chiemi, the movie star and famous singer who had come down from Tokyo.

And since she knew her reputation was that of an independent liberalized Westerner, Sachi decided to wear a kimono. Her seamstress created three, all works of art. The one Sachi selected was made of off-white fine silk that had a soft rose pattern of a very light blue in the bodice and sleeves, while the skirt had a virtual garden of baby blue roses around the bottom. The obi was of a richly brocaded silk that was only a bit darker blue. And in her ears, she wore Forster's tiny pearl earrings.

She and Mitsu, who was wearing a light lime silk kimono, were ready in the great room to receive guests when they began arriving at shortly after six—two strikingly beautiful women who could have been sisters.

The old story that army officers dressed in the dark when they wore civilian clothes certainly didn't apply to James Forster. Wearing a light wool flannel tuxedo that had been made by a master tailor in Saigon, the general could have stepped right out of *Esquire*. He was fifty-eight, and his brown hair was sprinkled with a touch of gray, but as he stood erectly before the huge wall of glass one might think that he was ten or fifteen years younger.

"Hard to believe it was almost obliterated once, isn't it?" Mitsu said softly as she walked up behind him.

He nodded. "Beyond comprehension. I was just trying to picture it, but pushed it away as too terrible, too unbelievable—even today."

Mitsu sighed. "Me too. It was rebuilt into this modern metropolis before I was old enough to know, so I can't relate."

Forster sipped his scotch. "I believe we—meaning the human race—can survive nearly anything as long as we have the will. This is certainly a prime example."

"Have you been through the Peace Park, the memorials and all?"

"Yes. A profound experience," he replied sadly.

Mitsu took his arm. "Is there any way you could be interviewed—I mean, the end of America's involvement, an American general in Hiroshima reflecting on the horrors of war—that sort of thing?"

Forster didn't need to see the corpses in the murals of the Peace Memorial Museum to tell him about the horrors of war—there were those of Guadalcanal, Bougainville, Iwo, Leyte, Okinawa . . . Dak To, Plei Me, Hue, Da Nang, a thousand rice paddies in Southeast Asia. . . .

"I don't suppose that would be possible, would it?"

Forster pushed it away. "Uh, no, I'm afraid not, my dear. They don't let us do those things. However, off the record, I'm glad it's over . . . for us, for me—"

"It'll be kinda tough not having any little brown people to trample on, won't it, General?" Billy Hoshi broke in sharply from behind them.

Forster tossed a quick glance at the startled Mitsu, then replied, "I'm afraid I miss your point, Mr. Hoshi." This was the first time he had met Sachi's cousin, though she had talked about him considerably over the years.

Billy had the same fault that plagued many Japanese men—he couldn't handle his liquor. And he knew it, almost always limiting himself to two or three drinks in public. If he wanted more, he made sure he got drunk in private. Tonight, he had had four scotches. "I mean, where are you going to start the next war against Orientals? Why don't you pick on China? Hell, you can't run out there." He laughed harshly.

Mitsu was angry. "Billy!"

Sachi glanced at them from a few feet away where she had stopped to chat with the publisher of the *Chugoku Shimbun*.

Excusing herself, she glided up to the huge window as Billy laughed. "Yeah, you bastards met your match down there, didn't you? Couldn't even handle a bunch of poor guerrillas, right?"

Sachi gripped Billy's elbow firmly, saying, "I want to talk to you."

He started to shake her off, but the control he had used so well over the years managed to push aside his resentment. "Okay, pretty cousin, but first I have to finish my scintillating conversation with Black Jack Pershing here." He started to turn back to Forster, but Sachi led him away.

Shortly they were in her spacious white study. She lit his cigarette, then leaned back against her massive desk. "What was that all about?" she asked quietly.

He wanted to shout it all out to her—tell her that a huge portrait of Ishiwara hung in his new apartment in Roppongi, that the Final War had already commenced, at least the skirmishes. He wanted to tell her about the Cherry Society and how its members had already infiltrated some of the higher echelons of Nippon's economic world. Yes, he wanted to grab her smug face in his powerful grip and roar that the first pitched battles were about to begin . . . that within a quarter of a century America would be *crushed,* relegated to a second-rate power, ready for self-destruction!

But he couldn't. Still—he *was* the head of the House of Hoshi. It was time for her to finally *learn* a few things. It had to happen sooner or later. "I'm afraid I just don't like American brass hats," he replied evenly. "And I plead alcohol in regard to disrupting the courtesy of your house. I apologize for my unwarranted and unworthy breach in custom. Okay?"

She watched him closely, ignoring the bright smile that spread over his face. "Forster is not only an important guest, he's a close friend," she replied coolly.

The drinks still had an influence on Billy's judgment. "Is he your lover?" he asked rashly.

Sachi drew in a sharp breath, "*That,* honorable cousin, is none of your damned business!"

Billy moved closer. "But it is," he said evenly. "As a member of my House, your conduct is my responsibility. And I won't have you cheapening yourself with a damned *hakujin!*"

Sachi glared at him. "I don't believe you're saying this. I—"

"Let me tell you something! The world marketplace is the next battleground, honorable cousin. And we're going to win the war. I've already seen the tools within Kishi, the tools of success that won't be denied."

He grinned, moving to within inches of her widening eyes. "The fruits of workers cooperating in intimate cells, communicating, interacting—the age-old Japanese custom of the family, the group . . . *these* are the tools that will make us winners. Our army and navy are in the factories now, pretty cousin, but they are every bit as dedicated—even more so than ever before because they will be *sharing* the victories on a more intimate level."

She shook her head, suddenly feeling ill.

"It will mean superior products that the lazy American worker in his greedy union won't be able to match. And it will mean a challenge that complacent, fat American management won't be able to meet. Now is the time to strike, my dear. Now is when we need admirals who will not flinch at the helm, now we need brilliant generals in the marketing field. . . ."

Surely, she told herself, surely it was the drinks.

He moved back, his eyes glowing, his hands coming up as if to grip a small globe of the world. "And there's more, dear one. Remember our beloved grandfather's great dream? Do you remember—get rich in America and come back as a big man to Nippon, a wealthy entrepreneur with two staunch sons at his back? You know, a general and a merchant prince . . . well, even he had no idea how real his dream actually was, did he?"

The dazzling smile returned. "You see," he announced in a hushed tone, "*I* am the general and merchant prince combined."

Sachi chalked her cue and absently stroked the cue ball at the purple four ball. She couldn't *believe* the bilge that had poured out of Billy's mouth. Yet, surely there had to be something to it. He made it sound like everyone was in on some kind of a master plot but her. *Her grandfather's dream—he had no idea!*

She shook her head and aimed at the five ball. The only light in the large game room hung over the green felt of that table, a setting she often came to when she was troubled. The total silence, except when the balls clicked, added to its feeling of isolation.

"Play you a game of eight-ball for a buck."

She turned as Forster, wearing a robe, stepped into the light. "Oh, I'm sorry, James," she replied quickly. "I wanted to wash away everything on my mind before I came down to your bedroom."

"I looked all over for you. The party was over an hour ago."

She nodded her head. "Yes, but I was troubled. Billy—"

"Forget what a little booze said." His arms were around her and his lips were nuzzling her neck. "All that matters is our love."

Tilting her head back and closing her eyes, she laid the cue on the table. He smelled and felt so good, so *strong!* Yes, he was all that mattered for the rest of the night . . . forever . . . for now.

His hand slipped behind her knees and in a moment she was cradled against his chest as he carried her from the room.

Fifty-four

November 1982

Sachi had visited Geneva for three days with her daughter when Mitsu was fifteen and they were traveling by auto from northern Italy to Paris. But that had been in mid-August, the time of the city's four-day Fêtes of Geneva holiday when the weather was pleasant. Now, the biting chill and early snow of November made a different place of the ancient and yet modern city that sat on the southwestern tip of Lake Geneva. Remembering the formal gardens as she gazed out the window of the taxi on the way in from the airport of Cointrin, she wished it were spring so James Forster might take her boating on the broad and lovely river Rhone.

She felt her breath quicken at the thought of seeing him within an hour. It had been over a year since they had been together and she missed him terribly. She would have been there that morning, but her flight out of Paris had been canceled.

He had called eight days earlier from New York. "Come to Geneva, darling. The GATT conference is bound to be interesting to someone who dabbles in the international trade game like you do. And then we can go on to Athens together for a few days. I have a conference there also."

The GATT was the General Agreement on Tariffs and Trade, essentially the eighty-eight-nation world trade organization that met infrequently in Geneva. Forster was attending as a special observer. Following seven years with WTI, he had left the huge company to become a special consultant to the White House on foreign trade, a position he insisted was more prestigious than important.

"If I need to entice you," he had added, "there are some

important things we must discuss.'' She made her reservations thirty minutes later.

She was soon at the President Hotel on Quai Wilson. Quickly going to their suite, she looked around with approval at the tasteful antique furnishings before unpacking. What a romantic place! She could stay here forever! Forty minutes later, Forster rushed in and swept her into his arms.

''When the weather is good, they serve outside in the park right by the lake shore. The view is lovely,'' Forster said with a shake of his head.

Sachi looked out the nearby window at the softly falling snowflakes. The La Perle du Lac on rue de Lausanne was one of the finest restaurants in the city. She laughed. ''The view is lovely in here. Warm.''

They had finished dinner and were sampling the fine cheeses. ''Yes,'' Forster replied. ''Well, I should have ordered better weather.'' He motioned to the waiter for more coffee.

''There were things you were going to tell me.''

''Yes, one is that I will be spending quite a bit of time in Japan in the next year or two.'' He smiled as he touched her hand. ''The boss feels we should make a more concerted effort at close, effective dialogue as a means of breaking down some of the trade problems. Something has to be done or there will be more protectionist bills on Capitol Hill than you can imagine. Every congressman with a constituency being hurt by Japanese imports will author a bill.''

Sachi raised an eyebrow. ''How romantic,'' she chided.

''All right, we'll go somewhere to dance and forget the world's trade idiocy.''

''No,'' she replied soberly, ''I really want to know what went on over at the conference center today. What do you call the place—'the bunker'?''

Forster nodded his head as he lit a cigarette. ''From your standpoint,'' he began quietly, ''it wasn't good. When the Japanese minister blandly told the assembly that Japan was one of the most open markets in the world, he was actually jeered. With every country feeling this recession, the feeling is running particularly deep against Japan. I had no idea it was so prevalent.'' He went on to examples like beef and orange import restrictions, tobacco, little things like aluminum baseball bats and described the French ire. ''They've retaliated by making the only port of entry for Japanese videotape recorders a seldom used customs house in little Poitiers. Have you ever *been* to Poitiers? If something isn't done, your recorders will take over the place while they wait to get in!''

He talked on for over half an hour describing the infighting, including the faults of the American approach. Suddenly, he snapped his fingers. ''I got so involved I almost forgot the most important point. . . . Darling, there's something that could be nothing more than idle rumor, or it could be serious. We have nothing concrete, so we can't take it to your government even if this were a good time to do so.''

He leaned forward, lowering his voice and speaking earnestly. ''A whisper has surfaced through our intelligence channels that the trading company of a major Japanese firm is going to start handling Soviet goods.''

She looked at him blankly, not certain what he was saying.

''As you know,'' he went on, ''the Soviets have a severe trading problem due to worldwide restrictions against them. Thus their marketing machinery isn't permitted in most parts of the Western world. Okay, what would be more desirable for them than using one of the powerful Japanese trading companies? It would be a *natural!*''

''What can I do?''

''Check it out. You've got all kinds of connections.''

She sipped her coffee. ''Any ideas who it might be?''

He shook his head. ''Not the slightest. I can't even imagine what motivation could be involved. Such a thing could create serious policy problems between our governments. Who could possibly want that?''

Sachi felt a sharp chill. One of the advantages of major Japanese firms was their use of powerful trading companies— independent entities within their corporate structures that were capable of representing any international company in the global marketplace. *Kishi, Ltd., had opened its own trading company in 1977 and Billy Hoshi was its president!*

Sachi arrived in Lodi on December 4. Although she was anxious to get back to Tokyo from her European excursion, Cedric's insistent plea for her to attend his birthday party took priority. And she hadn't seen her Aunt Haru in several years.

It was a warm, pleasant afternoon in the Valley, but the festivities were being held inside the house at The Other Cheek. At eighty-five, fat old Mario had defied medical science by remaining alive and was now fairly drunk in his wheelchair. In much the same condition were several of the town's oldest citizens who had been invited and inveigled into downing several tiny cups of fiery sake.

Sitting on a padded straight-backed chair in the center of the living room was the guest of honor. The number 100 hung down from a sign over his head. Leaning on his cane and holding a strong bourbon drink, Cedric smiled brightly whenever someone spoke to him. Heavy wrinkles around his even more pronounced beak of a nose couldn't hide his still avid interest in life. His high, bony cheekbones were covered with thin transparent skin, and while his neck didn't fill up his collar anymore, he was strong enough to still drive his car on occasion. Peering through the glasses he had finally given in to wearing in public, he growled at one and all and called himself the Valley's ancient curmudgeon.

Sachi smiled as she came out from the kitchen where Haru and the other women were fussing over a buffet. "How come you wouldn't let that damned Billy out of Tokyo?" Cedric snapped. "He so busy stealing business from us he can't fill his obligations?"

Sachi shrugged. "I'm sure he must have had something important keep him away." She knew her cousin had no use for Cedric or Lodi.

"Well," he said, hauling himself to his feet. "Get that skinny little aunt of yours and let's go out to the barn."

Haru, white-haired but healthy at eighty-two, had become a businesswoman in her own right in the years after she became a citizen. She bought Yoshi's small farm following the old man's death in 1959, as well as more vineyards and a larger farm which she had operated on shares for years. Each time Sachi tried to give her money, she'd refused. "My Noboru gave me everything," was her catchall reply. And while she never sought any position within the Japanese community, Sachi knew she was still regarded among the older members as the "young *oyakata*'s wife."

"We haven't eaten yet, Cedric," she said, wiping her hands on her apron.

"We've got all afternoon to eat," the old publisher replied crisply as he headed his cane toward the door. "I've been waiting ages for what we're going to do." He cackled merrily as he went outside. There was nothing else to do but follow him slowly to the barn.

Shortly, standing in the center of the sturdy old structure, Cedric turned to his listeners with the expression of one who was about to bestow a great gift. "I guess you might say the statute of limitations has run out," he began whimsically. "But I'm going to tell you folks a murder story. When Sataro left for Japan forty-one years ago, I promised to tell all on my hundredth birthday." He looked up and cackled. "Well, you old bastard— *here I am!*" Sobering, he looked at their curious faces and went on, "It was the first New Year the Hoshi family was here. Beginning of 1908 . . ."

Twenty minutes later, seated on a nearby bale of hay, he wound down to telling them about the sturdy floor beneath their feet. "Near as I can guess, those two bastards are buried just about . . . *there!*" he exclaimed, pointing his cane at Sachi's feet. He cackled as she quickly stepped aside. "No, we're *all* standing on them. And that's the story of the New Year's murders of The Other Cheek."

Haru stood hushed, staring silently at the floor. "My God, what a terrible thing for that wonderful man," she whispered.

Sachi, too, stared at the smooth hard stones. She felt her fingers tremble, sensing his presence more powerfully than at any time in recent years. She could see him pulling the trigger, hear the blasts . . . and she could see the body of Inspector Oishi going over the railing on the promenade of Brooklyn Heights. All these years there had been a slight guilt over his killing, a periodic qualm, a tiny nagging fear that she would somehow be found out.

And now she knew, she knew that her beloved grandfather had probably suffered some of those same anxieties. But he had lived right here with it! "Yes," she replied softly. "What strength it must have taken. I know." She wanted to tell them about Oishi, wipe it from her soul. But it was too involved and they didn't need to be burdened with it. They didn't even notice her moist eyes.

And yet Sataro's act of so long ago had just freed her, she thought with sudden relief. She was more than ever his granddaughter, his spirit. Hadn't they both killed when their backs were to the wall—each in defense of their children? It was the Hoshi will.

And now it must sustain her in what might be a most terrible confrontation with her cousin. As much as she hoped her fears from Geneva were wrong, deep down she sensed there was basis for them. Yes, and now was a good time to get some professional help. Now, when Sataro had given her the strength. Yes, if there were problems ahead, she would face them head on.

She would make the call to Tokyo.

She reached out and touched the quiet journalist's hand. "Thank you," she said quietly. "You don't know what it means to me."

Cedric smiled tiredly, going back to the sound of a shovel in the weak headlights of an old black Duesenberg.

Following Billy's shocking revelations the night of the huge reception in 1973, he had recanted with utmost charm, stating that everything he said was true to a certain extent but that it had been mostly whiskey talking. That had partially repaired the bridge between them, but Sachi had never been able to feel comfortable with him since that night. They saw each other perhaps twice a year at bank board meetings and possibly the same number of times in Tokyo.

Now, as she was required to wait in his outer office, she recalled the sheer violence that had crept into his eyes during the harangue. And much as she wanted her theory to be totally wrong, she was afraid it was all too logical. She had given it extensive thought in the month since Geneva and now it was time for the first step.

"Follow me, please, Mrs. Hoshi," the secretary said pleasantly.

The office was large, modern and quietly whispered success. The only painting in the room was a stark work of grays and blacks by Toko Shinoda and in the center, in front of the large window that revealed some view of the Imperial Palace, Billy Heigo Hoshi sat at a large abstract desk that held only one small pile of papers. He immediately got to his feet to bow and greet her.

She was adroit as she explained hearing a disturbing rumor in Switzerland. After talking around the point for several minutes, she asked, "Would you know of any Japanese trading firm foolish enough to consider working with the Russians on an intimate basis?"

His gaze across the coffee table never wavered as he replied, "The day is not far off when such a proposal may not be repulsive. It most certainly would be highly profitable. We've sold them products for years."

"And what about the government—wouldn't that pose a huge deterrent?"

He smiled. "I'm sure any firm attempting what you say would be on safe ground in that direction. Most probably even working in concert with some of those people who make things happen . . . if you know what I mean."

She nodded. The *zaikai,* of course—at least those who were conniving.

He smiled again, patronizingly. "And of course you know which tail wags the government."

"Then such a preposterous activity would not be impossible, right?"

His eyes were cold. "Precisely."

She got to her feet. "Well, then, I'm wasting both your time and mine, dear cousin. Give my best regards to your family, please."

A moment later, as she disappeared through the door, the smile froze on Billy's face. And a minute after that he was speaking on the telephone with his contact at the Soviet embassy. "I think it would be wise if we do not meet for a while, and then possibly it would be better away from Tokyo."

Sachi knew her warning visit would not deter Billy one iota—if indeed he were involved in such a scheme. They had merely sparred, she telling him she was onto something, he telling her to forget it because it was beyond her scope. Now she needed proof. And if ever discretion were paramount in a matter, it was in this grotesque charade into which she had been so suddenly thrust. As soon as she returned to her suite at the Imperial Hotel, she made the phone call that would get things started.

Minutes later, Mitsu arrived, well-groomed and vivacious as ever. She was now a leading talk show hostess at NHK and into other facets of television production. At first, Sachi had no intention of sharing her fears about the trading company matter with anyone until she had something concrete. But after much consideration, she decided her very bright daughter might be of some assistance—moral, if nothing else, since she had little use for their cousin.

She quickly explained what had transpired in Geneva and summarized her sparring session with Billy. When she finished, Mitsu shook her head angrily. "The bastard!" she snapped. "You know, he's been pretty quiet about it, but that man really hates the good old United States. Do you know that, Mother? If you're looking for motivation, you might think about that concept."

Sachi agreed, picking at the light lunch she had had served in the room. "But no one would go that far to strike back. It would take tremendous patience and unbelievable connections to even devise such a scheme." She frowned. "I've been out of touch with him. Do you know anything about his activities?"

Mitsu shook her head. "No. Except for reading where he had a hole-in-one out at Koganai about a year ago, and another article about the success of his trading company some time back, I haven't heard a thing. I suppose when I pay my New Year visit soon I can ask a few pointed questions."

"Just be careful. I don't want you openly involved."

*   *   *

The private detective was a soft-spoken little man, plain-looking enough to melt into any group of people—almost into a landscape, Sachi thought as he gave her an oral summary to accompany the written one. It was mid-March and already it seemed that spring was there to stay. They were alone at poolside, away from even the chance of prying ears.

"In summary, madam, the subject contacted no one whom we could connect to the Soviet Union until late January, when he went to Sasebo and met with the Rumanian. As you undoubtedly are aware, Rumanians have long done the Soviet dealing in the West. I was unable to get any tapes because the subject and his contact both flew on to Osaka by separate aircraft and met again two days later."

He sipped quickly from his teacup, then continued. "The next contact of which we are aware occurred in Hong Kong on February 23. The subject flew in and registered in a small English pension, the King Charles. There, he met with a Russian whom we've been able to identify only as Gresnokov, an agent for Soviet industry. Once more, we were unable to record their conversations."

The detective cleared his throat, handing several eight-by-ten photographs to Sachi. "One week ago the subject again met with Gresnokov, this time in Bangkok. In one instance, I was able to get close enough to use a high-powered recorder that picked up only a few phrases. You will have to listen to them to ascertain if they will be of any value. Most certainly they would not hold up in any court of law."

Sachi listened quietly as he went into more detail. When he finished, she felt as if a cold blanket had dropped over her head. She stared into the clear, glimmering water of the pool.

It was enough.

"Thank you," she said quietly. "I will notify your office if I wish any further surveillance."

The detective bowed. "Yes, madam."

After he left, Sachi continued to look into the water. There wasn't any doubt that Billy was arranging it, but why? His dislike of Americans was no longer any secret, but to actually court the Soviets as full trading partners in some kind of a surreptitious manner was totally illogical. Was it all part of this horrendous Final War possibility . . . some kind of a plan to obtain an ally to be discarded later? It was mad!

She shook her head as she climbed slowly away from the pool. It didn't make sense. She barely saw her beloved grounds as she made her way to the observation point. It had been ages since she had felt such profound sadness, such futility. Always, regardless of any setback, any fear or grief, she had been proud of every Hoshi that breathed. She clenched her fists. *And now suddenly a Hoshi posed a threat to everything that mattered, everything her grandfather had worked for, their great dream . . . everything!*

Putting her hand absently on the telescope, she slumped momentarily, then quickly drew herself erect. The distasteful task of unmasking him was hers alone, and there was no easy way to do it. It would be simple if he would just listen to reason—he was fifty-nine and could easily retire. It was the easiest solution, a matter of honor and keeping everything within the family.

But she knew he would never do it.

No, she had no recourse but Taku Kishi if Billy refused.

She sighed. A top-level conference regarding the fifth generation computer program was being conducted at Kishi headquarters in Tokyo for the balance of the week. Her unpleasant confrontations could wait until it was over. . . .

She headed slowly for the house, thinking of when she had flown from London to invest in a tiny electrical company headed by a thin, energetic little engineer. And now they were storming ahead on a development program that would require unimaginable sums to produce a computer that would nearly replace a human being.

What a brilliant man. God, she hoped she wouldn't have to tell him.

And she had brought Billy to him.

What a terrible disgrace.

She looked up to see a housemaid waving as she ran toward her. It was an emergency call from Tokyo. She hurried to the poolside telephone. Mitsu? What had happened—"Mrs. Hoshi," a vice president of Kishi said soberly through the receiver, "I have terrible news. Our beloved and honorable chairman and leader, Doctor Kishi, died two hours ago of a massive heart attack."

Fifty-five

Nothing is so fleeting as the cherry-flower,
You say . . . yet I remember well the hour
When life's bloom withered at one spoken word
And not a breath of wind had stirred.

—Tsurayuki, ninth century

The poem that had been chosen for Taku Kishi's memory was not only lovely but superbly fitting for one whose span of life and genius now suddenly seemed so fleeting. At least that was the consensus at the massive funeral and the following board of directors meeting in Tokyo four days later. In the midst of all the grief, the senior members of the firm closed ranks to assist in formulating the new leadership structure for Kishi, Ltd.

Taku Kishi had been chairman of the board and chief executive officer. All major departments, including the trading company and each overseas company, was headed by a vice president who was a stockholding director. Four outside major stockholders were also members of the board of directors. One of them was Sachi—the only woman to hold such a position in a Japanese firm of that size.

It was determined at the board meeting that selection of a new chairman would be delayed for thirty days so that the decision would be in keeping with custom. The wait would also permit the principle of *ringi* to be utilized among middle and junior management so that their wishes would be a valuable consideration in the choice.

Each board member would have one vote.

The new chairman would be one of the eleven vice presidents.

After the board meeting, Sachi caught an early evening flight down to Hiroshima. She felt immensely sad and depressed—not only had Kishi been a fine, long-time friend, but now she couldn't even go to him about Billy if the need arose. Staring down over the leading edge of the huge jet, she gratefully allowed herself to become hypnotized by the lengthening purple shadows below. Small lakes and ponds were turning into tiny mirrors as the last dark crimson of the setting sun faded out. There was a thin layer of cloud over which they were skimming so fast, now and then creating a white puff for the plane to burst through, and then disappearing long enough for the twinkling lights below to send up their greetings.

She had no strength for further discomfort on this day.

God, how she wished Forster were around.

Since he wished to cement her support in his run for the chairmanship, Billy interrupted his busy schedule to go to a morning bank meeting in Hiroshima ten days later. Following the meeting, they drove out to the villa for what Sachi said would be a business brunch about Kishi. At the conclusion of the meal, they went to her study where she removed the detective agency's folder from her safe.

A look of quizzical good humor was on Billy's face as she handed him an eight-by-ten black-and-white photo. It was one of him and the Soviet in Bangkok. "You're the handsome man in the neat gray hair," she said quietly. "The other man's name is Gresnokov. He's Russian."

As the mask slipped over Billy's face, she handed him a photo from Osaka. "This man is Roumanian, and you are with him in Osaka. The date is on the margin." She dumped the rest out on her desk. "There are more—Sasebo, Hong Kong. Do you wish to see all of them?"

He got to his feet. "What are you saying?"

"Come now, Billy, you most certainly remember my visit of a few months ago—about the rumor that a Japanese trading company was going to crawl in bed with the Soviets."

Collecting himself, he asked, "What are you saying—that it's

Kishi? Hell, I meet people from every part of the world. You know that."

Sachi shook her head, holding his gaze. "Don't waste your breath with lies, Billy. I want to know why you're doing this, and I specifically must know before the new chairman is selected."

He turned and walked away a few steps, then faced her. "Why are you meddling?" he asked softly. "These are vital matters that are none of your business."

She watched as he struggled with the mask, then settled into his salesman's tone. "The most natural arrangement in the world marketplace will be between a major trading company and the unrepresented Soviets. It will be worth billions! And there's no reason why it shouldn't be Kishi. This simply is beyond your comprehension. Like I've been trying to tell you, stick your dividends in the bank and stay out of such matters. I assure—"

"The Russians are not our friends."

"What are you saying," he shot back, "that communism is bad? How come your American friends are busy kissing the ass of Red China? No, cousin, don't dump that ideological crap on me!"

Sachi felt the anger coursing through her, but she held it back. "Now we're at the heart of it, aren't we? The culmination of years of hate, isn't that right? A master plot to strike back from a twisted mind with the patience of zen. Well, it has to stop here, now. I appeal to you. Think of your father, of your noble grandfather. I've told you about his search for peace. I—"

"My father was a *traitor!*" he snapped, his eyes glittering, all pretense at control now gone. "And I'm not so sure about our grandfather!" Reaching in his pocket, he jerked out the old silver disk and strode to the desk. "Even this is a farce, part of the lie that went with him to America!" He flung it down in front of her. "I'm tired of lies and traitors."

Sachi looked down at the worn disk for a moment. Sataro had told her so much about it. She picked it up with a firm nod. "You must alter your course or I'll have to step in," she said sadly. "And that would be a terribly uncomfortable situation for everyone."

His anger continued to flare as he reached for his hat. "This is beyond your prerogative!'' he said harshly. "You are still merely a woman in Japan!'' And he strode purposefully from her study.

She too was angry. Those were harsh and foolish words for one who knew her so well. She stepped outside her white study into the lovely small garden, pausing to watch the silvery trickle of water fall over a moss-covered stone and reach out with her finger to capture its sweet taste.

When had she last been intimidated?

But there was so much more involved than intimidation.

Reentering the suite, she went to the dressing area and quickly changed to a one-piece black bathing suit that accentuated the firm tone of her trim, shapely figure that had changed little from the days when she had turned men's heads from the Ginza to the Riviera.

Hopefully, a refreshing swim would cleanse away the smoldering resentment that lingered from the unpleasant encounter. It would also invigorate her for the next step, but first she had to face her moment of truth.

The water was cool, bracing, but all it did was clear her mind to the problem. Perhaps he was right, possibly what he was proposing and its rich profits for the company *was* the right course. Perhaps there were people in the *zaikai* and the government who agreed with him. It would be so simple to accede, to just sit back and let matters take their course without her interference . . . grow old peacefully.

She inhaled deeply as she rubbed the towel briskly over her short, tousled hair. That was the easy way, and no problems for anyone. On the other hand, fighting him could result in a horrible scandal. Mitsu would get drawn in and the Hoshi name would be dragged through all the mud in the empire. And what great and noble reward would that be for her grandfather, her beloved father and mother—was that what their memories deserved?

It was so painful. She looked up at the bright clear sky. "Help me, Grandfather, brace me and guide me.''

The chauffeur of the sleek black Mercedes stood by the rear door of the limousine as Sachi came out the front entrance of the hotel. Entering the company car, she thought of how the Imperial

Hotel—new and old—had played such a vital role in her march to this, most probably her greatest challenge. From its opening day of withstanding earthquakes to the present. . . .

She glanced at the bright blue-white, two-carat solitaire on her right hand. It matched the soft blue and white kimono that she had elected to wear instead of the trademark white suit and sable neckpiece that she normally wore to business conferences. She wanted everyone off balance today.

The driver moved smoothly into the heavy Tokyo traffic in front of Hibiya Park, then proceeded past the vast grounds of the palace toward Akasaka. Shortly, the vehicle stopped in front of the tall dark Kishi Building. Just inside the lobby, a deputy vice president whose name escaped her bowed deeply as he greeted her. Moments later, they stepped out of the elevator on the top floor, crossing thick carpeting to the chief executive officer's suite. The acting head of the company was a plump silver-haired little engineer who had been with Kishi since its inception. His name was Nokana. Two other vice presidents who were available— heads of the computer and chip companies—were also waiting. As she took a seat at the small conference table, she knew by the looks on their faces that they knew what she was going to say. Billy had obviously already talked to them.

Without going into his motives, she explained that she and her cousin had experienced a sharp difference of opinion regarding the Soviet marketing possibility. She then outlined matters of importance to Japanese trade with the West that were developed in Geneva, summarizing with, "Gentlemen, we don't need to make any more enemies."

Nonaka's response was pained but concise. "We are pleased that you brought this vital matter to our attention, Mrs. Hoshi, but there is nothing we can do. Only the chairman has the authority to interfere in a vice president's decisions. Therefore, the trading company's activities are the prerogative of Mr. Hoshi."

He shrugged. "And with the election of a new chairman coming soon, we cannot disparage our colleague. None of us can. You must remember that the company is watching us from below, and any break in solidarity or any form of disgrace would be seen in a very bad light."

She was beaten at this point, but she had expected it. It was now, as they said in America, time to call in some chits.

Departing the Kishi building, she told the limousine driver to take her to MITI—the Ministry of International Trade and Industry. Her appointment with its vice minister was next. She had helped him out of a minor jam many years earlier, and she was certain she could count on his discretion. His direct help would be another matter.

Settling back in the soft maroon leather of the seat, she glanced at the leaden skies and thought it looked like more rain. As the limousine waited for a traffic light, she focused on the curious blinking eyes of a small child trying to stare through the darkened window. He was no more than a year old and was slung to the back of a young woman on a bicycle. She smiled softly at him, thinking of how the outcome of this crisis might effect him and generations to follow.

For this Kishi matter had taken on much more impact. If what she was discovering through her cousin's plotting and manipulations were true, there was positive poison at the top. Was it the Final War she had heard about all these years? Were the generals and admirals in this conflict wearing pin-striped suits and were their war rooms the board rooms of giant corporations with the power to dictate to governments? If so, they were moving toward their Armageddon with heady success.

She sighed. She might not be able to deter it, but she could certainly throw herself in front of the impending Kishi disaster. That was her first dragon, and it loomed fearfully.

Fifty minutes later, she left MITI and again entered the Mercedes. There was one other connection she had hoped she'd never have to use. It went all the way back to her Grandfather Goto. "Take me to the Imperial Palace," she told the driver. "To the office of the Lord Privy Seal."

"How are you, Mother?" Mitsu sounded like she was in the next room, instead of her office in Tokyo.

"The wait is terrible," Sachi replied. "Do you have news?"

"Yes, according to word from three Kishi factories and one slightly drunk assistant vice president, our relative is doing very well with the rank and file. It seems he's a natural politician and convincing them that his marketing expertise over the years has made the company what it is.''

Sachi sighed, depressed at the news. "Yes, he has a nice smile,'' she replied sadly.

"Supposing I went to see him and told him I'd do a special show at NHK to expose him. Do you think that would help change his mind?''

Sachi caught her breath. "You stay out of this, Mitsu. We don't know how high this goes. No, I want you out of this completely, do you understand?''

"Okay. I just thought, well, do you realize he'll be unstoppable if he becomes chairman?''

"I'll still be around on the board.''

"Yeah, with one vote.''

The next morning, after visiting the bank, Sachi drove to the Peace Memorial Park. Walking by the highly spouting Fountain of Prayer, she continued around the Peace Memorial Museum, through the thousands of doves to the edge of the Pond of Peace. There, she stood before the abstract sculpture of two hands raised to the sky and the famous Flame of Peace it housed. She nodded—it would burn until the day all nuclear weapons disappeared from the earth.

She next visited the arched figure of an ancient Haniwa house that was the Memorial Cenotaph and sheltered a black stone coffin bearing the inscription, "Let All the Souls Here Rest in Peace; For We Shall Not Repeat the Evil.'' In the midst of 86,000 names of the dead attributed to the blast that were registered there, four were her Hoshis and one was her grandfather's Macnamara.

Her next brief stop was the Children's Peace Monument, and then it was back toward the museum. She smiled softly at the sight of a large class of wide-eyed junior high girls in their navy and white uniforms. They could have come from anywhere in the empire. Many Caucasian faces drifted by with cameras; everyone seemed to be taking pictures.

She decided against going into the museum. The photos of

piles of corpses, shreds of buildings and stark desolation would still be there. She didn't need a reminder. She would never need a reminder. Stopping by the statue of Mother and Child in the Storm, she turned for a parting glance. The fountain was again spouting to its peak height of ninety feet and a large flight of doves winged its way up into the late morning sunlight.

If she needed any reinforcement, that was it.

She had only two days to wait.

The next night at eight o'clock Sachi got out of the taxi and walked in the familiar driveway to the house that had been her home through the first half of her life. Tall trees that were old friends seemed to greet her, as did the welcome sight of the solid old building. Spring foliage abounded, but the half dozen cherry trees were at center stage, proudly showing the world that once more their bright blossoms had come for a brief stay.

She pushed away the nostalgia as she reached for the doorbell button. This was a business call, not a family reunion. She had been informed that no one was home but Billy, so there would be no pleasantries to surmount. She drew in a final deep breath as the door opened and a maid admitted her.

Billy was in the study, seated at the desk where her father had so often worked. She remembered her tragic father as he looked that last night, the night of the end. So handsome, sad, and gentle as they drank sake together, him telling her about her mother in soft and tender tones . . . with an empty sleeve at his side, and the touch of death on his fine head. How terribly wounded his soul had been.

Billy was casual as he fixed her a scotch and soda. "I'm sorry my wife was not here to greet you, but she is in Kyoto until tomorrow."

Returning to the desk with a brandy, he smiled pleasantly. "I assume you've given up on your witch hunt and are going to cast your vote for your honorable cousin tomorrow."

She watched him over her glass. Was he deluding himself, or was he actually so confident he refused to believe it? Ill? The thought had crossed her mind several times. It was certainly her premise. "No," she replied quietly. "My vote goes to Nokana."

The smile lingered on his face. "Then you and I will break even. But it won't matter—I expect to carry nearly all the other votes. The consensus opinion from lower management will take care of that."

She sat on the edge of the chair, erect, ready to make her last effort. "I have a written resignation for you to sign," she said crisply, removing a page from the thin briefcase she had brought along, and placing it on the corner of the desk. "It is an uncomplicated statement of bad health with the typical regrets about not being able to continue as the company moves on to greater accomplishments."

His only response was an audible chuckle as he reached for a thin cigar.

She waited as he made a deliberate effort in lighting it, then asked, "Did the vice minister from MITI talk to you?"

Billy grinned through the bluish cigar smoke. "Yes, we had quite a chat today. He certainly is interested in Kishi."

"And?"

"And I also talked to his counterpart in the Diet—a good friend of mine, by the way—and he feels that the matter can be resolved within the ministry. In short, my dear, the bureaucrat has been outmaneuvered. Now, do you have any more questions?"

She had been afraid the vice minister wouldn't be strong enough. She nodded, reaching into the thin briefcase again. "Very well, perhaps this will be of interest to you." She handed him an envelope embossed with the *mon* of the Lord Privy Seal.

He opened it and quickly scanned the enclosed letter. A frown creased his brow as he tossed it down, then picked it up and read it again.

"Oh, it's authentic," Sachi murmured. "I assure you. It was prepared by an old friend of my mother's family—who is, as you know, the secretary to the Privy Seal."

Slowly, Billy rose from the desk. Holding the letter at arm's length in front of her face, he flicked a flame to his lighter and touched it to the bonded page. As he dropped it to the floor, his face contorted with rage. *"I will not be stopped!"* he shouted. *"Do you hear? No one will sway me! Leave this house, you traitorous bitch!"*

Sachi got calmly to her feet and walked toward the door. Turning back, she said evenly, "The resignation is on your desk."

But she was worried.

The letter from the Emperor's closest aide should have convinced him.

"Arrived at 8:15. Call me. Love, James." Sachi stared in relief at his note as she rang his room on the house phone in the lobby of the Imperial.

"What are you doing here without warning me?" she scolded when he answered a moment later.

"Surprising you, my dear. In fact, I'm full of surprises tonight. And I have the feeling you need me around to hold your hand, right?"

"You are absolutely correct, James Forster. Except for pouring me a drink, don't move a single step. I'll be there in a moment."

Hanging up and hurrying toward the nearby elevator, she felt her pulse quicken. James Forster wouldn't solve any of her problems, but at least she'd have someone to discuss them with. And the thought of his firm body wasn't exactly unpleasant either.

Moments later she was in his arms, and minutes later they were in bed.

She awakened from her short nap at shortly after eleven as he brought the tray of tea and snacks to her side. Wrapping the sheet around her like a Grecian robe, she sat on the edge of the bed and ran her finger through his short gray hair. "What wonderful purpose brought you back to me at such an opportune moment, James?" she asked softly.

He looked up from where he sat by her feet. "I told you," he replied, "surprises."

She smiled. "Tell me. I like surprises."

"Okay, surprise number one—I'm moving to Japan. Hiroshima, to be precise."

Her breath caught as the words sunk in.

He grinned as he took her hand and kissed it. "Yeah, I'm going to write a book. Lots of old generals write books."

She sighed, nodding, not believing what she was hearing. How many years had she waited? How many years of dreaming of just such an announcement, yes, and even praying for it. . . .

"I've finally decided to get a divorce. There's plenty of money and her life won't change at this point. She has her activities in Washington and—"

"No, James!" She gripped his hand tightly as she looked with pain into his wide, uncomprehending eyes. "No . . . live with me in spurts, meet me anywhere . . . God, love me forever . . . but don't—" Her voice trailed off as she closed her eyes and brought his fingers to her lips. There wasn't a sound as the first tear slipped down her cheek. "I . . . I can't let you tear the dignity away from such a woman at this stage of her life," she whispered. "I just can't, James."

His eyes clouded over momentarily as he continued to stare at her.

She blotted her wet cheeks with the sheet and found the semblance of a smile. "Trust me," she whispered. "I know it's best."

Sachi arose early enough the next morning to take a thoughtful walk through the beauty of Hibiya Park, just across the street from the front of the hotel. It was fresh and cool after an early morning shower, and she wished she could just stay there and reminisce instead of going to the board meeting at ten o'clock. There she would meet with extreme unpleasantness, but here the memories of another time—of a young woman in love with a handsome, boyish colonel still lingered. And here were the faces of ambitious and conniving young Charlie Asaka, and of a young, bitter war widow doing what had to be done for the future . . . for the day she might need every iota of power she could muster. For a day such as this.

How clever and ruthless she'd been then, she thought as a woman jogger ran by her. Turning up a gravel path that led to the Hibiya auditorium, she wondered if she had enough of the same traits left to handle the coming encounter. She'd thought of going to the Yasukuni Shrine to pray to her father for help, but she only visited there once a year to revive her hatred for war. No, she would have to handle the confrontation head-on—that's what she had been preparing for all these years. It was what ancestors like Suiko and Itoko had given her—a female tenacity to overcome whatever was humanly possible. If it had to be with bare knuckles, no holds barred, so be it.

She had decided carefully on her ensemble, discarding the idea of wearing a new Miyake creation or a kimono. The only answer was her battle uniform. She settled on her finest white linen suit, set off by a single strand of large snowy pearls at the throat. On her head she placed a wide-brim, high-crowned hat of soft white felt. One side of its brim swept up in an Australian bush effect, providing just the touch of masculinity she desired. And on her hands, she wore merely the single large solitaire diamond. She wished only that it were fall or winter so she could set it off with her trademark sable neckpiece. But her high-heeled pumps would undoubtedly make her taller than anyone except perhaps her cousin. She would be intimidating enough.

"We're ready to call the meeting to order, Mrs. Hoshi."

She turned from the conference room's large picture window, where she'd been sipping tea and observing the magnificent view of sprawling Tokyo. Going to her seat in the middle of the table, she thanked the vice president from Brazil who held her chair. Looking up from her copy of the agenda, she met the blank gaze of Billy Heigo Hoshi. For some reason, perhaps a sense of the conflict that could unfold, they had been placed directly across the table from each other. He didn't even acknowledge her presence.

Without a word she extracted a copy of his resignation letter from her thin white briefcase and slid it across the table to him. After one quick glance at it, he threw her a single hostile look, then resumed his mask of pleasant expectations. After all, it announced, wasn't he soon to be the new chairman of mighty Kishi, Ltd.? She tried to settle her edginess by a series of long breaths.

Nokana was serving as acting chairman. From the head of the

long teakwood table he rapped his gavel at precisely ten o'clock.
"The meeting of the Kishi Limited board of directors will come
to order, please," he said in his deep voice. "Due to the nature
of this special business, we will dispense with reading the previous meeting's minutes. I will entertain a motion . . ."

Sachi tried to quiet her mounting tension as Nokana continued.
She watched Billy with quick glances, seeing that his eyes were
fixed on the pen he was slowly turning over and over on the table
in front of him. Round and round, over and over, like the turmoil
in her stomach. It was hypnotic.

The preliminaries were ending.

"And now to new business. The purpose of this meeting is to
select a new chairman and chief executive officer. Since all vice
presidents have been automatically nominated by our constitution,
the slate has been placed before each of you. I will now request
the reading of middle management's recommendation. . . ."

As Sachi anticipated, the long report praised each candidate,
but settled on the director of the Kishi Trading Company as its
consensus recommendation. Nods and calm looks followed its
end. Everything was going according to custom and the unofficial prognosis. Limited discussion followed. One of the more
senior vice presidents gave a five-minute presentation in favor of
Nokana, but Sachi knew it was only formality. It was her opening.

Her karma was at her fingertips. Nothing else mattered. This
was the climax, the peak of everything that had gone before . . .
the substance, the quintessence of her existence.

"Mr. Chairman," she began clearly when Nokana recognized
her. "It is my unfortunate lot to bring both discredit and discomfort to this most lofty and honorable meeting. And it is most
painfully difficult that I must be the means, since what I have to
present will bring the utmost of discredit upon the House of
Hoshi."

Billy's eyes were suddenly pinpoints of black hate.

She quickly explained Billy's connections with the Soviets and
his overall plan for the trading company. She then went on to
state that MITI and even the office of the Privy Seal looked with
displeasure upon the philosophy of full representation of the
Russians in the world marketplace. Holding up two letters, she

added, "I have here a letter from each agency verifying my statements."

Sipping slowly from her waterglass for effect, she quickly looked at each sober expression around the table. She knew what they were thinking—it was not the custom; these accusations should have been made beforehand, discussed at length in committee . . . she was a woman.

She looked back into Billy's cold mask. "I therefore suggest that Mr. Hoshi might withdraw his candidacy for the chairmanship," she said quietly.

Billy glanced slowly around the table, stopping with Nokana. With a sigh and a soft smile, he said, "I apologize to my honorable colleagues for the irrational statements of my well-meaning cousin, but we have discussed increased activity with the Soviets prior to this time." He gave them his most dazzling smile. "And I'm sure we can all reassess that position once Kishi is back on sound management footing."

It was a lie. Once he assumed control, nothing would stop him!

It was her turn again, time for the trumps.

"Mr. Chairman, I have no doubt that this wise and logical board will ensure what is right for both this company and our proud empire, but I'm afraid I must now insist not only on Mr. Hoshi's removal from the slate, but on his resignation from the company."

Every expression around the table was startled, angry.

She got to her feet, withdrawing a red-bordered file from her briefcase. "Gentlemen," she said evenly, "it took only a small group of intensely mad fascists with the cunning of genius to lead Nippon to the most utter stage of destruction known to man. Although the song they were selling fell upon receptive ears, and a vigorous empire eager to burst from its island confinement was easily led . . . a barely perceptible cell of fanatics was at the core of the movement."

She lowered her voice, slowly raising the red-bordered folder. "I have here the summary of another such cell—a subversive group based on hate for anything American, and dedicated to not only the most violent limits of revenge but to the eventual defeat of the United States in armed conflict by the new warriors of a *Banzai*-screaming Nippon . . . this group, this cell, calls itself the *Cherry Society!*''

The pen in Billy's fingers snapped as her eyes bored into his.

''Already this cancer's members have infiltrated the top levels of our government in both the political and bureaucratic channels. And even our shadowy and all powerful *zaikai* has some of its residue.''

She paused, unflinchingly staring into Billy's violent expression as he leaned forward in a threatening position. The eyes of all board members were fixed on the red-bordered folder that she now held high. The room was utterly silent. She was telling him it was his last chance and he was rejecting her with all the brutality in his being.

''Gentlemen,'' she went on softly, ''the Cherry Society's architect and leader is our *Mr. Hoshi!*''

The electric silence was broken by audible gasps as everyone turned to Billy, who slowly eased back away from the table, fighting to again assume the mask that admitted nothing. *Now she had to make her second strike!*

Before anyone could recover, her voice cracked again as she slammed the folder on the center of the table. ''Gentlemen, I must throw down my gauntlet! Not only do my stock holdings in this corporation exceed those of any other entity, but those of my daughter under her various names make her the *second* largest stockholder. Yet between us we have only one vote. The constitution of the company is illegal.''

She lowered her voice to almost a whisper. ''Gentlemen, if you do not guarantee Mr. Hoshi's resignation and the immediate suspension of any major Soviet trading agreements, we will be forced to sue for our rights. And my attorney is waiting outside this room with an injunction blocking any action by this board to select a new chairman—should I tell him to serve it.''

Billy's chair crashed to the floor as he bolted to his feet. The savagery that had marked him since childhood exploded. *''And I will sue you!''* he shouted, his eyes wild as he rushed around the table toward her. *''You traitor! You bitch! I—''* He took two more steps raising his hand as if to strike her, but the board members jumped to their feet in sudden response.

He stopped, staring at them in disbelief. Their eyes were flinty, their silence final. He shook his head in confusion as he read the decision, still not believing. He turned back to Sachi with a wounded look, almost beseeching her. But then the hate returned to his eyes as he whirled and stalked to the door.

Sachi held up her hands, her eyes flashing and her voice ringing out clearly. "There has long been talk of a final war, and this terrible incident within our own family most vividly illustrates its possibility. It is said that this final war will begin in the world marketplace, where Japan will crush all opposition by the turn of the century. . . . Now, we're all bright people—we *know* what goes hand-in-hand with trade imperialism! Already, there is a strong movement for major rearmament. . . . No, gentlemen, *it's just a taste of the same old romance that they fed us in the thirties!*"

She inhaled, pausing. "And we've all been to Hiroshima."

She waited once more for effect, then went on firmly, "I've dedicated the balance of my life to peace and specifically to the avoidance of *any* war with the United States. It's a solemn pact sealed with my noble grandfather when Nippon was last teetering on the brink of destruction. . . . And I assure you, gentlemen, I will enforce it with *every ounce of my considerable power!*"

Withdrawing a final page from her briefcase, she said, "This is my vote for Mr. Nokana. I assume an orderly and logical election will now take place."

And she walked erectly from the room.

Two mornings later at nine, Sachi drove into Hiroshima. It was warm and already muggy, promising that the soon-to-be-born clouds would provide afternoon showers when they reached maturity. Since it was Sunday, children were out skipping rope and enjoying the other games that such balmy weather invited. And everywhere the scent and beauty of the magnificent cherry blossoms dominated the landscape. She drove to a crest that was now a tiny park above the hillside that had once held Macnamara's Methodist mission. But Forster knew nothing about its history as she parked the white sports car and quickly jumped out.

Moving to the gate in the fence at the edge of the park, Sachi opened it and hurried down the rough slope. Forster followed, watching her stop momentarily then move quickly down the hill another ten yards. When he caught up, she was standing before a small stone monument. On its front in tiny, sober characters it read:

Sataro Hoshi
A Master of the World
and his wife,
Itoko
Died August 6, 1945

She knelt, removing a shiny silver disk from her pocket and bowing her head for several minutes before standing erect and directing her moist eyes down the hill toward the Inland Sea. The fresh breeze was on her cheek as she sniffed its salty smell and saw the city spread out between the verdant hills and the sparkling rivers. She looked down the River Ota and thought she could see where they had lived, a pretty house with a pleasant garden they had told her about. And she imagined a grim father entering the house to face a defiant mother as she held a small fearful son. Another sad son

622

watched. Angry words drifted up to her, terrible words, a peeping grandmother. The boys bowed to each other, a brave formal bow, a quick embrace. . . .

And she turned, forcing back the tears. She wanted to tell him—tell this man she loved but would never have—of the terrible loss when a son is torn away, when brothers are parted, of a great man's pride. But she couldn't.

It was all part of a man's dream.